The F... &

The Fisher Lass

Born in Gainsborough, Lincolnshire, Margaret Dickinson moved to the coast at the age of seven and so began her love for the sea and the Lincolnshire landscape.

Her ambition to be a writer began early and she had her first novel published at the age of twenty-five. This was followed by twenty further titles including *Plough the Furrow*, *Sow the Seed* and *Reap the Harvest*, which make up her Lincolnshire Fleethaven trilogy. Many of her novels are set in the heart of her home county, but in *Tangled Threads* and *Twisted Strands* the stories included not only Lincolnshire but also the framework knitting and lace industries of Nottingham.

Margaret's latest novels – *Wish Me Luck*, *Sing as We Go*, *Suffragette Girl* and *Sons and Daughters* – have all been set in her native Lincolnshire, known in World War II as 'bomber country'.

www.margaret-dickinson.co.uk

Margaret Dickinson

The River Folk
&
The Fisher Lass

PAN BOOKS

The River Folk first published 2010 by Pan Books
The Fisher Lass first published 1999 by Macmillan
First published by Pan Books 2001

This omnibus first published 2011 by Pan Books
an imprint of Pan Macmillan, a division of Macmillan Publishers Limited
Pan Macmillan, 20 New Wharf Road, London N1 9RR
Basingstoke and Oxford
Associated companies throughout the world
www.panmacmillan.com

ISBN 978-0-330-54544-0

1 3 5 7 9 8 6 4 2

A CIP catalogue record for this book is available from
the British Library.

Typeset by SetSystems Ltd, Saffron Walden, Essex
Printed in the UK by CPI Mackays, Chatham ME5 8TD

The River Folk

For Dennis, Mandy and Zoë

Acknowledgements

My birthplace, Gainsborough, is the inspiration for the setting of this novel although the story is entirely fictitious. I am very grateful to the members of The Delvers Local History Group (Gainsborough) and also to the Gainsborough and District Heritage Centre, for information and help received from their publications and exhibitions.

The *Maid Mary Ann* is modelled on the keel *Comrade*, now owned by the Humber Keel and Sloop Preservation Society. My sincere thanks to the members of the society and, in particular, to the crew of *Comrade* for a wonderful day's sailing on the Humber and for answering all my questions. (Any errors are mine, not theirs!)

My love and thanks to friends, Barry and Margaret Watson. Thank you for coming sailing on the Humber with me, Barry, and for not jumping ship when I was allowed to take the tiller!

I would also like to pay tribute to the book, *Humber Keels and Keelmen*, by the late Fred Schofield, formerly owner of *Comrade*. This book was a wonderful source of inspiration and information.

As always, my love and thanks to my family and friends for their loyal encouragement and support and special thanks to Zoë and Scott for setting up my web site. www.margaret-dickinson.co.uk

Prologue

1934

'Daddy, I'm sorry. Please, let me come up.'

The young girl stood at the bottom of the ladder leading up from the cabin on to the deck of the ship that was her home. The sliding hatch above her was open and through it she could see the stars. But tonight, they held no fascination for her.

'Daddy,' Lizzie cried again, her voice rising with fear. It was not being left in the dark confines of the cabin that frightened her, nor the sound of the water lapping against the side of the vessel, nor even the gentle rocking of the ship as it was lifted on the river's evening tide. The girl scarcely noticed any of these things, so much a normal part of her life were they. The terror that was gripping her heart, squeezing the breath from her body and making her legs tremble was the sound of her parents on the deck above her. They were quarrelling, shouting at one another and it was she, Lizzie, who had made her father so angry.

'Mam,' she tried again, but the cry froze on her lips as she heard her mother scream. And then, though she could hardly believe it, she heard the sound of a slap. In the lonely darkness, her chin trembled and tears filled her eyes. Surely her daddy wouldn't hit her mother. Not her daddy. He had never raised a hand to anyone in his life as far as she knew. He had never smacked her, Lizzie thought, not once. Not even when she was her naughtiest and stayed on the riverbank playing with her friend, Tolly, instead of coming on board ship when her father was ready to sail. More than once, he had missed the tide because of her. But even then, he would just look so disappointed, so hurt by her naughtiness, that she wanted to fling herself against him, bury her face in his neck and say, 'I'm sorry, Daddy. I will be a good girl. Truly, I will.'

It was what she wanted to do now, but, when they had come back to the ship from visiting her grandmother, her father had said sternly, 'Lizzie, go below.'

For once, she had not dared to disobey him but now, as she heard her mother cry out again, this time followed swiftly by a splash, she climbed the ladder calling out shrilly, 'Mam. Mam!'

Her father was leaning over the side, searching the inky water. He called her mother's name, a wailing sound that echoed across the river through the darkness and made the child shiver. She had never, in all her life, heard her father sound like that. So desperate, so stricken, so hopeless.

The long, drawn-out sound was borne on the wind and lost in the deep, shadowy waters of the river.

'Mary Ann. *Maaary Aaan!*'

Part One

Bessie

Part One

Hess

One

Bessie Ruddick slammed down her rolling pin and wiped her floury hands on her pinafore.

'I aren't having that racket coming through me kitchen wall,' she muttered. She stood listening for a moment to the sounds of a man and woman quarrelling in the house next door that had been empty for several weeks.

It must be let again, Bessie thought. The noise grew louder and now she could plainly hear the man's vulgar language. There was a thud and then a woman cried out, 'No, no, don't. Please, don't . . .'

'That does it,' Bessie said aloud. She marched out of her own house and, turning to her left, covered the few strides that brought her to her neighbours' door. Balling her fist, she thumped on it. She waited a few moments, but when no one answered, she bellowed, 'I know you're in there, 'cos I've heard you.'

Across the yard, Minnie Eccleshall appeared in her doorway. 'What's up, Bessie? Trouble?'

'You mind your business, Minnie Eccleshall, and let me mind mine.'

Minnie only grinned, folded her arms and leant against the doorjamb. Sparks were about to fly and there was, like as not, going to be a bit of fun.

A sash window grated upwards and Gladys Merry-weather poked her head out. 'Am I missing owt, Min?'

'Nowt to speak of, Glad. Just our Bessie on the warpath.'

'Right. I'll be down.' Gladys's head disappeared and seconds later she emerged from her own house to join her next-door neighbour. 'You told Phyllis? She wouldn't want to miss this.'

'She's out. Gone up town.'

'What's it about?'

Minnie shrugged. 'Dunno. But whatever it is, it sounds serious.'

Both women jumped as Bessie thumped the door again and shouted, 'Come on out here, mester, where I can see you, instead of skulking in there.' She raised her hand to batter the door once more, but as she did so it was pulled open and her fist almost met the nose of the man standing there.

'Oh. There you are,' Bessie said unnecessarily, for a moment caught off guard.

'Whaddo you want?' The man's voice was gruff and uncouth.

Bessie folded her arms across her ample bosom, behind her, she knew that Minnie and Gladys would be nudging each other. Of course, they knew the signs. Oh, this newcomer to Waterman's Yard was in for a battle royal.

'I want,' Bessie said slowly and clearly, 'a bit o' peace in me own house. I don't want to hear you shouting and bawling through me wall.'

She heard Minnie laugh and say in a voice deliberately loud enough for Bessie and the man to hear, 'That's nowt to what he'll hear when our Bessie gets going at her lot. She's a nerve.'

'Shush,' Gladys tried to warn Minnie. 'Don't let her hear you, else . . .'

Bessie ignored what was going on behind her and wagged her forefinger close to the man's face. 'This is a respectable neighbourhood, I'll have you know.'

His thin lips curled. 'Respectable? You don't know the meaning of the word, missis. You river folk, washed up with the tide, you were. All along the river.'

Bessie's glance raked him from head to foot. The man was unshaven with more than one day's growth of stubble on his gaunt face. He wore a grubby, collarless striped shirt, a black waistcoat with only one button and stained trousers. His thinning hair was black and, to Bessie's disgust, so were his fingernails.

'I want to meet your wife, mester.' A note of sarcasm crept into Bessie's tone that only her listening neighbours recognized as she tried a different tack. 'Just to make her feel welcome, like. See if there's owt we can do to help.'

'There ain't.' The man began to close the door but it was to find that Bessie's bulk had stepped firmly across the threshold.

Bessie Ruddick was a big woman in every way. She stood as tall as any man – taller than a good many. Her shoulders were broad, looking as if she could swing a sack of coal on to her back without a second's thought. Her face was round and jolly and, usually, her eyes shone with merriment. But at this moment her cheeks were blotched red with fury and her eyes sparked fire. Her voice was deep and resonant and when Bessie Ruddick got angry, her bellow could be heard by the ships passing by on the River Trent that flowed just beyond the road leading to the yards and alleyways.

''Ere,' he began, but, caught off guard, he was no match for the big woman.

'You there, love?' Bessie bellowed, calling into the dark interior of the house.

Unwisely, the man caught hold of Bessie's arm. 'Now look 'ere, you keep your nose out of our business and get your fat arse back to your own house.'

Slowly Bessie looked down at the dirty hand on her arm. Then, only inches away, her gaze met his. Suddenly, the man found his waistcoat and shirt grasped by two strong hands that almost lifted him off his feet.

''Ere . . .' he tried again, but found his breath somewhat restricted as the neckband of his shirt cut into his throat.

'No, mester. You look 'ere.' Bessie, though his nearness repelled her, thrust her face even closer to his. 'I heard you shouting at your missis and then I heard her cry out. Now unless I'm putting two an' two together and makin' five, you hit her, didn't you?'

The man's arms were flailing helplessly and his face was beginning to turn purple.

'Leggo, you owd beezum.'

'Now, now,' Bessie warned, tightening her hold. 'No rude names. Else you'll have my Bert to deal with when he comes home. When you hear his boots tramping down that there alley, you'd better hide, mester. My Bert doesn't like anyone being rude to his missis.'

Minnie and Gladys clutched each other, convulsed with laughter. Even from the other side of the yard they could sense the man's fear.

'He – he hasn't met Bert Ruddick yet, then?' Minnie gasped.

'Can't have, Min.'

The man, still in Bessie's grip, had found a little strength. 'Elsie,' he called weakly. 'Elsie. Come here, woman. Quick.'

As a thin, timorous woman appeared out of the

shadows, Bessie loosened her grasp and the man fell against the door. He backed away from her, his hand to his throat.

'You're mad, you are. We're not stopping here, Elsie. Pack yer things, we're going.'

The woman drooped. 'Oh Sid, I can't move again, I . . .'

'You'll do as I say . . .' he began, his voice rising, but when Bessie took a step towards him, he backed away and turned towards the inner room, almost falling over his feet in his haste to escape. 'She's mad, I tell you. Just get rid of her.'

Elsie tried to smile weakly at Bessie, but tears welled in her eyes and she touched her bottom lip where blood oozed from a gash.

Softly, Bessie said, 'Did he do that to you, love?'

'No, no. I – er – fell. Tripped over a packing case. You know . . .'

Bessie shook her head. 'No, love, I don't know. My feller'd not lay a finger on me.'

Despite everything, the little woman smiled as she murmured, 'No, I don't suppose your feller would, missis.' The smile faded as swiftly as it had come and she sighed heavily. 'I'm sorry if we disturbed you.' She glanced back over her shoulder and then moved closer as her voice dropped to a whisper. 'You haven't seen a little lass about the yard, have you?'

Bessie shook her head. 'No, love. Your lass, is it?'

The woman nodded. 'She's run off somewhere . . .' She jerked her head backwards. 'When he started. I'm worried she might get lost. And with the river so close . . .'

'Not from round here, then?' Bessie said. She was only trying to make friendly conversation, but Elsie's eyes widened in panic.

9

'No, no. Never even been to Elsborough before, till Sid . . .' She broke off and dropped her gaze. Then she mumbled, 'He's looking for work.'

'Aye well, it's not easy. Just back from the war, is he?'

She heard the woman pull in a sharp breath before she said, hurriedly, as if latching on to Bessie's question like a drowning person grasping for a lifeline, 'Yes, yes, that's it. Just home from the war.'

'Elsie . . .' Her husband's voice came warningly out of the shadows behind her.

The woman jumped and then stepped back nervously and made to close the door. 'I must go. If you see our Mary Ann, send her home, will you?'

'Aye,' came the man's rough voice again. 'You do that, missis, 'cos I'm going to tan her backside for her when I get hold of her, so you might hear a bit more yelling and screaming.'

Bessie raised her voice and shouted, 'I'd better not, mester, 'cos next time, I'll bring my Bert with me.'

Across the yard Minnie and Gladys leant against each other, tears of helpless laughter running down their cheeks.

'Bye for now, love,' Bessie was saying to the woman. 'I hope you're going to be happy here in Waterman's Yard.'

The woman closed her eyes and seemed, for a moment, to sway. 'Happy?' she murmured, for all the world as if she meant to add, 'What's that?'

Two

Bessie heard her husband's cheerful whistle echoing down the hollow-sounding arched passageway that led into Waterman's Yard.

Half the townsfolk of Elsborough lived in the yards – a conglomeration of houses that had been hastily built in the spaces behind the larger, grander buildings fronting River Road to accommodate a rapidly expanding population. Regarded by many as insanitary places and a breeding ground for disease, nevertheless the residents of the yards were a fiercely independent and proud community and none more so than the families who earned their living from the river.

The Waterman's Arms, for years a hostelry for sailors, keelmen and watermen of all description, stood proudly on River Road. Nestling behind it was Waterman's Yard.

As she heard his boots ringing on the cobbles of the yard where the sun rarely reached, Bessie bent to take the shepherd's pie out of the oven. Its potato topping crisp and brown, she placed it, piping hot, on the table as Bert stepped into the house and called, as always, 'Bessie, my angel, light of my life. I'm home.'

Bert Ruddick was a little ferret of a man, small and thin with sharp features and mischievous, beady eyes that missed nothing. His brown hair, turning grey now, was soft and silky. He had worked on, or beside, the river all his life, finding any kind of job he could. He was unskilled but his experience of the river and all her moods was second to none and it was a mark of his worth that whilst he had never had a regular job, he had never once been out of work. He was known as a purchase-man, whose casual labour was 'purchased' by the masters of the keels and sloops that plied the River Trent near Elsborough.

'Summat'll come in with the tide, Bess,' had always been his motto and it always had for even if there was no work available aboard ship, there was often plenty to be had on the wharves.

Bert loved his wife with a fierce pride and the marvel of it to him was that she loved him in return. What was it he'd heard someone say once? Something about love being blind and seeing with the heart and not the mind? Well, that must be the case with him and his Bessie. What she saw in him, a scrawny, pint-sized river dweller, he couldn't imagine. But as to what he saw in her, now that was a different matter. A fine figure of a woman she'd always been. Still was, in his love-blurred eyes. To him she wasn't the overweight, loud-mouthed woman that others saw. To Bert Ruddick, Bessie was a Boadicea and together they'd raised three strapping lads. Thank goodness they'd all taken after their mother for size, Bert would thank his lucky stars as he downed pint after pint in The Waterman's Arms and good-naturedly took the teasing of the men around him. Whatever they said about him, no one could deny that he had sired three handsome devils, who would break a few hearts around here before they were much older.

Smiling, Bessie went to meet him. Bert put his arms around her waist as far as he could reach and laid his head against the soft, well-known pillow of her bosom, whilst she clutched his head to her breast and planted a noisy kiss on the thinning hair.

'Tea's ready,' she said.

He lifted his head and sniffed the air appreciatively. 'Smells good, Bess.'

'Shepherd's pie. Just the way you like it.'

'You always do everything just the way I like it.'

Bessie chuckled, but only said, 'Wash your hands. The lads'll be home soon.'

As he soaped and scrubbed his hands vigorously in the deep white sink in the scullery, he asked, 'Any news?'

It was a question that had become a routine throughout the terrible war that had just ended, a question that had to be asked and yet the answer had always been feared. Now, perhaps, any news might be happier.

'We've got some new neighbours at last.'

'Really?' Bert straightened up and reached for the towel. 'You met 'em yet?'

Bessie pulled a face. 'Yes, but I aren't struck with 'em. I've had a run in with the feller already.'

'Oh dear,' Bert tried to look serious, but failed.

'You can smile, Bert Ruddick. I reckon he's a wife-beater.'

Now Bert's face was sober as he sat down at the table. 'I don't like the sound of that, Bess.'

'You should have heard the racket coming through this wall this afternoon. Swearing and carrying on. Then I heard a woman cry out and when I went round, she'd a gash on her lip. She said she'd fallen, but I didn't believe it. She's terrified of him, you can see it in her eyes.'

Shaking his head, Bert picked up his knife and fork. 'Well,' he said, knowing his beloved wife almost better than she knew herself, 'while they live next door, she might get a bit of peace from him.' He glanced up at her as he added shrewdly, 'Because you're not going to stand

13

by and see someone knocked into the middle of next week, are you?'

Despite the gravity of their conversation, Bessie laughed. 'You're right there, Bert, and—'

Whatever Bessie had been going to add was lost as the back door opened and they heard Dan calling, 'Mam, where are you?'

Tall and broad-shouldered, his dark brown hair curling on to his forehead, their eldest son appeared in the doorway of the kitchen. Dan's jaw was firm and square, his nose straight and his mouth wide and generous and, more often than not, smiling. But at the moment his face was serious, his hazel eyes worried. 'Mam, there's a little lass standing in the middle of the yard by the pump. She looks as if she's been crying. I tried to talk to her, but she shied away from me.'

Bessie followed him into the scullery and together they peered through the window at the young girl. Dressed in a dirty cotton dress, the hem ragged and uneven, her tangled black curls looked as if they hadn't seen a comb in days, let alone soap and water. Her face was thin and tears had washed pale streaks through the grime.

'I bet she's the little lass from next door,' Bessie murmured and went on to tell her son about the new arrivals. 'The woman asked me if I'd seen her.'

'How old do you reckon she is?' Dan asked.

'Anywhere between ten and thirteen. Difficult to tell.'

'But she's sucking her thumb. She's a bit old to be doing that, isn't she?'

Bessie gave a wry laugh. 'Aye, lad, and you'd be still sucking your thumb, I reckon, old as you are, if you had that feller next door for a dad. Come on, let's go and see what we can do.'

'Give us a minute, Mam,' Dan said, sitting down on a stool, 'while I get me boots off and I'll be right with you.'

Dan removed his flat cap and then eased off his heavy leather seaboots and thick socks, pushing his feet into a pair of slippers. Then he took off his gingham neckerchief and the thick woollen gansey that nearly all keelmen wore aboard ship and slipped on a checked shirt that Bessie kept hanging behind her scullery door for him to change into. His brown corduroy trousers he kept on. 'Right, Mam, ready when you are.'

Whilst Dan hovered near the back door, Bessie crossed the yard towards the girl. Closer now, she could see a faint bruise on the girl's jaw, purple turning yellow. And she was barefooted too. Bessie clicked her tongue against her teeth. Such neglect.

Bessie frowned. The girl was just standing there, motionless, with her thumb in her mouth. She was not even looking about her with a child's natural curiosity. She was silent and so still. That was what worried Bessie. At that age, Bessie's own lads would have been running riot about the yard, yelling and shrieking, with the neighbours appearing at their doors calling, 'Shut up, ya noisy little beggars. Bessie, can't you keep them lads of yours quiet?' But Bessie would only smile and lean against her doorjamb, arms folded, to watch her healthy, growing boys.

This child was quiet. Unnaturally so, to Bessie's mind.

'Take your thumb out your mouth, lass. You don't know where it's been.' Bessie was teasing gently, but the girl, apart from a darting glance upwards at the woman towering over her, made no sign that she had even heard.

15

The sight of this pathetic child touched Bessie Ruddick's big heart and her voice was soft as she asked, 'Are you the little girl who's come to live next door to us? Are you Mary Ann?'

Again, a swift glance from eyes that Bessie could now see were dark brown and fringed with long, black lashes. There was suffering in those soulful eyes, Bessie thought. She could see it, even in one so young.

'Poor little bairn,' the big woman murmured, resisting the urge to gather the child into her arms and carry her into her own home.

The girl had looked away again, but now there was a tiny nod of the head. Bessie thought quickly. She was obviously terrified to go home, and with good reason, if her father carried out his threat.

'I 'spect your mam's busy getting things straight. Tell you what, would you like to come into my house, seeing as we're going to be neighbours? You can have a bit of tea with us, if you like. My Bert's already tucking into his shepherd's pie. How about it, eh?'

The girl stared up at her for so long now that even Bessie felt disconcerted by the look. Still, she did not speak.

Bessie held out her hand and, after staring at it for a moment, slowly the girl put her own grubby hand into it and allowed herself to be led towards Bessie's door. Then, suddenly seeing Dan standing there, she hung back.

'It's all right,' Bessie soothed. 'It's only Dan. He's big, but he's as gentle as a lamb.'

He must have sensed the young girl's reluctance, for Dan moved away from the door and disappeared into the house.

'Now then,' Bessie said, leading her into the scullery. 'Sit up on that stool there and let's wipe them mucky

16

paws.' She reached for a damp cloth from the draining board. Gently, she took hold of the thin wrist. Feeling the bones, the big woman tutted to herself.

'You want feeding up a bit, lass, don't you? Come on, let's have that out of your mouth. A big girl like you didn't ought to be sucking her thumb, you know. It'll go all white and wrinkly and you'll end up with crooked teeth, an' all. Our Duggie – he's me youngest – used to suck his thumb when he was a bairn. The times I 'ad to creep into his room in the night and take it out of his mouth. But he's got the loveliest white teeth now you ever did see,' Bessie added proudly. 'And it's all thanks to me. There you are, all clean. Now, let's go and get you a bit of tea.'

Leading her into the kitchen, Bessie said, 'We've got a visitor, Bert. Make room at the table.'

Dan grinned at them. 'Already have, Mam. Come and sit next to me, little 'un.'

Slowly the child moved to stand next to Dan, but she didn't sit down. She glanced at the chair and then up at Bessie.

'You can sit down, love, it's all right,' Bessie said, aware that in many households, children stood to have their meals. Only the grown-ups had chairs. In the Ruddick household, Bessie's boys had all been provided with chairs from the day they left school and started work.

'You're a man now and earning, so you've a right to sit down to eat,' she'd said to each one in turn as they reached school-leaving age.

'You're a guest,' Dan smiled down at her.

The girl sat down gingerly on the chair. Bert laid down his knife and fork and picked up an empty plate. 'Like some pie, lass? And some peas?'

17

'My mam's shepherd's pie could win prizes,' Dan said and winked at her.

At that moment, Ernie, Bessie's second son, slipped quietly into the room and sat down at the table.

'This is Ernie,' Dan said. Ernie nodded shyly towards her, but then his gaze was firmly fixed upon his plate. 'He's quiet, too,' Dan went on. 'Never says much. But you wait till Duggie comes home. We'll none of us get a word in edgeways then.'

'I'll put Duggie's in the oven,' Bessie said, piling food on to a plate. 'And keep it warm. He'll be late, as usual.'

But only ten minutes later, the back door was flung open and the youngest Ruddick boy entered the house in a flurry of noisy greetings.

'Mam. Dad. I'm home.'

'Think we can't hear you, lad?' Bessie said, but she was smiling as she said it and already getting up again to take his meal from the oven. 'You're early, for you?' She glanced at Mary Ann and explained. 'Duggie's always late. I tell him, he'll be late for his own funeral.'

'Hello, who's this?' Duggie, his brown hair flopping on to his forehead, bright eyes twinkling and a grin that seemed to stretch from ear to ear, sat down opposite their visitor.

'The little lass from next door. They've moved in today,' Dan told him.

'Hello, little-girl-from-next-door,' Duggie said cheekily. At once the girl scrambled up from her chair and stood behind Dan, peering over his shoulder at the newcomer.

Bessie almost laughed at the comical expression on Duggie's face. Already, she understood the child's fear of men, but her youngest son, the noisiest, funniest scallywag of the three brothers, was staring open-mouthed at the girl's reaction to him. It was certainly not how girls, whatever their age, normally treated him.

'It's all right, love, he's a noisy devil, but he won't hurt you,' Dan patted the chair beside him. 'Come on, sit down.'

The girl slid back into her chair, her gaze still on Duggie.

'What's your name, then?' Duggie tried again and Bessie was touched to hear the gentleness in his tone. Even Duggie, bless him, had been quick on the uptake, she thought. 'That ugly brute you're sitting next to,' Duggie was saying, pointing his knife across the table, 'is Dan and this,' he added, nodding towards the taciturn figure beside him, 'is Ernie. And I'm Duggie, the good-looking one.'

There were derisory guffaws around the table from the rest of the family, apart from Ernie, but Duggie only laughed, the loudest of them all. Ernie, with neat dark hair and wearing a white shirt and tie, chuckled softly, but did not speak.

Duggie leant forward as if sharing a confidence. 'Ernie's got a posh job in an office in one of the warehouses on River Road. He keeps ledgers and things. He has to write down all what the ships bring in and take out. That's why he wears a smart white shirt to go to work, but he has a skin the same colour, 'cos he's always indoors, see? Me,' he added proudly, 'I work on Miller's Wharf at the moment but, one day, I'm going to be an engineer. I'm going to get an apprenticeship at Phillips' Engineering Works. Do you know it? They made tanks in the war and—'

'That's enough chatter from you, our Duggie,' Bessie said. 'Get on with your tea.'

As they ate, Bessie kept a surreptitious eye on the child. At last, the young girl took her thumb out of her mouth and picked up her knife and fork. Bessie noticed that she watched every movement Dan made and attempted to copy him.

Dear me, Bessie thought to herself, has the child reached twelve or so without having learnt basic table manners? Pity for the girl almost robbed Bessie of her own appetite as she watched the child eating very little of the food placed before her. She picked at the shepherd's pie and vegetables and played with the apple charlotte that followed, patting it with her spoon and then mixing it with the custard before spooning only a little into her mouth. Then she pulled a wry face.

'Give the little lass a spoonful of sugar, Bessie love,' Bert said kindly, noticing the girl's grimace. 'Mebbe the apple's a bit tart for her.'

Bessie rose from the table at once and went in search of the sugar, returning to heap generous spoonfuls over the girl's pudding. But still, Mary Ann pushed the food around her bowl and made little effort to eat it.

'So, are you going to tell us your name?' Dan asked when the meal was finished.

Again there was silence. Then, as they watched her, she raised her hand slowly and put her thumb into her mouth once more. Her huge eyes continued to stare at each one of them in turn, but returned each time, Bessie noticed, to Dan.

Dan leant forward, resting his elbow on the table, watching her with concern in his eyes. At eighteen, he was now a man, whereas the younger ones – even Ernie at only a year younger – still had boyish features.

Bessie Ruddick counted herself a lucky woman. None of her family had been involved in the dreadful war that had just ended the previous year. Her boys had been too young and her beloved Bert had been too old – just. They had felt the effects of the war, of course, as had the whole country, but she gave thanks every day of her life that her sons' names would not appear on the war memorial that the town was planning to erect in memory of its war dead.

The war had touched Waterman's Yard, though, for Amy Hamilton had lost her husband in 1916 and then her only son too. He had gone through four years of war to be killed with cruel irony only days before the armistice had been signed. Now Amy had locked herself in her house in the corner of the yard and rarely ventured forth. Not even Bessie had been able to prise her out. At least not yet, for Bessie was not one to give up a battle. She'd have Amy Hamilton out of that house and back in the land of the living one of these fine days or her name wasn't Bessie Ruddick.

For the moment, however, Bessie's attention was taken up with the little girl who sat at her table.

'Has she said anything, Mam?' Dan murmured.

Bessie, her gaze still on the girl, shook her head.

'Maybe she can't talk,' Duggie said.

With surprising speed, the thumb was pulled out of her mouth. 'Of course I can talk.' Then she popped her thumb straight back into her mouth and glanced around at them triumphantly.

Bessie laughed. 'There you are, our Duggie, that's telled you.' But Duggie only grinned, pleased that his remark had at least sparked a response.

'Come to live next door to us, have you?' Dan prompted. 'That's nice.'

'Well,' Bert stood up. 'I'm off for me pint, Bessie love. All right?'

''Course it is, Bert.' She heaved herself up from her chair and began to stack the dirty plates. 'I think it's time you went home now, love. Must be nearly your bedtime.' She paused before asking sensitively, 'Will ya dad have gone out, do you think? Does he go to the pub for a pint in the evening?'

There was fleeting fear in the child's eyes and all the Ruddick family saw it. Dan, for the first time, noticed the faint bluish mark on the child's jaw and glanced at his mother. A swift look of understanding passed between mother and son as Bessie gave a little nod. She saw her son's mouth tighten in a gesture so like her own.

'I'll take you home, little 'un, but first, are you going to tell me your name?'

She removed her thumb briefly and wriggled down from her chair. She moved to stand beside Dan and looked into his face on a level with her own. 'Mary Ann Clark and I'm twelve, nearly thirteen.'

Dan stood up. 'Well, Mary Ann Clark, twelve-nearly-thirteen, then you're quite old enough to allow me to walk you home in the moonlight.' He tapped the side of his nose and winked at her as he added, 'But don't you be telling my girlfriend, Susan.'

Bessie watched as Dan held out his hand to Mary Ann. The girl looked up at him, standing so tall above her now. Suddenly, a beaming smile illuminated the girl's face. Her brown eyes sparkled with mischief and two dimples appeared in her cheeks as she put her hand trustingly into his.

22

Three

'Mam, what's going on in that house next door?'

When he returned from taking Mary Ann back home, Dan's face was grim.

'You might well ask, lad.' Bessie's mouth was tight.

'This poor woman came to the door. She's got a cut lip that's swelling out here.' He held his hand about three inches from his own mouth, exaggerating the woman's discomfort but Bessie got the message. 'And wasn't that a bruise on the kiddie's jaw?'

Bessie nodded. 'I reckon so.'

'So? What are you going to do?'

Dan knew his mother well enough to know that she would not be able to ignore what they both guessed was happening within that household.

'Keep me eyes and me ears open,' she told him. 'And be round there like a shot.'

'She seems a nice little thing. Held me hand and skipped along at the side of me, she did.' He paused and then met his mother's gaze. 'But she didn't say any more. Not even to her mam. Do . . . do you think she's, er, well . . .?' He tapped his forefinger to the side of his head. 'Y'know? All right?'

Bessie frowned. 'I'd need to know her a bit more before I could be sure.'

'Mm.' Dan was thoughtful for a moment, then he

seemed to shake himself. 'Well, I'd best get mesen changed if I'm to see Susan tonight.'

'Mind how you go and don't be late in.'

The young man grinned at her, put his arm about her ample waist and kissed her cheek. 'Yes, Ma. No, Ma. Three bags full, Ma.' Then he stepped smartly back out of the way as Bessie's hand came up to smack his face. But the gesture was playful and affectionate with no strength or malice behind it.

'Go on with you,' she smiled at him. 'And give me love to Susan. Time you named the day with that lass, y'know, else you'll be losing her. She's a nice girl.'

'Oho, I'm not ready to tie the knot yet awhile. I want me own ship first.'

Bessie shook her head, but there was fond pride in her tone as she murmured, 'You remind me so much of me own father, Dan. He didn't marry me mother until he skippered his own ship. Mind you, he never owned it. But I reckon he thought of it as *his* boat. I was born on the river, y'know.' She grinned. 'Somewhere between here and Newark.'

Dan knew it only too well, as did all their family, but he listened patiently to his mother's reminiscing. 'Aye, it was me dad's life's ambition to own his own ship.' Her tone became wistful. 'But he never managed it.' Then she smiled at her eldest son as she added softly, 'Maybe you'll achieve it for him, lad.'

Dan grinned. 'I mean to have a damn good try, Mam.'

Bessie was dozing, her feet on the warm brass fender, when Bert came home from The Waterman's Arms.

'He was in the pub,' Bert said without preamble as he lowered himself into the chair opposite his wife.

Bessie opened one eye. 'Who was?'

Bert jerked his thumb towards the wall. ''Im from next door. Sid, er, Clark, was it the little lass said?'

Bessie nodded.

'He bought me a pint.'

Bessie closed her eye and said drowsily, 'I hope you didn't buy 'im one back.'

Bert spread his hands. 'Bessie, my angel, a chap's got to play the game, y'know.'

Now both Bessie's eyes flew wide open. 'You mean you did?'

Bert shifted uncomfortably. 'You've got to be sociable with the chap.'

'You may have to be, Bert Ruddick, but I certainly don't. Not if he knocks his missis about and clouts that bairn of his.'

'Are you sure about that, Bess? I admit I was a bit wary of 'im at first – after what you'd said. But I have to say, he seemed a nice sort of a chap.'

Bessie snorted. 'Well, he would be, wouldn't he, Bert Ruddick, if he bought you a pint?' Then she smiled as her husband had the grace to look sheepish. She cocked her head on one side, listening. 'Mind you, I don't hear any thumps and bumps from next door now, so mebbe I've got it all wrong. Mebbe that little woman really did fall over a tea chest like she said.' She shrugged her well-rounded shoulders. 'And as for the bairn, well, kids is always getting bumps and bruises, ain't they?'

Bert nodded, watching Bessie as she levered herself out of the chair. 'Come on, Bert. Time for bed.' She held out her hand and hoisted him to his feet. Then she smiled coyly down at him. 'Feel like a bit of a cuddle, Bertie?'

Bert shook his head. 'Oooh, Bess, light of my life. Now be gentle with me. I've got a headache . . .'

25

Bess gave a deep-throated chuckle and pulled him towards her, clasping his face to her bosom. 'It's not ya head I'm after, Bert Ruddick.'

It was a ritual they often played when alone and, giggling like two young lovers, they climbed the stairs to their bedroom.

It was two thirty in the morning when they heard the sounds coming into their bedroom through the thin wall. First a thud and then a woman's cries. A man shouting and then the chilling sound of a child's high-pitched screaming.

'I'm not having this,' Bessie muttered, throwing back the bedclothes and heaving herself out of bed. 'Bert – get the boys up. All of 'em.'

'Aw, Bess, do you think you should interfere? The feller'll be drunk. Why not wait till morning?'

Bessie rounded on him. 'Listen to that bairn. By morning, she could have been knocked into the next world. And if she hasn't, then that poor little woman probably will have been.' She wagged her forefinger at him. 'I'm not having it, Bert. Not in our yard.'

Bessie was pulling a shawl around her shoulders over her long nightdress and thrusting her feet into well-worn slippers. In the moonlight, shining fitfully into the room, she fumbled to light a candle.

'Are you shifting, Bert Ruddick, or do I have to face him on me own?'

Bert sighed and rolled out of bed. There was no denying his Bess. Every time she got into her battling mood, part of him shrank away, but the other half of him admired her spirit and wished he was more like her.

'Shouldn't we get the police?'

'Huh!' Bessie was scathing. 'What can they do? You know they don't like interfering. A man's home is his castle and all that rubbish. No, Bert, it's up to us to sort it out.'

Bert shrugged and gave in. Not for the first time, he smiled ruefully to himself as he opened the bedroom door to carry out his general's orders and marshal the troops.

The yard was alive with activity as if it were the middle of a busy day rather than halfway through the night. Candles flickered, sash windows were thrown open and heads peered out. Doors opened and men, dressed in vests and long johns, shouted, 'What's all the racket?' 'What's going on?'

Only Amy Hamilton's house remained in darkness.

From her bedroom window, Minnie Eccleshall shouted gleefully. 'It's our Bessie. Battling Bessie's on the warpath again. Eeh, but yon man doesn't know what's going to hit him.'

Gladys Merryweather was already at her door. 'She's got all her lads with her an' all. And Bert.' She raised her voice. 'You there, Phyllis? This'll be good.'

The Ruddick boys and their father formed a semicircle around Bessie as she thumped on the door of the neighbouring house. 'Come on out here, Sid Clark.' She waited and, for a moment, there was silence in the yard, as everyone seemed to be holding their breath. Then into the quietness came the rasping sound of a window being pushed upwards and, above their heads, Sid's slurred voice asked, 'Wha'd'you want?'

'You. That's who!' Bessie folded her arms as she looked up at him. 'Get yourself down here and open this door. I want to know if that kiddie's all right.' Her voice dropped a little as she added, 'And ya missis, too, if it comes to that.'

27

''Tain't none o' your business.' He shook his fist, not only at Bessie but at all the watchers around the yard. 'Get back to your beds all of you and mind your own business.'

Then he slammed the window closed and wrenched the thin, tattered curtains together but at that moment Bessie, close to the door, heard the child whimpering on the other side.

She knocked on it again, but this time quietly so that the man in the bedroom above would not hear. 'Mary Ann? Open the door, love.' Bessie tried the doorknob, but the door was locked. 'Unlock it, lass. Can you?'

There was a moment's pause whilst they all heard her fingers struggling with the lock. Then there was the sound of a key turning. Bessie tried the door again and it opened. Dressed only in a vest and knickers, her thumb in her mouth, the girl was shivering and sobbing quietly, trying, Bessie guessed, to keep the sound low so as not to anger her father more.

'Aw, me little love . . .' Bessie gathered her into her arms and, though Mary Ann was no longer a small child, Bessie picked her up. The girl wound her arms around the woman's neck and buried her face in her shoulder. For a moment, Bessie patted her back soothingly, rocked her and murmured, 'There, there. It's all right. It's all right.'

There was nothing else she could say, though even to Bessie the words had a hollow ring. Now, inside the darkened house, Bessie could hear the man lumbering down the stairs and through the rooms towards the back door, knocking furniture over in his path. Bessie prised Mary Ann's clinging arms from around her neck and handed her to Dan.

'Tek her into our house, Dan. Out of his way.'

Dan reached out, gathered the girl into his arms and

carried her away. As he went, Bessie heard him murmuring to her, 'You come with me, little 'un. I'll soon razzle up the fire in the range and you can have a nice drink of hot milk . . .'

Bessie turned to face Sid Clark, who was now standing in the open doorway, swaying from side to side, his hands against the doorjambs on either side for support.

'You interfering owd beezum. I'll have the law on you for this. Ab . . . abduct . . . abduction, that's what it is.'

Bessie spoke loudly and clearly. 'And I'll have the law on you. Knocking your missis about and frightening your lass half to death. Have you touched her, 'cos if you've laid a finger on that bairn, I'll . . .?'

'Oh aye.' The man was smirking now, confident of his ground. 'And what do you think the law'd do, eh? They can't touch a man in his own home. Not for chastising his own, they can't.'

'Oho,' Bessie said sarcastically. 'You know all about it, don't you? Had the coppers round to your house more than once, I bet.'

The man glowered. 'I told you – mind your own business.'

'If a child's getting hurt, then it is my business. I'll make it my business.'

'Well, she ain't. I never laid a finger on her.'

'What about your wife?'

'That's nowt to do wi' you. A man's got a right—'

'No man's got a right to belt anybody,' Bessie thundered, her voice carrying through the black night and echoing round the yard to the listeners. 'Least of all, a little thing like her, who can't stand up to you.'

'Like to take me on yourself, would you?' the man sneered. 'Reckon you could, do you, missis?'

Bessie pushed up the sleeves of her nightdress. 'Oho,

29

wouldn't I just, mester . . .' she began, and took a step towards him.

'Bess . . .' came Bert's warning voice, but either side of her, her two remaining sons moved closer.

The man blinked, and glanced around at the menacing faces. Swiftly, he stepped back and slammed the door. From behind its comparative safety he shouted, 'I'll have me day with you, missis, you see if I don't.'

'Not if I see you first, mester, you won't,' Bess shouted back and gave the door one last thump, whilst Bert shook his head worriedly and muttered, 'Leave it now, Bess.'

'But I want to see his wife's all right, I—'

'You've done enough, lass,' Bert said firmly. Then beneath his breath, he added, 'More than enough.'

Four

'You go back to bed, all of you. You too, Bert. You've all got work in the morning. I'll stay down here with Mary Ann. I'll make her a bed up on the couch in the front room and sit with her.'

Bert knew there was no sense in arguing, so he reached up to kiss his wife's cheek and then pattered back up the stairs to his cold bed. He hated sleeping without his Bess beside him. Her presence was warm and comforting. His sons, too, yawning now that the excitement of the night was over, went back to their beds.

The child was soon drifting off and Bessie watched over her, tenderly stroking her hair and carefully removing her thumb from her mouth. When Mary Ann was asleep, Bessie tiptoed back into the warm kitchen to sit in her armchair by the glowing coals. She left the door between the two rooms open so that she could hear the child if she stirred. Bessie leant her head back and closed her eyes. She sighed heavily. She knew Bert didn't agree with her interfering, but she could not stand by and see a child at risk. Nor that poor woman if it came to that, although where she was concerned Bessie felt a trace of irritation. Why did Elsie put up with such treatment? Why didn't she up and leave him and take her child with her?

Bessie's innate honesty answered her. You've never been in that situation, Bessie Ruddick, nor are you ever likely to be, so don't judge others till you know how

you'd be yourself. 'I know one thing, though,' she murmured aloud. 'I wouldn't put up with it.'

The following morning, when the menfolk had gone to
work, including Sid Clark, Bessie wrapped the child in a
shawl and took her next door.

'You there, Mrs Clark?' When no answer came, Bessie
opened the door and walked into the house.

Smashed crockery littered the floor of the scullery. As
Mary Ann still had no footwear, Bessie lifted her over the
sharp slivers of pottery and moved towards the living
room. There she glanced around her and then shook her
head in disbelief. The contrast between this house and
her own home was stark.

Bessie kept her house lovingly polished and although it
lacked natural lighting, like all the houses in the yards,
which were hemmed in by other buildings, Bessie's home
was never gloomy. In some houses, the front door led
straight into the main room of the house. In the early days
of their marriage, however, Bert had built Bessie a scullery, so that entry into the Ruddicks' house was through
this and then into the kitchen. Here, her family had their
meals at the table in the centre of the room and sat around
the warm fire in comfortable easy chairs in the evening.
Beyond the kitchen was Bessie's front parlour, used only
at Christmas and on special occasions. In this room were
Bessie's family heirlooms. A glass-fronted china cabinet
holding her treasures. A grandfather clock in a mahogany
case with a brass face and a pendulum that swung with a
comfortingly dependable rhythm. On the sideboard was
Bessie's most prized possession; a model of a keel with its
one large, square sail and smaller topsail, patiently made
by Bessie's own father.

But in this house, where Bessie was standing, looking about her with growing unease, there were no such comforts, no family possessions of any kind. The grate in the range was cold and the few bits of furniture scattered about the room looked as if they had come straight from the scrap heap.

'Mebbe they have,' Bessie murmured, shrewdly.

She set the child gently on the one sagging armchair and straightened up. Then she glanced at the door she guessed led to the stairs. Was the woman still in bed? Bessie bit her lip, wondering if she should venture upstairs. She glanced down at the child, but Mary Ann had curled up and fallen asleep again.

Bessie opened the inner door and peered up the stairwell. 'You there, missis?' Silence. Bessie frowned. 'Mrs Clark?' Still no answer, but as she put her foot on the first step and took hold of the banister, she heard a movement above and glanced up to see Elsie Clark approaching the top of the stairs. Relief at seeing the woman alive and on her feet flooded through Bessie. 'I've brought your little lass home.'

The woman was hiding her face with her hand and her voice croaked as she said, 'Thank you.'

Bessie sighed. 'Come on down here, love, and I'll make you a cup of tea.'

'There's no need. I'm fine.'

'You don't look it,' Bessie said with blunt kindness. ''Ow about I put the kettle on while you get dressed.'

Even from the bottom of the stairs, Bessie heard the woman's heavy sigh. Flatly, Elsie said, 'No point. I've no tea or milk or sugar. I – I'll be going shopping later. Just moving in, an' that. Y'know . . .'

Her voice trailed away and now, as if she could not be bothered to hide the truth any longer, her hand fell away from covering her face. Bessie, in the light from the window near which the woman was standing, could see her bruised and swollen cheek, one eye almost closed.

'You get dressed, love, and let me have Mary Ann's clothes. Then you're both coming round to my house.'

'Oh, but I—'

'No "buts",' Bessie said firmly. 'You're coming.'

Half an hour later, Mary Ann was tucking into a bowl of porridge whilst her mother sat beside Bessie's range, holding her hands out to the warmth and gratefully sipping a cup of tea.

Forthright as always, Bessie asked, 'Why do you put up with it, love?'

Elsie's shoulders sagged. 'What else can I do?'

'Leave him.'

'Where would I go?'

'Haven't you any family?'

Elsie's head drooped so low, her chin was almost resting on her chest. Her voice muffled, she said, 'They don't want to know me. You see . . .' She bit her lip and then glanced anxiously towards Mary Ann. Her voice little more than a whisper, she went on, 'They all tried to warn me against him. My mam and dad, even my two brothers and my sister. But I wouldn't listen. You might not believe it . . . Bessie, is it?'

Bessie nodded.

'Well, you might not believe it, Bessie . . .' Elsie Clark shook her own head as if she did not quite believe it herself. 'But fifteen years ago, Sid was a good-looking feller. A real charmer, smart and, I thought, quite ambitious. He was a drayman for a brewery.' Her eyes misted over as she remembered her youth and falling in love for the first time. 'But he didn't intend to stay a drayman forever, he said. Oh, he was handsome then,

Bessie, sat up on the front of his dray, driving them two great horses that were dressed out with horse-brasses and bedecked with ribbons.' Now she sighed heavily as she dragged herself back to her unhappy present.

'What went wrong, Elsie?' Bessie prompted.

'The war. That's what went wrong.'

'Ah.' Bessie's tone was suddenly more understanding. 'Well now, I can sympathize, but only a bit mind you, 'cos even if he has been to Hell and back – and by all accounts that's what it was for a lot of 'em – it doesn't give him the right to batter you about.'

'He . . . he had a bad time.'

'So did a lot of 'em. Them that's lived to tell the tale.' Briefly Bessie's thoughts went to Amy Hamilton shut away in her house of sorrow. 'And a lot never even had the chance to live to remember it. It's still no reason why you should put up with the treatment he's handing out to you now.' She jerked her thumb towards Mary Ann, still sitting at the table. 'And what about yon little lass? Does he hit her, an' all?'

Swiftly Elsie said, 'No, no. At least . . .' Her gaze met Bessie's momentarily and then fell away again in embarrassment. 'Not like he goes for me.'

'But he does hit her?' Bessie persisted, determined to get at the truth.

Elsie nodded. 'When she's naughty.'

'Naughty? Her?' Bessie was scandalized. 'I wouldn't think the bairn's got it in her to be naughty. Not what *I'd* call naughty, anyway.'

'Oh, she can be quite a cheeky little madam at times. And disobedient.'

Bessie sniffed, disbelievingly. 'Well, personally, I like to see a child with a bit of spirit.'

There was silence in the kitchen for a moment until

Mary Ann pushed back her chair and came to stand beside Bessie. Her thumb in her mouth, she leant against her and rested her head on the comforting shoulder. Bessie put her arm about the child. 'Now then. Feel better?'

Mary Ann nodded.

'And now we'd better get you to school, hadn't we? You'll just make it in time, if we hurry.'

Mary Ann's brown eyes regarded Bessie solemnly. She removed her thumb from her mouth and declared, 'I don't go to school.'

''Course you do. Everybody's got to go to school.' Bessie turned towards Elsie. 'Does she think she's old enough to leave? She isn't, you know, because they've just put the leaving age up to fourteen, haven't they? Won't she have to stay on?'

'I – she can't go to school. I haven't had the chance to get her into one. What with the move and everything . . .' Elsie's voice trailed away yet again.

Mary Ann's voice piped up. 'I haven't been to school for a year.'

'Mary Ann – please . . .' her mother began and then, defeated, glanced at Bessie. 'We – we've been moving about a lot. I had to go where I could find work and since he's been home . . .'

She said no more but the unspoken words hung in the air. 'Since he's been home, it's been worse still.'

'Right then,' Bessie said decidedly. 'If you like, Elsie, I'll take her to see a friend of mine who runs a little private school.'

Elsie's eyes widened in fear. 'We can't afford . . .' she began, but Bessie held up her hand.

'Don't worry about that. Miss Marsh is a lovely lady and she'll tell us what we ought to do. You won't have to pay a penny, love, so don't worry. Now, come along,'

Bessie said, at her happiest when she was taking charge of a situation. 'Let's get that grubby little face washed and that hair combed and I'll take you along to see my friend, Miss Edwina Marsh.'

Five

'Bessie. What a lovely surprise. What brings you here?'

Edwina Marsh herself opened the heavy oak door set between white pillars. The large, three-storey house was situated near the town's bridge over the River Trent.

'This little lass, Miss Edwina.'

Edwina looked down at the girl clutching Bessie's hand and smiled at her. She pulled the door wider open and said, 'Come in, please. Come into my study and I'll get some tea sent up.'

'Well, if it's no trouble, Miss Edwina, I'm fair parched. We've had quite a long walk, 'aven't we, Mary Ann, all along River Road? And, of course, we had to stop and look at the ships, didn't we?'

Edwina smiled. She knew how Bessie loved the river and how she would use any excuse to walk along its banks, smell the dampness and relive her memories of her young life aboard her father's vessel.

'Did you see Dan aboard Mr Price's ship?'

Bessie shook her head. 'No, they should be away downriver by now. They've gone to Hull.'

'Sit down, Bessie.' Edwina indicated a chair whilst she pulled on a tasselled rope to summon her maid.

'What would you like to drink, my dear?' she asked Mary Ann, but the girl only sucked hard on her thumb and regarded the stranger with large, solemn eyes.

'A glass o' milk, Miss Edwina, if you please.' Bessie

nodded wisely. 'She could do with a bit of building up, if you ask me.'

'So?' Edwina sat down behind her leather-topped desk. 'How can I help you?'

Bessie hesitated and glanced at the girl beside her, unwilling to speak in front of her. At that moment a knock sounded on the door and a maid, dressed in a lacy cap and a white apron over a black dress, entered. Bessie looked at her and then towards Edwina. 'Could Mary Ann go with your lass to the kitchen? I – er – I'd like to talk to you in private, if you know what I mean.'

Edwina glanced at the young girl and then met Bessie's gaze. 'Ah, yes, I understand. Of course. Mary Ann, would you like to go with Sarah? She'll take care of you and give you—'

The thumb was dragged out of her mouth as Mary Ann said, 'No, I'm staying here. With her.' And she pushed her arm through Bessie's and hugged it to her.

'Now, now,' Bessie said gently, but there was a hint of firmness in her tone. 'Be a good girl for me, eh? It's only down to the kitchen.'

Sarah stepped forward and bent to speak to the girl, who was acting like a truculent child. 'Cook's just taken a batch of scones out of the oven. Maybe she'll let you have one, thick with lovely butter and strawberry jam.' She held out her hand. 'You come with me, pet.'

Mary Ann stared up at the maid for a moment and then very slowly put out her hand to take Sarah's. Then she looked back at Bessie. 'You won't leave me here? You won't go home without me?'

'Well, I've come to see about you going to school somewhere, love, but I promise not to leave you here without telling you first.'

Mary Ann pouted. 'I don't want to stay here. I want to

go home to my mam. I've got to see if my mam's all right. You know I have.'

For the first time, Bessie saw a side to the girl that she had not seen before. Suddenly, Mary Ann seemed much older than her years. With a shock, Bessie realized now that that was what she had seen in the depths of those brown eyes, experience and knowledge beyond her years. This child had seen things that no twelve-year-old ought to have witnessed.

Bessie patted Mary Ann's hand. 'You go with Sarah, love. Everything will be all right.'

'Promise?'

'I promise.'

For a long moment she stared into Bessie's eyes, gauging if this woman was to be trusted. Satisfied, Mary Ann turned and allowed herself to be led from the room.

As the door closed behind them, Bessie let out a huge sigh. 'If ever I needed help, Miss Edwina, I need it now.'

The two women regarded each other solemnly across the desk and then the younger one reached out with both her hands and Bessie put her own into them. 'Oh Bessie, you know I will do anything – anything I can – to help you. I owe you such a debt of gratitude I'll never be able to repay if I live to be a hundred and fifty.'

They smiled at each other, but the anxiety that was in Bessie's eyes was still there, just like the sorrow that never quite left the blue eyes of the young woman sitting opposite her.

'I'll never forget what you did for our family, Bessie. And for me, especially.'

Bessie's thoughts went back to the dreadful time when Edwina's brother, Arthur, had been killed on the Somme.

Only a week later, Edwina had learnt that her fiancé, Christopher, had been killed too.

'I thought my world had ended,' Edwina murmured softly. 'And I couldn't be any help to poor Mother, grieving over her firstborn.'

'She was always very kind to me.' Bessie smiled fondly, remembering the time Edwina's mother had come to live at The Hall as a young bride. For a time, Bessie had been her personal maid, until she had left service to marry Bert. 'She even seemed to understand why I was so homesick for the river.'

At fourteen Bessie had been forced to find employment ashore. 'I could've been mate for me father aboard his ship, but I had a younger brother and me dad wanted him.' Bessie looked mournful for a moment, recalling the time when she had hated the fact that she had been born a woman. But her life in service had been made all the easier by the young Mrs Marsh.

'So,' Bessie went on, 'when I heard about Arthur being killed – such a lovely little chap, he was, as a bairn – and then you losing your young man too, well, I had to come to The Hall. Just to see if there was owt I could do. Though,' Bessie sighed heavily, 'what can anyone do in such circumstances?'

Edwina closed her eyes for a moment as if feeling again the searing grief. 'You did more for us than you can possibly know, Bessie. I was so glad to see you that day.'

They glanced at each other and Bessie knew their memories were the same. Edwina's mother had been hysterical with grief. Her father had locked himself in his study to deal with his sorrow in his own way and her brother, Randolph, had disappeared for several days. Even now, no one knew exactly where he had gone.

'There we were,' Edwina said, with a trace of bitterness in her tone. 'Supposed to be pillars of Elsborough society. Father, a leading businessman in the town. Mother, with her charitable works. And what happened? We all went to pieces. Countless other families were losing fathers, husbands, sons and . . . and fiancés and managing to get on with their lives, yet we couldn't cope. Do you know, Bessie, I truly believe that without your strength, I wouldn't have come through it.'

'Oh Miss Edwina, 'course you would. You're strong. You'd have come through right enough.' Bessie was flattered by the compliment and knew her cheeks were glowing pink, but she felt she didn't deserve it. She squeezed Edwina's hands, then released them and sat back in her chair. 'How is your mother now?'

'Bearing up, as they say. But I don't think she'll ever get over it, Bessie. I don't think any of us will.'

'No, lass,' Bessie said softly, 'you don't get over a thing like that, you just learn to live with it and carry on as best you can.' Briefly her thoughts flitted to Amy Hamilton, locked away in her house in Waterman's Yard. She hadn't seen her for two days, Bessie realized with a jolt. She really must . . . But Edwina's next words were dragging her back to her present problem.

'Now, tell me about Mary Ann.'

By the time Bessie arrived back home, she felt a lot happier. Edwina had offered to take the girl, at least for a few weeks, without payment and Mary Ann, won over by cook's buttered scones, had agreed to stay for the rest of the day, provided that Bessie promised to fetch her home in the late afternoon.

'I'll be able to assess her, Bessie, and even if she has to

go to another school, it'll make the transition easier for everyone,' Edwina had said. 'There won't be so many awkward questions asked about where she's been before. The less anyone knows about the poor child's home circumstances, the better.'

Bessie had looked at the sweet face in front of her. Edwina's golden hair was piled high on her head and soft curls fell on to her forehead. She was a pretty girl, with delicate features that belied an underlying strength of character. But in the blue eyes, there was always a sadness now that Bessie knew only time could heal. Was this lovely young woman destined to fill her lonely life educating other people's children?

'You'll meet someone else, one day,' Bessie had said aloud, gently.

Edwina had shaken her head. 'Even if I wanted to, Bessie, a whole generation of fine young men – *my* generation – has been wiped out. There are going to be a lot of war widows and spinsters, who'll never find a husband. They simply won't be there.'

With that Bessie had not been able to argue.

Bessie's contentment with her morning's work was short-lived. No sooner had she sat down in the armchair near the range, and eased her feet out of her shoes to rub her bunion, than there was a knock at the door.

'Come in, whoever you are,' she called out. 'Can't a body have five minutes' peace around here?'

Minnie Eccleshall popped her head around the door leading into Bessie's kitchen. 'There you are, Bessie. Where've you been?'

'That's for me to know and you to find out, Minnie Eccleshall. What do you want?'

Minnie, small and thin with sharp features, came and sat down opposite her. 'Any tea on the go, Bessie?'

'If you make it, Minnie. I'm fair whacked out. I've walked nearly to the bridge and back . . .' And I've got to do it again this afternoon, she thought to herself.

'Whatever for?'

'I've just told you, that's—'

'All right, all right.' Minnie jumped up again, reached for the kettle and went out into the scullery to fill it. She set it on the fire and then busied herself setting cups on the table and fetching tea, milk and sugar. Then she set the teapot to warm on the hearth.

Again she sat down. 'Have you seen Amy, 'cos neither me nor Gladys have seen her for two days?'

'No, Minnie, I ain't, so let's have this tea you're making and then we'll go across. That's if I can get me feet back into me shoes,' she added wryly.

Half an hour later the two women were banging on the door of Amy Hamilton's house.

'I didn't see a light on last night, either, now I come to think of it,' Minnie whispered, though exactly why she was whispering she could not have explained. It was as if she had a sudden foreboding. She clutched hold of Bessie's arm. 'Oh Bess, you don't think we're going to find her hanging from the ceiling, d'you?'

'Don't talk daft, Minnie,' Bessie snapped, but for a brief moment even Bessie's usual confidence deserted her.

Amy had been so depressed, and although all the neighbours had rallied round when the dreadful news had first come through that poor Amy had lost not only her husband but, later, her son too, there was a limit to their goodness. Time had passed and their patience with the grieving woman was exhausted. Only Bessie still waddled across the yard most mornings, to knock on Amy's door to make sure she was up and about and facing the day.

Bessie sighed. Even she was beginning to think that it was high time Amy pulled herself together. Nevertheless, as she felt under the loose brick near the door to retrieve the key, Bessie couldn't help thinking for the second time that day, 'It's not happened to you, Bessie Ruddick, so don't judge others till you know how it feels.'

As she turned the key in the lock and pushed open the door, she found she was holding her breath and praying silently, 'Please let her be all right. Don't let her have done anything daft.'

Six

'You there, Amy?' Bessie called.

They were creeping through the gloomy house like a couple of criminals.

'What if she's taken a bottle of pills or summat and she's lying in bed,' Minnie, close on Bessie's heels, whispered. 'Dead for two days and not one of us knew.'

Or cared enough to know, Bessie's conscience smote her, so that once more she snapped back, 'Give it a rest, Minnie. You should have been a writer with that imagination of yours.'

Huffily, Minnie said, 'I'm only trying to warn you, Bessie. That's all. I don't want you to walk into her bedroom and get a nasty shock.'

'All right, all right,' Bessie said testily. In truth, she was beginning to get even more anxious. The grate was cold, the ashes not even cleared out, and on the table stood a jug of milk, turning sour, and a loaf of bread with green mould on it.

'Come on, we'd better look upstairs, Min.'

'You can go first, seeing as you think me so fanciful.'

Outside the door of the front bedroom, Bessie, her hand on the knob, paused and exchanged a glance with Minnie. 'Here goes,' she murmured and pushed open the door. The room was in darkness but, nevertheless, they could see a mound beneath the bedclothes.

Behind her, Minnie let out a piercing shriek, startling Bessie so that every nerve in her body jumped.

The mound of bedclothes too seemed to leap in the air, bounce and then sit up with a cry of its own.

Bessie recovered the quickest and lumbered across the room to drag open the curtains. Then she turned to look at the woman in the bed. 'Oh, so you are still in the land of the living, Amy Hamilton.' She eyed her sceptically and then sniffed. 'But by the look of you, only just! You ill?'

Amy clutched at her chest and flopped back against the pillows and pulled the covers up to her chin. 'What have I got to get up for?' she said piteously and allowed the tears that filled her eyes to trickle down her temples and into her matted, unkempt hair. 'Go away and leave me alone. I just want to die.'

'Really?' Bessie said dryly. 'Not if I have anything to do with it. We can't afford flowers.' She pushed her sleeves up her arms and then turned to heave the sash window upwards. The morning air blew freshly into the stale room. Shivering, Amy burrowed beneath the covers.

'Come on out of it.' Bessie grasped the bedclothes and flung them back, revealing the thin woman curled up into a ball. 'Just look at the state of you! What would your George say if he could see you now?'

'Oh Bess, that's cruel.' Minnie's eyes were round, whilst Amy started to wail.

'Sometimes, Minnie Eccleshall, you've got to be cruel to be kind. Now, are you going to help me get her out of this bed or do I have to do it on me own? Because, mark my words, Minnie . . .' Bessie wagged her finger across the bed at her friend and neighbour. 'Out she's coming, whether she likes it or not.'

Minnie sighed and shook her head. 'You're a hard woman, Bessie. A hard woman.'

'Aye, but I'm right, aren't I? If we let her lie here . . .' Bessie said no more as with one accord they grasped hold of Amy and dragged her bodily out of the bed.

''Ere, wrap this blanket round her and tek her downstairs. In fact, tek her across to my house. It's warm there. Make her a cup of tea and there's some porridge on the stove. Get some of that into her. I'm going to strip this bed . . .'

Ten minutes later, Bessie waddled into her own back scullery, scarcely able to see where she was going above the mound of washing she was carrying. 'Good job I was planning on lighting the copper in the wash-house today.'

There was a communal wash-house in Waterman's Yard and every week, usually on a Monday, the women gathered together to boil, wash, rinse and mangle their washing and exchange gossip. All except, in recent weeks, Amy Hamilton.

'Mind you,' Bessie was grumbling, 'with all that's been going on this morning, it's a bit late on in the day for starting a washday now.'

Minnie sniffed unsympathetically. 'Well, if you will go off on secret missions – so secret you can't tell your best friend – then . . .'

Bessie's eyes twinkled. Poor Minnie didn't like being left in the dark about what was going on in the yard. 'I'll tell you, Min. All in good time, but . . .' She lowered her voice. 'Let's see to poor Amy first, eh?'

Minnie grinned at her friend. 'Right you are, Bess. Whatever you say.' She paused and then asked, 'Er . . . what, exactly, are we going to do?'

'There's plenty of hot water in me back boiler, so you fetch me tin bath out the wash-house and . . .'

'You're not going to give her a bath in the middle of the day, Bess. And it's not even Friday.'

'And how many Fridays in recent weeks do you reckon she's given 'ersen a bath? Did you see 'er feet? Black, they are.'

'Oh but, Bess . . .'

'Don't "Oh but, Bess" me. And another thing. Have you got any clothes she could borrow while I get all hers washed? Dear oh dear, I've never seen a body in such a state in all me born days.'

'Well, I don't know about that . . .' Minnie said doubtfully.

Now Bessie laughed out loud. 'I could lend her some of mine, but she'd be able to wrap 'em twice round 'ersen, wouldn't she?'

As Minnie turned to go, Bessie called after her, 'And don't go telling Phyllis. It'll be all round this yard and the ones on either side of us, if you do. You might as well splash it across the weekly *Elsborough News* as tell Phyllis Horberry.'

Minnie grinned over her shoulder. 'All right, Bess, I won't. But you have to admit, Phyllis does bring home some choice bits of gossip now and then.'

Bessie chuckled, then her face sobered. 'Aye, but I don't want poor Amy being one of them.'

'All right, Bess,' Minnie said again and trotted off to do as her friend bade her.

The sight of their neighbour stripped naked tore at the hearts of the two women and pricked their consciences.

'Ya nowt but skin and bone, Amy lass,' Bessie whispered as she gently soaped the woman's hair and Minnie tipped a jug of water over it to rinse the suds away. 'Whatever have you been doing to let yasen get in such a state?'

Amy said nothing but submitted meekly to their ministrations, her arms wrapped around her knees drawn up to her chin. Her crying had stopped and, just once, Bessie thought she saw the ghost of a smile on Amy's mouth as Bessie's motherly hands washed her. She sat staring into the glowing coals in the fire, a faraway look in her eyes. Then the smile faded and tears welled once more.

'They had to sleep in the trenches, you know. Just where they were. In the cold and the wet and the mud. And rats, as big as cats, would snuggle up under their armpits at night.'

Bessie shuddered inwardly and glanced at Minnie. She had turned white. Stoically, Minnie said nothing but bent her head, continuing to soap Amy's feet.

They let Amy talk, hoping that unburdening her terrible memories might help her. 'And sometimes, they hadn't proper food. Just bully beef and biscuits were all they had. Just think, Bessie . . .' Amy gave a sob. 'My boy – my baby – dying out there in all that. He was crying for me – I know he was crying for me. And I wasn't there to look after him, to keep him warm and safe. I wasn't there, Bessie. I wasn't there.'

'Stand up, love,' Bessie ordered gently, but found that together they had to lift Amy bodily to stand up and step out of the tin bath. Then Bessie wrapped a thick, warm towel around her. For a moment she put her arms about Amy and held her close, trying to transmit some of her own strength into the frail, grieving woman. 'There, there. You sit by the fire here. That's it. Now, did you eat some porridge?' When Amy did not answer, Bessie turned to Minnie. 'Did she?'

'Only a couple of spoonfuls.'

Bessie nodded and bent towards Amy. 'Now come on, lass. Let's get you into these clothes Min's brought across for you. Then you can sit here for the day and have a bit of dinner with us. It'll only be cold meat and pickle, 'cos me and Min's going to give your place a good going over.'

'Oh Bess, I don't know about that,' Minnie began. 'My ol' man'll be home for his dinner and—'

'Your Stan won't mind. He's got the kindest heart I know in a man.' She grinned broadly, ''Cepting for my Bert, of course.'

Minnie smiled back. 'Oh, of course, Bess.'

The smiles faded on the faces of both women when they looked back again to their friend.

'We've got to help her, Min,' Bessie said quietly. 'We'd never forgive ourselves if . . .' She left the words unspoken but Minnie, her friend of many years, understood perfectly.

The two women had a busy day, but by the time Bessie had to go to meet Mary Ann from school as she had promised, Amy's house was positively gleaming. A fire burned brightly in her range. There was hot water in the boiler behind it and food on her table.

'Sorry, it's not more, Amy lass, but I've a regular army to feed at my house.' As she said the words, Bessie heard Minnie's sharp intake of breath and knew the woman thought her tactless. As she had worked through the day, Bessie's thoughts had not been idle ones. At first, she had dwelt on the woman Amy had once been.

She remembered the Hamilton family coming to Waterman's Yard. It was in the spring of 1900. Bessie remembered the date clearly because she had been expecting Dan when Amy and George had arrived to live in the corner house with their little boy, Ronald, who was just learning to walk. She had thought at the time, a playmate for my boy, so certain had Bessie been that her firstborn would be a boy.

The Hamiltons had been a quiet family. George did not work on the river but had a job in the local engineering works. He was a reserved man and didn't mix much with the other men in The Waterman's Arms. He was friendly enough and always so polite, touching his cap when he met any of the women who lived in the yard and smiling his slow, gentle smile. Ronald, as he had grown, had resembled his father. He had been timid and studious and had rarely joined in the rough and tumble games of the other children. Who would have thought, Bessie shook her head sadly, that he would have been one of the first in the town to volunteer in 1914 and him only sixteen?

His mother, too, at first had seemed shy but Bessie had drawn her into the small community of Waterman's Yard. Soon Amy had revealed a lively sense of humour and a sharp wit that, on a Monday morning when they all worked together in the wash-house, had had all the women reeling with laughter. Before long she was exchanging banter with Bessie and the others and was well able to defend herself when the occasional quarrel broke out.

Bessie longed to see the poor woman Amy had now become restored to the person she had first known, and by the time she and Minnie closed the door on Amy's now spotless house, Bessie had a plan of action. In fact, she had two, one concerning Amy Hamilton and the other Mary Ann Clark.

As regards Amy, Bessie had no intention of pussyfooting around her, minding every word she said for fear of upsetting her. Amy, she had decided, would have to come back into the real world and she, Bessie Ruddick – with the help of Minnie and everyone who lived in their yard – was the woman to do it. She remembered Edwina's mother clinging to her and wailing aloud, 'Oh Bessie, what shall I do? What shall I do without him? My boy. My baby.'

'You've Master Randolph and Miss Edwina to think of, madam,' Bessie had said. 'Miss Edwina's hurting too. She needs you.'

But Mrs Isabella Marsh had been so lost in her own anguish that she had been unable to give comfort to her daughter, who was grieving for two men in her life she had loved. For a while, Bessie had mothered both the sorrowing women.

And now it seemed she had to start again with Amy.

Bessie's plans for Mary Ann were less straightforward. This would be interfering in the lives of people she hardly knew and she doubted she would have the backing of her own family or neighbours.

Then she smiled to herself. She wasn't nicknamed Battling Bessie Ruddick for nothing.

'So, how did you enjoy your first day back at school, Mary Ann?'

The girl, though still sucking her left thumb and clinging on to Bessie's hand with her right, nevertheless was hopping and skipping alongside her.

'Tek that thumb out of your mouth and talk to me properly 'cos I know you can. And walk nicely, Mary Ann. You're too big now to be acting like a two-year-old.'

Mary Ann promptly removed her thumb and glanced up coyly at Bessie. A smile touched her mouth and the two dimples deepened. 'It was nice. That lady you know, she was ever so kind.'

'And did you make some friends?'

Mary Ann pulled a face. 'Not really. They all seem a bit posh and stuck up.'

Well, they would, Bessie thought to herself, seeing as the children who went to Miss Marsh's school came from the moneyed folk in the town.

She felt a tug on her hand as the girl said, 'Let's see the boats. We might see Dan.'

'Not this afternoon, Mary Ann. He's gone to Hull.'

'I want to see them anyway.'

Bessie didn't need asking twice. Any excuse, her Bert always said, and she was down to the river like a water rat making for its home.

They went down the slippery steps of one of the staithes, almost to the water.

'Be careful,' Bessie said, gripping the young girl's hand. 'I don't want you falling in the river. You'd get carried away by the current and caught amongst the weeds, else be swept under the wharf there. Then we'd never get you out.'

'Has there ever been anyone drownded?' Mary Ann asked.

'Oh aye, one or two,' Bessie said, 'so you just hang on tight to me.'

They stood on the step above the water line and looked up and down the river.

'What a lot of boats.'

Bessie beamed, her gaze taking in the riverside scene. 'Aye, there is, an' all. See that down there? That's the packet boat just coming back from Hull. It goes every day and calls at several places down the river as well as teking folks all the way to Hull and back again at night.'

'Where's Hull?'

'It's a big port on the Humber. This river . . .' Bessie pointed to the water flowing past just below their feet, 'is the River Trent. It flows into the Humber and then that river flows into the North Sea.'

'Oh.' Mary Ann did not seem to understand.

'You ask Miss Edwina tomorrow at school. She'll show you on a map and then you'll be able to see just where Dan has gone.'

Mary Ann smiled up at Bessie and the older woman was amazed, yet again, to see how the smile altered the child's face. It was suddenly alive with fun and mischief. Bessie's kind heart longed to see that look on the young girl's face all the time, in place of the haunted, frightened look that fear of her own father caused.

Further down the river, men off-loaded sacks from a ship on to the wharf, running with a wheelbarrow up and down a long gangway from ship to shore. Beyond that, a crane lifted heavy cargo on to the land.

'When I was your age, I lived on a ship. The one me dad skippered. In fact,' Bessie added, with pride, 'I was born on board.' She laughed. 'Somewhere between here and Newark.'

'I'd like to live on a boat.'

'A ship, Mary Ann. A vessel that size is called a ship. Their proper name is a keel. My dad was a keelman and so's Dan. And then there are sloops. But they're all ships. Don't you let our Dan hear you calling them boats. Boats are the little ones you row . . .'

Bored now with Bessie's explanations, Mary Ann tugged at her hand. 'If Dan's not here, then let's go home, Auntie Bessie.'

With a stab of guilt, Bessie realized that the child no doubt wanted to see her mother, wanted to know that she was all right.

'Come on, then.' They turned and began to climb the steps, Bessie taking one last, lingering look at the water and the ships and busy wharves.

'Will Dan be home tonight? Which way will he come?'

'Upriver. Up on the tide. There'll be a fair one tonight. I'll be down later to see the Aegir.'

'What's that?'

'The tidal wave that comes up the river all the way from the sea. It comes twice a day, just like the sea goes in and out, but you can't always see it clearly. Sometimes the waves are only like ripples. But when it's what they call a spring tide, then we get lovely big waves.'

The girl frowned uncomprehendingly. 'I've never seen the sea. At least, only in pictures.'

'You ask Miss Marsh tomorrow,' Bessie said again. 'She's got some nice pictures of the Aegir. She'll show you. She'll explain it all to you.'

'Can I come with you tonight to see it?'

'Oh well, now, I don't know about that. It might be past your bedtime.'

The girl pouted and then put her thumb in her mouth.

As they reached the top of the steps, Mary Ann said solemnly, 'I'd like to see the ogre tonight, Auntie Bessie. I might not be here after tomorrow. Maybe we'll have moved again.'

Bessie stared down at her. 'Moved again? But you've only just got here.'

The girl shrugged, accepting the inevitable. 'We don't stay nowhere long.'

'Oh, I see,' Bessie said. But she didn't. She didn't see at all. And to her amazement the little girl's words had brought the older woman a strange sense of loss.

She might not have known Mary Ann for many days, but already the child had wound her way around Bessie Ruddick's heart.

Seven

At about half past eight the following morning, when the communal wash-house was full of steam from the bubbling brick-built copper in the corner and Bessie's raucous singing could be heard echoing round the yard, Mary Ann, thumb in her mouth, appeared at the door. She said nothing but waited until Bessie spotted her.

'Hello, love. You just off to school, then?'

The large brown eyes regarded Bessie soulfully. Then she removed her thumb briefly to ask, 'Are you going to take me?'

'I'm a bit busy this morning, love, as you can see. Can't your mam take you?'

The girl shook her head. 'She's in bed.'

Bessie tutted to herself. 'All this staying in bed,' she muttered. 'Must be catching.' She sighed. 'All right. We'll just run across and ask Mrs Eccleshall to keep an eye on the copper. I'll take you this morning, but after that, you'll have to go on your own. You're a big girl now. By rights, you ought to be working. It's only 'cos they've upped the age you leave school that you're stopping on.'

'My dad says I can't. He says I've got to earn some money.'

'Oh aye,' Bessie said wryly, 'for him to spend in the pub, I suppose. Well, he'd better think again because it's against the law and they'd have him in prison if they

57

found out he was sending you out to work instead of to school.'

'Would they? Would they really send him to prison?'

Bessie turned and stared at the girl in surprise. There was no fear in Mary Ann's tone, no dread that her father might be sent to jail. Bessie blinked and stared harder. If she hadn't been so young, Bessie would have said that on Mary Ann Clark's face was a devious, scheming expression.

The older woman shook her head, castigating herself for such thoughts. 'She's only a bairn,' she murmured. Yet Bessie was beginning to see that Mary Ann was a mixture of childishness and worldliness. So used to her own sons, who had always shown surprising maturity for their ages, Bessie found it unusual. But when she thought about it, Duggie could leap in seconds from being the hardworking lad on the wharves, with dreams of becoming an engineer, to a mischievous prankster, playing tricks on the unsuspecting Bessie and even, though not very often, putting one over on his older brothers. The thought crept into her mind now that perhaps, young though she was, this perceptive child realized that if Sid Clark were sent away, life for her mother and for her would be a whole lot easier.

When she returned from the long walk along River Road almost to the toll bridge, Bessie's first thought was to check on Amy Hamilton. Finding that she was up, dressed and had eaten some breakfast, Bessie crossed the yard again to knock on the door of the house next to her own. When she got no response, as was her usual habit with her near neighbours, she opened the door and went inside.

'And if she dun't like it,' Bessie murmured to herself as she did so, 'she can lump it.'

Remembering how she and Minnie had startled Amy – and themselves – Bessie mounted the stairs calling out, 'Elsie? Are you there?'

She glanced in the first open door and saw that there was no proper furniture at all in the room, just what looked like a straw mattress on the floor, the only covering a dirty grey blanket. In the far corner sat a doll and one jigsaw puzzle. Bessie shook her head in disbelief. Is this how that poor child was obliged to live? Angry and disgusted, she turned away and lumbered towards the closed door across the landing. Flinging it open, she called again, 'Elsie, where are you?'

This time the shape beneath the bedclothes did not leap up in fright – it did not even move. Bessie stood a moment, her hand to her mouth. 'Oh dear Lord,' she whispered, 'don't say he's done for her.'

She was lying with her face to the wall and, from where Bessie was standing near the door, Elsie Clark did not appear to be breathing, although in the light from the dirty window Bessie could not see clearly. She tiptoed across the room, went around the end of the bed to bend over the woman, whose head was buried beneath the thin blanket. Gently, she touched her shoulder. 'Elsie?'

To Bessie's great relief the form stirred and a muffled voice said, 'Go away. I've got flu or summat. You don't want to catch it.'

Bessie laughed aloud in relief. 'A bit of the sniffles doesn't bother me. I haven't had a day's illness in me life. Not that I can remember, anyway. Great strapping lass like me,' she joked. 'Come on now, sit up and I'll make you a cuppa.'

'Please . . .' The woman's tone was pleading, fearful almost, Bessie thought. 'Leave me alone. If Sid finds you here . . .'

'And I aren't frit of him, neither,' Bessie snorted, 'so come on, let's be having ya.'

She tugged at the blanket until, with a sigh of resignation, the woman gave in and sat up with a wince of pain.

'Oh, my good night!' Bessie exclaimed. She didn't need to ask what had happened. She could see.

Elsie's face was a mass of bruises, some older than others. The most recent injury appeared to be to her left eye, which was so swollen it was closed. She sat up in the bed holding her left arm and, through a lip that was still swollen from two days previously, murmured, 'I reckon me arm's broken.'

Bessie, staring at her, sat down heavily on the end of the bed as she asked, yet again, 'Aw lass, why do you put up with it?'

The woman shook her head. 'You don't understand. And I can't explain it all. He doesn't mean it. I know he doesn't and he's so sorry afterwards.'

'Huh, I'd make the bugger sorry,' Bessie muttered and added to herself, and I probably will. Aloud, she said, 'I'll make you that tea I promised and a slice of toast and then I'm calling the doctor to you, me girl.'

'Oh Bessie, no. I can't afford . . .'

'Ne'er mind about that. I'll pay, if necessary. If that arm is broken, it's got to be seen to.'

That evening, Bessie was waiting for Sid Clark to arrive home. When she saw him with a pathetic bunch of flowers in his hand, she stepped out of her door and barred his way.

'Oh aye, and where did you pinch them from, eh? Off some poor beggar's grave in the churchyard?'

'Get out of me way. The missis'll have me tea ready.'

'She will, will she? She'll have a job. She's in hospital.'

'Eh?' To Bessie's satisfaction, the man had the grace to look startled and even a little afraid. 'What's up with her?'

Bessie let out a wry, humourless laugh as she felt, rather than saw, Bert and two of her sons appear and come to stand behind her. Out of the corner of her eye, she saw Minnie and Stan Eccleshall emerge from their house across the yard, to be joined by their neighbours, Gladys Merryweather and her husband, Walter. And Phyllis Horberry, never one to miss a bit of drama, peered out from her half-open door.

'What's up?' Bessie raised her voice so that it was loud enough for the whole yard to hear. 'You have the gall to ask, "what's up?"'

Sid Clark shifted uncomfortably from one foot to the other, glancing around him at the watching faces, but Bessie continued without pity. 'She's black and blue from head to foot, Sid Clark, and her arm's broken. That's what's up.'

There was a murmuring around the yard like a cool breeze of disapproval and the Eccleshalls and the Merryweathers moved closer.

Sid dropped the flowers to the ground and stepped back, glancing fearfully about him. Bessie stepped towards him and wagged her forefinger in his face. 'Now listen here, you. It's got to stop. While you live in this yard, you don't lay another finger on her, you hear? Else you'll get a taste of your own medicine.'

Sid glared at her and then, with a sudden movement, dodged around Bessie and made for his own door.

'Oh,' Bessie shouted after him, almost as an after-thought but in fact it was calculated as a barbed parting shot. 'If you're interested where your daughter is, she's in our house. And that's where she's staying till her mam gets home. And even then, well, we'll see, won't we?'

From the doorway of his own home, the man turned and, feeling safer now, sneered. 'Yer welcome to the little bitch. Yer can keep her as far as I'm concerned.'

He slammed the door and Bessie heard the key turn in the lock.

'Aye, you lock yasen in, Sid Clark,' she bellowed. 'That's the only place you're going to be safe from now on, and even then, I wouldn't be too sure, if I was you.'

Eight

Dan returned home late that same night.

'I hope you don't mind, lad,' Bessie said, almost as soon as he stepped through the door, 'but I've put that little lass in your bed.' Then she explained to him what had been happening during his absence.

''Course I don't, Mam. I'll sleep on the couch tonight. It's only for one night anyway. We'll be off again on tomorrow afternoon's tide.'

'It might be a bit longer than that,' Bessie pulled a wry face. 'I daren't let her go home until her mam's out of the hospital.'

Dan shrugged his broad shoulders and smiled at his mother's anxious face. 'I don't mind. When I'm home for a longer stretch while she's here, me and the lads can play musical beds and all take turns on the couch.'

Bessie nodded, relieved. 'You're a good 'un, Dan. You all are. I just can't let mesen send her back to be on her own with 'im.'

Dan patted her round cheek with a display of affection. 'And you're the best of us, Mam. You and that big heart of yours.'

'Go on with you.' Bessie smacked his hand away playfully, but the flush on her face showed her pleasure at his compliment.

The following morning, Mary Ann was up early and much to Bessie's surprise and delight was soon trotting back and forth between the back scullery and the kitchen carrying the plates from Bessie to the table for the men's breakfast. Then, when all were tucking in to bacon, egg and fried bread, Mary Ann stood beside Dan's chair watching him eat.

'Aren't you going to sit down and have some breakfast, love?' he asked.

Mary Ann nodded and pulled her chair close to his. She looked at him coyly out of the corners of her eyes and then reached out to take a piece of bacon from his plate.

'Oi, I didn't mean take mine,' he laughed, amused by her audacity.

Bessie appeared from the scullery, carrying two more plates. 'What's going on?'

'She's nicking our Dan's breakfast,' Duggie spluttered.

Bessie placed a plate of food in front of Mary Ann. 'There's no need for that, lass. Here's yours.' Then she sat down herself and picked up her knife and fork.

But Dan only grinned and winked at the young girl, to be rewarded with the most dazzling smile that Bessie had seen from her yet, the dimples in her cheeks deepening prettily.

By heck, Bessie thought, she's going to be a stunner, this one, when she's older. She'll break a few hearts before she's done. Just as long as it isn't one of my lads. Aloud, she said, 'Eat up, love, time you were setting off for school. Give my love to Miss Edwina if you see her.'

The brown eyes widened. 'Aren't you going to take me?'

'You know the way. You're big enough to go on your own.'

Mary Ann's lower lip trembled. 'I'll get lost.'

'No, you won't,' Bessie said, gently but firmly. 'You turn left at the end of our alley on to River Road and keep going until you get nearly to the bridge and it's the

64

big red house with the white pillars on the right hand side of the road.'

'It's all right, Mam, I'll walk along with her. I'm going to see Susan.'

Bessie sniffed. 'Think I was found under a Christmas tree, lad? That's in the opposite direction.'

'Who's Susan?' Mary Ann asked at once.

'She's his young lady,' Duggie volunteered. 'They're walking out together.'

'Are you going to marry her?' The question was a natural one, yet to Bessie's knowing ears, there was a sharp edge to the girl's tone. Poor bairn, the older woman thought, her view of marriage can't be a happy one. Maybe, she thought, while she stays in this house, we can show her a different kind of family life.

'He'll be daft if he doesn't,' Duggie said, tapping the side of his nose and winking. 'Her father owns the ship he works on.'

'Now, Duggie, you young scallywag, don't go putting ideas into the bairn's mind that aren't true,' Bessie scolded. 'Susan's a lovely girl and our Dan wouldn't go marrying someone he wasn't in love with. 'Sides, there's some might think it was a disadvantage marrying your boss's daughter.'

Dan grinned good-naturedly at his brother and punched him lightly on the shoulder.

Bert rose from the table. 'Well, Bessie, light of my life, much as I'd like to stay home with you all day, I'd better get myself off to work.'

Heaving herself up from her chair, she fetched her husband's jacket and scarf and held it for him to slip his arms into the sleeves. Tenderly, she wrapped the muffler around his neck. Then she planted a loud kiss full on his mouth. At once Bert responded: his hands resting on her well-rounded hips, he kissed her in return. 'Bye bye, my angel. Be a good girl . . .' he chuckled. 'At least till I get home.'

'Oho,' Bessie patted him playfully on the cheek. 'Chance'd be a fine thing, with all the work I've got to do looking after you lot.'

The young men were used to this kind of affection between their parents, but Mary Ann was staring open-mouthed at the older couple, and her astonishment grew as all three sons also kissed their mother before leaving the house themselves to go to their various occupations. Even at her tender age and despite her unfortunate home circumstances, Mary Ann could see that it was not an action made out of duty, but given with true affection. Close on Dan's heels as he made to leave the house, she too stopped in front of Bessie, threw her arms around her and pressed her face into Bessie's bosom.

Bessie stroked the girl's hair, but instead of silkiness, Bessie felt it thick with dirt and grease. She cupped Mary Ann's face in her hands and kissed her forehead. 'We'll wash your hair tonight, love. I've some lovely shampoo you can have a bit of. It'll make it ever so pretty. Off you go now with Dan. You'll be all right walking home on your own tonight, won't you?'

For a moment, Mary Ann's eyes clouded but then she nodded. As Bessie watched them go and heard their footsteps echoing down the alley, she heard Mary Ann's high-pitched voice chattering to Dan.

Suddenly and with pleasant surprise, Bessie realized that not once that morning had she noticed the child with her thumb in her mouth.

'You didn't get lost then?' Bessie greeted Mary Ann when she appeared in the yard late in the afternoon. 'Here, you can make yasen useful. Put these pegs in the peg bag for me while I get this washing in. We're going to give you a nice bath and wash your hair before the menfolk come home. And then,' she added hastily as she saw the doubt in the girl's eyes, 'I've got a present for you.'

'A present for me? What is it?'

'Ah, now you'll have to wait and see.'

Bessie bundled more of Amy Hamilton's sheets and pillowcases into her basket and picked it up. Earlier in the day Bessie had had to coax Amy out of her bed once more. Helping her to wash and dress, Bessie had discovered a bundle of dirty bed linen stuffed into the bottom of a wardrobe.

'I don't know,' she grumbled to Mary Ann now, but without any real grudge, 'I seem to be doing nowt but wash this week. Come on, lass. I can iron these later.'

A little later, as she knelt beside the tin bath in front of the fire, it also crossed Bessie's mind that she had not bathed so many people in one week since her boys had been little.

'What did you do at school today?' Bessie asked as she lathered Mary Ann's hair, massaging the child's scalp with her strong fingers.

'Miss Edwina's learning me 'broidery.'

'Is she now? That's nice. Miss Edwina does lovely embroidery. I'll tek you to the church some time and show you the altar cloth she's done. It's beautiful. There now, bend your head while I pour this jug of clean water over you to rinse off the soap.'

As she stood before the fire, submitting herself to Bessie's vigorous towelling until her skin glowed, Mary Ann asked, 'Where's me present then?'

'There on the fireguard. I thought you'd have noticed by now. Not very observant, are you?'

The girl twisted round to look at the clothes warming on the fireguard. Undergarments and a blue cotton dress with smocking at the neck.

'I did see them,' Mary Ann said, 'but I didn't think they were for me.'

Bessie laughed. 'Well, I don't think I could squeeze into them, do you?'

Mary Ann put her arms round the woman's neck as Bessie knelt on the peg rug and kissed her cheek. The towel slipped from her naked body and Bessie was pleased to see that, whilst she was thin, the girl's skin was a healthy colour and her body firm and supple.

'Come on,' Bessie said, 'let's try them on. Minnie – Mrs Eccleshall – brought them across. She has a daughter. She's away working in service now. But Min's a terrible hoarder and she hasn't thrown her daughter's old clothes out. They're not new, of course, but there's plenty of wear left in them. Put your arms up. That's it.'

Bessie sat back on her heels to look at the girl. 'Fits you a treat. I thought it might be a bit big, but Min's girl was tiny so it's not bad. Not bad at all. Now let's rub your hair dry.'

Towelled dry, Mary Ann's hair fell in curls and waves to her shoulders.

'Black as a raven's feathers and just as shiny now. You've got lovely hair, lass. You ought to learn how to take care of it yourself. Still, enough for now . . .' Bessie pulled herself up. 'I must get the tea. My Bert and the boys'll soon be home.'

'And Dan? When will Dan be home?'

'He's gone back on his ship. Up to Newark this time, I reckon he said. He'll not be back for a day or two.'

'Oh,' Mary Ann said and put her thumb into her mouth.

Nine

After tea, when Bert had gone for his nightly pint and Ernie and Duggie had disappeared, Bessie glanced at the clock on her mantelpiece and said, 'Come on, Mary Ann, I'll take you to see the Aegir. Tonight's a big one. So come on. I don't want to miss it.'

When they arrived at the Miller's Staith, there were already several people lining the steps that led right down to the water's edge.

'There you are, Bessie, I thought you wouldn't miss tonight's tide,' a voice called.

'Saved me a place, have you, Min?' Bessie lumbered down the slippery steps to stand beside her neighbour. 'I thought you'd have called for me.'

'I would've,' Minnie said, 'but I've only just got here mesen on me way back from town. If I'd come home first, I'd have missed it.'

'Oh well, in that case,' Bessie's eyes twinkled with mischief, 'I forgive you.'

'Ta very much, I'm sure.'

The two women smiled at each other and then, as someone shouted, 'It's coming,' they turned, like everyone else, to look downriver, leaning dangerously forward to get a better view.

Bessie grabbed hold of Mary Ann. 'Don't you go falling in the water and get swept away. We'd never find you.'

''Course the best place to see it,' Minnie said, 'is Bourton corner.'

Bessie nodded excitedly. 'Yes, yes, it is. It swirls round that corner and you think it's going to come up and over the bank.'

'Wouldn't be the first time,' Minnie muttered and then, her excitement rising too, she clutched Bessie's hand and said, 'Here it comes, Bessie. Here it comes.'

The tidal wave, foaming at the crest, swept majestically up the river, rippling up the banks on either side and rocking the boats moored at the wharves. Behind the first wave front, which raised the level of the whole river until the tide ebbed, came smaller ripples, the whelps, like young following their mother.

'I don't like it,' Mary Ann cried, clinging to Bessie.

'Don't be silly, it won't hurt you.' For once Bessie was irritated by the girl's childishness. Nevertheless, she held on tightly to the girl's hand, afraid that Mary Ann might try to get away and, in so doing, topple into the water. 'Don't you think it's lovely? Just look at that big wave. Come all the way from the North Sea, that has, Mary Ann. Right up our river for miles and miles.'

The water surged just below where they were standing and splashed up the steps, sending spray on to their feet.

'I don't like it,' the girl wailed. She pulled herself out of Bessie's grasp, turned to scramble back up the steps and pushed her way through the watchers.

'Mary Ann, wait. Wait for me,' Bessie cried and turned to follow her, but felt Minnie's hand restrain her.

'Let her go, Bess. She'll find her way home. It's only across River Road. Don't let her spoil your fun. We shan't see another one like this for a while. Just you enjoy it.'

Bessie turned back towards the river, but Mary Ann being so silly had spoiled her excitement and her pleasure, and the wave was gone now, leaving only ripples in its wake. The onlookers began to disperse.

'I suppose,' Bessie said to Minnie, thinking aloud, her generous nature forgiving the girl's foolishness already, 'I shouldn't have expected her to love the river like we do, Min. The Aegir can be a bit frightening if you've never seen anything like it before.'

'I 'spect she's not used to the water,' Minnie suggested.

Bessie shook her head. 'Probably not. She told me she'd never even seen the sea.'

'There you are then,' Minnie said, as if that explained everything.

The two friends reached the top of the steps and turned to smile at each other.

'I'd better go and find her and see if she's all right,' Bessie said as they approached Waterman's Yard.

Minnie sniffed. 'She'll be all right, Bess. Do you know, I've never seen you fuss after anyone so much in all me life? An' that's saying summat.'

'Mebbe it's because I've never had a little girl of me own,' Bessie said wistfully.

'That little madam's got you wrapped around her little finger, Bess. You want to watch it.'

But Bessie only smiled.

A week later, Elsie Clark was still not home from the hospital and Mary Ann continued to stay with the Ruddick family.

'What gets me, Bert,' Bessie murmured sadly as they lay side by side in bed, 'is that Mary Ann doesn't seem bothered about either of them. Her dad or her mam. Now 'im, I can understand, but you'd've thought she'd have wanted to go to see her mother in the hospital.'

'I thought you took her on Sunday afternoon?' Bert murmured sleepily.

'I did, but I nearly had to drag her there.'

'Wasn't she pleased to see her mam when you got there then?'

There was a moment's silence whilst Bessie lay staring into the blackness, thinking. 'I suppose so,' she said at last. 'But it was odd. Not like I'd have expected a young girl to act when she hadn't seen her mam for several days. I mean, I wouldn't have liked my lads to act like that if I was in hospital, Bert.'

Bert's soft chuckle came through the darkness. 'Bess, my angel, if you were ever in hospital – God forbid,' he added with fervent reverence, 'me and the lads would be camping outside that hospital door, I can tell you.' Then he went on, 'And was her *mam* pleased to see *her*?'

'Well, yes,' Bessie said slowly. 'Sort of, but even then it wasn't how I would have been if I hadn't seen one of me own for a few days. Elsie thanked me for looking after Mary Ann and told her to be a good girl and that, but there wasn't the affection there, the love. You know?'

'Mm, I can guess what you mean.' He turned on his side, preparing for sleep. 'Ne'er mind, Bess, we've enough love in this house to spare a bit for that little lass, haven't we?'

Not for the first time in her life, Bessie thanked the good Lord who had brought Bert Ruddick to her. As a young girl Bessie had been obliged to leave the river to go into service, yet she had always hankered to return to life afloat. Her marriage to Bert had put an end to those dreams, but her happy years with him had been worth the sacrifice. Although, Bessie chuckled to herself softly in the darkness, it wouldn't do to tell him that too often.

*

One afternoon, Edwina accompanied Mary Ann home from school, stepping into Bessie's kitchen and sitting down, completely at ease in surroundings that were very different to her own home.

She drew off her gloves and said, 'I'm lending Mary Ann an embroidery frame. May we fix it to the edge of your table, Bessie?'

'Of course you can.'

From her bag, Edwina took out a small circular frame with two rings of wood, which fitted over each other, the outer one with a tightening screw. She fitted the frame to the table by means of a clamp and then she stretched a piece of canvas over the smaller of the two rings and placed the larger one over it so that the material was trapped between the two and stretched tightly.

'That leaves you free to work with both hands,' she explained. Taking a blunt-ended embroidery needle, she threaded it with coloured silk and took a couple of running stitches through the fabric to secure it.

'Now, Mary Ann, watch carefully. We call this cross-stitch or gros-point. You make a diagonal stitch like this and then you bring your needle back up through there and then down again through that tiny square, crossing over the first stitch you've just made,' Edwina explained. 'But all the top stitches must lie the same way, usually from the bottom left to the top right corner. See? Now you try.'

The young girl's black hair, which Bessie had washed again earlier that day, was shining, tied back now from falling in unruly curls around her face. Her expression was one of rapt concentration as she followed the gentle guidance of the young woman sitting beside her. Edwina's fair head bent close to the young girl's and Bessie was pleased to see that the sombre black which Edwina had worn for more than a year following the deaths of her brother and her fiancé had now been replaced by a smart, close-fitting costume of deep purple. It was still too dark a colour for Bessie's liking, but it was a start, she told herself. She liked to see Miss Edwina in royal blue, a vibrant colour that complemented her hair colouring and accentuated the colour of her eyes. But those eyes had not sparkled with joyous laughter for a long time now. Edwina was still the gentle, kind young woman she had always been, but the light had gone out of her eyes and out of her life.

Bessie sighed. So many lives lost in that dreadful war with scarcely a family untouched by its tragedy.

She fervently hoped that what they said was true, that it was the war to end all wars.

'That's very good, Mary Ann,' Edwina was saying. 'Come and see, Bessie, how neat Mary Ann's stitches are.'

Bessie stood behind them, peering over to see the girl's work. 'They are,' she said, unable to keep the surprise from her tone. 'Have you done sewing before? Has your mam taught you?'

Mary Ann shook her head.

'I reckon you've got a natural talent then, lass. What do you say, Miss Edwina?'

'It's a little early to say that, I think, but she's certainly a fast learner.' Edwina smiled. 'At least, at sewing and embroidery.'

The girl looked up and her own smile transformed her face. Her brown eyes sparkled with mischief and the dimples in her cheeks deepened. 'I like doing this much better than horrid sums and reading stuffy books. And who'd I want to be writing to anyway? Only Dan.' She giggled. 'And the postman doesn't deliver to his ship.'

Edwina laughed and, as she rose from her chair, she touched the girl's hair in an affectionate gesture. 'Well, as long as you promise me you will still try hard with your sums and your reading and writing, I'll promise to teach you all I can about embroidery. How's that, eh?'

The girl pulled a wry face, but then smiled. 'All right, as long as you promise that I'll be able to sew as good as you. I'll be able to make an altar cloth like the one Auntie Bessie showed me in the church that you'd done, won't I? I'll be able to dedicate to all sailors like Dan?'

For a moment Edwina's eyes were bright with tears. Bessie held her breath. The child had unwittingly touched a raw nerve.

During the time Mary Ann had been staying with them, Bessie had taken her into the parish church to see the beautiful altar frontal that Edwina had worked.

'She did it after she lost her brother and the young man, Christopher, she was going to marry,' Bessie had told Mary Ann as they stood admiring the beautiful purple brocade material with intricate embroidery worked in gold thread. 'They were killed in the war and she presented it to the church in their memory.'

The girl had been silent as they walked down the long path from the church. As they crossed the road, Bessie had pointed and said, 'And that's where Miss Edwina's family lives.'

The Hall was a large, timber-framed medieval manor house, the centre of which was the great hall, with wings of smaller chambers to the east and west. At one corner stood a brick tower with turrets and ramparts and arched leaded glass windows.

'They reckon Henry the eighth once slept there.'

'Who's Henry the eighth?'

'Ah well, now, you'd better ask Miss Edwina that, lass. All I know about him is that he had six wives.'

'Six? All at once?'

'Oh, I don't think so.' Bessie had scrabbled back in her

mind, trying to recall her scant lessons in history. Failing to remember more, she took refuge in Edwina's name again. 'You ask Miss Edwina. She'll know.'

Mary Ann had glanced back before the church disappeared from their view as they turned a corner. 'I'd sooner she learnt me how to 'broider,' Bessie had heard her murmur.

'I'm sure she will if you ask her nicely.'

That was how it had started. Since that day Mary Ann's only interest in her education had been centred solely on learning how to embroider. Bessie and Edwina contrived together to encourage the girl as much as they could and yet at the same time coax her to try harder at her other lessons.

Now, they moved away from Mary Ann, whose head bent over the frame and whose nimble fingers threaded the needle in and out of the canvas with amazing sureness.

'I think you're right, Bessie,' Edwina said in a low voice as the two women moved into Bessie's back scullery so that the girl should not overhear their conversation. 'I think she could well have a natural talent. I noticed it the very first time I gave her some sewing to do at school.' Edwina smiled. 'It's just a shame that her interest in writing and sums isn't as great.'

'Oh well, we can't be good at everything. I'm not much good with sums mesen.' Bessie smiled broadly. 'I leave all that to Bert. He's the clever one.'

'Now come, Bessie, don't belittle yourself. You're a wonderful wife and mother. A marvellous homemaker and . . .'

'Go on with you, Miss Edwina,' Bessie laughed.

'It's not flattery, I assure you. Mary Ann could do a lot worse than follow your example.'

Bessie sighed. 'Well, I'll try to help the little lass as

much as I can as long as they're here, 'cos I've really taken to her. And so have Bert and the lads.'

'She certainly seems to have taken to your Dan.'

Bessie laughed. 'She idolizes him. Trots after him everywhere he goes when he's home, given half a chance. And when he's away, she brings his name into every conversation nearly.'

'She talks about him a lot at school, too, and when I give her an essay to do, it's always about Dan or this family.' Edwina paused and then asked, 'What did you mean just now when you said, "as long as they're here"?'

Bessie shrugged. 'It seems the Clark family move about a lot. They've been here a month now and according to what Mary Ann says that's about the longest they've stayed anywhere recently. I had a run in with her dad when they first came and one or two since then, too.' Bessie's mouth tightened. 'You know she's in hospital, don't you? Her mam?'

Edwina nodded. 'How is she?'

Wryly, Bessie said, 'Doesn't seem too anxious to come home. And who can blame her? But when she does, he'd better watch out 'cos I'm not putting up with 'im knocking her about any longer. These walls . . .' she jerked her thumb towards the wall between her own home and the Clarks' house, 'are pretty thin. I can hear everything that goes on, so I'll be keeping me ear out for any more bumps and thumps.'

'Do you get a chance to talk to Mrs Clark?'

Bessie shook her head. 'I've talked to her more in the hospital than I do when she's here. Keeps hersen shut away in the house. Only comes out now and again to go to the shops and then she scuttles in and out of the yard as fast as she can. Bert has a pint now and again in The Waterman's . . . with him.' Bessie's voice was scathing as if she could not bring herself to give her neighbour even the common courtesy of using his name. 'Mind you, I don't hold with him being pals with the feller.' Her shoulders lifted again as she added reflectively, 'But maybe my Bert's right in what he says.'

Edwina hid her smile and asked, 'And what does your Bert say?'

'That if we're friendly with them, then maybe we can help all the more.'

'I think he has a point,' Edwina said softly. 'It certainly means we – and I do mean "we", Bessie – can help Mary Ann more.'

'I'd like to try and help her mam, but I can't get close to her. I have tried. I've been to visit her a couple of times in the hospital without Mary Ann and tried to talk to her, but she just clams up.'

'I'm sure you've done your best,' Edwina soothed.

'I can't be doing with these folks who shut themselves away. There's another one across there.' Bessie nodded towards the house in the corner of the yard. 'Amy Hamilton. I know she's suffered a terrible loss. But she's not the only one.' Bessie's eyes softened and briefly she reached out and touched Edwina's hand. 'I wish she had more of your spirit, lass.'

The sadness in Edwina's eyes deepened and there was a catch in her voice as she said softly, 'To lose a husband and a son must be even harder than the loss I've had to bear. I know my own mother and Christopher's mother too are devastated. It – it just seems such a tragic waste of young lives.'

Bessie was frowning. 'From the bit I did glean from Elsie Clark, it's something to do with the war that's made her husband act the way he does.'

'The men suffered some horrific experiences. Perhaps Mr Clark is to be pitied rather than blamed, Bessie.'

Bessie was not prepared to be quite so understanding. 'Mebbe you're right, Miss Edwina. Even so, I don't reckon it gives him the right to knock his wife and bairn about, do you?'

In that Edwina had to agree. 'No, Bessie, I don't.'

Mary Ann was still sitting at the table late in the afternoon when Dan flung open the back door with a flourish and called, 'Mam, Mam, you there? I'm home and I've brought Susan to see you.'

Bessie straightened up from the range oven where she had just placed a steak and kidney pie to cook for her family's tea, but she had no time to move to meet her son and his young lady or even to call out a greeting, before Mary Ann gave a delighted shriek, dropped her needle and jumped up from her chair, knocking it backwards on to the floor in her haste. As Dan appeared in the doorway, Mary Ann flung herself at him so that the big man lifted her up into his arms and swung her round.

'Hello, little 'un. My, you're looking bonnie. That's a pretty dress. It suits you.'

He set the girl on the floor and stood back to admire her. Mary Ann preened and twirled around in front of him, holding out the skirt of her yellow cotton dress like a dancer pirouetting before an appreciative audience.

'Your mam got it for me from the market and Miss Edwina shortened it for me because it was too long.'

'It looks very nice.' He smiled down at her. 'Very grown up.'

Nothing he could have said could have pleased her

more, but as he stepped aside and drew the girl standing behind him forward, the smile on Mary Ann's face faded.

'This is Susan. We're . . .' The tall, good-looking young man seemed suddenly embarrassed. 'We're walking out together.' He glanced towards his mother. 'I talked to Susan's father yesterday and he's agreed we can see each other.' He put his arm around Susan. 'So now we've come to tell you.'

Bessie lumbered towards them, throwing her arms wide, trying to embrace them both at once. She let out such a bellow of laughter, it seemed to shake the walls. 'That's wonderful. You're very welcome, love. Make yourself at home. You'll stay and have tea with us, won't you, 'cos my Bert'll want to see you?'

As Bessie chattered on excitedly, she was uncomfortably aware that Mary Ann was standing very still and silent now, staring resentfully at the newcomer.

Ten

'When's the wedding, then?' Duggie teased, as the Ruddick family sat around the table. The stranger in their midst blushed. She was not really a stranger, for she was the daughter of the owner of the ship on which Dan served as mate, but it was the first time she had visited their home as the girl Dan was courting.

'Take no notice of him, love,' Bessie said and lightly pinched her youngest son's ear lobe. 'You just behave yourself, our Duggie.'

But Dan only grinned. 'Not for a while yet. Not until I've got me own ship.'

Duggie let out a guffaw. 'Reckon you'll be waiting a long time then, Susan.'

Ignoring him, Dan turned to her. 'We could live aboard then. You wouldn't mind that, would you?'

Susan's blush deepened and she glanced up shyly. In a soft voice, she said, 'Of course not. I was born aboard the *Nerissa*. It was only when my elder brother reached school age that we got a house on shore.'

Bessie beamed, but before she could open her mouth there came a chorus from all her family, who knew her so well that they could predict her words. 'Eh, that'd be grand, our Dan. It'd be just like the old days.'

Bessie let out such a loud laugh that soon the whole family was convulsed. Even Susan, her shyness forgotten

81

amidst such warmth, leant against Dan's shoulder, laughing until the tears ran down her face.

The only person at the table not joining in the merriment was Mary Ann.

'I hear your Dan's courting, then?'

'Aye, I thought you'd be first to know, Phyllis, but keep
it to yasen for a day or two, will you? I haven't even had
chance to tell Min and Gladys, let alone Amy.'

Phyllis smiled. 'My lips are sealed.'

Bessie cast her a wry glance and gave a grunt of
disbelief as she thrust a peg firmly over Bert's long johns
on the washing line. Phyllis Horberry couldn't keep a
secret no matter what dire threats were made. A grapevine
was nowhere in it, Bessie thought. Phyllis was more like
a town crier when there was a choice bit of gossip going
the rounds. Bessie sometimes wondered whether Phyllis
herself didn't sometimes start the rumours.

'I reckon she sits up at night making it all up,' Bessie
had said to Bert on more than one occasion when Phyllis's
latest bit of tittle-tattle seemed particularly incredible.

On this occasion, however, Bessie could not, nor
indeed had she any wish to, refute Phyllis's statement.

Phyllis Horberry seemed to consider herself a little
above the other inhabitants of Waterman's Yard. She
always dressed smartly and, as much as her purse would
allow, tried to follow the fashion of the day. Her husband,
Tom, was the local lamplighter and Phyllis worked in a
draper's shop in Pottergate. Neither of them had any
connection with the river whereas both Minnie's husband,
Stan, and Gladys Merryweather's Walter worked, like
Bert Ruddick, as casual purchase-men.

'So when's the wedding?'

'Give 'em half a chance, Phyllis. They've only been walking out officially for a couple of days. You'll have me with grandbairns before I can turn round.'

'You'd like that, though, wouldn't you, Bessie?'

Bessie's expression softened. 'Aye, I would.'

Phyllis nodded beyond Bessie's shoulder. 'Looks like you've got a ready made one already, the time she spends at your house.'

Bessie smiled. She had no need to turn round to see Mary Ann coming towards them.

'Hello, love,' Phyllis smiled. 'How are you? How's your mam? I haven't seen her about lately. Is she poorly?'

Bessie hid her smile. It was by no means the first time she had witnessed Phyllis swinging into action. This was how she found out all her news. A barrage of questions so that her 'victim' felt obliged to answer.

Not so Mary Ann. The girl merely stared up at the woman, her thumb in her mouth, and said nothing.

'Cat got ya tongue?' Phyllis said, though not unkindly. 'Well, I'll have to be off. Can't stand here chatting all day. See ya, Bessie.'

'Bye, Phyllis. Now, love . . .' she turned to Mary Ann. 'You off to school then?'

Mary Ann said nothing but continued to stare, now at Bessie.

'Off you go, then. Your mam's coming home today but you can still come and see me when you get home tonight. I'll be doing me ironing if this lot manages to get dry today.' She pulled a comical face. 'And I'll be very pleased to be interrupted.' Still there was no response from the girl. 'You can stay to your tea with us if your mam doesn't mind, although I 'spect she'd like to see you herself, wouldn't she?'

Her brown gaze still steadily upon Bessie, Mary Ann asked, 'Will *she* be there again? With Dan?'

'Amy.' Bessie banged on her neighbour's door. 'Amy, love, are you there?'

The door flew open. 'There's no rest for the wicked when you're around, is there, Bessie?'

Bessie grinned and stepped across Amy's threshold. 'I've brought you a steak and kidney pie, love. It's nice and hot so pop it in your oven to keep warm while you do yourself a few taties.' Bessie looked at her neighbour. Amy was looking much better, so she risked a gentle jibe. 'You ain't forgotten how to peel a few taties and boil 'em, 'ave ya?'

The smile, so long unused, began tentatively at the corner of Amy's mouth and then, quivering, spread across her face. Then she reached up and put her arms about Bessie and laid her head against her shoulder. 'Oh Bessie, what would I do without you? What would any of us do without you?'

Embarrassed by the unaccustomed display of affection, Bessie patted Amy's back. 'There, there, you'll be all right, Amy love. You'll be all right.'

Her voice muffled against Bessie's shoulder, Amy said, 'It'll only be thanks to you if I am.'

'Come on, now, before I drop this pie.'

Amy stood back and wiped the tears from her eyes. 'You're right, Bessie. I know you are. My George wouldn't have wanted me to carry on this way. I will try, really I will.'

Bessie beamed with delight and relief. 'I'm pleased to hear it,' she said, as she bent to put the pie in the oven of Amy's range. She closed the door and straightened up again. 'And your Ron wouldn't want to see his mam grieving like this either, Amy. He were a lovely lad – bright as a button and never without a smile for you, even if he was a bit on the shy side. He'd not have liked to see you this unhappy for the rest of your days, now would he?'

Amy's lower lip trembled and she caught it between her teeth. Tears welled in her eyes again and Bessie thought for a moment that she had pushed things too far too soon. But then, Amy nodded and said, 'You're right, Bessie. I know you are. But it's just . . . so hard.'

Bessie patted her friend's arm but for once could find no words. She couldn't say, 'I know,' because she didn't. She didn't know what it would be like to lose her Bert and one of her lads. At the mere thought of it happening, Bessie could feel her throat constrict and tears prickle at the back of her eyelids, but she could only guess at the devastation this poor woman must be feeling at the loss of both her husband and her only child. That was the reason that Bessie's patience for Amy's grief was unlimited.

'You know, Min,' Bessie said a short while later to her friend, 'I reckon Amy's really on the mend. Oh, she'll never get over it. I 'spect you never do get over something like that, do you? But I reckon she's starting to pull herself together a bit.'

'Not before time,' Minnie replied tartly.

'Don't be too hard on her, Min.'

Minnie smiled across the kitchen table as the two women, their week's washing hanging together on the lines outside in the yard, took a well-earned break over a cup of tea and a biscuit. 'You're a funny woman, Bessie

Ruddick, and no mistake. Ranting and raving one minute and soft as a brush the next.'

Bessie shook with laughter. 'That's me, Min. That's me to a tee.'

Min laughed with her. 'But I wouldn't change you, Bessie. Not one hair of your head. Life's certainly never dull when you're around.' She took a sip of her tea and then asked, 'So, what's your next project? The woman next door, I take it, 'cos you seem to have taken charge of the little lass already.'

Bessie sighed heavily. 'D'you know, Min, for once in me life I don't know what to do. I have to admit I've never come across a feller before who knocks his missis about. I know we've got a few ruffians living in the yards, I can't deny that. One or two drunks, the odd gambler here and there and one or two not quite as honest as they might be, but in the main, the river folk are a hard-working lot and I've always been proud to be one of 'em, but him, well . . .'

'He's not one of us, though, is he? I mean, he's nowt to do with the river, is he?'

'No. He's a drayman. So she says. But where he works now, I don't know. He goes off every morning as if he's going to some sort of work somewhere, but that's all I know.'

Minnie laughed. 'It's a mystery, all right. But I know the very woman to solve it.'

Both women laughed as together they said, 'Phyllis!'

Eleven

'Hello, Elsie. How are you?' No one was more surprised than Bessie to see their new neighbour struggling up the alleyway between the houses and across the yard laden with shopping bags. 'Been doing your Christmas shopping? It'll soon be on us now, won't it? Only three weeks to go.'

Elsie Clark lowered her bags and put her hand on her thin chest. But there was a smile on her face as she said, 'This is going to be our best Christmas ever. Sid's got a good job and he likes it here.' She nodded towards Bessie. 'Your husband's made him feel welcome, having a pint with him in the pub, an' that. I'm very grateful. He's settled down a lot now.' She gave a nervous laugh and added, 'If you know what I mean. And as for our Mary Ann, I never have seen her so happy.'

In the weeks since Elsie had been home from the hospital, Bessie had not once heard the Clarks quarrelling. Elsie's arm was better and there were no bruises on her face.

'I'm glad, love. Here, let me help you with those.'

'Oh no, no, it's all right,' Elsie said quickly. She bent and picked up the bags again. 'I didn't get cleared up before I went out. Me kitchen's a tip.'

Bessie laughed. 'You've no need to feel embarrassed on my account. You should see mine sometimes. Looks like it's been hit by a tidal wave. I remember sometimes on board ship when I was a bairn, 'cos the weather can be rough, 'specially in the mouth of the Humber near Hull, y'know. Well . . .'

'I'm sorry, Mrs Ruddick . . .'

'Call me "Bessie". Everyone else does.' Bessie gave a raucous laugh. 'I hardly know who you're talking about when you say "Mrs Ruddick".'

'All right, Bessie, then. But I must go. Sid'll be back soon and I haven't got his tea ready. Is Mary Ann home? Have you seen her?'

Bessie shook her head. 'Now you mention it, I haven't. I hadn't realized it'd got so late.'

'I wonder where she's got to?' Worriedly, the woman murmured almost beneath her breath so that Bessie had to strain to catch the words, 'I hope she's home before Sid, else there'll be trouble.'

'I bet I know where she is,' Bessie said suddenly as she remembered. 'Dan's ship's unloading at Miller's Wharf. Look, you go and see to your shopping and start your old man's tea and I'll go and look for her. I bet the little minx is there.'

'But what about your own tea?'

'In the oven keeping hot. They all come in at different times, my menfolk, so I have it ready early, all plated up for when they decide to appear.'

'Well,' Elsie said, doubtfully, 'if you're sure, I would be grateful.'

'Off you go, love. I'll go and find her.'

Mary Ann was not at the wharf.

'Hello, Mam. What are you doing here?' Dan greeted his mother. 'Come to hold me hand on the way 'ome, have ya? We're just about done, so if you hang on a minute . . .'

Bessie's laugh echoed across the dark waters of the

river. 'I don't reckon it's your old mam's hand you want to be holding, is it, lad? Not now. No, I'm looking for Mary Ann. She's not come home from school. I thought she'd be here waiting for you. Have you seen her?'

Dan shook his head and a worried frown creased his forehead. 'It's a bit late for her to be out, isn't it, now it's dark so early? School finished ages ago, didn't it?'

Bessie nodded. 'Yes. I thought she'd be here. I told her mam not to worry, that I'd come and find her. I was so sure she'd be here.'

'We'd best get looking for her then, hadn't we?'

'Well, yes, but you must be tired and hungry.'

'No "buts", Mam, I'll help you find her.'

They had walked away from the wharf and were now standing in River Road.

'Do you think she could still be at school?' Dan asked.

'She could, I suppose. But it wouldn't be like Miss Edwina to keep her there this late. Not without letting her mam or me know.'

'Could she have got lost?'

'She shouldn't have. She knows the way home well enough by now, unless . . .' Bessie pondered and bit her lower lip.

'What, Mam?'

'It is nearly Christmas and all the shops in the town are so pretty. I shouldn't think the poor little mite's expecting to get much for Christmas. Maybe she just went to have a look, you know.'

'And she might have got lost, you mean?'

'I don't think she knows the town very well. She's been into Pottergate and the Market Place with me a couple of times, but if she took a wrong turning . . .'

'Come on, we'll go and see if we can find her.'

Together Bessie and Dan wound their way through the

narrow streets where the houses were so tall on either side that the alleyways were dark even on the brightest day. Now, they would have been pitch black if Phyllis's husband, Tom Horberry, hadn't been round already to light the lamps on the brackets set high on the wall. Twisting and turning, they came to one of the town's main streets. Pottergate ran down to the river ending in the Packet Landing, where boats and the steam packet to Hull moored. Rounding the corner by the Woolpack Hotel, which stood close to the Packet Landing, its clientele travellers on the early boats to Hull, Bessie suggested, 'We'll walk up towards the Market Place. That's where she might be.'

Now they were passing shops which, tonight, were all keeping late hours to catch the Christmas shoppers. A baker's where mince pies, Christmas cakes and chocolate Yule logs filled the window. Then a flower shop where Christmas trees stood on the pavement outside, leaning drunkenly against the windows, whilst holly wreathes and bunches of mistletoe adorned the inside.

Past the shoemaker's, the grocer's and a china shop they walked without even glancing in the windows. Usually, Bessie loved ambling down Pottergate and would dawdle to look in every shop, but tonight she was anxious and hurried on, panting a little, as fast as she could. Dan, with long, easy strides, kept his pace to match his mother's. He too ignored the shops, his worried glance scanning the milling crowd.

'Happy Christmas to you, Bessie.' A voice came out of the shadows and she turned to see Tom Horberry wobbling down the middle of the street on his bicycle.

'And to you, Tom,' Bessie replied automatically and then added swiftly, 'have you seen Mary Ann?'

Tom dismounted and wheeled his bicycle towards

them, and in the glow from the lighted shop windows, Bessie could see the puzzlement on his face.

'You know,' she said, unable to keep the impatience from her tone, 'the lass who's come to live in the yard. Next door to us.'

Tom's expression cleared. 'Oh aye, I know who you mean now.' Then he shook his head. 'No, sorry, I haven't. Lost, is she?'

'I hope not,' Bessie muttered. Already she was moving on.

'I'll keep a look out on me way home, Bessie,' Tom called after them. 'If I see her, I'll take her home with me.'

Bessie waved her hand in acknowledgement and called back over her shoulder. 'Right you are.' Then in a lower voice she murmured to Dan, 'But I doubt she'll go with him. I don't think she even knows him. And she's funny with men, isn't she?'

'I think she's getting better. She was laughing with our Duggie the other day.'

Despite her anxiety, Bessie grinned. 'Well, who wouldn't?'

On they went again until they reached the jewellers' on the corner where the street opened out in the Market Place.

'There she is,' Dan said suddenly.

'Where? Where?'

He pointed. 'Over there. Just coming out of that draper's shop.'

'That's where Phyllis works. Mebbe she's been talking to her. And just look at her,' Bessie said, 'skipping along as if she hasn't a care in the world and us worried half to death.'

She felt Dan's hand on her arm. 'Now, Mam, don't have a go at her. That little lass doesn't get a lot of fun in her life and you're only mad at her 'cos you've been worried. After all, she's old enough to go into the town by herself now, isn't she?'

Bessie's anger subsided in a second. 'Yes, you're right, lad. But even so, she ought to know just to tell one of us where she's going. Even if her mam wasn't at home, I was. Or one of the other neighbours.'

She saw Dan's white teeth as he grinned at her in the dim light. 'Let me tell her, she'll take it better from me.'

'You're right there, lad. All right, you just give her a gentle ticking off and I'll say no more about it.'

As they neared Mary Ann, Bessie raised her voice. 'There you are, love. We thought you'd got lost.'

At the sound of her voice, Mary Ann stopped, and when she saw Dan, she gave a little hop of delight and ran towards them. 'Dan, Auntie Bessie. Were you looking for me?'

She pressed herself between them and linked her arms through theirs.

'We just wondered where you'd got to, love,' Dan said gently, looking down at her. Bessie noticed that there was a note of firmness in his tone as he added, 'You ought to let one of us know where you're going, though, if you're not coming straight home from school. 'Specially now it's getting dark earlier. All right?'

Bessie saw the girl glance up at him, adoration in her eyes. 'All right, Dan. I'm sorry if you were worried . . .' She turned her head briefly to include Bessie. 'I won't do it again.'

'Good girl, but just say you're sorry to your mam as well, won't you?'

Mary Ann laughed. 'She'll not care. She'll not notice I'm not there.'

'That's where you're wrong,' Bessie couldn't stop herself from saying now, 'because it was the first thing she asked me when she got back from shopping. Were you home?'

Mary Ann stopped suddenly and, with her arms through theirs, both Bessie and Dan were brought to a halt too. 'Shopping? Me mam? Me mam's been out shopping?'

Puzzled, Bessie looked down at her. 'Well, yes. It's nearly Christmas.'

'But me mam never goes out shopping. She . . .' For a moment Mary Ann hesitated and then blurted out, 'She hasn't any money.'

'She must have. How does she buy food and that?'

In a small voice, Mary Ann said, 'Me dad gets the food.'

Bessie was quick to notice that the girl said 'gets' and not 'buys' and for a brief second she wondered if Mary Ann was implying that her father stole what they ate.

Her next words refuted this. 'Me dad goes to the market last thing, when the stall-holders are closing up, you know. He gets bargains and he haggles with the stall-holders till he gets things for . . . for next to nothing. He says me mam's too weak to argue. She'd give in and pay them what they asked.'

Above her head Bessie exchanged a glance with Dan as they moved on again.

'She's been out shopping this afternoon 'cos I saw her come back mesen loaded with heavy bags.'

'Maybe she's been out buying your Christmas present, eh?' Dan grinned down at her.

Mary Ann grimaced as if she did not believe it, but then she smiled coyly up at him as she said, 'That's what

I've been doing. I've been getting you a Christmas present.'

'Me? Now why should you go spending your money on me, love?'

''Cos I wanted to.'

The uneasy feeling crept over Bessie again. 'Getting' not 'buying' the girl had said.

Keeping her tone deliberately light, she asked, 'Been saving your pocket money, have you?'

'Oh no, I don't get any pocket money.'

There was silence before Bessie was obliged to ask, 'So where did you get the money to buy Dan a present?'

Mary Ann replied promptly without a hint of hesitation. 'Miss Edwina gave me some.'

'Oh,' Bessie said, unsure now what to say. Had the girl asked Miss Edwina or had that kindly soul realized that poor Mary Ann would have no money of her own with which to buy presents? She resolved to have a quiet word with Edwina, but now all she said was, 'That was very kind of her.'

Bessie felt Mary Ann squeeze her arm. 'I'll show you later, Auntie Bessie, but you've to promise faithfully not to tell Dan.'

Beside them, Bessie heard Dan's deep chuckle.

'I reckon we'll have a party on Boxing Day evening. What d'you say, Bert?'

'Whatever you like, my angel.' Bert knew better than to point out that it would be a lot of expense and hard work for his Bessie. He didn't mind the cost so much; the lads were all very good and chipped in with extra housekeeping money for their mother at such times. But he did worry about all the extra work it would mean for his wife. He knew she worked from dawn to dusk – and beyond – to look after him and their three sons, besides involving herself with the neighbours and their problems. To his Bessie, the inhabitants of Waterman's Yard were one big family, even, he smiled to himself, Sid Clark.

It was as if she could read his mind, for her next words were, 'I suppose we'll have to ask *him* from next door?'

'You can't very well leave him out, can you, love? After all, Mary Ann's bound to be here and I expect you'll want to ask Elsie. So . . .' He spread his hands.

'Yeah,' Bessie sighed, but planted a kiss on the top of his thinning hair as she passed his chair. 'You're right, Bert. I couldn't bring mesen to miss him out, 'specially not at Christmas.'

Bert chuckled and asked impishly, 'So, have you bought him a present?'

'No, I have not,' was the swift retort. Then, realizing he was teasing her, she grinned and added, 'I'll leave that to you. An extra pint in the pub, eh?'

Bert pretended to groan. 'Why do I dig a hole for myself every time?'

''Cos you're an old softie and I always have to have the last word.'

Bert looked up at her coyly, 'Well, most of the time, my angel. Only most of the time.'

'Talking of presents, Mary Ann's embroidering a handkerchief for Dan with a big curly "D" in one corner. She says that she's doing something for me at school. Miss Edwina's helping her, but she won't tell me what it is. Says it's to be a surprise. And that reminds me,' Bessie murmured more to herself now than to Bert, 'I still haven't had a word with Miss Edwina about the money. Reckon I'll have a walk up to the school tomorrow morning.'

Twelve

'So did the little minx ask you for money to buy a present for Dan?'

Edwina bit her lip. 'Er, well, not exactly.'

Bessie nodded and smiled, 'Ah, I thought so. You gave her some. Oh Miss Edwina, you are good, you—'

Edwina was shaking her head. Softly she said, 'No, Bessie, I didn't give her any money.' She met Bessie's gaze steadily and the sadness that was always in her eyes deepened, but now for a very different reason. 'Two shillings went missing out of my purse last Thursday.'

Bessie closed her eyes and groaned. 'Oh no.'

'I thought, at first, it was the kitchen maid. But she's been here six months and nothing has ever gone missing before. Then I remembered I sent Mary Ann from the classroom to fetch a book from my office.' Edwina waved her hand to indicate the bookcase standing against one wall of the room where they were sitting. 'My purse was lying here on my desk.' She spread her hands. 'I know, I know, it was careless of me. I shouldn't have left it lying about, but I didn't think that anyone here would . . .' Her voice trailed away sadly.

'What are you going to do? Bring the police in?'

'Oh no, Bessie. Heavens! Not for two shillings.'

Bessie shook her head. 'It's not the amount that matters, Miss Edwina, if you don't mind me saying so. It's the principle.'

'Well, yes, but . . .' Edwina put her hand to her fore-head. 'Oh dear, how silly of me to have put temptation in that poor child's way. She has so little in her life. I should have realized.'

Bessie gave a wry sniff of disapproval. 'Don't blame yourself, Miss Edwina. You're not used to having children in your school whose parents haven't a ha'penny to scratch their backsides with. If anyone's to blame, then it's me for bringing her to you. Besides, she should know better than to go stealing. Her circumstances aren't *that* bad. Mind you,' Bessie's kind heart forced her to reconsider, 'with Sid Clark for her dad, it isn't any wonder really.'

'What do you know about her background?'

'Very little. I haven't learnt any more about the family since the day I brought her here. They're a close lot. He doesn't even loosen his tongue when he's having a pint with my Bert.' Grimly, she added, 'Mebbe they have got summat to hide.'

Edwina sighed heavily. 'Do you want to be here when I speak to her?'

Bessie considered for a moment. 'No. 'Tain't my place, really. If anyone ought to be here it's her mother. Or her father, God forbid! But not me.' She heaved herself to her feet. 'What are you going to do, Miss Edwina? Expel her?'

'Goodness, no!' Edwina was shocked. 'I'm going to try to help her.'

'It's very good of you. Maybe too good. I hope she won't throw your kindness back in your face.'

Edwina, too, rose and walked with Bessie to the door. 'Leave it with me. I'll give the matter some thought before I do anything.' She sighed as she added, 'It's at this sort of time that I miss Christopher the most. He was so calm and level-headed in a situation like this. He would have known exactly the best way to handle it. And he was kind as well, he wouldn't have wanted to be too harsh on the child, I know.'

Bessie patted Miss Edwina's hand. 'You'll do the right thing, I know you will.'

When Mary Ann arrived home that afternoon, Bessie saw her crossing the yard and going straight to her own home instead of skipping into the Ruddick house as she always did.

Oh dear, Bessie thought, it looks like Miss Edwina's said something already and the girl daren't face me. But half an hour later Mary Ann appeared at Bessie's back door, holding two badly wrapped small parcels in her hand.

Bessie noticed at once that although there was a smile plastered on the girl's face, her eyes were red, but all Mary Ann said was, 'I've brought your presents round. One for you and Uncle Bert and one for Dan.'

Bessie smiled. 'I thought you'd have kept them until the party.'

'Oh no, I want you to have them on Christmas morning.'

'You won't see us open them, though, will you?'

The disappointment showed plainly on the girl's face. A smile tugged at the corner of Bessie's mouth. The little minx, she thought, she's angling to be asked here for Christmas Day. Then she relented. Bending down she said, 'Tell you what. As long as ya mam doesn't mind, you can come round after dinner on Christmas Day. About three o'clock and we'll all save our presents and open them then, eh? How would that be?'

The girl's eyes shone and she flung her arms around Bessie and pressed her face against her. 'Oh Auntie Bessie. Thank you. That would be wonderful.'

'But you must remember to ask your mam,' Bessie said firmly and then added, 'and then you're all coming to our little party on Boxing Day, aren't you?'

'Now, Amy, I won't take no for an answer. You're coming to our party.'

'I will if I'm back, Bessie.'

'Back? Back where from?' Bessie asked, surprised.

'I'm going to me sister's in Lincoln on Christmas Eve and staying over. I was planning to come back on Boxing Day, that's if I can get here. I don't know if there'll be any trains running.'

Bessie nodded. 'In that case, I'll let you off, 'cos I'm glad to hear you're going to your sister's. It'll do you good to get away for a bit.'

A ghost of a smile lit Amy's tired face. 'I don't know about that, Bessie. I daren't stay away too long. What'd I do without you to bully me?'

Bessie chuckled and the two women smiled at one another.

'So? What happened? Did you speak to her, 'cos she's said not a word to me.'

Once more Bessie was sitting in Edwina's study, a cup of tea in her hand and, under cover of the desk, easing her feet out of her shoes.

'Yes, I did. She was heartbroken, Bessie, that I'd found her out and begged me not to tell you or Dan. I didn't tell her that it had been you who had alerted me. She doesn't think you know anything about it.'

'But she admitted taking it?'

'Oh yes. She wanted to buy Dan a Christmas present.

You see . . .' Edwina sighed again. 'I suppose I must have put the idea into her head in a way.'

'I wish you'd stop trying to take the blame, Miss Edwina. There's no excuse for her being light-fingered.'

Edwina smiled. 'No, no, you're right, Bessie. Of course you are. But as I was saying, I suggested that she make something for you – I can't tell you what, I don't want to spoil her surprise – but of course I provided her with the materials. I actually gave her some money to go into town one lunchtime and buy what she needed. So,' Edwina spread her hands, 'I suppose when she wanted to get Dan something, she thought I wouldn't mind.'

'I know you wouldn't, but did you tell her that she should have asked you?'

'Oh yes, I was very firm about it. I said what she had done was stealing and that if she ever did such a thing again I would have to get the police in and tell her father and . . . and you and Dan.' Edwina shook her head. 'Do you know, she didn't bat an eyelid when I mentioned the police or her father. But when I threatened to tell you and Dan she became almost hysterical.'

'I could see that she'd been crying when she got home, but she never said a word to me about it.'

'Of course she wouldn't. Nor will she. The last thing she wants is for you or Dan to find out.'

There was silence between them for a moment before Edwina added, 'The thing that shocked me the most was when she said, quite offhandedly, that if her father found out he'd take his belt to her.'

Bessie placed her empty cup and saucer down on the desk. 'He would,' she said shortly. 'There's no doubt about that.'

'Then we'll have to make sure he doesn't find out, won't we? I think she's learnt her lesson.'

'I hope so,' Bessie said, with feeling. 'I really hope so.'

Thirteen

'Bert, this has been one of the best Christmas Days we've ever had. An' that's saying summat, 'cos we've had some good 'uns.'

'It's all thanks to you, my angel.' Bert kissed his wife soundly. 'I don't think I've ever eaten so much in my life.' He patted his stomach, though there was not an ounce of spare fat on his thin frame. 'I'll be as round as you are soon, if you keep feeding me like that.'

'Eh, watch your cheek, m'lad, else you'll not get your last present of the day when we get to our bed.'

Bert chuckled happily, safe in the knowledge that his wife would not carry out her dire threat. They were sitting contentedly by the fire's last glow at the end of a hectic and happy day. Early in the evening, Dan had left to go to Susan's house and the other two boys were out, continuing the day's merrymaking in their own way.

'Aye, it's been a grand day, love. We've not been able to make merry properly for a few years now, have we?'

'Not while the war was on, no. And even last year, with it only having just finished a month or so before and all those poor lads trickling home, well, it was difficult, wasn't it?'

Bert nodded.

'But this year,' Bessie smiled. 'It's different. Even Amy's bucking up now. And when we get into the New Year. Fancy, 1920 already. Makes me feel old, Bert.'

'Old?' Bert grinned. 'You'll never be old to me, light of my life.' Then his smile faded a little as he added, 'There was only one sad moment.' He sighed and shook his head. 'When that poor little lass came in from next door and sniffed the air and said how good your dinner smelt.'

'Oh dear, yes. I never thought for a moment that her mam wouldn't have cooked a proper Christmas dinner.'

'Ne'er mind, love.' Bert was smiling broadly again now. 'She got one, didn't she?'

Bessie laughed, remembering the plate she had set before Mary Ann, piled high with turkey, stuffing, sausage and bacon rolls, potatoes and Brussels sprouts. 'Where she put it all, I don't know. She must be like you, Bert, got hollow legs.'

'I don't know about that, love. But one thing I do know, she's got clever fingers.'

Bessie's eyes followed his gaze to the framed sampler now hanging in pride of place above their mantelpiece. It had been Mary Ann's gift to Bessie. Worked in cross-stitch on canvas were Bessie and Bert's names with the date of their marriage and beneath it were listed the names of their three sons with their dates of birth. Round the edge were tiny images of things that were important in their lives: wedding bells, a house, a ship and a cradle.

'And them hankies she gave our Dan. I suppose she embroidered them an' all,' Bert said.

'Er, yes.' Bessie's pleasure at the sight of the gift that the girl had given Dan had been marred by the memory of how she had acquired the money to buy it.

'What is it, Bess?'

'Bert Ruddick,' Bessie smiled at him, 'you know me a mite too well, don't you?'

'Well now, I could see a little cloud come into those sparkling eyes of yours when I mentioned the lass's gift to our Dan. What is it that bothers you, eh? Think she's getting a bit too attached to him, d'you?'

Bessie's eyes widened in astonishment. That thought had never entered her mind.

Bert nodded, understanding at once. 'You hadn't realized, had you? She's growing up, love, and young girls of her age start to look at young fellers, now don't they? She's fallen for our Dan and no mistake.'

'Oh Bert,' Bessie said. 'I never gave it a thought. I just thought, well, that she'd taken to him. You know, her being an only child an' that . . .' Her voice trailed away. 'Oh dear,' she murmured.

'You still haven't told me what's bothering you. If it's not that, then what is it? And don't try telling me "nothing".' He wagged his finger at her in playful admonishment.

So Bessie told him the full story, but at the end all Bert said was, 'Poor bairn.'

Bessie opened her mouth to remonstrate with him, but before she could utter a word, he said, 'I know, I know what you're going to say, my angel, and of course you're quite right. Nothing gives anyone the right to take another's belongings, but even so . . .' He gave a huge sigh. 'Even so, I still say, "poor bairn."'

Bert heaved himself up and held out his hand to his wife. 'Come on, light of my life. If you're to give the lass and her mother and father, to say nothing of half the neighbourhood an' all, a good party tomorrow night, you'd best be up the wooden hill, down sheet lane and into blanket fair. Come on.'

It all began so well. Mary Ann was the first to arrive for the party, dressed in a red dress that Bessie hadn't seen before.

'Miss Edwina gave it to me. It's brand new. I've never – ever – had a new dress before. Isn't it lovely?'

'It most certainly is,' Bessie agreed, marvelling yet again at Edwina's generosity of spirit.

Everyone in the Ruddick family complimented Mary Ann on her appearance and Duggie chased her round the front parlour, in use in honour of Christmas, with a sprig of mistletoe. Next came Minnie and Stan Eccleshall closely followed by the Merryweathers and the Horberrys.

Last of all Elsie and Sid Clark appeared at the back door and were ushered in to join the throng. Bert put a glass of beer into Sid's hand and Bessie steered Elsie in the direction of Minnie. 'You know everyone, don't you?' Bessie said and then carried on without waiting for an answer. 'Here, Min, you look after Elsie for me while I see to things. Mary Ann, you come and help me carry the sandwiches through. Dan, get Stan a drink, will you? Duggie, put that mistletoe down and make yasen useful.'

At first the atmosphere was a little strained but as the beer flowed, everyone began to relax. All, that is, except Phyllis Horberry and her husband, Tom. Bessie could not help noticing, despite being so busy looking after every-one, that whenever Sid Clark turned to speak to one of them, they coldly ignored him and turned away.

'Phyllis,' Bessie said in a loud voice above the chatter. 'Give us a hand in the kitchen, will you? I'll get to the bottom of this,' she muttered as she headed back towards the kitchen hoping Phyllis would follow her. At that moment a knock sounded at the back door.

'That'll be Amy, I 'spect. I'll just let her in.'

'I'll go,' Phyllis said swiftly.

From her scullery as she cut more bread and butter, Bessie could hear the low murmur of their voices and then, as she emerged carrying two plates, the two women glanced at her and their conversation ceased abruptly.

'Hello, Amy,' Bessie said cheerily and, careful how she phrased her words, asked tactfully, 'Have a nice time with your sister, did you?'

'Nice time? Nice time, you say?' Amy's voice was shrill and with more fire in it than Bessie had heard in a long time.

Bessie smiled. 'Oh dear, got sore knees, have you, love?' The extent of Bessie's tactfulness was limited. Amy's sister, Clara, was a devout Catholic who would no doubt have spent much of the Christmas period attending services and dragging a reluctant Amy with her. Amy, once a regular churchgoer herself, had had her own Christian beliefs badly shaken by the loss of her husband and son. Since that time she had never, to Bessie's knowledge, set foot in the parish church, a defect which was high on Bessie's list of priorities to remedy.

Amy was stepping towards her, her thin neck stretching forward, like a chicken about to peck a rival. 'Is it true?'

Bessie blinked. 'Is what true?'

'What Phyllis says?'

Bessie glanced at Phyllis, who was wearing a strange expression. It was a cross between her usual, self-satisfied smile when she had just imparted a particular juicy piece of gossip and a sudden look of panic.

'Amy, no, don't say anything.' Phyllis put out her hand to restrain Amy. 'I only told you in case you'd rather not come in. But don't spoil Bessie's party. Me and Tom were just going. He doesn't want to stay. Not now he knows.'

'Knows?' Bessie said sharply. 'Knows what?'

'About that Sid Clark,' Amy spat. 'Where is he? I'll tell him a thing or two . . .'

Before either of the women could stop her, Bessie hampered as she was by carrying two plates of bread and butter, Amy whirled about, rushed through Bessie's kitchen and into the front room.

'Oh law. I'm sorry, Bessie, I didn't mean . . .' Phyllis began, but Bessie was too busy hurrying after Amy to stay and listen to her.

Amy flung open the door with such violence that it crashed against Bessie's prized china cabinet and the glass in the doors shattered. Amy, however, was unaware of what she had done.

'Where is he? Where is that bloody coward?'

Everyone in the room seemed turned to stone as Amy launched herself forward towards Sid Clark, her fists flailing. Dan was the first to recover his senses and leap into action. He caught hold of Amy around her waist, but not before she had landed one punch at Sid's shoulder.

There was little weight behind it for Amy, though like a wild thing at this moment, had little real strength. Sid staggered backwards more from shock than from the blow, the pint of beer he held in his hand slopping over on to Bessie's best square of carpet, which had taken her and Bert ten years to save up for.

'Here, here, what's got into you, Amy?' Bessie crashed the plates she was carrying down on to the table and rushed to help Dan.

'He's a bloody conchy, that's what he is. Phyllis has just told me.'

All eyes turned to look at Sid Clark and then suddenly the room seemed to erupt. He swung his beer mug round, smashing it into his wife's face, sending further splashes of liquid up Bessie's wallpaper. 'You bloody bitch. You and your big mouth.'

Before anyone could reach her, Elsie had crumpled into

106

a heap. Then Sid lunged, hand outstretched, towards Mary Ann. Catching her by the hair, he yanked it viciously. 'Or was it you, telling these fancy friends of yours?'

Now Bessie swung into action, her family behind her. Only Dan, still struggling to hold Amy, did not move forward.

'Leave her alone,' Bessie bellowed, and whilst Bert and her three younger sons grasped Sid Clark, Bessie reached out for the girl and pulled her into the safety of her arms. 'What's all this about? Phyllis . . .' Bessie looked around the room, but the person who had thrown this particular stone into the pond and caused more than a ripple was nowhere to be seen. 'Tom, get that wife of yours in here this minute. I want to know what has caused all this.'

A moment later, Tom brought a reluctant Phyllis in.

'Now, everyone calm down and let's sort this out. Bert, help Elsie up, will ya, and sit her in that chair. Are you all right?'

The woman, still dazed, nodded. Her face was not cut, miraculously after such a blow, but a red and ugly swelling was beginning to show.

'And you,' Bessie ordered Sid. 'You sit down, an' all.'

Against her Bessie could hear Mary Ann's soft whimpering and the sounds of her thumb being sucked vigorously. She bent over her and whispered, 'There, there, love, it's all right. It's all right.' They were only words of reassurance, for Bessie was well aware that things were far from all right. 'Now, Phyllis, just tell us what this is all about.'

Phyllis glanced at Amy, who, though quiet now, was still staring at Sid, hatred in her eyes, before saying, 'He was a conchy in the war. He spent most of the war in a prison cell in Lincoln jail. Someone at work told me. A friend of hers told her because her husband is a warder at the jail. Somehow, he even got out of being sent to the Front as a stretcher-bearer.' Phyllis, warming to her story now, nodded knowingly. 'That's where most of the conchies ended up, but not him.'

'That was a job and a half,' Bessie muttered. 'It'd take some guts to go out picking up the wounded and—'

'How would you know anything about it, Bessie Ruddick?' Amy screeched suddenly. 'When your husband and all yer sons stayed safe at home here?' The pitch of Amy's voice rose. 'Were they conchies an' all?'

Bessie's face flamed. 'You know very well they weren't, Amy, and if you say any such thing about my Bert or my lads, you an' me are going to fall out.'

'Your Dan could have gone,' Amy persisted.

'No, he couldn't. He weren't old enough. He's only just eighteen now.'

Amy's mouth was tight with resentment. 'My lad volunteered and he was only sixteen. *Sixteen*, Bessie. All the way through he went. Four years of hell and then he gets killed only days before the peace is signed. And then I have to live alongside folks like *'im*.' She flung her arm out towards Sid. 'If I had my way, he'd have been shot.'

'Aw, come now, Amy . . .'

'Don't you "come now, Amy" me, Bessie Ruddick. I've seen it all. Palling on with 'em. Having them here, in your own home and taking their kiddie to Miss Edwina's school. Oho, I bet your fancy friend won't be so ready to help when she finds out just what the kid's father is. Not when she lost her brother and her fiancé. Oh no, Miss Edwina will understand, even if you don't.'

With that parting shot, Amy pulled herself free of Dan's hold and marched out of the room, slamming the door so that the already battered china cabinet yielded up yet more broken glass.

For a moment there was silence in the room, then Bessie turned her look upon Sid. 'Is it true? What she says?'

'A man's got a right to follow his own conscience,' he growled. 'I don't hold with war and killing other folks. I'm a peaceful man – if I'm left alone.'

Bessie's eyes narrowed and her lips tightened as she struggled with her own feelings. She'd no time for the men who hid away at home whilst others gave their lives for their country, but a tiny part of her could sympathize with someone who genuinely believed that war was wrong and that they should take a stand against it. She had heard that some very eminent people had suffered abuse because of their beliefs. It took a courageous man to stand alone against family, friends and neighbours and even the world at large. For that very action meant ridicule, hatred and imprisonment. In some cases, they had given their own lives in the cause of peace, for she had heard that many had been shot for cowardice.

Bessie frowned. She had never met a conscientious objector before and, of course, she didn't know Sid Clark well enough, didn't know him at all, but he didn't strike her as a man of unshakeable principles. She regarded him thoughtfully. There was a veiled threat in his final words and his sentiments didn't quite ring true. Not to her ears. Here he was, she thought, bold as brass in her front room claiming to be a peaceful man when he was a wife beater and not above ill-treating his daughter. Oh no, Bessie couldn't see it and she prided herself on being a good judge of character.

'Get him out of here, Bert,' she said quietly now. 'Tek him to the pub while I see to Elsie and this little lass.' She glanced around the room. 'The party's over, folks.'

109

Fourteen

'Well, did you ever?' Minnie had managed at last to close her gaping mouth. 'What do you make of all that, then, Bess?'

The rest of Bessie's guests had gone, but Minnie had stayed to help clear up the remnants of the shattered party.

At Bessie's bidding, Bert and his sons had taken Sid to the pub.

'Try to find out more of his side of the story, Bert. I don't like to condemn a feller afore he's had chance to defend himself. But we've got to get at the truth if we're to help 'em.'

Bert had nodded. He didn't hold with conchies. Hadn't a scrap of sympathy for them, but he knew his Bessie was thinking more about the man's wife and daughter than about Sid. If it meant living next door to the feller for the sake of that little lass and her mother, then Bert – and his sons – would do it.

Phyllis had scuttled away as if she couldn't get leave quickly enough, her husband close behind her, and they were soon followed by the Merryweathers and Stan Eccleshall. Bessie herself had taken Elsie and Mary Ann back to their own house. The girl had begged to stay, tears running down her cheeks, but Bessie had been firm. She needed time to herself for once, although she was glad to have Minnie's company and help now.

In answer to Minnie's question, Bessie said slowly, 'I

suppose it could account for his behaviour. He must have had a tough time.' She was trying to be fair to the man, but it was hard to be rational and, for once, even Bessie's tender heart failed. 'But it don't give him the right to knock his wife and bairn about.'

'I've never seen Amy so riled,' Minnie said, as she swept up the broken glass whilst Bessie scrubbed at the stain on her carpet.

'As far as Amy's concerned, you know what they say, Min?'

Minnie looked up. 'No. What?'

'It's an ill wind that blows nobody any good.'

'How d'you mean?'

'It could stop Amy wallowing in self-pity. Now she's got someone to direct her anger at, it might drag her out of that terrible depression.'

Minnie shook her head. 'Oh, you're getting too deep for me, Bess. All I know is, I don't reckon this is over. Not by a long chalk, I don't.'

Two hours later when the men were still not home, Bessie went next door to check on Elsie and Mary Ann.

'Can I come in, love?' she called, but pushed open the door and stepped inside without waiting for an invitation.

Elsie was sitting huddled near the range, even though there was no fire in the grate. There was no sign of Mary Ann.

'Little lass in bed, is she?' Bessie asked, moving to sit down in the chair opposite the woman.

Elsie nodded.

'Eh, but it's cold in here,' Bessie shivered. 'I'd light you a fire, but it's a bit late now. The room'll hardly get warm afore you go to bed, will it?'

'There's no wood or coal,' Elsie murmured.

'I'll bring you a bucketful round in the morning, then,' Bessie said, trying to be cheerful. 'Always difficult to gauge what you're going to be needing over the holidays, ain't it?'

She knew she was making excuses to save the woman's pride. There was no coal in the house, Christmas or not, and, she suspected, very little food. Before the fracas, Bessie had noticed Sid Clark tucking into her sandwiches as if he hadn't eaten for a week. And she hadn't forgotten Mary Ann's round eyes at the plateful of Christmas dinner Bessie had placed before her. She had thought the Clark family was going to have a good Christmas when she had seen Elsie loaded with shopping. She must have been wrong, Bessie thought.

'Now, love, do you want to tell me about it? Maybe, if I know the full story, I can help.'

Elsie shrugged her thin shoulders. 'I doubt it, Bessie. We'll just have to move on again. Everywhere we go, somehow, someone seems to find out about us and we have to go.'

Bessie gave a wry snort of laughter. 'I could have warned you about Phyllis Horberry. A ferret's got nothing on her when it comes to a bit of gossip.' She put her head on one side and regarded the pathetic little woman. She felt sorry for her and for the young girl upstairs, who was probably lying on that old mattress, sobbing herself to sleep and sucking her thumb until it was white and wrinkly.

'Maybe if the folks round here knew the truth, they could sympathize a bit. Worth a try, ain't it?'

Again, the disconsolate shrug. 'You can't expect someone like poor Amy Hamilton to understand,' Elsie said reasonably. 'Can you?'

Bessie sighed. 'Not really, if I'm honest with you.'

'Sid never used to be like he is now, Bessie. I want you to believe that. He was quite a good husband and father. Oh, he always drank a bit and it always made him nasty tempered, but he never knocked me and Mary Ann about. Not . . . not until he came out of prison.' Elsie sighed. 'After the war finished and he came home, it still wasn't over.' Flatly, she added hopelessly, 'It never will be over. Everybody thinks that in Sid's case he was hiding behind the name of being a conscientious objector just to get out of going to the Front.'

'I suppose,' Bessie said thoughtfully, 'folks think that, if he'd been genuine, he'd have gone as a stretcher-bearer, like Phyllis said.' She paused and asked softly, not wanting to bring this poor woman any further pain, but needing to get at the truth. 'Wouldn't he?'

Elsie gave a deep sigh. 'It grieves me to say it, Bessie, but I have to agree with you. That's what he should have done.'

'Then I'm sorry for you, Elsie,' was all Bessie could say. 'Very sorry.'

As she went home, Bessie had the uncomfortable feeling that Minnie's words were prophetic.

This wasn't over by a long chalk.

Fifteen

Minnie's prediction came true a week later.

Bessie and Bert woke with a jump at two o'clock in the morning on New Year's Day to hear the screams coming through their bedroom wall from the house next door.

The Ruddicks' New Year celebrations had been quiet and just within their own household. Their sons had stayed at home to see the New Year in with their parents and Susan had been invited to spend the evening with them. Dan had set off to walk her home just after midnight. The rest had gone to their beds soon after one o'clock, although Bessie had slept fitfully, listening with half an ear for Dan to arrive home.

'Daft, you are,' she had muttered to herself. 'He's a grown man now.'

'What, love?' Bert had murmured sleepily. 'What d'you say?'

Bessie had chuckled. 'Nothing, sweetheart, just me worrying about our Dan.'

'He'll be all right, he's . . .' Bert had begun, but the sentence ended in a gentle snore.

Bessie had lain awake for a while, staring into the darkness imagining, quite irrationally, all the different sorts of trouble Dan could get involved in if he encountered revellers roaming the streets. But gradually her heavy eyelids had closed and she had fallen into a half sleep.

114

Then the commotion had begun and, at once, she was fully awake.

'Oh no,' she groaned as she levered herself out of bed and lumbered across the room to light the candle on the mantelpiece. 'I've been afraid of this. Come on, Bert.'

Although he sat up and lowered his legs to the floor, Bert said, 'Do you really think we should interfere, my angel?'

'I aren't lying here listening to that racket and doing nothing about it.'

There was another cry of pain followed by a thump and, plainly through the wall, they could hear Sid shouting obscenities.

'Just listen to the man. Have you ever heard owt like it?'

Bert gave a wry smile. 'Well, yes, I have, love, amongst sailors and workmen.' He shook his head. 'But it's not the sort of language you like to hear a man using to his wife.'

There was a thud against the wall and the sound of splintering wood. Then, suddenly, there was silence. An eerie, uncanny silence that sent a chill through Bessie.

'Oh Bert, what's he done?'

But Bert was swinging his legs back into bed and lying back against the pillow.

Shocked, Bessie said, 'You're not just going to lie there and do nothing, Bert Ruddick, are you?'

'What can we do, Bess? If we go round and bang on his door, he'll not answer it. So, short of breaking it down, how are we to get in?' He paused and then asked quietly, 'Do you want me to call out the police?'

Bessie shivered and got back into bed, though she did not, for the moment, blow out the candle. 'I don't know. I really don't know what to do, Bert. I just hate to think of that poor woman – and Mary Ann – having to

115

put up with that lot.' She nodded her head towards the wall.

Bert snuggled down further beneath the covers. 'It seems to have settled down now. I expect he got blind drunk. She told you he was worse then, didn't she?'

'Mm,' Bessie murmured, her hearing still tuned to any sound coming from next door. 'What worries me now is, why has it gone quiet so suddenly?'

Despite the gravity of their conversation, Bert chuckled. 'That's the trouble with you, my angel. Never satisfied, are you?'

For once, worried as she was, Bessie did not pick up on his teasing innuendo. Bert turned on his side, his back to her, but Bessie still sat up in bed, a shawl around her shoulders, listening intently.

'I can't hear anything,' she muttered. 'It's *too* quiet now.'

She waited a few moments more and then, exasperated, swung her legs out of the bed again, saying, 'I'm wide awake now. I'm going down to make some cocoa. D'you want some?'

There was no answer from her husband, so, pushing her feet into her slippers and taking the candle, Bessie plodded down the stairs and into the kitchen. Minutes later she had just settled herself into Bert's armchair near the dying embers in the range when she heard the back door open and close very quietly. The inner door opened and a shadowy figure stepped silently into the room. Bessie saw him start as he saw the lighted candle on the table and her sitting in the chair.

'You waiting up for me, Mam? Am I going to get a clip round the ear for being late home?'

He stood over her, towering above her, this big, handsome son of hers, her firstborn.

116

Bessie chuckled. 'I don't think I'll bother. You're a bit big for that now.' Then she added, wagging her finger at him playfully, 'But don't think I wouldn't if I thought you deserved it.'

Dan, too, laughed softly and sat down opposite her. 'Any cocoa going? It's cold out and I've had a long walk home.'

As Bessie got up to get him a mug of cocoa, she asked, 'Did you get your ear clipped yon end for Susan being late home?'

'No, the Prices were still merrymaking. The house was ablaze with light and they'd got friends and neighbours round. I reckon it'll go on till dawn.' He grinned at her in the flickering candlelight. 'But I thought seeing that her dad is me boss and I'm due to sail one of his ships downriver tomorrow on the afternoon tide, I'd better look willing and get to me bed.'

'You mean today, lad,' Bessie said. 'It's New Year's Day now. The first of January 1920. Can you believe it?'

'So, what are you doing still up?'

'Oh, I've been to bed once, but then there was this unearthly racket from next door. He's been at it again.'

Dan cocked his head on one side and listened. 'Seems all right now, though. Drunk, was he?'

Bessie handed him his cocoa and sat down heavily with a sigh. 'I 'spect so. He was shouting and swearing and carrying on. There was thuds and bangs and then she was screaming.'

Dan looked suddenly worried. 'Who? Mary Ann?'

'No, I don't think so. I think it was his missis. Elsie.'

Dan relaxed slightly, but angry disapproval was still in his eyes. 'He's still got no right . . .' He broke off and sighed. 'Still, it seems to have stopped. Let's hope he's fallen into a drunken stupor.'

'It went quiet all of a sudden, though. That's what's worrying me.'

'But you've not heard the little lass? You've not heard Mary Ann?'

Bessie shook her head. 'No.'

'I reckon if it had been anything really bad, she'd have come round here. Don't you? She knows by now, surely, that she can come to us for anything, doesn't she?'

'I think so,' Bessie agreed. 'I hope so.'

'Come on then, Mam,' Dan said, draining his mug and standing up. 'Let's both get to our beds, eh?'

'Aye, you're right, lad,' Bessie said as she got up, and then she added, with feeling, 'At least I hope to God you are.'

Sixteen

'I ain't seen hide nor hair of any of 'em this morning, Min, and I'm worried sick now.'

'Mebbe he's sleeping the booze off and she and the little lass are having a lie-in while he's quiet.'

Bessie sighed. 'Sounds reasonable, I suppose, after all the shenanigans last night, but . . .' she bit her lip. 'I'd feel better if I just saw one of 'em.'

They were standing outside Minnie's door, arms folded and looking across the yard towards the Clarks' house.

There was not a movement to be seen. No curtain moved, no window or door opened.

'I can't stand it any longer,' Bessie said. 'I'm going across there and I don't care if I do wake 'em up.'

'If you rouse the sleeping tiger,' Minnie warned, 'you'll get more than you bargained for. And she'll not thank you neither if she's gettin' a bit o' peace.'

Bessie had taken a step forward but now she stopped again and groaned. 'Oh Min, I don't know what to do.'

'Leave it till dinner time and then if we've seen nowt by then, well, I'll come with you.'

Bessie considered. 'All right. Good idea. Yes, that's what we'll do.'

Midday came and still there was no sign of life from her neighbours, so Bessie crossed the yard once more and rapped sharply on Minnie's door. 'Come on, Min, if you're coming, 'cos I'm going to see what's what.'

Minnie opened her door, untying her apron. 'I'm right with you, Bess.'

Together, they approached the house and Bessie raised her hand to knock, but before she could do so, Minnie clutched her arm and said, 'Listen, can you hear summat?'

Bessie was motionless with her arm still raised in the air. From behind the door came a whimpering like an animal in pain.

'Oh my God,' Bessie breathed. She grasped the door-knob, turned it and pushed, but the door did not yield.

'It's locked.' Instead of raising her arm again, she put her face close to the door and called softly, 'Is that you, Mary Ann?'

The whimpering beyond the door grew louder until it became a wail.

'It is her,' Bessie said. 'I'm sure it is.' Raising her voice again, she said, 'Mary Ann, love, open the door.'

The two women standing outside saw and heard the doorknob move, but still the door did not open. The girl's crying increased. 'I can't. There's no key.'

'What? But there must be,' Bessie said, getting more and more agitated by the minute. Something was dread-fully wrong behind that door and now she was castigating herself inwardly for having waited so long before trying to find out just what had happened.

'Look on the floor, love. Has it dropped out?'

There was a scrabbling sound and then, 'I can't find it.'

Then Bessie jumped as Mary Ann thumped on her side of the door. 'Get me out, Auntie Bessie, get me out.'

'I wish Bert or one of the lads was here.' Bessie bit her lip and then said suddenly, 'I know. Min, what time is it?'

'Dunno. About twelve, I think.'

'Right. You stay here. I'm going for Dan. With a bit of luck, he won't have sailed yet.'

120

She was halfway across the yard before Minnie called after her, 'He'll not come, Bessie, if he's ready to sail.'

'He'll come,' Bessie muttered, pulling her shawl closely around her as she hurried through the alleyway between the houses. 'When he knows it's for that little lass, he'll come.'

Only minutes later, she was hurrying back again to Waterman's Yard, Dan loping along beside her.

'You're sure it's Mary Ann behind the door, Mam?'

'Certain,' Bessie puffed. 'Called me Auntie Bessie, didn't she? "Get me out, Auntie Bessie," she said. "Get me out." Like a trapped animal. Poor little mite.'

'But where's her mam?'

'I daren't think, lad,' Bessie said grimly.

'Right then,' Dan said, equally adamant. 'Break down the door, it is.'

When they arrived back, other neighbours had gathered.

Gladys had joined Minnie outside the Clarks' house and, from her doorway, Amy Hamilton was shouting unwanted advice. 'Leave 'em to it. I don't know what you're bothering with them for. If I'd my way I'd . . . I'd lock the house up and set fire to the lot of 'em.'

Minnie, imbued with some of Bessie's spirit, rounded on her. 'Shut up, Amy. It's the little lass and her mother we're bothered about. Not him. I'm with you there. He can go hang, for all I care.'

'Tarred with the same brush, the lot of 'em,' Amy ranted.

'You can't blame the bairn. Be fair, Amy.'

'Be fair, you say. Is it fair that my Ron threw his life away to save the likes of his miserable hide?' She jabbed her finger towards the house. 'Who thought about my Ron, eh?'

121

'We all thought about your Ron and your George, Amy,' Bessie said, coming across the yard and catching the gist of the conversation. 'You know we did. We still do, but it doesn't mean we have to turn our backs on Mary Ann just because of what her father is.'

'And what would you know about it, Bessie Ruddick?' was Amy's parting shot as she slammed her door with such force, it seemed to rattle on its hinges.

Dan went straight to the door and called out, 'Mary Ann? Are you there, love?'

At once they heard her cries. 'Dan, oh Dan. Help me, please help me.'

'Listen, love. Calm down. We'll get you out. But first of all, try to stop crying and tell me, can you really not find the key?'

'No, no, it's gone. Dad's locked the door and gone. And me mam. I can't find me mam.'

Dan turned and his eyes met his mother's terrified gaze as she murmured, 'Oh my dear Lord, what has he done?' Then with renewed vigour, she said, 'Get that door down, son.'

Again Dan put his mouth close to the door and shouted, 'Mary Ann, listen to me, love. Get right away from the door, 'cos I'm going to break it down and I don't want to hurt you. Do you hear me?'

'Yes, Dan.'

'Do you understand, love? Stand right back out of the way.'

Her voice sounded fainter now, further away, as she said again, 'Yes, Dan.'

Dan gave a small nod of satisfaction and stood back. First he kicked at the door near the lock, trying to break it and then he put his broad shoulders against it and heaved until the wood splintered and gave way. Pushing it aside, he stepped inside and held out his arms.

The girl rushed to him and he picked her up and held her close. She wound her arms about him and buried her face against his neck, sobbing wildly.

For a few moments he just held her, patting her back and soothing, 'There, there. You're safe now. It's all right.' Then gently he prised himself free of her clinging arms and set her on the ground. 'Now you go with Mrs Eccleshall to our house.'

'No, no . . .' Mary Ann began, but when Dan said, firmly, but kindly, 'Please do as I ask, Mary Ann, because I want me mam to come upstairs to see to your mother. Understand?'

Biting her lip, the tears still running down her face, the girl nodded, 'But you'll come in a minute.'

'As soon as we can,' was all he would promise.

As Minnie led her away, Mary Ann looked back at Dan, stumbling as she did so instead of looking where she was going. Only Minnie, holding her hand, prevented her from falling.

'Right, Mam,' Dan said soberly and with no relish for what they had to do. 'We'd better have a look-see.'

'Oh lad, what are we going to find?'

'I daren't think, Mam,' Dan said, but nevertheless he led the way into the house and, following Bessie's direction, went upstairs and into the main bedroom.

As he pushed open the door, Bessie knew, like her, Dan was holding his breath.

The bowl and jug on the washstand had been smashed on the floor and the stand overturned. Two spindly-legged chairs had been broken as if they were matchwood and the bed had been overturned and rested at an angle against the wall.

'I bet that was the loud thud we heard,' Bessie muttered, her wide eyes taking in the scene of devastation before them.

'But where is she?' Dan said, looking round. 'Where's Mrs Clark?'

'Mebbe she's gone with him.' Her voice hardened. 'Mebbe they've both scarpered and left the little lass . . .'

'No,' Dan shook his head. 'Surely no mother would leave her child.'

Bessie cast him a wry glance but said nothing. Dan might be a man now, but in some ways he still had a lot to learn about the world and its cruel ways.

'You don't think . . .' he was saying and pointing with a finger that shook slightly, 'that she's under there?'

They exchanged a glance that said, 'Well, if she is . . .'

Dan heaved the bed away from the wall and it fell with a crash on to the floor. Elsie was lying face downwards, squashed against the skirting board, and before Dan even turned her over very gently, they both knew that there was little or no chance of her being alive.

Seventeen

Now, of course, they had no choice. The police had to be called.

'I'll have to go, Mam. If I miss the tide, Mr Price might sack me.'

'What? When you're walking out with his daughter?'

Dan sighed. 'That wouldn't make a scrap of difference to Mr Price. In fact, it would make it worse, because he'd think I was deliberately taking advantage.'

Bessie sighed. 'You're right, Dan. Jack Price is a hard man. I know him of old.'

'Mam, tell the police when they come that I'll be home tomorrow and I'll go straight to the station and give them a full statement. It'll only be the same as yours anyway.'

Bessie nodded. 'You go then, lad. I'll give you a few minutes to get aboard, else if your ship's not halfway down the river, they'll likely fetch you back.'

Despite the gravity of the moment, Dan smiled. 'Thanks, Mam. Good luck.'

Wryly, Bessie said, 'I reckon I'm going to need it, lad.'

As Dan's heavy boots clattered across the yard and away down the alley, Bessie went towards her own house, biting her lip. 'I wish my Bert was here,' she muttered to herself. 'I could do with him here right this minute.'

How on earth was she going to break the dreadful news to Mary Ann?

The girl's first question, however, was not about her

mother, nor her father. 'Where's Dan?' she demanded the moment Bessie set foot in the kitchen.

'He's had to go back to his ship, love. Come and sit down with me a minute. Min, have you got that kettle boiling? I could do with a strong cuppa.'

'Yes, Bess.' Minnie scuttled between kitchen and scullery and only when they were all sitting around the roaring fire in the kitchen range did Bessie say gently, 'Mary Ann, we've found your mam, love.' She glanced at Minnie, but her neighbour was looking even more round-eyed and fearful than the young girl was. 'I'm afraid . . .'

'She's dead, isn't she?' Mary Ann took the words from her and Bessie held her breath, unable to guess exactly how the girl was about to react.

Bessie nodded. 'I'm so sorry, love, but yes, she is. And . . . and I must call the police. You understand that, don't you?'

Mary Ann was staring at her. Her calmness was unnerving. Bessie had steeled herself to cope with hysterics, but Mary Ann sat quietly and it was obvious by her next words that she was thinking rationally and, for her age, with adult logic.

'My father killed her, didn't he?'

Bessie gulped. 'I'm afraid it does look that way, yes.'

'And now he's gone?'

Bessie nodded.

'He locked me in, didn't he? Locked me in that house with my mother lying dead somewhere . . . Where was she?'

'Did you look in their bedroom?'

Mary Ann nodded.

'So, you saw the bed against the wall?'

Again the girl nodded.

126

'She . . . she was under that.'

Beside her Bessie heard Minnie gasp and, turning to glance at her, saw that she had turned white.

'Here, give me that cup before you drop it,' she said, getting up at once. 'Now, head down between your knees. I can't do with you fainting on me just now, Minnie Eccleshall.'

A little roughly, though not unkindly, Bessie took the cup and saucer out of Minnie's shaking hands and thrust her head into her own lap. 'Now, just stay like that till you feel better.' She glanced at Mary Ann. 'You all right, love?'

Although the girl nodded, Bessie was still worried. Her reaction was unnatural. Although it would be hard to deal with, she almost wished Mary Ann would cry, rage even. At least that would be more normal. But she just sat there, staring ahead of her, her face expressionless, her hands lying idly in her lap, as if her mind was completely blank.

Perhaps it was, Bessie thought. Perhaps that was going to be the girl's way of dealing with it. Just not to think about it.

Slowly Minnie sat up. 'I'm all right, Bessie, honest. Sorry. Now, what do you want me to do?'

'Finish your tea first,' Bessie said, sitting down again herself and picking up her own cup. She glanced at the clock. Dan had had a good half an hour's start now. Time enough, she thought. She mustn't be much longer fetching the police or they would want to know why she had delayed calling them. 'Then,' she went on, 'if you'd look after Mary Ann, I'll see to everything else.'

Minnie nodded gratefully and gave another little shudder, pleased not to have to go into the house next door. 'You can come home with me, Mary Ann.'

Bessie nodded her approval. Although it was only just across the yard, at least in Minnie's home, Mary Ann would hear less of the comings and goings next door.

As she saw them out, Bessie whispered to Minnie, 'Keep her the far side of your house, if you can. The less she sees the better, poor bairn.'

Minnie nodded. 'There's only me scullery window looks over this way. I'll do me best, Bessie.'

Bessie patted her friend's shoulder. 'I know you will, Min. Thanks.'

As Bessie stood in the middle of the yard awaiting the arrival of the police, Amy opened her door. 'What's going on, Bessie? What are you standing there for?'

Bessie glanced over her shoulder towards the alleyway, but there was no one emerging from its shadows into the yard yet.

She moved towards Amy and said in a low voice. 'There's trouble at the Clarks' house. The police are on their way. I've just been to the station to fetch them.'

Amy smiled maliciously. 'Good for you, Bess. Get the bugger arrested, that's what I say. Sling him back in jail where he belongs. Let him rot . . .'

'He's not there, Amy. He's gone.'

Amy's mouth dropped open. 'Gone? Gone where?'

Bessie shrugged. 'Dunno.'

'So why . . .?' Amy began and then her eyes widened. 'You don't mean he's done for her?'

'Well, she's dead. That's all I know for certain. But it looks like it.'

Even Amy, for a moment, was shocked. Then her mouth was a grim, tight line. 'I can't say I'm surprised. That's all his sort are good for, battering defenceless women. I told you he was no good. That's what comes of having a conchy in our yard. I hope they find him and hang him.'

Grimly, Bessie said, 'If they do find him, that's exactly what they will do. Hang him.'

'Hanging's too good for him,' Amy said now, perversely. 'They should throw him to the women. All us women, who've lost someone in the war. We'd soon show him what we thought of a conchy.'

'Oh Amy,' Bessie sighed sadly. 'Don't be so bitter, love.'

'Bitter? Bitter, you say? Don't you think I've got good reason to be bitter?'

With that Amy slammed the door just as Bessie heard what sounded like an army of heavy boots thundering down the alleyway and into the yard.

'So, Mrs Ruddick. You and your son found the body, did you?'

Bessie faced the burly, solemn-faced policeman. He was not in uniform but had introduced himself as Inspector Chapman. He seemed to be in charge of a sergeant and several younger constables, who were dashing about doing his bidding.

Bessie licked her dry lips. 'Yes. My son Dan has had to go back to work. He said to tell you that when he gets back tomorrow, he'll come straight to the station to see you.' She tried to smile winningly at the man. 'I'll tell him to ask for you, shall I?'

The man was unmoved and said sternly, 'He should not have done that, Mrs Ruddick. He should have waited here.'

Bessie bristled. 'He's on one of Mr Price's ships and

he'd have missed the tide, else. Expect him to lose his job, do you?'

'This is a very serious matter, Mrs Ruddick.'

'I know that,' Bessie snapped. 'I've got eyes in me head, ain't I? But, like I said, he'll come and see you just as soon as he gets back tomorrow. Besides, I was with him. He can't tell you any more than I can.' Craftily, she added, 'Not as much, really.'

'Oh? Why is that?'

'Because me and Bert heard all the rumpus going on in the night.'

'And who might Bert be?'

'Me husband, of course.' Bessie was fast losing her patience. She had got off on the wrong foot with this man, she knew, so she took a deep breath and tried to hold on to her composure. 'Dan wasn't even here.'

'Really?'

'No. His young lady had been here with us to see the New Year in and he'd taken her home.'

'I see. We shall need her name and address to verify that.'

'Whatever for?'

'To confirm your son's alibi.'

'Alibi? What on earth should my Dan need an alibi for?'

'No need to get alarmed, madam. It's just routine.'

'Is it, indeed. Well, it sounds a very silly routine to me, if you start accusing innocent folk, who just try to help. It's obvious who's done it, ain't it?'

'Maybe. Maybe not,' the man said carefully. 'We have to make our inquiries and you'd do better to assist us, Mrs Ruddick.'

'I'm trying to,' Bessie snapped again, 'if you'll let me get a word in edgeways to tell you.'

Now the man listened whilst Bessie explained in detail all that had happened the previous night. When she fell silent he asked, 'Had you heard such noises before last night?'

Bessie's mouth tightened. 'Oh yes. From the day they moved in, we knew what he was, but I had a go at him . . .' She was about to recount how she had threatened Sid Clark on his own doorstep, but she was fast becoming very wary of this policeman. She doubted that he would see her side of such a situation. He might even run her in for menacing the man, or something as daft.

For once, Bessie held her tongue, but it was, even she realized, with great difficulty.

'Do you know anything else about the family? You mentioned a girl?'

'Yes, Mary Ann. She's across at my neighbour's house.'

'Does she know what's happened?'

'I told her.'

'And?'

Bessie shrugged. 'I don't think it's sunk in yet. She's only thirteen.'

'I shall have to have a chat with her, since she was in the house all night.'

Bessie shuddered inwardly. What this dour man's questioning would do to poor Mary Ann she dare not think.

Eighteen

'Now then, me little lass, you come and sit down in Mrs Ruddick's kitchen with me and we'll have a little chat, shall we? Perhaps this nice lady would make us a cup of tea. Should you like that, eh?'

Bessie's mouth dropped open. Inspector Chapman was like a different man. Mesmerized by the sudden change in him, she watched as he took hold of Mary Ann's hand and led her across the yard, walking on her right hand side so that his tall, broad frame shielded her from even having to see her home.

'Now,' he said kindly, as they entered Bessie's house. 'You sit there. My word,' he spread his large hands out towards the warmth as they sat down either side of the range. 'This is a nice fire, isn't it? Get yourself warm, love. Cold old day, isn't it? And this little bit of trouble doesn't help, does it?'

Little bit of trouble, he called it. Well, that was one way of looking at it, Bessie supposed. Just about the worst that could happen to anyone had happened to Mary Ann and he was calling it 'a little bit of trouble'.

Bessie went into her scullery and set about making a cup of tea, but she kept her ears attuned to what was going on in her kitchen.

'I'm sorry to have to ask a lot of questions, love, but you're old enough to understand that we have to find out what's happened, don't we?'

132

Bessie could not hear if Mary Ann answered, but she heard the man continue. 'So, were you there last night? All night?'

Again there was a pause and Bessie presumed Mary Ann was merely nodding or shaking her head in response.

The big man's voice was very gentle now as he asked, 'And can you tell me what happened?'

There was a long silence before Bessie, carrying a tray of cups through, heard Mary Ann say haltingly, 'Me dad came home drunk. It was very late. Later than usual. Gone midnight.'

'Does he get drunk very often?'

Now Bessie was in the room setting the tray on the table and saw Mary Ann nod.

'And then what happened?'

'We'd gone to bed, me mam and me.'

'And where did you sleep? In that little room at the top of the stairs?'

Again, she nodded.

'And your mam?'

'In the big bedroom. With . . . with me dad.'

'Yes?' Gently Chapman encouraged her.

'Well, he was banging about. Falling up the stairs, you know.'

Now the man nodded, but Bessie noticed that he never took his gaze away from Mary Ann's face. He was watching her intently.

'Then I heard him get into bed. It creaks, their bed. And I heard her crying out, "No, no, please don't." Then I heard him making funny noises, sort of grunting and the bed was creaking and me mam was still crying.'

Chapman and Bessie exchanged a look but neither said a word as the girl continued, recounting now things she didn't perhaps fully understand, but the older man and woman understood only too well.

'After a bit it went quiet and I thought he must have fallen asleep but then I heard him shouting at her. "Shut up, you silly bitch, I've every right."' Mary Ann paused and wrinkled her forehead. 'At least, I think that's what he said. Then he said, "What sort of wife are you, eh?" And then he was swearing and . . . and hitting her. I heard the slaps and her crying out. Then . . . then it got worse. There was thumps and bangs and . . . and then I didn't hear me mam no more.'

She was sitting rigidly upright, twisting her hands together in her lap, her eyes wide in her pale face, as she was obliged to relive the nightmare.

'And your father?'

Bessie was very tempted to intervene to save Mary Ann any further anguish, but she knew the policeman was only doing his job and she had to admit that he was handling a very sensitive situation in the best way possible.

'After it all went quiet, he went out.'

'Did he come into your room? Did he say anything to you?'

Mary Ann shook her head. 'No, I had a chair lodged under the doorknob. I . . . I thought he might. Sometimes . . . sometimes he's hit me an' all. But I don't think he even tried my door. I think he just rushed out. I heard him going down the stairs and then the back door slammed. A bit later, I went into me mam's room but the bed was tipped up and she wasn't there. I didn't go downstairs because I was frightened he'd come back and catch me. I'd have been in for a belting if he had.'

Bessie and Chapman exchanged another grim look.

Now Mary Ann looked from one to the other. 'Me mam was under the bed, wasn't she?'

Chapman nodded.

'If . . . if I'd found her, could I . . . I mean . . .?' Mary Ann's voice broke and faltered.

Catching her meaning, Chapman reached forward and patted her hand. 'No, no, love. I'm sure you couldn't have done anything by then to help her. You mustn't think that.'

Bessie was feeling her own stab of guilt. If she had gone round there when the noise had first started, maybe she could have prevented the catastrophe. Then she sighed. Unlike Mary Ann, Bessie was old enough and wise enough to know that whatever she had done, it had been a tragedy waiting to happen.

All she could do now was to help Mary Ann.

When Dan didn't arrive home the next day, Bessie began to worry.

The previous twenty-four hours had been, Bessie thought, probably the worst she had experienced in her whole life.

The whole afternoon had been taken up with Inspector Chapman and his questions. Then he had asked a young constable to come into Bessie's kitchen and write everything down, so that both Bessie and Mary Ann had to go through it all again.

Poor Elsie's body had been taken away and there would be a post mortem, Chapman told them, and an inquest. The house had been sealed up and no one – not even Mary Ann – would be allowed to enter it.

'If the child needs anything,' Chapman said to Bessie as he left, 'get one of my men to get it for her. There'll be someone here, certainly for the rest of today.'

Bessie nodded. 'Just her clothes. If they could just bring her clothes out. She's only in her nightie.'

'Right, I'll see to that for you. Thank you, Mrs Ruddick, you've been most helpful.' His voice became stern again. 'But please make sure your son comes straight to the station and asks for me personally, will you?'

'I will,' Bessie replied shortly, beginning to bristle indignantly again.

When Bert and her other sons had arrived home that night, they had been shocked to hear the dreadful news, but Bessie was comforted by their presence. She no longer felt as if she were carrying the burden alone.

'You couldn't have done anything, my angel,' Bert reassured her in the privacy of their bedroom in the early hours of the morning, when neither of them could sleep. 'I doubt we could have got into the house anyway.'

'We should have broken the door down and got in,' Bessie said.

'We know that now, Bessie love. But law-abiding citizens can't go breaking folks' doors down.'

'We had good reason, Bert. We could hear what was going on.'

Bert sighed. 'I know how you feel, love. I feel the same, but I still don't think there's anything more we could have done.'

Bessie could not answer him, for she knew that as long as she lived she would never entirely rid herself of the prickle of guilt she felt. If only . . .

'They want to see Dan. He's to go straight to the station when he gets home. I hope he won't get into trouble with the police. That feller, Chapman, was mad he'd gone.'

'Well, he would be,' said Bert reasonably. 'He's only doing his job.' He chuckled then. 'Poor Dan. It was a rotten choice to have to make. Risk the wrath of your employer and maybe the sack or get on the wrong side of the law. Not an enviable choice.'

Bessie snorted. 'You'd think Jack Price would be a bit more understanding.'

'He isn't and he never will be. He's a hard case, Bessie. And I should know 'cos I've worked for him on and off for twenty years.'

'I like his lass, though. Susan. She seems a nice girl for our Dan.'

'Mm,' Bert said thoughtfully. 'She is. I'll grant you that. But I'm not so sure Dan isn't stacking up a load of trouble for himself by getting involved with his employer's daughter. That's not going to be an easy situation.'

'That's the least of my worries at the moment, Bert,' Bessie said wryly.

'I know, love, I know.' Bert had kissed her then and had added, 'Now, let's try and get some sleep because tomorrow's not going to be a lot easier than today's been. Let's just hope that the police aren't too hard on our Dan, eh?'

But now, by late the following afternoon, Dan had still not appeared.

'Shall we take a walk down to the river and see if we can see Dan's ship?' Bessie suggested.

Mary Ann jumped up, a spark of interest brightening her eyes for the first time. 'Ooh yes, let's.'

'Right, get ya coat, then.'

They crossed the yard without even glancing at the house next door, walked down the alley and out on to River Road.

'Now then, let me think,' Bessie paused a moment. 'Where's he likely to be? Dixon's Wharf today, I reckon. Let's try there anyway, shall we? Come on, it's this way.'

The wharf was busy and Bessie and Mary Ann had to be careful not to get in the way of the men unloading the cargo from the ship moored there.

'Is that Dan's ship?'

'Yes, that's the *Nerissa*.' Bessie squinted against the bright winter sun glinting on the ripples on the river. 'But I don't see Dan.'

'He'll have gone to the police station, won't he?'

'He might have, but I'd have thought he'd have come home first.'

'Mrs Ruddick. Mrs Ruddick.'

They both heard the voice calling Bessie's name and turned to see Susan hurrying towards them.

The young woman held a handkerchief to her face and was obviously very distressed. It was clear that she had been crying. Automatically, Bessie put out her arms to catch hold of her. 'Why, lass, whatever's the matter?'

'Oh, Mrs Ruddick. It's Dan. He's been arrested.'

Nineteen

'I want to see that feller, Chapman.' Bessie faced the desk sergeant in what her neighbours would have called her 'Battling Bessie' mood. 'And I want to see him now.'

'I'm sorry, madam. Inspector Chapman is not available. Can I help you in any way?'

'Then I want to see my son.'

'Your son, madam?'

'Dan Ruddick. You've got him here, haven't you?'

The man leafed through a large book in front of him. 'I don't believe so, madam. What makes you think he's here?'

'Susan,' Bessie jerked her thumb over her shoulder towards Susan and Mary Ann standing behind her, 'says he's been arrested.' She turned towards Susan now. 'That's what you said, didn't you?'

'I . . . it's what my father said.'

'And when was this, miss?'

'Well, I – er – don't know when, exactly. I just presumed it was when they docked back here this morning.'

'Docked, you say? Ah now, wait a moment. If you'll just sit down over there . . .' He turned away towards an open door leading into a room behind the reception area.

'Oi, wait a minute . . .' Bessie began, but Susan pulled at her arm and whispered, 'I think he's gone to ask someone. Let's sit down and wait.'

With ill grace, Bessie sat down on a wooden bench seat

set against the wall. 'I don't know. What a carry on. As if our Dan has done anything wrong.'

They waited for what seemed like an age, but, in fact, it was only a few minutes, before the sergeant returned.

'Yes, I thought so,' he began as if answering his own unvoiced question. 'It seems our colleagues in Hull arrested two men yesterday in connection with an incident which has taken place in – er . . .' He consulted a piece of paper he held in his hand. 'Waterman's Yard.' He looked up. 'Would that mean anything to you?'

Bessie heaved herself up and lumbered towards the desk. 'Yes,' she replied shortly, only just managing to hold on to her temper. 'It would.'

'The inspector is at this moment travelling to Hull to bring back both prisoners.'

'Prisoners? What on earth do you think you're doing arresting my lad? You've no right. No right at all. All he did was to go to his work. All right, all right, I know mebbe he should have stayed and seen the policeman before he went, but he'd have missed the tide and probably got the sack.' She glowered at the man behind the desk. 'Not that that would have bothered any of you, I suppose. You probably don't have any idea how important it is.'

'I can't tell you any more than that, Mrs – er . . .?'

'Ruddick. Mrs Ruddick. I'm his mother.'

'Well, Mrs Ruddick, I am sorry but I'm not at liberty to tell you any more than that.'

Bessie's frown deepened. 'Oh, so you could then. I see. Like that, is it?'

The sergeant said nothing. 'If you call back later today, maybe I'll have more information for you then.'

Muttering, Bessie turned to go. 'Come on,' she said to

Mary Ann and Susan. 'We're wasting our time here. We're not going to get anything else out of him.'

She had begun to move towards the door when she stopped suddenly and turned to face the man again. 'Wait a minute. You said they'd arrested two?'

'That's right.'

'Who's the other one?'

The sergeant pursed his lips and began, 'I'm not at liberty . . .' but Bessie finished his sentence for him.

'. . . To tell you. Thanks, mester, for nothing.'

Bessie's anger carried her along the street and back towards the river.

'Does your father know anything?' she asked Susan.

Susan walked quickly beside her whilst Mary Ann had to take little running steps to keep up with them. Despite her size, Bessie was remarkably nimble on her feet when she was seething with indignation.

'I don't know,' Susan said worriedly. 'He was awfully angry. I . . . I didn't stay to ask him much.'

'Right then,' Bessie said. 'I'll see him.'

'Do be careful, Mrs Ruddick,' Susan said worriedly. 'Please don't make it any worse for Dan. Father's very cross about it all.'

But Bessie was too furious herself to listen to Susan's warning. 'Well, he's no right to be. I'll give him a piece of my mind.'

As they approached the wharf they saw Susan's father coming down the gangway from his ship.

'Jack Price,' Bessie bellowed, her voice echoing along the riverbank. 'I want a word with you.'

'Oh you do, do you?' The man was glowering as they neared each other. 'I could have lost a valuable contract through your son and his shenanigans. I've a good mind to sack him.'

141

'It's putting you and his job first that's caused the trouble,' Bessie snapped.

Jack Price gave a wry laugh. 'Oh no, it isn't. That's not even the half of it.'

Bessie stared at him blankly.

'He's been arrested, Bessie, for aiding and abetting a wanted man to evade arrest.'

'Eh?' Bessie said and now her voice was a high-pitched squeak of disbelief.

'Clark had stowed away on my ship.' Jack's tone was indignant. 'And the police think that your Dan had something to do with it, being as how you're neighbours and Clark is a drinking pal of your Bert's.'

Bessie spluttered with rage, hardly able to get the words out. 'How can they . . . how dare they . . . you don't think that?'

When Jack did not answer, Bessie gasped, 'Jack Price, you can't think that of Dan. Not of my boy. We've known each other years, Jack. Why, we went to school together.'

'When you were there, Bessie.' Even amid his anger, Jack could smile at the memory of the time when school and Bessie had not seen much of one another. Living on her father's ship had not been conducive to regular education. But Bessie was at this moment in no mood to be humoured, not even by being reminded of her own fond memories.

Jack's mouth hardened again. 'I'm sorry, Bessie, but I've to think of my own business. You must see that.' He turned towards his daughter, standing a little way behind Bessie. He pointed at her and said, 'And you, my girl, are not to see Dan Ruddick until all this business is cleared up. I don't want you involved. You hear me?'

Though tears ran down Susan's face, she did not argue.

'Get yourself home, now, and help your mother,' Jack ordered. With one look of desperation at Bessie, Susan, without a word, did as she was bid.

Bessie's anger flared again. 'So you think he's guilty, do you?'

'Bessie, go home, will you? If the lad really had nowt to do with it, then his job's here for him. But if he did . . .' Jack Price did not finish his sentence, but the unspoken words were clear enough as if he had shouted them from the rooftops.

'If he did, Jack Price, then you'd better keep your head down, because you'll see pigs flying past.' Bessie turned and grabbed hold of Mary Ann's hand. 'Come on, lass. We're going home.'

Later that afternoon, Bessie returned to the police station but once more all they would tell her was that Sid Clark and Dan had been brought back to Elsborough police station and were now in the cells.

'You'd better get your lad a solicitor,' was the only advice they would give her.

'A solicitor!' Bessie wailed later to Bert. 'How on earth can we afford to pay for a solicitor?'

'Have you spoken to Miss Edwina?' Bert asked. He was as worried as Bessie, but had taken the news much more calmly. 'Her father's a magistrate. Perhaps he can help?'

'Oh Bert . . .' Dramatically, Bessie flung her arms around him. 'I never thought of that. Mind you, I ain't been thinking straight all day. What would I do without you, Bert? I'll go first thing in the morning. I know she'll do what she can. She'll believe in my lad, even if that rat,

Price, doesn't. Do you know?' she went on indignantly. 'He's told Susan that she's not to see Dan any more. Now that tells you a lot, doesn't it?'

Behind her, Mary Ann smiled.

Twenty

'Of course, I'll do whatever I can.'

In her own way, Edwina was as indignant as Bessie. 'It's unthinkable that Dan would be involved in any way. I'll speak to my father as soon as I get home.' She reached out and took Bessie's hand. 'Try not to worry, Bessie. The police had to do their job and just remember, they don't know Dan like we do. But it'll be all right. I promise you. Sid Clark must have known that Dan's ship was leaving the following morning.'

Bessie nodded, hope lighting her eyes now as she listened to Edwina's calm and rational explanation of what might have happened. 'Mebbe he heard someone talking about it in The Waterman's,' she suggested.

'There you are, then. Maybe he even thought, in his twisted mind, that Dan *might* help him. Not that he would, of course,' Edwina added hurriedly. 'What happened in Hull? Do you know?'

Bessie shook her head. 'They won't tell us anything.'

'I'll try to find out for you. In the meantime, have you brought Mary Ann to school?'

Bessie nodded. 'Yes, I thought it best for her.'

'I'm sure you're right. I'll make sure all the staff know what's happened and we'll look after her. I'll walk home with her tonight. You know what other children can be like and the news will be spreading like the proverbial wildfire by now.'

Bessie nodded sadly. 'Poor little lass. I wonder what's going to happen to her?' She felt Edwina's thoughtful gaze on her and looked up. 'What?'

'Can you look after her for a few days at least?' Edwina asked. 'Just until we can find out if she's any relative, who would take her in?'

Bessie's answer was swift. 'Of course we can. As long as it takes.'

It was already dark in the enclosed confines of Waterman's Yard when Edwina and Mary Ann arrived at Bessie's home late that afternoon.

'Come in, come in. The kettle's boiling. Mary Ann, you nip across to Minnie's. She's been baking and promised me one of her apple pies.' Bessie winked at Edwina. 'Minnie Eccleshall's pastry is legend around here. Not even I can get it as light as she does. Come in, Miss Edwina. Here, let me take your hat and coat. Go on, Mary Ann, there's a love.'

When the girl was safely across the yard, Bessie said, 'I arranged all that with Minnie earlier, just in case you had owt to tell me.'

Edwina nodded. 'I have. I managed to see my father at lunchtime. It appears that Dan has been arrested because they believe he helped Sid Clark to escape by allowing him to stow away on the *Nerissa*.'

Bessie nodded, but held back her impatience. That much she knew already.

'Naturally, Dan is protesting his innocence and pointing out – and there are witnesses to this, Bessie – that it was he who raised the alarm when he saw the man trying to sneak off the ship at Hull.'

'But they don't believe him?'

'Not yet, but they will,' Edwina said confidently. 'I've got in touch with our solicitors and Mr Riggall promised to go to the station and see Dan this very afternoon.'

Bessie let out a sigh of relief. 'Thank you, Miss Edwina.' She wrinkled her forehead. 'I expect we can scrape up for his fees.'

Edwina waved her hand as she removed her gloves and sat down in Bert's sagging armchair. 'Don't worry about that, Bessie, please. My family retains Riggall and Bates on a permanent basis.' She smiled impishly. 'I'm sure that little bit won't be noticed on the account.'

'Oh Miss Edwina, but we couldn't . . .'

'Yes, you can and you will, Bessie Ruddick. You're looking after the girl, aren't you? If we all do our bit, then . . .'

She said no more as the door opened and Mary Ann appeared, carefully carrying an apple pie, hot from Minnie's oven.

'Now, doesn't that look a treat?' Bessie said. 'What say we all have a piece, eh? With a nice helping of cream?'

Dan arrived home about eight o'clock that evening to a rapturous welcome from his family and a tearful, clinging one from Mary Ann.

'There, there, love. It'll be all right,' Dan patted her awkwardly and looked over the girl's head for help from his mother.

Briskly, but not unkindly, Bessie said, 'Now, now, Mary Ann. Let our Dan get inside the door. I bet you're hungry, lad, aren't you?'

'What happened?' Duggie demanded. 'Is everything all right?'

Dan pulled a face. 'Sort of. I'm released on bail pending

147

further inquiries. They haven't dropped the charges yet, but Mr Riggall seems sure they will. It's thanks to Miss Edwina that I'm here at all. If it wasn't for her, I'd still be locked up in that awful cell.' He gave a dramatic shudder and glanced sympathetically towards Mary Ann. He wondered if she was thinking about her own father, locked up in a similar cold, dank place. 'Worst of it is,' Dan went on, 'I'm not allowed to leave the town, so I can't sail.'

Bessie exchanged a glance with Bert, who said, 'That's a blow, lad, because the way Price is feeling at the moment, I doubt he'll find you work elsewhere.'

'No,' Dan said gloomily, 'and I don't expect he'll let me see Susan either.'

Bessie put her hand on his shoulder. 'There are other ships and other employers. Once all this business is over, it'll be all right.'

'Maybe,' Dan murmured. 'But don't say it, Mam. Don't say there's other girls, 'cos I don't want to hear it.'

Quietly, Bessie said, 'I wasn't going to, lad. I wasn't going to.'

Mary Ann, sitting next to Dan, slipped her arm through his and leant her head against his shoulder, smiling gently.

The tiny community of Waterman's Yard rallied around Mary Ann. Even Amy grudgingly acknowledged that whatever had happened was not the girl's fault. But she could not and would not have a scrap of sympathy for the man.

'If I had my way,' she said loudly for all to hear, 'they'd not only hang the devil but draw and quarter him an' all and stick his head on a pike near the bridge for all to see his shame.'

Bessie smiled wryly at the change in her neighbour. At least, Bessie thought, she's showing a bit of spirit at last. Anything's better than that dreadful wallowing in self-pity.

'Aye,' Bessie murmured to herself more than once. 'It's an ill wind that blows nobody any good.'

The police were now satisfied that they had the right person in jail awaiting trial for murder and, to everyone's relief, all charges against Dan were dropped. With the examination of the crime scene complete, the authorities gave permission for the house the Clarks had occupied to be cleared, cleaned and re-let.

'I can't see anyone wanting to come and live there,' Minnie Eccleshall shuddered. 'I don't even want to set foot in the place.' She eyed Bessie fearfully. 'You weren't going to ask me to come with you, Bessie, were you?'

Bessie weighed the key she held in her hand thoughtfully. 'The owners have asked me to see to the clearing out. Everything belongs to Mary Ann by rights, though there's nothing in there that's worth a brass farthing, if you ask me. Still, there might be some bits and pieces she'll want.'

Appalled, Minnie said, 'You're not expecting that poor little lass to go in there, are you?'

'Heavens, no. What do you think I am, Minnie Eccleshall? No,' she added grimly. 'I'll see to it. And when you've got a rotten job to do, then I always say it's best got over and done with. So, if you're not going to be a help, Min, at least don't be a hindrance.'

'Sorry, I'm sure.' Min said huffily as she stepped back smartly out of the way. But still, she did not offer to help Bessie.

Even Bessie's stout heart quailed a little as she opened the door that had been repaired and stepped inside. Hands on hips, she stood in the centre of the kitchen and surveyed the broken chair, the rickety table, the dirty curtainless windows. There was nothing here that made a home, nothing worth keeping for Mary Ann. And despite Miss Edwina's endeavours to find someone, it seemed that Mary Ann had no relatives who were willing to take her.

'I made contact with her mother's family,' Edwina had told Bessie only the previous day and shook her head sadly. 'They won't have anything to do with her. They just don't want to know. Can you believe it?'

Bessie had shaken her head sadly. 'I can believe it, yes. Because it happens. But I don't understand it.'

Now, as Bessie stood in the silent, tragic house, she said aloud, 'Well, Bessie Ruddick, me girl, you always did hanker after a daughter. And now it looks like you've got yourself one.'

Part Two

Mary Ann

Twenty-One

1921

'Now you remember all I've told you. Miss Edwina's given you the most marvellous chance, Mary Ann. Taking you on as an upstairs maid, and as her personal maid too. You don't know how lucky you are. I started work at The Hall when I was thirteen as a scullery maid and I had to work me way up. And the cook they had there then was a right tartar, I can tell you . . .'

Beside her, Bessie prattled on, but Mary Ann was listening only with half an ear. Her mind was busy with her own plans for her future – plans that certainly included what Bessie and Miss Edwina had mapped out for her, but Mary Ann's own ambitions went much further than either of them could guess.

Bessie was right about one thing though, the girl conceded. She was lucky, very lucky, that Miss Edwina had offered her a job in her own home, for The Hall was only just a few streets away from Waterman's Yard and a mere couple of hundred yards from the river.

Mary Ann smiled. From today on, she was a working girl, a grown up and, best of all, she would be living and working only a short distance from Dan.

'Are you listening to me, lass?' Bessie prodded her arm.

'Of course I am, Auntie Bessie,' Mary Ann answered

with pretended obedience. 'I'm to be a good girl and work hard and be a credit to you and to Miss Edwina.'

'Aye well, that an' all, lass.' Now Mary Ann felt Bessie's comforting hand take hold of her arm. Her voice was gentle as she added, 'But most of all, lass, I want you to be a credit to your poor mam. Don't ever forget her, will ya?'

They stopped on the path outside the entrance to The Hall and turned to face each other. Although she had grown rapidly in the past year, Mary Ann still had to stand on tiptoe to reach up and kiss Bessie's cheek. The girl had, as Bessie put it, 'filled out in all the right places'. Now she was no longer the skinny little waif, but a pretty young girl with an impish smile and a sparkle in her eyes, on the brink of womanhood. Mary Ann said nothing in response to Bessie's plea, but merely smiled, stepped back and with a little wave moved towards the back door of The Hall.

'See you on Sunday afternoon, Auntie Bessie. Give my love to Dan when he comes home tonight.'

Then she was gone, running lightly across the grass towards the stately building that was now to be her home.

Mrs Nellie Goodrick was nothing like Mary Ann had expected the cook at The Hall would be. She had pictured someone like Bessie on baking day. Tall, maybe, but round and jolly and red-faced from the constant heat of the oven. So the appearance of the woman standing before her, hands on hips, her steely, unfriendly gaze raking Mary Ann's appearance from head to toe, was a surprise – and not a pleasant one.

Nellie Goodrick was certainly tall, but with little shape to the bony body covered by her copious white apron.

The apron and the white cap were the only things, Mary Ann thought, that made her look like a cook. She had cold grey eyes and a nose like a bird's beak above a thin-lipped mouth that seemed constantly pursed in disapproval.

'So you're the new girl, are you?'

Mary Ann decided meekness would be her greatest ally, at least on her first day.

'Yes, ma'am,' she answered, keeping her voice low and deferential.

'I hope you know how lucky you are? This position should have been young Clara's by rights. She's been here long enough to be promoted from just a general maid.' The woman gave a quick shake of her head. 'But there you are, life isn't always fair, is it?'

Life had been decidedly unfair to Nellie Goodrick. Not only had she not even been in the queue when the looks were given out, but she had also allowed bitterness to warp her personality. Her forty-six years of life had been spent solely trying to please others. Firstly her parents, from whom she had never managed, not once, to illicit an endearment or a gesture of pride towards her. Secondly, her husband, whom, in a short-lived marriage, she had also, it seemed, failed to please. And so, it had been her lot to be in service from the age of thirteen, the last twenty years in the employ of Bertram Marsh and his wife, Isabella, here at The Hall.

Mr and Mrs Marsh kept themselves aloof from their servants. They were kindly, always fair, but distant. Their eldest son, Arthur, who had been killed on the Somme, had been quiet and shy and had scarcely spoken more than a few dozen words with the woman who prepared all the food he ate. As for Randolph, the second son, who was now, because of the death of his brother, the heir to the Marsh estate, well, what Nellie Goodrick thought about him was best left unsaid. Her opinions, if ever voiced, would earn her instant dismissal from this household.

There was really only one person within the household for whom Nellie had any affection, such as her unloved and unloving heart was able to feel – Miss Edwina. And it was for this reason alone that Nellie Goodrick strove to keep her resentment at the arrival of this girl in check. And this girl especially, for they all knew of Mary Ann's tragic circumstances. Unlike the inhabitants of Waterman's Yard, the servants at The Hall believed in the saying 'bad blood will out'. There was certainly bad blood flowing through Mary Ann Clark's veins in Nellie's opinion and, as she had remarked at the supper table in the kitchen only the previous evening, 'Miss Edwina will regret bringing her here. You mark my words.' Everyone around the table from Peter Deakin, The Hall's one and only manservant, to Clara Dobson, the general maid, and the kitchen maid, Jessie Banks, had indeed 'marked her words'.

Now she saw the subject of her words standing before her in person, Nellie felt no compunction to change her mind. The girl had a bold look, she thought, and she was pretty, far too pretty to work here. Nellie sighed. No doubt within a very few months she would be the third girl to depart hastily in tears and without a reference, having believed Randolph Marsh's seductive protestations of love. It was on the tip of her tongue to warn the girl, but the bitter resentment against anyone who was even remotely attractive rose in her throat and choked her warning.

Mary Ann stared back at the woman unflinchingly. Far from being daunted by the cook's animosity, she saw it as a challenge.

In the last year or so since the tragedy of Waterman's Yard, as it had been headlined in the local newspaper, Mary Ann had changed. Welcomed into the Ruddick family household, she had been spoiled and petted by them all. Bessie and Bert had immediately treated her as their daughter, as if she had been born to them late in life, the gift of their dreams.

For the boys, she had been a younger sister to be teased and spoiled and protected and each, in their own way, had done so. The extended family, the other inhabitants of the Yard, had shown her nothing but sympathy, and Mary Ann had blossomed in the warmth of their affection like a flower under the sun's warm rays. Her life would have been perfect if it had not been for the dreadful shadow of her father's crime. There was not a person in the town who did not know all about it and who she was. Whilst the residents of the Yard might be kindly, other people were less understanding. There was no escape unless she went right away, but that would mean leaving Dan and the rest of his family.

'The best way,' Miss Edwina had counselled, 'is to hold your head high and live through it. I know it's difficult, especially when you're so young, but it's the only way. You can't run all your life, Mary Ann. Wherever you go, however far away from here, people have a habit of finding out about you, and you would have to run again and go on running.'

Mary Ann had agreed. 'I don't want to leave here, Miss Edwina. You and Auntie Bessie and everyone in Waterman's Yard have been so kind to me,' she said winningly. But the real reason why she wanted to stay in Elsborough Mary Ann had kept to herself.

During the time that the trial of Sid Clark and the impending death sentence upon him were constantly in the news, there had been no respite from people's interest in her. Not until the sentence had been carried out could Mary Ann begin to build her new life.

'I want to go, Auntie Bessie,' she had declared the day before her father was due to be hanged at nine o'clock in the morning at Lincoln prison.

Bessie had looked at her aghast. 'Oh love, whatever for?'

The girl had shrugged. 'I just need to go. I need to be there.'

'You mean . . .' Bessie had faltered, for once completely lost for words. 'You want to see him once more before . . .?'

At this, Mary Ann had shaken her head vehemently. 'Oh no, I never want to see him again.' Her dark eyes had held Bessie's and her mouth had hardened as she said, 'I just want to be there to know he's really dead and never coming back.'

Bessie had put her arms around her and tried to draw the girl's rigid body close. 'Aw love, he's been found guilty. Even if he was to get a last-minute reprieve and they didn't hang him, he's never going to get out of jail again. I promise you, he's never coming back.'

It had been Dan who had taken her, very early the following day, to Lincoln. They had stood in the grey, dank morning outside the grim walls of the prison on top of the hill. There was a small gathering and Mary Ann caught brief snatches of the murmured conversations around her.

'They reckon he's not shown a scrap of remorse at what he's done.'

'The bastard!'

'Aye, well, he were a conchy, weren't he? What can you expect?'

'Too cowardly to fight the enemy, eh, but he could batter his poor wife to death . . .'

'There's a kiddie, isn't there? A girl?'

'Aye, poor wench. She'll be an orphan after this morning's work.'

''Spect it'll haunt her for the rest of her life.'

Mary Ann stood stolidly silent. Not so much as the twitch of a muscle or the flicker of an eyelid betrayed the fact that she had overheard. Only Dan, squeezing her hand in comfort, knew.

The words went on, floating around her head.

'He's not long now. It's gone eight. The chaplain will be with him now.'

'Then he'll be taken from the condemned cell to a room right next to the scaffold,' one man said, and added, almost with a note of pride, 'I've seen the place.' Then he gave a dramatic shudder. 'By heck! I wouldn't want to be in his shoes at this moment.'

Now Mary Ann's fingers tightened on Dan's hand, although neither of them spoke or even glanced at each other.

At a quarter to nine, they heard the distant tolling of the prison bell and then, just as the hour of nine o'clock struck, they saw a black flag being hoisted on the prison tower.

'That's it, then,' a voice behind them said. 'That's him done for. And good riddance, I say.'

The murmuring amongst the crowd seemed to grow louder and when, a few minutes later, a warder appeared at the door and attached two notices to a board on the wall outside, the onlookers surged forward. The declaration, signed by the Under Sheriff of Lincolnshire, the Governor and the Chaplain of the prison, stated that 'the judgement of death was this day executed on Sidney

Clark'. Beside it, another notice announced that a surgeon had examined the body and pronounced the said Sidney Clark dead.

'Come on, love,' Dan said softly. 'Time we went home.'

Mary Ann slipped her arm through Dan's and turned her back on the place where her father had died. She would never, she vowed silently, think of him again.

'Well,' Nellie Goodrick said, 'I suppose Clara had better take you up to Miss Edwina's room.'

Mary Ann smiled her best smile and even dropped a tiny curtsy. 'Thank you, Mrs Goodrick,' she said prettily.

Clara Dobson was as sour-faced as the cook and took no pains to conceal her resentment of the newcomer. 'Miss Edwina's never had a maid before. What she wants to bring you here for, I don't know. I've always done everything for her.'

For the moment, Mary Ann kept her mouth tightly shut, even pressing her lips together to stop them mouthing the retort that sprang to her lips.

The other girl grumbled on. 'You needn't think yourself above the rest of us. You'll have to muck in and help with the housework, like everyone else has to.' Mary Ann felt her belligerent glance. 'We're not exactly overloaded with servants here. It's a big old house and takes a lot of looking after.'

She's right there, Mary Ann thought, as she followed the girl. It is a very old house.

They passed through the great hall, which was the very centre of the medieval house. There was little furniture in the room, but the vast timber arched roof was awesome. Each roof-truss was cut from a naturally curving oak tree and carved by craftsmen long since gone.

Mary Ann gazed about her. For a brief moment, she felt strangely in awe of the room's size.

'Through here,' said her unwilling guide sharply, leading the way up a wooden spiral staircase towards the east wing, where the furnishings gave the old rooms a more modern appearance, along passages that nevertheless still creaked with age, until Clara opened a bedroom door and stood aside for Mary Ann to enter. 'Here you are, then. You'd best get busy being Miss Edwina's personal maid. And don't ask me what you're to do, 'cos I aren't helping you. Not ever. So don't ask.'

Mary Ann passed close to her, entered the room and looked about her. Whilst the walls and ceilings could not hide their age, the furnishings were pretty and feminine, indicative of the young woman who slept there.

Mary Ann turned and, with a smile that dimpled her cheeks and lit up her eyes, said in response to the sullen maid's statement, 'I won't, Clara. Believe me, I won't.'

Twenty-Two

'How've you got on, then? Everything all right?'

Bessie was waiting at the door for her on the following Sunday afternoon, just like any anxious mother awaiting the return of her daughter for the first time since starting work.

Mary Ann gave a little skip and ran the last few steps across the yard to throw her arms around the woman she thought of as her mother now. 'It was all right. I don't see much of Miss Edwina because she's at school all day. But I clean her room from top to bottom, just like you've taught me. And I sort out all her clothes and tidy all her drawers.' Mary Ann laughed and the merry sound echoed around the yard. 'For someone who's so good at needle-work, there's a lot of her things need mending. Miss Edwina might have shown me how to do pretty stitches, but you've shown me how to darn and mend, Bessie, and that's going to be a lot more use to me now.'

Bessie hugged the girl to her. She had missed her. Even though she was only a street or two away, the house where Mary Ann now lived and Bessie's home in Water-man's Yard were worlds apart. But Bessie knew every inch of the inside of The Hall and she had been imagining Mary Ann's every move during the days she had been away.

'What were the rest of the staff like with you? And the master and the mistress?'

'I only saw the master striding through the great hall,' Mary Ann began as Bessie drew her into the warm kitchen and fussed over her. 'The mistress came into Miss Edwina's room once to see what I was doing. She seems a nice lady, but she always looks so sad and . . . and vague, somehow. As if she's not quite aware of what's going on around her.'

Bessie's face was sober. 'She's lost her boy. Her eldest son. Her firstborn. Think how I'd feel if I lost Dan.'

Mary Ann's eyes were horrified. 'Don't, Auntie Bessie. Don't say such a thing.'

'It's all right, love.' Bessie patted the girl's arm, angry with herself that she had touched on even the thought of a personal tragedy. Mary Ann had already had more than her share of trouble without imagining more. Swiftly, bringing the conversation back to safer ground, Bessie said, 'What did the mistress say to you?'

'She just asked me if I was all right and that she hoped I'd be happy with them.'

'That was kind,' Bessie murmured and added, 'and the rest of the staff. What was Nellie Goodrick like with you?'

Mary Ann laughed. 'I reckon her face'd turn milk sour.'

Bessie chuckled. 'Poor Nellie. She came as a kitchen maid just before I left to marry my Bert and she was a poor scrawny thing then.'

'And,' Mary Ann went on, 'Clara Dobson reckons I've taken her job so she's very unfriendly.'

'Oh dear, that's a shame.'

Mary Ann shrugged and there was a tight determination to her mouth. 'She doesn't bother me.'

'What's your own room like?'

Mary Ann, like all the other servants at The Hall, was obliged to live in. She pulled a face. 'All right, except that

I have to share with Clara and neither of us are happy about that.'

'And, er . . .' Bessie seemed hesitant now. 'And what about Mr Randolph? Have you met him yet?'

'No. He's away.'

'Ah. Now, you just be careful of him, love. He's got a bit of a reputation where pretty young housemaids are concerned.'

'Don't worry about me, Auntie Bessie. I can take care of myself.' Mary Ann put her head on one side and listened. Hearing no other movement in the house except for the sounds in the kitchen, she said, 'Where is everyone?'

'Bert's upstairs on the bed, snoring his head off after the big Sunday dinner I've just given him. By the way, I've saved you a plateful if you want it, love.'

'And the others?'

'They're off out somewhere. Don't ask me where.'

'And Dan? Where's Dan?'

'So you're the new little maid?'

Mary Ann, sitting in a window seat, her back to the latticed, leaded window, her head bent over her needlework, looked up to see a man standing a few feet in front of her. Without doubt, he was the most handsome man she had ever seen. Handsomer, even, than Dan, she had to admit. He was tall with smooth fair hair and a broad forehead. His nose was long and straight and his jaw strong and square. Indeed, his features were so well balanced they could have been carved by an artist's chisel. His mouth curved in a mocking smile and he held his head slightly on one side, one fair eyebrow raised in a sardonic question.

He moved closer. His voice was rich and deep as he asked her, 'And what is your name, young lady?'

She stood up, laid her work aside and bobbed a little curtsy. 'Mary Ann, sir. You must be Mr Randolph.'

He laughed softly. 'So you've heard about me?'

'Miss Edwina has spoken of you, sir.'

This was quite true, for Edwina had said only that morning before leaving to go to her school, 'My brother returns today.' She had smiled and added, 'He's a handsome devil, Mary Ann, and unfortunately he is only too well aware of it. He's also a shameless flirt with pretty young girls. You, my dear, fall into that category, so please be warned.'

Her words had been spoken with humour and yet there had been an underlying caution in them and they had echoed Bessie's earlier warning. Standing before him now, Mary Ann could see why. Young though she was, she could see the interest sparking in his eyes as his glance travelled slowly and appraisingly up and down her slim body. Mary Ann returned his stare steadily, not in the least fazed by his interest in her.

'You're a bold one,' he murmured. 'New maids usually blush and simper on meeting me.'

Mary Ann smiled, knowing that her own brown eyes were full of mischief.

He moved closer still and reached out, touching her chin with his forefinger. Nearer now, she could see that his eyes were a startlingly bright blue.

'We shall have to become better acquainted, Mary Ann.'

'Randolph.'

He let his hand fall away as they both heard Edwina speak behind them. She entered the long room and came towards them smiling. 'Now, now, you leave my little

165

Mary Ann alone. Besides, unless I'm much mistaken, Mary Ann has eyes for no one but Dan Ruddick. Isn't that right, Mary Ann?' Without waiting for confirmation or denial, she continued, holding her face up to Randolph for his brotherly kiss, 'And he's a big burly skipper of one of Mr Price's keel boats that goes up and down the river. So you'd better beware.'

She patted her brother's chest playfully and then moved to pick up Mary Ann's needlework.

'That's very good, my dear. Excellent, in fact.' She looked up and smiled. 'I think you'll achieve your dream one day of being able to embroider a banner for the church. What do you say, Randolph?' Edwina held out the circular embroidery frame, which held the stretched piece of peach-coloured satin upon which Mary Ann had been working in coloured silks.

Randolph cast a disinterested glance upon it. 'Yes, very nice. Well, I must be off. I'll see you at dinner, Edwina.' Then he turned and strode away down the room.

For a moment both young women stood watching him and then Edwina touched Mary Ann lightly on her arm and said, 'Come, it's time I taught you how to outline this silk work with gold thread.'

Together they sat on the window seat, their heads bent over the delicate embroidery, but before her eyes, all Mary Ann could see was the handsome face of Randolph Marsh.

Randolph filled The Hall with his presence.

'Whenever he comes into the house,' Mary Ann told the Ruddick family one Sunday afternoon when she had been working at The Hall for several weeks, 'it's like a whisper runs through the house. "Mr Randolph's home,

Mr Randolph's home." And everyone scuttles about like he's some god.'

They were all sitting around the table for Sunday afternoon tea. It was a family ritual that they all enjoyed. They exchanged their news, reported what had happened to them in their working life the previous week. Told funny stories or found sympathy and, often, advice for their problems too.

'His mother indulges him,' Bessie remarked, as she poured the tea from the huge teapot and handed the cups around the table. 'In her eyes he can do no wrong. And since he's a chip off the old block, as they say,' she smiled and explained, 'just like his father was when he was that age, well, Mr Bertram isn't going to find fault with him either, is he?'

'That's not always the case, though, is it, my angel,' Bert remarked. 'Sometimes when a son is exactly like his father and they're both strong characters, then there can be a clash of personalities.' His grin widened as he winked at Mary Ann. 'Mind you, with my lot, I know my place.'

Mary Ann smiled back. Bert Ruddick was what she would call a lovely man. Kind, generous, sensible and down to earth, but when it came to strength of character, then there was really only one member of the Ruddick parents' incredible partnership that could be called 'strong' and that was Bessie. But Mary Ann was beginning to realize that Bessie was a wise woman. Whilst she took the lead in almost everything, she always acted as if she deferred to her husband's wishes and she never allowed anyone to voice the notion that it was she, and not he, who wore the trousers in their house.

'You're quite right, Bert,' Bessie was saying now. 'But your boys respect you, don't they? I'm not sure that Mr Randolph respects anyone.'

'He seems very fond of Miss Edwina,' Mary Ann put in. 'He's always very kind to her.' She wrinkled her forehead thoughtfully. 'In fact, he treats Miss Edwina better than anyone else. Even better than his mother. He's a bit . . . a bit . . . sort of . . .' The young girl sought for the right words to express what she felt. 'Offhand with her. Do you know what I mean?'

Bessie nodded, her mouth tightening for a moment. 'I do. It's because Mrs Marsh is so soft with him – always has been – and he knows it. Miss Edwina, now, she stands up to him. She sees right through him and won't stand for his nonsense. So,' Bessie shrugged at the perverseness of human nature, 'he respects her far more than he does his indulgent mother.'

'Do you think Miss Edwina will ever get married?' Mary Ann asked.

Before Bessie could answer, Duggie said, 'Didn't you know? She's waiting for me. Tall, dark and handsome. I'm just what she's looking for.'

Bessie's laugh rang out. 'Dark, I'll grant you. But as for the rest, well . . .'

Duggie laughed the loudest of them all. He was the shortest member of the Ruddick family, but his shoulders were broad and strong from his work on the wharves along the river. He was not conventionally good looking; his nose was a little too large, his jaw slightly too square, but his dark eyes sparkled with mischief and good humour. His black curly hair, an unruly mop, coupled with his weather-beaten skin gave him a gypsyish appearance. 'I never liked school when I had to go,' he was saying now. 'But if I could go to Miss Marsh's, I'd go back tomorrow.'

'Aye, and it'd do you some good an' all,' his mother teased. 'Mebbe you'd have got that apprenticeship at the engineering works you're always going on about, if you'd worked a bit harder at school, m'lad.'

There was a moment's silence around the table and Mary Ann held her breath, but then Duggie adopted a hangdog expression and pressed the palm of his hand over his heart. 'Aw, Mam, cut me to the quick, you have.' Sitting next to Mary Ann, he pretended to dissolve into tears and hid his face against her shoulder.

'The truth sometimes hurts, lad,' Bessie said.

Duggie raised his head, gave an exaggerated sigh and then grinned amiably. 'Yeah. You're right, Mam. Of course, you are.' He glanced at Mary Ann and winked. 'It's me own fault if I'm going to have to work on the river all me life.'

'You could do a lot worse.' At once, Bessie sprang to defend not only Bert, but Dan too. 'If truth be told, lad, I'm proud that you *do* work on the river. Much better than being in a smelly old factory.'

'Ernie works indoors. You're proud of him and his posh office job, aren't you? Even if it is still only a stone's throw from the river.'

Bessie opened her mouth to reply but to everyone's surprise Ernie spoke. 'I sometimes wish I was out on the river instead of stuck indoors.'

The whole family and Mary Ann stared at him, waiting for him to go on, but a flush of embarrassment crept up the young man's neck. He looked down at his plate, crumbling a piece of bread between his fingers. Then, as if to cover his discomfort, everyone seemed to speak at once.

'You're doing well there, Ernie,' his father said. 'You stick at it, lad. Maybe one day you'll be office manager.'

'I envy you in winter,' Dan grinned. 'Nice and warm indoors. I'll swap you, if you like.'

'Can you get me a job there?' Duggie joked.

'We were talking about Miss Edwina,' Bessie said, glancing at Mary Ann. Her smile faded as she added, 'And no, I doubt she will ever get married now, if I'm honest, because I don't know whether she'll ever meet anyone who will match up to Mr Christopher in her eyes. It was a match made in heaven. They were ideally suited and were so in love. You could see it in their eyes.' She sighed heavily. 'It's a cruel world.'

Now there was silence around the table for a few moments, the only sound the clatter of knives and forks against plates.

At the end of the meal, Dan stood up. 'I'll be on me way then.'

Everyone looked up at him and then Mary Ann rose too and slipped her hand through his arm. 'Are you going to walk me home, Dan?' she said, her head coyly on one side. 'But I don't have to go yet. I don't have to be back at The Hall until nine.'

For a moment Dan looked embarrassed. 'Well, I . . . er . . . I've arranged to go out tonight, Mary Ann. Perhaps Duggie . . .?' He looked hopefully across at his younger brother.

'Yeah, I'll walk you back, Mary Ann.'

Mary Ann pouted. 'You always see me back on a Sunday night, Dan.'

'Maybe he's meeting someone. A girl,' Duggie tormented. 'Oho, I'm right. Look at his face.'

Under their scrutiny, Dan's face reddened even more.

'Who is she, Dan? Come on, you can tell us.'

Bessie stood up and began to gather the plates into a pile. 'Leave the lad alone. He's big enough and ugly enough to look after himself. He'll tell us when he wants us to know.'

170

Dan shot his mother a grateful look, but even so he said, 'You might as well know, I suppose. I'm seeing Susan.'

'Susan!' came a chorus of surprised voices and Bessie added, 'Not behind her father's back I hope, lad, else you're stacking up trouble for yourself.'

'No, no. He's given his permission. She was waiting for me yesterday on the wharf. I thought it was all over – for good – but it seems she asked him if she could see me again and he agreed. So . . .' He shrugged and then glanced down at Mary Ann, seeming about to speak to her. But she, after staring at him in shocked silence for a moment, snatched her hand away from his arm and sat down heavily on her chair. For the first time in ages, Mary Ann's hand crept up towards her face and, almost of its own volition, her thumb crept into her mouth.

She was aware that Dan was still hovering close by, looking as if he didn't know whether to go or to stay. Mary Ann felt his hesitant gaze upon her but, stubbornly, she refused to look at him.

'Don't stand there dithering, lad,' Bessie was saying briskly. 'Get off with you, if you're going. And you, Mary Ann, can stop that sulking this minute and come and help me with the washing up.'

But Mary Ann continued to sit quite still, sucking her thumb and staring into the fire.

Twenty-Three

Mary Ann walked quickly through the dark streets with Duggie trying to keep up with her.

'By heck, you walk quick for a girl. What's the hurry? Got a train to catch, have you?'

'It's cold and I'm getting wet,' she snapped.

Duggie laughed. 'Little bit of rain won't hurt you. You ought to work outdoors in all weathers like me.'

'Well, I don't and I don't want to.'

'Oho, getting used to the soft life, are we?' he teased, but there was no malice in his tone. Duggie hadn't a drop of spite in him, but Mary Ann was in no mood for his jocularity.

She stopped suddenly. 'You needn't come any further.'

'Our Dan'd knock me head off if I hadn't seen you to the door and summat happened.'

Through clenched teeth Mary Ann said, 'If "your Dan" had been so bothered, he'd have come with me himself.'

There was a moment's silence before Duggie said, 'By heck, you're jealous. You're jealous of him going to meet Susan, aren't you?'

Mary Ann glared at him. Through the darkness she could not see his face, but she knew he was laughing. She could hear it in his voice.

'What would you know about it, Duggie Ruddick?' With that parting shot, she whirled about and was gone, running along the wet pavement to get away from him as fast as she could.

She heard him calling behind her, 'Mary Ann, Mary Ann. Wait. I didn't mean . . .'

She rounded the corner, and before her loomed the dark shape of The Hall, lights twinkling from its leaded windows. He wouldn't follow her any further now. He would know she was home. Near the door leading into the kitchens and thence to the servants' quarters, Mary Ann leant against the wall to catch her breath. She rested her head against the rough brickwork, closed her eyes and gave a low groan.

Now the whole Ruddick family would know of her love for Dan. Duggie was the last of them to be able to keep a secret. She could imagine him telling them all, could see them sitting round the fire laughing together at her foolishness. Maybe Dan would laugh the loudest. The thought wounded her and she let out another low moan.

'What's the matter? Are you hurt?'

Mary Ann jumped as the voice came unexpectedly out of the darkness.

'Oh! Mr Randolph. No – I mean . . .'

'What are you doing out here in the dark?' He moved closer, towering over her. 'Waiting for a young man, perhaps?'

'Oh no, sir.'

'Really? You surprise me. A pretty little thing like you must have a string of admirers.'

'No, sir,' Mary Ann said again, trying valiantly to make her tone sound prim. 'Mrs Goodrick would flay me alive if I had a follower.'

'Indeed?' He paused and then asked, 'So, what are you doing out here, skulking about in the dark?'

'I'm not skulking,' Mary Ann flashed indignantly, quite

forgetting for the moment to whom she was speaking. 'I've just come back from my afternoon off and – and . . .' Ingenuity came to her rescue. 'I – I think I've twisted my ankle coming up the path. I was just resting against the wall for a moment. I . . .' She began to embroider the tale. 'I felt a bit dizzy with the sharp pain.'

'Pray allow me to assist you.' The words sounded concerned and yet his tone held a hint of derision, as if he didn't quite believe her and yet was willing to play along.

'I'll be all right, sir, thank you. If I can just get inside.'

'You didn't ought to put any weight on it, if you have sprained it, my dear.'

Before Mary Ann realized what was happening, Randolph had bent down, put one arm beneath her knees and the other about her waist and lifted her up into his arms. She gave a cry of protest, but his only answer was a soft laugh.

Moments later, they were in the room that Randolph called his den and he was setting her down gently into a leather armchair at the side of a crackling fire.

The room, at the far end of the east wing of the sprawling old house, had been the boys' playroom. As they had grown older they had called it their den, where they could be alone together or where they could invite their friends without disturbing the rest of the household. Sadly, only Randolph now enjoyed its privacy. Not a day went by when he did not miss his quieter, more sober, brother, although not for one instant would he ever have admitted what he believed to be a sign of weakness – that of pure, unadulterated affection for another human being.

'Which foot did you hurt?'

'The . . . the right one.' Mary Ann was feeling apprehensive. What if he could tell that she had not hurt her ankle at all?

Randolph sat down on a footstool and took Mary Ann's foot into his hands. He unlaced her boot and gently slipped it from her foot. Then his hands slid up her leg to find the top of her stocking. Mary Ann's eyes widened. 'Don't . . .' she began, but he only smiled in the firelight.

'If I'm to be your doctor, then you must allow me to examine you properly.' His voice was deep and somehow hypnotizing, silencing her protests almost before they had begun.

Gently, he eased her stocking down and drew it from her foot. With strong fingers he gently pressed around her anklebone. His head was bent over her foot and Mary Ann noticed that his hair was thick and springy and that, despite his efforts to smooth it, there was a tiny, wayward curl behind his ear. For some irrational reason, she had the urge to reach out to touch it.

'There doesn't seem to be anything broken, nor is it swollen.' He looked up at her then, his eyes, shadowed and unfathomable depths in the flickering light from the fire, the only illumination in the room. In little more than a whisper, he asked, 'Where does it hurt?'

Mary Ann ran her tongue around her lips, which were suddenly dry, naïvely unaware how provocative her action was to the man kneeling before her. 'It doesn't now,' she said. 'It must have felt worse when . . . when I did it than it really was.'

Randolph smiled in the dim light. 'I'm sure it did.' He spoke the words so softly that she was unable to tell whether he believed her or not. He was still kneeling in front of her, stroking her foot with his fingers in a caress that suddenly became stronger, more urgent. 'Perhaps a little massage will help,' he murmured.

He was stroking the area around her ankle and then smoothing the top of her foot and gently wriggling each of her toes. His touch, intended to heal her imaginary hurt, was, in fact, driving that other hurt from her heart and her mind. He leant towards her, looking up into her face. 'Is that better?' he asked, his voice soft and deep.

'Yes . . .' Mary Ann gulped at the strange feelings enveloping her. A tingling sensation was coursing through her, making her feel as if she was blushing all over her body. Her heart was beating faster than normal and now it had nothing to do with having run the last few yards to the back door of The Hall. 'Yes, thank you, sir.'

She tried to pull her foot out of his grasp, but his hands held it and his fingers continued to fondle her toes. 'You have a very delicate foot, Mary Ann. And such trim ankles. I wonder – I long to know – are your legs as perfect? Are you every bit as perfect all over?' His hand was creeping once more beneath her petticoat.

Mary Ann reached forward and pushed away his searching hand. 'Please, sir. I must go.' With a sudden, sharp movement, she wrenched her foot away from him and bent forward to retrieve her boot and stocking, but before she could reach them, he had taken her by the shoulders and was drawing her gently up.

'Can you stand on it without pain?'

Pretending to test her weight upon it, Mary Ann nodded. 'Yes, sir, I think so. Thank you for your kindness, but I must . . .'

The rest of her words were silenced as he bent his head and found her mouth with lips that were hungry for the taste of her. 'You sweet, pretty little thing,' he murmured against her mouth. 'What kind Fate brought you to me?'

It was the first time that anyone had kissed her with the passion a man has for a woman. It frightened her, yet at the same time exhilarated her. The blood was pounding in her ears, her heart was thudding beneath her ribs as Randolph kissed her and stroked her hair.

Then he was straightening up, drawing away from her and leaving her bereft, washed upon the shore by the tide of a shared passion and then abandoned. He took both her hands in his and gently, reverently, kissed each of her fingers in turn. The touch of his lips sent a shudder through her.

'My dear, I would not hurt you for the world. You are far too sweet and innocent. Come, sit with me.' He sat down in the huge armchair himself and drew her, unresisting now, on to his lap. 'I've seen you about the house, Mary Ann, and oh . . .' He rested his cheek against her breast and she felt sure that he must hear her heart, taking wild, leaping somersaults. 'How I've longed to hold you, to touch you. And then, tonight, there you were. A damsel in distress and me, your knight in shining armour. Sweet, sweet Mary Ann.'

Mary Ann said nothing. She did not know what to say. She had not the words to express the excitement, the heady emotion that filled her heart and tore her rational mind to shreds.

Somewhere a door banged and Mary Ann jumped, pulling away from him. He reached out and caught hold of her. 'Don't be afraid. No one will come in here, I promise you.'

'I . . . I must go, sir. I must.'

He nodded and stood up too, towering over her. Resting his hands lightly on her shoulders, he looked down into her upturned face. Then he traced the outline of her cheek with his forefinger.

'Sweet, sweet girl. This is our secret. You know that, don't you?'

177

Mesmerized, Mary Ann nodded. 'Yes, sir. Of course, sir.'

Tenderly and with great gentleness, he kissed her once more, then held her hand as he led her across the room. He opened the door a little to stand listening for a moment before whispering, 'The coast is clear. Off you go. And remember, this is our secret. Our very own wonderful secret.'

Blushing, Mary Ann smiled and passed through the doorway, carrying her boot and her stocking. The door closed behind her and, as she paused, she thought she heard his deep, soft laugh beyond the panels. She smiled and hugged her arms around herself. She, too, felt like laughing aloud and shouting with sheer joy. Instead, she crept away, hurrying swiftly along the passages and corridors with the silence of a wraith until she reached the safety of her own room.

Luckily for Mary Ann, Clara was asleep, lying on her back, her mouth wide open and snoring noisily.

Mary Ann wrinkled her nose in disgust. It seemed so unfeminine for a girl to snore. True, Clara had adenoidal trouble and couldn't help it, but still . . .

Mary Ann stretched her arms above her head and let out a sigh of sheer delight. Slowly, she began to undress in the moonlight shining in through the skylight that afforded the only natural lighting in their attic bedroom. Running her hands over her body, savouring the feel of Randolph's hands upon her, Mary Ann smiled to herself.

I can do better for myself than you, Daniel Ruddick.

Twenty-Four

The following morning Mary Ann was disappointed to find that Randolph was not in the dining room waiting for her to serve his breakfast.

Keeping her tone devoid of any particular interest, she asked, 'Will Mr Randolph be in to breakfast, Miss Edwina?'

'I don't think so, Mary Ann. I understand he left early this morning for Yorkshire. He'll be gone a few days.' Edwina rose from her place at the table and smiled. 'Would you like to come to the school this afternoon? I was wondering if you would like to teach the little ones a few basic embroidery stitches.'

Mary Ann swallowed her disappointment and smiled brightly. 'I'd love to, Miss Edwina.'

'Good. Then we can walk home together later and call to see Bessie.'

Mary Ann nodded, although the smile faded from her mouth. She avoided meeting Edwina's gaze and busied herself clearing away the breakfast dishes. She would love to see Bessie, but, for the first time ever, she hoped that the rest of the family would not be at home.

That afternoon, Mary Ann sat surrounded by seven eager little girls. Each held a piece of linen, some coloured wool and a needle.

'Now,' Mary Ann began, smiling around at them all. 'I don't know all your names, so each time I speak to you, you must tell me what your name is until I can remember it for myself. All right?' Seven small heads nodded. 'First of all, I must warn you about the needle. You must be very careful not to hurt yourself or anyone else. When you are not working with it, you must fasten it on to the corner of your piece of work. Like this.'

She held up a small piece of linen and threaded the needle in and out of the material until it was securely fastened. 'Never leave your needle lying about and always keep a piece of thread in it and attached to some material. Now, let's begin . . .'

For the next hour, Mary Ann worked happily with the children, showing them firstly how to make small, neat running stitches about an inch in from the edge of the material. Then she taught them how to do buttonhole stitch about the very edge of the fabric. Some of the tiny fingers found this very hard, pulling the thread too tightly so that it puckered the material. Mary Ann seemed to spend most of her time picking out the stitches and then showing them again and again.

Towards the end of the afternoon, Edwina slipped into the room and sat at the back of the class watching and listening. As the bell sounded and Mary Ann allowed her charges to put their work away, Edwina moved forwards.

When the girls had trooped from the room to retrieve their coats from the cloakroom, she smiled and asked, 'Now, did you enjoy that?'

Unable to keep the surprise from her voice, Mary Ann said, 'Yes, I did. I didn't think I'd have the patience, but they were so keen and willing to learn.' She pulled a face. 'Even though some of them don't seem to have held a needle before.' She blushed a little as she remembered.

'Still, I can't say much about that, can I? I didn't do any sewing until I met Bessie and then you.'

Edwina smiled kindly. 'You have a natural talent for it, Mary Ann. Always remember that not everyone is lucky enough to have your gift. You must be very patient with those who have not.'

Mary Ann nodded. 'Do you mean you want me to do it again?'

'Would you like to?'

Mary Ann's eyes shone. 'Yes, please, Miss Edwina.'

With school over for the day and the children gone, Edwina and Mary Ann walked along River Road towards Waterman's Yard. For a while they walked in silence for Mary Ann's thoughts were busy. At last she said, 'Do you think I could be a teacher?'

To her, a teacher was someone of standing, someone to be admired and looked up to. It would make her more equal to Miss Edwina. More equal with her brother, Mr Randolph.

Carefully, Edwina said, 'I don't see why you shouldn't. But it would mean a lot of hard work, Mary Ann.' Edwina did not like to tell the girl that because of her background, Mary Ann's early education had been badly neglected, and that to become a fully fledged teacher, one had to pass examinations. But the girl had intelligence and was quick to learn. There was no telling what Mary Ann could do if she put her mind to it.

When they arrived at Bessie's home, she and Minnie were sitting in the kitchen enjoying a cup of tea.

'I'll be going,' Minnie said, standing up at once.

'Please don't let us drive you away, Mrs Eccleshall,' Edwina said, but Minnie insisted.

'No, no, miss. It's time I was going. If my Stan's tea isn't ready when he steps through the door . . .' She pulled a comical face, but they all knew that she was only joking. 'I'll see you tomorrow, Bessie. Going into town, are we?'

'Of course. It's market day.' Bessie heaved herself up. 'I'll be ready. Now then.' She turned to Mary Ann with her usual greeting. 'How are you, love?'

'Fine, Auntie Bessie,' Mary Ann said, and plunged into recounting her afternoon at the school, ending by saying, 'Miss Edwina thinks I might be able to be a teacher, if I work hard.'

She saw the two women exchange a glance, but all Bessie said was, 'That'd be nice, love.'

They drank tea and ate a slice of Bessie's plum bread. Then Edwina rose and pulled on her gloves. Mary Ann, too, put down her cup and made to rise.

'You can stay for the evening if you wish, Mary Ann. I'll tell Mrs Goodrick I've given you permission. But please, be home by nine o'clock.'

Instead of leaping at the chance to remain in the Ruddick household, and especially taking the opportunity to see Dan, Mary Ann hesitated. If Duggie had told the rest of his family about her feelings for Dan, then she could expect to be teased unmercifully. And if Dan knew, then she would wish the floor to open up and swallow her whole. Then Mary Ann raised her head defiantly. What did it matter now, anyway? She could laugh it all off as one of Duggie's japes. For Dan was seeing Susan again, and hadn't she, Mary Ann, got someone now who was really interested in her? Someone far more handsome and dashing and eligible than a man who sailed up and down the river on a barge. You've missed your chance, Dan Ruddick, she thought. I've got better fish to fry.

She smiled. 'Thank you, Miss Edwina. I'd love to stay.'

'Right then,' Bessie said. 'You can make yourself useful and lay the table.'

They all laughed as Edwina said, 'I'll be on my way before I'm given a job. Please give Mr Ruddick and the boys my regards.'

'I will,' Bessie said going to the door with her. 'And I know they'd send you theirs.'

The Ruddick menfolk came home one by one, each greeting Mary Ann in their different ways. Bert with quiet affection and with serious enquiries as to her health, her wellbeing and her happiness in her situation, Ernie with shyness and only a few, hesitant words and Duggie with his usual ebullience. But now, there was an extra twinkle in his eyes that teased her without a word being spoken.

And then Dan, the last to come home, how would he greet her? Mary Ann held her breath.

His pleasure at seeing her unexpectedly was genuine and his manner towards her the same as ever. Affectionate and concerned for her – just like any elder brother. She knew now – now that she had experienced how a man behaved when he was attracted to her – that Dan looked upon her as he would a sister. He had never kissed her or touched her in the way that Mr Randolph had. He didn't love her in the way that Mary Ann had imagined she loved him.

Had she really loved Dan or had her adoration of him been just because he had shown her tenderness when she had been starved of love?

'Hello, fancy seeing you here!' He was smiling down at her. 'Everything all right?'

Mary Ann nodded and swallowed. He was the same as ever and it seemed that perhaps she had maligned Duggie in thinking he had told his family about her feelings for Dan.

Margaret Dickinson

As they all sat down to eat, Mary Ann began to tell them about her day, her visit to the school and the class of little girls to whom she had begun to teach embroidery.

But she was careful that not once did she mention Mr Randolph's name.

Twenty-Five

Randolph returned to The Hall three days later.

Mary Ann, passing through the great hall carrying a tray, heard his boots echoing on the tiled floor behind her.

She stopped, turned to face him and waited whilst he glanced around him to make sure there was no one else there. Then he came to her.

'Have you missed me?' His left eyebrow rose in question.

'Oh yes,' she breathed, her knees trembling. 'Where have you been?'

'Just away,' he said idly. 'On business.' He glanced around again and then leant closer, his lips brushing her hair. 'I've thought about you every minute I've been away. Come to my room this evening. I've brought a little present for you.'

There was the sound of voices and he turned from her abruptly and strode away.

The dishes on the tray she was carrying rattled together as her hands shook. Mary Ann bit her lip and tried to steady her leaping heart, and for the rest of the day her lack of concentration earned her a sharp reprimand from Mrs Goodrick, which brought a satisfied smirk to Clara's face.

*

It was late when Nellie Goodrick allowed her to leave the kitchen and, having gone to her room first, Mary Ann waited until she thought the way was clear for her to creep down to Randolph's den.

The master, Bertram Marsh, was in his study, locked away with his cigars and a bottle of port. Mrs Marsh had retired to her bedroom. She wasn't sure where Edwina was, but as she hadn't seen her since dinner, Mary Ann hoped she would not run into her as she tiptoed through the house towards the east wing. Nervously, she tapped on the door and heard him bid her enter.

He was sitting in the deep armchair and when he turned his head and saw her standing in the doorway, he rose at once and came towards her.

Closing the door softly, he drew her towards the fire. 'I thought you weren't coming.'

'I couldn't get away before, sir,' she said breathlessly.

'Oh Mary Ann, please don't call me "sir". Not when we're alone.' He pulled a face. 'Of course we must keep up the pretence outside this room. No one must know. You do understand that, don't you?'

'Yes,' she said, though her tone was hesitant with disappointment. She wanted to tell everyone. She wanted to wipe away Clara Dobson's smug expression and see the look of disapproval on the cook's face that she knew would be there. But most of all, she wanted to see Dan's face when she told him about Mr Randolph.

Randolph put his arms around her and drew her into his embrace, resting his cheek against her hair. 'Oh Mary Ann, you don't know how much I've missed you. Everywhere I went, I kept seeing your sweet little face, those dark, magnificent eyes and those pretty little dimples in your cheeks when you smile.'

He bent his head then and lifted her chin with his finger

so that she was looking up into his face. Then he began
to kiss her and the room reeled around her and she was
borne along on a tidal wave of a new and exciting
emotion.

Gently, he pressed her down on to the thick rug in
front of the warm fire. He turned down the gaslights so
that the only illumination in the room came from the
flickering firelight. Removing his jacket, he lay down
beside her. Propping his head on one hand, he let his gaze
roam all over her, until she felt disconcerted and embarrassed by his scrutiny. With his right hand he stroked the
hair from her face and caressed her cheek, then he allowed
his hand to stray to her bosom where, deftly, he unbut-
toned the topmost three buttons of her blouse, with her
hardly being aware of what he was doing. Then his hand
travelled down to her waist and thence to her groin where
it rested.

He bent over and as his lips pecked gently at her
mouth, he murmured endearments, such words of love
and longing that Mary Ann had never heard before.

'You adorable little creature. Don't be afraid, my sweet
Mary Ann. I won't hurt you. I promise I won't hurt
you . . .'

It was two o'clock in the morning before Mary Ann
stumbled up the back stairs to her room. She was sore
and bleeding, for despite his promise, it had hurt when he
had entered her, for she was a virgin. Despite the traumas
of her early life that had left her with a worldly knowledge, she was nevertheless still ignorant and naïve in the
desires of men and women carried away by tumultuous
passion.

She was shaking now with a mixture of fear and yet

exhilaration too. She was loved and desired and by such a man as Randolph Marsh.

'Let's keep this to ourselves, my darling, for now. I want you just for myself. But one day the whole world will know how much I love you and want you.'

At his words, her heart sang. He didn't mean to keep their love hidden like some grubby little secret. He really loved her and he wanted to parade his love for everyone to see. Sleep was impossible. In the cold, dark attic room Mary Ann lay in her narrow bed a completely different person to the girl who had lain there only the previous night. Now she was a woman. Her body had responded to his like a woman's and the next time there would be none of the pain. Randolph had told her so.

'Next time,' he had said, as they had lain together in the aftermath of his violent lovemaking, 'it will be just as wonderful for you. I promise.'

It was their secret – a wonderful, exciting, daring secret – and Mary Ann hugged the knowledge to herself. She would tell no one. Not even Bessie. For somewhere in the dark recesses of her mind, buried deliberately deep, Mary Ann knew that Bessie would be shocked and angry at what she had done this night.

'You're looking a bit peaky, love. Are you all right?'

Mary Ann was startled and her heart began to thump at Bessie's question. She knew the cause, but how was she to avoid telling the truth? Bessie was far too sharp not to know a lie when it was being told to her. So Mary Ann decided that the truth, but not the whole truth, was the best policy.

'I've not been sleeping very well. I'm tired.' She did not, however, add that the reason she was missing her sleep was because she spent the late hours of most nights in Randolph's arms.

'Are they working you too hard?' Bessie persisted. 'Is this teaching thing, as well as all the work you have to do at The Hall, too much for you? It'd be just like Nellie Goodrick to work you all the harder just because you're Miss Edwina's favourite.'

And Mr Randolph's favourite, Mary Ann was thinking, but she shook her head and said, 'No, no. I love doing that.'

She was silent now, her eyes downcast. It was not only the lack of sleep, but the fear too. Mary Ann was not so ignorant – Bessie in her matter-of-fact way had seen to that – that she did not know the risk she was taking. Any day, she might become pregnant. What would happen then? Would Randolph stand by her as he had promised?

'Don't be afraid,' he had whispered. 'I'll always take care of you.'

But would he marry her? The words had never been spoken. He had never said as much, but he had promised not to hurt her and, always, to look after her. So, didn't that amount to the same thing? Didn't that mean that one day she would be his wife?

'I adore you,' he told her constantly. 'I've never known anyone like you before. I've been waiting the whole of my life for someone like you.'

Starved of love for most of her young life, Mary Ann's hungry soul fed on his words. Even in the warmth of Bessie's kitchen, the memories made her shiver with desire for him, the feel of him, the smell of him and the sound of his whispered words.

'Are you catching a chill, love?' Bessie persisted in her concern.

Mary Ann forced a smile on to her mouth. 'Me? Ill? I've never been ill in me life, Auntie Bessie.' She put her head on one side as she deliberated. She must act as normally as possible or this wise, perceptive woman might start to probe a little too deeply.

So, as she always had done when she visited Waterman's Yard, Mary Ann asked, 'Where's Dan?'

Dan walked her back to The Hall that night and insisted on seeing her right to the door the servants used. Mary Ann's heart was skipping wildly, afraid that Randolph might be waiting for her in the shadows. But no, she reasoned inwardly. Randolph would be waiting in his room, their little love nest, for her to come to him.

'Are you really happy at The Hall, Mary Ann?' Dan asked her as they walked along. He reached out and took hold of her hand in the darkness and put it through his arm so that they walked closely together. 'We want you to be happy. You know that, don't you?'

Only a short time ago, Mary Ann would have been ecstatic at his action. She would have read far more into his affectionate gesture than perhaps he meant. Now, knowing that he was once more seeing Susan, she realized it was no more than a brotherly protectiveness.

Added to that, she now knew so much more about desire and she had the love of a man of position in the community, a man of standing. Oh, if she were to become Mrs Randolph Marsh and live at The Hall as its future mistress . . .

'Of course I'm happy there. Why wouldn't I be?'

'I just wondered, that's all. You've often said that Mrs Goodrick is very severe with you, and that you and Clara don't get on.'

'Huh,' Mary Ann expressed derision. 'Who are they, anyway? I don't care about them.'

'Perhaps not,' Dan said reasonably. 'But they could make your life very difficult.'

In the darkness, Mary Ann smiled to herself, hugging her delicious secret. She couldn't wait to see the look on the faces of the cook and that uppity housemaid when Randolph made the announcement that they were to be married.

'Are you going to marry Susan?'

'Oh, well now,' Dan sounded embarrassed. 'It's early days yet. Her father has only recently given permission for us to see each other again.'

'Permission? What on earth do you need his permission for?'

'Susan's not twenty-one yet. And besides, she wouldn't want to go against her father. Nor would I,' he added wryly. 'Don't forget, he's my employer. Not only that, if he were to sack me, he's got a lot of influence amongst the river folk. I'd be hard pressed to find another job round here.'

Her clear laugh rang out in the night air. Now that her sights were no longer set on Dan, she could joke about such things. 'Then you should marry me,' she said, with teasing flippancy. 'I don't have any parents to object.'

Dan did not answer and for a moment both of them were silenced by bitter memories flooding back. She felt him squeeze her hand closer to his side in the gesture of comfort.

As they rounded the corner and the dark shape of The Hall loomed before them, Dan asked, 'When shall we see you again? Next Sunday?'

'Unless Miss Edwina and me call on our way home from school in the week. We do that sometimes.'

'Are you enjoying that? The teaching, I mean?'

Mary Ann's reply was swift and genuine. 'Yes. I'm quite surprised how much I like the children. I never had much to do with other kids, being an only one and not going to school an awful lot.'

Again, the reference to her past life made Dan bring the conversation round to looking forwards, not backwards. 'Should you like to be a teacher?'

Her answer this time did not come so quickly. She had other plans now, plans that meant she would be a lady of leisure with no need to earn her own living or have any occupation.

'I wouldn't mind teaching embroidery, but to be a proper teacher, well, I don't think I could. I mean, I haven't been to school enough myself and there'd be a lot of examinations to take.'

'Would there be so many if you were just to teach embroidery?'

'No, I don't think so. Miss Edwina says that a lot of those would be practical exams and she thinks that maybe I could scrape through the written ones.' She was playing a part now, with no real intention of ever taking such examinations. She wouldn't need to as Mrs Randolph Marsh.

'Here we are then, safely to the door. You're not late are you? You won't get into trouble with Mrs Goodrick?'

'No, no. I'm in good time.' But it was not Mrs Goodrick she was thinking of. She was in good time to go up to her room and then to slip down the stairs again to see Randolph.

The windows of his room were just across the lawn between the two wings of the house and Mary Ann could not resist glancing across towards the soft lighting shining beyond the leaded panes. He was there. He was waiting for her. In fact, she fancied she saw the outline of his shape standing at the window.

With a spark of devilment, she stood on tiptoe and kissed Dan's cheek. 'I'll see you Sunday, if not before. Thank you for seeing me home, Dan. Goodnight.'

'Goodnight, Mary Ann. God bless.' To her surprise, he reached out and took her by the shoulders. Then he bent his head and kissed her firmly on the mouth.

He released her so quickly that she was caught off balance and put out her hand to steady herself against the wall. She gave a small gasp of surprise, but he had turned away and before she could utter a word he had disappeared into the darkness.

Half an hour later, Mary Ann was tapping softly on the door of Randolph's room. She put her hand on the knob in readiness for his soft, 'Come in.'

Suddenly the door was flung open, wrenched from her grasp and she found herself being pulled roughly into the room, the door being slammed behind her. Now he was gripping her shoulder so strongly that his fingers dug into her flesh.

'Who was that with you? I saw you. I saw you kissing him. I'll kill him. Tell me . . .' He shook her. 'Who was it?'

Mary Ann gave a nervous laugh and tried to make light of it. She was afraid and yet a feeling of exhilaration flooded through her. He must really love her to get so jealous.

'It was only Dan.'

'Dan who?' he shot back.

'Dan Ruddick. He walked me home, that's all. One of them always does.'

'What do you mean?' he asked harshly. 'One of them?'

'One of the Ruddicks. I lived with them before I came here. Didn't you know?'

His grip began to slacken a little, but a new fear was creeping through Mary Ann's veins now. Did he not know who she was? Did he not know her background or her terrible past?

He was calmer, but his tone was still sharp as he asked, 'Why did you live with them? Are they your family?'

'Sort of. They took me in after my parents . . .' She hesitated only momentarily before adding, 'Died.'

'The Ruddicks?' he said slowly and thoughtfully. 'They live in Waterman's Yard, don't they?'

Quietly, Mary Ann said, 'Yes.'

'And your surname is?'

Almost inaudibly, she said, 'Clark.'

'Mary Ann Clark.' He said the name as if realization had just come to him.

She looked up at him, desperately afraid now that she was going to see his face twisted with anger and revulsion, but it was expressionless as he stared down at her for what, to Mary Ann, holding her breath, seemed an interminable age.

Then slowly, he cupped her face in his hands and kissed her forehead. 'You poor little thing. I never realized who you were. What a dreadful thing to happen to anyone. And to someone as sweet and lovely as you.'

Joy and relief flooded through her. She put her arms about his waist and buried her face against his chest. 'Oh Randolph, Randolph. You do love me.'

He drew her to the hearth and they lay down together. That evening his lovemaking was gentle and giving and, more than ever, Mary Ann believed herself secure in his love.

Twenty-Six

'Mary Ann? Whatever are you doing creeping about the house at this time of the night?'

In her flight from Randolph's arms back to her own room, Mary Ann froze at the sound of Edwina's voice.

It had to happen. Night after night, she had been going to Randolph's room for several weeks now and it was only a matter of time before another member of the household caught her. Mary Ann didn't know whether to be pleased or sorry that that person was Miss Edwina.

'Are you ill, my dear?' Edwina came towards her and then, as she saw her more clearly, 'Why, you're still fully dressed.' Mary Ann saw Edwina's mouth tighten as she asked, 'Have you only just come in? Oh really, Mary Ann. No wonder you are so tired sometimes during the day. And there I was blaming myself for having perhaps expected too much of you, involving you in teaching too. You really must come home earlier than this. I shall have to speak to Bessie—'

'No,' Mary Ann interrupted. 'No, please don't do that. I . . . . I won't let it happen again, Miss Edwina. I promise.'

'Well,' Edwina said doubtfully. 'Just mind you don't. Run along now and get to bed.'

Her heart still thumping, Mary Ann sped along the corridor and up the back stairs. She would have to tell Randolph what had happened. Maybe he would agree to tell everyone the truth now.

But in the morning, Mary Ann rose with tired eyes to hear from the servants' gossip that Mr Randolph had left The Hall early that morning and would not return for four or five days.

'Where's he gone?' Mary Ann asked, without thinking.

'That's no concern of yours,' Mrs Goodrick snapped, 'or of mine.' A slow smirk stretched her mouth, but what purported to be a smile did not reach the woman's eyes. 'Not that I don't know, of course.'

'So?' Mary Ann stood her ground. 'Where has he gone?'

Mrs Goodrick raised her forefinger to wag in Mary Ann's face, but before she could do so, Clara said smugly. 'He's gone to Yorkshire again, I bet.'

Mary Ann wheeled around upon the hapless housemaid. 'Yorkshire? Why? Why's he gone to Yorkshire?'

'Ah,' Clara said. There was a glint in her small, piggy eyes that sat in her round, podgy face. The girl suffered from facial acne and, this morning, the crop of spots around her chin was particularly fiery. 'That'd be telling.'

At that moment the bell above the door tinkled and Mrs Goodrick smoothed down her white apron. 'That's the mistress wanting me in the morning room. You two, get on with your work and be quick about it.'

Clara turned away, but as the door closed behind the cook, Mary Ann reached out and grasped the girl by her hair, almost wrenching the white lace cap from the girl's head. 'You just tell me what you mean, Clara Dobson, else I'll pull your hair out by its roots.'

Clara let out such a shriek and then began to scream so loudly that Mary Ann let go of her hair at once. 'Shut up,' she hissed. 'You'll have the whole household down here.'

Clara backed away from her, her mouth wide in a

series of shrill cries. 'Get away. Get away. Don't touch me.'

The kitchen door burst open and Mrs Goodrick hurried in again, swiftly followed by Edwina.

'Whatever's going on?' the cook began. 'Stop that silly noise, girl.'

'She was going to kill me. She's a bad 'un. She'll murder all of us in our beds. Just like her father did.'

'Clara!' Edwina's voice was shocked. 'I will not have such talk in this house. You will apologize to Mary Ann this instant.'

Clara was crying now. Great wracking sobs were shaking her whole body. 'It was 'er, Miss Edwina. She pulled me hair. Just 'cos I wouldn't tell her where Mr Randolph has gone.'

'Mr . . .?' Edwina began, astonishment in her tone. Then Mary Ann felt her questioning gaze upon her. Quietly now, Edwina said, 'I think you'd better come with me, Mary Ann. Mrs Goodrick, will you deal with Clara, please?'

With that, Edwina turned and left the kitchen. Subdued now, Mary Ann followed her. Edwina led the way up the stairs to the privacy of her own bedroom. She opened the door and stood aside for Mary Ann to enter the room. Then she closed the door.

Mary Ann stood in the centre of the pretty bedroom, a mutinous look on her face. Edwina leant against the door for a moment and Mary Ann felt her watching her. Edwina crossed the room to the window and sat down in a chair. She did not invite Mary Ann to sit down, but left the girl standing where she was.

'Now,' Edwina began. Her voice was still low. Edwina rarely raised her voice but now there was steeliness to her tone. 'Are you going to tell me what this is all about?'

Mary Ann glanced at her. Edwina's eyes were shrewd and knowing and for a moment Mary Ann held her breath. There would be no point in lying to Miss Edwina, she thought. Edwina would know and she would then be in deeper trouble.

If only, she thought, Randolph had not gone away. And without telling her too. He might have said something last night, but as she remembered the previous evening, she knew that all such thoughts must have been driven out of his mind. Just like there had been no room for anyone else in her mind but him.

'Why are you smiling, Mary Ann?' Edwina's voice cut into her erotic memories of their passionate lovemaking.

'I just . . .' Mary Ann began hesitantly. 'I just wanted to know where Ra—, where Mr Randolph had gone, miss. That's all.'

Edwina's eyes narrowed, and even Mary Ann, for all her boldness, found the young woman's gaze disconcerting.

'And why should that concern you?'

Mary Ann manufactured a disinterested shrug, but she knew that she could not deceive Edwina. Not for long. Already, Mary Ann could see the realization dawning in Edwina's face. Then Edwina closed her eyes momentarily and gave a low groan and murmured, 'Oh no. Not again.' She sighed and stood up and then she crossed the room towards Mary Ann and put her hand out to take the girl's arm gently. 'Come. Sit down with me. We must talk and I want you to be absolutely truthful with me, Mary Ann. For your own sake, my dear, as much as anyone else's. Do you understand me?'

Mutely, Mary Ann nodded and allowed herself to be led towards the window where Edwina pushed her gently into a chair. Then she sat down beside her. 'Tell me, am I right in thinking that you had been to Randolph's study last night when I bumped into you on the stairs?'

Edwina's gaze was penetrating, yet not angry or unkind, just dreadfully anxious.

Mary Ann swallowed and her eyes widened. There was nothing else she could do but whisper, 'Yes.'

'And?'

Now Mary Ann turned rebellious. 'And what?'

'What happened? Did he try to . . . try to . . .?'

The truth burst from her lips. Why should she keep it secret any longer? Why shouldn't the whole world know the truth?

'He didn't *try* anything. Randolph loves me. He said so. We're to be married. I know he wants to marry me.'

Edwina gasped and the colour drained from her face. 'Did . . . did Randolph say that to you? Did Randolph ask you to marry him, Mary Ann?'

The girl stared at her. For a brief, terrifying moment, a sliver of fear crept into her heart. 'Not yet. He hasn't actually asked me yet. But he will. I know he will. That's what people do when they're in love. They get married.'

She knew her words must be like shafts through Edwina's heart, reminding her of her own lost love, but at this moment Mary Ann didn't care about anyone else's feelings. She was safe in Randolph's love. It was an armour that shielded her, protected her and gave her strength against the likes of Mrs Goodrick and Clara. Even against Miss Edwina.

Edwina was shaking her head sadly. 'Oh my dear Mary Ann. I am so sorry my brother has deceived you in this way. I should have known. I should never have brought you here. Into this house.' Her mouth tightened and now there was a flash of anger in her fine eyes. It was not directed at Mary Ann, but at her absent, callous rake of a brother. Her next words were like a death knell to all Mary Ann's hopes and dreams.

'Randolph is engaged to a girl in Yorkshire and has been for the past twelve months. He will never marry you, my dear.'

Twenty-Seven

Mary Ann flew to her attic bedroom and slammed the door. She threw herself on to the bed and gave way to a storm of hysterical weeping.

'Mary Ann, let me in. I've got to change my clothes.' Clara's plaintive voice was at the door, but Mary Ann did not answer.

A few minutes later there was a sharp rap on the door and Nellie Goodrick shouted, 'Open this door at once or it'll be the worse for you, miss.'

Still, Mary Ann made no reply. Only when Edwina knocked and said in her gentle way, 'Please, Mary Ann, let me come in. Let me talk to you, my dear,' did she respond, her voice muffled with tears, 'Go away and leave me alone.'

She refused even to open the door so that Clara could come to her bed. She neither knew nor cared where the girl spent the night. Not until lunchtime the following day, when she heard that Randolph was back, did Mary Ann wash her face, tidy her hair, smooth down her dress and open the door to go downstairs. She marched straight through the great hall to Randolph's den. Anger now carrying her along, she was determined to face him.

She didn't even bother to knock but flung the door wide and stepped into the room.

'What the . . .?' he began, rising from his chair behind the desk. 'Oh,' he said then, sinking back. 'It's you.'

'Yes, it's me,' she said and stood before his desk. 'Is it true? Are you going to marry a girl in Yorkshire?'

Frowning, Randolph stood up again. 'That has nothing to do with you.'

'Nothing to do with me,' she screamed at him. 'When you seduced me in this very room. There . . .' She flung out her arm towards the hearthrug. 'Right there. You made love to me and whispered promises you didn't mean to keep. How dare you say it has nothing to do with me?'

He moved around the desk to stand in front of her. His eyes glittered with anger and his mouth twisted in a sneer. His handsome face, even to the besotted Mary Ann, was suddenly ugly. 'You didn't really think I would marry you, did you? Not even you could be so naïve, surely?'

Mary Ann gasped, staring up at him, shocked now at the change in the man she loved. Then she narrowed her eyes calculatingly as she said, 'What if I was to tell you I'm expecting your child?'

He returned her gaze with equal calculation. 'Are you?' he asked dispassionately.

'What if I was?'

He shrugged. 'You'd be taken care of.' Then with a cold smile, completely devoid of any feeling, he added, 'Just like several before you have been.'

'I hate you,' Mary Ann spat between clenched teeth, and she balled her fists and pummelled his chest. 'I hope I never see you again as long as you live.'

He caught hold of her wrists and held her fast. 'Mary Ann, my little Mary Ann.' Now his voice was soft and seductive and his sudden change of tone was her undoing. She was trembling at his touch. She loved him, she couldn't help it. However badly he treated her, she could not stop loving him. She gave a sob and fell against him. He put his arms around her and kissed her hair. 'My dear,

dear girl, you must understand, in my world, in my family, one cannot always marry where one's heart lies. It is my duty, but I will always . . .'

She dragged herself free of him, anger surging through her once more. She was on a seesaw of emotion – one moment she loved him – the next she hated him and the violence of her passion frightened her. She wanted to hit him, to wipe that arrogant, self-confident smile off his face. She really felt in that instant as if she could kill him. 'Duty?' she screamed at him again. 'What do you mean, duty? If you loved me, you wouldn't be planning to marry someone else.'

Randolph spread his hands, as if in helplessness. 'I have to, Mary Ann, but it doesn't mean . . .'

'Oh yes, it does. I'm leaving and I'll never see you again.'

She whirled around and made for the door, but his voice followed her mockingly, 'I don't think you mean that, my dear. If I so much as crooked my little finger, I think you'd come running.'

'Aw lass, whatever's the matter?'

Mary Ann flew into Bessie's open arms, weeping hysterically.

'There, there,' Bessie tried to soothe her.

Mary Ann clung to her, burying her face against the stout woman's shoulders. 'Oh Auntie Bessie, Auntie Bessie. He said he loved me. I know he loves me. They're wrong. They're all wrong.'

'Who? Who are you talking about? Now come, lass. Stop that crying and tell me what's happened.' Bessie was firm now.

'Perhaps I can enlighten you, Bessie.' Edwina's calm

voice spoke behind them. Her tone was flat with disappointment and concern.

'Oh Miss Edwina. I didn't know you'd come with her. Come in, come in. Sit down. I'll make some tea.'

Edwina held up her hand. 'Please don't trouble, Bessie. We need to talk to you before your menfolk come home. Mary Ann.' Her tone took on a note of firmness, too. 'Now stop that crying.'

But Mary Ann only wailed louder.

Bessie disentangled herself from the girl's clinging arms and took hold of her. Gently she shook her. 'Stop that this instant and sit down.'

Mary Ann's cries rose hysterically until, with a desperate glance at Edwina, Bessie raised her hand and slapped the girl smartly on the cheek. The noise ceased and for a moment Mary Ann seemed not to breathe. Shocked, she stared at Bessie and then collapsed weeping into Bert's big armchair.

'I think I'll make that tea, miss, if you don't mind. I could do with some, ne'er mind anyone else.'

Edwina nodded and, whilst Bessie swiftly mashed a pot of tea from the kettle that was already boiling over the fire in the range, she patted Mary Ann's shoulder and talked quietly to her. By the time Bessie had poured out three cups of tea, the young girl's sobs had subsided to inconsolable hiccups.

'Now,' said Bessie briskly. 'Will one of you please tell me what is going on?'

'I'm afraid it's my brother, Randolph, up to his old tricks, Bessie,' Edwina began as she took the cup and saucer handed to her.

Mary Ann felt them both look at her and then exchange a knowing glance between them. Then they began to talk almost as if Mary Ann were not present.

Edwina sighed heavily. 'You know what he's like. What he's always been like. Two young girls have been dismissed in the past because they were pregnant, and in each case they swore that Randolph was the father of their babies. Another left, also pregnant, but loyally refused to name the father.' Edwina sighed. 'But I always had my own suspicions. Goodness knows how much my father must be paying out even now to help those poor girls.'

Mary Ann saw Bessie's lips tighten and felt her glance upon her, but for the moment, she said nothing.

'It seems,' Edwina went on sadly, 'that he has filled Mary Ann's head with the notion that he is in love with her. The poor child believed he would marry her. Then she found out that he had gone to Yorkshire. She locked herself in her room. Not one of us could get her to come out. I was on the point of coming to you for help, Bessie, but then Randolph returned.'

'Yorkshire?' Bessie looked puzzled.

Edwina nodded. 'That's where Celia Thompson lives. Randolph's fiancée. He'd gone to see her to . . . to discuss plans for their wedding.'

'And does this Miss Thompson know about his philandering?' Bessie asked harshly.

Edwina smiled wryly. 'You don't mince your words, do you, Bessie?'

'Never have, miss, and I doubt I'll start now.' For a brief moment the two women shared an intimacy borne of their long knowledge of each other, which excluded Mary Ann. Then Edwina sighed heavily. 'I doubt it. And I expect he'll carry on just as before even once they are married.'

Bessie gave a snort of disapproval.

'You know how it is, Bessie. Randolph is now the son

and heir to our family's estates. He must make a good marriage.'

'I thought all that sort of thing had been swept away by the war. Seems I was wrong.'

'I wonder if it will ever be completely swept away, as you put it. Not in our – forgive me, dear Bessie – in our class.' She reached out and touched Bessie's hand and for a moment, despite the gravity of their conversation, she smiled impishly. 'You know I have always considered myself most fortunate to have been born the girl in the family. At least I can choose whom I marry. And I did.' Her eyes clouded. 'My only misfortune was to lose him.'

'Yes, miss. I know. Your Mr Christopher was a lovely man.' Bessie leant closer to her. 'But what would have happened if you had chosen someone of whom your family disapproved, eh? Just you tell me that.'

Edwina wrinkled her forehead and sighed. 'Yes, I suppose you are right. Things might have been very different then, if father had not approved of Christopher.'

'I'm sure they would have been,' Bessie said wryly. 'And it happens in other walks of life, an' all. Look at our Dan, for instance. It's taken Jack Price long enough to decide that Susan can start walking out with him again.'

'Is that what you're saying,' Mary Ann blurted out now. 'That Randolph won't marry me because his father won't approve?'

Mary Ann saw them turn to look at her, surprise in their eyes as if they really had forgotten, for the moment, that she was sitting there listening to every word they said.

Carefully, Edwina put her cup on its saucer and set it down on the table. 'My dear, I cannot hide the fact that Randolph is entering into something of an arranged marriage. There has been an understanding between our families for years that, eventually, Celia would make a suitable bride for . . . for . . .' she faltered and tears came to her eyes, 'for the heir to the Marsh estates. She has no brothers and her father wishes her to marry into a family of equal standing to the Thompsons, who have extensive estates in Yorkshire.'

'She was promised to Mr Arthur, wasn't she?' Bessie put in.

Edwina nodded. 'But after Arthur was killed, Randolph agreed to marry her instead.'

'And she agreed?' Even Bessie, who was versed in the ways of the gentry, sounded amazed. As for Mary Ann, she could scarcely believe what she was hearing.

Edwina shrugged. 'Evidently, yes.'

'So he doesn't love her then?' Hope sprang briefly again in Mary Ann's breast. 'He can't do, if it's all been arranged by their parents.'

'I expect they have become very fond of each other,' Edwina said carefully. 'I'm sure neither of our families would press them into a loveless marriage.' Though she said the words, even Mary Ann could detect that Edwina's tone lacked conviction. Always a truthful woman, Edwina was obliged to add with ill-concealed disapproval, 'Although I expect that Randolph, once he has produced an heir and a spare, will still feel able to find his pleasures elsewhere.'

Mary Ann shuddered. The revelations of the past hour had been a dreadful shock to her. She had understood nothing of the ways of the gentry, yet she knew that Miss Edwina would not lie to her. And Bessie, too, understood every word that was being said and, worse still, accepted it as being the truth.

Although she was calmer now, tears poured down Mary Ann's face as she said bitterly, 'With the likes of me, you mean?'

Neither of the women answered her and Mary Ann bowed her head in shame and cruel disillusionment.

'Hello, love. What are you doing here?'

Dan came into the house, the first home. As he looked more closely at her, his welcoming smile faded. 'Whatever's the matter?' he said at once, unknowingly echoing his mother's first question.

'There's been a bit of bother at The Hall,' Bessie said, bustling between her scullery and the table as she set the tea. 'Can't tell you now, Dan. Bert'll be home in a minute and his tea's not ready.'

Dan sat down opposite Mary Ann, who was sitting huddled close to the range, shivering miserably and, from time to time, still shedding tears.

'Are you poorly, love?'

Again Bessie spoke for her. 'No, she's not. At least, I hope she's not. I'll have to sort that out later. Oh lor', heaven forbid we've that to deal with an' all.'

'Ma? What are you on about?'

'Later, lad. We'll tell you later.'

Suddenly, Mary Ann jumped up. 'Stop talking about me as if I'm not here. And I'm not staying here while you tell them all. I don't want them all laughing at me. Duggie and . . . and . . .'

Bessie set a meat and potato pie on the table and turned to face her. 'Now you just look here, m'girl. There's no one in this house going to laugh at you. You're part of this family. They're like brothers to you and don't you forget it. Duggie may be a little scallywag at times,

208

but 'is heart's in the right place and, besides, it's no more than you deserve. You've been a silly little girl and—'

Mary Ann covered her ears. 'Stop it. Stop it. I won't listen.'

With that she stumbled towards the door, knocking against furniture as she went. 'I won't stay here another minute. I won't stay where I'm not wanted. I'll chuck myself in the river. Nobody cares . . .'

She flung open the back door and flew across the yard, her running feet echoing back into the house as mother and son stared at each other, stunned into silence.

Twenty-Eight

Mary Ann hid behind a stack of barrels on Miller's Wharf. She curled herself into a ball, hugging her knees to her chest and burying her face in her skirt.

She heard Dan's urgent, frantic voice. 'Mary Ann? Mary Ann, where are you?' Then she heard Bessie, puffing and panting, arrive. They were standing just the other side of the barrels now and Mary Ann could hear every word they said quite plainly.

'I've just passed ya dad coming home. He'll leave a note for the lads to follow us and he'll be here himself in a minute.'

'She can't have got far.' Dan's tone was distracted. He was hardly listening to what his mother said. 'I was right behind her.' He was moving away from Mary Ann's hiding place, his voice fading as he neared the edge of the wharf over the water.

'She wouldn't really do what she said, Mam, would she? I'll never forgive myself if anything happens to her.'

'It's not your fault, lad. It's that devil at The Hall up to his tricks again. Ee, it's me to blame if anyone is. I should have known better than to let a pretty little thing like her go up there, but – well – I thought with Miss Edwina looking after her, he'd leave her alone.'

There was a pause and then very faintly, so that Mary Ann had to strain to hear her, Bessie said, 'Poor little lass. She only wanted to be loved. That's all it'd be.'

210

Mary Ann held her breath as she heard Dan say, 'That's what I mean. That's why I feel so badly. I should have . . .' His voice faded completely as they moved on, searching the riverbank.

She stayed hidden for a few moments longer, then she crept out and tiptoed towards the edge of the wharf, standing right on the tip of the planking. She looked down at the dark, swirling water, wondering just how deep it was. She couldn't swim and it would be very cold. She might get swept away by the current, but Dan was only a few yards away anxiously scanning the banks of the river. She could see them, vague shapes in the gathering dusk.

Mary Ann tensed herself, gave one last glance towards Dan and Bessie, and then drew in a deep breath. As she jumped into the water, she let out a piercing shriek that penetrated the night and brought Dan running.

The dark, cold water swirled around her, the strong current carrying her downriver, dragging at her clothes and sucking her beneath the surface. She struggled, pushing upwards, her lungs bursting. She didn't mean it. She hadn't meant to die. She didn't want to die. She just wanted . . .

And then strong arms were reaching for her. Safe hands held her and pulled her upwards and she gulped in the sweet, cold air.

There were no angry words as Dan carried her home, Bessie puffing alongside. No recriminations. Only loving, tender concern from each member of the family. Even Duggie fetched the tin bath and filled it with water from the boiler and then stood outside in the scullery whilst Bessie stripped Mary Ann's wet clothes and helped her

211

into the bath. Then the older woman knelt on the peg rug and soaped her gently.

'There, there, lass. It's over now. You must forget all about him. He's not for you.' She gave a snort of condemnation. 'He's not for any nice girl, if you ask me. But then I suppose that poor lass they've chosen will have to take him on. Me heart bleeds for her, whoever she is.'

Mary Ann had been silent from the moment Dan had plunged into the river and pulled her out, spluttering and coughing. She had clung to him, burying her face against his neck as he had carried her home. She had not cried, had not spoken, but now she lifted her face and looked into Bessie's eyes as she said, 'Celia. Her name's Celia and she lives in Yorkshire.'

Bessie nodded. 'Aye, I know. Celia Thompson.' Her mouth was a tight, grim line.

'But why, Auntie Bessie? Why's he going to marry her if he doesn't love her?'

Again Bessie snorted in a most unladylike manner. But Bessie Ruddick would have been the first to admit that she was no lady and, by her next words, it was clear that she had no wish to be. 'Love's got nowt to do with it, lass. Not in their circles. Arranged marriages, that's what happens in their class. Well, all I can say, Mary Ann, is that I'm glad I was born on a ship on the river to plain and ordinary folk. Miss Celia Thompson's got my sympathy.'

'Do . . . do you know her? Have you ever seen her?'

'No. I haven't been up to The Hall since Mr Arthur got killed. 'Course I see Miss Edwina. I'm very fond of her, but I haven't much time for some of the others. Mrs Marsh is all right, in her way, and Mr Arthur was a nice young man, but he's gone now, poor feller.' She paused and then sniffed disparagingly. 'I never did think much to the master, to tell you the truth, and as for that other devil, Mr High and Bloody Mighty Randolph Marsh, well, I wouldn't spit on him if he was on fire.' She levered herself up from her kneeling position and added, 'Come on now, lass. Get yasen out of that water. Let's get you dry and let poor Dan get into the bath. He'll catch a chill, else, and you wouldn't want that now, would you?'

An hour later, the whole family was seated around the fire, Mary Ann holding a steaming mug of cocoa with a drop of whisky in it that Bert had fetched for her from The Waterman's Arms. Dan sat close by Mary Ann, casting anxious glances at her every few seconds.

'You can have my bed tonight. I'll sleep on the couch in the front room.'

'Up you go, then, lass,' Bessie said kindly and, as if adding the second part of the same sentence, Bert said, 'And have a good night's sleep, love. You'll feel better in the morning.'

Mary Ann put her mug down and stood up. She swayed a little and put her hand to her forehead. She gave a little gasp and, immediately, Dan was at her side.

'I'll carry you up.' Without waiting for any protest, he picked her up in his strong arms. 'Duggie, open the doors for me, will you?'

Duggie sprang up and leapt towards the door leading to the stairs. Then he bounded up the stairs ahead of them to open the door to his brother's room, Dan being the only one of the three brothers who now had a room to himself since Mary Ann had moved out to live in at The Hall. He went to the bed and pulled back the covers so that Dan could lay her down. Then gently he pulled the bedclothes over her, tucking them warmly around her.

'Thanks, Duggie,' Dan said, 'I'll be down in a moment.'

For the first time that evening, Duggie grinned, knowing himself dismissed. He nodded down at Mary Ann. 'Good night, Mary Ann. Sleep tight. Watch the bugs don't bite.'

Mary Ann smiled weakly at him, but she did not speak.

As the door closed behind Duggie, Dan sat on the edge of the bed and took her hand into his. His touch was warm and comforting and Mary Ann closed her eyes.

'Now promise me, Mary Ann,' Dan said, his voice even deeper with anxiety, 'that you won't ever do such a thing again. No man's worth that.'

Mary Ann squeezed two tears from her eyes. Her chin quivered and then she opened her eyes and looked at him, hoping she looked the picture of abject misery. 'I . . .' she began, her voice cracked and thick with hurt. Then latching on to the words she had heard Bessie utter, she said, 'I just wanted someone to love me.'

She felt him squeeze her hand even tighter. 'We love you, Mary Ann. You know we do. All of us. Even,' he smiled slightly, 'that young rascal Duggie.'

'I know. I know you do. But I meant . . . I mean I want someone to love me more than just . . . just like a brother.'

'Mary Ann,' he breathed and leant towards her.

She sat up suddenly and flung her arms around his neck, pressing her cheek to his face. 'Oh Dan, why couldn't you love me when I wanted you to? Why couldn't you fall in love with me? If only you had, then this might never have happened. I would never have fallen for Mr Randolph. I just wanted someone to love me and take care of me.'

His arms were around her slim waist and she could feel the warmth of his hands on her body. 'Mary Ann, Mary Ann,' Dan whispered, burying his face in her hair. 'I'll take care of you. I'll never let anyone hurt you again. I promise you.'

She felt a shudder run through him as he kissed her neck and she felt once more the shiver of delight run through her own body as his hands caressed her.

And then he was kissing her, cupping her face between his hands and murmuring, 'You're so sweet. You're so pretty. My little Mary Ann.' His lips were seeking her forehead, her eyes and, lastly, her lips.

Exhilaration coursed through her. Dan would love her. Dan would take care of her. Dan would never hurt her like Randolph had done. She would forget all about Randolph Marsh and, from this moment on, it was Dan she would love.

'Now, lass,' Bessie began briskly the following morning when Mary Ann at last appeared downstairs, bleary-eyed and yawning. 'Bert and the lads have gone to their work, but they all said I was to give you their love. Feeling a bit better, are you?'

Mary Ann nodded and yawned again. She pulled the shawl around her shoulders and sat in Bert's armchair, putting her bare feet on the warm brass fender.

'Here, get this down you. A nice bowl of porridge. Put hairs on ya chest, will that.'

Mary Ann took the proffered bowl and spooned the porridge slowly into her mouth, hunching her shoulders and bending towards the fire.

'Here, let me stir that fire up a bit, if you're cold.'

Having done so, Bessie sat down in the chair opposite and Mary Ann felt the woman's thoughtful gaze upon her. 'Now, lass. What are you going to do? Miss Edwina called this morning. She says it'd be better if you didn't go back to The Hall, but she can find you extra work at the school, if you'd like that.'

Mary Ann said nothing.

'What about it, eh?'

Mary Ann shrugged, but still she remained silent.

'Have you a better idea?'

Mary Ann shook her head.

'Well, then?'

Mary Ann lifted her shoulders again and then, looking straight into Bessie's eyes, she smiled as she said, 'It won't be for long anyway. Whatever I do.'

'Aw now, come, lass,' Bessie flapped her hands. 'Don't talk that way. You mustn't think of—'

'No, no, I didn't mean that Bessie. What I meant was, I won't be able to work for much longer.'

Bessie's mouth dropped open and then she groaned and closed her eyes. 'Oh no. Not that. I was afraid you might be. Aw lass, no.'

'Dan's told you? I didn't think you'd mind. I thought – I hoped you'd be pleased.'

'Pleased? How can I be pleased? You no more than a bairn yasen and now you're going to bring another into the world.' She frowned as if she had suddenly realized what Mary Ann had said. 'Dan? What's Dan got to do with it? Did you tell him last night? Does he know?'

Mary Ann shook her head. 'Auntie Bessie, I don't think we're talking about the same thing. You think I'm carrying Mr Randolph's child. Is that it?'

Bessie nodded.

'Well, I'm not.' That much she was sure of and now she hoped to bluff it out that she had ever lain with Randolph Marsh. That wasn't the sort of thing Bessie would like if Mary Ann were to become her daughter-in-law.

Bessie let out a huge sigh of relief. 'Oh, thank the good Lord for that.' Then she frowned. 'So if that's not it, just what are you on about?'

Mary Ann set her empty bowl down on the hearth and then smiled at Bessie. 'I'm not going to be able to work for Miss Edwina much longer because I'm going to be too busy looking after my husband.'

'Oh now, look, Mary Ann. You must get it into that head of yours, he's not going to marry you. His sort . . .'

Mary Ann shook her head. 'I'm not talking about Mr Randolph. I don't want to talk about him ever again. I don't even want to hear his name mentioned.'

'Then . . .?'

Bessie was clearly puzzled and Mary Ann's smile widened as she added, 'I'm going to marry Dan.'

If Mary Ann had hoped to drop a bombshell into Bessie's lap, she had certainly succeeded.

'Dan? Our Dan?' Bessie blustered, her round face reddening. 'But . . . but he's courting. He's walking out with Susan Price.' She shook her head and then leant towards Mary Ann, taking the girl's hand gently into her own. 'Look, love. You've got it all wrong. Our Dan was just being kind to you last night. He loves you, yes. Like we all do. Like a daughter or a sister. But if he's going to marry anyone, love,' her tone became even gentler, 'it's Susan.'

'No,' Mary Ann shook her head firmly. 'No. He's going to marry me. I know he is.'

That evening when Dan stepped over the threshold, his mother's tirade hit him with a force that was almost a physical blow. From the bedroom, Mary Ann heard the raised voices and crept downstairs to listen.

'Whatever are you thinking of, Dan Ruddick? I'm surprised at you. Leading the poor girl on after all she's been through. First, that rotten home life she had as a bairn and then that bastard at The Hall and his philandering ways, taking advantage of a young and vulnerable lass. But you! I'd have thought you'd have had a bit more sense.'

'Hold on, Ma, hold on.' Mary Ann heard his deep voice and could imagine him holding out his hands, palms outward, to fend off his mother's onslaught. 'What are you on about?'

'You! That's what I'm on about. Leading that little lass on to believe you're going to marry her. How could you?'

'Marry her?' Dan sounded surprised, as if the thought had not even occurred to him.

'That's what she said, but how she's got that idea into her head, I don't know, unless you've put it there.'

There was a moment's silence whilst Mary Ann held her breath before she heard Dan say again, 'Marry her.'

Now the words were spoken softly, as if he was rolling the idea around in his mind, pondering, even savouring, the notion.

'Well,' Mary Ann heard him say at last. 'Why not? Why shouldn't I marry her, Ma?'

Twenty-Nine

The wrangling within the Ruddick household went on for days. Whilst, in the main, the argument occurred when she was out of the room, Mary Ann was usually somewhere in the cramped house and could scarcely fail to overhear most of what was said.

'You're not serious, our Dan,' Bessie persisted. 'I don't want you hurting her. She's had enough broken promises to last her a lifetime. Tell her the truth now, lad, before it's gone too far. Tell her that she misunderstood you. That you were just feeling sorry for her because she was so upset. She'll understand. But tell her now, Dan.'

'I'm telling her no such thing, Mam. Besides, she needs someone like me to take care of her.'

'What about Susan, lad?' Bert asked in his quiet and thoughtful way when he was being serious.

'Oh, she'll be all right.' There was an unusual trace of bitterness in Dan's tone as he said, 'She'll always have her *father* to take care of her.' Gently, now, he asked them, 'But who's going to take care of little Mary Ann?' Then his voice hardened as he added, 'The likes of Randolph Marsh?'

To this, his family had no answer.

Bert shook his head sadly, 'You'll likely lose your job with old man Price if you jilt his one and only daughter. Besides, you've waited months, years almost, to get her back after that bit of trouble.'

219

'It was she who came back to me, if you remember, Dad. And to be honest, if Susan had thought that much about me, she'd have stood by me at the time it all happened, never mind what her father said.'

'Oh, now you're being unfair, Dan,' Bessie said.

At this moment Mary Ann stepped into the room and went straight to stand by Dan.

Keeping his voice low and his anger in check, although Mary Ann could see that his eyes were sparkling with defiance, Dan said levelly, 'No, I don't think I am, Mam. Susan knew very well that her dad was being unjust, that I had nowt to do with Sid Clark being aboard our ship.'

'You can't expect a lass like her to go against her father, though.'

Now Mary Ann, putting her hand on Dan's arm, spoke up. 'I would have done. I'd have run away with Dan sooner than do what me dad told me.'

Bessie and Bert glanced at her, looked at each other and then away.

'Aye well,' Bessie murmured. ''Appen you would, lass. But in your case, no one would have thought any the worse of you. But . . .' Bessie bit her lip, hesitating to hurt this young girl, whom she loved like one of her own, any more than she had been wounded already. But it had to be said and Bessie Ruddick had never been one to shirk saying what needed to be voiced. Gently, she added, 'But you do see, don't you, that Susan comes from – well – a loving, caring home. Her father was bound to be cautious for her, and though I could have hit him mesen for not believing in our Dan, even I could see how Jack Price must have felt. D'you see?'

Mary Ann shook her head. 'No. If Dan loves me and he doesn't love Susan, then what's the problem?'

'The problem,' Duggie, for once very serious, put in, 'is

that Dan will be without a job. And Price will see to it
that he doesn't get another round here.' Then his impish
sense of fun got the better of him, even in the midst of all
the wrangling. 'I think you'd do a lot better to marry me,
Mary Ann, than this old sobersides, anyway.' He leant
across and tweaked her nose playfully. 'What do you
say?'

Coyly, Mary Ann put her head on one side. 'Why,
thank you, kind sir. But I must decline your offer. I am
already spoken for.'

Dan, covering her hand where it lay upon his arm,
smiled down at her. 'There, it's settled then. We'll be
married as soon as you're sixteen.'

And they were. There was nothing Bessie or Bert or his
two brothers could do to dissuade Dan from his decision.
Even Susan, visiting Waterman's Yard, her eyes red-
rimmed from weeping, could not break his resolve.

Mary Ann, listening outside the door into the kitchen,
overheard her pleading with him.

'My father says he will give you your own ship. You
can be a skipper, Dan.'

'That's bribery, Susan,' Dan said harshly, his tone
implying how shocked he was that Susan should resort to
emotional blackmail.

'It's not,' Susan cried. 'If you were his son-in-law,
there's nothing my father wouldn't do for you. He just
wants me to be happy.'

'It's not so long back that he wouldn't have had me as
a son-in-law if I'd been the last man on earth.'

'You can't blame him for that. He was only trying to
protect me.'

Mary Ann heard Dan's deep sigh. 'I know and I don't
blame him. Not really. Not any more.'

'So why? Why are you marrying this girl? Everyone

knows she's been Randolph Marsh's latest . . .' She hesitated before adding scathingly, 'Piece.'

'Susan . . .'

'Well, it's true. She's no better than she should be. Why are you marrying her? Because I know you don't love her. Is she expecting his child? Is that it?'

'No, she isn't,' Dan said sharply.

'Are you sure?' Susan asked quietly, almost pityingly as if she believed Dan was being duped by Mary Ann's wiles.

Grudgingly, as if feeling disloyal in having to offer proof, Dan said, 'I am sure because me mother told me she wasn't. I don't think she's even – well, you know – been with him.'

Susan gave a humourless laugh. 'If you believe that, Dan Ruddick, you're even more gullible than I thought you were.'

'Susan, please, try to understand. I have to take care of her. She needs someone to love her and look after her.'

'And you're the only poor fool around to do it, are you, Dan?' Susan's tone was filled with sadness now as she said, 'If there's nothing more I can say to you, I'll go.' Her voice softened as she added, 'I wish you well, Dan. I hope you will be happy. I mean that, because I love you and I always will. You might not believe that it grieves me to say it, but I think she will only bring you unhappiness, my dear.'

Susan must have turned away from him, for the kitchen door opened so suddenly that Mary Ann was caught eavesdropping. Susan's eyes narrowed as she looked into Mary Ann's startled eyes. Then she leant closer and whispered so that Dan, still in the other room, would not hear. 'Just you look after him, Mary Ann Clark, else you'll have me to reckon with. You hear me?'

Then before Mary Ann could think of a sharp retort, Susan was gone, running across the yard, her hand to her face as if she could no longer hold back the tears.

Mary Ann watched her go.

Who would have thought that quiet little Susan Price would have had quite so much spirit? For a brief moment, even Mary Ann admired her.

Once the news got out, of course, the other residents of Waterman's Yard had their say too. Battle lines were drawn with Bessie, now defending her son to outsiders, and Minnie Eccleshall on one side. Opposing them were Gladys and Phyllis. But most vociferous of all was Amy Hamilton.

Monday morning brought them all into the yard's communal wash-house, face to face. And from Dan's bedroom window where she was sleeping now, Mary Ann heard it all.

'What's it got to do with you anyway, I'd like to know?' Bessie said, declaring war.

'Can't abide to see a good man go to waste on a little trollop like that,' Amy said primly. 'We all know what she's been up to with *him*.' She jerked her thumb in the direction of The Hall.

'She's not in the family way, if that's what you're thinking. She's not having to get married.' Bessie picked up her washing basket and turned to go indoors before her sharp tongue could say more.

'You bitch, Bessie Ruddick,' Amy muttered, her face fiery red.

'Here, here, there's no need for that sort of talk,' Minnie sprang at once to Bessie's defence. 'She only said—'

'I know what she said,' Amy spat. 'She's got a long memory and an even longer knife. And she knows how to wound with it, an' all.' Amy turned and stormed towards her own back door.

Inside the Ruddicks' house, Mary Ann ran down the stairs as Bessie came in.

'What was all that about?' she asked.

'Something and nothing,' Bessie said. 'Get the kettle on. I could do with a cuppa after that.'

Mary Ann busied herself and they were sitting at the table pouring out the tea when Minnie poked her head round the door. 'Any left in the pot?'

'Come on in, then.' Bessie sighed and rested her arms on the table.

Minnie sat down. 'You going to tell us then?'

'I don't know if I should,' Bessie murmured. 'Doesn't seem fair. 'Specially now.'

'Oh, go on, Bess. You know I can keep a secret. I'm not like Phyllis. And Mary Ann here, well, she'll not say owt, will you, lass?'

Mary Ann, having witnessed Minnie defending her alongside Bessie, smiled. ' 'Course not, Mrs Eccleshall.'

Bessie sighed. 'It's a long time ago. Me and Bert had been married nearly two years and I was expecting our Dan when the Hamiltons came to live in the yard. George had got a job at Phillips' Engineering and they'd moved here from Lincoln. Their little boy, Ron, was about eighteen months old, I think.' Bessie paused a moment and smiled sadly, remembering the golden-haired little boy learning to walk on the uneven cobbles of Waterman's Yard. 'But living in the yard then was old Mrs Jaggers and she was *the* biggest gossip I have ever met in me life.'

'What? Worse than Phyllis?' Minnie asked incredulously.

'Oh, ten times worse than her. Anyway, only a few weeks after the Hamiltons moved in, Mrs Jaggers was spreading it around that they'd had to get married. That Amy was six months gone when she walked down the aisle.'

'How had she found that out?'

Bessie shrugged. 'How does Phyllis find things out? They know someone, who knows someone, who knows.'

Minnie was thoughtful for a moment before she said, 'I'd never have thought it of Amy, though, of all people. She's always seemed so prim and proper.'

'It can happen to the best of us,' Bessie said, and then she winked at the other two like a guilty conspirator. 'I have to admit, even I was lucky not to get caught 'afore Bert put the ring on me finger.'

The two women laughed together and Mary Ann joined in, though her laughter was with relief, realizing now, even more than before, just how lucky she had been that she was not at this moment carrying Randolph Marsh's bastard.

Thirty

'So what are you going to do now that you're married?'

Once all the legalities, because of Mary Ann's age, had been satisfied, they were married quietly in the parish church. The only witnesses present were the Ruddick family members and Minnie and Stan Eccleshall.

Once back in Waterman's Yard for the 'reception', for which Bessie had spent the whole of the previous day baking, she asked the question and went on, 'It's high time you were making some decisions. All I've heard so far is a lot of talk. But you know you can both stay here, Dan, in your room, if that's what you want?'

Dan smiled at his mother. 'I know, I know. You'd like to keep all your chicks under your roof, wouldn't you, Ma?'

'She can't wait to be a grandma,' Duggie teased. 'That's what it is. So you'd best get up them stairs, our Dan, and get cracking.'

Everyone laughed, though Mary Ann lowered her head, pretending to be shy at the mention of their wedding night. In truth, she was rather nervous at the thought of what would happen when she and Dan climbed into bed together. Not because she was ignorant, for she knew all too well what to expect. But Mary Ann was desperate to deceive Dan into thinking that for her it was the first time. She thought back to the night Randolph had first made love to her. To her chagrin, she felt the familiar thrill run through her when she remembered his touch and his seductive words.

No, no, she must not think of him. She must think only of Dan now.

Thoughtful as ever, Dan was drawing the conversation away from such delicate matters, though Mary Ann hoped fervently that he did not even begin to guess at the real cause of her blushes. That night, she knew, she would have to be a very good actress.

'I shall have to start looking for a job tomorrow.' He glanced apologetically at his new wife. 'I'm afraid a honeymoon is out for us at the moment, love.'

Mary Ann slipped her hand into his and squeezed it. 'I don't mind. As long as we're together.'

Duggie made a sound as if he was going to be sick, which earned him a gentle clout from his mother. 'Don't you mock it, son,' she laughed. 'You'd do better to find yasen a nice girl.'

Duggie put his hands over his heart and threw back his head dramatically. 'But my heart is broken, Mam. Dan has stolen the only girl I've ever loved.'

The whole family laughed and Duggie's grin was the widest of all. 'There's one good thing about it, though,' he said. 'She's really our sister now, isn't she?'

Mary Ann felt a warm glow run through her, and inside her head she repeated the vows she had so recently spoken in the church. She would be a good wife to Dan. Lovingly, she smiled up at him and he reached out and touched her face gently with the tips of his fingers.

'Aye,' Bessie was saying. 'And we've got a daughter, 'aven't we, Bert?'

'Yes, light of my life, we have.' He beamed across at the couple, but then his smile faded a little as he added, 'But you're right, Dan. You should start looking straight away for a job. I've asked around for you already, but everyone is so frightened of Price's hold on this stretch of the river, you might have to go further afield.'

The interview with Mr Price a week earlier, Dan had told them all, had been short but nasty. 'He's a vindictive old devil, but I have to hand it to Susan that she hadn't told him before now.'

That had surprised Bessie. 'That day she came here, I thought she'd run straight home and tell him. I thought you were for the sack then, lad.' Bessie had glanced at her son and then away again. She had said no more, but her look had said, 'Susan must still care for you if she has kept it hidden from her father all this time.'

Understanding, Dan had nodded. 'I feel guilty enough about it, without her old man having a go at me.'

'You've no reason to feel guilty,' Mary Ann had said. 'It's no good marrying her if you don't love her. You love me now, don't you?'

'Yes, yes. Of course I do.'

'And it's not as if you were engaged to her or anything, is it?'

That had prompted a wry grimace from Dan. 'Good job I wasn't. Do you know what he said to me? If we'd been officially engaged, he'd have had me up in court for breach of promise. Can you imagine that?'

Bessie had nodded. 'Aye, with Jack Price I can believe anything.' She had looked, then, at her husband. 'What about you, Bert? Is your job safe?'

Bert had wrinkled his brow. 'I reckon. We go back a long way, Jack and me.' Bert tapped the side of his nose and winked at his wife. 'There's things I know about Jack Price that perhaps he wouldn't like aired in public. I reckon he'll let me alone.'

'Couldn't you make him give Dan his job back, then?' Mary Ann asked. 'Couldn't you sort of threaten him?'

Bessie had answered swiftly for her husband. 'It's not in Bert's nature to do things like that.'

'I think it'd be best,' Bert said quietly, 'for you to make a clean break, Dan. It'd only make things very awkward for you if you were to stay on with him, now wouldn't it?'

'Yes,' Dan was forced to agree. 'Yes, you're right, Dad.'

Mary Ann continued to help Miss Edwina at the school, both in teaching embroidery and helping out generally. They had been married for two months and Dan had still not been able to find work.

'I know how difficult things must be for you, Mary Ann,' Edwina said, 'so there'll be a little extra in your pay packet each week until Dan has found another job.'

'Oh thank you, miss. You are kind.' Mary Ann paused and then added, 'You heard then?'

Edwina smiled. 'Not much remains a secret in this town, not even from the so-called gentry.' She pulled a wry face against herself. 'But seriously, how is Dan's search for work progressing?'

Now it was Mary Ann's turn to pull a face and say, 'Not very well. So many people have business with Mr Price and they're not prepared to upset him by giving Dan a job. Mr Price has let everyone know that he believes Dan jilted his daughter and broke her heart.'

Edwina sighed. 'Oh dear.' She was thoughtful a moment and then said, 'There's someone my father knows. A boat owner near Newark. I'll see what I can do. Leave it with me, Mary Ann.'

229

A week later, Mary Ann ran nearly all the way home, arriving breathless and holding the stitch in her side. 'Dan. Where's Dan?'

'He's out. Why, whatever's the matter?'

Mary Ann's face was overjoyed. 'Miss Edwina's found him a job. At least, she's arranged for him to go and see a boat owner near Newark and she's put in a good word for him, so he can't fail to get it.'

'Here, here, slow down. I can't keep up with you, lass. Sit down and tell me slowly.'

Mary Ann sat down, taking huge gulps of air to steady herself. 'Miss Edwina's father knows a man who owns several boats . . .'

'Ships, love, ships,' Bessie, out of habit, corrected her.

'Ships, then.' Mary Ann was impatient to impart her news. 'And Dan's to go and see him. It's a Mr Sudbury. One of his skippers has just been taken very ill and he's desperate to find someone.'

'That's a bit of luck,' Bessie began and then she clapped her hand to her mouth. 'Oh, that sounds awful towards the poor feller who's ill, but you know what I mean.' Her face clouded. 'Dan's not a skipper though. He hasn't the experience.'

'Mr Price was going to make him a skipper if he'd married Susan, so he must have thought he was capable of being one.'

Bessie was frowning. 'How d'you know that? I didn't know that.'

'Oh, er . . .' Mary Ann realized suddenly that in her excitement she had let her tongue run away with her. 'Dan told me.' Mentally, she crossed her fingers, hoping the lie would not catch her out. She was sure Bessie would not have approved of her eavesdropping.

'Well . . .' Still, Bessie did not sound too sure, but she

smiled and nodded and said, 'At least he can go and see this Mr Sudbury. That's something, ain't it? But I shouldn't get your hopes up.'

Dan travelled to Newark the following day, leaving Mary Ann in a turmoil of excitement until she heard his footsteps in the alleyway that evening. She flew out of the house and across the yard to meet him, Bessie waddling after her as fast as she could. Dan caught Mary Ann in his arms and swung her round.

'I've got a job. I've got a job and what's more, we've got a home, an' all. Mr Sudbury says we can live aboard the ship I'm to skipper. There now, what do you think of that?'

Mary Ann gave a squeal of delight and Bessie clapped her hands. 'I'm that glad for you, I don't know where to put mesen. Wait till Bert hears. And to live aboard, an' all. Oh, I'm that envious. It's a wonderful life, Mary Ann. You'll love it.'

Mary Ann was still hugging him. 'I don't care where we live, as long as I'm with Dan.'

That evening the house was alive with chatter as Dan related all that had happened and everyone plied him with questions.

'Whatever did you tell him?'

'Does he know you've not skippered before?'

'Did he ask for references, 'cos I doubt old Price'd give you the time of day.'

'It's all thanks to Miss Edwina. Oh, but she is good.' This was from Bessie.

'One at a time, one at a time,' Dan grinned happily. 'I

told him the truth. Everything. There was no other way, really, was there? But he's a really nice chap. I took to him and I think he took to me. He's a real, larger-than-life character. He wears a check jacket and trousers and a top hat all the time and always has a cigar in his mouth. And you should hear him laugh. It's so loud it's a wonder we can't hear it from here.' If it was possible, Dan's smile broadened even further. 'It seems that John Sudbury had a run in with Jack Price some years back. He can't stand the man and they're bitter rivals now for trade on this part of the Trent. So, he's very happy to put one over on him. He said he'd heard of me. You know how river folk talk? And he'd heard nowt but good, how I was a good worker and that I was more than ready to take on my own ship. He wants me to take on all the work I can get downriver, to Hull, even into Yorkshire, if I can.'

'How's he paying you, lad?'

'Thirds, Dad.'

Everyone nodded approval, except Mary Ann who looked puzzled. 'What's that mean?'

'It's the way the earnings are shared between the owner and the captain. The owner pays certain expenses out first, then the money that's left is split one-third to the owner, that's Mr Sudbury and then two-thirds to the captain.' Dan grinned, as if he could not, even yet, believe his good fortune.

'And that's all yours?'

'Well, yes, but I'll have a lot of expenses to pay out of my portion. Casual labour, towing, horse-hauling, even lock pennies when we have to go through locks or bridges that have to be operated to let us through and then of course there's our living expenses . . .'

'Oh stop, stop. I don't want to know,' Mary Ann laughed.

Now Dan glanced apologetically at Mary Ann. 'There's just one thing. I had to tell him about the bit of trouble a while back. I thought it best to be completely honest with him. And it was a good job I was, because he'd heard all about it. He put his hand on my shoulder and said that clinched the deal as far as he was concerned. If I could be that honest about that, then he had no more worries.'

'There you are. Haven't I always told you, honesty is the best policy?' Bessie reminded him.

'You have, Ma. You have.'

'It's all down to you and your upbringing that's got Dan that job today, our mam,' Duggie teased, but Bessie only pretended to preen herself and agreed, 'Of course it is.'

The whole house shook with their laughter.

Thirty-One

'Mary Ann? Mary Ann, where are you?' Dan's voice echoed through the house on his return from another trip to Newark a week later.

'Here, Dan, upstairs. I'm just packing,' she called, then scrambled to her feet and hurried down the stairs carrying the pillowcase containing their clothes. 'What is it? Is something wrong?' But when she saw his face, she knew that there was nothing wrong at all. In fact, everything was very right.

His face was a picture of happiness and pride as he held out his hand to her. 'Come with me. I've something to show you. And Mam too. Where is she?'

'Across at Mrs Eccleshall's, I think.'

'Come on . . .' Dan was like an excited schoolboy. He grasped Mary Ann's hand and pulled her outside and across the yard. 'Let's get her. I want her to see it too.'

'What, Dan? What are you on about?'

He turned a beaming smile upon her. 'My ship, of course. Our new home, Mary Ann.'

Mary Ann gasped. 'You've brought her home already?'

Dan nodded as he rapped on Minnie's door, calling impatiently, 'Mam, Mam, are you there?' Unable to wait even the moment it took for the door to be answered, he opened it and called again. 'Mam?'

Bessie appeared. 'Whats the matter?' For a moment her eyes were worried, but she too, on seeing his face, saw she had no cause for alarm. She, quicker to guess than Mary Ann had been, said, 'You've got her? You've brought her home?' She stepped out into the yard and began at once to move towards the alley. 'Let's be 'aving a look-see, then.'

Minutes later, the three of them were standing on Miller's Wharf staring in awe at the sleek lines of the keel.

'She's not new, of course, but she's just been repaired, overhauled and repainted.'

'She looks as good as new.' Bessie's round face was aglow with delight. 'Just look at that paintwork. I like the colours. Blue, white and orange. Very smart. You'll be able to embroider him a pennant in those colours for the mast, Mary Ann.'

'So, how about it, Mam?' Dan asked. 'Are you coming aboard?'

Bessie shook her grey head. 'Oho, I don't know about that, lad. I'm a bit too broad in the beam now to be clambering up and down ladders.'

'Come on,' he coaxed. 'I want you to explain things to Mary Ann.'

'Well . . .' Bessie said, still doubtful, but she allowed Dan to help her aboard his first ship as master.

'I can't get down there,' she said looking askance at the companion down into the stern cabin. 'I'd forgotten how narrow they are.'

'Aw, come on, Mam. Your dad was a big feller, wasn't he? And he managed it.'

'Oh, go on, then,' Bessie said, 'I'll have a go, but don't blame me if I get stuck and have to stay there for your first voyage.'

Dan laughed. 'That's all right. You'd be good ballast if the weather gets rough, Mam.'

'Oh you!' Bessie said and took a swipe at him, but Dan ducked out of the way.

Dan went down the vertical ladder first and helped his mother climb down, followed by Mary Ann.

'Oh Mary Ann, she's beautiful. Just look at this lovely wood.' Reverently, Bessie ran her hands over the varnished mahogany of the cabin's interior. Every panel was a cupboard door, which Bessie was now opening and closing with excitement. 'So compact,' she enthused.

Next to the ladder down which they had climbed was a tiny stove complete with a hob on the top bar of the fireplace for the kettle or pans. It even had a minute brass fender and fire irons. On the opposite side of the ladder, on the port side and round the after end of the cabin, was a locker with cushions on it for seating.

'And that's where you put your coal,' Bessie said, pointing to a part of the locker on the port side. 'And then your pans go under there.' Now she was pointing at the lockers across the end of the cabin. Above this was a drop-leaf table and above that, the polished, built-in cupboards. On the starboard side of the cabin was a double bed.

'And look here.' Bessie was pointing to the opposite side again. 'This is what they call the spareside. It's a spare bed.' Her smile widened. 'This is where your bairn'll sleep. See?'

'Oh, so you think there's going to be one then, Mam?'

'There'd better be, our Dan,' Bessie said, closing the drawer. 'Else I'll want to know the reason why.'

Dan put his arm around Mary Ann's shoulders and gave her a squeeze.

'Oh Mary Ann,' Bessie was saying ecstatically. 'You're going to be so happy here.'

Mary Ann was not so sure. It all looked so small and

cramped and she still had to experience her first trip on the water.

They climbed back up the ladder, Bessie heaving and grunting as she did so, until they all three stood on deck again.

'You'll have to learn how to scull the cog boat,' Bessie said, leaning over to look at the tiny boat moored aft of the ship.

'The what?' Mary Ann gaped at her.

'This little boat.' Bessie beckoned her. 'It's called a cog boat and it's only got one oar and you scull it. Like this.' Bessie demonstrated as if gripping the oar in both her hands and sculling the little boat through the water.

'You'll soon learn how to do it. I used to be a dab hand at it. I could scull faster than me dad by the time I left the river.' She sighed and gave one last look at the small vessel bobbing gently on the rippling river. 'But I reckon my sculling days are well and truly over.' She laughed, but there was a tinge of nostalgia in the sound. 'Reckon I'd capsize it now. It's handy for you to get to shore to do your washing and fetch supplies, an' that. You'll soon get the hang of it all, love.'

Mary Ann thought about the cramped conditions of the cabin, the enclosed bed she would share with Dan, no doubt squashed by his broad shoulders against the side of the bunk, the tiny stove where she would be expected to do all the cooking. Then she looked down at the boat, which was her only means of transport to the shore and, she could not help the thought from entering her mind, her only escape from the ship.

'Mm,' was all Mary Ann said in reply to Bessie, but in that one sound were all the doubts and fears she was feeling inside.

Of course she had realized how different her future life

with Dan aboard this ship would be from the one she had planned as the wife of Randolph Marsh and lady of the manor. But now she was facing the reality of it.

Bessie was dragging her back from her daydreams. 'What you want to do is this. On wash days, you take all your washing in the cog boat and you scull up to the next lock or wherever there's a wash-house. If you time it right, by the time Dan gets there, you're done. And then, when he's travelling without a load you can string a line up in the hold, peg all your washing on it, open the fore and aft hatches and, as you sail, your washing dries lovely.' Bessie beamed with pride. 'And not so much as a smut or speck of dirt to be seen.' She sniffed derisively. 'Not like I have to put up with in the Waterman's Yard. I reckon half the time, me washing comes back in dirtier than what it went out.'

Bessie moved towards the gangway from the ship on to the jetty. 'See you Sunday and don't be late for yar dinner. Twelve o'clock sharp. By the way, Dan.' Bessie paused at the head of the gangway and turned briefly to ask, 'What's this little beauty called?'

Dan's laugh echoed across the river. 'I reckon it's a good omen, Mam. I thought so the minute I saw her. At the moment, she's called the *Maid Marian*. Mr Sudbury calls all his vessels after something to do with Robin Hood, but he's given me permission to alter the spelling a bit.' Dan put his arms around Mary Ann's shoulders and hugged her to him. 'From now on she'll be the *Maid Mary Ann*.'

Mary Ann fell in the river three times before she could scull the cog boat properly.

'I reckon I ought to have learnt you how to swim first,'

Dan laughed as he fished her out of the river for the third time.

'I'll soon have no dry clothes left at this rate,' Mary Ann wailed, standing, dripping, on the deck of the ship and looking the picture of misery. 'I'll never get the hang of the wretched thing,' she muttered, casting a malevolent glance at the little boat bobbing innocently a few feet away.

'You will. You're doing fine. Really you are. It's all a matter of keeping your balance. One day you'll be sculling up and down this river faster than I can sail.'

Mary Ann glanced at him disbelievingly and squelched away to find some dry clothes yet again. Laughing, Dan followed her.

'I've brought you a little present, Dan,' Bert held out a brown paper parcel. 'It's from me and yar mam.'

'Just to let you know how proud we are of you, son,' Bessie beamed.

'Oh Dan, open it, open it,' Mary Ann said, excitedly. She was still a child when it came to presents. Maybe it was because she had had so few in her young life.

Dan unwrapped the gift, a seaman's peaked cap.

'I reckoned now you're going to be a captain, you'd better look the part,' Bert said.

'Thanks, Dad.' Dan grinned and put on the cap. 'It fits perfectly.'

''Course it does,' Bessie said with pretended indignation. 'I took one of your old caps to be sure the size was right.'

'So how's married life then?' Duggie asked as they all sat down to Sunday dinner. 'Recommend it, do you? Reckon I ought to try it?'

'It'd be a brave girl to take you on,' Bessie remarked, setting the joint of beef in front of Bert whilst he sharpened the carving knife on a steel.

Mary Ann joined in the good-humoured teasing, saying, 'Who do you think would have him, Auntie Bessie?'

Before Bessie could answer, there was a knock at the back door and a voice called, 'Coo-ee. Anybody in?'

'It's Phyllis. Now what does she want? Just as we're sitting down to dinner, an' all.' Things had never been quite the same between Phyllis and Bessie since Phyllis had caused the trouble at the Boxing Day party. Ever since then, Phyllis had always seemed to take sides against Bessie in any argument.

'Minnie's my only real friend,' Bessie had said to her family after Phyllis had once again sided with Amy concerning Mary Ann's marriage to Dan. 'The rest of 'em, I can take 'em or leave 'em.'

Bert had smiled and put his arms around her waist. 'But, my angel, if one of them were in trouble, you'd be there, now wouldn't you?'

Bessie had chuckled. 'You know me too well, Bert Ruddick. That's your trouble.'

Now, as they heard Phyllis calling again, 'Anybody home?' Bessie said, ''Spect it's a bit of choice gossip she can't wait to pass on.' She raised her voice and called, 'Come in, Phyllis, if you must.'

Phyllis appeared in the kitchen doorway. 'Oh, I'm sorry. You're having your dinner. I'll come back later.'

'No, no. You might as well say what you've come to say. Bert's not carved yet and I'm still dishing up.' She turned to face her neighbour, hands on hips, and asked, 'What's the Horberry Gazette got for us this week, eh?'

'If you're going to be like that, Bessie Ruddick, I'll keep what I know to myself.'

'Pigs might fly,' Bessie murmured.

'Hush, my angel,' Bert warned softly.

Phyllis appeared to be struggling with her desire to impart her titbit of news and her need to withhold it to spite Bessie. Her desire won. She pulled out a chair and sat down at the table. 'Have you heard the news?'

'Shouldn't think so,' Bessie said and paused as she bent to lift out two tureens of vegetables, keeping warm in the oven. Placing them on the table, she added, 'Not afore you, Phyllis.'

Phyllis beamed. 'There's to be a big wedding at the parish church in June. Mr Randolph and Miss Celia Thompson have announced the date of their marriage. By, it'll be a posh affair, won't it? Nellie Goodrick says she doesn't know how she's going to cope with all the catering. Mind you, she's already made the wedding cake.'

Her news was greeted with silence. Phyllis's glance darted from one to another, coming to rest at last upon the newly married couple. 'And that's not all,' she added, and now there was a sly note in her voice. 'I've heard that Ted Oliver . . . You know him, don't you, Dan? He's the ferryman at Eastlands?'

Dan said nothing, but gave a curt nod.

'They say he's got his feet well and truly under the table with Jack Price. He's courting Price's daughter, Susan. 'Course he's quite a bit older than her, but they say Jack Price is singing his praises to the rooftops.' Again, she glanced around but, when no one spoke, she got up. 'I'll leave you to it, then. Enjoy your dinner.'

Suddenly, Mary Ann's appetite seemed to have deserted her. She glanced at Dan, fearful that he would notice, but he, too, seemed lost in his own thoughts.

Thirty-Two

'I've got my first cargo. Cement from Hull to be 'livered to Lincoln.' Dan seized Mary Ann's hand as if he couldn't wait to set off. 'Are you ready, my pretty little mate?'

'Yes, yes,' she said, trying to look as if her excitement matched his, but, inwardly, her heart was plummeting. This was it, then. Today – right this moment, it seemed – she would have to go aboard the ship, which was to be her home. They'd come back to Bessie's at weekends whenever they could, she knew, but for most of the week they would be travelling up and down the river carrying cargoes this way and that.

'Come on,' Dan was urging. 'We must catch the tide.'

From now on, Mary Ann thought, her life was going to be ruled by the tides, the currents and the wind.

The ebb tide was running strongly and as soon as they were aboard and had cast off, the current began to take them steadily downriver. From the cabin where she was stowing away their belongings, Mary Ann heard Dan calling her. She climbed the ladder and made her way carefully to him.

'When we get into the Humber, Mary Ann, you'll have to help me.' He put his arm around her. 'You're my "mate" now.'

'Oh Dan, I can't. I don't know what to do.'

Dan's arm slipped from her shoulders. 'You'll have to, love,' he said and whilst his tone was still gentle, there was a firmness in it too now. 'I can't manage everything on my own. You'll have to do exactly as I tell you. Look, we'll take our time going downriver, go with the tide and I'll show you what you have to do . . .'

The next few hours were a mesmerism of sails and sheets, rollers, lee boards and bowlines.

'I'll never learn all that, Dan,' she said at last, appalled at what he expected of her. Now Dan's reply was terse. 'You'll have to, Mary Ann. Like I said, you'll have to act as "mate".'

She stared at him. 'I thought when you talked about me being your mate, I thought you meant I was your wife. I didn't think you meant I had to help sail the boat . . .'

'Ship, Mary Ann. It's a ship,' Dan frowned, but she ignored him and gestured vaguely in the direction of the cabin below.

'I knew I'd have to cook and wash, but I didn't expect . . .' Her voice trailed away as she glanced help-lessly around her. 'I can't do all this.'

She heard Dan sigh heavily and then, though he seemed to have to make a deliberate effort, he put his arms around her. 'We can't afford to employ anyone else. At least, not yet. Besides, wives often act as mates.'

There were only the two of them aboard ship and whilst keels the size of the *Maid Mary Ann* could nor-mally be handled by a captain and mate, it was not going to be so easy when one of them was a complete novice. The son of a woman who had been born on the river and brought up almost from the time she could walk to help out aboard her father's vessel, Dan, in his excite-ment at having his first command, had failed to remem-ber that his new wife was totally ignorant of life on the water.

When they got into the Humber, somehow Dan

managed to heave the sails up with Mary Ann doing exactly what he told her.

'There,' he said at last, a little breathless but smiling. 'That wasn't so bad, was it?'

Mary Ann looked down at her hands, roughened and sore with rope burns, and said nothing.

The wind filled the sails and the ship sped forward.

'Now, you ought to learn how to steer. Come here, Mary Ann.'

Gingerly, Mary Ann took hold of the carved wooden tiller.

'There,' Dan said, 'just get the feel of it.' He put his hand over hers and guided her to move the tiller to the right, then to the left, so that she could see in which direction the ship responded. 'See,' he said, 'nothing to it.' But Mary Ann could detect that the confidence he was trying to exude was forced.

'See that tall building on the far bank?' he said. 'Now, try to keep that in line with the bow of the ship.'

Mary Ann, biting her lip with concentration and with the wind from behind them blowing her hair across her face, only nodded.

That first trip to Hull was a near-disaster.

The first time Dan decided to change tack, Mary Ann went for'ard and waited for his commands.

'Stand by,' she heard him shout above the noise of the wind in the sails and the lapping water. Tensing herself against the motion of the ship, she saw him making ready, saw him push the tiller hard over to port and then release one of the ropes on the same side. She heard the rattle as he released the starboard lee board, but when she heard his command, 'Rise ya tack,' instead of operating the tack roller as he had shown her, she released the bowline.

Too late, she heard his bellow, 'No, no, Mary Ann . . .'

The sail flapped and for a moment the ship rocked and Mary Ann knew she had done something wrong, but could not, for the life of her, remember what.

'I'm sorry, I'm sorry,' she screamed, tears blinding her as she fought to keep her balance.

He came to her and, for a moment, held her close. 'It's all right, it's all right. We'll just let the ship come around and we'll try again.' Patiently, he explained again that she should not release the bowline until he commanded 'Let go'.

'I feel sick,' Mary Ann wailed. 'Take me home, Dan. Please, take me home. Take me back to Auntie Bessie.'

Dan took her by the shoulders and held her firmly. 'Now look, Mary Ann, we've got to do this together. You have to try again . . .'

By the time they reached the safety of the port of Hull, Dan was trembling with exhaustion and Mary Ann was crying hysterically. 'I hate it. I'm never coming with you again.'

'That was nothing,' he shouted back, fear at what might have happened snapping his patience. 'What do you think it would have been like if there'd been a real gale blowing?'

'Oh,' she wailed. 'I hate you, Dan Ruddick.' She flung herself away from him and almost fell down the ladder into the cabin, where she scrambled into the bed and buried her face in the pillow.

She heard him follow her down and then felt his touch on her shoulder.

'Don't cry, love,' he said wearily, the anger gone from

his tone now. 'It's not your fault. I should have realized. Mary Ann, I'm sorry. Please don't cry.'

She sniffed, but turned over and sat up, facing him with red and swollen eyes. 'What are we going to do? How are we going to get home again?'

Dan sat down and rested his arm on the table. 'I'm going to send a telegram home and ask Dad, or Duggie, to come to Hull on the train.'

'What are you going to put? "Mary Ann useless. Send help"?'

Dan actually laughed as he said, 'Something like that,' and then added swiftly as he saw her tears begin again, 'No, no, I'm only joking. I'll think of something.'

What he did put Mary Ann never knew, but the following day, whilst the cargo of cement was being loaded at a wharf not far from Hull, Duggie arrived at the station and took a hansom cab to find them.

'I've only come to help out, y'know. Just temporary. Just until you get the hang of it, Mary Ann,' he said. She had expected Duggie to tease her, to make fun of her ignorance of life aboard ship, but to her surprise, he did not. 'Because I'll soon be getting me apprenticeship at Phillips, y'know.'

'Of course you will, Duggie,' Dan said, 'but in the meantime, you can fill in the time helping me.'

'Well, that's all right then. Just so long as everybody knows.'

'You'll be all right sleeping in the fo'c'sle cabin, won't you?' Dan asked.

''Course, I will.' Duggie grinned. 'Won't be the first time, will it?'

'Nor the last,' Dan murmured, but only Mary Ann heard him. Duggie had served with Dan before as mate and there would be no need for words of command to pass between them. Each knew exactly what to do and the ship would be safe in their expert hands.

Louder, Dan said, 'Now, Mary Ann's been busy all morning down in the cabin. We'll go down and see what she's been cooking up, eh? We'll have a bit of dinner and then we can be away on the afternoon tide.'

'We'll need a tow up to Torksey,' Duggie said. 'But if the wind's fair we should be all right once we get into the Fossdyke.'

'How are we going to get towed?' Mary Ann asked, her curiosity overcoming her wish not to be involved with the sailing of the ship at all.

'Sam Bryce runs a daily service with his tugs from Hull all the way to Newark and all points in between,' Duggie explained to her.

'Right,' Dan said, climbing down the ladder into the stern cabin, with Duggie following. 'I'll see to it. But first things first. Me stomach feels as if me throat's been cut.'

Mary Ann went down after them. As she stepped off the last rung and turned to face them, it was to find them both looking at the cold grate in the stove and then at the table on which were three empty plates and, in the centre, a plate of sandwiches.

Dan lifted the edge of one and then turned to Mary Ann in horror. 'Cold fat bacon sandwiches?' he said, unable to keep the disgust from his tone. 'And not even the kettle on for a mug of tea. What on earth have you been doing all the morning, Mary Ann? I thought at least you'd have made us a nice hot stew in the beef kettle.' Before she could answer, Dan caught sight of the piece of embroidery Mary Ann had been working on. He picked it up and thrust it towards her. 'Is this what you call work? Sitting sewing all the morning?'

Easy tears filled Mary Ann's eyes. 'I . . . I didn't know how to light the fire. I couldn't find . . .'

'There's sticks and paper and coal in the locker there.' Dan pointed to the coal locker on the portside of the cabin. 'You could have asked. Duggie hasn't had a bite to eat since leaving home this morning.'

Mary Ann stared at Dan as he ranted on. She had never seen him so angry. Where was her kind, understanding husband? Her own temper flared. 'I can't cook on that silly little stove.'

'Plenty of women do,' Dan thundered, his rage filling the cabin. 'My mam's taught you to cook, hasn't she?'

'Yes, but in her kitchen range. Not on that – that *thing*.'

'It's perfectly adequate. My grandmother cooked for her whole family on just such a stove.'

'Look, it's all right,' Duggie interrupted. 'Mam packed me some grub up and I ate it on the train. And you'll soon get the hang of it, Mary Ann. Look, Dan, let's eat these sandwiches then you go and arrange about a tow and I'll show Mary Ann how to light the fire and she can cook us a meal for tonight.' He looked from one to the other, his good humour and sensible suggestions lightening the atmosphere.

Dan, still glowering, sat down. He picked up a sandwich and ate it in two mouthfuls as if to say, 'Hardly a man's meal, is it?'

Duggie sat on the other side of the table, munching happily and looking around the cabin.

'Snug as a bug in a rug, down here, aren't you? They've fitted it out nice, haven't they . . .?' Duggie prattled on saying nothing in particular and yet keeping up a constant chatter to which neither Dan nor Mary Ann replied.

When he had finished eating, Dan rose and climbed the ladder on to the deck.

'Right, then,' Duggie winked at her. 'Let's get this fire lit.' He leant towards her and, in a conspiratorial whisper, added, 'It'll be all right, love. It must all be very strange for you. And old Dan, well, he's got a lot on his mind. It's a big responsibility, being a captain, you know. Just take no notice of him. I'll help you get a meal started, an' all, and you'll soon get the hang of it.' He winked at her again, patted the bed and said saucily, 'You just give him a cuddle when you get him into this bunk tonight and he'll be all right.'

For the first time since they had left Elsborough, Mary Ann smiled. Suddenly, she threw her arms around Duggie's neck and kissed his cheek. 'Oh Duggie,' she said. 'You are good to me.'

Embarrassed, Duggie released her arms and gently pushed her from him. He laughed, trying to make a joke of her action. 'Give over, Mary Ann, you're a married woman now.'

Mary Ann put her head on one side, her cheeks dimpling prettily. Coyly, she said, 'And you're my brother now, so I'm allowed to kiss you.'

'Come on,' he said again, deliberately changing the subject. 'Let's get this fire lit.'

'Are we going home now?' Mary Ann asked when the cement in bags had been put ashore by the *Maid Mary Ann*'s derrick, straight on to the drays belonging to the builder who had bought the whole shipment. They had passed Elsborough on their way upriver to Lincoln and Mary Ann had sulked because Dan had refused to let her off the ship to go home to Bessie.

'Not yet,' Dan said. 'We're going further upriver, almost to Newark, for a load of Trent gravel.'

'Oh.' Mary Ann turned away before he could see the disappointment on her face.

'But we'll be home on Saturday,' he promised. 'And then you can have a nice hot bath in Mam's kitchen and see all your friends.'

Mary Ann held her breath, afraid that somehow he had guessed her thoughts. Oh, it wasn't the bath she was hankering for, although it would be nice to sink into the tin bath full of deliciously hot water and to smell the scented soap that Bessie shared with her. There was someone Mary Ann wanted to see, even more than she longed to see Bessie again, but her husband was the last person she could tell who that someone was.

'Is it true? Is he really going to marry this . . . this Celia?'

Mary Ann was standing before Edwina's desk in her study at the school.

'Oh, my dear.' Edwina stood up and came around the desk. She put her arms about Mary Ann. 'You must forget all about him and get on with your own life with Dan.' She stood back a little, but still clasped Mary Ann by the shoulders. Her steady gaze held Mary Ann's. 'Dan's a fine man.' Edwina sighed as she added, 'A far better man than Randolph, I have to admit it, even though he's my brother. You should be very happy with Dan. He'll not hurt you.'

'No, I know,' Mary Ann whispered, sorry that she had come here now on an impulse that had made her take a detour from shopping for supplies in the town before returning to the ship. She had thought that she could perhaps talk to Miss Edwina. Although she could talk to

Bessie about anything else, it was impossible to confide in her mother-in-law about her memories of Randolph Marsh.

'I was so happy for you when I heard you were to marry Dan Ruddick. I thought – well – that whatever had happened between you and Randolph had been just an infatuation. You're not the first young girl to fall for his flattery.' Her mouth was tight as she muttered, 'I wish I could say that you would be the last, since he is to be married at the end of this month, but if I'm honest, I can't even say that.' Edwina sighed and let her hands fall from Mary Ann's shoulders. 'Forget about him, my dear. Get on with your life with Dan and be happy. That's all we want for you. That you should be happy.'

Mary Ann lifted her chin and smiled, knowing now that she must never again speak of Randolph in this way to Edwina. Oh, she would continue to see Miss Edwina, for she loved her dearly, and she could perhaps ask after him in a casual manner, just like anyone would ask after her brother. But never again must she speak aloud her secret thoughts of Randolph.

'I will,' she said bravely, hiding the despair she was feeling inside. 'And can you keep a secret?'

She saw the wariness in Edwina's eyes as the young woman nodded.

Mary Ann's smile broadened as she said, 'I think I'm going to have a baby.'

For a moment, fear and disbelief clouded Edwina's eyes. She swayed a little and caught hold of the edge of the desk for support as she gasped, 'Oh no.'

'It's all right, miss,' Mary Ann took hold of her arm gently and led her to a chair. 'It's all right. Really, it is.' She leant over her and, looking straight into Edwina's eyes, she said softly, 'It is Dan's baby, I promise you.'

For a moment, Edwina gazed into her eyes, desperately trying to see if she was telling the truth. Mary Ann couldn't blame Miss Edwina for doubting her. In the past she had told lies when it suited her, had even stolen from Miss Edwina. And only Mary Ann knew how many times she had pinched fruit and cakes from the market stalls in the town when she had been hungry as a child. No, Mary Ann could not blame her. But for once, she was telling the truth. The child she was carrying was indeed Dan Ruddick's.

Though in her heart of hearts, how Mary Ann wished it was not.

Thirty-Three

'I'm going to be a grandma. Oh Bert, do you hear that?'

A month later, Mary Ann's suspicions were confirmed by the doctor.

Bert smiled and winked at Mary Ann. 'I hear, my angel. I hear.' He put his arms about his wife. 'But you don't look old enough, light of my life. No one will ever believe you.'

'Oh, go on with you,' Bessie said, smacking him playfully, her smile so wide, Mary Ann thought, you could tie it at the back of her head. 'And you're going to be a grandpa, Bert. How shall you like that, eh?'

'I shall like it very well. Very well, indeed. When is it due, Mary Ann?'

'In the spring. About the end of February or the beginning of March, I think.'

Bessie clapped her hands. 'It might be born aboard the *Maid Mary Ann*. Somewhere on the river, just like I was. Maybe Dan'll deliver his own bairn, just like my dad helped deliver me. Or, if you're near here, he can fetch me. I hope it's a girl. Oh, you will give me a granddaughter, Mary Ann, won't you?'

Mary Ann laughed. 'I'll try, Mam.' Since her marriage to Dan, Mary Ann had begun to call Bessie 'Mam' rather than addressing her as an adoptive 'Auntie'. It made her feel even closer to the woman, who had been more of a mother to her than her own had ever been. Bessie was delighted. She had allowed the girl to come to it in her own good time, but Mary Ann knew that every time she called Bessie 'Mam' it gave the older woman a little thrill of pleasure.

'But don't you think,' Mary Ann was saying now, 'that Dan will want a boy?'

'You can give him a boy later. There's plenty of time for that. No, we want a girl first, Mary Ann. And you can tell Dan I said so.'

Mary Ann smiled. 'Yes, Mam.'

The winter months passed comparatively uneventfully. Duggie was still mate aboard the *Maid Mary Ann*, although hardly a week went past without him saying, 'Well, I might not be here much longer. I've to see Mr Phillips about an apprenticeship . . .'

Often without Dan's knowledge, he helped Mary Ann. To her surprise it had been Duggie who had patiently helped her to learn what to do aboard the ship; Duggie not Dan, who relit the stove in the cabin for her if it went out; Duggie who praised her first culinary efforts and hung over the side of the ship to help her aboard when she returned in the cog boat.

'You come up, love,' he would call out. 'I'll get the washing . . .' or the shopping or whatever she had been ashore to do.

He had even coaxed her to learn how to take the tiller.

'It'll not happen often, Mary Ann,' Duggie told her. 'But you ought to be able to, just in case we ever get a time when we really need you to help out.'

As her pregnancy advanced Duggie fetched and carried for her more and more. He even sculled the cog boat for her, taking her ashore whenever she needed to go. If Dan didn't need him on deck, Duggie helped with the cooking whilst Mary Ann sat on the seat with her embroidery or sewing tiny garments for the expected baby. Then, when they were all three eating the meal later he would say, with pretended innocence, 'This stew's lovely, Mary Ann.'

Two weeks before Mary Ann's expected confinement, Dan said to her, 'I've got to go to Hull with a cargo, I think you should stay at home with me mam.'

'Oh I can't, Dan. She wants me to have the baby aboard the ship.'

Mary Ann had come to terms with her life afloat, although she had to admit to herself that it was only because of Duggie's presence aboard. She told herself that she was happy, that she should be grateful to Dan, and to Duggie too, for taking care of her. But she could not love her husband in the same way that she had loved Randolph Marsh. When they lay together in the bunk bed and Dan made love to her, the only way she could respond to him was by closing her eyes in the darkness and remembering those times with Randolph. Only then would her body ripple with desire and move in unison with Dan's hunger. Sometimes she bit so hard on her lower lip to stop herself from calling out Randolph's name that she drew blood.

When Dan said, 'You really have taken to the life now, haven't you, Mary Ann? I was so worried at first that you would find it so cramped aboard ship. That you'd feel . . . restricted,' Mary Ann had to bite back the hasty retort that it was only thanks to Duggie if she had. Instead, she shrugged and said, 'I've got used to it.'

Tenderly Dan reached out and spread his hand over her rounded belly. 'You're getting very big, aren't you? It can't be long now.'

Mary Ann smiled up at him. 'Do you think it could be twins?'

Dan laughed. 'What, a boy *and* a girl. That'd please Ma, wouldn't it?'

Mary Ann grimaced. 'Maybe, but I don't know how I'd cope with two.' She glanced around the tiny cabin. 'It's going to be hard enough with one. Still,' she yawned, 'I'll have to manage. And I'm coming with you to Hull. Your mam would never forgive me if I gave birth to her grandchild in Waterman's Yard instead of on the River Trent.'

Still, Dan looked doubtful. 'It's a cargo of potatoes and you know what that means.'

Mary Ann nodded. Dan would be stopping at several berths at villages along Trentside to pick up their cargo. The farmers brought their potatoes in sacks, which had to be loaded by hand, and the trip to Hull would take much longer than a straight run.

'And it can get very rough on the Humber, you know.'

'Don't remind me,' Mary Ann said at once with feeling, and Dan grimaced apologetically as he added, 'Still, you're not due for another couple of weeks, are you?'

'No. I'll be fine.'

Dan cupped her face in his hands and kissed her forehead. 'Oh Mary Ann, I do love you. I'm so proud of you the way you've learnt how to do everything. Do you know that? I'm sorry if I was a bit sharp with you at first. It was a big thing, you know, getting my first command. Am I forgiven?'

Mary Ann put her arms about him and buried her face in his chest. Unseen, she screwed up her face, for a brief moment riddled with guilt that she could not love this good man as he deserved to be loved. And there was something else too. She didn't know how to tell him the piece of news that she had heard the previous day in the town.

256

A week earlier, whilst they had been upriver near Newark, Susan Price had married Ted Oliver.

'Dan. Dan! I'll have to go below.'

'Not now, Mary Ann,' he yelled at her above the noise of the wind. 'I need you on deck. You'll have to stay at the tiller.'

The wind was driving up the Humber from the North Sea. Squalls of rain lashed the ship, stinging Mary Ann's face until she screwed up her eyes, unable to see, but still, doggedly, she clung to the tiller. 'I have to,' she gasped, the rain cold in her mouth. 'I have to go below.'

They were on their way back from Hull with a cargo of wheat, loaded in bulk, for one of the waterside mills in Elsborough.

'I've got dreadful pains. The baby's coming.'

Dan, his face wet with the rain, stared at her, horrified. 'For God's sake, Mary Ann. Not now.'

'I can't help it,' she screamed back at him as another pain wracked her body. She bent double, still hanging on to the tiller with one hand but clutching at her stomach with the other and gasping.

'Another half an hour, Mary Ann. Hang on if you can. Another half an hour and we'll be into the Trent.'

'Oh aye,' she countered bitterly. 'Never mind me. We've got to make the Trent. It's got to be born on the Trent.'

'Don't be stupid. I didn't mean that. It'll be calmer there. More sheltered. That's what I meant.'

Mary Ann didn't answer. As the contraction eased, she stood up and resumed her task.

'All right?' Dan's face was anxious, but he dared not let her leave yet. True, like his mother, he wanted his son or daughter born on the water, but not in it.

When they reached the calmer waters of the River Trent, the ship was stable. The wind still rocked her from side to side and flapped her sails, but now the *Maid Mary Ann* was in no danger of capsizing.

'You can go below. Duggie and I can manage now.'

'Oh thanks.' Mary Ann's tone was heavy with sarcasm. As she began to move towards the companion, another spasm of pain shot through her. She doubled over and fell to her knees.

Dan was beside her in an instant. 'Oh, love, I'm sorry. I didn't realize.'

Tenderly, now, he held her until the pain subsided, then he lifted her up and together they staggered towards the ladder. Dan went down first and then Mary Ann followed, Dan guiding her feet on to each rung. Another pain creased her and she cried out, her foot slipping so that she fell heavily against him.

'There, I've got you,' he gasped. 'You're all right. Here, let me help you get these wet clothes off.'

'I can manage,' Mary Ann snapped. 'Just go back and sail your blasted boat.'

Dan looked for a moment as if she had slapped him physically in the face, but then he said quietly, 'We'll sail a little further and then we'll drop anchor.'

Without waiting for her to argue, he climbed the ladder and disappeared. Left alone, Mary Ann leant on her hands on the side of the bed and groaned. Then, feeling another twinge, she stripped off her wet clothes and prepared the bed for giving birth. As she climbed into it, she wondered just how long it would be before she would get out of it again.

*

When Dan came down to her again, she said, 'It seems to have quietened down now. The pains aren't coming so often.'

'Perhaps it was a false alarm,' Dan said hopefully. Much as he wanted the child to be born on the river, he would have liked to have been a little nearer Elsborough, a little nearer some knowledgeable help. 'Can I sail a bit further upriver, then?'

Mary Ann ran her hands over her stomach then she nodded. 'Can we get near home do you think? So you can fetch Bessie?'

Dan leant across the bed and kissed her. 'We'll try. Hang on, Mary Ann.'

But they had only gone a few miles when Mary Ann was crying out, 'Dan, Dan. My waters have broken. It's coming, oh it's coming.'

Once more Dan anchored and came down to the cabin. 'We've only got as far as Eastlands' Ferry. Can't you hang on a little longer?'

'No, no.' Now she was writhing on the bed, her whole body bathed in sweat, her dark hair plastered to her face.

'Oh, let me die. I just want to die,' she moaned. As the pain gripped her once more, she screamed, 'I don't want it. I don't want it.'

Dan was beside himself, feeling helpless and ignorant of what to do.

There were towels and hot water all ready, but he had no idea what they were for.

'I'll go for help. I'll take the cog boat and go for help.'

Mary Ann clutched at him, her grip vice-like in her agony. 'No, no, don't leave me. I'm going to die. Don't leave me.'

'Duggie will go then.'

Once Duggie had gone, Dan sat with her, holding her

hand, wiping her forehead, his agony almost as bad as hers as he watched her suffer.

'Oh, why doesn't it come?' she moaned, lying back exhausted against the pillows.

Dan stood up suddenly. 'Where the hell has Duggie got to? He can't have been daft enough to try to go all the way to Elsborough, surely?' He stared down at her, anxious and afraid. He'd sooner face a mountainous sea than this. 'Something must be wrong,' he muttered. 'You need a midwife or a doctor and you need one now.'

'Don't leave me. Please, don't leave me.'

'Mary Ann, I have to. I'll have to swim to the bank and . . .'

Desperate now, he was already climbing the ladder as she called out weakly, 'Don't leave me, Dan. Oh, don't you leave me too.'

As she heard him step on to the deck and begin to run across it, Mary Ann whimpered, 'Why does everyone leave me? What have I done so wrong?' Then, as pain seized her again, she cried out, 'Mam. Mam!' not knowing whether it was for her own mother she called, or for Bessie.

Out of a haze of pain, she heard voices and then Dan saying loudly, 'There you are. I was just about to set off myself. Thank God . . .'

Mary Ann closed her eyes and offered up a silent prayer. Duggie had come back. Duggie had brought Bessie. Everything would be all right now. Bessie was here. Bessie would take care of her . . .

She heard Dan's boots scraping on the ladder and his voice calling out to her. 'Mary Ann? Duggie's back and he's brought someone to help you.'

Bleary-eyed, Mary Ann turned her head to see Dan coming towards her. Behind him, coming carefully down the vertical ladder, was Susan.

Thirty-Four

'Get her out. I won't have her here.' Mary Ann screamed, trying to push herself into the farthest corner of the enclosed bunk bed, away from the woman coming towards her.

'Don't be silly, Mary Ann.' Dan, in his anxiety, was frowning and his voice was unusually sharp. 'Susan's come to help you.'

'I want Mam,' she cried, the sweat shining on her face. Then, lest he should think her half-demented with the pain, she added, reverting to her childhood name for the woman she now thought of as her own mother, 'I want your mam. I want Auntie Bessie.'

Susan leant over the bed. Gently and with infinite kindness, she said, 'Mary Ann, it was too far for Duggie to go for Mrs Ruddick. Let me help you, now that I'm here. I'm sure I can, but Duggie can set off to go for his mother, if you want him to.'

Mary Ann's eyes were huge in her red face. 'How can you help?' she asked harshly. 'You haven't had a baby.'

She saw Susan wince at the deliberate shaft, but calmly she replied, 'No, my dear, but when I was fifteen, my mother had my little brother. I was there at the birth. Admittedly, I don't know as much as Mrs Ruddick, but,' she smiled now, 'I think I can safely say I do know a little more than Dan or Duggie.'

At that moment, a pain gripped Mary Ann with such

261

ferocity that she threw herself backwards on the bed and arched her body. Her screams echoed down the river.

'Dan,' Susan said, taking charge without any further permission or otherwise from Mary Ann, 'I need hot water, a bowl, soap, plenty of clean towels ... Ah, I see you've already made a start. Good.'

Dan, thankful to have something positive to do, hurried to do as she asked, although there was barely room in the small cabin for them to move around each other. At last, Susan said, 'I think you'd better go on deck now, Dan. Out of the way.'

But Dan shook his head. 'No, I'm staying here. I want to see my son born.'

Mary Ann, through a haze of pain and near delirium, saw Susan smile and heard her say softly, 'And if it's a girl?'

Dan's voice came clearly to her. 'I'll love her just the same.'

'Sit over there, then, and keep out of the way, Dan Ruddick. This is women's work.'

At that moment, Duggie poked his head down the companion. 'How's she doing? Anything you want?'

'We're fine, Duggie ...'

Panting between contractions, Mary Ann gasped, 'You speak for yourself,' but Susan only smiled and went on, 'But you could take the expectant father out of my way.'

'I'm staying here,' Dan declared and Duggie grinned. 'He's too big for me to shift, Susan. Sorry, you'll have to put up with him. Just watch he doesn't pass out, though.' He laughed and added, 'I'll wait up here, though, if it's all the same to you.'

Then Susan was bending over Mary Ann again. 'Now, my dear, the next time you get a strong pain, I want you to push.'

Mary Ann, between spasms, blinked at her. 'Push? Push what?'

'Well, sort of . . . bear down. You've got to help the little mite. It can't come into the world without a bit of help from you. You've got to push it out.'

'Have I?'

Susan nodded and as Mary Ann's face began to twist with the pain once more, she said, 'Come on, Mary Ann, push!'

An hour later a baby girl made her way noisily into the world. Mary Ann, weak and exhausted, was scarcely aware of Dan's triumphant shout and of Susan's smiling face as she cut the cord, lifted the child and put the red and bawling infant into its father's arms.

'You have a daughter, Dan. So you'd best forget all about having a son for this time.'

Even through her fatigue, Mary Ann was aware of Dan and Susan standing close together, their heads bent over the child, marvelling at its lusty cry and its waving limbs.

'By, she's a little fighter, ain't she?' Dan was grinning broadly.

'She's a little beauty. And just look at all that black hair.'

'Oi, what's going on down there?' A shout from above made both Dan and Susan look up with startled eyes. 'Out of me way, Duggie Ruddick. It's not you I'm after.'

'Oh dear,' Susan said, suddenly agitated. 'That's Ted. He must have come looking for me. I must go.'

'Wait a minute. You can't leave her like that.' Mary Ann saw Dan nod towards her and Susan turned back with a little start, almost as if she had completely forgotten about the mother.

'Oh dear, no. You're right, I can't. The afterbirth hasn't come away yet.' For a moment, Susan seemed uncertain, and when another shout from on deck filtered down to them, she jumped visibly.

'Susan? Are you down there?'

'Look, Ted . . .' Now they could hear Duggie trying to reason with him.

Susan whispered to Dan. 'Give the child to me. She can lie beside Mary Ann. You go up there and tell him what's happened while I see to her.'

Mary Ann lay back against the pillows. She was beginning to shiver now. All she wanted was to be wrapped up warmly and left to sleep and sleep. And she certainly didn't want the yelling infant beside her.

'It's not coming away. Can you push again, Mary Ann?'

Weakly, Mary Ann said, 'Whatever for? She's born now.'

'Yes, but there's what they call the afterbirth. It has to come away. If it doesn't, you could be dreadfully ill.'

'I am dreadfully ill now,' Mary Ann moaned, and lay with her eyes closed. 'I just want to die.'

'Don't talk like that,' Susan said, sharply. 'You've got a baby to think about now.'

'I don't want it. You can keep it.'

' "It" is a "her",' Susan reminded her brusquely. 'Now, come along. We've got to get this afterbirth out. Just sit up a minute, Mary Ann.'

Mary Ann did not move, making no effort to assist the woman who was trying so hard to help her, limited though her own knowledge was.

'Mary Ann . . .'

'Susan,' Ted's bellow came down the companion. 'You come home now. Do you hear me? I won't have you on this ship a moment longer.'

'Oh dear,' Susan muttered, wringing her hands. 'Oh Mary Ann, please . . .'

'Look . . .' Mary Ann raised her head and then heaved herself up on to one elbow. She opened her mouth to speak again, but caught her breath and was seized by a fit of coughing.

'Oh!' she cried, as she felt something slither out of her and rest, wet and sticky, between her legs.

'Thank goodness!' Susan said with relief. 'It's come away.' Then she raised her voice. 'I'm coming, Ted. I won't be a minute.'

'You'll come now, woman.'

But Susan remained where she was, busily washing Mary Ann. 'I'll be in trouble with him,' she murmured, 'but I can't leave you like this.'

Despite her exhaustion, Mary Ann was intrigued. 'What do you mean? Why should he mind?'

Susan glanced at her and then away again. In a low voice she said, 'Ted told me I was to have nothing to do with Dan again.'

'Well, you aren't. I mean, you're only helping me, aren't you?'

'Yes. But I'm aboard Dan's ship, aren't I?'

The two young women stared at each other as Mary Ann said shrewdly, 'You mean he's jealous of Dan?'

Susan nodded. 'Oh Mary Ann,' she whispered and suddenly there were tears in her eyes. 'You don't know the half of it.'

Mary Ann saw her brush the tears away impatiently and plaster a brave smile on her face. 'There. That's all I can do. But I think Dan should get his mother to have a look at you as soon as you get to Elsborough. I must go.' But even then, she could not resist putting out a gentle finger and touching the cheek of Dan's baby girl.

As she turned away and put her foot on the first rung of the ladder, Mary Ann said, 'Susan . . .'

Susan paused and looked back at her.

'Thank you,' Mary Ann said. 'I know it must have been hard for you.'

Susan nodded, smiled and then climbed the ladder. Mary Ann lay back and closed her eyes, but a second later they flew wide open as she heard Ted Oliver's voice again. 'What the hell do you think you're doing?'

Mary Ann let out a startled gasp as she heard distinctly the sound of a slap and Susan's cry.

'Now, look here . . .' began Dan's voice.

'Don't you "look here" to me, Dan Ruddick. You just keep away from her now. You hear me. She's *my* wife now. You cast her off when you took up with that little trollop down there. So you leave Susan be. She's mine.' A pause and then, 'Come on. We're going home.'

Another startled cry from Susan and Mary Ann imagined that Ted had grasped hold of his wife and was pulling her after him. Straining her ears, she heard them climbing down the rope ladder and into a rowing boat that bumped gently against the side of the ship. Then she heard the splash of oars as Ted pulled away. The sound became fainter and, at last, Dan descended the ladder and came to the side of the bed.

His face, showing none of the earlier exultation at the birth of his child, now looked grim with shock and despair.

'He hit her, Mary Ann. Right in front of me. The bastard actually hit her. We couldn't stop him.'

Mary Ann lay back and closed her eyes, memories of her early life flooding back to her. Fleeting pictures of the beatings her mother had suffered at the hands of her father. She could almost feel the bruises once more that she had received from him.

'Maybe he'll finish up at the end of a rope,' she said, bitterly.

As she drifted into an exhausted sleep, the last words she heard Dan say were, 'I'll hang the bastard mesen if I catch him hitting her again.'

Thirty-Five

'Oh Mary Ann, she's beautiful. What a little treasure. Look, Bert. Look at those big eyes.'

The new grandmother was drooling over the baby, whilst the mother was lying listlessly on the bunk, refusing to even try to get out of it.

'What's her name?'

Mary Ann, still weak and uninterested in her daughter, shrugged. 'Haven't thought of one yet.'

'Not thought of one!' Bessie was scandalized. 'Why, I'd have thought you'd been discussing names for weeks. We did, didn't we Bert? Rosemary was a favourite. Every time we picked Rosemary, didn't we?'

Bert grinned. 'Aye. Good job we never used it though, eh?' He tickled the baby under her chin. 'She's smiling at me. Look, she's smiling at me.'

'Wind,' said Bessie knowledgeably.

'Never,' Bert insisted. 'She knows who her grandpa is. She's smiling at me.'

Bessie looked at him fondly. ''Course she is, Bert.'

Mary Ann listened to them and silently ground her teeth. Why didn't they go away and leave her alone? And they could take the squalling brat that pulled and sucked at her and made her breasts sore with them.

They were looking at her, watching her, concern on their faces. 'Do you want to call her after your mam, love?' Bessie asked gently.

Mary Ann lay against the pillows and closed her eyes, remembering the thin little woman who had been so dominated, so overpowered by Sid Clark that she had not had the strength for her own survival, yet alone that of her only child. Mary Ann could scarcely remember affection or any kind of care from her mother. She opened her eyes and turned her head to look at Bessie and Bert standing there. These two warm-hearted souls had been far more like proper parents to her than ever her own had been.

'Or you could call her after yourself, or even after our Dan. Danielle. That's a nice name.' Bessie pulled a grimace. 'Bit posh, mebbe, for the likes of us. But it'd be nice.'

Briefly, the question flitted through Mary Ann's mind. Was there a feminine form of Randolph? But, of course, she did not voice the question aloud, although the thought of even suggesting it made her smile impishly.

Misreading it, Bessie said, 'You like that? Danielle?'

Mary Ann moved her head on the pillow. 'No. I'd like to call her after you, Mam.'

A flush of pleasure crept up Bessie's neck and suffused her face. Bert put his arm around his wife and squeezed her waist. 'Aw, now that's nice. Isn't that lovely, lass?'

Mary Ann was touched to see tears in their eyes.

'Me proper name's Elizabeth,' Bessie said.

Mary Ann sighed and closed her eyes again, but, seeing how much pleasure her sudden decision had given them both, the smile stayed on her mouth. 'That's settled then. Elizabeth it is. We've already asked Duggie to be her godfather. Do you think Miss Edwina would agree to be her godmother?'

'I'm sure she'd love to be,' Bessie said, as she laid the child beside Mary Ann and added softly, her voice breaking with emotion, 'Thank you, Mary Ann, for giving us a beautiful granddaughter. You've made me and Bert very happy, to say nothing of our Dan. He's fair puffing out his chest like a pouter pigeon.'

Bert moved forward too and leant over the bed to kiss Mary Ann's forehead. 'We're very proud of you, lass.'

Mary Ann felt a peculiar lump in her throat. She looked down at her baby daughter. She had been so locked away in her own discomfort that she had turned against her child, blaming its arrival for feeling so dreadful. Now, she really looked at her for the first time, seeing her through the eyes of the besotted father and the doting grandparents.

They were right, she was a pretty little thing, Mary Ann saw now. With dark wisps of hair and dark eyes, round cheeks and a surprisingly smooth skin. Her small mouth worked in sucking movements yet she made no noise and merely gazed up, unblinkingly, at the face of her mother.

'Hello,' Mary Ann said softly, gently tracing the shape of the tiny face with her finger. 'Hello, my little Lizzie.'

Mary Ann could see the relief in Dan's face when he climbed down the ladder into the cabin later to find her out of the bunk bed and sitting on the bench seat feeding her child.

'Feeling better, love?' he asked tenderly and reached out to touch the baby's head.

'Much better. I'll soon be up and about.' There was a pause before she added, 'Did your mam and dad tell you her name?'

Dan shook his head. 'Mam said you'd decided, but she said you'd tell me yourself.'

Mary Ann smiled up at him. 'We'll christen her after your mother, Dan. Elizabeth. All right?'

She didn't need to hear Dan's answer – it was written in the broad smile that wreathed his face. 'But I thought,' she went on, 'that we'd call her Lizzie. What do you think?'

Dan nodded. 'Fine by me.' He paused a moment, watching them, then he said, 'If you're really feeling better, Mary Ann, we should take the ship back to Newark. Mr Sudbury has been very kind – very understanding – but it's time I was earning us all some money again.'

'Of course,' Mary Ann said at once. 'But I can't do much just yet.'

'Oh no, no,' Dan held up his hand in protest. 'I wouldn't expect you to, my love. Besides,' he smiled down fondly at them with love and pride in his voice, 'You've enough to do looking after our daughter. Duggie says he'll do the cooking for a few days.'

Dan was a good husband, Mary Ann thought, and he would make a wonderful, loving father. She did love him, she told herself. She really did. She glanced down at the infant in her arms. Lizzie's blue gaze was fastened upon Mary Ann's face as she sucked contentedly. The baby's tiny fingers fluttered, uncontrolled, and touched her mother's breast. Mary Ann trembled beneath the feather-light touch and in that moment she vowed, I will be a good mother to you and a better wife to Dan.

And so doing, she locked away the memories of Randolph Marsh and determined to think of him no more.

Their life together – the three of them that had now become four – evolved into a pattern. Most of the time,

Mary Ann and the growing child travelled aboard the ship. She worked hard and kept the promise she had made to herself, and only when the child was fast asleep and all her chores done did she allow herself to pick up her embroidery. Now her work had a purpose, for she learnt how to smock and to make intricate delicate lace, too, with which she decorated her daughter's little dresses.

Duggie's presence still lightened Mary Ann's days and he was a second father to Lizzie. His good humour never flagged. Rarely was Duggie Ruddick seen without a smile on his face and a quick-witted quip from his tongue. And his teasing was never cruel, never barbed. He was like the brother Mary Ann had never had and she could have wished for none better.

He seemed to have a succession of girlfriends, but no one serious. Whenever they moored to load or unload, or went home to Waterman's Yard for the weekend, there always seemed to be a girl on the wharf waiting to catch a few moments with Duggie.

'You're a right Jack the lad,' Mary Ann teased him. 'Aren't you ever going to settle down?'

Duggie pretended to frown and drew in breath in a whistle. 'Not me, Mary Ann. I'm not going to stay here all me life, you know. I'll be away to seek me fortune one of these fine days.'

'Leaving? You're going to leave us? Have you got an apprenticeship?'

He pulled a face. 'I reckon that's passed me by, Mary Ann. I'm getting a bit too old now.' Then he laughed. 'Don't worry. I'm not leaving yet. Besides, it's only a pipe dream. I'll probably end me days on this stretch of river. But sometimes . . .' His face took on a dreamy expression. 'Just sometimes, when we're at Hull, I look out down the Humber and out into the North Sea and wonder what's out there beyond the horizon. I wonder what I'm missing. I get a bit restless and long to pack a few belongings on me back and head off into the unknown.' Then he gave a mocking sigh. 'But, like I say, I'll probably never do it. I like me mam's cooking – and yours,' he added hastily, 'to go too far away.'

'You needn't spare my feelings, Duggie. My cooking isn't a patch on your mam's or on yours, if it comes to that. Even I look forward to Sunday dinner in Waterman's Yard.'

'Your cooking is a lot better than it used to be, Mary Ann, and it's amazing how you manage in that little cabin, so don't belittle yourself.'

Mary Ann coloured at his praise. For all his teasing, Duggie was always truthful.

So the routine of their lives continued. Whenever they were moored in Elsborough, they spent time with Bessie and the family, and Mary Ann always tried to see Edwina. Her visits to the school, she told herself, were to keep up her learning, and to prove this to herself as much as to Edwina – and to Bessie – every time they went there she insisted that Edwina should teach her a new embroidery stitch. But when their heads were bent together over the fine stitches, Mary Ann had to bite upon her lips to stop them from asking, 'How is Randolph? Where is he and what is he doing? Is he happy?'

Then came the day when Mary Ann stepped into Edwina's office unannounced to find that Edwina already had visitors.

A smartly dressed woman was sitting on the chaise longue set against one wall of Edwina's study. She was reclining languidly against the cushions and smoking a cigarette in a long, ebony holder. She was not particularly good looking, Mary Ann thought, her eyes drawn to the

273

stranger as she stood in the doorway, but with the skilful use of cosmetics, her hair trimmed in the short haircut of the day, and her fashionable clothes, the woman oozed sophistication. But her mouth had a petulant twist to it and her eyes, squinting at Mary Ann through the haze of her cigarette smoke, were dull with boredom.

There was a young boy, no more than a year old, sitting on Edwina's lap. As he turned to see who had come into the room, Mary Ann was startled by the brightness of his blue eyes. For an instant, Mary Ann trembled. The child's eyes were so like Randolph's that there could be no mistaking the little boy's parentage.

Edwina raised her head and smiled. 'Mary Ann, how nice. Come in, my dear. Come and meet my nephew, Lawrence.'

Thirty-Six

Edwina made the more formal introductions as Mary Ann moved forward into the room.

'This is Celia, my sister-in-law.' Tactfully, Edwina cleverly avoided mentioning Randolph. 'And this is Lawrence. He's only a couple of months younger than your little Lizzie.'

Mary Ann drank in the sight of the child. He had Randolph's fair hair and blue eyes, and as she glanced between them she could see that, although the child had inherited the shape of his mother's mouth, whilst hers wore a sulky expression, his was upturned in a cherubic greeting.

She moved forward, squatted down in front of the little boy and held out her finger for him to grasp. 'How do you do, Master Lawrence? What a handsome little man he is.'

'He's like his father.' The woman spoke behind her, her tone bitter. 'He'll no doubt break a few hearts when he's older.'

Mary Ann drew in a breath sharply. Did Celia know who she was? Did she know all about Mary Ann's affair with Randolph? And if so, who had told her? She was sure he would not have done so, so that left only one person. She glanced resentfully at Edwina, but Edwina gave a little shake of her head. Aloud she said, 'He has some of your features, Celia, surely, and he's so placid. Such a good baby.'

'He doesn't take after either of us for that, Edwina. I'm sure Randolph was a demon as a child and my mother never tires of telling me that I dispatched twelve nannies single-handedly.' Celia stubbed out her cigarette in a glass ashtray and stood up. Smoothing down her skirt, she said, 'I'd better be going. Are you sure you don't mind looking after him, Edwina? His wretched nanny has a dreadful cold and has taken to her bed.'

'Much the best thing. You don't want the little man to catch it.'

'I suppose not.' The woman sounded as if she didn't care one way or the other, only that her own life should not be disrupted. 'It's really most inconvenient. I have a luncheon appointment with Mrs Phillips.'

Mrs Phillips was the wife of one of the town's most influential men. He owned the huge engineering works that was one of Elsborough's major employers. So, thought Mary Ann, Celia had wasted no time in ingratiating herself with the town's elite.

Edwina, with no such pretensions, smiled. 'It'll be a real pleasure. If it didn't sound so horrid, I could wish that the nanny might catch a cold more frequently if it means I get the chance to look after him.'

Celia shrugged her slim shoulders. 'If that's the case, you can have him on her afternoon off and welcome.'

'But that's the only time you get to spend with him,' Edwina protested.

'I'm not very good with young children, Edwina. I don't pretend to be. I'll get on better with my son when he can hold an intelligent conversation.'

She slipped on her coat and picked up her handbag and gloves. She stood a moment looking down at the sweet picture Edwina and the child made. 'You're very maternal, aren't you, Edwina? You really should get married and have children of your own before it's too late.' Then, losing interest, she said, 'I must go. Deakin can pick Lawrence up at four o'clock in the Bentley.'

'Very well,' Edwina murmured, her attention captivated by the child in her lap. 'I'll take good care of him.'

Since her brother's marriage, Edwina had moved out of the family home and now lived in an apartment at the top of the school building. Mr and Mrs Marsh senior, of course, still lived at The Hall.

'My dear Edwina, of that I can be sure,' Celia said, as she reached the door. 'Goodbye and thank you again. You're such a treasure. Goodbye – er . . .' She hesitated, trying to recall the name she had just been given. 'Goodbye – Mary Ann, is it?'

Mary Ann nodded as she said quietly, 'Goodbye, Mrs Marsh.'

As the door closed behind Celia, Mary Ann said, 'She didn't even say goodbye to him.'

Edwina sighed. 'No. Like she said, she isn't very good with young children. She never takes a lot of notice of him. It quite upsets me to see how offhand she is with the little chap. I'm just praying that she will change once he gets a little older and, to her mind, more interesting.'

Mary Ann allowed the boy to clasp and unclasp her finger and only resisted when he tried to draw it towards his mouth. 'No, no, you're not going to chew my finger,' she laughed.

'He's still teething. See how he dribbles,' Edwina said adoringly.

Mary Ann's face sobered. 'Does she . . . does Mrs Marsh know who I am?'

Edwina shook her head again. 'If you mean does she know about your . . .' She paused briefly struggling to find an appropriate word. 'Association with Randolph. No, she doesn't.' Then she added wryly, 'At least, not unless Randolph has told her himself and I doubt that very much.'

Mary Ann said nothing, her gaze on his child as the boy played with her fingers and smiled playfully up into her eyes.

'He is a lovely little boy,' she murmured, but now Edwina was trying to draw the conversation away.

'Tell me, how is Lizzie, and, of course, Dan and Duggie? And do you see anything of poor Susan?'

Susan Oliver had become known, all along the riverbank, as 'poor Susan'. Though Dan and Mary Ann had probably been the first to know, it was now common knowledge that her husband Ted was wildly and irrationally jealous of her. She was a virtual prisoner in the cottage near the ferry, which Ted operated between the two villages on either side of the Trent, appropriately named Eastlands and Westlands. The ferryman's cottage was at Eastlands and so it was always known as Eastlands' Ferry.

Susan had no friends and saw little of her own family. It was a disastrous marriage, but Susan was trapped. Her father would not countenance the scandal of a divorce.

'He's a hard man, that Jack Price. Thank God I don't work for him any more,' Dan said often. 'He seems to blame Susan. Says she must be giving her husband cause for jealousy. What chance has she got, locked away in the middle of nowhere?'

Mary Ann would glance at him and wonder. Whenever they passed by the tiny white cottage on the riverbank, Dan would be on deck, and she knew he stood looking across the expanse of water hoping to catch sight of Susan.

But Susan was never to be seen. Very occasionally,

as they had come upriver, they would see her in the distance, pegging out the washing on the line, but by the time the *Maid Mary Ann* drew level, Susan had scuttled indoors.

Did Ted see Dan watching out for his wife, Mary Ann thought, and did he, too, wonder?

In answer to Edwina's question, Mary Ann shook her head. 'Not much. I haven't seen her to speak to since the night Lizzie was born.'

'She's got a little boy now, hasn't she?'

Mary Ann nodded. 'Yes. Tolly. He was born about ten months after Lizzie. When was Lawrence born?'

'Two months after Lizzie.'

'And I never knew,' Mary Ann murmured.

For a moment, Edwina looked embarrassed. 'I'm sorry. I should have told you. But – it was, well, awkward.'

'Is that why no one told me? Not even Bessie.' Mary Ann looked straight into Edwina's eyes. 'She knew, I suppose?'

Edwina nodded and said again, 'I'm sorry, Mary Ann, we should have told you.'

As she walked home, back to the wharf where she knew Dan would be waiting, anxious to catch the tide, Mary Ann pondered on the strange quirk of Fate that had brought three children into the world within the space of a year. Three children, who were linked in a strange way by their parents' pasts. What did life hold for each of them? Mary Ann wondered. Would their paths cross? Would they even know one another? Perhaps Lizzie and Tolly would, she mused. As long as his father didn't guard him as jealously as he did his wife. But would Lizzie ever know Lawrence?

A smile played mischievously upon Mary Ann's mouth. If Edwina was to look after her nephew on the nanny's day off, she thought, then she must try to bring Lizzie to visit her godmother on one of those days.

Thirty-Seven

Lizzie was almost nine when Mary Ann met Randolph Marsh again.

The intervening years had been kind to Mary Ann and her little family, although there had been no more children. She had found a kind of contentment with Dan and, after the shaky beginning, had grown to love her daughter although her displays of affection towards the child were spasmodic. One moment she would lavish kisses and cuddles upon Lizzie, the next she would be offhand with her and lost in a world of her own memories. To a less confident infant, such erratic behaviour would have been disastrous, but Lizzie, sure in the love of a large, extended family, appeared to take her mother's mood swings in her stride.

Lizzie was a delight to all who knew her. In looks, she resembled her mother: dark hair, deep brown eyes and dimples in her cheeks, which seemed ever present for the child smiled constantly. She was bright and intelligent and quick to learn. In her character, she took after the Ruddick family. She was forthright, even from an early age, in her opinions like her grandmother, Bessie. Yet any bossiness was quickly dispelled by her lively, teasing manner which echoed her Uncle Duggie's nature.

Her father, her grandfather and her two uncles, especially Duggie, doted on her and spoiled her. In their eyes she could do no wrong and any necessary correction had to come from Mary Ann or Bessie.

Lizzie learnt to walk on the deck of the *Maid Mary Ann* and to swim under Duggie's tuition, not in the river for the currents were too strong and treacherous, but in the town's swimming baths when they moored for a few hours at one of the wharves.

'She's not to swim in the river. You must teach her that, Mary Ann,' Dan commanded. 'Folks throw all sorts of rubbish and muck into the river.' Before she reached school age, he had built her a miniature cog boat of her own. He taught her to scull in the shallow waters of the River Trent, paying out the rope from the ship with the little craft attached to it. Then, with a mixture of concern and pride, he and Duggie hung over the side as the tiny hands manoeuvred the oar with a deftness that was in her blood.

When she reached school age, Mary Ann was adamant that Lizzie should attend Edwina's school.

'She's going to be a lady when she grows up,' Mary Ann declared, and even Bessie, who normally despised anyone trying to 'rise above their station', backed the decision. If she had been fully aware, however, of all that lay behind Mary Ann's scheme, Bessie might not have been so ready to agree. But wanting the very best for her granddaughter, Bessie even persuaded each member of the Ruddick family to contribute to the fees.

Dan missed his little girl dreadfully from the moment she stepped off the ship in her smart new uniform. Mary Ann, holding Lizzie's hand, had known that Dan was watching them as they walked the length of River Road that first school morning.

'Turn and wave to your daddy,' she had said to Lizzie before his tall, still figure was lost from their sight.

Lizzie had turned and blown him a kiss from her tiny

hand. Then she had skipped ahead of her mother, anxious to begin her new life.

Edwina, Lizzie's godmother, had loved her from the first time she had seen her, and now having the child in her charge, she found it difficult not to favour her over her other pupils.

'She's so bright and quick,' Edwina extolled Lizzie's virtues to anyone who would listen. Then she would smile fondly and say, 'But she's a little mischief at times and is often in trouble with her teacher. It's difficult to be angry with her for long, though. She makes you laugh just when you're trying to be stern with her.'

Mary Ann's secretly cherished hope that Lizzie would meet Lawrence Marsh did not happen. Often, when they were small, Mary Ann would take her daughter to see Edwina hoping they might meet the boy by chance. But Fate never decreed their meeting. And by the time Lizzie attended the school, Lawrence already had a tutor at home and then, at the age of seven, he was sent away to boarding school. In the school holidays when perhaps he visited Edwina, there was no plausible reason for Lizzie to be there.

Lizzie did, however, know Tolly Oliver.

Almost from the time she could walk, she would stand at the ship's rail and wave to the boy who lived in the ferryman's cottage.

'That's Tolly,' Mary Ann had heard Dan tell her. She had watched Lizzie staring at the boy and then dimpling as she laughed and waved to him.

It became a ritual that every time they passed by on the river, Lizzie would run to the side and wave.

'Wave to Tolly, Mamma,' Lizzie would shout. 'We must all wave to Tolly. Daddy, wave to Tolly.'

'Poor Tolly,' Dan would murmur, but it wasn't until Lizzie grew a little older that she asked her mother, 'Why does Daddy always call him "poor Tolly"? Is it because he always looks so lonely? Or is it because they haven't much money?'

Mary Ann looked down at the young child and marvelled at her perception.

'A bit of both, I think,' had been her answer. Mary Ann could not explain to the child that because Tolly's mother was 'poor Susan', it seemed natural to call her son a similar name.

'He looks so thin, doesn't he?' Lizzie mused, with an unusual understanding from one so young.

Hearing their conversation Dan had come to stand alongside them. In his hand he held a potato from the cargo they were carrying.

Thoughtfully, he tossed it up and down in his hand like a huge cricket ball.

'Wants feeding up a bit, poor lad. Shall we throw him this?' Dan smiled down at his daughter and then, above her head, he caught Mary Ann's glance.

Quietly, Mary Ann said, 'They say, in the wash-houses, that Ted hasn't much time for his lad.'

Dan pulled a face. 'Doesn't surprise me. The man's so eaten up with jealousy, I don't think he's got a loving bone in his body. He can't stand anyone to come between himself and Susan – not even his own son.' And he said yet again, 'Poor Tolly.'

Mary Ann glanced at him and was sure that secretly her husband was also thinking, 'Poor Susan.'

'Throw it, Daddy. Throw that big potato to Tolly. His mam can cook it for his dinner.'

Dan raised his arm, drew it back and hurled the

unusual missile across the rippling water to the bank. The garden of the ferryman's cottage came down to the river with no fencing or hedge between it and the slope of the bank. They watched Tolly stare in surprise as the potato landed close by him and rolled almost to his feet.

Lizzie jumped up and down and clapped her hands. 'It's for your dinner, Tolly,' she shouted, her piping voice bouncing on the breeze to him. 'It's for your dinner.'

Slowly the boy bent and picked it up. He stood a moment with it in the palm of his hand and then, even from a distance, they could all see the broad grin on his face. He waved and then turned and dashed into the house. They heard him calling, 'Mam, Mam, look . . .' But the rest of his words were lost.

Even Mary Ann was touched by the boy's pleasure. She smiled at Dan. 'That was a nice thing to do, Dan Ruddick.' She reached up and touched his cheek. Dan caught hold of her hand and kissed her fingers tenderly.

'Look, there's Tolly's mam,' Lizzie said, and Mary Ann and Dan turned back to see Susan standing in the doorway of her home. She was holding the potato and as her hand fluttered briefly in a nervous gesture of thanks, Mary Ann felt Dan let go of her hand.

It became another ritual that, as long as Ted Oliver was not around to see, every time the *Maid Mary Ann* passed Ferry Cottage, they would throw something to Tolly if the cargo they were carrying was suitable. In winter, if they were carrying house coal to the Co-op's yard in Elsborough, both Dan and Duggie would pelt enough coal to keep the cottage fire burning for a week. They watched with amusement and delight as Tolly scurried about the grass picking up the coal and putting it into a bucket.

'The lad can hardly carry it,' Duggie would laugh, but Dan would only smile and say, 'It'll keep him warm for a day or two.'

Potatoes and other vegetables were regularly hurled across the water and sometimes they even carried canned fruit, imported into Hull and distributed via the rivers and canals. Lizzie would laugh aloud as she watched Tolly picking up the cans and staring at the labels in amazement.

'Are you sure you're not making more trouble for Susan?' Mary Ann asked. 'How is she going to explain the appearance of canned fruit on her pantry shelves to a man like Ted Oliver?'

Dan shrugged. 'She'll think of something,' he said confidently.

'Well, I'm not so sure. I don't think a tin of pineapple or peaches is worth a black eye or a broken jaw.'

She turned away to go below, but she knew Dan was looking after her thoughtfully, trying to gauge whether his wife's comment was justified or whether it was really because she didn't like him giving presents to Susan.

'He can work that out for himself,' Mary Ann muttered to herself as she sat down in the cabin and picked up her embroidery. She sighed and gave a wry smile. She wasn't even sure of her motives herself, so how was Dan to guess?

As soon as she could scull safely, Dan allowed Lizzie to take her little cog boat along the shallows of the river as long as the current wasn't running too strongly, keeping pace with the ship but always in sight of her father. It was on such day that Mary Ann, watching her from the slowly moving ship, saw Tolly standing on the bank near his home. She watched Lizzie manoeuvre her little boat towards the muddy riverbank. Above the breeze and the flapping of the square sail above her, Mary Ann heard her daughter's clear voice. 'Hello. You're Tolly, aren't you? I'm Lizzie.'

Mary Ann could not hear the boy's reply, but she saw him nod and she could only guess at the conversation that followed as the *Maid Mary Ann* moved on upriver. 'It's a funny name, Tolly, isn't it?' Mary Ann knew her daughter well enough to be sure of that first question.

His cheeks would redden as he admitted, 'It's short for Bartholomew.' He grimaced. 'I'm called after me dad's father.'

Lizzie's laughter rang out and Mary Ann watched her daughter gesticulating with her small, capable hands towards the ship and then to her own little boat. Mary Ann smiled. Now Lizzie was proudly telling Tolly how her father had made the craft himself, especially for her. The boy moved closer, right to the water's edge, so that he could see the boat properly.

Mary Ann cupped her hands around her mouth and called, 'Lizzie. Lizzie.'

When the girl looked up, Mary Ann beckoned. But the child only waved and turned her head away to talk to Tolly again.

'The little minx,' Mary Ann murmured. 'She's deliberately ignoring me.'

The ship moved on and there was nothing Mary Ann could do as she watched the boy hold out his hand to help her daughter step ashore. Then giving a little laugh herself, Mary Ann shrugged. Oh well, she thought, if that's what she wants to do, she'd better get on with it.

Mary Ann turned away and went below and it wasn't until half an hour later that she heard Dan calling frantically. 'Mary Ann, Mary Ann. Where's Lizzie? I can't see Lizzie.'

Mary Ann climbed the ladder. 'She's with Tolly. I called to her and beckoned her but the little madam took no notice.'

'And you left her there?'

'She'll be all right. She'll—'

'Why didn't you take the cog boat and go after her? You know she's to stay in sight of the ship. I don't want her sculling on the river without one of us watching her.'

'The last I saw of her she was climbing out of the boat and on to the bank,' Mary Ann told him. 'They'll be playing together. She'll be all right.'

'How's she going to catch up with us or hadn't you thought of that?'

Mary Ann blinked. She hadn't.

'I thought not,' Dan muttered and his face was dark with anger. 'You'd better take the cog boat and go back for her.'

'I haven't time . . .' she began, but Dan said harshly, 'Now, Mary Ann.'

Irritated by both her daughter's misbehaviour and what she saw as Dan's fussing, Mary Ann sculled back downriver towards the ferryman's cottage. Lizzie's cog boat was tied to a post set in the riverbank at the bottom of the garden, but there was no sign of the children.

Mary Ann drew level with the cottage. 'Lizzie. Lizzie!' she called, balancing herself in the small boat, her hand on the oar. Susan appeared in the doorway. 'Why, Mary Ann. Is something wrong?'

Exasperated, Mary Ann answered sharply. 'Lizzie

stopped to talk to your boy and now they've disappeared. I'll tan her backside for her when I catch up with her.'

Susan stepped out into the sunshine and, shielding her eyes, glanced up and down the river. A little way downstream, the ferry, with Ted Oliver at the winding gear, was leaving the opposite bank, bringing its passengers from Nottinghamshire into Lincolnshire. Swiftly, Susan stepped back into the doorway of her home so that she could not be seen from the ferry.

'He . . . he might have taken her salmon fishing, Mary Ann.' She pointed in the direction of the approaching ferry. 'Further downstream, beyond the ferry crossing. At the bend in the river. D'you know where I mean?'

Mary Ann nodded. 'Thanks, Susan.' She looked again at the woman. It was years since she had seen Susan this close and she could see, even from this distance, that the woman, who was still only young, had changed noticeably. She was thinner. Her hair, drab and untidy, was pulled back into an unbecoming bun at the back of her head. Beneath the apron she wore, the hem of her dress was uneven, as if part of it had become unstitched and she had neither the time nor the energy to mend it.

Mary Ann's clever fingers itched to repair the garment and then she laughed at herself for wanting to help the girl who had always been a rival for Dan's affection. Well, she didn't look much of a rival now, poor thing, Mary Ann thought, with a rare moment of genuine sympathy for Susan.

'I'd better go and look for them,' she called and then, pausing only to allow the ferry to pass by and the ripples it made to subside, she began to scull further downstream.

She found the children side by side, lying flat on a ledge over a shallow part of the river, their gaze intent on the water. Mary Ann sculled closer and saw them look up in disgust as her paddle disturbed the stillness.

Lizzie leapt to her feet. 'You've frightened them away, Mam. Tolly was going to show me how to catch one with his net.'

'I'll frighten you, me girl, when I get me hands on you.'

Tolly glanced fearfully from one to the other. 'I . . . I'm s-sorry,' he stammered, but Lizzie only grinned saucily at her.

'You'll have to catch me first.'

'Why, you cheeky little . . .' It was at that moment that Mary Ann became aware of a rider on horseback in the meadow behind the children, coming slowly towards the riverbank. A tall, handsome man, dressed in a black riding habit.

Mary Ann felt the breath squeezed from her body as she gazed for the first time in almost ten years on Randolph Marsh.

Thirty-Eight

'I only wanted to catch you a fish, Daddy.' Mary Ann listened with only half an ear to her wayward daughter's excuses. 'I won't do it again. At least, not without asking you first.' The child was incredible, Mary Ann thought, though her mind was still reeling. She argues like an adult, justifying her naughtiness. 'Please don't take my boat away, Daddy.'

Every nerve in her body still jangling, Mary Ann wandered away down the deck towards the bows leaving Dan to admonish the child for once.

So often Mary Ann had thought about what she would do, what she might feel, when she saw Randolph again. Would she hate him, want to fly at him and pummel him or scratch his eyes out as she had the last time they had been together? Now she was in turmoil because it had happened and she had felt none of those things. She had been totally unprepared for the thrill that ran through her. It was still there, the power that he exuded over her. The mere sight of him had made her whole being quiver.

She leant on the rail and gazed back down the river, hungry for another glimpse of him, but though she scanned the fields on either side she could see no galloping horse.

Had he recognized her? Had he known her?

He had made no move of acknowledgement. He had

merely reined in his horse and sat there, high up in the saddle, watching them.

Maybe the children had been poaching. Mary Ann didn't know if anyone owned the rights to fishing in the river. Perhaps Randolph did, for since his father's death quite recently, he had inherited the Marsh estates and all that went with them. The fields of golden corn, the meadows, streams and woodlands that stretched along the Trent valley, even the villages and many of the homes of the people who lived there were owned by the Marsh Estate. So, maybe he even owned part of the river, certainly the right to fish there.

Dan had once hinted as much when they'd all heard of Bertram Marsh's death one Sunday lunchtime in Waterman's Yard. 'That family's got too much power, if you ask me. They nearly own the folk around here. 'Tisn't right. Not in this day and age. It's nineteen thirty-three, for heaven's sake, and we're still living in a system that's almost feudal.'

'Fancy yasen as Lord of the Manor, do you, our Dan?' Bessie had asked.

'I'd make a darn sight better job of it than *he's* going to,' he'd responded, waving his fork at his mother.

'It's a shame young Mr Arthur was killed,' Bert had put in quietly. 'He'd have made a much better squire than his brother.'

'Be better still if women had the same chance as the menfolk. Miss Edwina would be perfect.'

Duggie, as ever, had teased, 'I don't know. We gave 'em the vote and now they want to rule the world.'

The family had laughed and the conversation had turned away from the Marsh family. Mary Ann had said nothing, but she had listened and now, as she stood on the deck of the *Maid Mary Ann* shading her eyes against

the glare of the sun sparkling on the water, she thought,
And now he's master of it all.

She saw him again one day when she was alone at the
wash-house a mile along the river south of Eastlands'
Ferry. She heard the pounding of a horse's hooves and her
heart missed a beat as she dropped Dan's shirt back into
the tub of rinsing water and hurried outside. He was
galloping across the field and, as she watched, he took a
hedge in a flying leap, horse and rider suspended in mid-
air for a heart-stopping moment until he landed with a
thud on the opposite side. Mary Ann stood watching him
until he was a speck in the distance.

The day he spoke to her, once more at the wash-house,
Lizzie was with her.

'Good day, Mrs Ruddick.' Sitting high above her on
his restless stallion, he looked down upon her, smiling
that slow, sardonic smile that still had the power to twist
her heart and make her pulse race.

'Mr Marsh,' she murmured and tried to turn away,
pushing Lizzie before her towards their two cog boats
moored against the small landing stage.

He leant forward, resting his arm on the front of his
saddle. 'So formal, Mary Ann,' he said softly and she
glanced over her shoulder, looking up once more into
those blue eyes, and she knew herself lost.

She tried, oh how she tried, to turn away, to step into
the boat and scull back down the river to Dan and to
safety. And maybe, just maybe, she would have managed
it if Lizzie had not refused to respond to her mother's
little push urging her towards the river. Instead, she stared
up at the stranger and then smiled prettily.

'Hello,' Lizzie said. 'Who are you?'

'Lizzie . . .' Mary Ann began, but Randolph's laugh rang out. 'Don't scold her, Mary Ann. I like a child with spirit. My own son could well take a lesson from her. In fact, I must bring him to meet her. Maybe . . .' his voice was suddenly deep and low, 'maybe they will become good friends.'

Mary Ann's head shot up as she said tartly, 'Surely you wouldn't allow your son to consort with the likes of us?' Then she added pointedly, 'Mr Marsh.'

'I wasn't suggesting they should be married, Mary Ann.' Again, his voice was soft as he added, 'Though times are changing. I doubt my son will be obliged to marry where his father chooses.'

His blue eyes were holding her gaze now and in that brief moment, there passed between them explanation, sorrow; even, Mary Ann believed, a plea for forgiveness, though not a word was spoken.

'I must go,' she said hoarsely.

'I'll see you again though?'

Now there was no mistaking the entreaty in his tone. But all Mary Ann would allow herself to say, was, 'Good day, Mr Marsh.'

As they sculled, side by side, downriver, Mary Ann was aware of him keeping the pace with them as he rode along the riverbank, matching their speed. But before they came to a bend in the river and within sight of Dan's ship, Randolph turned and galloped away towards the woodland on the other side of the meadow bordering the river.

'Who was he, Mam?' Lizzie called.

Mary Ann tried to quieten the thudding of her heart, so strong that it seemed to echo the sound of his horse's hooves. She thought quickly and said, 'Miss Edwina's brother,' and as they neared the ship, she said, 'Don't tell your father or Uncle Duggie that we met him, Lizzie.'

The child's eyes were innocent. 'Why not?'

Mary Ann swallowed and then, knowing that the child would do nothing to hurt her beloved father, she answered deviously, 'Your daddy doesn't like him and it would only upset him to think we had even been talking to him.'

Lizzie's cheeks dimpled. 'All right, then. I promise.'

Their meetings became frequent and, soon, were planned.

Whilst Lizzie was at school, there was no danger of discovery, for Mary Ann waited until the ship reached the part of the river where the wash-house was situated.

'I'll catch you up,' she would say gaily to Dan as she clambered down into the cog boat, loaded with their weekly wash.

'I don't know why you don't come ahead and then let me pick you up when I get here like most watermen's wives do?' Dan remarked more than once, but the comment was said idly with no thought in his trusting mind that Mary Ann might have her own devious reasons.

Mary Ann never answered him, just waved goodbye and sculled towards the bank, her heart thumping in anticipation, knowing that in the shadows of the trees at the edge of Raven's Wood, only a field's width away, Randolph was waiting.

Thirty-Nine

'I never wanted to hurt you, you must know that, Mary Ann.'

They were sitting together with their backs against a tree trunk, hidden deep in Raven's Wood, the scent of bluebells all around them, the sound of rustling leaves and busy, twittering birds above them.

'I wish you hadn't left The Hall,' he said. 'Why did you run away?'

'How could I stay?' she asked simply.

'I would have cared for you. Looked after you. I said I would.'

'And what would your bride have said,' she asked bitterly, 'if you had installed your mistress just down the corridor?'

Randolph sighed and swished his whip at a passing bumblebee. 'You're right, of course. You couldn't have stayed there, but if only you'd given me a little time. Time to work something out.'

'Such as?'

'I would have found you a little cottage somewhere.'

The idea appalled and yet thrilled her at the same time. 'I'd have been a kept woman, you mean? Your mistress?'

'At least we could have been together.'

'You *could* have married me,' she retaliated.

He was shaking his head sadly, 'No, I couldn't Mary Ann. Not then. If I was free now, maybe. But then . . . No.'

'Because of your father?'

'Partly.'

'What then?'

Again, he sighed. 'My family name and the Marsh Estate mean everything to me. There was a clause in Great-Great-Grandfather Marsh's will that should any heir marry against the wishes of the family, then he would be cut off with a shilling.'

'They really put that? In the will?'

Randolph nodded. 'Oh, yes. And they meant it.'

'And it still counts today?

'Yes.'

'And Lawrence? He'll have to marry someone of whom you approve or he will be "cut off with a shilling"?'

'Yes.'

Remembering the word that Dan had used, Mary Ann said, 'It sounds positively feudal to me.'

'It is,' Randolph agreed blandly. 'But then in our world, it works. Of course I might . . .' he smiled down at her, but his tone had a tinge of sarcasm, ' . . . try to be a little more understanding where my son's concerned.'

Mary Ann looked deep into the blue eyes that were so close to hers. She had seen those eyes afire with passion and she had seen them cold with rejection. Now they were calculating.

Perceptively, she said, 'And you might not.'

'It would depend, of course,' Randolph said glancing away. 'He is my only son and heir. My only child. And now, it is highly unlikely there will be any more.'

Her eyes widened and her gaze met his again as he added in a whisper, 'If you know what I mean.'

She did. Oh, she did, and her heart began to sing.

She tore her gaze away from his, fearful of what he

would be able to read in her eyes. 'Why did you never tell me yourself that you were engaged to Celia?'

'Who was it who told you?' Even after all these years his voice was harsh with anger against whoever had enlightened her.

Mary Ann, glad that she had kept Edwina's name out of the conversation thus far, said quite truthfully, 'It was common knowledge amongst the servants.'

Randolph sighed. 'Ah yes. Servants gossip. I sometimes think they know more about our lives than we do ourselves.'

Mary Ann giggled. 'I hope they don't know about us now.'

They sat together, their fingers entwined, until she said slowly, 'So, you're telling me that your marriage to Celia was a marriage of convenience? The union of two land-owning families.'

'It's the done thing, my dear, in my world.'

'Do you love her? Your wife?' She thought about Celia, the bored, discontented woman, whom she had met just that once in Edwina's apartment at the school. She certainly had not looked happy then, Mary Ann remembered. So were things any better now? 'Are you happy together?'

Randolph gave a wry laugh. 'Hardly. Haven't I just told you as much?' Again she dared to glance at him and, suddenly, the old passion, the remembered fire was still there in his eyes. 'We did our duty and produced a son and heir.' He grimaced. 'I suppose we should have provided a "spare" as well, but after Lawrence's birth, Celia flatly refused to go through the whole disgusting process, as she called it, again.'

Mary Ann rested her head against his shoulder. 'You'll have to take good care of him, then.'

'Mm,' Randolph murmured. 'Let's just hope there's not

another war.' His tone was bitter as he added, 'They have a nasty habit of devastating future generations.'

He put his arm around her and pulled her close. 'And what about you, my sweet Mary Ann, are you happy with Dan Ruddick?'

Carefully, Mary Ann said, 'He's a good man. He's kind and loving, but . . .'

He touched her chin with a gentle finger. 'But?' he prompted.

'But he's not you,' she said simply and raised her face for his kiss.

The school holidays presented problems for their trysts.

'You stay with your daddy,' Mary Ann said one wash day when she knew Randolph would be waiting, but Lizzie would not be coerced. 'I want to come, Mam. I like turning the mangle.'

'Let her go with you,' Dan said, unwittingly making matters worse. 'She doesn't want to be stuck on board ship all the holidays.'

'Besides,' Duggie called across the deck from where he was hauling on a sheet to bring in the sail, 'you might see young Tolly.' And he winked at his niece.

It was not Tolly whom Lizzie met that day, but Lawrence Marsh.

'There's a motor car coming,' Lizzie said, as she helped Mary Ann to fold the wet sheets. Dropping the end she was holding on to the dirty floor, she dashed to the door.

'Oh Lizzie, now look what you've done.' Exasperated already by the mere presence of the girl, Mary Ann snapped, but Lizzie was not listening.

'It's that man. The one we saw on horseback. He's got a boy with him.' The sound of the motor came nearer until it drew up outside the whitewashed building. The noise of the engine petered out as it was switched off and Mary Ann heard Randolph's voice.

'Good day to you, Miss Ruddick.'

Mary Ann held her breath. She hardly dared to move to the doorway. She was sure that if anyone saw them together, they would guess the truth. Then she let out her breath in a long sigh. She was being foolish. What could a couple of children know about the craving she had for this man? The mere sight of him made her knees tremble and her stomach churn. And when he touched her, the world seemed to explode in a firework of dazzling lights.

She swallowed the excitement that rose in her throat and moved to the door.

'Mr Marsh,' she managed to say, outwardly calm. 'Good morning.'

Her glance went to the boy, who was climbing out of the passenger seat.

'Mrs Ruddick, may I present my son, Lawrence. And this, I presume, is your daughter.' He was holding out his hand to Lizzie as he added, 'And what is your name, my dear?'

He was playing the part just as she was, Mary Ann thought. He knew very well what Lizzie's name was, just as she knew who Lawrence was. Mary Ann hid her secret smile as she watched Lizzie dip her knee and hold out her hand. The girl dimpled at the tall man and her eyes twinkled, but she swiftly lost interest in the adult and turned her attention to the boy.

'Hello. How old are you?'

Lawrence blinked at her directness, but after a moment's hesitation, he answered, 'Nine – at least nearly.'

Lizzie's smile widened. 'Me, too.'

The two adults watched in amusement as the youngsters eyed each other. 'You're tall for your age, aren't you?' Lizzie appraised. 'You're taller than me.'

The boy was thin, but his child's face promised to be handsome in adulthood with a straight nose and firm jaw.

'So what do you say to a ride in my motor car, little lady?' Randolph said. Turning towards Mary Ann so that the children should not see, he winked at her and added, deliberately offhand, 'And, of course, your mother may come too if she wishes.'

Five minutes later the car was speeding along country lanes, frightening squawking chickens and filling the quiet air with noise and smoke. The children bounced on the back seat, laughing, whilst Mary Ann clung on, terrified when Randolph hurled the car around corners throwing his passengers from side to side.

He brought the car to a halt at the edge of the wood and turned to the children.

'Run and play in the woods.' It was a command rather than an invitation.

Mary Ann felt Lizzie's eyes question her. 'Mam?'

'It's all right,' she reassured her. 'But only half an hour, mind.' Then she added primly like any good and dutiful wife should, 'We must get back then or your father will wonder where we've got to.'

The children clambered out of the car and ran shrieking and yelling into the wood and disappeared amongst the trees.

Still sitting in the car, Randolph reached for her. 'Oh Mary Ann, Mary Ann.'

An hour later, Mary Ann went to the edge of the woods and called, 'Lizzie, Lizzie. Where are you?'

She heard their laughter and then their footsteps

crunching through the undergrowth towards her. 'Come
along. We're late,' she said briskly, pretending to be cross.
'We'll never catch the ship up at this rate.'

'Sorry, Mam. But Lawrence and me were building a
den.'

As they walked to the car, Mary Ann held Lizzie back
a pace or two behind Lawrence. 'Lizzie, we won't tell
your father about this. About riding in a motor car. He
might be worried. And you don't want to worry your
daddy, do you?'

She felt Lizzie glance at her. 'No, Mam,' the girl said
quietly.

'It would be best not to mention that we met Mr
Marsh and his son. That way, you can't let it slip, can
you?'

'No, Mam,' Lizzie agreed, but there was reluctance in
her tone. She hated deceit of any kind and not being
truthful with her father especially would cause her pain,
Mary Ann knew. But she could not take the risk of the
child letting out her secret.

As they climbed into the car, Lawrence was asking
eagerly, 'Can we take Mrs Ruddick and Lizzie out again,
Father?'

Coyly, Mary Ann glanced at Randolph. 'Well, I don't
know about that. I expect Mr Marsh has better things to
do than take us for rides in the country.'

She heard his low chuckle and then as he swung the
starting handle and climbed back in beside her, beneath
the noise of the engine he said, 'I can't think of anything
I'd rather be doing.'

He took them back to the wash-house and even helped
to load the heavy basket of washing into Mary Ann's cog
boat. Already, Lizzie was sculling ahead down the river
and Lawrence had remained in the car.

'When will I see you again?' he whispered.

'Next week,' she replied.

'A whole week,' he moaned. 'Oh, I can't bear it.'

'No. Neither can I.' For a moment as he handed the basket down to her, their eyes met each other's and held. There was such passion in his eyes that it seemed to burn into her. 'I know,' she breathed. 'I know. But there's nothing I can do.'

'There must be,' he whispered intensely. 'There has to be.'

'I must go,' she said, desperate to stay but knowing she had no choice.

'Mary Ann,' he said urgently, but already the boat was inching away from the bank.

'Thank you, Mr Marsh,' she called out for the benefit of Lawrence's young ears. 'Thank you for your kindness.'

As she sculled away, she knew he stood watching her, but she dared not look back.

If she had, she might well never have returned to the ship.

Forty

'Wherever have you been?' was Dan's greeting as they climbed aboard the *Maid Mary Ann*, weighed down with wet washing to be dried. 'I was worried. I thought something must have happened. I nearly had to anchor.'

'Oh, what a catastrophe that would have been,' Mary Ann snapped. 'Well, you can thank your daughter. She ran off playing and I couldn't find her.' She avoided looking at Lizzie, knowing that the girl would be gazing open-mouthed at her mother's lies. 'I shan't take her again.'

'But, Mam, I . . .' Lizzie began, but Mary Ann rounded on her. 'Not another word, miss, if you know what's good for you.'

She picked up the basket and walked along the deck away from them, praying very hard that her daughter would not give her away.

'Never mind, love,' Mary Ann heard Dan say behind her. 'You stay with me and Uncle Duggie.' He laughed, indulgent as ever. 'You can't run away far on board, can you?'

Their meetings went on through the summer and, despite her threat, Mary Ann was obliged to take Lizzie with her. Sometimes, Randolph brought Lawrence, at other times he came alone, but on those occasions there was no opportunity for a jaunt to the woods; there was no one to keep Lizzie occupied. On such days, Mary Ann could see her own frustration mirrored in Randolph's eyes but there was nothing they could do. One day, when Lizzie had been in mischief, Mary Ann used her naughtiness as an excuse to leave her with Dan, hoping to snatch a brief time alone with Randolph. But, not knowing, he brought Lawrence along.

They both heaved a sigh of relief when the school holidays were over and they watched in amusement as the two young people said goodbye to each other.

'I've got to go away tomorrow,' Lawrence told Lizzie haltingly. 'Back to boarding school.'

Lizzie pulled a face. 'Poor you. I go to your auntie's school. I stay with me grandma in the week when Mam and Daddy are away. It's nice there. Do you like school?'

Mary Ann saw the boy glance towards his father. With obvious diplomacy, Lawrence said, 'It's all right.' Then he turned back to Lizzie and in a low voice, added, 'But I'll miss you. We've had a great time this hols, haven't we?'

As the children continued to talk, promising to write to each other, Randolph murmured, 'Do you think this is the start of a romance? Is it going to be the romance of the century?'

'Oh no,' Mary Ann whispered, touching his hand discreetly. 'No, ours is the romance of the century.'

Randolph grasped her hand impulsively and said, 'Next week when we're alone, try to stay as long as you can. I want to take you for a drive.'

'I'll be here,' she promised. 'Same time, same place.'

But the following week, when she knew Randolph would be waiting for her in the shadow of the trees, she was aboard the ship in Grimsby docks waiting whilst a cargo of barley was loaded to be 'livered to a malt kiln in

Elsborough. She was angry and frustrated, but there was nothing she could do. She could not send a message and all she could do was hope and pray that he would be there the next week.

'I don't like to be made a fool of, Mary Ann,' Randolph said stiffly.

'Would you have liked me to have sent a telegram to The Hall?' Her tone was brittle, hiding her own fear that he would not come to meet her again. ' "Sorry, can't meet you on Monday. Love from your mistress." '

'Don't be ridiculous, Mary Ann,' he snapped.

'Ridiculous, am I? Randolph, I am at the mercy of the tides, the wind, Dan's cargoes and where they have to be loaded. It's a miracle that we have been able to meet as often as we have. It's only because he usually has a regular run on a Monday, and we pass here at about the same time each week, that I've managed it until now.'

'So what went wrong last week?'

Mary Ann shrugged. 'An urgent delivery that they were prepared to pay over the odds for.'

'And, of course, your thrifty husband couldn't miss such an opportunity, could he?'

'No,' Mary Ann said shortly, disliking the sarcasm in Randolph's tone that was directed at her husband. It was quite bad enough that she was deceiving Dan. In spite of all her faults – and she knew there were many – she couldn't bear to hear Dan ridiculed too. He didn't deserve that. In fact, Mary Ann realized in a fleeting and rare moment of honesty, he didn't deserve any of it. Dan Ruddick was a good man, too good for the likes of Mary Ann Clark.

'Come . . .' Randolph was holding out his hand to her,

all smiles now. 'Don't let's waste our precious time together in quarrelling. How long have you got?'

She couldn't resist him. As he had said, so long ago now and so prophetically, he only had to crook his little finger and she came running.

Pushing away uncomfortable thoughts, Mary Ann smiled impishly now. 'I told him I had a lot of extra washing to do this week, with having missed my turn at the wash-house last Monday.'

Randolph's returning smile was wolfish. 'Good, because I am going to take you on a long car ride.'

They took the country lanes and back roads where there was less likelihood of being seen by anyone who knew them. The car was bouncing down a long, rutted cart track towards a small, white cottage, on the far side of Raven's Wood, set against a backdrop of trees. They came to a halt outside the door and switched off the engine. Leaning back in his seat, he said, 'Here we are.'

Mary Ann looked at the cottage. It was painted white with a pretty garden and a climbing rose tree around the green-painted front door. Then she looked at Randolph. 'Here we are – where?'

'Home,' he said.

Her heart was racing and the blood was pounding in her ears. 'What . . . what do you mean?'

He leant towards her and took hold of her hand. Softly, he said, 'This could be yours, Mary Ann, if only you'll say the word.'

'You mean – it's yours?'

'Of course I do. It's part of the estate. It's really a gamekeeper's cottage, but I don't have need of as many gamekeepers as I used to have. So, it's been empty for a while. Oh, Mary Ann, Mary Ann . . .' He moved nearer and began to kiss her neck, urging her, tempting her between his kisses. 'Leave him, Mary Ann. Come to me. Be mine. You know how I need you, how I want you . . .'

For a while she gave in to his passion but afterwards, in the cold light of reason, she said, 'You know I can't.'

It was over Sunday lunch in Waterman's Yard that the trouble began.

'Have you seen Randolph Marsh's new car? It's a monstrosity of a thing.' Duggie, still interested in all things mechanical, laughed. 'But what I'd give for a ride in one.'

Mary Ann glanced worriedly at Lizzie, but she was concentrating on eating her favourite pudding – treacle sponge that Bessie always made for her – and didn't appear to be listening to the adult conversation going on around her.

'It'll have set him back a pretty penny. I think it's a Rolls Royce.'

'No, it isn't.' Lizzie took another mouthful before she said, 'It's a Bentley.'

Duggie laughed. 'How do you know that, our Lizzie?'

Lizzie scraped the spoon around her bowl to get the last drop of treacle. 'Lawrence told me.'

There was silence around the table as all eyes turned to look at her. Suddenly, Lizzie was motionless. Then her spoon clattered into her dish as she gazed, horrified, at her mother.

'Lizzie, go below.'

When they arrived back at the ship, Dan's voice was stern. Nothing more had been said around the dinner table, but there had been an awkward silence. Bessie had opened her mouth and Mary Ann had felt her heart begin to thump with fear. Nothing got past her mother-in-law, but then she saw Bert put out his hand to touch his wife's. Bessie had glanced at him, met his steady gaze, seen the slight shake of his head and had closed her mouth. But she had got up quickly from the table and began to clear away the pots, crashing them dangerously together so that Mary Ann was in no doubt that Bessie smelt trouble.

Even Duggie, usually blithely unaware of undercurrents, kept silent and, when the time came for them to return to the ship, he made an excuse that he was meeting some cronies in The Waterman's Arms.

Now Mary Ann was alone on deck with her husband.

'What's been going on?' Dan demanded. There was a tension in his voice, but she could tell that he was struggling to remain calm. 'How does my daughter – a child of ten – know the difference between a Rolls Royce and a Bentley? And how come she knows the boy?'

Mary Ann's laugh was brittle as she tried to bluff her way out. 'She's met him. Just once.'

'When? How?'

Mary Ann shrugged. 'That day she ran off and I couldn't find her. You remember? Well, that's where she was. They'd been driving past and stopped to speak to her. Mr Randolph and his son.' Embellishing her story, Mary Ann went on. 'They took her for a ride in their motor car.'

Dan was appalled. 'Took her . . .? She got in a car with strangers?' He paused and Mary Ann glanced away from him, her resolve wilting under his keen scrutiny. Now he was shaking his head. 'Oh no. I don't believe it. She wouldn't do that. Not my Lizzie. Not after all I've told her. She wouldn't get into a car with complete strangers.'

He paused and said slowly, 'Not unless she knew them.' There was a long pause before he asked, his voice now deceptively quiet, 'Did she know them, Mary Ann?'

'Of course not. How could she?'

'Mary Ann, I want the truth and I mean to have it. Either you tell it to me or I shall ask Lizzie. She will tell me the truth, I know she will, but I don't want to have to put a child in the awful position of having to tell me her mother's secrets.'

There was silence between them, the only sound the lapping of the water against the side of the ship, a fitful moon their only light in the darkness of the night.

'Mary Ann?'

Her resolve snapped. Her voice was a high-pitched shriek. 'All right. All right. You want the truth. All right. I've been meeting him. Randolph. He's my lover.' She paused and then, plunging the knife in even further, added, 'Again.'

He lunged at her and, grabbing her shoulders, shook her. He was shouting now. 'Why? Why, Mary Ann? Haven't I been good to you? Haven't I looked after you and cared for you?'

'I love him,' she screamed at him. 'I always have. And he loves me.'

'No. No. You can't believe that. He's just amusing himself with you. How can you allow yourself to be taken in by him? How can you be so stupid?'

Mary Ann pulled herself free of his grasp and ran to the side of the ship. 'Let me go. What do you know about it? What do you know about love?'

'How can you say that to me, Mary Ann? I gave up Susan for you.'

Appalled, they stared at each other through the darkness. He moved towards her. 'Mary Ann, I didn't mean it.

I love you. Really I do. Forget about him. We'll say no more about it, if you promise me not to see him again.'

'No, no,' her cry was anguished. 'I can't live without seeing him. I'm sorry, Dan. I don't mean to hurt you, but—'

'Listen to me. He'll leave you again, just like he did before, when he tires of you.'

Her voice rose hysterically. 'It's not like that. It wasn't his fault. He had to marry Celia. His family made him.'

'Don't be ridiculous. A man in his position can't be made to do anything he doesn't want to.'

A seed of doubt crept into her mind, rooted itself there and began to grow. But instead of gratitude, Mary Ann hated the person who had sown it.

She flew at Dan and pummelled his chest shrieking at him. 'I hate you. You don't want me to be happy. You want to keep me a prisoner on this blasted boat.'

Dan tried to catch hold of her, but she struggled free, crying hysterically. He raised his hand and slapped her face, not in fury, but to bring her to reason.

She fell back against the rail and at that moment the Aegir, moving majestically upriver, lifted the ship at its moorings.

Mary Ann, caught off balance, felt herself falling backwards over the side. Her arms flailed helplessly and her mouth opened in a terrified scream as she splashed into the black, swift flowing water.

She rose to the surface and heard, just once, the desperation in Dan's voice as he called her name.

'Mary Ann. *Maaary Aaan!*'

Then the dark waters closed over her head.

311

Part Three

Lizzie

Lizzie

asked in the tu—

"Aye, but ... soon, and will be a lass ... Dimple ...

... and Finn ... ly he ... said tr ... and Liz ...
... of Mackin ...

... good, of the ... stem and that on ... thing, it had
never held much ... for her. And now t ... though still
... probative of ... arry daughter, was ... ne to accept
... this with her ... edge of the river ... ly moods,
... and her bonnie, common sense, he said slowly, her a
... aster breed ...

... he long ... comes to be extra ... ho ... r, and
two ... all righ ...

Forty-One

1939

The rowing boat bumped gently against the side of the ship and Lizzie heard Tolly's voice calling, his face upturned as her father leant over the side. 'Mr Ruddick? Can Lizzie come fishing with me?'

'Where are you going, lad?'

Stifling her giggles, Lizzie watched as her uncle, Duggie, joined his brother to peer down at the boy, too. For a moment, Tolly seemed fazed by the two stern, weather-beaten faces staring down at him and his stammer became suddenly more pronounced. 'N-not far. Just – just to the bend in the river.'

'The Aegir's due soon and it'll be a big one,' Duggie warned.

'I know. That's why it's a good time. C-can Lizzie come, Mr Ruddick?'

The two men exchanged a glance. Lizzie, at fifteen, was a child of the river. Born and bred on the water, it had never held any fears for her. And now Dan, although still protective of his pretty daughter, was obliged to accept that, with her knowledge of the river and all its moods and her innate common sense, he should allow her a greater freedom.

'As long as you promise to be extra careful,' he said. 'Then, all right.'

Lizzie, already dressed for the expedition for she had known Tolly would come, climbed the last few steps of the ladder from the cabin and stepped on to the deck. The two men turned at the sound and Duggie laughed out loud. 'You little minx,' he said, holding out his arm and drawing her to him to hug her. 'You've arranged all this, haven't you? What if your dad had said, "No"?'

Lizzie, so like her mother in many ways, with dark unruly curls and dancing dark eyes, laughed, 'I'd have gone anyway,' she teased, although they all knew she would have done no such thing. Already, the girl seemed older than her years, far more mature than most girls of her age, and it seemed as if she had been blessed with the best traits of character from each of her parents. She had her mother's looks and her sunny nature and impish ways, but from Dan she got her honesty and, although this was probably a throwback to her grandmother, Bessie, she was forthright and afraid of no one.

'I've fried you a piece of steak each and there are potatoes, swede and carrots in the boiling pan.'

'Now, don't be late,' her father frowned. 'I want you home before dark.'

'Yes, Dad,' Lizzie called gaily as she swung herself over the side and down the rope ladder towards Tolly's boat. 'I'll bring you back a salmon.'

She sat in the bows of the small boat, whilst Tolly rowed strongly away from the ship and, reaching the middle of the river, rested a moment on the oars, allowing the boat to drift with the current. Lizzie gave a contented sigh, leaning back in the boat and allowing her hand to trail in the water. It was a balmy evening, a quiet time, when everyone seemed to be waiting for the swell of the Aegir surging up the river. The willow trees planted along the riverbank to strengthen it, the ducks swimming in convoy, the ships and the smaller boats, moored at the wharves or at the landings all seemed to be waiting for the great wave.

'I've got a job,' Tolly told her. Now that they were alone, all sign of his stammer had vanished.

Lizzie sat up and clapped her hands. 'That's wonderful. Is it with Mr Bryce, the basketmaker?'

On the Nottinghamshire side of the river, near the shipyard, were the workshops of Harry Bryce. Harry had served in the Great War and had been blinded, but he now ran a small cottage industry, weaving willow baskets with intricate skill. It was the root of the willow that strengthened the bank, the tree itself only serving as nature's ornament. So, with the permission of the authorities, Harry Bryce harvested the willow he needed from along the side of the Trent. Because of his blindness he was unable to do that work himself and so an army of schoolboys worked for him in their spare time, and to some, like Tolly, he had taught the rudiments of his trade.

To Lizzie's surprise, Tolly said, 'No. It's at the shipyard.' His face sobered. 'I wanted to work for Mr Bryce and he would have taken me on, if he could have afforded it. But,' he added hastily, 'I shall still be able to help him if he needs me.'

Lizzie smiled at him warmly. She knew he was very fond of old Mr Bryce, who had been very kind to him. The basketmaker's workshop had been a haven from the boy's unhappy home life.

As if reading her thoughts, Tolly said, 'He's like another dad to me.' He coloured a little and the stutter was temporarily back as he added, 'In fact, he's n-nicer to me than me real dad is.' Only to Lizzie did Tolly ever speak of his bullying, aggressive father, and she told no one, not even her own beloved daddy and uncle, although she was aware that they knew much of what went on inside the ferryman's white-washed cottage.

Tolly was smiling as he said, 'I shall row up the river to work every day and Mr Bryce has already said that if the weather's ever really bad, then I can stay with him for a night or two.'

'What will you be doing there? At the shipyard, I mean?'

'I'm to be an apprentice carpenter. Me dad's signed the papers already.'

'Is it what you want to do?'

Tolly shrugged. 'I don't know. I can't think of anything else.'

She leant towards him. 'Why don't you leave home? Why don't you get away from him?'

Tolly pressed his lips together and shook his head. 'I don't want to leave me mam. Now I'm older, maybe I can get between them a bit more.'

'Yes, and look what happens when you do. Like last week, you got the black eye.'

'I'd sooner that, than me mam get hit.'

'Oh Tolly,' Lizzie's eyes filled with tears. 'Why does he do it?'

The boy shrugged his thin shoulders and then smiled. 'Come on, it'll be here soon. Let's not think about him. Not tonight. Tonight, we're going fishing.'

He rowed a little further and then they sat waiting until they saw the wave coming towards them around the curve in the river.

'She's a big 'un. Hold on tight, Lizzie.'

As the Aegir rolled towards them, Tolly positioned the rowing boat bows into the wave. They clung on as the little boat crested the foaming wave and rode on top of it before meeting the smaller waves – the whelps, as the locals called them. The wave had stirred up the mud from the river bottom, so that fish were choked and swam about in panic.

The two youngsters waited patiently until the water began to settle and clear a little.

'There! Look!' Lizzie cried, 'I can see one. There's another – and another.'

'They're exhausted now,' Tolly said, reaching for his salmon net. He dipped the round hoop into the water and drew it along, scooping up the disorientated fish.

'Well, it's certainly fish for tomorrow night's supper,' Lizzie laughed, as fish after fish landed in the bottom of Tolly's boat.

'Just made it.'

Duggie was leaning down over the side of the ship to help her aboard. 'Your dad was starting to get twitchy because you weren't back and it's almost dark.'

'I'm sorry, but just look how many fish we caught.'

'My word, that is a fine catch. We'll be able to take some to your gran, Lizzie. She and your grandpa love a bit of fresh salmon. Here, Tolly, let me help you.'

'Where's Dad?' Lizzie asked, excitedly. 'I want him to see how many we've caught.'

'He's below in the cabin. He's in one of his moods.'

The delight fell from Lizzie's face. 'Is it my fault? Because I'm late.'

'Nah,' Duggie said, lifting the fish on to the deck. ''Course it isn't. Just go and make him a cuppa, lass, and put plenty of sugar in it.' He grinned. 'Sweeten the old grump up a bit.'

Lizzie sighed as she went towards the companion, feeling again the burden of guilt. For five years Lizzie had secretly carried the belief that she had been to blame for that fateful night when her mother had disappeared.

For weeks afterwards, she had cried, 'I'm sorry, I'm sorry, Daddy.' Her father had stroked her hair and though the sorrow never left his eyes, he had comforted her. 'It's not your fault, sweetheart. It's nothing to do with you.'

Five years later the haunted look was still there in his eyes. He never spoke about Mary Ann and no one had ever told Lizzie what had happened to her mother. Perhaps they didn't know, she thought, for all anyone would say was, 'She's gone away, love.'

Night after night, Lizzie would dream that she heard her mother's voice and would wake with the name on her lips, 'Mam?'

A girl at school – one who had never liked Lizzie, thinking her not the type who should attend a select private school – had said, 'They might hang your father. One day they'll find your mother's body floating in the river, all bloated and ugly, and then they'll hang your father for killing her. Just like they did your grandfather.'

Lizzie had run, crying, to Miss Marsh. Edwina had held her and comforted her, but even she had offered no explanation. Afterwards, the rest of her class had refused to include Lizzie in their games and, worse still, had ignored her completely, refusing to speak to her.

'She's a tell-tale-tit,' they mocked. 'Run and tell teacher, why don't you, Cry Baby?'

Lizzie had run home to the safe arms of her gran in Waterman's Yard. She had had nightmares for weeks, waking screaming in the night until Bessie had said one morning, 'You're not going to that school any more.'

So she had gone to the town's school, and there, Tolly had become her friend. Though the nightmares had lessened, Lizzie, deep within her, still believed herself to blame for the quarrel between her parents that night. And worse still, now, was implanted the terrifying thought that perhaps her mother had drowned in the river and that her father had been to blame. But Lizzie dared not ask, dared not put such a terrible thought into words. So she remained in ignorance. Outwardly, she was the sunny-natured, pretty girl she had always been, but deep in her heart she carried a leaden weight of sorrow. And what frightened her the most was that when she looked into her father's eyes, she saw that same fear mirrored there.

So Lizzie kept quiet and asked no questions lest she should bring more shame and sorrow upon her family.

She could not even talk to Tolly about it.

Forty-Two

From leaving school in 1938, Lizzie lived permanently aboard the *Maid Mary Ann*. She had always helped to look after her father and her uncle ever since her mother had gone, but, as she got older, she had taken on more and more of the domestic chores. Now, the only time she spent ashore was at the weekends when they all stayed with her grandparents in Waterman's Yard.

'There's going to be a war, you know.' If he said it once during the early part of 1939, Duggie said it a hundred times. But there were no clouds, war or otherwise, in the skies for Lizzie and Tolly that summer. Besides fishing for salmon and blobbing for eels, Lizzie would scull to meet him early in the morning before he went to work and together they would pick wild mushrooms, returning to the ship with a basketful. She made a rich, tasty pink sauce and served them hot to her father and uncle.

In early summer the two youngsters sought out the nests of plovers and moorhens, taking one or two eggs for their breakfasts.

'As long as you leave at least one egg in a moorhen's nest,' Tolly told her, 'she'll lay more. Just like a hen does.'

'I don't feel so bad about taking them, in that case,' said the tender-hearted Lizzie, who hated to think of the poor mothers robbed of their eggs.

On Sundays, after attending morning service in the

parish church with her family, Lizzie would often find
Tolly waiting in Waterman's Yard.

'Are you c-coming blackberrying, Lizzie? I've f-found
loads near Bourton.'

'As long as you don't go near Raven's Wood,' Dan
would say and his frown would deepen. 'I don't want you
going there.'

'All right, Dad,' Lizzie would agree cheerfully and off
they would go for the afternoon, returning with their
mouths and fingers stained with blackberry juice and
refusing Sunday tea.

'Little scallywags, not eating that trifle I've spent hours
making.' Bessie would pretend to be offended.

'Don't worry, Mam,' Duggie would say, winking at
Lizzie. 'There's all the more for me.'

Then Bessie would gratefully accept the basketful of
blackberries they had brought her. 'These'll make lovely
jam and I'll have some apple and blackberry pasties ready
for you next week to take back to the ship, Lizzie.'

'You enjoy yourselves,' Duggie said each time Lizzie
went off with Tolly and, helping her climb down into
Tolly's rowing boat, added, 'while you can.'

'Oh shut up, Duggie,' Dan said at last irritably. 'Anybody'd think you wanted a war the way you keep going
on about it.'

Duggie only laughed and said, 'Well, it's the navy for
me if it does happen.'

Lizzie stared at him. 'You wouldn't join up, Uncle
Duggie, would you? Not really. What'd we do without
you?'

Duggie put his hands across his heart. 'Ah, at least
there'll be one pretty girl pining for me.'

Duggie had never married. Although he had come
dangerously close once or twice he had always escaped

'the net', as he called it. He had never been without a girlfriend for very long, but as soon as rings and wedding bells were mentioned, he tactfully disentangled himself. It was to his credit that he had never left a girl pregnant, nor even particularly heartbroken. He was, at heart, a kind man and with his never failing good humour, he was genuinely liked by everyone as much as they loved him. The girls he jilted could never bring themselves to hate him and, in fact, he remained on good terms with most of them.

'I'll not be the only one,' Lizzie teased him. 'What about Janice?'

Duggie feigned ignorance. 'Janice? Who's Janice?'

Lizzie, joining in the fun, pretended to sigh. 'I see. Behind the times again, am I? Who's the latest then?'

'Well, there's this very nice girl who works in the jewellers' on the corner of Pottergate. Sheila, I think her name is. I was thinking of asking her out on Saturday night.'

'You want to be careful, Uncle Duggie. If she works in a jewellers', she might be able to buy things cheaper. She could have a ring on her finger before you know it.'

Duggie laughed loudly. 'She might well, Lizzie, my love, but it won't be me buying it for her.'

'Aren't you getting a bit old for all these young girls?' Dan said.

'I'm only thirty-four. They like an older, more mature man.'

'Older, yes,' Dan said. 'Mature – never!'

'You're just . . .' Duggie began, but then Lizzie saw him catch his lip. She guessed he had, in his teasing way, been going to say, 'You're just jealous,' but even Duggie stopped short of such a barb.

Dan walked away down the deck, a lonely figure, his

shoulders hunched. Lizzie stared after him and felt the familiar lump in her throat. Poor Dad, she thought, her love for him swelling in her breast. Whatever had happened that night, he was not to blame. She had to believe he was not to blame.

Now she murmured to Duggie, 'Will Dad have to go to war, Uncle Duggie?'

'Shouldn't think so, love. For a start he might be too old and even if he isn't, there are what they call "reserved occupations". He does a very useful job moving supplies about on the water. You never know, business for ships like ours might even pick up. Strange old world,' he mused more to himself than to the girl at his side. 'A catastrophe like a war can even be the making of people.'

'In business, you mean?' Lizzie asked.

'Aye, that and in a personal way too.' He grinned at her. 'Very character-building, is a war, young Lizzie.'

Soberly, Lizzie looked at him. The wind ruffled his dark hair, blowing it on to his forehead. For once his eyes had a serious, faraway look, as if already he was imagining himself sailing the high seas in a smart naval uniform.

Lizzie shuddered and reached out to touch his arm. 'If – if you do go, Uncle Duggie, you will be all right, won't you?'

The smile was back on his face as he patted her hand and looked down at her. ''Course I will, little Lizzie. It'll all be over by Christmas anyway. I'll be back before you've even missed me. You'll see.'

Everywhere the talk was of the war, but towards the end of August the annual regatta still took place. It was held, as always, on the stretch of river between Westlands and Eastlands, near where Ted Oliver ran his ferry.

'I've built a sea horse.' Proudly, Tolly showed Lizzie the barrel with the wooden horse's head he had made attached to one end. 'Are you entering the cog boat race, Lizzie?'

She nodded and her eyes twinkled with mischief. 'The blindfold race.'

'You're not!'

'I am.' She laughed. 'The worst thing that can happen is that I end up rowing down the middle of the river and have to be towed back by a motor boat.'

'No, no, you won't. I reckon you know this river as well as any of the men.'

'Are you going in for the greasy pole? My dad's having it on his ship this year.'

Every year one of the keel ships had a fifty-foot pole fixed in the bows pointing out over the water with a flag attached to the end of it. The pole was well greased, or soaped, and the person who walked along it and retrieved the flag won a prize and, later, it was also used for a pillow-fighting contest.

The day was bright and breezy and everybody seemed determined to enjoy themselves. Lizzie lined up in her cog boat with six other contestants. Tolly was not one of them as he had promised to try to shout instructions to her. Duggie would do the same from the opposite bank.

Solemnly, the brown paper bags were given out to each participant to put over their heads and the starter fired a pistol. Lizzie began to scull her boat away from the bank, but above the noise made by all the watchers, she could not distinguish Tolly's voice. For a moment she stopped sculling and let the boat drift, catching the feel of the current. Then, beneath the paper bag, Lizzie smiled and began to scull strongly in the direction she believed the opposite bank to be. It seemed to be taking her a long time and, for a moment, Lizzie thought she had miscalculated and that she was blithely sculling downstream to the amusement of all the onlookers. Then, quite clearly, she heard Duggie's voice.

'Come on, Lizzie. You're winning, lass. Just another two yards. Come on.'

A few more strokes and Lizzie felt the boat jolt against the bank and a huge cheer went up from the crowd. She removed the bag and turned to look back at her competitors. Three were tangled up with each other in the middle of the river, shouting and swearing, to the vast enjoyment of the watchers. One was rowing vigorously upstream against the current and another was sculling, supremely unaware, downstream. The last one hadn't even got away from the opposite bank and seemed to be going round in circles. Then, on the far bank she saw Tolly jumping up and down with excitement and waving his congratulations at her win.

Later, Duggie won the greasy pole competition and Tolly won the barrel race and everyone enjoyed the ale and sandwiches aboard a barge anchored in the middle of the river.

Although no one knew it at the time, it was to be the last time the regatta was held, for on Sunday 3 September war became a reality. The news was greeted by a lot of people with a sense of relief. At least the dreadful waiting was over.

'Well, now we know. Now we can get at 'em.' Duggie rubbed his hands gleefully as his father turned off the wireless and sat down in his chair. The whole family was squashed into Bessie's kitchen to hear the Prime Minister's broadcast.

'We'll just be left with young boys and old men to run the country,' Dan grumbled, 'whilst all the able-bodied men are away playing soldiers.'

There was silence until Bert's quiet voice said, 'It'll not be a game, son.'

Usually, it amused Lizzie to hear her daddy addressed as 'son' by his own father, but this morning, she was not smiling. Her face was serious, her eyes wide with anxiety as she listened intently to the conversation around her.

'Women did all sorts of things in the last lot,' Bessie murmured. 'Drove ambulances, worked in factories, even went to the Front as nurses. 'Spect they will again.' Lizzie felt her grandmother's gaze upon her. 'Even Lizzie here. She'll have to do her bit.'

'She's far too young,' Dan said quickly. 'Besides, I need her, 'specially if Duggie's going.' A strange bitterness crept into his tone as he added, 'At least she's capable of being a good "mate", even though she is a woman. She won't sit in the cabin all day doing her embroidery.'

Lizzie didn't understand his words or the look that passed between him and Bessie.

'Of course I'll stay with you, Dad,' she said, leaning against Dan's shoulder and smiling up at him.

Dan returned her smile and for a brief moment the haunted look went from his eyes. 'Aye, you'll never leave your old dad, will you, love?' he murmured softly.

'If it lasts as long as the last lot,' Bessie still insisted, 'she'll have to do as she's told in another three or four years' time and it won't be you doing the telling, our Dan. Not this time.'

When Duggie volunteered and was accepted into the Merchant Navy, Lizzie became her father's official mate aboard Mr Sudbury's ship, which he had skippered for the last sixteen years.

328

'You'll not always be able to take the lass with you, Dan,' his employer had warned. 'We shall more than likely get asked to go on some very odd missions, so just be prepared. By the way, I'm going to have the ship fitted out with a small diesel engine. You can still make use of the sails whenever possible, but it'll cut out wasted time waiting for a tow. Things are going to change, Dan,' Lizzie heard Mr Sudbury say to her father. 'And if we're to survive, we'll have to change with them.'

Dan bemoaned the fitting of a noisy, smelly engine to his beloved keel, but Lizzie loved its rhythmic phut-phut-phut. 'Wouldn't Uncle Duggie have liked it, Dad? I know just what he'd say. "Should have had one years ago." '

Dan's only reply was a baleful glance. 'I don't know why Mr Sudbury's bothered to have one fitted. Trade's dropped off that much, we look like being laid up for weeks. Everything's coming in by the ports on the west coast now. Besides, we're not allowed to move in the hours of darkness, so where's the point? The only cargo I've got this week is fifty tons of cement for building air-raid shelters.'

'It'll pick up again, Dad. It's bound to.'

A cold spell during the early months of 1940 kept the *Maid Mary Ann* moored at Elsborough and though Lizzie could find plenty to do ashore, Dan chafed at the enforced idleness. But when warmer weather came, with it returned some of the trade to the east coast ports.

Towards the end of May, Dan said, 'You can't come with me tomorrow, Lizzie.'

'Why not? Where are you going?'

Her father seemed tense and anxious and his answer was evasive. 'Oh, just into the Humber, but Mr Sudbury said you were not to go. He's sending one of his men down to go with me.'

The following morning, Lizzie helped her grandmother pack a basket of food for Dan.

'I think we'd better pack him a bit extra, love,' Bessie murmured. 'I reckon he's going to be gone a few days.'

'A few days?' Lizzie stared at her. 'Where's he going and why can't I go? And who's this man going in my place? Do you know more than he's told me?'

'Calm down, calm down,' Bessie smiled, but Lizzie noticed that the anxiety in her eyes was still there. 'All I know is that Mr Sudbury told ya dad it's something to do with the government or the War Office, or somebody.'

'What? Some sort of job for them, you mean?'

Bessie shrugged. 'I don't know and I don't even think your dad does. Mebbe this bloke who's joining him will know more. Now,' she added briskly, closing the lid and putting the peg through the fastening, 'can you carry this, love, 'cos I've packed enough to feed an army?'

'I know, I'll borrow Mr Eccleshall's pram wheels.' Lizzie darted out and across the yard to knock on Minnie's door. When their children had outgrown their old pram, Stan Eccleshall had removed the body and had fitted a sturdy wooden box on to the wheels. Through the years, it had seen good service for all his neighbours in Waterman's Yard.

At Miller's Wharf her father came down the gangway to help her lift the heavy basket aboard.

'I ought to be coming with you,' Lizzie grumbled. 'Who's going to look after you?'

'I wish you could come, Lizzie. I'll miss you, but he seems like a nice chap who's come. He's lost three fingers off his right hand so he didn't pass his medical for service, but it doesn't seem to stop him being able to handle a ship.'

'You . . . you will be careful, won't you, Dad?'

'Of course, now give us a hug and off you go back home to your gran.'

Lizzie watched him board and then cast off for him, waving to both him and the stranger on the deck of the *Maid Mary Ann*.

'Lizzie.' A familiar voice spoke behind her and she turned to smile at Tolly as he came to stand beside her. 'You not going on this trip, then?'

Lizzie shook her head. 'They won't let me.'

Tolly was gazing thoughtfully after the ship as it moved out into the middle of the river and began to sail downriver. Lizzie's gaze was still on her father's vessel, but Tolly glanced back upriver and then suddenly, he gripped her arm. 'Look. Just look!'

Lizzie turned to see several more of Mr Sudbury's ships coming down the river, following the *Maid Mary Ann*.

'Now just where,' Lizzie murmured, 'are they all going?'

'I don't know,' Tolly said, his gaze on the unusual sight. 'But it must be for something very important.'

Forty-Three

'You're like a cat on hot bricks, Lizzie,' Bessie grumbled. 'For heaven's sake find yourself something useful to do.'

'I'm just worried where Dad's gone, Gran. He's been gone three days.'

'Well, you're often away longer than that. How do you think I feel when I don't hear from you for days on end?' Bessie's needles continued to click as she sat beside the range, knitting a pair of socks.

'That's different. You know I'm with him then. You know I'll look after him.' She caught her grandmother's comical expression and laughed too. 'Oh, you know what I mean. We look after each other.'

Bessie chuckled softly, 'Aye, I know what you mean. You're a good girl, Lizzie.' There was a slight pause as she appeared to be thinking. 'I tell you what, love. You can go up to Miss Edwina's school for me. I'm running short of wool. She's become one of the mainstays of the local branch of the WVS and she's organizing all this war work that us housewives can do at home and still feel we're "doing our bit", as they say.'

Bessie, at sixty-five, now found it difficult to get about and rarely left the confines of the yard. She still struggled to the river now and then to watch the ships and she managed to get into the town once a week to do her shopping. But the effort exhausted her and her legs and feet pained her constantly.

Lizzie, despite her youth, realized that her grandmother still needed to busy herself to blot out the worry over Duggie. She jumped up, relieved to have something to do herself, something that might take her own mind off worrying about her father for a little while. She was missing, not only him, but the river too. She longed for the open air, the breeze in her face and the sounds and smells of the river. In Waterman's Yard, she felt stifled.

'Right,' she said. 'I'll go now.'

At the school, the door was opened by a tall, young man of a similar age to herself, who was vaguely familiar. Lizzie stared at him and he stared back. His fair hair was smoothed back and he was smartly dressed in a suit, white shirt and tie. But it was his bright, blue eyes that made her remember him.

'Hello, Lawrence,' she said at the same moment that his face broke into a grin, creasing the lines around his eyes, and he said, 'Lizzie!'

He pulled the door wider, inviting her in. 'I presume you've come to see Aunt Edwina?'

'Well, yes,' she conceded, but, greeting his smile with impish mischief, she added, 'But, of course, if I'd known you were going to be here . . .'

They laughed together.

'You've grown,' he said, as he led the way upstairs.

'So have you,' she countered and teased. 'However tall are you?'

'Six two in my stockinged feet.'

Tolly was tall, too, she thought, taller than she was, but Lawrence dwarfed even him.

He was opening the door into his aunt's study and ushering her in. 'You have a visitor, Aunt Edwina.'

333

Edwina rose from behind her desk and took off her spectacles. She came round the desk and held out her hands. 'Lizzie. My dear girl. How lovely to see you. I hear about you, of course, from Bessie. But it's ages since I saw you. Let me look at you.' Still holding her hands, she stood back and looked Lizzie up and down. For a moment there was a strange look in her eyes as if the sight of the pretty, dark-haired girl, with the sparkling brown eyes and cheeks that dimpled so easily with her ready smile, reminded her so poignantly of someone else.

Lizzie held her breath. She knew, without being told, that she reminded Edwina of her mother, Mary Ann. She remembered the closeness that had once existed between them, though the memories themselves were hazy now, mere fleeting childhood images that had left an impression rather than solid knowledge.

'I was just telling her that she's grown since I last saw her.'

Edwina looked startled as she glanced at her nephew and then back to Lizzie again. 'You – you know each other?'

Now it was the young ones who looked embarrassed. They glanced at each other and then swiftly away again. Lawrence cleared his throat. 'We met once or twice as children.' His voice dropped to a murmur. 'A long time ago now.'

Edwina let go of Lizzie's hands and turned away. 'Yes, yes, of course,' she said absently and then, gathering her wits, said briskly, 'Now, my dear. You've come to collect some wool for your gran, have you?'

She led the way across the room to a pile of boxes in one corner. Picking one up she handed it to Lizzie. 'There are two more. Bessie said that Mrs Eccleshall and Mrs Merryweather have offered to help too.'

'And Mrs Hamilton,' Lizzie said. 'She was the first to knock on Gran's door and offer.'

'Was she indeed?' For a moment, Edwina was lost in her own memories of the last war that gave her an empathy with the woman in Waterman's Yard. 'Well, every little helps,' she murmured.

'Lizzie can't carry all that lot on her own. Look, I'll walk home with her.'

'Oh Lawrence, I don't know . . .' Edwina began, but already he was picking up the other two boxes, resting his chin on the topmost one and smiling over the top of them at Lizzie, refusing to take no for an answer.

They walked the length of River Road laughing and talking just as if the intervening years since they had chased each other in the woods had never happened.

'Remember the den we built in the woods?' he asked. 'I wonder if it's still there?'

Lizzie laughed. 'We might need it, if we get invaded.'

'Oh, that'll not happen.' Lawrence was full of confidence. 'At least, not once we've got ourselves organized. I just wish I was a bit older and could do my bit too.'

'Here we are,' Lizzie said and led the way down the narrow alleyway between the houses and into Waterman's Yard, calling out as she pushed open the door of Bessie's home, 'I'm back, Gran.' She turned to Lawrence. 'I'll just put this down and come back for those two,' but Lawrence shook his head and followed her into the house.

'It's all right,' he said. 'I'll bring them in for you.'

Placing the boxes on the table in the kitchen, Lizzie watched as he went towards Bessie sitting in her chair by the range.

'Good day, Mrs Ruddick. I'm pleased to meet you.'

Bessie gaped up at him and then made as if to heave herself to her swollen feet.

'Please – don't get up. I don't wish to disturb you. I've only walked along with Lizzie to carry the boxes.' He smiled at her, his eyes crinkling. 'It looks as if they've set you a lot of work.'

Bessie, recovering her senses, said, 'Oh, I can still manage a bit of knitting, young man. It's just a pity I can't get about like I could.'

Without invitation, Lawrence sat down opposite her and leant forwards to talk to her, resting his elbows on his knees and linking his fingers. 'It must be very difficult for you.'

Lizzie watched in amazement as he sat there in her grandfather's chair, talking so easily and so naturally to her grandmother.

'Make this young feller a cup of tea, love,' Bessie said, her knitting needles never faltering.

As Lizzie busied herself, she listened to their conversation.

'It's sad that Holland and Belgium have surrendered, isn't it?' Lawrence began.

'Aye, and the papers are now saying that our lads are being driven back in France.'

'Right to the coast. They say the enemy has almost got them surrounded.'

At least, Lizzie thought, as she carried in the tea tray, there's no one belonging to us trapped on the French beaches and facing German guns and war planes. Uncle Duggie won't be there. For once, he was better off being out at sea.

'What a nice young man,' Bessie said, when Lawrence had taken his leave. 'Such nice manners and genuinely charming. Who is he, Lizzie?'

Lizzie gaped at her in surprise. 'Don't you know, Gran? He's Miss Edwina's nephew. Lawrence Marsh.'

Now Bessie did drop her knitting and struggled to her feet. She stood in front of Lizzie and, panting from the effort, wagged her finger in her face. 'And if I'd known that, girl, he wouldn't have been allowed across me doorstep. You're to have nowt more to do with him. Do you hear me, Mary Ann?'

Lizzie stared at her grandmother, but seeing how agitated the old lady had become, she said quietly, 'I hear you, Gran. I hear you.'

Bessie sank back into her chair with a sigh of relief, though whether from being able to rest her huge body once more or because her granddaughter had, as she believed, given her word, Lizzie couldn't tell.

She stared down at the grey head now bending over the box on her knee as she sorted through the wool.

Mary Ann, Lizzie was thinking. *She called me Mary Ann.*

Forty-Four

They were walking through the woods together. He had found her that morning at the wash-house just beyond Eastlands' Ferry, almost two weeks after he had met her again.

'I didn't know if you still came here.' Lawrence said, standing uncertainly in the doorway.

Lizzie straightened up from bending over the rinsing tub and pushed the damp hair from her face, shiny with sweat.

'Hello.' She smiled at him and then laughed. 'Yes. Modern inventions like washing machines haven't reached us aboard ship yet.'

He stepped into the steamy atmosphere. 'Have you time for a little walk? I thought we might take a trip down memory lane.'

'How have you got here? On horseback?'

'No. Bicycle.'

'A steed of sorts,' she teased, then added, 'I'll be finished in a couple of minutes when I've mangled these sheets.'

'Can I help?'

'You could turn the handle if you like.'

He stepped over the puddles on the brick floor and grasped the handle of the mangle. 'Tell me when.'

Lizzie fed in the folded wet sheets as he turned, the water flooding back into the rinsing tub.

'Thanks.' She laid the sheets on top of the other wet washing in the basket that Tolly had made for her in Mr Bryce's workshop and then she stepped outside into the sunshine. Although it was a warm day, Lizzie still shivered coming out from the steamy heat of the wash-house.

At once Lawrence removed his own jacket and slipped it around her shoulders.

'I heard about your father. I'm glad he got back safely.'

Lizzie beamed with pride. 'Yes, wasn't it a wonderful thing to do? All those little boats going across the Channel to rescue all those men off the Dunkirk beaches. And to think my father was there.' She shuddered again, but this time not from the cold. 'And there I was thinking he was perfectly safe somewhere on the Humber or on one of the rivers.'

Dan and his ship had taken part in the humiliating, and yet at the same time, glorious evacuation of Dunkirk. The British troops and their allies had taken their retreat badly, their pride wounded. Yet the way in which the country had rallied to bring thousands home had been a triumph of grit and determination. When the call had gone out for Operation Dynamo, Mr Sudbury, along with many boat owners, had responded with every seaworthy vessel he owned.

'However did he get down to Sheerness?' Lawrence asked. 'I didn't think keels went out to sea.'

'He was towed down there, I think.' She wrinkled her brow and added slowly, 'From what I can make out – though he won't say much about it – not many ships went from as far north as this, but Mr Sudbury and my dad were determined not to be left out.'

'Well, I can sympathize with that. I know how they feel,' Lawrence agreed. 'You must be very proud of your father.'

'Oh, I am.' Then she added jokingly, 'But I'm never going to trust him again when he says he's just going away for a couple of days without me.'

They walked on in silence for a while and when they came to the edge of the wood, she asked him, 'You know when we were younger and used to play here?'

'Mm,' Lawrence said. 'What about it?'

'Well . . .' She hesitated, knowing she might be treading on dangerous ground. Dangerous not only for him, but for her too. 'What were our parents doing?'

He glanced at her and for a moment he looked much older than his fifteen years, much older than she was, even though they were almost the same age. Whilst she did not think herself stupid or ignorant, she could see that he understood the ways of the world far better than she did.

He took hold of her hand and, instead of answering her question at once, he said, 'Let's sit down against this log, shall we? It'll be cooler still in the woods, but it's nice and warm here in the sun.'

As they sat down, side by side, still he did not let go of her hand. His touch was warm and dry and gentle.

'I expect they just sat and talked,' he began hesitantly, but now he was not meeting her eyes.

'Why?' Lizzie was every bit as direct as her grandmother. 'Why would a man like your father – a man in his position – want to spend his time with someone like my mother?'

Now Lawrence smiled. 'Same reason I came to find you today. Because I like you. Because I enjoy being with you and I want to get to know you better.'

'But – but they were both married.'

'That's never troubled my father,' Lawrence said wryly. 'My parents are barely civil to each other now. He's hardly ever at home and when he is, they quarrel. Oh, it's terribly civilized. No raised voices, no shouting. Just icy politeness, sitting at either end of the dinner table with me in between them. Sometimes, the only way they will communicate with each other is through me. You know, "Lawrence, will you ask your father to pass the salt," and "Tell your mother I shall be away on business for the coming week." That sort of thing.' He paused and then, his tone gentle and concerned now, asked, 'What about yours? Do they get on?'

Lizzie stared at him. 'Don't you know?'

'Know? Know what?'

'My mother . . .' She hesitated, choosing her words carefully. If her father had had something to do with her mother's sudden disappearance, Lizzie could unwittingly get him into serious trouble. So she repeated what the family had told her. 'She . . . she went away. Six years ago.' She found she was gripping Lawrence's hand tightly as she went on, haltingly, 'It was my fault. We were at my gran's. All the family was there and one of them, Uncle Duggie I think, was talking about your father's motor car. I didn't think what I was saying and I let it out that we'd had a ride in it. When we got back to the ship my father sent me below to the cabin. And on deck, they had a huge quarrel.' She shuddered as she brought back the dreadful memories of that night and Lawrence put his arm around her shoulders. 'I'd never heard them quarrel like that. Never.' Her voice broke as she finished, 'And then she . . . she went away.'

She had never been able to speak to anyone about that night, not even to Tolly, and yet now she found herself telling this comparative stranger all about it.

With gentle intuition, he said, 'You've kept all that locked inside you all this time, haven't you?'

She nodded.

'And you've no idea what happened to her?'

Pressing her lips together, Lizzie shook her head.

He pulled her to him in a swift, understanding hug. 'Poor you.'

It was nice sitting here in the sunshine with him; the only sound was of birds flying in and out of the trees. It was hot and she felt suddenly sleepy. Everything seemed so quiet and she couldn't remember having felt so at peace for a very long time. Even the war with its blackout and air-raid warnings seemed very far away at this moment.

'I must go,' she said, but with no real conviction.

'Must you?'

'Well . . .' Her eyelids felt heavy. It was so warm and comfortable sitting here in the quiet warmth of the day, resting her head against his shoulder. 'Just a few more minutes then . . .'

Something was tickling her cheek. Sleepily she brushed it away, but then was startled awake by a voice that said, close to her ear, 'Lizzie. I think you should wake up now. You've been asleep an hour.'

Lizzie sat up suddenly and then scrambled to her feet. 'An hour? Oh no! Dad will be miles upriver.'

Lawrence, getting up, said, 'Come on. I'll help you.'

She put out her hand, palm outwards as she said swiftly, 'No. I'll be fine.' Then realizing she had sounded abrupt, added, 'Thanks all the same. It's . . . it's been lovely to see you again. But I must go.'

Even before he had time to say another word, she had whipped his jacket from around her shoulders and flung it at him. Then before he could try to stop her, she was running across the field towards the wash-house. His voice drifted across the growing distance between them. 'I'll see you again, Lizzie.'

Lizzie didn't think she had ever paddled so furiously in her life. As she passed by the shipyard where Tolly now worked, she saw him waving to her from the bank. She sculled nearer and shouted to him. 'Can't stop. I'm late catching up with me dad. See you tomorrow. We'll be back then.'

Even from a distance, she could see the disappointment on his face, but he waved and smiled. 'See you then, Lizzie.'

When at last she caught up with the *Maid Mary Ann*, she was sweating both with the effort and with fear that her father would ask awkward questions.

Lizzie was a very honest girl and would only bend the truth a little if it was to save another's feelings. She would never lie to protect herself. Now, it was her father whom she wished to protect. Instinctively, after what her grandmother had said, she knew he would not be happy that she had spent time in the company of Lawrence Marsh. Deciding that it was best to stick to the truth as near as she could, even if it was not the whole truth, Lizzie said, 'I'm sorry, Dad. I fell asleep.'

'Asleep?'

'It was so warm in the sun when I'd finished the washing, I just sat down and next thing I knew I was waking up without any idea of how long I'd slept. I am sorry.'

Dan was smiling at her now and saying, teasingly, 'Am I supposed to believe that, you little minx? I expect you've been talking to Tolly, eh? Now just you be careful.' He tapped her lightly on her nose. 'Don't you go getting that lad the sack if he's seen talking to you when he should be working.'

Lizzie grinned up at her father. 'No, Dad, I won't.'

'You can hang the washing in the hold, Lizzie. There's room this trip.'

As Lizzie went forward and down into the hold to string lines from one side to the other, she breathed a sigh of relief. Then she opened two or three hatch boards fore and aft so that, as the ship moved forwards, the breeze would dry her lines of washing.

Her father had never minded Lizzie spending time with Tolly and, as long as she caused no trouble for Tolly at his place of work, it seemed Dan still had no objection. She wondered, though, just what his reaction would be if he knew with whom she really had been.

Forty-Five

Three times during the week that followed, Lawrence found her. Once, at the wash-house again and twice, as she sculled down the river, he appeared, on his bicycle, on the bank.

'Are you following me, sir?' she teased as her cog boat, the full-sized one now of course, bumped gently against the muddy bank.

Lawrence smiled. 'Yes.'

Lizzie laughed, delighting in his boldness that held no hint of apology or explanation.

He dismounted and slithered down the bank.

'You'll get muddy,' she warned, but took the hand he held out to her as they scrambled back up the steep slope.

'Now you look a real river urchin, just like me,' she told him.

'But not half as pretty,' he said gallantly. Then his teasing manner sobered as he added, 'Lizzie, I'm going away tomorrow. Back to school.'

'I thought you'd left. I mean, it's term time now, so why have you been at home?'

'The school got bombed and we were all sent home. But now they've fixed up some temporary accommodation, so we've got to go back. But I'll be home again at the end of July, for six weeks then. So,' he said, without any of the usual hesitance in a youth of his age, 'I'll see you then.'

A teasing retort sprang to her lips. She almost said, 'Not if I see you first,' but suddenly she realized that she wanted, more than anything, to see him again.

Lawrence reached out and touched her face, leaving a streak of mud on her cheek. 'You will take care of yourself, won't you? I mean, no going off in your father's ship to rescue soldiers.'

She pulled a wry face. 'I wasn't allowed to go last time.'

'But you would have gone, wouldn't you, if they had let you?'

Without hesitation, she nodded. 'Oh yes, I would.'

'I thought as much. See, I was right. So, I'm asking you, please take care. The bombing's going to get worse, you know.'

'It sounds as if it's you that ought to take care, in case they bomb your school again. Was anyone hurt?'

Lawrence shook his head. 'Not seriously. They'd had some very good shelters built in the grounds and we'd all crowded into them.'

There was a pause and they stood looking at each other until Lawrence said, 'I'm sorry, I'll have to go.'

'So will I,' Lizzie said, but neither of them made a move.

'I'll see you, then. Can I write to you?'

Lizzie thought quickly. 'Best not,' she said and pulled an apologetic face. 'We move about such a lot, you know.' There was only Waterman's Yard as a permanent address for her, and her grandmother was bound to ask questions. Swiftly, Lizzie added, 'Besides, it's only a few weeks until the end of July. You'll soon be home again.'

'Yes, of course,' Lawrence agreed, but the expression on his face seemed to mirror her own feeling that it still seemed an awfully long time. Aloud he said, 'I'll see you then.'

'Right. I ought to be going, too.'

Still, neither of them moved. Then he came towards her, put his arms about her and bent his head to kiss her firmly on the mouth. Surprised, Lizzie gasped. For a youth of only sixteen, he seemed amazingly experienced.

He released her, stepped back and picked up his bicycle. Throwing his leg over the cross bar, he paused a moment to look at her, then he gave a quick nod and began to pedal away. When he reached the far side of the meadow, just before disappearing amongst the trees, he braked, turned and waved once more to her.

Lizzie, standing motionless where he had left her, her fingers against her lips, now raised her hand in return.

At the end of July, Lawrence came home for the school holidays. He was waiting for her outside the wash-house as she sculled from the ship to the wooden landing on the riverbank. Fearfully, Lizzie glanced back to see if her father had seen him, but Dan had gone below to see to the engine.

'How are you? Oh, it's good to see you again, Lizzie. I've missed you. Is everyone all right? All your family?'

'Here . . .' Playfully, she thrust the heavy basket of washing at him. 'You can make yourself useful and carry this.' Then she marched ahead of him to the safety of the wash-house in case her father should reappear on deck.

'So?' he asked again. 'How have you been?'

'Fine, thanks.'

To Lizzie's surprise, Lawrence removed his jacket,

rolled up his shirtsleeves and said, 'Now, what can I do to help?'

Later, as they were walking through the cool shade of the wood, they heard the drone of aircraft overhead. Lawrence stood very still, listening intently. After a moment, he said, 'It's all right, they're ours.'

Lizzie's eyes widened. 'Can you tell just by listening to them?'

'Oh yes. The enemy planes sound very different. Those are British bombers, all right. That's what I'd like to be in when I join up. I want to go into the RAF and train to be a pilot.'

Softly, Lizzie said, 'Then it will be me telling you to take care of yourself, won't it?'

'I s-saw you. I saw you w-with him.'

Tolly's face was a mixture of hurt and anger and anxiety for her.

Lizzie glanced at him, noticing that his stammer was always more pronounced when he was upset or angry.

She almost said, 'Who?' but that would have been silly. She knew very well whom he meant.

'So?' she said, resentful at his intrusion. 'What's it got to do with you?'

The hurt on his face deepened. 'I'm s-sorry,' he mumbled and turned away. At once contrite, Lizzie grabbed his arm. 'No, it's me who should be sorry. I know you're only thinking of me. Sorry, Tolly.'

'He'll only hurt you, Lizzie. He . . . he's not for you.'

'But he's nice, Tolly. I'm sure you'd like him if only you met him.'

Tolly gave a rueful grin. 'I doubt it.'

'Why do you say that? You don't even know him.'

'I know enough about him. If he's anything like his father—'

'You shouldn't judge him by the name his father has got,' Lizzie cut in angrily.

Tolly looked at her strangely. He shook his head slightly. 'You really don't know, do you?'

'Know what?'

'About . . . about his father and your mother.'

'His . . .? My . . .?' she faltered, her eyes widening.

'Before she married your father, there were rumours that she . . . she was involved with Randolph Marsh. She . . . she worked at The Hall then.'

'How do you know all this?'

'M-my mother told me.'

'And how does *she* know?'

Embarrassed, Tolly looked away. 'She's very bitter about your father marrying your mother.'

Lizzie said nothing now, but the question was in her eyes.

'My mother was walking out with your father and he threw her over to marry Mary Ann.' Tolly moved nearer to her and tried to take her hands in his, but she snatched them away. 'I'm sorry. I shouldn't have told you. I thought you knew.'

'No,' Lizzie said slowly. 'It's evidently a big family secret.' Her mind was whirling and the terror which she tried to keep locked away – that her father had had something to do with her mother's disappearance – was pushing its unwelcome way to the forefront of her mind. Was that another terrible family secret?

Lizzie sat down on the bank and Tolly dropped beside her. She plucked absent-mindedly at the grass, her thoughts reeling. Clinging to a desperate hope, she said, 'If I ask you something, will you tell me the truth?'

''Course I will.'

'And will you also promise to tell no one that I've asked you such a thing?'

Tolly nodded.

The question that she had longed to ask for such a long time, but had never dared to voice before, came haltingly. 'Do . . . do you know what happened to my mother?'

His eyes full of compassion, Tolly shook his head. 'I don't think anybody really knows. There's always been a lot of talk, of course.'

'Has there?' None of it had ever reached her ears. Had the family protected her yet again, shielding her from the gossip? The only thing that had ever occurred – and she could never forget it – had been the cruel teasing at school. And then she had been quickly removed from its influence.

Tolly volunteered no more, so she prompted. 'What did they say?'

He shrugged. 'Oh, you know. That she'd run off with someone. That . . . that she'd drowned that night in the river.'

Lizzie shuddered. That was her biggest fear, for if it were true, then her father had been involved in some way, maybe innocently, but he had been there.

Tentatively, Tolly put his arm around her and when she did not throw him off, he held her close. 'Oh Lizzie, I'm sorry. But you do see now, don't you, how it would hurt your family to know that you were – well – meeting Lawrence Marsh?'

'We're only friends,' she murmured, but immediately in her mind's eye was his face – a face she knew already so intimately.

'You're going to go on seeing him, then?'

'It's not fair to judge him by his father,' she burst out angrily again and, before she could stop herself, she added, 'Can you be blamed for what your father does?'

Tolly looked as if she had physically slapped him in the face and immediately, she said again, 'Oh Tolly, I'm sorry.' She touched his face with her hand and he put his own over the top of it and held it, pressed to his cheek.

'You're right, of course,' he whispered. 'But I just don't want to see you get hurt. I couldn't bear it if . . .' He turned his head away from her and his voice was muffled as he added, 'If he ever hurt you. If he does, he'll have me to reckon with. And you can tell him that.' Then, with a sudden, coltish movement, Tolly kissed her. It was a clumsy, boyish bump against her cheek, rather than a kiss and, pulling back, his face flushed, he mumbled, 'Sorry.'

Before she could say a word, he scrambled to his feet and stumbled away.

Forty-Six

As the months went by, trade returned slowly to the River Trent and now the *Maid Mary Ann* was as busy as she ever had been. The Humberside ports were prime targets for enemy bombers, and stocks of food and other goods were moved to inland ports. The warehouses along the Trent, and particularly those at Elsborough, soon became storehouses for food and other essential items.

The engineering works in the town now produced the weapons of war.

'Do you know,' Lawrence told Lizzie excitedly, 'one of the firms in our town is building a gunner's turret that's going to be used on bombers?'

And, quite separately, Tolly said, 'We're working continuous shifts at the shipyard now, building barges and small coasters.'

In the town, the queues, caused by food rationing, grew longer.

'There's a British Restaurant opening in town,' Bessie told Lizzie, 'but they say the meat they use is whalemeat.' She pulled a face. 'Reckon I'll stick to fish and chips from our chippy. At least they haven't rationed that yet.'

It wasn't until 1941 that Elsborough got its own real taste of the Blitz, and bombs fell quite close to Waterman's Yard, but, thankfully, never in it. The Ruddick family had one narrow escape however. Aboard the *Maid Mary Ann*, Dan and Lizzie were approaching the town to moor at Miller's Wharf when a bomb fell into the river a hundred yards or so ahead of them. Dan stopped the engine as the swell of the ripples reached them.

'I'm going to drop anchor right here, Lizzie,' Dan said. 'I'm not going to risk going over that. We'll wait until morning.'

They waited through the night, but no explosion occurred. Only at daylight did they, very gingerly, dare to proceed to the wharf, holding their breath, as they sailed over the place where the bomb had fallen.

'I expect it's buried itself deep in the mud.'

'Will it explode?' Lizzie asked, leaning over the side to look into the murky water.

'Who knows?' was all Dan could say. 'It's a risk we'll all have to take.'

In May, enemy bombers dropped their bombs on a village on the Nottinghamshire side of the Trent. Speculation as to the reason for this was varied. Some believed that the enemy aircraft had seen the short stretch of light-coloured dual carriageway that ran through the village shining in the moonlight and had thought it to be the river. Accordingly, they had dropped their bombs on to farmland and isolated houses, believing that they were targeting the Elsborough factories. Others thought that the bombers had followed the railway line to the village and, when this disappeared abruptly, had calculated that they must be over an industrial area. Dropping incendiaries to illuminate the zone, they had accidentally ignited a dry gorse fox covert and, thinking they had hit something big, had then dropped their 'heavies'. But one ARP Warden on duty in Elsborough that brilliant, moonlit night insisted that he had seen an enemy pathfinder circling over the town and that an RAF night fighter had pursued it westwards over the River Trent. The enemy aircraft had then jettisoned its incendiary bombs, which resulted in the fires that led the larger force of enemy aircraft arriving later to bomb the burning area.

The village was relatively unscathed, although the railway line was hit, but one farmhouse about a mile outside was severely damaged. Watchers said later that the house seemed to jump up in the air when a landmine buried itself in the grass field a hundred yards or so away. A mother and her two children were the only occupants of the house, the father being away on night work.

'They'll not survive that,' the villagers said, but miraculously, the mother, hearing smaller bombs dropping earlier, had taken the children downstairs. As the huge landmine descended, whining through the night sky, she pushed the children under the kitchen table and crawled beneath it herself. The blast was terrifying, shattering every window in the house, breaking crockery and blowing doors off their hinges. Surrounded by broken glass and covered in soot that had been blasted down the chimney, the family stayed there for the remainder of the night.

'Poor things,' Bessie said, when she heard the story. 'They got it instead of us. Thank the good Lord they're not hurt.'

His shadow filling the doorway of the wash-house, Lawrence said for the umpteenth time that summer, 'Come for a walk?'

'I shouldn't really.' Lizzie's eyes twinkled at him. 'But I will.'

His face seemed to light up with pleasure. 'You little minx. You do like teasing folk, don't you?' He balanced himself on the balls of his feet. 'Come on, I'll race you to the woods.'

She dropped the wet sheet back into the rinsing tub, splashing her apron, but she scarcely noticed as she ran to the door and began to race after him across the meadow behind the wash-house and towards Raven's Wood.

Breathless and laughing, she fell into his arms. 'That's not fair. You had a head start.'

His arms were tightly around her and he was looking down into her eyes, his face serious now. 'Oh Lizzie, Lizzie, how I love you.'

And then he was kissing her as if he would never stop.

When, at last, they paused for breath, Lawrence whispered, 'Let's find our den, deep in the woods. Let's make it our own special place.'

Hand in hand, they went deeper amongst the trees until the sunlight was almost blotted out.

'Where is it? I can't remember.'

'No, I can't.' He stopped and looked about him, then leading her towards a clump of bushes, he added, 'But this will do . . .' Pulling aside the foliage, she saw that the centre of the undergrowth had been cleared. A blanket was spread on the ground and to one side stood a picnic hamper.

Through the dimness, she stared at him. 'Lawrence Marsh, you've planned this.'

He was smiling at her, sure and confident, but Lizzie's eyes narrowed thoughtfully as she said bluntly, 'I hope you're not thinking of trying anything.'

Lawrence laughed. 'Would I?' But his jocular sarcasm implied that he meant to do just that. She stepped into the clearing and he allowed the branches he was holding to fall back into place. Now they were cocooned, deep in the heart of the wood with only the birds for company.

'Champagne, madam?' Lawrence said, kneeling and throwing back the lid of the basket with a flourish.

Lizzie gasped. 'Wherever . . .?'

'Raided my father's cellar. I'm getting rather good at it.'

He pulled out a bottle, dusted it. It opened with a loud, echoing pop, startling birds who rose into the air calling alarm to each other. The liquid frothed out of the neck of the bottle as he tipped it into a narrow glass.

'I've never tasted champagne before,' Lizzie said, as she sat on the rug, took the glass and sipped the sparkling liquid.

'Well, life with me will be one long taste of champagne.' He filled his own glass and sat down beside her. Then, touching her glass with his own, Lawrence said, 'Here's to us, Lizzie.'

They ate cold chicken legs and hardboiled eggs with lettuce and tomatoes. There were even individual trifles in small glass bowls.

'Who packed all this up for you? Your mother?'

'Heavens, no. My mother wouldn't be seen dead in the kitchen. No, I smiled nicely at Cook and she packed it all up in a basket that I could carry on the back of my bicycle.'

Lizzie giggled and then hiccuped. 'Fancy having servants that you can just order to do whatever you want them to. Oh dear, I feel all funny. My head's sort of woozy.'

Lawrence took her glass and set it on the ground. 'There, lie back and close your eyes.' He lay down and put out his arm. 'Rest your head on my arm.'

'Mm,' she murmured, drowsily. 'This is nice. So cool out of the sun. I could stay here all day.'

'Then,' Lawrence was leaning over her now, 'why don't

we?' He bent his head and kissed her, gently at first but then with a growing ardour. 'Lizzie, oh Lizzie. I want you so much. Please, let me . . .' He was unfastening the buttons of her blouse and slipping his hand inside.

'No!' At once Lizzie was fully awake. She pushed his hand away and sat up. She looked round at him angrily, but Lawrence only lay there, his hands behind his head, smiling up at her. 'I'm not that sort of girl,' she said crossly. 'If that's what you're after, then you can find someone else.'

'I don't want anyone else, Lizzie,' he said lazily. 'I want you. I always have.'

'Well, not without a ring on my finger. And a wedding ring at that.'

She began to scramble to her feet, but he caught hold of her and pulled her down again so that she landed on top of him. 'I love you when you're angry, it makes me want you all the more. So, Lizzie Ruddick, will you marry me?'

'What? You're not serious.'

He put his arms around her, holding her to him. 'Lizzie, I love you. I want to marry you. Say you'll marry me. Please?'

Lizzie's heart somersaulted. 'Oh Lawrence. You know we can't. Your family would never allow it.'

His face darkened. 'My family aren't going to rule me. I can promise you that. I've no intention of having a marriage like my parents. I'm going to marry for love. It's you I love, Lizzie, and you love me, don't you? I know you do. Let me hear you say it. Please, darling Lizzie?'

Suddenly, overcome with tenderness, she stroked his hair and said, 'I do love you, Lawrence, but we're so young. We couldn't possibly marry until we're of age. They wouldn't let us.'

'We could run away.'

She laughed at the thought. 'Elope, you mean?'

Lawrence was serious. 'Yes, why not?'

But Lizzie was still teasing. 'To Gretna Green?'

He gripped her arms excitedly. 'I don't think we'd have to go as far as that. There are couples getting married all the time now in a hurry. Because of the war, I mean. Maybe we could find someone who wouldn't ask too many questions.'

'But we're only seventeen.'

His face sobered. 'I know and next year, I'll be called up. If I'm old enough to die for my country, then surely I'm old enough to get married.'

She laid her cheek against his chest and heard the beat of his heart, loud in her ear. 'Oh Lawrence, don't say such things. Don't even think them.'

He stroked her hair and whispered, 'I mean it, Lizzie. I have never been more serious about anything in the whole of my life. I love you and I want to marry you. And soon.'

A little later as they emerged from the shadow of the trees, brushing leaves and grass from their clothes, a man on a bicycle rode along the pathway that ran alongside the woods.

'Hello, Lizzie. All right?'

Startled, Lizzie looked up as the man passed close by them. He winked at her and then nodded knowingly towards Lawrence.

'Oh yes, thank you,' Lizzie said weakly to the retreating figure. As he rode away, the man was whistling, and the strains of 'Who were you with last night?' reached Lizzie.

When he was out of earshot, she sank to the ground as her legs gave way beneath her. She closed her eyes and groaned. 'Oh no.'

Lawrence dropped to his haunches beside her and stared at her in concern. 'What is it? Have you hurt yourself? Did you twist your ankle, or something?'

'No, no. But, that was Mr Horberry.'

'So?'

'His wife is only the biggest gossip in Elsborough and they happen to live in Waterman's Yard.'

Forty-Seven

'What's Gran doing on the wharf, Dad?'

Lizzie's sharp eyes had already spotted the lonely figure of Bessie standing on the edge of the wharf where the *Maid Mary Ann* was expected to dock. Throughout her childhood the sight of her grandmother waiting for them had not been unusual, but now, since her bad legs kept her almost a prisoner within Waterman's Yard, she hardly ever came to greet them.

As soon as the ship bumped gently against the planking, Lizzie scrambled ashore. 'Gran? Are you all right?'

'No, I'm not all right.' Bessie was seething with anger as she wagged her finger in her granddaughter's face. 'Not if what I've been hearing from Phyllis is right. And don't lie to me, girl, like your mother used to do.'

Lizzie returned the older woman's stare steadily. Quietly, she said, 'No, Gran, I won't lie to you, if you'll promise to believe me.'

'Ah, so you do know what it's about then?'

Lizzie nodded.

There was a pause before Bessie agreed, 'Very well, then. But you'd best come home. I aren't washing me dirty linen in public for the world and his wife to hear.'

Lizzie felt her grandmother's fingers, still surprisingly strong in their grip, grasp her arm. 'Come on.'

'Lizzie. Lizzie, where are you going? I could use a bit of help here.'

She glanced back over her shoulder towards her father, but before she could answer him, Bessie turned and shouted, 'She's coming with me, Dan. There's things we've got to talk about.'

'Can't it wait? We—'

'No, lad, it can't wait.'

'What's the matter? Is something wrong?' Now Dan was worried.

'I hope not, lad,' his mother said darkly. 'But that's what I aim to find out.'

Without waiting for any further protest, Bessie began to move away, grunting at the pain in her legs, but still keeping fast hold of her granddaughter. 'You just come with me, m'girl.'

Meekly, Lizzie went.

'Now then,' Bessie began as she sank into her armchair with obvious relief. 'Are you going to tell me what's been going on or shall I tell you what I've heard?'

'It's about Lawrence, isn't it?'

Bessie nodded.

Lizzie licked her lips. 'Well, it's true I've been meeting him and going for walks with him . . .'

'And?'

'And he's kissed me.'

'That all?'

Lizzie's eyes widened. 'Yes, Gran. I promise you. Except . . .'

'Go on.' The anger had not left Bessie's face.

'Except that the last time I saw him, he told me he loves me and . . . and that he wants to marry me.'

Bessie snorted. 'Did he, indeed? I hope you weren't daft enough to fall for that sort of talk.'

When Lizzie did not answer, Bessie sighed. 'Oh Lizzie, love. His sort don't marry the likes of us.' She wiped a tear from her eye as she murmured, 'Your poor mam could have told you that.'

'That's what I told him,' Lizzie said.

'You did?' Bessie's face brightened and some of the strain left her features. 'There, I knew you were a sensible girl. Oh, but you had me worried, 'specially when Phyllis said her Tom had seen you together coming out of Raven's Wood.' She frowned severely again as she asked, 'And were you, like he said, buttoning your blouse and him pulling up his trousers?'

Lizzie gasped. 'No, we weren't. Brushing the grass off our clothes, mebbe, but we'd only been kissing and cuddling. Nothing more, I swear.' Her eyes glittered with anger too now. 'I'm not that daft, Gran.'

'Aye well, there's no harm in that, as long as that's all it was.' Bessie smiled suddenly. 'I wasn't past a bit of kissing and cuddling in me day, neither. But don't you tell your grandpa that.' She wagged her finger again at Lizzie, but this time her mood was playful. 'And it never went any further than that. Your grandpa's the only man I've ever – you know – with, and I happen to be proud of the fact. And if you take my advice, m'girl, you'll not let any man have his way with you until you've got a wedding ring firmly on your finger. Oh they'll sweet talk you, ask you to prove that you love them and all that, but when it's over, they've no respect for you then.'

Lizzie was quiet. She knew her grandmother was right, but she still couldn't think that Lawrence would treat her so shabbily even if she did allow him to make love to her.

She felt Bessie's keen gaze on her. 'So, lass, are you going to promise me that you won't see Master Lawrence again?'

Lizzie returned her grandmother's gaze steadily. Quietly, she said, 'No, Gran, I can't promise you that. You see, I think I'm in love with him too. And if he asks me to marry him again, I'm going to say, "yes".'

The lines on Bessie's face seemed to sag. She shook her head and closed her eyes. 'Oh Lizzie, you'll break your poor dad's heart. You can't do it, lass. You just can't.'

'So what was all that about?' Dan wanted to know the moment Lizzie set foot back on board. 'Is everything all right? No one's ill, are they?'

'No,' Lizzie answered, trying to keep her voice light. 'Everyone's fine.'

'So what was all the secrecy and the hurry?' The smile that was not often evident these days lit his face briefly and drove away, for a moment, the sadness that rarely left his eyes. 'I bet Phyllis Horberry had a choice bit of gossip to impart, was that it?'

Lizzie stared at her father, her eyes widening, but then she realized that he was just joking. He couldn't possibly know how very near the truth he was. She took a deep breath. She'd never have a better opening and, knowing that she would have to tell him – wanted to tell him herself before someone else did – Lizzie said, 'As a matter of fact, it was about something Phyllis had found out . . .'

The dark, haunted look was back in his eyes and the smile was gone from his face. His frown deepened as she added, 'About me.'

'You? What on earth could Phyllis Horberry find to gossip about you?' Then his face cleared and he actually laughed as he said, 'Oh, you and Tolly, I suppose. Is that all?'

'No, Dad,' Lizzie said, trying to tell him as gently as

363

possible, but there was no easy way. 'Not me and Tolly. Me and Lawrence Marsh.'

There was a moment's silence, save for the sounds of the river all around them.

'Oh no. I don't believe it. No, oh no. My God! Not again.'

'Dad, please listen to me. Let me explain . . .'

'Where've you been meeting him, eh?' He took a step towards her and grasped her roughly by the shoulders.

'Dad, you're hurting me,' Lizzie squirmed in his hold.

'Tell me where?'

'In . . . in Raven's Wood.'

'You'll keep away from there. Do you hear me?' He shook her to emphasize his command. 'You're not to go anywhere near those woods.' Then, in what sounded almost like an afterthought, he added, 'And him. You'll keep away from him, an' all. From this moment, you will not leave your grandmother's house or this ship without someone – another member of the family – with you. Do you hear me? You are never, ever, to see him again.'

'Dad, please . . .'

'Not another word.'

He released her, turned and strode along the deck away from her as if he could not put a distance between them fast enough.

Lizzie watched him go, tears blurring her vision. She felt so alone. There was no one she could turn to. 'Oh, Uncle Duggie, I wish you were here,' she murmured. 'You'd understand, wouldn't you? You'd help me?'

And then she thought of Tolly. Tolly was her friend. He would understand. She must find Tolly.

*

When the cargo had been off-loaded, and she and her father had eaten their supper in the cabin amid a stony, uneasy silence, Lizzie lifted her chin and said, 'I'm going out in the cog boat. I'm going to find Tolly.'

Her father glowered and said gruffly, 'All right then. Just so long as you give me your word that it is Tolly you're going to meet.'

Lizzie's brown eyes regarded him steadily. 'Yes, Dad. It is.'

His voice was no more than a whisper, but there was a threat in his words. 'Don't you ever lie to me, Lizzie. Don't you *ever* lie to me.' And the unspoken words lay between them 'or else'.

Lizzie shuddered inwardly and the nightmare fears were back. Her mother had lied to him and then she had disappeared.

Lizzie sculled downriver until she came level with the shipyard where Tolly worked. She saw his small rowing boat moored beside the landing and manoeuvred hers alongside it. She did not have long to wait before she heard the hooter sound and saw the men begin to pack up for the day. Then she heard Tolly's boots clomping along the wooden boarding of the landing and saw him looking down at her.

'Lizzie!' Delight spread over his face and he jumped down into his boat and together they rowed away from the yard, a little way downstream. Then they rested, Tolly leaning on his oars.

'I haven't half missed you this summer. I expect you've been busy now you're full-time mate for your dad. And of course, I've been working long hours, but I have missed us going fishing and blackberrying and, oh just everything.' He brushed back the untidy flop of hair from his forehead and added, 'So where are we going tonight then? What about—?'

'Tolly,' she interrupted. 'Please, listen. We are friends, aren't we? I mean, you've always been my very best friend.'

The boy, several months younger than Lizzie, coloured. ''Course we are. Don't be daft.'

'So, if I tell you something, you will try to understand? You will be on my side?'

There was a sudden wariness in his eyes. 'I s-suppose so.'

'I've been meeting Lawrence Marsh. Tolly, we've fallen in love and we want to get married, but—'

'Married!' Tolly's harsh tone and the shock on his face were almost worse than either her grandmother's or even her father's. 'Marry him? You must be out of your mind.'

Shocked, she saw that there were tears in his eyes. 'Tolly, listen to me, please. I need your help. Will you find Lawrence for me? I must see him. I've got to talk to him.'

He pressed his lips together into a hard, tight line. 'No,' he said shortly. 'I won't.'

Lizzie gaped at him. 'You won't?'

'No, I won't. Lizzie, forget him. He's no good for you.'

'Don't you start. I've had enough from everyone else. I thought I could count on you. I thought you were my friend.'

'I am your friend. That's why I'm saying what I'm saying. And if everyone else is saying the same, doesn't that tell you something?'

Tears of rage started in her eyes. 'It tells me that not one of my family, nor even my best friend, wants me to be happy.'

'We do. That's all we want. You know that, Lizzie. But he won't make you happy. Not in a million years.'

Angrily, she picked up her oar and stood up in the cog boat. As she began to work the oar and the boat began to move away from his, she cried, 'I should have known better than to come to you. What would you know about being in love, Tolly Oliver? You're too young to understand.'

Then she turned her back on him and began to scull her way back up the river.

'Lizzie, Lizzie, wait . . .'

She heard him calling her, heard the anguish in his tone, but she did not look back, not once, for she knew he would be sitting there in his boat, watching her go, looking lost and forlorn.

She did not dare to look back and, for the first time in her life, Lizzie hardened her heart against Tolly.

Forty-Eight

The following week there was another occasion when Lizzie was not able to accompany her father aboard the *Maid Mary Ann*.

'You'll stay here with your grandmother and you will not leave the yard,' her father commanded. 'At least that's one thing I can be sure of. He won't come here looking for you.'

But Dan was wrong. The day after the *Maid Mary Ann* left for Hull, Lawrence knocked on the door of Bessie's house in Waterman's Yard. Lizzie, unsuspecting, opened the door. Startled to see him there, all she could utter was a surprised, 'Oh!'

Behind him, across the yard, she could see that already Minnie was standing in her doorway and Gladys was shaking a feather duster out of an upstairs window with such vigour that all the feathers threatened to come loose and flutter down into the yard. Their voices drifted across to her.

'Posh company yon lass is keeping now, ain't she, Min?'

'That's right, Glad. Bessie'll have to get her best tea set out to entertain young Mester Marsh.'

Recovering her senses, Lizzie pulled him inside. 'Come in, quick.'

She was thrilled to see him, bowled over to think that he had come to Waterman's Yard to see her, yet she asked sharply, 'Whatever have you come here for?'

'Well, that's a fine way to welcome your fiancé when he comes a-courting.' Lawrence was smiling at her, his eyes sparkling with teasing laughter. 'I'm relieved to see you're all right. I was worried when you didn't come to the wash-house yesterday.'

'You went there? You waited for me?'

'Of course I did. I saw your father's ship go by but you never came.'

'Lizzie,' Bessie's voice came from the kitchen. 'Who is it? Who's that you're talking to?'

'You'd better go,' Lizzie whispered. 'They've found out. I'm not allowed to see you.'

'Not allowed . . .?' Lawrence began. 'Oh well, in that case, I'll just come in and have a word with your grandmother.'

Before Lizzie could make a move to prevent him, Lawrence had stepped through the scullery and into the kitchen and was moving into the room, his hand outstretched in greeting. 'Mrs Ruddick, I trust I find you well.'

If the moment had not been so serious, Lizzie would have been convulsed with laughter at the look of astonishment on her grandmother's face.

'Well, he's got a nerve, I'll give him that.'

Bessie was lying back in her armchair as the door closed behind Lawrence and they heard his footsteps crossing the yard.

Lizzie sat down opposite her grandmother. She smoothed sweaty palms down her skirt. 'Don't you think he's nice, Gran?'

'He's very polite, but it's all fine talk, Lizzie love.'

Lizzie felt the stab of disappointment like a physical pain. 'Oh Gran, I thought you liked him. You've been sat here talking and laughing with him for more than half an hour.'

'He's nice enough, I grant you. Takes after his auntie, I expect.'

'There you are, then.'

'But that doesn't mean I want you to have anything to do with him, because I don't. I've told you before, Lizzie, it's not on. And what your dad'll say when he knows he's actually had the nerve to come here and me entertaining him in here an' all. He'll have me guts for garters. I must be getting soft in me old age. And what Miss Edwina will say if she gets to hear about it, I don't know. She'll be horrified.'

Lizzie's heart sank. Was no one, not even her dear friend, Tolly, on her side? But she shied away from thinking about Tolly. It was strange, but his disapproval hurt her more than anyone else's, more even than her father's.

'Of course I had to be civil to the lad. He was a guest in my house, but I left him in no doubt as to how we feel, now didn't I?'

Lizzie, the lump in her throat growing, merely nodded, for her grandmother's parting words to Lawrence had been, 'I'm sorry, lad, but her dad won't allow her to see you and there's an end to it.'

Miss Edwina called the following afternoon, but it was Bessie who was in for a surprise.

'So,' Edwina began, sitting down and withdrawing her gloves from her elegant fingers. 'You don't think my nephew's good enough for your granddaughter, Bessie?'

'Eh?' Bessie gaped at her visitor whilst Lizzie stood

quietly behind her grandmother's chair listening to the exchange, amazed herself at what she was hearing.

Calmly, Edwina went on. 'I understand that Lawrence wishes to marry Lizzie, but that you, and I presume Dan, too, object. Quite violently according to Lawrence. I believe you have forbidden Lizzie to see him. Isn't that a little extreme, Bessie?'

'Well, I never did.' Bessie was open-mouthed with astonishment. 'You of all people, Miss Edwina. Why, it was you who put a stop to all that business between Mary Ann and your brother and yet now you seem to be condoning what's going on between his son and her daughter.'

'It's completely different and you know it is, Bessie. Lawrence is very different from his father. Randolph was a rake and I knew he would only hurt Mary Ann.'

Lizzie watched as the two women exchanged a long look, before Edwina went on more briskly, 'But this is different. Very different. Lawrence is a good boy. He's not the sort to lead a girl on and besides . . .' She glanced up at Lizzie now and smiled. 'I don't think your granddaughter is the sort to allow herself to be "led on", do you?'

Bessie snorted. 'Huh, she's her mother's daughter too, don't forget.'

'Gran . . .?' Lizzie began, but Bessie only snapped, 'Be quiet, miss, and speak when you're spoken too.'

Lizzie bit her lip and retreated to sit in a chair by the window, although she could still hear every word that was being said.

'I'm sorry, Miss Edwina,' Bessie was saying stiffly, aware that the years of their friendship could be wiped out in a single moment. 'But Dan and the whole family are against this. There's no more to be said.'

'So, you're going to deny these young people a chance of happiness?'

'They wouldn't be happy, Miss Edwina. Are you going to tell me that your nephew would go and live on a boat with Lizzie?'

'Of course not. She would go to live at The Hall.'

Bessie's reply was grim. 'Exactly. And how do you think she would fit in there?' She leant forwards towards her visitor. 'Our sort are servants at The Hall, not mistresses of it.' With blunt sarcasm, she added, 'Unless it's the other sort of "mistress" he wants.'

Calmly, refusing to be goaded, Edwina said, 'I think that's the root of the matter. You don't really believe that he intends to marry her.' She stood up. 'Well, I'm very disappointed, Bessie. I had thought that in this uncertain world you would have allowed two young people a little happiness.' She stood looking down at the older woman as she added softly, 'Lawrence will be called up very soon now and who knows what will happen then.'

'And you'd have her left a widow? Mebbe with a child?'

Slowly, Edwina nodded, 'Yes, I would. If I had had the chance, I would have married Christopher and had his child. At least I would have had something, instead of a lifetime of loneliness.'

'That's as maybe,' Bessie's tone was still harsh. 'But you've money behind you. You would never have had to struggle to raise a child. It'd have been easy for you. What would she do, eh, left with a bairn?'

Edwina's face turned white and, shocked, she whispered, 'That's a cruel thing to say, Bessie. Cruel and heartless. I'd never have thought it of you.'

Unrepentant, Bessie said, 'I've never been one to shirk the truth, Miss Edwina, not even when it hurts.'

Edwina let out a shuddering sigh as she said flatly, 'I'm sorry, more sorry than you'll ever know, after all the years we've known each other and been friends. We have been friends, haven't we, Bessie?'

Lizzie could hear the sorrow in Edwina's voice, and her grandmother must be feeling it too, she thought as she watched and listened, for Bessie only nodded as if she did not trust herself to speak now.

Edwina went on. 'I'm sorry we have to part like this. Please think it over. Because you are wrong about Lawrence, truly you are.'

Lingering just a moment longer, Edwina stretched out a trembling hand to touch Bessie's shoulder, but the older woman remained seated in her chair, her head bowed, and did not utter a farewell or even look up as Edwina left the house. Only when she had been gone several minutes, and Lizzie got up from her chair and went to sit opposite her grandmother, did Bessie look at her, tears in her old eyes, and say bitterly, 'See what trouble you've caused? You've lost me one of the dearest friends I ever had.'

With a sob, Lizzie jumped up and ran from the house, through the yard and out into the street. For once, Bessie made no attempt to call her back.

Forty-Nine

Lizzie knocked at the back door of The Hall.

'Is Lawrence here?' she asked the young kitchen maid, who opened the door.

The girl gaped at her. 'The young master, you mean?'

'I suppose so, yes.'

'Wait a minute, miss. I'll ask Cook.'

The girl looked flustered, wondering why someone dressed as poorly as Lizzie and coming to the back entrance should be asking to speak to the young master and calling him 'Lawrence' in such a familiar way too. Understanding the girl's dilemma, Lizzie smiled to herself as she realized her own mistake. She should have walked boldly up to the main entrance, where the door would no doubt have been opened by a manservant.

'Come in, please, miss. Cook says she'll have a word with you.'

Lizzie stepped into the warm kitchen, where the smell of freshly baking bread was like a heady perfume.

'So,' the cook began without preamble. 'You're her daughter, are you? Setting your cap at the young master like your mother before you, eh?'

Lizzie drew herself up. 'Is that any of your business?'

'Oho, Miss Hoity Toity. Just like your mother, aren't you? You even look like her. Well, she came to a bad end, didn't she? And you will, an' all. You mark my words. And yes, anything that goes on in this house is my

374

business. When your mother worked here, she caused us all a lot of trouble. I got a right roasting from Miss Edwina for not having kept me eye on her. I'll never forget that. So you can turn yourself about and get out of my kitchen.'

Lizzie glanced about her. There were several doors leading out of the kitchen, presumably to pantries and cellars and store cupboards, but which one, she wondered, led to the upper part of the house?

'Do you hear me? If you know what's good for you, you'll be on your way and . . .'

At that moment one of the doors opened and a man, dressed like a butler, appeared. Lizzie sprang forward, dodged beneath his outstretched arm and was through the door before anyone could scarcely draw breath.

She entered a vast hall and stood a moment to stare around her in fascination. Then, behind her, she heard the sound of the man following her and she hurried on again, running the length of the room. She scampered along passages and up staircases, her heart thumping and yet she was enjoying the game of hide and seek. It was a wonderful old house, with nooks and crannies and plenty of hiding places. How the children of the house must have loved their games within its walls, she thought. What fun, what glorious fun life must be like to live in a place like this.

Her pace was slower now, for she had given the butler, or whoever he was, the slip and now she had time to peep into the rooms on either side and to marvel at the solid furniture and oil paintings hanging on the walls. In one room, she saw an embroidered wall hanging.

'Miss Edwina's been busy,' she murmured to herself, and then a door at the end of the passage opened.

'Lizzie.' She heard his voice and turned to see him coming towards her, his arms outstretched.

She ran to him and threw herself against him. 'Oh Lawrence, I had to come. Please don't be angry.'

'Angry? My darling, I'm delighted. I couldn't think how to get to see you, if you were being held prisoner by the dragon.'

'The . . .?' she began. 'Lawrence, please, don't call my gran that. She's wonderful, really. It's just that she doesn't think . . .'

'I know, I know. I'm sorry. I didn't mean to be rude towards her. But they won't listen to us, will they?'

The manservant was hurrying down the corridor towards them. 'Master Lawrence, I'm so sorry you've been troubled. I really don't know what Cook was thinking of to even let a gypsy woman into the house.' His voice was harsh as he spoke now directly to Lizzie. 'Come along, young woman . . .'

He was already stretching out his hand to take hold of her by the shoulder when Lawrence put up his hand. 'It's quite all right, Deakin. Miss Ruddick is a friend of mine.' Pointedly, he added, 'A very good friend. In fact, if I have my way, she could well be your future mistress at The Hall.'

For a moment, the man's face was a picture, and it was a credit to his professionalism that he managed with a supreme effort to mask his feelings, give a little bow and say, obsequiously, 'I am so sorry, sir. I had not realized. Pray forgive my intrusion.'

He turned away and marched, stiff backed, down the corridor whilst both Lawrence and Lizzie fought to stifle their laughter.

'Come in here. We won't be disturbed.'

He led her into the room at the end of the corridor. Intrigued, Lizzie glanced around. It was Lawrence's bedroom.

'Now my reputation will be in tatters,' she teased, but nevertheless she allowed him to lead her to the window seat. They sat together, holding hands.

'Oh Lizzie, let me look at you. It seems ages since I saw you.'

'I must look a mess.' She tried to smooth her tangled hair and scrubbed at her face. 'No wonder he thought I was a gypsy.'

'Darling, have you been crying?' Tenderly, he touched her face with his fingers and then drew her into his arms.

'They're all against us, Lawrence, everyone. At least, everyone except your Aunt Edwina.'

'Aunt Edwina?'

She drew back from him a little and looked up into his face. 'She came to see my grandmother. Came to plead our cause.'

Lawrence's eyes lit up. 'She did?'

Lizzie nodded. 'Yes, but she didn't get anywhere. They . . . they fell out. After all these years, they quarrelled and I feel so guilty about us being the cause of it.'

'They'll get over it,' Lawrence said, airily unconcerned. 'But don't let's waste precious time talking about them. Oh Lizzie, I've missed you so much.' He held her close again. 'I want to be with you for every minute of every day.'

He stood up and pulled her to her feet. Then he was kissing her, with an urgency that made her gasp. 'Darling . . .' he whispered and she felt his hands begin to caress her waist. His fingers moved up to unfasten the buttons of her blouse and with his other arm he was pulling her across the room towards the canopied old-fashioned four-poster bed.

'No, Lawrence, no.'

His eyes were ablaze with passion. 'Why, Lizzie? Why

not? I love you and we're going to be married. We're engaged now. Or as good as. I thought you loved me.'

'I do, you know I do, but . . .'

'Then prove it. Prove you love me as much as I love you. Oh, I want you so much. I've dreamed about this moment. Please, Lizzie . . .'

She pulled away from him, with tears of frustration. She wanted him too, just as much, but there were tears of bitter disappointment too. 'You're just like they said. That's all you want. You don't love me. Not really, or you wouldn't ask.'

Her words were like a douse of cold water to him. 'What do you mean? I don't understand.'

She was crying openly now. 'If I let you, you'd hate me afterwards.'

'I wouldn't. I swear I wouldn't.'

'Well, I'd hate myself and probably you too. I'm not going to give you or anyone else the chance to say that I'm just like my mother.'

'Lizzie, oh Lizzie.' She could see that his dismay was genuine as he reached out for her again, but this time only to take her gently in his arms to comfort her. 'I'd never even think such a thing.'

Her sobs, muffled against him now, began to subside as he stroked her hair and murmured, 'Then we'll be married, my darling. As soon as I can arrange something, we'll be married.'

She lifted her face to his. 'Oh Lawrence. Darling Lawrence, you really do love me.'

As he bent his head to kiss her once more, he whispered against her mouth, 'Never doubt it for a moment, my dearest love.'

Fifty

Lizzie was lucky that neither her grandmother nor her father, when he returned home, asked her if she had seen Lawrence. She didn't want to lie to them and, had they asked her outright, she would not have done so. She would have told them the truth. But, as they did not ask, she did not volunteer the information.

Her father, often morose and distant in the years since her mother had gone, was even more silent than usual. He very rarely smiled now and requests to her aboard ship became orders. It was as if she were merely an employed mate rather than his beloved daughter.

They made a trip to Newark where the ship was laid up for three days whilst necessary repairs and painting were carried out. Normally, her father would have suggested she stay at home, in Waterman's Yard, but this time he insisted she went with him, and she spent a miserable three days in a small hotel in the town with nothing to do, whilst her father was busy at the boatyard. Even when he was with her, they hardly spoke to each other.

When they set sail downriver once more, it was a relief.

'We're going straight through to the Humber,' her father said, 'before we go home.' Lizzie glanced at him, but said nothing. She could hardly ever remember a time when they had passed by Elsborough without calling.

Only when they were being towed in the days before they had an engine had they not stopped.

It was all a deliberate ploy, Lizzie fumed inwardly, to keep her away from Lawrence. He would be returning to boarding school soon. His father was adamant that he should sit his higher school certificate before joining the RAF.

'I'm not going back,' Lawrence had told her, but Lizzie believed that, when the time came, he would have no more choice in the matter than she had in obeying her father.

The trip to Hull was uneventful and on their return home, as they neared the Miller's Wharf, Lizzie could see her grandmother standing there.

'Oh, not again,' she breathed and sighed, bracing herself for more trouble. 'I suppose she's heard that I went to The Hall. Better get it over with, I suppose.'

No doubt, Lizzie thought to herself, Phyllis had heard the choice bit of gossip about this gypsy girl knocking at the back door of The Hall, demanding to see the young master. But as she jumped ashore and moved towards Bessie, Lizzie could see there was something dreadfully wrong. Something far worse had happened. Tears streamed down the old lady's face and she suddenly looked even older than her sixty-six years.

Lizzie stretched out her arms towards her. 'What is it? What's happened? Is . . . is it Grandpa?'

Unable to speak, Bessie shook her head. She clung to Lizzie and pressed her face into the girl's shoulder, sobs wracking her huge frame.

'Oh Gran, darling Gran. What is it?'

'Mam?' Dan was beside them now.

'It's . . . it's our Duggie. He's gone. He's lost at sea. His . . . his ship was torpedoed.' Her voice rose to a wail of untold grief and desolation. 'We've lost him, Dan. I've lost one of my boys. My baby.'

Dan put his arms around her and the three of them stood there clinging together, trying to find mutual comfort when nothing and no one could bring any kind of consolation. Lizzie was crying too now, 'Oh no. Not Uncle Duggie. Please say it's not true?'

Dan was the first to recover and said quietly, 'Come on, love. Be strong now for your gran's sake. Take her home and I'll come as soon as I can.' He looked down at his mother with such tenderness on his face that it twisted Lizzie's heart afresh. 'Come on, Mam. Lizzie will go home with you. Where's me dad? Does he know?'

Her body still heaving with tearing sobs, Bessie only nodded. 'He's sat at home by the fire. Won't move. Won't say a word. And Ernie. He's hardly said a word, either. And when he does, it's to say summat daft, like it ought to have been him and not our Duggie. He's just pacing up and down the yard, running his hands through his hair as if he'd like to pull it from his head.'

Dan said nothing, sparing a moment's thought for his taciturn brother, the one they always seemed to forget. Yet Ernie had been the first in their household to volunteer, only to be turned down by the medical board.

'You'll have to be strong, Mam. You always have been.'

Bessie shook her head. 'Not this time, lad. I'm done for. I'm too old to take any more. Mary Ann going fair broke me heart, but this . . .'

Her tears were unceasing as Lizzie helped her homewards. Bessie leant so heavily on her that the girl felt as if she were almost carrying her. But she was strong physically and now she had to be strong emotionally for all their sakes, for the woman who had always been the rock in their midst, the one to whom everyone, family and neighbours alike, had always turned in their troubles, was shattered and heartbroken.

When they entered Waterman's Yard, Ernie was nowhere to be seen, but Minnie rushed forwards. 'Oh Bessie, we've just heard. We're so sorry.' She dissolved into tears and covered her face with her apron.

'Thank you, Mrs Eccleshall,' Lizzie said. 'But I just want to get Gran home.'

'Of course, love. But if there's anything I can do, you've only to say. Oh, it's dreadful. It really is.' And she wailed afresh.

But what was there she could do? Lizzie thought sadly, as she helped Bessie, stumbling, across the yard. What was there any of them could do?

Amy Hamilton was standing by the door of Bessie's home, her arms folded across her thin chest. 'Well, Bessie Ruddick, now you know, don't you? Now you know how it feels.'

Feeling a shudder run through Bessie and hearing her groan, Lizzie braced herself as her grandmother leant even more heavily against her. Anger flooded through Lizzie and gave her a fresh spurt of strength. 'Excuse us, Mrs Hamilton, if you please,' she said with icy politeness. 'I want to get Gran into the house.'

Amy, with a strange look of surprise on her face, stared at Bessie, but she stood aside as Lizzie manoeuvred Bessie through the door and the scullery and into the kitchen.

'Sit down, Gran. I'll mash us a pot of tea.'

'I'll do it,' a voice said behind her, and Lizzie turned in surprise to see that Amy had followed them into the house.

'There's no need for you to trouble yourself, Mrs Hamilton . . .' she began, but the woman cut her short.

'There's every reason, lass. Every reason, but you wouldn't understand.'

Surprise robbed Lizzie momentarily of speech, and she sat down suddenly beside her grandmother, staring at Amy, who was busying herself about Bessie's kitchen and back scullery as if she were in her own house. Lizzie's glance went then to her grandfather sitting in his chair by the range. He looked in a worse state than her grandmother did, Lizzie thought, anguished. She felt helpless in the face of such grief. Her own sorrow was bad enough, but to see these two dear people so devastated broke Lizzie's young heart. It would have been bad enough for one of them to lose the other, their life's partner, but to lose one of their children went against nature. It wasn't the right order of things.

'His ship got torpedoed,' Bessie murmured again as if, only by repeating it, could she begin to believe what had happened to her beloved boy.

'It's a waste,' Amy said, placing a tray of teacups and saucers on the table and picking up the teapot. 'A tragic, senseless waste. That's what it is.' There was anger in her tone and even when she said, 'Here, Bessie girl, drink this,' it was said brusquely. She held out a cup of tea, but Bessie appeared not to have heard. Lizzie took it and gently patted her grandmother's arm.

'Mrs Hamilton's made you some nice tea, Gran. Come on, try and drink it.'

'Here you are, Bert.' Amy was standing over him, issuing an order she would not allow him to disobey. 'Drink this.'

Suddenly, Lizzie remembered and understood. This was the woman who had lost her husband and only son in the Great War. Lizzie felt her resentment towards Amy drain away. This woman, brusque though she seemed at this moment, was probably the only one of them around here who truly understood how Bessie must be feeling.

'Am I going to have to feed you, Bert Ruddick? Come on, rouse yasen.'

Tears running unashamedly down his face, Bert looked across at Bessie, who was lying back in the chair, her eyes red in a face pale with exhaustion. He closed his eyes and groaned.

Lizzie watched as Amy bent down towards him. 'Come on, Bert. You've got to be strong for Bessie.'

He shook his head. 'She . . .' he began haltingly as if even speaking was an effort. 'She's the strong one.'

Quietly, Amy said, 'Not this time, Bert. Poor Bessie's going to need you to be strong for her this time.'

Bert looked up at Amy and then slowly he reached out to take the cup of tea she held out to him. Though his hand shook and the cup rattled in the saucer, he picked it up and gulped the strong, hot liquid like a man thirsting in the desert.

Satisfied, Amy turned her attention to Bessie. 'Now then, let's be 'aving you an' all.' She smiled at Lizzie and her tone became gentle as she said, 'You go into the scullery, lass, and get a bit of dinner ready. I'll stay with them.'

At the sink in the scullery, as she peeled potatoes and washed vegetables, her own tears falling into the bowl of water, Lizzie could hear the low murmur of Amy's voice, although she could not hear what was being said. A little while later, Dan arrived and Amy came out into the scullery.

'I'm going now, lass, but I'll be back.'

Lizzie turned and opened her mouth to express her thanks, but Amy held up her hand. 'Don't say anything, lass, 'cos I might not like what you're be going to say.'

'I wasn't—' Lizzie began, but Amy interrupted.

'I lost me husband and son in the last lot and it was your gran who pulled me through. I'd have done for mesen for sure, if it hadn't been for her. I might sound a bit hard, a bit unfeeling, but I'm only giving her a taste of her own medicine.'

Lizzie gasped, astonished to think that the woman could be so vindictive after all these years. But once more, Lizzie had to admit that she was wrong as Amy explained. 'It's medicine that's hard to dish out and it's bitter to take, lass, but it works. It worked on me. I thought Bessie Ruddick was the hardest, most callous bitch around, but she knew what to do. Oh, she knew how to shake me out of me self-pity. I'm still alive today only because of her, Lizzie. And I'll never forget it. So, now I'm going to be here for her when she needs help.'

Lizzie's voice was unsteady as she said, 'Thanks. Thank you, Mrs Hamilton.'

If it hadn't been for Amy Hamilton, Lizzie thought later, the Ruddick family might well have lost Bessie and probably Bert too.

For days and weeks, Bessie hardly ate. The weight dropped from her and loose skin sagged beneath her jaw. Bert tried his best. He cajoled and pleaded with her, but to no avail. Even the taciturn Ernie was heard to plead, 'Come on, our Mam, try to eat something.'

Bessie retreated into a world of her own. Sitting beside the range, staring into the fire, she stirred only to answer the call of nature. She didn't even undress at night or go upstairs to bed, and soon her unwashed grey hair was lank and greasy, her clothes stained and crumpled.

It was Amy who finally broke through the wall of

misery. Once more she stood over Bessie. 'Are you going to sit there, Bessie Ruddick, till you rot? You're beginning to smell now.'

For the first time since they had received the dreadful news, Lizzie felt herself wanting to laugh. And yet she wanted to cry at the same time. Holding her breath, she watched as, slowly, Bessie raised her face to look at Amy. Suddenly, there was a spark of anger in her grandmother's eyes. 'What right have you to tell me what to do, Amy Hamilton, I'd like to know?'

'Oh you would, would you? Well, I'll tell you what right I've got.' She leant down so that her eyes were on a level with Bessie's. 'Same right as you had to save my miserable life all them years ago. Remember?'

The two women stared at each other, a lifetime of memories between them. 'And think about it, Bessie. You have got other family. There's poor Bert here, and your other lads, to say nothing of this poor lass who's bewildered and lost by it all. They're all hurting, Bessie. I had no one left, no one to live for, and yet you still wouldn't let me go, so I'm damned if I'm going to let you shrivel away and bring more grief to your family. You hear me, Bessie Ruddick. By heck, if you weren't so big and fat, I'd shake some sense into that stupid head of yours.'

Amy straightened up and turned to Lizzie and Bert, who were standing by listening, first shocked and then amused by Amy's antics.

'Lizzie, see if Mrs Eccleshall's at home. Tell her I need her help across here, but tell her to leave her tears at home. I don't want her coming in here weeping and wailing and making matters worse. And you, Bert, get the tin bath, bring it in here and fill it with water. It's time me and Min gave Mrs Smelly here a good bath. I'm just going to my house to fetch her some clean clothes.'

It had been the turning point and whilst the whole family still grieved, once Bessie started to recover, they all began to come to terms with their loss.

'I miss Uncle Duggie so much,' Lizzie told Tolly, who, their previous quarrel forgotten in the wake of such a tragedy, had been one of the first to arrive on the doorstep to offer his sympathy. 'He was always so happy and cheerful.' She smiled wistfully. 'I even miss him teasing me.'

They were sitting on the riverbank, watching the fish, but today neither of them had the heart to try to catch any.

'I expect there's a lot of people who miss him. Your uncle was what they call a lovable rogue. A bit of a lad with the women, but everybody liked him.'

'Yes. Yes, they did.' She sighed. 'I suppose that should be a comfort, but it isn't.'

'No.' Tolly reached out and took her hand. 'Nothing's a comfort really, because nothing can bring him back.'

'We're not the only ones to have lost someone, though, are we?'

'No,' Tolly agreed again. 'But that doesn't make it any easier either.'

She leant her forehead against his shoulder. 'Oh Tolly, thank goodness you're too young to be called up. Let's hope it's all over before you reach eighteen.'

He did not answer her and she could not tell him everything that was in her heart. Much as she loved Tolly – he was like the brother she had never had – she could not tell even him that with each passing day her fear grew that, before long, Lawrence would have to go to war.

Fifty-One

'Lizzie, I want to go to church this morning. Will you come with me?'

Bessie was standing in the kitchen, dressed in her best black hat and coat.

'Of course, Gran. I'll get my coat.'

'And find a hat,' her grandmother murmured. 'Doesn't do to go into church without a hat.'

The church was packed – every seat seemed to be taken.

'What's going on?' Lizzie whispered. 'I've never seen the church as full as this for a normal morning service.'

'It isn't a normal service,' Bessie said. 'It's a special service for all those families who've lost someone. That's why I wanted to come.' She nodded towards the congregation in front of them as they squeezed into a pew near the back of the church. 'Just look at all these poor folks who've lost loved ones. I'm not the only one and it's time I realized it.'

'Oh Gran,' was all Lizzie could say as tears threatened to choke her. She put her hand through her grandmother's arm and kept it there throughout the service. By the time it was over and the people were filing out, Lizzie wasn't sure whether coming had been such a good idea. Throughout the prayers and the hymn singing there had been the sound of people crying. Even Bessie, usually loath to let strangers witness her emotions, had dabbed at her eyes and blown her nose vigorously.

'Come on, Gran, time to go,' Lizzie urged, when Bessie made no move to leave.

'Hang on a minute, love,' Bessie said. 'There's something I want to see when everyone's gone.'

'What?' Lizzie asked, sitting down again.

'Amy reckons someone's embroidered a banner of some sort. It's on the wall near that little chapel at the side there. She says it's got Duggie's name on it.'

'Really?' Lizzie said, intrigued too, now.

When everyone except the verger, who was still busy, had left, Bessie and Lizzie walked to the front.

'There it is,' Lizzie said, pointing to the wall at one side. They moved closer and saw, embroidered in silks and gold thread upon satin, the emblems of the Merchant Navy and the words 'In loving memory of Douglas Ruddick, who gave his life in the service of his country, September 1941'.

'Who do you think has done it?' Lizzie asked.

'I suppose,' Bessie said slowly, her gaze never leaving the beautiful piece of work, 'there's only one person who could have done it.'

'Miss Edwina?' Lizzie suggested.

'I suppose so,' Bessie said, thoughtfully. Then, more briskly, she added, 'Come on, time we were going.'

But just before they turned away, Bessie reached out and touched the name of her son worked in gold thread.

In the spring of 1942, Lawrence volunteered for the RAF long before his call-up papers came.

'If you won't marry me, Lizzie, I might as well die the hero.'

Lizzie turned pale. 'How can you say such a thing to

me? You know how difficult it's been for me, losing Uncle Duggie and my gran and grandpa needing me.'

'I need you too, Lizzie.' There was a frown on Lawrence's handsome face. 'I'm beginning to think you don't really love me.'

They were in the shadows of the woods, deep amongst the trees where no passing cyclist could see them and, this time, they would be more careful when they left their secret place. Meeting at all had still been difficult, yet since the awful news about Duggie, Lizzie's grandmother had not once mentioned her involvement with Lawrence Marsh. The only time the matter had ever come to the surface again had been the time when Edwina had called at Waterman's Yard to see Bessie.

She had knelt on the rug in front of the grieving woman and taken hold of her hands. 'I'm not going to let a silly argument spoil our friendship, Bessie. I'm so very sorry about poor Duggie. You know, if there's anything I can do, anything at all . . .'

But Edwina had gone away without Bessie saying a word to her, for she had called at a time when the older woman was so lost in her grief she was speaking to no one. Since that day, Edwina had not called again and Bessie, either too proud or not even aware that Edwina had been, did not make the first move to restore their former friendship.

Slowly, the old couple had begun to come to terms with their loss, though their lives were altered forever. Lizzie was able to go back aboard the *Maid Mary Ann* to cook and care for her father, but there were still times when she was not allowed on a particular trip. It was only on these occasions, when she stayed in Waterman's Yard, that she had the opportunity to slip away to meet Lawrence.

'You know that's not true,' she said now, winding her arms around his neck.

'How do I know it's not true? You won't let me make love to you. You won't run away with me to get married. What am I supposed to think?'

'How could I leave my family after what happened?'

'Most families around here have lost someone. They don't all go to pieces. You have to get over it. Get on with your life. Our lives, Lizzie.' He took her gently by the shoulders and looked down into her eyes. 'I'm going away soon. I've joined up and I'm going to train to be a pilot, probably on bombers. I really want to be on Lancasters.' His eyes were afire with a passion in which she had no part.

Lizzie drew in a horrified breath at the thought of the danger he would be in.

'Before I go,' he was urging her, 'I want you so much. I want to make love to you so badly, it hurts. If you really love me, you wouldn't send me away not knowing, not having tasted such happiness.'

'Lawrence, I . . .' she began, but he cut her short, pulling her against him and resting his cheek against her hair.

'I know. I know what you're going to say, Lizzie, and I'm trying to understand. Truly, I am. So . . .' He paused and pulled back a little from her, looking down into her face once more, and now he was smiling gently. 'So, I've found us this vicar, miles from here, who will marry us.'

'Marry us? But he can't. We're not old enough to get married without parental consent.'

'He's a doddery old fool who hardly seems to know what day of the week it is, let alone still compos mentis enough to think to ask us our ages. All we need are some witnesses. I'm sure one of his church wardens would oblige and I thought we might ask Aunt Edwina.'

Lizzie eyes opened wide. 'Miss Edwina?' She shook her head. 'Oh no, that wouldn't be fair.'

'Why not? She and your grandmother aren't on speaking terms now. So she tells me. So what does it matter?'

'Aren't . . .? Oh no, you've got it wrong. Your aunt called just after my uncle was lost at sea, but it was at the time that Gran hardly knew what was happening. I don't think she was even aware that your aunt had called.'

Lawrence shrugged. 'Anyway, she might do it. Oh Lizzie, what do you say? Please – please, will you marry me?'

Swept along on the tide of his passionate pleading, and fearing that so very soon she might lose him, just like she had lost her dear uncle, Lizzie heard herself saying, 'Of course, I will.' And then he was kissing her so ardently that all thoughts of her father, her grandmother, even of Tolly, were driven from her mind.

Lawrence gave her no time for second thoughts or for doubt of any kind. He planned it all with such meticulous care that nothing could go wrong.

'We won't tell Aunt Edwina,' he decided later. 'She's such a one for truth and honesty that she might disapprove, not of what we're doing, but the way we're doing it. Now, are you sure there's nothing else you want? I've bought you a pretty dress . . .' He grimaced. 'Not a white one, darling, I'm afraid, but a very pretty one nonetheless. And flowers. I've ordered you a bouquet. And afterwards . . . oh darling, afterwards, I'm taking you away to a lovely little hotel in the country, where we can be com-

pletely alone. There'll be no bombs, no talk of war. Just
the two of us, I promise.'

As she slipped home through the dusk of early evening, a
shadow loomed from the entrance to the alleyway leading
to Waterman's Yard.

'Tolly! What on earth are you doing skulking about in
the dark? You frightened the life out of me.'

'Sorry,' he muttered.

There was silence between them before she said, 'Why
are you here? Is something wrong?'

'You tell me.'

'What do you mean?'

'What do you think I mean?'

'Oh, do stop being so irritating,' she snapped.

She heard him take a deep breath. 'All right, if that's
the way you want it. You've been seeing him again,
haven't you?'

Her voice rising, Lizzie said, 'What's that got to do
with you?'

'Ah, so I'm right.'

'I didn't say so.'

'You didn't deny it either and since you ask, it's got
everything to do with me. Do you think I want to see you
throw yourself away on someone like him? Someone
who'll cast you aside like an old shoe when he's . . . he's
had his way with you and then tired of you. He'll never
marry you, Lizzie . . .'

'Well, that's just where you're wrong.' Angry beyond
reason now, Lizzie's tongue began to run away with her.
'We're getting married this coming Saturday, so there.'

With that parting shaft, she strode away from him

down the alleyway. His voice echoed through the darkness, 'Oh Lizzie, no. Think what you're doing. Please.'

Tolly must have been waiting on the wharf the following morning when her father's ship docked. Or he might even, Lizzie thought bitterly, have rowed downriver to meet him.

'What's this all about?' her father thundered, when he stepped over the threshold of Bessie's house in Waterman's Yard, without a word of greeting to her after two days away. 'Is this true what Tolly tells me? That you've been seeing young Marsh again and that you're going to marry him?'

'Dad . . .' Lizzie began, but Dan was in no mood to listen.

'Well, just let me tell you, my girl, it'll be over my dead body if you do. Haven't I had more than enough trouble from that family? Hasn't his father caused me enough grief? To think that you could do this to me, Lizzie.' His anger seemed to die as he shook his head and said sadly, 'I thought you were different, but I see you're not. You're just like her. In looks, in everything. You're just like your mother.'

'Dad, don't say that.' Lizzie was crying now as she flung herself against him, trying to wrap her arms around his big frame, but, hurt beyond understanding, he flung her away from him as if he could not bear to touch her. 'Why won't you listen to me?' she cried. 'Why won't you try to understand?'

''Ere, 'ere, what's going on?' Bessie appeared in the doorway leading from the kitchen into the scullery where they were standing. 'What's all the shouting about?'

'She reckons she's going to marry young Marsh, that's

what's the matter,' Dan shouted. 'I thought you were going to keep an eye on her. Are you behind it? Has she wheedled her way around you, just like Mary Ann used to do?'

'Don't you take that tone with me, lad,' Bessie wagged her finger at him, some of her old spirit returning. 'Besides, she's isn't old enough. Without your consent,' Bessie added, calmly matter-of-fact, 'it wouldn't be legal.'

'I shouldn't think that'd bother *him* for a minute,' Dan sneered. 'It'll make divorcing her all the easier, won't it?'

'Doesn't anyone care about me?' Lizzie almost stamped her foot with anger. 'Don't you want me to be happy? He's joined up. He's going in the RAF in a few weeks. Going to be a bomber pilot. Don't you think he deserves a little happiness? Don't you think we have to snatch what happiness we can, while we can?'

She saw them glance at each other, but now they were silent, as if each were thinking the unspoken words. Had poor Duggie snatched what happiness he could in his life, cut short by an enemy torpedo?

Dan ran his hand distractedly through his hair. 'Oh Lizzie, it's because we love you so much and because there's so much you don't understand.'

'I'm sorry, Dad. The last thing I want to do is to hurt you, or Gran, but I'm going to marry Lawrence.'

His expression hardened again as he stared at her. Then through tight lips, he said, 'Then you'd better get on with it, but don't come running back to me when he casts you off like an old shoe.'

She shuddered at his words. They were the very same ones that Tolly had used.

395

Fifty-Two

Lizzie refused to let the rift between her and her family spoil her wedding day. The April sun shone brightly on the tiny church set high on a Yorkshire hillside as, dressed in her finery and carrying a bouquet, Lizzie walked up the narrow path, clinging to Lawrence's hand.

'However did you find it?' she asked.

He chuckled. 'It wasn't difficult. The church is on land belonging to my mother's family, to her brother now, actually. And he pays the vicar, who's as deaf as a post and can't see too well either. He hasn't even asked awkward questions about our ages or anything. So, there's no problem. Although making several trips up here to arrange it all did take rather a lot of my father's precious petrol coupons.' He looked down at her and any doubts she had were swept away. There was no denying the look of love and desire in his eyes.

They were wrong, she told herself, her heart singing with happiness. They were all so wrong. Lawrence loved her and they would be so happy together that her father and her grandmother would see it for themselves. And then they would forgive her. Lizzie was so confident in their love for her – she knew they were only concerned, like they said, for her happiness – that she knew they would all come around one day.

The old man in a dirty surplice shuffled forward to meet them. Twice during the service, he dropped the book and Lizzie had to bend down to retrieve it and place it back into his shaking hands. He stumbled through the words, squinting through grubby spectacles whilst the organist thumped out a hymn on the wheezing organ.

'I don't know who is the oldest,' Lawrence whispered. 'The vicar or that organ.'

'Ssh,' Lizzie hissed, but was soon in danger of being overcome with a fit of the giggles.

The service was over far sooner than she had expected and, once the register had been signed – the verger and the gravedigger having been commandeered as witnesses – they were outside in the sunshine.

'Could I prevail upon you to take a picture of us?' Lawrence stopped the organist as he hurried out of the church.

'Oh – er – yes, of course, but I am in rather a hurry.'

The man fumbled with Lawrence's camera. 'What do I press? Oh yes, I see.'

Quickly, he snapped three photographs and then said, 'That do? I really must be going.'

'Thank you,' Lawrence said, taking the camera, and then whispered to Lizzie, 'We'll take some more at the hotel. I'll take some nice ones of you. They've got a lovely garden there, with a little bridge over a stream . . .'

'I'm sorry, darling,' Lawrence said, as he rolled away from her after their first attempt at making love. 'I just wanted you so badly. It'll be better the next time . . .'

As he drifted into sleep, Lizzie lay, tensed and unsatisfied. If that was all there was to making love, she thought, all that heaving and pushing and grunting, then she didn't know what all the fuss was about. In the early hours, when Lawrence stirred and woke her, he whispered, 'It'll be better for you this time, darling, I promise.'

But still, despite his efforts to think of Lizzie's feelings, wanting her to experience the heights of passion along with him, he came to a shuddering climax long before her body had begun to respond to his caresses.

He tried to make light of it and pretended to leer as he murmured, 'It's going to take a lot of practice. An awful lot of practice . . .' Again, he slept.

By the fourth day of their honeymoon, Lawrence said, 'Things'll be better when we get home. We'll be among familiar surroundings then.'

Familiar to you, maybe, Lizzie thought, but she said nothing.

'And I expect you're still upset about your family,' Lawrence added. 'Once you've made up with them, you'll feel more relaxed.'

'Are you saying it's my fault?'

'Of course not, darling. You're just tense, that's all. It's only natural.' He took her in his arms and kissed her gently. 'I do love you so much, Lizzie. I just want everything to be so perfect.'

She kissed him in return and said, 'I'm sorry. Perhaps it is my fault. I . . . I mean it is the first time, for me. You're right, things will be better when we go home.'

He caught at her hands. 'Then let's go. Right now. Let's go home and begin our proper married life. With you as mistress of The Hall.'

Lizzie caught her breath. 'Don't be silly. Your mother is mistress of The Hall.'

Lawrence shrugged. 'In name only. Rather like their marriage. I think it's been "in name only" for years.'

'But she still lives there. And your father.'

'Supposedly. But he's hardly ever at home. God only

knows where he goes. I think he's got a fancy woman somewhere.'

Lizzie gasped. 'And ... and doesn't your mother mind?'

'No, she couldn't care less.' He grinned. 'Maybe she's got a fancy man somewhere too.'

'Well, I hope you don't think you can do that when you get tired of me,' Lizzie said, her eyes flashing.

'Oh darling.' He stroked her hair. 'I'll never get tired of you. For as long as I live.'

Their homecoming was unheralded and, consequently, devoid of welcome, although Lizzie doubted there would have been much of one anyway.

At dinner that first evening, when Lawrence had instructed her on how she was expected to dress, Lizzie was seated on one side of an enormous table, with Lawrence's father and mother at opposite ends, with far more than the length of the table between them.

The meal passed almost in silence, the rattle of cutlery and the chink of china the only sounds in the vast, cold dining room. If it hadn't been for the pressure of Lawrence's foot against her own beneath the table, Lizzie would have fled.

At the end of the meal, Lawrence cleared his throat and said, 'Father, Mother, there is something I have to tell you. *We* have to tell you.' He reached across the wide table to take her hand as he said, 'Lizzie and I were married last Saturday.'

Randolph stood up so suddenly that his heavy chair crashed to the floor and his red wine spilled over on to the table, the glass rolling towards the edge. Deakin hurried to catch it before it smashed on the floor. Then the manservant picked up the chair and set it behind his master before retiring to stand discreetly in the shadows of the corner of the room. He stood like a statue, ready to serve if needed, but more likely, Lizzie thought shrewdly, anxious to hear this latest piece of scandal with which he could regale the other servants.

'You did what?' Randolph, purple with rage, shouted.

Lizzie's fingers trembled but Lawrence's hand, she noticed, was warm and firm and steady. At a slight sound from the other end of the table, Lizzie turned to see that his mother was leaning back in her chair and holding her ribs. To Lizzie's amazement, the woman was laughing. 'Well done, Lawrence, my dear. You've finally shown you have got a spark of spirit in you after all. I was beginning to wonder.'

'Have you taken leave of your senses, boy? Married at your age. And about to go into the forces. What on earth were you thinking of?' There was a pause before Randolph added, 'Oh I get it. In the family way, is she?'

Quietly, Lawrence said, 'No, father, she isn't. Though I hope . . .' He smiled across the table at Lizzie. 'That she might be very soon.'

He released her hand then and stood up, turning to face his father. 'Wouldn't you like a grandson, father?'

'Of course I would,' the man thundered, and then flung out his arm towards Lizzie. 'But not with *her* as its mother.'

Randolph turned, pushed the chair that Deakin had so carefully placed behind him out of his way so that once more it toppled to the floor, and then he strode from the room. The only sound that followed him was his wife's laughter.

*

'He hates me. He doesn't think I'm good enough for you,' Lizzie said mournfully, when they were alone in their room later.

Lawrence sat beside her on the bed and put his arm about her shoulders. 'Well, your family hate me, don't they?'

'Perhaps they're all right. Perhaps we do come from such different worlds that it'll never work.'

'Lizzie, please don't say that. We'll make it work. We'll prove them all wrong. You do love me, don't you?'

'Of course I do.'

His lips were against hers. 'Then prove it, Mrs Marsh. Prove it.'

Fifty-Three

On 29 April 1942, a bright, moonlit night and only days after Lawrence and Lizzie had returned to The Hall after their marriage, Elsborough suffered one of its worst air raids of the war. A Dornier dropped bombs on the centre of the town, killing thirteen people and injuring many more. Gas pipes were fractured and fires broke out. Smashed water pipes gushed water into the streets and hampered the efforts of the rescue services.

Huddled in the deep cellars below The Hall with Lawrence, his mother and the servants – of Randolph, there was no sign – Lizzie could only listen to the distant thuds and worry about her family in Waterman's Yard. 'Dad's probably away,' she murmured to Lawrence, 'but what about Gran and Grandpa?'

'You've an uncle still living at home, haven't you?' Lawrence said, sounding unconcerned. 'He'll look after them.'

'No,' she said worriedly, feeling a fresh stab of guilt. 'Now I'm not there, he's gone with my dad aboard the *Maid Mary Ann* to take my place as mate.' She chewed her lip as anxiety gnawed at her. 'They'll be on their own.'

'Well, there's plenty of folk around who'll look after them.' Lawrence chuckled. 'That Horberry fellow, for a start. Time he did something useful instead of stirring it for others, eh?'

She was irritated by his seeming lack of concern for her

elderly grandparents, but she had to admit that what he said was true. There were plenty of people in Waterman's Yard who would look after Bert and Bessie Ruddick. They didn't really need her.

Strangely, the thought hurt her.

Her mother-in-law's voice, coming through the gloom, interrupted Lizzie's thoughts. 'What did you say your father's boat is called?'

'The *Maid Mary Ann*.'

'Shouldn't it be the *Maid Marian*?'

'It was,' Lizzie explained, pleased to have something to talk about; something to take her mind off the thud of bombs still falling somewhere above them. 'But because my mother's name was Mary Ann, the owner allowed my father to change the name slightly.'

'Mary Ann, you say?' Although Celia Marsh still spoke with her usual, seemingly disinterested, drawl, there was suddenly a different edge to her tone. 'Your mother's name was Mary Ann?'

'Yes.' Now Lizzie's answer was short. She had no wish to be drawn into searching questions about her mother.

'How strange,' Celia murmured. 'How very strange.' Then, with definite interest now, she asked, 'And where is your mother now, dear? Still aboard the boat named after her?'

'Er ... no, she ... I mean ...' Lizzie floundered, knowing that in the shadows The Hall's servants were listening intently.

Lawrence came to her rescue smoothly. 'Lizzie lost her mother some years ago. She doesn't like to talk about it.'

'Lost, you say? You mean, she died?'

'Lizzie was very young. Her people just told her that her mother had "gone away".'

'Ah,' Celia said. 'I see.'

403

And to Lizzie, flushing uncomfortably in the darkness, it sounded very much as if Celia Marsh understood perfectly, perhaps even better than Lizzie herself had ever done.

With the dawn came Lizzie and Lawrence's first real quarrel.

'I'm must go to Waterman's Yard.'

'You're not going. It's too dangerous. I forbid it.'

'You . . . what?' Lizzie was scandalized. 'How dare you speak to me like that?'

'Of course I dare, you're my wife. And, if you remember, not many days ago you promised to obey me.'

'That has nothing to do with it . . .'

'It has everything to do with it. I won't allow you to go running back to the yards. They don't want you, they've said as much, and now that you're my wife, your home is here, at The Hall. And soon, with the help of my mother, you will have something of a position in the town.'

'A position? What sort of a position?' Lizzie was aghast, horrified at what his words implied. That she was to cut herself off from her family and, worse still, regard herself from now on as one of the gentry.

'A position in society. Mother knows everyone in the town who is worth knowing. She'll make sure you meet all the right people . . .'

'Lawrence, do you know what a prig you sound?' she flung at him, turned and walked out of the room, slamming the huge door behind her. Around her the old house seemed to creak in protest.

*

'Darling, I'm sorry.' That night, in bed, Lawrence took her in his arms. 'Please, don't let's quarrel. I have to go away next week. I'm to report to training camp.'

'Oh Lawrence.' Lizzie, contrite now, kissed him and put her arms around him. 'So soon? I thought you weren't going for another month. Darling, I'm sorry. I'm so sorry.'

'Well, my eighteenth birthday's next week, so I suppose the RAF think a few days doesn't make any difference.'

'You mean you won't be at home for your birthday?'

'No.'

'Oh Lawrence . . .' Full of remorse now for her behaviour, she gave herself to him, thinking nothing of her own needs now, only of his.

'You've made yar bed, lass, now you'll have to lie in it. It's no good coming back here because he's gone away to war and your ma and pa-in-law won't speak to you.'

Lizzie was in her grandmother's kitchen watching the older woman standing at the table kneading bread. Every so often Bessie winced and shifted her feet, trying to ease the pain.

'Let me do that, Gran. You sit down.'

'I'm not a cripple yet, thank you,' Bessie snapped and glowered at Lizzie. 'Hadn't you better be about your wifely duties? Aren't there luncheon parties and good works you should be attending to in your smart new clothes?' Bessie glanced resentfully at the new, well-cut costume Lizzie was wearing.

'Oh Gran, how long are you going to keep this up?' She sat down at the table and leant her elbows on it, though she was careful to avoid the scattering of flour.

'Who asked you to sit down, Mrs Marsh?'

Lizzie gaped at her and then stood up slowly. 'Well, if that's how it is. If I'm not welcome here . . .'

'That is how it is.' Bessie wagged her finger towards Lizzie, sending a further shower of flour over the table. 'You've hurt your dad more than I can find the words to tell you. It was bad enough what Mary Ann did to him, but you . . .' Words did, indeed, seem to fail her for the moment. 'You were the apple of his eye. He thought you could do no wrong. And you've done about the worst thing to him you could have done. Now he's all alone with his memories. And what bitter memories they are, an' all.' She shook her head. 'Poor Dan. My poor Dan. And don't you go running to him, either. He doesn't want to see you.'

Lizzie felt the tears spring to her eyes. 'I love Dad, he knows I do. I love all of you.'

'Well, you've a funny way of showing it, that's all I can say.'

Now anger spurted in Lizzie. 'And you've all a funny way of showing you care for me. You don't seem to want me to be happy.'

With that, she whirled around and ran out of the house and across the yard, almost bumping into Amy Hamilton coming down the alleyway loaded with heavy shopping bags.

'Oh morning, Mrs Marsh, ma'am. Doing a bit of slumming, are we?'

Lizzie gave a sob, dodged around her and hurried on, the sound of Amy's laughter echoing down the passageway after her.

Fifty-Four

Lizzie felt as if she didn't belong anywhere now. At The Hall, Randolph Marsh ignored her completely and the servants were barely civil to her. To their minds, as well as to her own family's, she had betrayed her class. She was no longer one of them, but neither did she belong to the family she had married into. If only Lawrence had not gone away, Lizzie thought, things might well have been different.

Edwina might have become her friend, for she alone out of all of them had not been against the marriage. But Edwina rarely came to The Hall and Lizzie hesitated to visit her home.

Almost daily, Lizzie found herself going down to the river to stand on the wharves, watching the ships coming and going. Sometimes, she saw the *Maid Mary Ann* and her father or Ernie in the distance, but not once did they raise their hand in greeting or come to speak to her, even though she was sure they had seen her standing there. She longed to go aboard. Her need for sight of the cabin, so recently her home, for the feel of the ship beneath her feet and to breathe the damp smell of the river, to feel again its every mood, was like a hunger within her.

At nights, alone in her bed, Lizzie slept fitfully, dreaming that she was back on board in the middle of the River Humber on a calm, sunny day. Out there, away from everything, there was such peace and tranquillity, the only sounds the ship carving through the water, the wind billowing the sails and the seagulls calling overhead. She could hear her father's commands, 'Rise ya tack' and his long, drawn-out 'Let gooo', so clearly that she awoke with a start, her limbs already tensing to obey him. Then, with a sense of disappointment, she realized where she really was.

She was homesick for the river and its folk, but she was no longer welcome there.

At other times she wandered along the riverbank until she was opposite the shipyard. Once, she saw Tolly rowing homewards but, though she waved and shouted his name, he did not even glance towards her.

She felt so bereft, so cut off and alone.

Strangely, it was Lawrence's mother, Celia, who, in her cool, offhand manner, extended the hand of friendship. 'If you've nothing to do, my dear, there's plenty of voluntary work in the town you could help with. The WVS could certainly use another pair of hands.'

The 'good works' that her grandmother had spoken about so scathingly, Lizzie thought. She sighed inwardly, but summoned a smile. 'I'd be glad to help. Please tell me what I have to do.'

For the first time since Lizzie had known her, Celia became animated. 'You can join the local branch of the WVS. There are all sorts of jobs they do.' She ticked off a list on her fingers. 'Helping out at the rest centres and mobile canteens, providing hot drinks and food for Civil Defence workers. Then there's all the work we do for people who've been bombed out. Some of them have lost everything, all their possessions, clothes, absolutely everything. So we have a centre for the collection of clothes. You could help sort the bundles that come in there, perhaps.'

'I had been wondering whether to join up, too,' Lizzie murmured.

'Oh no,' her mother-in-law said swiftly. 'Lawrence wouldn't want you to do that. But he wouldn't mind you helping out in the town. I'm sure he wouldn't. Just so long as you're always here when he comes home on leave . . .'

Lizzie found the women volunteers were a mixed bunch: from the smart, town ladies, dressed in their fitted costumes with padded shoulders and pork-pie hats with long, curling feathers, to the housewives from the terraced street who came along to the centres in their aprons and their overalls. Yet there was camaraderie amongst them.

'We all muck in together,' Barbara, a young housewife from the backstreets of the town, told Lizzie, and she nodded towards one or two of the grander ladies, who were delving their well-manicured hands in amongst the grubby second-hand clothing without turning a hair of their neat heads. 'Who'd have thought it, a few years back to see the likes of them working alongside us, eh?' Then she laughed. ''Spect I shouldn't say such things to you, should I? You've just married Mrs Marsh's son, ain't you?'

Lizzie nodded.

'Bet you miss him, love, don't you? Ne'er mind, he'll soon be home on leave again. My old man's coming home next week.' She winked broadly at Lizzie and said, 'So I won't be here for a day or two. I'll be flat on me back giving comfort to the troops. Well, one of 'em, anyway.'

The raucous laughter echoed around them and Lizzie smiled.

'I'm off into town this dinner to get some frilly underwear,' Barbara went on. 'There's a man on the market selling knickers made out of parachute silk. That'll give my Harry a thrill. Why don't you come too, Lizzie? Give that new husband of yours a nice surprise when he comes home, eh?'

Lizzie thought about the fancy underwear that Lawrence had bought her for their honeymoon. Her lips tightened a little as she remembered his words. 'There's everything you need, my dear. I didn't think you'd be used to going into such shops.' It had been kind of him, she told herself, but she would have liked the chance to choose her new clothes for herself. With a spark of rebellion now, Lizzie nodded. 'All right, I will,' she told Barbara.

'Oho, madam from The Hall buying frilly knickers off the market. Whatever will Lady Celia say?' said a voice close by.

'You shut it, Vi. She's all right, is Mrs Marsh.' Barbara glanced at Lizzie and grinned. 'Both the Mrs Marshes are.' She linked her arm through Lizzie's. 'You stick with me, gal, I'll show you how to put a bit of spice into your marriage.'

'She don't need it,' said someone else. 'They've only been married a few months. They're still at the dewy-eyed stage.'

'Then she'll be ready to keep her old man from straying when the time comes, won't she?' Barbara countered, refusing to be shouted down. 'Come on, Lizzie, take no notice of them. We're going knicker shopping.'

'What on earth are you wearing?' Lawrence said, as they dressed for dinner on the first night of his leave.

Turning from the dressing table with a smile, Lizzie told him about her shopping expedition with Barbara. 'I was lucky to get them.'

'Lucky? I wouldn't call it that. Take them off this minute.'

Misunderstanding, Lizzie giggled. 'Oh Lawrence, not now, we haven't time.'

'I don't mean that,' he snapped. 'Get them off and put something decent on.' He strode across the room to the chest and dragged open one of the drawers. 'Where is all the nice underwear I bought you? That's real silk. Mind you,' he glanced at her over his shoulder as he added scathingly, 'I suppose I can't expect you to know the difference.'

Lizzie sprang to her feet. 'How dare you . . .?' she began, but he was walking calmly towards her holding out the undergarment of his choice. 'Here, put these on and mind you throw that rubbish where it belongs.'

For an instant Lizzie contemplated rebellion, but his eyes were suddenly so cold that she knew he was utterly serious. Remembering that he only had a few precious hours at home, she gave way and removed her knickers and put on the pair he had brought her.

'Is that better?' she asked tartly, and began to turn back to the dressing table.

He stepped close to her and put his arms about her, nuzzling his face against her hair. 'Much,' he murmured, and she could hear in his tone that at once his good humour had been restored. 'I shan't be able to eat for thinking about you dressed in those beneath your demure dress. And those stockings and suspenders. Oh,' he pretended to groan in ecstasy. 'Oh Lizzie . . .'

With a swift movement he picked her up in his arms and carried her to the bed.

'Lawrence, no. We mustn't. We'll be late for dinner.'

'It'll wait,' Lawrence murmured, his mouth searching

hers and his fingers pushing their way beneath her bras-
siere. 'This won't . . .'

Their coupling was soon over. Taken by surprise,
Lizzie had no time to begin to enjoy it, even if she had not
still been seething with anger at Lawrence's high-handed
attitude with her over her underwear. But Lawrence did
not seem to notice. He rolled off the bed, straightened his
clothing and said, 'Hurry up and get ready. We'll be late.'

During the time Lawrence had been away, Lizzie had
given a great deal of thought to what might be wrong
between them in the marriage bed. She had listened to
how the other girls had talked about their husbands and
young men and she had been to the cinema twice where
she had watched, fascinated, as the heroine seemed to give
herself to the hero with complete abandon.

Later that night, lying beneath him once more, Lizzie
closed her eyes and imagined she was Hedy Lamarr or
Rita Hayworth. She caressed Lawrence and moaned and
writhed, simulating pleasure.

'Oh darling, darling,' he murmured at last, panting
against her neck in the aftermath of desire, 'that was
glorious.' He raised his head and looked into her face.
'You felt it too, didn't you?'

She nodded, guilty at the lying, yet feeling it was
justified for she had made Lawrence so happy.

He kissed her gently. 'You were wonderful – wonderful, my dearest love.'

They made love constantly throughout the week of his
leave, seeming to spend most of the time in their bedroom.

'What must your mother think?' Lizzie said, feeling
embarrassed.

'She'll understand, though . . .' he pulled a face, 'I

doubt their marriage has ever been as good as ours. Mind you,' he grinned cheekily at her, 'it did produce me, so perhaps they were happy at first.'

He laid his hand against Lizzie's stomach. 'Do you think you might be pregnant? I do so want a son.'

Lizzie glanced at him coyly, pushing away the guilty knowledge that, for her, their week of passion had been only an act. 'It won't be for the want of trying, will it?'

He was pushing her back against the pillows. 'One last time, Lizzie, please, just one last time before I have to go . . .'

Perhaps in time, she could not help thinking as his hands caressed her and his mouth found her breast, I will feel what he feels. Perhaps in time, it won't be just an act. She dug her fingers deep into his thick hair and held him close, arching her body to meet his, but as she moaned in pretended ecstasy, a tear squeezed its way from beneath her eyelids and ran down her temple.

Fifty-Five

Christmas 1942 was the most miserable Lizzie had ever spent. Lawrence could not get leave to come home. It was not the lack of traditional fare, for the Christmas dinner at The Hall was almost the same as in peacetime – roast turkey with chestnut stuffing and roast potatoes and Brussels sprouts, followed by Christmas pudding and brandy butter, made with real butter. There were trifles with real cream and real coffee to follow. How many other households would be able to afford, or even have access to, such luxuries? Certainly not her family in Waterman's Yard. Yet, with all the deprivations that the Ruddick family would be suffering, Lizzie longed to be there. She knew her grandmother would be fortunate indeed if she had managed to acquire a chicken for their dinner. More than likely the pudding would be a sugarless Christmas pudding from a wartime menu issued by the Ministry of Food, and the coffee would be made with acorns.

But Lizzie would have given anything to have been in Waterman's Yard amidst the laughter and the teasing, rather than sitting at the long table, handling the fine silver and eating off the expensive china plates between the silent Randolph and Celia Marsh.

It was a relief, after Christmas, to return to the WVS centre and to join in the lively chatter once more.

'Have you heard the latest?' At times, Barbara was almost as big a gossip as Phyllis Horberry, yet her tales were told with kindness. There had always seemed to be a hint of malice in Phyllis's tattle. 'You know the Olivers that live in the ferryman's cottage at Eastlands?'

Lizzie stiffened and found she was holding her breath. She listened, but said nothing.

'He used to be the ferryman, didn't he? Works in Phillips Engineering now, doesn't he?'

'Yeah, since the beginning of the war.'

'Who runs the ferry now then?'

Barbara shrugged. 'Not so much call for it nowadays with motor transport using the bridge, though I think a few of the locals still use it to get from Eastlands to Westlands across the river. I 'spect his wife operates it or his lad. They've got a lad with a funny name. Ollie or summat like that.' Lizzie bit back the reply that sprang to her lips as Barbara continued. 'Well, me and Ted Oliver were walking out together years ago, but I soon packed him up. He was a violent bugger, he was. He only ever hit me once, mind you, but that was quite enough for me.'

'He married Susan Price, didn't he? Old man Price's daughter?'

'Tale went,' someone else said, 'that someone jilted her. I forget who, but they say she married Ted Oliver on the rebound.'

'Aye,' Barbara said grimly, 'and I bet the poor woman has lived to rue the day, an' all.'

'What about him?' another, impatient for the juicy morsel of gossip, prompted.

'He's buggered off,' Barbara said bluntly.

Lizzie felt herself reddening, not at the language – she had heard far worse on the river – but her heart went out at once to Tolly.

'What do you mean?'

'What do you think I mean? He's run off with another woman.'

'He never has.'

'It's true. He's had a fancy piece for years, they say. In Westlands. She was married an' all, but her husband's been in the army since the beginning of the war and he's been killed. So Ted's moved in with her.'

'The bastard,' someone murmured. 'Didn't waste any time, did he? That's not nice, that.'

'It's the war,' said another. 'You've got to take your happiness where you can find it.'

'Mebbe, mebbe not,' Barbara said. 'But in this case you can't blame the war. This time, it's Ted Oliver.'

'I feel sorry for his wife. She's a nice little woman, by all accounts. The only good thing she's ever had in her life is her lad and now he's going in the RAF any day . . .'

The gossip flew around her head, being chewed over and digested, but Lizzie heard no more. Her mind froze. Tolly, her dear Tolly was going away. He'd be eighteen in a month or so's time, just after Christmas. And she hadn't realized. Wrapped up in her own life, she hadn't remembered that soon he, too, would be going to war.

Tears blurred her vision. Oh Tolly, Tolly, her heart cried. How could I have forgotten?

Lizzie's hand trembled as she knocked at the door of the small white cottage on the riverbank.

Susan opened the door. 'Why, Lizzie, how nice.' Her smile was warm and genuine and she looked happier than she had looked for years. 'How smart you look. Come in, come in.'

Lizzie stepped across the threshold and said, 'Has he gone?'

Susan's smile widened and her eyes twinkled. 'Who? Ted?'

Lizzie felt the colour creep into her face. 'Oh I'm sorry, I didn't mean . . .'

Susan reached out and touched her hand. 'I know you didn't, love. But I expect everyone knows – or they soon will. Yes, he's gone and to be honest, it's good riddance, Lizzie, 'cos he's made our lives hell at times. Mine and Tolly's.' Her smile faded and her mouth tightened. 'It was the biggest mistake I ever made. But my father was so for me marrying Ted and he wouldn't ever believe what was going on in this house. He sided with Ted against me, his own daughter. Can you believe it?'

Lizzie shook her head and fought to swallow the lump in her throat. 'It . . . it was Tolly I meant. I heard he'd been called up.'

Now Susan's face was sad as she nodded. Her voice dropped to a whisper. 'Not called up, exactly. He volunteered, but he doesn't go till January, until after his birthday. He's still here. Do you want to see him?'

'If . . . if he wants to see me.'

Susan smiled again. 'I'm sure he will.'

As she followed Susan through into the next room, Lizzie was not so sure, but the smile that lit Tolly's face when he looked up and saw her was reassuring. As he rose to greet her, he seemed to Lizzie to have grown even taller, and he had filled out so that the gangly youth had gone. Now his shoulders were broad and the floppy hair had been cut short and was smoothed back with hair cream.

'He's getting ready to be one of the Brylcream boys,'

417

Susan teased and her glance caressed her son fondly, although she could not quite hide the anxiety that lay deep in her eyes.

'Shall we go for a walk along the bank?' he said and minutes later, as they strolled beside the river, Lizzie murmured, 'It's just like old times.'

'Not quite,' Tolly said, in his gentle voice that was now deeper. He glanced her up and down. 'You're not quite dressed for salmon fishing, are you?'

She gave him a rueful smile and they walked on in silence for several minutes before she burst out, 'At least you're speaking to me. My family won't have anything to do with me. I haven't seen any of them for months.' She turned and looked up at him. 'Is my father all right? Have you seen him recently?'

Tolly nodded. 'He's fine as far as I know. Always gives us a wave as he passes by.' He grinned briefly. 'He doesn't chuck coal or veg or tins of fruit at me any more, but he always looks out for us.' His voice was even deeper as he added softly, 'Both of us. Mam and me. He always has done.'

Again there was a long silence before Lizzie said, 'You will take care of yourself, won't you?'

As if by silent, mutual consent, they stopped and turned to face each other. Tolly put his hands on her shoulders. 'Are you happy, Lizzie?'

She answered swiftly, too swiftly. 'Of course I am.'

Tolly said nothing, but he raised his eyebrows in an unspoken question. Then he let his hands fall heavily away from her and he thrust them deep into the pockets of his trousers. 'That's all right, then,' he muttered glumly.

Lizzie had the feeling that he would have been far happier if she had told him that she was lost and lonely and utterly miserable in her new life.

And it would not have been so far from the truth either, she acknowledged to herself, though the words remained unsaid as they walked on together.

Lizzie didn't see Tolly again before he went away, although she continued to visit his mother in the ferryman's cottage. She heard that he had completed his basic training and was learning to be a rear gunner on Lancasters.

'Isn't that dreadfully dangerous?' she asked Susan fearfully. Lawrence had told her that the rear gunner's turret was the most vulnerable part of the aircraft that he now piloted.

Susan had tried to smile bravely, but had failed miserably.

'I'm so proud of him, Lizzie, but I'm so dreadfully afraid for him. So terribly afraid . . .'

By the time Lawrence came home on his next leave, Susan had already heard that the aircraft in which Tolly had been flying had been shot down and that all the crew had been posted missing, presumed killed.

Lizzie sobbed against Lawrence's shoulder. 'He was my friend. My very best friend ever since we were at school.'

He held her but the soothing words she sought, needed, were not forthcoming. 'Aren't I your best friend now?' he asked, sounding hurt.

'That's different,' she murmured, her words muffled against him.

He led her towards the bed, tried in the only way he knew to take her mind off her sorrow. But lost in her grief for Tolly, Lizzie could not even make the effort to put on the act. She lay acquiescent beneath him, but not participating, whilst he took his pleasure, using her body.

At last he rolled away, frowning. 'You could at least pretend you're enjoying it,' he said bitterly, and she gasped wondering if he had guessed the truth.

Then, spiritedly, she flashed back, 'And you might show a little more concern when I'm so upset.'

They stared at each other, dismayed to find they were in the middle of another quarrel.

Fifty-Six

Although they had tried to make up, by the time Lawrence's brief forty-eight-hour leave was over, there was still a constraint between them.

'I'm sorry, Lawrence,' Lizzie said, genuinely contrite.

'It's all right,' he said, but she could see from the tightness around his mouth and the resentment in his eyes that it was anything but 'all right'. 'I don't know when I'll get leave again,' he went on. 'I'm being posted to Scampton to a newly formed squadron, six one seven. You mustn't tell a soul, Lizzie, it's all very hush-hush. We're to have special training, low flying over water at night. They won't tell us why, but it must be something big.'

'Oh Lawrence . . .' Now she clung to him, feeling a surge of concern. 'I do love you. I'm so sorry about . . . about everything. Try to get home again, soon. It'll be better, I promise.'

But it wasn't. When he came home again – for Scampton was only a few miles away and he could easily get home even for only a few hours – if anything, the situation was worse. Lizzie had been lonely and miserable with no one to turn to for comfort. She had visited Susan, but had found herself in the role of comforter. Now she had no one. Her father and grandparents were lost to her and Edwina was far too occupied with keeping her school running and all her pupils safe from the bombing, to say nothing of the war work in which she involved herself.

Even the work that Lizzie did for the war effort had become monotonous and now she was without the friendly camaraderie of the other girls. The one or two with whom she had formed a casual friendship, Barbara in particular, had moved on. Some had gone on to do other work, one or two of the younger ones had joined the forces and the new batch of women and girls seemed to view the wife of Lawrence Marsh from The Hall as an outsider. Lizzie was listless and mourning the loss of her friend. Then she was riddled with guilt because it should have been her husband and his safety that dominated her thoughts.

But all she could think was, *Oh Tolly, Tolly. I've lost you.*

When Lawrence arrived home again, looking wide-eyed with exhaustion, Lizzie tried hard to hide her feelings. She fussed around him, running a bath for him and using double the regulation amount of water. She laid out his suit herself on the bed and helped him tie his bow tie, although in fact, he was far more expert at tying than she was.

He smiled down at her, resting his hands lightly on her waist. 'I've missed you so much, Lizzie. How . . . how have you been?'

She realized he was trying to show concern for her feelings and yet not wanting to open up the raw wound again.

'Fine,' she said brightly, but there was a brittle quality in her voice, a forced gaiety that she was afraid he could not help but notice. She patted his chest as she completed the tie and stood back. 'How about you, darling? You look awfully tired. Is it very dreadful?'

He nodded. 'We've been taken off all other operations, just to concentrate on this wretched special training.

We're getting such a lot of stick from the other chaps now. We just all wish something would happen.'

There were only the three of them at dinner: Lawrence, his mother and Lizzie. Celia made polite enquiries about his life in the RAF, but her interest was superficial and made out of the need for civilized, dinner-table conversation.

'Father away on business, is he?' Lawrence asked towards the end of the meal.

Celia leant back in her chair and fitted a cigarette into a long black holder. Deakin moved forward to light it for her and she inhaled deeply and blew smoke rings into the air, watching them float and then dissolve before she turned her limpid gaze on her son. 'My dear boy,' she drawled, 'your guess is as good as mine. I doubt the war is going to make your father change his ways.' She smiled, but the smile did not reach her eyes. 'Do you?'

Lawrence looked down at his plate and, beneath the table, Lizzie felt his foot find hers and press it. He needed her, she knew. He needed her to put her arms around him and hold him close and love him. He needed her to tell him that everything was going to be all right.

Lizzie rose from the table and smiled at her mother-in-law. 'That meal was delicious. I don't know how Cook manages it with all the rationing.'

Celia blew out the blue smoke again. 'It's what she's paid for.' She rose from the table, her movements languid, and moved towards the door. 'Good night, my dears,' she said offhandedly over her shoulder. 'If you're leaving early in the morning, Lawrence, please don't disturb me. I need my beauty sleep.'

Lizzie watched as Lawrence, who had risen to his feet the moment she had got up from the table, stared after his mother. 'Good night then, Mother,' he murmured. 'And

I'll say "goodbye" too . . .' but already the door had swung to behind her.

Lizzie held out her hand to him. 'Come on, darling. Shall we go up?'

He walked around the table and took her hand, clinging to it like a drowning person.

She tried, oh she tried so very hard, to respond to his desperate need of her. She willed herself to be swept along on the tidal wave of his passion, but there was a shadow between them, the shadow of a lost soul whom Lizzie could not forget.

At last, they lay in each other's arms in the huge bed against a mound of pillows. He buried his face against her neck and Lizzie could feel the wetness of his tears on her skin.

His voice was muffled as he said, 'It's over, isn't it?'

She held him tightly. She closed her eyes but her own tears squeezed their way from beneath her eyelids and ran down her face. She stroked his hair as sobs shook him. But she said nothing. There was nothing she could say.

She lay amidst sumptuous surroundings, her every whim pandered to by lackeys. She had no need to work for her living; she had no need to do anything. She had a wardrobe full of fine clothes, enough food set before her each day that would have fed the whole family in Waterman's Yard. And she was in the arms of a handsome young man who, she knew, loved her. And yet . . . All she wanted was to be back on the river, on her father's boat, standing at the prow, the wind in her hair, and watching for Tolly on the bank.

The truth came slowly, only moments before Lawrence lifted his head and, in the half-light, looked down into her eyes. 'Lizzie, my darling Lizzie,' he whispered. 'It's not me you love, is it? It's Tolly.'

She drew in breath. 'No, no . . .' she began to say, but very gently he laid his finger against her lips.

'Hush, my darling. Just let me love you one more time. For the good times, Lizzie. And we have had some good times, haven't we?'

'Yes, oh yes. Oh Lawrence . . .' Her tears flowed unchecked now and she clung to him. Now their loving was tender and giving, but they were crying, sobbing against each other, both knowing that the next time Lawrence came home, Lizzie would no longer be at The Hall.

Tomorrow morning, after Lawrence had gone, Lizzie was going home.

Fifty-Seven

Lizzie was waiting on Miller's Wharf when the *Maid Mary Ann* arrived. As soon as the gangplank was in place, Lizzie, her heart thumping in her chest, her mouth dry, ran up it and for the first time since before her marriage, she stepped on to the deck of her father's ship.

'Hello, Uncle Ernie.'

The quiet man nodded and said only one word, 'Lass.' It was both a greeting and a question. Lizzie looked about her and saw her father standing at the tiller. He was staring at her, but from here she could not read the expression in his eyes.

'Dad.' She made her way to him, tears stinging her eyes at the sight of him. He seemed to have aged since she had last seen him. His hair was liberally sprinkled with white, and lines of sorrow were etched deeply into his face. A few feet away from him, she hesitated, found she had to swallow a lump in her throat before she could begin to speak.

Then the words tumbled out, jumbled, scarcely making sense. 'Oh Dad. I'm sorry. Forgive me. I've come home. You were right. Please, will you forgive me? I was so dreadfully wrong. Please . . .'

For a long moment, in which Lizzie's hope plunged into despair, her father stared at her, his face expressionless. Then slowly, as if the action, so long unused, was rusty, he opened his arms wide to her.

With a sob of thankfulness, Lizzie ran into them to be enveloped in the safe embrace of his strong and loving arms.

Later, in the tiny cabin, they talked. 'Oh, it's so good to be back here,' she murmured, her glance roaming lovingly around the confined space, the polished cupboards, the tiny stove where she had cooked so many meals for her father and Uncle Duggie, the bed where she knew she had been born. 'I've missed it all so much.'

Already, Dan was able to tease her gently as they sat together on the bench seat, holding hands, almost like reunited lovers. 'All that grand living and you hankered for this?'

She nodded and pressed her lips together hard to try to stop the tears that welled in her eyes. But they spilled over and ran down her cheeks. Dan reached over and, with a callused hand that was surprisingly gentle, he brushed them away. 'Don't Lizzie, love. Don't cry. You're safe home, now. No more need for tears.'

'But I hurt you so. I hurt everyone. Gran and Grandpa. And . . . and Tolly.' Now the sobs shook her and she buried her face against his chest. 'I can't ever tell him, Dad, how sorry I am. How wrong I was.'

'Ah.' She felt the breath sigh from her father's chest as he said softly, 'Ah, Tolly, is it?'

It was all he said and all he needed to say, for they both knew what lay behind that simple statement without another word being spoken.

He held her close whilst she cried out her sorrow and then, when she sat up slowly and dried her eyes, he asked gently, 'What about Lawrence?'

It was the first time he had spoken his name in gentleness.

'He's gone back to Scampton. He's . . . he's involved in some sort of special training. I don't know what. He . . . he couldn't tell me.'

'Of course he couldn't, love.'

'He . . . he knows I've come home. He knows it's over.'

Her father nodded. 'Poor lad.'

Lizzie's eyes widened as she stared at him. 'You . . . you feel sorry for him? For Lawrence? But . . . but I thought you hated him.'

Her father sighed heavily, releasing a lifetime of bitterness. 'No, I don't hate the lad. He can't help being his father's son.'

'What is it about his father that you . . .?' she began, but Dan patted her hand and said, 'Not now, Lizzie love. Maybe one day, I'll tell you it all. But not now. Now, I just want to enjoy you being back with me.' He put his arm about her again. 'For good, is it, Lizzie?' he asked softly.

She nodded and then, closing her eyes, she laid her head against his shoulder. The question could rest for now. There would always be another time to ask. She was home where she belonged.

'Now listen, Mam,' Dan began the moment he stepped over the threshold of Bessie's home, with Lizzie hovering uncertainly on the doorstep, nervous even to enter the house that had once been as much of a home to her as had the ship. 'Before you start, just let me have me say first, for once, will you? Me and Lizzie have sorted everything out between us.' He put his arm out and drew her in. 'She's sorry for what's happened. And she's home to stay and . . .' As Bessie opened her mouth, Dan held up his hand. 'That's all there is to be said.'

Bert had come to stand behind Bessie. He slipped his arms halfway around her ample waist – it was as far as they could reach – and peered around her shoulder. He was grinning happily. 'Bessie, my angel, isn't that just the most wonderful news? Come away in, Dan. You, too, love. Come and give your old grandpa a kiss.'

'Now just you wait a minute, Bert Ruddick . . .' Bessie twisted herself round in his embrace. 'I'm not having her—'

'Bessie, my angel, light of my life . . .' He reached up and kissed her full on the mouth. 'You have the loveliest mouth, but it don't half run away with itself – just now and again.' He lowered his voice, trying to hide what he was saying, but Lizzie's sharp ears caught the gist of his whispering. 'The lass is sorry . . . we don't know what's happened . . . taken a lot of courage to come back . . . just be thankful . . .'

There was a moment's silence before Bessie gave a shriek of laughter and clasped Bert to her, burying his face in the softness of her bosom. 'You're a good man, Bert Ruddick. The best. The very best.' Then she turned and held her arms wide to embrace Lizzie, the tears coursing down her plump cheeks.

It was on Bert's wireless that they all heard the news bulletin later that same week. The modulated tones of the announcer told them that a squadron of Lancaster bombers, flying at a very low level, had attacked the dams in the Rhur valley. Devastating flooding had been caused to the industrial region and the mission had been hailed as a great success, one that could possibly turn the tide of the war.

'Nine of our Lancasters are missing,' the announcer concluded in solemn tones.

Lizzie gasped and turned white, but she could not speak, not even when all her family turned to look at her.

Without waiting for the news that would surely follow in a few days' time, Lizzie knew, instinctively, that Lawrence would not be coming back.

It was Edwina who brought the official news to Waterman's Yard. She stood hesitantly on the doorstep, unsure of her welcome. The last time she had visited her old friend had been to offer comfort on the news of Duggie's death. Edwina had not come again to the Yard, but now, further tragic news had brought her unwillingly to Bessie's door once more.

But now Bessie drew her inside and hugged her. Any constraint between them fell away. 'We can guess why you've come, Miss Edwina,' Lizzie heard her say. 'Lizzie's in a right state, blaming herself.'

Lizzie looked up as they came into the kitchen. Edwina came straight to her, holding out her hands to take Lizzie's. 'You know, don't you, my dear?'

Lizzie, unable to speak, nodded.

'His plane went down over the target. It . . . it blew up. There was not the slightest chance of any survivors. I am so sorry.'

Shaking, Lizzie clung to Edwina's hands. 'I feel . . . so guilty. I should have carried on the pretence. I tried. I tried so hard, but he knew. He guessed. I . . . I feel as if I sent him to his death.'

'You mustn't think like that,' Edwina tried to reassure her. 'You probably gave him more happiness in these last few months than you will ever know.' Tenderly, she stroked a tendril of hair back from Lizzie's face and said, very quietly with a world of regret in her voice, 'It's more than I did for my man before he went away to war.'

'He wanted a child,' Lizzie sobbed. 'Lawrence so much wanted to ... to leave a son to carry on, if the worst happened. I haven't even been able to do that for him.' She raised her face to look into Edwina's. 'I would have done, if I could.'

'I know, I know.' Edwina put her arm around the girl and held her close. 'But it's over now,' she said, unwittingly echoing Lawrence's own poignant words. 'And now you must go on with your life, but before you do, can I ask just one more thing of you, Lizzie?'

'Of course. Anything.'

'Randolph is arranging a memorial service in the parish church. Will you attend as Lawrence's widow?'

Lizzie shook her head. 'His father won't want me there.'

'Oh, but he does,' Edwina said, surprising both Lizzie and the listening Bessie. 'It was Randolph who wanted me specifically to ask you to come.'

Fifty-Eight

There were fewer mourners at the memorial service than had been expected. Family members and local dignitaries, who attended out of duty only, made up the congregation. Once, the church might have been packed with the townsfolk paying their respects to a member of the unofficial squire's family, but Randolph was not liked and Lawrence hardly known. A few ladies from the committees upon which Celia served attended and only one person represented the river folk: Lizzie.

At the end of the service, Lizzie made her farewells to Edwina, who had sat with her throughout, but as she walked away down the long path to the gate, she heard a man's voice calling her name. 'Lizzie. Lizzie, a moment, if you please.'

With surprise, she turned to see Randolph Marsh following her. She stopped and turned to wait for him.

'My dear,' he said, taking her arm and urging her further down the path away from the small gathering outside the church door. 'You no doubt know that you will receive Lawrence's airforce pension, but . . .'

'I don't want his money,' her voice was shrill. 'That's not why I married him. I want nothing from you. Nothing.'

She could tell that he was fighting to hold on to his patience. 'Now, my dear, don't be so hasty. You are entitled to it and I certainly have no objection to make. What I wanted to ask you, my dear, was . . .'

Lizzie ground her teeth together, wishing he would stop calling her 'my dear', for there was not an ounce of affection in the endearment. But she said nothing as his next words shocked her. 'I don't suppose, by any miraculous chance, you could be pregnant?'

She stared up at him, her eyes wide with amazement. The audacity of the man, she thought. What an unfeeling, hard bastard Randolph Marsh was. Everything she had ever heard about him was true. Here he was at his own son's memorial service, and all he was concerned about was, was there any possibility of an heir for his family's fortune?

Lizzie's mouth was tight as she said shortly, 'No, I'm not.'

She pulled her arm free of his grasp and marched away from him, glad to be leaving the Marsh family for good.

'Oh Dad, Gran's waiting on the wharf again.' Lizzie turned towards her father standing at the wheel guiding the ship towards its mooring. 'Something must have happened. She only ever comes now when there's trouble.'

Lizzie had slipped back into her former life as if she had never been away. Her brief marriage to Lawrence Marsh was now never spoken of and the affection between herself and her father was, if that were possible, even stronger than before. As for Lizzie herself, she was as happy as it was possible for her to be, but deep inside she carried a heavy burden of regret. She felt such guilt that she had not been able to love Lawrence, as she should have done. She could not forgive herself for having hurt him. And worse still, when she realized at last where her true feelings lay, it was too late. Tolly was gone. She would never be able to make up her quarrel with him, not properly. Even though, that last time, they had parted on better terms, there was still so much that had been left unsaid. There was so much she wanted to tell him. And now she would never be able to. She would never be able to tell him how much she really loved him.

Lizzie and her father exchanged a troubled look as the vessel drew nearer to the wharf. Bert had been a little under the weather two days ago when they had left and the same thought was obviously in both their minds. Had something happened to him?

But as the ship drew nearer and Lizzie leant over the side, she could see that although her grandmother's face was anxious, she did not look devastated, as she no doubt would have done if something had happened to her beloved husband.

Lizzie was the first off the ship and running towards her. 'What is it, Gran? What's happened?'

Without the usual greeting, Bessie nodded her head beyond Lizzie towards Dan. 'It's yar dad I have to talk to, lass. Not you.'

'Just tell me, Gran, it's not Grandpa, is it?'

A brief smile chased away some of the anxiety on Bessie's face. 'No, lass. Your grandpa's fine. Better than he was.'

'Thank goodness,' Lizzie breathed. 'Then, what is it?'

Doggedly, Bessie said, 'You'll know soon enough, but your dad has a right to know first.'

Several minutes passed before Dan was able to step ashore. Lizzie could hardly contain her impatience and then, to her disappointment, as her father came towards them, Bessie waved her away. 'Just let me tell yar dad, there's a good lass.'

She opened her mouth to protest, but seeing the look

on her grandmother's face, she turned away and walked
to the far end of the wharf. She watched them converse,
although it was Bessie who was doing all the talking. Dan
was just listening, staring down at his mother in disbelief.

'Whatever can it be?' Lizzie muttered to herself, standing first on one foot and then on the other.

She saw her father nod, say a few brief words and then
her grandmother turned and, leaning heavily on the walking stick she now used, made her painful way from the
wharf and towards her home.

Dan came towards Lizzie and stopped in front of her.

'What is it, Dad? What's happened?' She could guess
nothing from his face, for his expression was a strange
mixture of shock and disbelief.

His words came at last, halting and disjointed. 'She's
come back. She's at your gran's house. She's very ill. She
. . . she . . .'

Lizzie took hold of his hand. 'Who, Dad? Who's come
back.'

For a long moment, unable to believe it himself, Dan
stared at her. Then, his voice breaking with emotion, he
said, 'Mary Ann. Your mother. She's come back.'

Lizzie felt as if her legs were going to give way beneath
her, but whether from shock or relief that her mother was
alive – and therefore the dark secret she had always
dreaded had been entirely unfounded – she did not know.

'Where has she been all these years?'

Her father was looking down at her strangely now.
'You mean, you don't know, Lizzie?'

Lizzie shook her head and now, for the first time,
she could whisper, 'I thought she might be dead. That

night . . .' The question she had so desperately wanted to ask for so long, and yet had not dared, could now be voiced. 'I thought she'd drowned.'

'What?' His tone was scandalized. For a moment Dan closed his eyes and then groaned aloud. 'Oh, my dear girl, I never realized. Lizzie, I'm so sorry. I should have explained it to you. But at the time, you were so young and then, well, I couldn't bear to speak her name. I just wanted to blot it all out, to forget it. To forget her.'

But he hadn't been able to. Lizzie knew that. The haunted look in his eyes that had always been there told her so.

'It's all right,' she said now. It wasn't, but it was all she could say. She couldn't add to this poor man's burden any more. He was already suffering. He had suffered for years because of that night, and now . . . What now? Lizzie thought. Aloud, she said, 'So, where did she go?'

'She's been living in a little cottage just the other side of Raven's Wood.'

Lizzie gasped, understanding, at last, why there had been such anger when her father had learnt that that was where she had been meeting Lawrence. As if reading her thoughts, Dan smiled wryly. 'Yes, when you started meeting Lawrence there, I was always afraid you'd find out where she was.'

'But why – I mean, why was she living there?'

'Can't you guess?'

Mystified, Lizzie said, 'Not really. Unless she became tired of living on the ship and wanted a little house of her own.'

Dan sighed so heavily that she felt the waft of his breath on her face. 'If only that had been the case.' The hurt of years was in his tone as he added, 'No, your mother left me to go to her lover. She's been a kept

436

woman, his mistress, hidden away near the woods all these years. All I can presume is that he no longer wants her now. So, she's come back.'

'Her ... her lover?' Lizzie began, and then it all fell swiftly into place. It was suddenly so blindingly obvious, that Lizzie was astounded at her own naïvety.

'Oh, my God,' she breathed and, not usually given to blasphemy, her father understood the depth of her shock. 'It was Randolph Marsh, wasn't it?'

Her father nodded and then added, his voice deep with emotion now, 'And that's not all. Your gran says she's expecting a child.'

Fifty-Nine

'You've told her?' was Bessie's greeting as Lizzie and her father stepped into the house.

Dan nodded. Then his voice was husky as he asked, 'Where is she?'

Bessie gestured with a slight movement of her head. 'Front room. I've had to rig up a bed in there for her. She's in a bad state.' There were tears in Bessie's eyes as she added, 'I couldn't send her away, Dan.'

The big man reached out and touched his mother's wrinkled hand. 'Of course you couldn't, Mam. I . . . I wouldn't have wanted you to.'

Woodenly, he moved towards the door leading into the front room. Big and strong as he was, Dan looked suddenly so vulnerable and afraid. Impulsively, Lizzie followed him, caught hold of his hand and smiled up at him. 'Do you want to go in on your own or shall I come in with you?'

He looked down at her and she felt his hold on her hand tighten. 'Come with me, Lizzie. Please,' he said hoarsely and, together, they went into the room.

Lizzie would not have recognized the woman lying in the bed. Apart from the bulge beneath the bedcovers that pronounced her pregnancy, she was thin to the point of emaciation. Her cheeks were hollowed, her eyes bulging from their sockets, and her hair hung, lank and unkempt, about her shoulders. Her face was an unhealthy pallor, devoid of any colour.

'Oh Dan!' Her voice was weak, little more than a whisper. Then her gaze came to rest on Lizzie. 'And Lizzie.'

With what appeared to be a great effort, she lifted her arm from the bed and reached out with trembling, skeletal fingers.

'There isn't long. Dan, please, will you forgive me? Please say you forgive me. I couldn't bear to go without making my peace with you.'

Dan moved suddenly, dragging Lizzie with him as he went towards the bed, his other hand outstretched to take Mary Ann's. 'My dear, don't say anything. You're home now and we're going to take care of you.'

He released Lizzie's hand and, sitting down on the edge of the bed, took hold of Mary Ann's with both his strong, warm hands. Lizzie, unable to speak, stood behind him, but her gaze never wavered from the woman in the bed.

'Oh, Dan,' Mary Ann breathed and closed her eyes. Tears pushed their way from beneath her eyelids and ran down her face. 'You're such a good man. I was such a fool. A stupid, naïve fool. So often, I've wanted to come back to you. You don't know how much I've missed you and . . . and Lizzie. And Duggie. I even missed Duggie and his teasing, too.' She opened her eyes now. 'I . . . I was so sorry about Duggie. Did you see the banner?'

Dan was puzzled. 'Banner? What banner?'

'The banner I embroidered in his memory. I gave it to the parish church. I thought they would put it up some-where . . .'

'You? You did that, Mary Ann?'

Weakly, she nodded. 'It was the least I could do. It was

the only talent I ever had, wasn't it?' she said bitterly. 'Being able to embroider. I was useless at everything else. I even loved the wrong man.'

Lizzie watched as Dan said nothing now, but merely patted Mary Ann's hand.

'Dan, I was so wrong. So wicked . . .'

'Don't say that, my dear. A little foolish, maybe, but wicked, no.'

'I was. It was so wrong of me to leave a good and generous man like you. And I took you away from poor Susan too, didn't I? I did it deliberately, Dan. I couldn't bear to see you loving her, while no one seemed to love me. And then, to leave my child, my own flesh and blood. What sort of a mother does that? That was unforgivable.'

Her glance lifted now to rest on Lizzie and the slightest of smiles touched her mouth. 'She's pretty, Dan. Like I used to be, isn't she? And from what I've heard, she's been just as silly as her mother.'

Dan shook his head. 'No, no. She's come home. She's back with me now.'

'Since Lawrence was killed?'

'Well, no.' There was embarrassment in Dan's tone and he glanced apologetically at Lizzie before adding, 'She came home before that. She'd . . . she'd realized things weren't working out.'

Mary Ann gave a little nod and murmured, 'Maybe she's got a little more sense than me, then. I hope so.'

Lizzie was listening with a kind of bemused, shocked fascination. She had not seen her mother for nine years and yet Mary Ann knew all about her. She knew about her marriage, about her young husband's death – everything. But then, she would have heard it all from her lover. No wonder Randolph Marsh had been so incensed over Lawrence marrying Lizzie.

If it hadn't been such a tragic situation, Lizzie thought, it would be funny. But looking at the poor creature in the bed, there was nothing to find amusing.

'You've come home now, Mary Ann,' Dan was saying. 'And when you're better . . .'

Mary Ann was shaking her head. 'I'm not going to get better, Dan. This child is going to kill me.'

'Don't talk like that. I won't listen to such talk. You'll have the child and then, when you're stronger, we'll see what's to be done.'

Mary Ann was smiling at him sadly. In her huge, dark eyes Lizzie could see a depth of knowledge, a premonition, that what she said was the truth.

She had no will to survive any longer.

'I've come back, Dan,' Mary Ann whispered, 'for one reason only. To beg your forgiveness, so that I can rest in peace. Just say it, Dan. Please. Say I'm forgiven.'

His voice broke then and he lifted her hand and pressed it to his cheek. 'Oh Mary Ann. You're forgiven. You are forgiven.'

A week later, Mary Ann gave birth to a strong, healthy boy, who yelled constantly for the sustenance his sick mother could not give him. For the three days following the difficult and protracted birth, whilst the life drained out of Mary Ann, Lizzie sat beside her mother's bed, holding her hand.

Most of the time, Mary Ann was barely conscious, but Lizzie stayed there anyway. On the third night, at about three in the morning, Mary Ann awoke. Lizzie, dozing fitfully and uncomfortably in the chair, was instantly awake too.

'Is there anything you want, Mam?' she asked softly.

The room was illuminated softly by a tiny nightlight on the mantelpiece.

'No,' Mary Ann whispered. 'Just . . . hold my hand, Lizzie. And tell me you love your wicked, silly mother.'

'I do love you. We all do. Just get well and we'll be so happy together.'

'No, Lizzie. It's not going to happen, my darling.'

'Why not? You're not going back to *him*, are you?'

Mary Ann's smile was weak, but for a brief moment some of the suffering left her face. 'No, my love. I wouldn't go back to him. Not ever again. He's a cruel, harsh man. He uses people. But I couldn't see it. I was dazzled by his sophistication, his charm. I thought he loved me, but I doubt very much if the man is capable of love. And yet, I still couldn't seem to stop loving him.'

With an effort that was obviously painful, Mary Ann turned herself to face her daughter. For a moment her gaze lingered on Lizzie's face as if she were drinking in every feature of it to carry with her into eternity.

'Dan is a hundred times the man Randolph Marsh is. It's my tragedy that I didn't see it when I had his love. I did love your father, Lizzie, truly I did, but in a very different way. My feeling for Randolph was a kind of madness, a passion that wouldn't die. Dan's love was the true love. It was gentle and kind and good. Perhaps that sounds a little boring, but it's the only sort that lasts.'

She lay back against the pillows again, for a moment exhausted by the effort. 'You know,' Mary Ann said softly, 'I always thought you and Tolly might end up together.'

Suddenly, there was a lump in Lizzie's throat and she closed her eyes and pressed her lips together to prevent them uttering a sound.

'He always seemed so devoted to you, even as a little boy.'

Again there was a long silence before Mary Ann whispered, 'Find yourself a good man, Lizzie. A man like your father. A man who truly loves you for yourself . . .'

Her voice faded away and Lizzie could see that her mother had fallen asleep.

She sat back in her chair and closed her eyes, but the tears came anyway. Tears for her mother, who, despite Lizzie's own brave words, knew she was dying. Tears for Lawrence too, but most of all, the tears she wept were for Tolly.

Lizzie woke with a start as she heard a movement in the next room and knew that the house was stirring. The pale light of dawn was creeping in through the gap in the curtains. Lizzie stretched and then glanced towards her mother.

She was lying just as she had fallen asleep. She looked very peaceful and there was the ghost of a smile on her mouth. The lines of suffering had fallen away from her face and, though it was still thin, she looked more like the woman Lizzie remembered as her mother.

It was then she realized that the life had ebbed away from Mary Ann whilst Lizzie slept.

Sixty

'So, what are we going to do with this young man, then?'

Blunt as ever, Bessie was the one to voice the question that had been in everyone's mind, but the one that no one had dared to broach. They had buried poor Mary Ann in a corner of the town's cemetery the day before and now the most pressing question was, what was to happen to her baby son?

'I'd look after the bairn mesen,' Bessie added, tickling the wriggling infant fondly as he lay in his makeshift crib – the bottom drawer of the chest of drawers from Bessie's bedroom. 'But I'm really too old now.'

'I suppose I should go to The Hall,' Dan said, reluctantly.

'Oh no,' Bessie said fiercely. 'You aren't going there. No, I tell you what. Lizzie can go and ask Miss Edwina to come to see me.'

'Miss Edwina?' Lizzie and her father chorused together.

Bessie nodded firmly. 'Why not? She's the bairn's aunt.'

Lizzie glanced at her father, who shrugged. 'Aye, run along, lass. If your gran thinks it's the right thing to do.'

Lizzie walked the length of River Road deep in thought. What a muddle it all was, she thought. The child was her half-brother and would have been half-brother to Lawrence too. He was no blood relation to either Dan or to Bessie and yet they were concerning themselves over the infant's welfare.

444

Her mother had been right, Lizzie thought with a sad smile. Her father really was a good man. Despite the sorrow in her own heart, she felt a surge of happiness that she, at least, had been reconciled with her loving family. If only . . .

No, she told herself determinedly, I mustn't think of Tolly. Not today. Today I must think of that poor, nameless little boy. My half-brother. I mustn't think of Tolly now . . .

She was ushered into Edwina's private apartment at the top of the house.

'Lizzie, my dear.' Edwina came towards her, her hands outstretched. 'How are you? Yesterday must have been awful for you all.'

Lizzie nodded. 'We saw you in church. Why didn't you come back to the house?'

Edwina sighed. 'I was in two minds what to do.'

'It must have been difficult for you, too.'

Edwina pressed her lips together and nodded. She led Lizzie to the window seat and they sat down side by side.

'We used to sit here together, your mother and I. I used to teach her embroidery.'

Lizzie nodded. 'I know. There's a trunkful of it in Gran's house. Everything my mother ever made. Even the little baby dresses with the fancy smocking she made for me. Gran was showing me them only yesterday. She's kept it all.'

'Has she really?' Edwina was surprised, as she added, 'Fancy that.'

There was a moment's silence and then they both spoke at once.

'How is . . .?'

'Gran's sent me . . .'

They smiled and then Edwina said, 'You first.'

'Gran wonders if you could call to see her? She . . . they . . .' Lizzie bit her lip.

'Go on,' Edwina prompted gently.

'It's about the baby. They don't know what to do.'

'Baby?' Edwina's eyes widened. 'What baby?'

'You . . . you didn't know?'

Edwina continued to stare at Lizzie and, robbed of speech, merely shook her head.

Lizzie swallowed. This was proving to be even more difficult than she had imagined. 'When my mother came back to us, she was expecting. Almost on her time, in fact. The baby was born ten days ago and she died three days afterwards.'

Edwina let out a long sigh. 'I didn't know. Bessie sent word about her death and when the funeral was, but she said nothing about a child.' Again they stared at each other as Edwina added softly, 'Of course, it's Randolph's child, isn't it?'

Lizzie nodded.

'So,' Edwina said, so quietly that Lizzie almost didn't hear her words, 'Randolph has an heir after all.' Then, shaking herself from her reverie, Edwina stood up and said briskly, 'I'll come at once. Just wait a moment while I get my hat and coat.'

They walked side by side back to Waterman's Yard without speaking, each lost in their own thoughts.

As she stood looking down upon the infant, a look of love and adoration drove away all the sadness that had for many years been in Edwina's face. Joy sparkled in her eyes as she bent and carefully lifted the baby boy into her arms.

'Oh,' she breathed, stroking his head with gentle fingers. 'He's just like Lawrence was as a baby and my mother always said that he was the image of Randolph as a child.' She gave a light laugh and added, 'There's no denying whose this baby is.'

'Aye,' Bessie said bluntly as she and Lizzie watched. 'But will his father acknowledge him?'

'Not at once, no. I know my brother well.' Edwina's voice hardened. 'Too well. But I think in time, he will. His desperate need for an heir will override anything else. Eventually.'

'And in the meantime?' Bessie asked.

'In the meantime,' Edwina said firmly, 'if Dan will help me, I will adopt the child legally.'

'Dan? Why does it concern Dan?'

'Because, Bessie,' Edwina explained gently, 'Mary Ann was still legally Dan's wife, wasn't she? I think I'm right in saying that in the eyes of the law, this is Dan's child.'

Bessie sniffed, but said nothing. Edwina went on, 'But there's nothing to stop Dan allowing me to adopt him. I'll make sure everything is done legally and properly.'

'What shall you call him, Miss Edwina?' Lizzie asked quietly.

Again Edwina's loving eyes roamed over the baby's face, drinking in every tiny feature. 'Oh, there's only one name I could call him, Lizzie. Christopher.'

So it was all settled between them and the following day, Edwina came to collect her nephew, soon to be her adopted son.

'I'm surprised she's being allowed to adopt him,' Dan said, and added hastily, 'Not that I'm not delighted she is, but with her not being married . . .'

Bessie shrugged. 'We're in difficult times. There'll be a lot of poor little mites left orphaned because of the war. I expect the authorities have been able to allow this particular adoption because of the special circumstances. Besides,' Bessie added shrewdly, 'she knows all the right

447

people, doesn't she? Moves in the right circles, so to speak.' She tapped the side of her nose. 'I 'spect it's a case of "not what you know, but who you know".'

'Now, now, Mam,' Dan teased.

'No, lad, don't get me wrong. I'm only too pleased she does. In this case, it's fully justified, however she's managed it.'

Dan put his arm around Lizzie's shoulder. 'Well, lass, are you ready? Time we were getting aboard.'

'I'm ready, Dad.' She bent and kissed her grandmother. 'Take it easy, Gran. Give my love to Grandpa. Tell him we'll see him on Wednesday.'

'Ta-ra, love. Take care.'

They were sailing past the ferryman's cottage when they saw Susan standing at the very edge of the riverbank, waving a piece of paper and shouting.

'I can't hear what she's saying,' Dan said. 'Can you?'

'No,' Lizzie said, shading her eyes against the sun. 'But she's looking very pleased about something.'

'I can't steer any nearer the bank, Lizzie. Take the cog boat and have a word with her.'

Minutes later, the cog boat was bumping against the bank, but before Lizzie had even the chance to climb out of it, Susan was reaching out towards her.

'Lizzie, he's safe. He's alive, Lizzie.'

Lizzie gaped up at her and the breath seemed knocked from her body as her heart began to thud painfully. 'Alive?'

'Yes. Tolly's alive. He's a prisoner of war. He's in a prison in Germany. But he'll be coming home, Lizzie. One day, when it's all over, he'll be coming home.' As Lizzie scrambled up the bank, Susan, tears coursing down her face, clasped her hands. 'Oh Lizzie, Tolly will be coming back to us.'

They hugged each other, there on the bank, dancing round with joy and singing together, 'He's coming home, he's coming home.'

Lizzie waved and shouted to her father, but still he could not hear the wonderful news. 'I'll go back in a minute,' she said to Susan. 'But tell me, is he all right? Was he hurt?'

'He broke a leg when they crash landed behind enemy lines, but he says he's received good treatment and his leg has mended well. They won't let him come home yet, of course, so we'll have to be patient until the war is over. Oh pray God, it isn't long.'

The war dragged on for another eighteen months, and for those who waited for loved ones with fear and longing, it seemed much longer. But then in May of 1945 came VE Day and soon afterwards, prisoners of war began to arrive back home.

'When will he be home?' Lizzie asked Susan constantly. Although she had written to him during his captivity and received a few letters in return, his words had been stilted and distant.

'It'll be because of the censor,' Susan tried to comfort her. 'They know every word is going to be read by the Germans. Mine are just the same.'

But his mother never showed Lizzie her letters from Tolly, so Lizzie could not be sure that the woman was not just being kind.

'He'll be home very soon now,' Susan was able to say

at last. 'But he's to go into hospital first to have a thorough check. He's fine. His leg's healed well, but he has been ill. Nothing serious, though.'

'Just prison camp conditions, I suppose,' Lizzie said, thinking of one or two men who had already come home after being imprisoned. Their skeletal figures had shocked Lizzie, but at least, she had told herself at the time, they are alive and home again, and she mourned for all those who would not be coming back. Uncle Duggie, Lawrence and so many more. Once, she had believed that Tolly, too, was lost to her forever. But now, her heart lifted as she thought that soon, very soon, she would see him again.

The weeks that passed before his arrival dragged interminably. Susan had received a letter from him and told Lizzie, 'He hopes to be home next week. When you come back from Hull, Lizzie, he'll be here.'

Now that day had arrived. They were returning home, sailing upriver towards Elsborough, closer and closer they came to the white cottage and Lizzie was standing at the bow of the ship, shading her eyes, squinting to catch sight of him.

And then there he was standing in the garden of his home, his mother hovering in the doorway of the cottage behind him. He was thin, Lizzie could see that even from this distance, but he looked resplendent in his RAF uniform, tall and with his hair blowing in the breeze. She waved but there was no answering wave from him. He just stood there, watching her.

Lizzie swallowed. He was still angry with her. He no longer loved her, if, indeed, he ever had done. Had her love for him coloured her imagination and made her believe that perhaps he had loved her too? Lizzie felt the tears prickle her eyelids and the lump in her throat grew, threatening to choke her.

Her father was at her side. 'Throw him this, love,' he said gently as he handed her a piece of coal from the cargo they were carrying.

'It's no use, Dad,' she said, her voice breaking. 'He . . . he's not forgiven me.'

'Go on, love. Just try it.' He pushed the piece of coal into her hands and hurried back to the tiller.

Lizzie balanced it in her hand and then threw it towards Tolly. It landed a little way beyond him, then rolled down the slope, coming to rest at his feet.

If he picks it up, she told herself, he loves me still. Or even if he smiles, or just – just waves. Anything, she found herself praying, just to show me that he forgives me. Please, oh please, Tolly. Don't you know how much I love you? Don't you know it was you all the time? Only I was too blind, too stupid to see it.

She found she was holding her breath as slowly the ship slid by the man standing on the bank. Tolly was perfectly still, his gaze upon her following the movement of the vessel as it carried her by him. Across the expanse of water, they stared at each other. The young man, solemn-faced, the girl, her dark eyes anxious, her lips parted.

Then slowly, oh so slowly, Tolly bent down. His fingers grasped the piece of coal and then, just as slowly, he straightened up. A smile spread across his mouth as he raised his hand to wave to her.

For a moment, tears blurred her vision as she raised her own trembling hand.

Behind him, Susan moved out of the cottage doorway and came to stand beside her son, linking her arm through his.

Susan waved too, although she was looking not at her, Lizzie noticed with surprise, but at Dan.

Lizzie turned to glance at her father, standing with his hand resting on the tiller of his ship. His gaze, however, was not, for once, on the river ahead, but on the woman standing on the riverbank.

The smile, which lit his eyes with a happiness for so long unknown, spread across his face and, as Lizzie watched, Dan raised his hand and waved to Susan.

The Fisher Lass

*With the deepest admiration this book is
respectfully dedicated to the fishermen of Grimsby,
their wives and families.*

Acknowledgements

Grimsby is the inspiration for this novel although the story is entirely fictitious. I am very grateful to Mr Richard Doughty, Director of Museums, Archives & Archeology, and all his staff and volunteers at the National Fishing Heritage Centre in Grimsby for their interest and help, especially Mike Cullum and Doug Richards for sharing with me their experiences aboard minesweepers during World War II; Ray Smith for his wonderful tours of the *Ross Tiger*; Bob Roach, Craig Lazenby, Fisheries Historian, and Russell Hollowood, Fisheries Officer, for general background information and patiently answering innumerable questions.

My special thanks to Mike Coulson, of Skegness, who served as a radio operator aboard trawlers for two and a half years in the early 1960s and so kindly read the whole script for me.

My love and thanks as always to my family and friends, especially those who read and helped edit the script in the early stages; my sister and brother-in-law, Robena and Fred Hill; my brother and sister-in-law, David and Una Dickinson; my friends, Pauline Griggs and Linda and Terry Allaway. Thank you all so much for your hard work!

Part One

One

'Let me go. I'm not what you think.' The girl's terrified voice echoed along the dark, wet streets. 'Please – no – please don't.'

'Don't lie to me. You're one of Aggie Turnbull's sluts.' The man holding her laughed cruelly. 'I saw you come out of her house just now.'

'No – no. I'm not.' The girl struggled but was no match for his grip.

From an alleyway opposite, Jeannie watched the figures silhouetted against the light that spilled out from the windows of the Fisherman's Rest.

She had been hurrying along the deserted streets, anxious to find lodgings, when she had seen five or six young men lurch out of the pub on the corner. The sound of laughter from inside followed them into the night. Immediately, she had melted into the shadows until they moved on. But the group stood on the pavement, gathered around one of their number who seemed even worse for drink than the rest.

'We should get him home,' one of the young men said. 'If he doesn't get to the church for eleven in the morning, upstanding and sober, there'll be hell to pay.'

'Oh give it a rest, Edwin,' was the disdainful answer. 'It's his last night of bachelorhood. Let the poor chap have a good time, eh?'

'Sorry, I'm sure. But I'd have thought you of all people,

3

Francis, ought to be looking after Robert. That's what a best man is supposed to do, isn't it?'

The other laughed loudly. 'Maybe, but it's high time our brother cut loose the apron strings and had a little fun. And if tonight's his last night of freedom then . . .'

Jeannie heard the one addressed as Edwin mutter some reply, but, from across the street, she could no longer distinguish exactly what he said.

His brother's voice was clear. 'Then you run along home to dear Mama, Baby Boy, and leave us men to drink this town dry before the morning.' She saw him raise his hand and pat Edwin on his cheek with such a condescending gesture that Jeannie herself almost stepped out of the shadows and slapped him back.

They were beginning to move off down the street, half carrying, half dragging the befuddled bridegroom-to-be between them. Still Jeannie stayed hidden. Then she noticed the figure of a girl emerge from one of the houses a few yards down the street. Pulling her shawl about her head and hunching her shoulders, the girl tried to scuttle past the young men, but a hand shot out and grasped her arm.

'Oho, what have we here?' Jeannie heard Francis's languid voice raised again. 'A little bit of skirt for you, Robert, my boy. One of Aggie's girls.'

It was then that Jeannie heard the girl's frightened denial. Instinctively, she moved forward out of the shadows.

'Leave her be, Francis,' came Edwin's voice, but his protests were drowned by the general shout of approval.

'If she's one of Aggie's trollops, she's fair game.'

There was laughter now from all except Edwin and the bridegroom who seemed barely conscious. He was unable

4

to stand without support and his head lolled against one of those who held him upright.

The girl began to struggle, her screams echoing down the street.

'Leave her alone,' Edwin persisted. Still fast hold of the girl with one hand, Francis turned and shoved his brother in the chest. Edwin fell backwards into the road as the others dragged the girl and the semi-conscious bridegroom towards an alley between two houses.

Jeannie dropped the bundle of her belongings and ran forward.

Pausing only a second, she heard their crude comments. 'Prove yourself a man.'

'Your bride'll thank you tomorrow night, Robert.'

'My turn next.'

And then again came the petrified girl's screams that now went on and on.

Enraged and without thought for her own safety, Jeannie ran past Edwin, struggling to rise from the roadway, and plunged into the blackness of the alleyway.

She pushed and shoved her way amongst them, her fists flailing, not caring whom she hit, just forcing her way through. 'Let her go. You're animals . . .' She was standing now above the two on the ground. The young man lay motionless, sprawled on top of the girl. Squatting beside them, Francis was tearing at the girl's clothing, ripping away her blouse to expose a white mound of flesh and then pushing the face of his drunken brother into her bosom. 'How's that feel, eh, Robert? Good, is it?'

Jeannie reached out and grasped Francis's hair with her strong fingers, jerking him with such unexpected force that he gave a cry of pain and fell backwards, clattering against a bin and its surrounding mound of rubbish. Then she bent and pushed the inert young man away. There was not an ounce of resistance in him and he slid off the girl and rolled over on to his back, his eyes staring up at Jeannie with a glazed, stupid look. She bent over him, straining in the darkness to see his features. She intended to remember him and all his cronies. He blinked once or twice as if trying to focus on her face.

'I dinna know who you are, but I'll no' forget you,' she hissed at him. 'You should be ashamed of yoursel'.'

She straightened and now pulled the girl up. Turning, she made to return to the street, but Francis had regained his feet and was barring their way.

Through clenched teeth, Jeannie said, 'Get oot of ma way.'

There was a strange silence for a moment and then Francis threw back his head and laughed. 'Why, it's only a fisher lass. A Scottie. And we all know about them, don't we, chaps? Following the herring fleet down the coast, like camp followers . . .'

'How dare you—' Jeannie began and then she did what she had been wanting to do since she had seen this man's attitude towards the young man called Edwin. She smacked Francis's cheek so hard that it stung her own hand.

For an instant he gawped at her, unable to believe her audacity. 'You little—' he began, but whatever he had been about to say, or do, was cut short by Edwin stumbling into the alleyway and calling urgently, 'Come on, there's a policeman walking down the street. Let's get out of here.'

Suddenly, there was a lot of pushing and shoving and scrambling towards the opening into the road and Jeannie and the girl found themselves pushed backwards so that they fell over the prostrate young man and sprawled on the cobblestones beside him.

The superior voice of Francis rang through the night air. 'Just a little fun, constable. Out on a stag night and we encountered these two street girls . . .'

Red rage misted Jeannie's eyes as she struggled to her feet once more. 'I'm no such thing. I'll tell you what happened . . .' Emerging from the darkness, she pushed her way through to stand facing the black-uniformed officer.

'Now, now.' The man held up his hand, palm outwards, placatingly. 'We don't want any trouble. You and your friends be on your way, Mr Francis, and as for you, young woman, you'd best not let me catch you on any street corners for the rest of tonight.'

'How dare—' she began again, but felt a warning hand on her arm and heard Edwin whisper, 'Leave it. For heaven's sake leave it, else he'll run you in.'

Jeannie clamped her mouth shut but her eyes flashed in the darkness. Edwin was pulling her arm and saying quietly, 'Come on. Let's get them out of that alley and home.'

To her surprise, when she walked back into the alley-way, it was to find the girl trying to help the young man up.

Jeannie paused. Had she made a terrible mistake? Was this girl what the young men had implied? Maybe she was known to them. At Edwin's next action, this thought seemed to be confirmed.

'Here,' he said to the girl. 'I'm sorry about tonight. You're not hurt, are you? Please.' He pressed something into her hand. 'Please take this. We – your dress is spoilt. I – I am sorry, truly I am.'

Silent now, Jeannie stood back, just watching as Edwin

pulled his brother to his feet. The young man stood there swaying, shaking his head as if trying to clear it.

'Come on, Robert old chap. What Mother will have to say about this, I dread to think.'

Staggering a little as the one leant heavily upon the other, they moved towards the street. As they passed close to Jeannie, the bridegroom-to-be raised his head and looked straight into her eyes. She saw him open his mouth, lick his lips and then in a cracked whisper, he said, 'I'm so sorry.'

'So you should be,' Jeannie muttered, still outraged. 'But I dinna suppose you'll mind anything about it by the morning.'

'I'm hoping very much that he won't remember,' Edwin said with feeling.

As they emerged from the shadows, the constable said, 'Oh 'tis you, Mr Robert and Mr Edwin. Ah well, I see now . . .' The man laughed and nodded towards Francis. 'But you'd best be getting him home, Mr Francis, if you're to get him to his wedding tomorrow.'

And then they were gone, lurching down the street to hail a cab on the corner and disappear.

'Good riddance,' Jeannie muttered and then turned to the girl, who was still standing in the shadows, sniffling miserably and trying to cover herself with the torn fabric of her dress.

'Come on,' Jeannie said, kindly but with a hint of the exasperation one might use to a wayward child. 'Let's get you home. Where d'you live?'

'Baldock Street.'

'Where's that? Is it far?'

'No, no. It's the next street but one.'

'Right. I'll see you safe home and then . . . Now, where did I drop ma things?'

Two

On her arrival in Havelock earlier that evening, Jeannie had felt compelled to go down to the docks, to walk along the quays out to the end of one of the piers until she stood surrounded by the sea, willing her father's boat to appear on the horizon. But in the gathering dusk, there was not a single vessel coming in from the heaving sea, past the lightship and into the mouth of the Humber.

Behind her, alongside the jetties, a forest of masts and funnels swayed with the motion of the water beneath them and the wind that howled around them. The local trawlers had all made safe harbour on the evening tide and already their crews were gone, enjoying their brief time ashore before sailing for the fishing grounds once more. But now came the lumpers, the men who unloaded the fish on to the pontoon for the early-morning fish market on the dockside. Already several were beginning to gather in the hope of a night's work.

And with the morning tide would come the Scottish herring boats. Perhaps her father's little steam drifter would be amongst them.

Jeannie clasped the shawl that was in danger of being whipped away and drew it around her head and shoulders. Instead of giving warmth, the sodden garment made her shiver and, with sudden determination, she picked up her bundle, turned and marched along the pier, without glancing back, even just once more, towards the sea. She hurried along the quayside, taking care to keep her bright red hair hidden beneath her shawl. Maybe this far south, she told herself, the fisherfolk did not have the same superstition, but back home in Scotland, she knew of two fishermen who refused to put to sea if they saw a red-haired woman just before they were about to set sail. Jeannie had no wish to upset the folk here. She needed to find work and even if it meant tying a scarf around her head so tightly that she appeared bald, then she'd do it. There was no way she could hide the peppering of freckles across her nose, nor her green eyes, but in the dusk of the September evening she was just a tall, slim figure hurrying home, even though, as yet, she thought ruefully, she had not found a place to call 'home'.

Ignoring raucous shouts from the men, she turned in the direction of the streets of back-to-back houses close to the docks where the fisherfolk lived. It was beginning to rain and, in the narrow streets, darkness had already closed in. She regretted her foolishness in staying so long looking out to sea for a boat that she knew, in her heart of hearts, would never come home again. Yet the compulsion was still strong. She could not believe, even yet, that the big, laughing man who had been her father – who *was* her father, she told herself fiercely – could be gone for ever.

Now, with her arm about the sobbing girl, Jeannie hurried her along, patting her shoulder every so often and murmuring, 'There, there, hen. You're safe now.' But inwardly she was cursing her own stupidity for having lingered so long at the docks. It was getting late and, soaked to the skin and still trembling with anger, Jeannie doubted she would find a place to stay for the night.

She glanced down at the thin little figure cowering against her and clinging to her arm. The girl only looked fourteen or fifteen. She ought to have more sense than to be wandering the streets alone at this hour, Jeannie thought. What sort of family allowed such a young girl to be out alone?

'This is where I live,' the girl said. 'Down here, second house in the row. Number four.'

'I'll see you to your door, then I must be away.'

'Go the back way, down the alley,' the girl said. 'Me mam'll have a fit if we knock at the front door.'

Your mam'll have a fit anyway, Jeannie wanted to say, when she sees the state you're in. She said nothing but rapped sharply on the back door of the girl's home and, when it was flung open, she found herself facing the tallest, broadest man she had ever seen. She had thought her father big, in every sense of the word, but this man would have dwarfed even Angus Buchanan.

'Grace.' His voice was as cavernous as his frame. He reached out towards her with huge, calloused hands, taking her into his arms as she threw herself against him and burst into a storm of weeping.

'It wasn't my fault, Dad,' Grace was sobbing. 'They – they attacked me. They – they thought I was – that I was . . .'

His mouth tightened and swift anger darkened his eyes as, over her head, his stern gaze met Jeannie's. The man didn't need to speak for her to read from his expression just what he was thinking.

Lifting her chin defiantly, she said, 'I ken your daughter is no' what they thought and neither am I. But if that's a' the thanks I get for trying to help her, then I'll be on ma way.'

'Wait!' The word was like the crack of a sail in a force nine gale. 'I'm sorry if I misjudged you, girl. Please come in. I want to know what happened.'

His arm still about Grace's shoulders, he turned and led

the way through the scullery and into the kitchen of the terraced house, leaving Jeannie to step inside and close the door behind her.

A woman straightened up from bending over the range and looked towards them, her glance taking in, with a look of horror, the young girl's dishevelled appearance. Now Grace pulled herself from her father's arms and flung herself towards the older woman, sobbing wildly, 'Oh Mam, Mam.'

The woman did not at once take her into her embrace, but held her firmly by the shoulders at arm's length. 'Are you hurt, hen? Tell me at once, now?'

The girl shook her head. 'No, no. Not the way you mean. Not – not that . . .'

Jeannie was staring at the girl's mother. In the warm room after the cold of the wet night and added to the fact that she had not eaten all day, Jeannie's legs felt suddenly weak. She passed the back of her hand across her brow and the room swam before her.

'George,' she heard the woman's voice say again. 'George, yon lassie's about to pass out. Catch hold of her . . .'

She felt as if she were waking up from sleep, but as she stirred and consciousness returned, Jeannie became aware that she was lying on a hard, horsehair sofa and that faces, in shadow from the light behind them, were bending over her. She struggled to rise, but gentle hands pressed her back. 'Lie still, hen. And drink this. Why, you're soaked to the skin.' The woman's motherly hands touched her shoulder.

Gratefully, Jeannie pulled herself up to a sitting position

and took the proffered steaming cup of tea. Sipping it, the sudden warmth to her cold body made her shiver.

'You'll be catching a chill. Drink that and then we'll get you out of those wet things.'

The woman turned now and addressed someone standing behind her. Looking beyond her, Jeannie saw a young man, his shoulders broad beneath his fisherman's jersey, who was almost as tall as the man who had opened the door to them. He even had the same colouring. Fair, springy hair and blue eyes, but without the beard that the older man had. He was obviously the son and so, Jeannie realized, the girl's brother.

Standing a little way back from the couch, the young man seemed uncertain what he should do or think. Every so often he glanced worriedly at the grim expression on his father's face.

But it was the mother who took charge. Small, with a well-rounded, comforting sort of body and with grey hair pulled back into a neat bun at the nape of her neck, she was quick and decisive in her movements. She wore round, steel-rimmed spectacles which constantly slipped down the bridge of her nose, so that for most of the time she seemed to be peering over the top of them. With a gesture that was obviously a habit, she pushed them back up her nose with her ring finger.

'George, fetch some blankets from upstairs.'

'I'm not moving, Nell, until I've heard what happened.' The father's voice was deep and booming but for all that, the woman shooed him away with a flap of her hand. 'Away with you,' she ordered, adding sharply, 'and do as I say.'

To Jeannie's amusement, her husband turned away to do his wife's bidding. When the older woman once again

13

bent over her, her tone was gentle, all severity gone, and the concern in her voice made tears spring to Jeannie's eyes.

'There, there, hen,' she patted Jeannie's hand. 'You're safe now. Both of you. Tom will see you home when you're ready to go.'

'I'll not be seen walking the street with the likes of her, Ma, so . . .'

The woman straightened up again and said fiercely, 'Away and fetch more wood for the fire, Tom.'

For a moment the young man's face was mutinous, but then, with a glance towards his sister and a glower towards the stranger in their midst, he, too, turned to do as he was told.

As the back door slammed behind him, the woman winked at Jeannie. 'He thinks himsel' beyond being ordered about, but he's still ma bairn and I'm no' about to let him forget it.'

Jeannie, revived by the warmth of the room, the tea and even more than that, by the warmth of the woman's kindness, smiled.

'What made you pass out, hen, because you look a strong lassie to me, not the fainting kind at all?'

Jeannie looked up at her and her smile widened to a grin. Now she was over the initial shock of hearing the woman speak, she could laugh about it.

As she opened her mouth and said, 'It was hearing another voice from home . . .' it was the older woman's turn to draw in a sharp breath and stare down at her. Then she, too, laughed and said, 'You're one of the fisher lasses, are you?'

They were the same words that one of the young men in the street had used, but there was a world of difference

14

in the way it was said now. 'Well, you're very welcome in my home, hen, and not only because you helped our lassie.'

She jerked her head towards where the young girl was huddled close to the range, still trying to pull her torn garments together to hide her shame and embarrassment. She was a pretty girl, Jeannie saw now she had time to look at her properly, with a small nose, a sweet mouth and large, blue eyes that, at this moment, filled with easy tears. Her long, fair hair was coming loose from its pins and her face, streaked with dirt, was unnaturally pale from the shock she had just suffered.

Answering the girl's mother, Jeannie said softly, 'Then you don't think I'm a – a . . .'

'A Scottish fisher-lass a whore? Never,' the woman bridled indignantly. 'Never in a million years. And Tom will get a piece of my mind for even thinking such a thing.'

At that moment both men returned.

For the next half-hour, the kitchen of the small terraced house was a bustle of activity. The men were dispatched once more whilst the girls took off their wet, soiled clothes and wrapped themselves in the blankets and Mrs Lawrence set a pan of thick broth on the range to heat.

A little later, Mr Lawrence demanded yet again to be told the truth of what had happened.

'Ya should have told us straight away,' he said to Grace, but his glance of reproach was towards his wife. 'Then I could have gone out and found them.' He said no more, but he pounded one fist into the palm of his other hand and no one in the room was in any doubt as to what he would like to do to his daughter's attackers.

'Now, hen,' Nell Lawrence was saying to her. 'Tell us what happened?'

The girl gulped and, for a moment, hung her head. 'I

15

was just on me way home, Mam. They came out of the Fisherman's Rest and – and – well – they were drunk and . . .'

'Are you sure they didna hurt you? They didna . . .'

Grace shook her head. 'No, no, but – but they might have done if – if it hadn't been for her.' She looked across towards Jeannie who was now sitting up on one end of the couch and gave a shudder. 'I daren't think what might have happened if you hadn't come along when you did.' She gave a ghost of a smile. 'And I don't even know your name.'

'Jeannie. Jeannie Buchanan.'

Now it was the turn of the two men to look surprised and then George Lawrence let out a guffaw of laughter that lightened the tension and, for a moment, had everyone in the room smiling. 'There you are, Nell, one of your own. I didn't notice it when I opened the door to you, lass. I was too teken up with Grace. Well, well, a Scottish lassie, eh? I'll be damned!'

'And well you might be, George Lawrence, but . . .' His wife wagged her finger in the direction of Tom. 'But your son there certainly will be if he doesna apologize to this lassie for thinking what he did.'

Tom shuffled his feet awkwardly. His swarthy face reddened and then there was a sudden sheepish grin. 'I'm sorry, miss. No offence. I were just that mad – worried – about our Grace.'

Jeannie smiled and nodded. 'It's all right.'

'What I want to know is,' Mrs Lawrence said turning back to her daughter, 'what were you doing anywhere near the Fisherman's?'

Again the girl hung her head and, at once, Jeannie knew that she should not have been there.

'I was walking down Harbour Road.'

16

'Why? What were you doing down there? That's out of your way?'

'I – I'd been to Aggie's.'

'Aggie Turnbull's?' Now the mother's voice was raised in anger. 'I've told you to keep away from there. I won't have you going anywhere near *that woman*.'

Then Jeannie saw that Mrs Lawrence was looking, not at her daughter, but directly at her husband.

'You still haven't told us who the men were,' Tom was saying, emulating the older man's outrage. 'Cos if I know any of 'em, I'll . . .'

'No, no.' The girl's voice was shrill with terror. 'No, you mustn't do owt, Tom, please. Nor you, Dad.'

Her father was frowning at her. 'Why? Why ever not?'

'Because – because it was – they were out to celebrate – one of them, the one they were trying to – to make . . .' She gulped.

Jeannie, feeling a stab of sympathy for the young girl, said quietly, 'It was obviously a stag night. A group of young men were out on the town. One of them – Robert, I think I heard him called – is getting married tomorrow . . .' She glanced up at the clock on the mantel-piece above the range and, smiling wryly, added, 'Well, today now and . . .'

She became aware that the two men and the mother were exchanging glances, then George Lawrence leaned towards his daughter and demanded, 'Robert – and getting married tomorrow? You don't mean it was Mr Robert Hayes-Gorton and his pals?'

The girl nodded miserably and her voice was no more than a whisper as she said, 'Yes, Dad.'

In unison, the two men let out a long breath and George sat back in his chair. 'Oh well, that's it then, lad, there's nowt more to be said or done.'

Grimly, Tom said, 'No. Not now, there ain't.'

Jeannie was mystified. 'Nothing to be done? But surely, you're no' going to let them get away with it? I mean, what if . . .' She hesitated as three pairs of eyes glanced in her direction.

'What? What is it?' she asked.

Nell Lawrence said, 'There's nothing they can do, Jeannie. Not if they want to keep their livelihood. Mr Robert's father is a trawler owner and he owns the ship my husband skippers. He's his employer.' She sighed and added, her voice flat now with defeat, 'And Tom's too. He's a deckie on another Gorton boat.'

In a sudden, jerky movement, Tom got up, thrusting his chair away so that it fell backwards on to the floor with a clatter. 'It's ya own fault, Grace,' he said harshly, all sympathy gone now. 'You shouldn't have been anywhere near the pub at that time of night. Or going to Aggie Turnbull's. You brought it on yasen.'

He turned away and dragged open the back door, slamming it behind him as he left so that the pots on the shelf rattled.

Scarcely able to believe what she had just heard, Jeannie stared after him.

Three

Robert Hayes-Gorton woke with the feeling of a cold wetness around his neck. It was still dark and the room was illuminated only by a pale light that filtered in through the half open bedroom door from the landing. He raised his head but the room seemed to be spinning around him. Then he became aware of a vile smell and, putting his hand to his face, felt the sticky thickness of vomit caked around his chin.

He groaned aloud. In the dim light he could see the dark stain over the pillow and the sheets. Gingerly he put his feet to the floor and levered himself upright, but the feeling of nausea so overwhelmed him that he sat down again quickly and put his hands to his head. The vomit was all over his face, even in his hair, and the feel and the smell of it made him retch again. He grasped the bedpost and hauled himself upright and staggered towards the bathroom adjoining his bedroom. He bumped into the door jamb and then lurched towards the bath, banging his knees against it. Then he reached out and grasped the gold tap. Water poured into the bath but it was only lukewarm. Shivering he made himself climb into it and lay down, completely submerging his whole body. Then, sitting up, he soaped himself vigorously, furious now that he had allowed himself to get into such a state the previous evening.

'Bloody Francis,' he muttered. 'Some older brother he is.'

He couldn't remember drinking so much to get this drunk. But then, he couldn't remember much about last night at all. Suddenly he was still, his hands, covered in lather, suspended in the action of soaping his hair. Last night! Oh Lord – he could remember. At least, there was something . . . A wave of shame swept over him and yet he couldn't quite remember the actual reason for such a feeling. What was it that had happened last night that he couldn't recall and yet his subconscious mind was telling him that it was something awful? Was it just because he'd got so drunk? No, it couldn't be that. He'd been drunk before, though never as bad as this, he had to admit. No, there was something else. There was something shameful about the previous evening's escapades.

Slowly, he rubbed his hands over his hair, washing away the stench and massaging his aching head at the same time. Then carefully he stood up and stepped out of the bath, still a little unsteadily but feeling much better than when he had stepped into it. He dried himself vigorously until the roughness of the towel made his skin glow. Then dropping the towel to the floor he stepped back into the bedroom, wrinkling his nose in disgust at the smell coming from the bed. There was no way he was going to sleep there.

The eiderdown had slipped to the floor from the end of the bed and, thankfully, was unmarked. Picking it up, he wrapped it around himself and went towards the couch set beneath the window. First he opened the top of the sash window and then lay down on the couch, settling himself for what was left of the night. He closed his eyes and tried to will sleep to claim him. In only a few hours he'd be standing at the altar waiting for Louise and if he looked half as bad as he felt at this moment, there'd be hell to pay. His mother would have something to say about all this, never mind his bride and *her* mother.

His head still pounded, but the cooling draught from the window soothed his brow and he began to feel drowsy. But in the final moments before sleep overcame him, pictures flashed into his mind. Fleeting, disturbing images.

Darkness, shouting and laughing and then a girl. She was bending over him, saying something. Shouting at him. Yes, that was it. She was shouting at him.

'You should be ashamed of yourself.'

'Tom'll see you to your lodgings, hen,' Mrs Lawrence said, levering herself up. 'Your clothes'll soon be dry, except your shawl, that is. I'll put that in the tub for you and you can call for it another time. I'll lend you one of mine.'

'Thank you,' Jeannie said, but she made no move to divest herself of the blanket nor to rise from the sofa. She glanced up. 'There's just one snag. I've no place to go. I was on my way to find lodgings when . . .' she gave a slight gesture with her head towards Grace, 'it happened.'

'I see. Well, you can bide here for the night if you dinna mind sharing with Grace, that is. But we'd best be awa' to our beds. It's late and they're . . .' she gestured towards the two men, 'awa' on the morning tide.'

'That's kind of you, but . . .'

'No "buts",' the woman said quickly. 'We're grateful for what you did. It's the least we can do.'

The small terraced house bulged when the two men were home at the same time. With only two bedrooms upstairs, the son slept downstairs on the couch.

At five o'clock the following morning, Nell Lawrence tapped on the door of the bedroom where the two girls had shared the narrow bed. 'The herring boats are in, Jeannie. Get up. You too, Grace.'

Jeannie swung her legs to the floor and padded on bare feet to the window. Bending, she lifted the corner of the curtain and looked down into the street below. Already, the fisher-girls were emerging from the houses in ones and twos, tying the cotton rags around their fingers as they walked, laughing and calling to each other. Swiftly, Jeannie washed in the pink and white bowl and dressed. Carrying her heavy boots in one hand and her gutting knife and cotton bandages in the other, she went down the stairs to find a bowl of thick porridge awaiting her on the kitchen table.

'There you are, hen, made the Scottish way.'

'This is kind of you,' Jeannie said, picking up her spoon with relish. 'But I ought to be away down to the docks. The girls'll be getting together and if I'm no' there, I'll be left out.'

The herring girls worked in teams of three, two gutters and a packer. As one who had arrived a little later than the rest, Jeannie knew it was difficult to find work. She was an outsider, one who was not already part of a team.

For many years now, the Scottish herring girls had travelled together down the east coast, even as far as Great Yarmouth, keeping pace with the fleet as it followed the shoals of herring, beginning in the Shetlands in the spring and early summer and then drifting southwards through summer, ending up off the English south-east coast by November. The fisher lasses were a close-knit band and each girl jealously guarded her place within a team and each team fought to stay together. They knew one another's ways, each relying on the other's skill; the packer on the gutters to work swiftly and cleanly, the gutters dependent upon the packer to lay layer upon layer of salted silver fish neatly and tightly in the barrels so as to pass the foreman's strict standards. From the days of the luggers and their great flapping sails to the modern steam-driven drifters the fisher lasses had followed the herring fleet.

'What job do you do then, lassie?' Nell wanted to know, sitting down at the table opposite Jeannie and wrapping her hands around a mug of steaming tea.

Jeannie shrugged and said, between mouthfuls, 'I don't mind, just so long as I find work. Gutting or packing. I've done both, though I like the gutting best.'

Nell nodded. 'Aye, the packing's a back-breaking job. I was a gutter.' She smiled. 'Not tall enough to be a packer bending right down to reach into the bottom of the barrels.'

Jeannie pulled a face and laughed with her. 'Well, I canna make that excuse, Mrs Lawrence. But I dinna mind. I'll take what comes.' She did not add aloud, if anything does come. She would liked to have stayed chatting, to have asked Nell more about how she came to be living here in England, but reluctantly she rose and said, 'I must be away. I've lodgings to find and . . .'

'Ah, now about that, hen . . .' Mrs Lawrence interrupted. 'I had a word with George this morning and we're agreed. You can stay here, if you like. Just whilst you're with the fisher lasses. You'll be moving on soon anyway and our menfolk'll be awa' now for a while. And even if you're still here when they come back, well, you wouldna mind sharing the couple of nights they're home with Grace, would you?'

'It's kind of you, Mrs Lawrence,' Jeannie said again, but in her own mind she was doubtful about accepting the woman's offer. As a fisher lass, she needed to be with the other herring girls. When the boats came in, she had to be there, ready to work at once as part of a team, even in the middle of the night. Being separated from the others might mean that she would not be fetched and might be left out. Aloud, she said, 'I'll be away to the docks to see if there's work to be had.'

As if reading her thoughts and understanding her dilemma, Nell Lawrence nodded. 'Aye well, hen. See what happens. You're welcome to come back here if you want.' Then, almost as an afterthought, she added, 'I'll come with you, if you like? If Billy McBride is still one of the foremen, then . . .' she winked broadly at Jeannie, 'he'll find you a job.' Then, almost playfully, she wagged her forefinger, 'But dinna tell my George I said so.'

The herring boats had been sighted nearing the mouth of the Humber, the chugging of the coal-fired engines accompanied by the screeching of seagulls driven wild by the banquet of fish.

The fisher lasses were gathering on the dockside, standing in small groups, binding each other's fingers and chatting amiably together. Some had their hair drawn back into a bun on the back of their head; others, like Jeannie, covered their hair completely with a square of cloth. But they all wore oiled cotton skirts and aprons and short-sleeved, hand-knitted jerseys. A few had thick scarves wound around their necks against the cold wind that whistled in from the river and along the dock.

As they drew near, Nell stopped and looked about her. 'If I hadna seen it with ma own eyes, I wouldna have believed it,' she murmured shaking her head. 'There's hardly anyone here.' Puzzled, Jeannie too glanced around.

To her, there seemed to be a great many girls here – and all waiting for work.

'In my day,' Nell was saying. 'The place was just seething.' She waved her arm in a broad arc to encompass the area where the wooden troughs – the farlanes – stood awaiting the day's catch of fish and where the herring girls would stand at their work for the next twelve hours or so. Beyond them were row upon row of empty barrels where a few men – the coopers – stood waiting for the work to begin. They all seemed to be dressed in a similar fashion: open-necked shirts, the sleeves rolled up above their elbows; braces, holding up their trousers, covered by a waistcoat. Sturdy boots and a cloth cap completed their workaday attire.

As Nell seemed to be lost in her own memories, Jeannie squared her shoulders, lifted her chin and marched up to the nearest group. ''Mornin'.'

The girls glanced her up and down and then nodded in return to her greeting.

'D'you ken if there's work to be had?'

'Gutting or packing?' was the brief question.

'Either,' Jeannie said.

One of the girls jerked her thumb over her shoulder. 'See Billy McBride. He's the foreman. He'll know.'

Jeannie turned back to Nell Lawrence. 'He is here. Somewhere.'

The woman blinked and, pulled out of her reverie, gaped at Jeannie for a moment. 'Och aye, aye,' she said, suddenly remembering exactly what she was doing here. 'I thought he would be, but it'll be finding him that's the problem.' Nell chuckled. Then she glanced at Jeannie and pointed to her hair that curled waywardly on to her forehead, however tightly she tied it back beneath the triangle of cloth. 'Tuck your hair well oot of sight, hen. Billy's one of the old fishermen. He doesna trust red hair.'

Jeannie smiled and did as she was bade. She had every respect for the superstitions of the fisherfolk. Maybe, she thought sadly, I brought my own father bad luck when I went down to the harbour to wave him off that last time. The thought hurt, but she swallowed her private feelings, lifted her chin with a tiny gesture of determination and followed Nell.

They wandered amongst the throng asking, 'Billy McBride?'

A shake of the head, a shrug, and 'I havena seen him,' until one girl said, 'He was here a minute ago. Och, there he is.'

Jeannie looked where the girl pointed, but could see no one. Nell, however, threaded her way through and Jeannie followed in her wake until she came up behind Nell almost bumping into the woman as she stopped suddenly.

'Well, well, Nell MacDonald. Yer've no' altered a scrap, young Nellie.'

Jeannie watched the woman's shoulders shake and heard her laughter. 'You auld rascal, Billy McBride. You're still a right blether.'

Over Nell's shoulder Jeannie saw the man they were seeking. No wonder, she thought, he had been so difficult to find. Whereas on her first sight of Nell Lawrence's husband, Jeannie had thought him the biggest man she had ever encountered, now she found herself facing perhaps the smallest man she had ever seen. He was no more than four feet tall and whilst at the present moment he was greeting Nell like a long-lost friend, Jeannie could see that the man's sharp, beady eyes would miss nothing and that his mouth, at the moment stretched wide in a smile, was capable of contracting into a hard, thin line.

The girls who mingled around them were certainly in awe of this little man, for their jobs depended upon his say-so.

He would have hired the teams in Scotland, bringing them down the east coast, probably even arranging their travel and accommodation, keeping the girls tightly under his control. It was doubtful that there would be any work to be had, Jeannie realized with a sinking heart, yet he was her only hope, so she smiled at him and stood meekly behind Nell whilst the older woman chatted and almost flirted with her old friend.

Then his glance came beyond Nell to appraise Jeannie. 'And who's this, then, Nell? Your lass, is it?'

Nell shook her head. 'No, Billy. I have a daughter – and a son – but they're working. No, this is Jeannie Buchanan. She arrived last night and . . .' Nell's swift glance at Jeannie silently asked that she should not recount the circumstances of how she came to meet the Lawrence family. 'And,' Nell went on, 'I was wondering if you could find work for her.'

'Och, well now, Nell, that might be difficult.' The man stroked what looked like a three-day growth of grey stubble on his chin. 'The girls are already in teams, ye ken.'

'Aye, but if you could, Billy . . .?' Nell left the plea hanging.

Now the man addressed Jeannie. 'Gutting or packing, lass?'

'I dinna mind. I've done both.'

'Your first time in England, is it?'

Jeannie was obliged to nod, 'Aye, but,' she added swiftly, 'I went to the Shetlands last year.'

'Well, you're tall enough to do the packing, but, as it happens, it's a gutter we're short of. The lass cut herself

27

badly and it's gone septic. She didna bind her fingers properly. Now – let me see your hands.'

Smiling with a sense of pride, Jeannie obediently held out her strong hands for inspection, knowing that the tiny faint scars on her fingers were her passport to employment. Taking them into his own, he turned her hands over, his glance keen and knowledgeable. Jeannie knew that the foreman would be able to tell, just from looking at them, if she were speaking the truth. If she were a practised gutter, Billy McBride would know.

Then Billy looked up into her face, staring at her, shrewdly assessing her character. Her clear green eyes returned his scrutiny steadily and she allowed her mouth to curve in the hint of a smile, not so much as to be thought too forward, but just enough to give a small sign of self-confidence in her own ability. She was dressed like all the other girls mingling on the dockside and now as a final proof, if proof were still needed, from her pocket she pulled out the binders for wrapping around her fingers to protect them from the sharp gutting knife.

The man was nodding. 'You'll do, lass. Shall you be following us down to Yarmouth?'

There was the only slightest hesitation before Jeannie said, 'Aye,' but it was enough for the man to glance sharply at her once more. 'I need to be certain, Jeannie.'

'Yes, yes,' Jeannie said swiftly, but Billy McBride was still not wholly convinced.

'Some man here?' he probed bluntly.

If her heart had not been so heavy within her, Jeannie would have laughed out loud. She swallowed and, with a fleeting glance towards Nell, who was quietly watching and listening, said, 'Only my father.' As she said the words, she nodded seawards, towards the homecoming fleet.

'Och, I ken.' The man smiled now, satisfied.

It was not that she deliberately intended to mislead the foreman, who, though brusque in his manner, seemed fair enough, but Jeannie found it difficult to confide in anyone.

As he raised his voice and shouted to two girls standing together, binding each other's fingers, 'Flora, Mary, you've got a new gutter . . .' Jeannie lifted her head, smiled and moved forward to meet her new workmates.

'See you tonight, hen,' Nell called after her and Jeannie turned, waved and said, 'Thanks, Mrs Lawrence.'

Their glances held each other's for a moment as the older woman said softly, 'Thank *you*, Jeannie Buchanan.'

Four

The organ music seemed so loud. It reverberated through Robert's head, louder and louder, until he wanted to put his hands over his ears and run out of the church.

'You look awful. For God's sake don't pass out on me again,' Francis hissed at his shoulder.

'Thanks,' Robert muttered wryly. 'You do wonders for a chap's morale. Besides,' he added morosely, 'it's you I've to thank if I do look a mess.'

To the unobservant eye, Robert would have looked no different from what the guests might be expecting to see in a nervous bridegroom. Both he and the best man, indeed all the gentlemen of the wedding party including Edwin as usher, their father and the bride's father, were attired in black suits and waistcoats, with silk ties around stiff, winged collars. They each wore highly polished black shoes and white spats and carried a top hat and white gloves. A snowy handkerchief, neatly arranged in the top pocket, and a white carnation in the lapel completed the look and if the bridegroom's face was pale, his dark brown eyes shadowed, then they would say fondly that it was the occasion overwhelming the young man of only twenty.

But his brother was not so sympathetic. 'Serves you right,' Francis retorted. 'I can't abide a chap who can't hold his liquor.'

Robert glanced sideways at him, but the darting pain

behind his eyes made him turn his head back to face the altar.

'Nor,' Robert heard Francis snigger, 'a chap who can't rise to the occasion when he has a member of the fair sex – er – just handed to him.'

'Oh, for goodness sake, Francis. Don't be so crude. Not here, of all places.'

But his elder brother had no reverence in his being and Robert regretted having asked him to stand as his best man. In fact, now he came to think of it, he had not himself asked Francis nor even wanted him. It had all been taken for granted, all taken out of his hands by his parents and his future in-laws.

'Of course your elder brother must be your best man,' their mother had decreed and there had been an end of it.

He wondered if the fact that Francis, the first-born son and heir, had been the only one of the three Hayes-Gorton brothers to be sent away to boarding school, had set him apart. Robert, three years younger than Francis, and then Edwin, born a year after Robert, had both attended the local Grammar School as day pupils.

'I will not allow you to send all my sons away,' their mother had insisted.

But had Francis's time away from home given him his supercilious manner? And had he learnt there, too, from unsuitable peers, the dissolute life he now led? Francis had stated, with such determination that allowed no argument from their parents, that he had no intention of marrying. With a rare flash of insight into his own character, he had said, 'I suppose I could be quite fond of Louise, but I would not be cruel enough to marry her. My way of life would break her heart in a couple of weeks.'

And so Samuel's desire for a grandson had become a duty for the second son to fulfil.

Robert had been swept along on the tide of his family's machinations and in this bemused state he found himself standing before the altar in St Michael's Church at eleven o'clock on the morning of the fourth of September in the year of Our Lord Nineteen Hundred and Twenty-four waiting for the organ to strike the first triumphant chords in the music that would herald the arrival of his bride.

A girl, he realized with a shaft of horror, whom he hardly knew.

How on earth had it all happened? He wondered if she too had been inveigled into this marriage. Was she also feeling as he did at this moment? Utterly panic-stricken.

'I can't go through with it, Francis. I can't marry Louise. I—'

His brother's grip was vice-like on his arm. 'My dear boy, of course you must go through with it. Just cold feet, that's all.'

But this was more than cold feet, more than just wedding-day nerves. Robert made to pull away, to pull free, but Francis held him fast.

Now the older brother spoke through gritted teeth. 'It's all gone too far now. Think of the trouble you'd cause. If nothing else, think of the company.'

'The – the company? Is – is that all you can think about?'

Slowly Francis turned his head, his cold blue eyes a steely gaze upon his younger brother. 'The Gorton Trawler Company – and what this marriage will mean to it – is all that matters.'

Robert felt a cold sweat. It wasn't that he didn't like Louise. She was a sweet girl, with blonde hair cut short to frame her delicate features that were like those of a fine porcelain doll. Though he did not, he thought as another spasm of fear gripped his insides, love her.

'Francis, I really can't . . .' he began but when he turned his head again, the pain stabbed once more. Robert groaned aloud and then tried to stifle the sound that seemed to echo around the rafters of the church roof. 'I've never been this bad before.'

Francis gave a snort of laughter. 'Well, I lost count how much ale you had and then,' he paused significantly, 'you went on to the rum.'

Now Robert groaned again, making no effort this time to conceal the noise. 'Oh hell,' he said under his breath. 'You know rum makes me bad. Why didn't you stop me?' There was a pause, then bitterly, Robert added, 'It was you giving me it, wasn't it? Pouring it down my throat.'

'I thought you ought to have a good time on your last night of freedom.'

'You call that a good time?' the bridegroom said with feeling. 'When I can't even remember leaving the pub let alone anything after that.'

'What a shame. Then you have no recollection of the girl?'

'Girl? What girl?' Robert turned towards him again, ignoring the stab of pain this time. 'What – what happened? What did I do?'

At that moment, the organ broke into the bridal march and there was a stirring through the church as the congregation rose to its feet.

'Forget it,' Francis said. 'I think Edwin took care of it anyway. And if there's any further bother—'

'Bother? What sort of bother? Tell me,' Robert demanded as they got up.

'I said, forget it. It'll be all right. You're getting married and your beautiful bride is walking up the aisle behind you at this very moment. Just forget about what happened last night.'

33

'But I don't know what did happen . . .' he began but Francis was pushing him forward to stand before the steps at the end of the aisle.

As Robert fixed his gaze upon the huge stained-glass window above the altar, he was thinking, not of his bride walking slowly to stand beside him, but of a girl in the darkness of the alley bending over him and shouting at him.

Jeannie soon slipped into the work as a gutter alongside the other fisher lasses standing at the farlanes – the waist-high troughs overflowing with slippery herring. Mary and Flora were friendly, laughing and joking as they worked, but their hands moved like lightning. Flora was the other gutter in their team of three, slicing open the fish with a long, easy motion from head to tail, scooping out the insides and then tossing the fish to Mary, the packer. It was a bright, warm morning and soon the girls were taking off the thick scarves from around their necks. The fish dock rang with their laughter and their Scottish voices. Jeannie felt good to be amongst her own kin. The Lawrences had made her welcome in their home and not just because of the gratitude they felt but also because she was a Scottish lassie too and far from home. Nell would remember, even after all these years, what that felt like.

Jeannie half-listened to the gossip flying around her as she worked, but when Flora said, 'It's the Hayes-Gorton wedding today,' her interest sharpened.

Mary was laughing. 'Aye, and the bridegroom'll have a thick head this morning. They were pouring the drink down his throat last night in the Fisherman's . . .' And then, lest anyone should think she had been present, she added quickly, 'So I heard.'

'Och aye,' Flora teased, quick on the uptake. 'I bet you were there, Mary Fraser, with your man.'

Joining in the repartee, Jeannie winked at Flora and called back over her shoulder to their packer. 'You got a man then, Mary?'

'No, I havena,' came the quick reply, a little too quickly to be convincing and Jeannie and Flora laughed aloud.

'She'd've liked to be marrying Robert Hayes-Gorton hersel' this morning.'

'Who wouldna?' Mary's voice was dreamy but her busy hands never slackened their pace.

Careful to make her tone sound deliberately off-hand, Jeannie asked, 'What's he like then, this Robert What's-'is-name? Who is he anyway?'

Flora actually paused for a moment in her work and stared at Jeannie. 'You mean you dinna ken who the Hayes-Gorton family are?'

Jeannie shook her head. She had a shrewd idea from the conversation that had passed between the members of the Lawrence family the previous evening, but by feigning ignorance now, she realized she could learn more.

Behind her, Mary giggled. 'You'd better tell her, Flora.' She lifted her head and shouted to the other girls working close by. 'Listen, everyone. Story time.'

'Go on, then, Flora,' called a voice nearby. ' "*Once upon a time* . . ." ' There was a ripple of laughter, but then those within earshot fell silent, ready to listen.

The centre of attention, Flora preened herself. 'The Gorton Trawler Company is the second biggest trawler owner in Havelock . . .'

'And the biggest is the Hathersage Company,' put in another voice.

'Ssh, let Flora tell it.'

'Aye, she's a born storyteller. Go on, Flo.'

All the while a thousand bound fingers never stilled, sharp knives flashing. Hands plunged into the brine-filled farlanes to pick up the fish. Herring, their scales sparkling in the sunlight, were ever on the move being gutted, tossed and packed. The coopers moved amongst the girls, inspecting the packers' work, removing the full, heavy barrels and bringing empty ones. Thirty-five barrels a day, Billy McBride demanded from each team and with eight hundred to a thousand fish to each barrel, the fisher lasses stood there hour after hour with not a moment to waste. Banter and laughter, or a story, were welcome diversions.

Like an actress centre-stage, Flora began. 'The Gorton Company was founded in the 1880s by Thomas Gorton. He was just an ordinary fisherman then, but he married the daughter of the feller who owned the boat he skippered. The girl's father was against it.' She laughed. 'I s'pose he thought Thomas was just after his boat.'

'And was he?'

Flora shrugged. 'I like to think they really loved each other.'

'Did they elope?' a voice asked and the listeners laughed.

'To Gretna Green?' someone else joked.

'I dinna ken if they went to Gretna, but they did run away to be married.' Now Flora held their attention once more. 'They were awfu' happy together in their wee terraced house near the docks. But she was an only child so when her father died, she and her husband inherited the trawler.'

'I thought so,' muttered a voice, more cynical than the rest, but Flora ignored the interruption.

'Thomas Gorton skippered it himself for a while but then he bought another boat and another until he had a fleet of ten or so. They say he was a nice old man. A real fisherman through and through. Tough, but always fair. And he stayed all his life in the same house.' She nodded briefly in the direction of the rows of terraced houses where the fisherfolk lived and where the Scottish girls found lodgings. 'Old Thomas died about twenty years ago and his son, Samuel, took over the company.' Flora paused for effect, knowing she had her listeners spellbound, so she began, as all good storytellers, to embellish the truth a little.

'He was a different kettle of fish altogether.' She smiled at her own pun.

'And still is,' muttered a voice thick with resentment.

'He bought a posh house on the outskirts of the town and began to live the life of a laird. True, he carried on building up the company, but he cut the men's basic wages and their share of the catch to buy more ships.'

'Hathersage is worse, though,' came the voice again. 'He's a tyrant.'

Flora went on. 'The Hayes-Gortons now own fifteen boats and about a hundred-and-eighty families depend on them for a living.'

'Oh, good at arithmetic, isn't she?'

'Hathersage has got twenty boats.'

'And don't forget, if a catch is bad, or the price drops, the deckies barely earn a living wage.'

'I've heard of men coming back from two or three weeks at sea and they owe the company money because they've already borrowed against their wages.'

'Aye, and then the wages they expected don't come, so they're in debt,' another voice complained bitterly.

'How did it come to be *Hayes*-Gorton?'

The remarks flew back and forth, but Flora only

answered the last question. 'Samuel married a girl fu' of airs an' graces. She insisted on adding her maiden name to Gorton and making it a double-barrelled surname.'

There were groans of derision all round.

'That's not the young ones' fault,' Mary put in. 'The three brothers. Is it, though?'

Now the laughter was turned on Mary. 'Sweet on them, are you, Mary? Which one do you fancy then?'

Jeannie risked a brief glance back at their packer. The girl was blushing, but still she answered her tormenters. 'They're so good-looking. A' three o' them. I'd take me chance with any one o' them.'

'The younger two are fine, but the eldest . . .' Flora shook her head. 'His eyes . . .' She held up a fish. 'They're as cold as this herring's. And it's dead.'

Then slicing her knife through the flesh, she tore out the guts and held it up again. 'And he's as much "heart" as this has got now.'

She tossed the fish behind her as if flinging the man away from her too.

'You sound bitter about him, Flora?' Jeannie said quietly.

The girl glanced at her. Dropping her voice so that the conversation was now only between the three of them, herself, Mary and Jeannie, she said, 'He's nothing to me, if that's what you're thinking. Thank God. But two years ago, on my first trip down here, I worked alongside a girl called Rose. Bonnie wee thing she was, though not ever so quick at the gutting. Still, the men liked her and I reckon that's why she kept her place. Well, she got in with Francis Hayes-Gorton. You'll see him, in a day or so, strutting about the fish dock. He'll mind to keep his fancy clothes away from the fish, but he's eyeing up the girls. You'll see,' she said and nodded wisely. 'But if you pay heed to me,

38

you'll keep away from him. Handsome he may be, but he's as rotten as a barrel of fish left out in the sun.'

'So it's no' him who's getting married today then?' Jeannie said, still feigning ignorance.

'I'm coming to that,' Flora said and raised her voice again to continue her tale. 'Samuel Gorton married into money, some say – and I would agree with them – deliberately. And,' she wagged her knife dramatically in the air to emphasize her point, 'today, he's making his second son, Robert, do just the same thing.'

Now there was a chorus of disbelief.

'Never.'

'Who's he marrying then?'

At Flora's side, Jeannie said, 'Well, he's the fool for allowing himself to be pushed into doing it.'

Flora laughed wryly. 'You dinna ken Samuel Hayes-Gorton, Jeannie. Nobody, but nobody, including his own sons . . .' She paused and then added with emphasis, '*Especially* his own sons, dare to defy him.'

Jeannie was silent, thinking of her own father. A big, gentle-hearted giant of a man, with a mane of fair hair with a tinge of red in it and a beard and moustache that covered most of his face. But not his eyes that twinkled and sparkled with mischief and merriment. Her mother's death seven years earlier had threatened to devastate the big man, but he had put aside his own grief to support his eleven-year-old daughter in the loss of her mother.

And now he, too, was gone. One day soon, Jeannie knew, she would have to come to terms with the awful truth. But not yet, not yet. Not until someone found a piece of the boat or . . .

The voices around her were invading her private thoughts.

'Who's he married then?'

'Why do you say Robert's marrying for money?' Mary put in. 'He's too nice to do that.'

There was a chorus of laughter. 'Och, Mary, you missed out there. You should have netted him. It could have been you in the church today all dressed in white with all of us making an archway of gutting knives.' Gales of laughter echoed along the dockside.

'Because,' Flora said, enjoying creating the suspense, 'he's uniting the two biggest trawler companies on the east coast of England. Today, Robert Hayes-Gorton is marrying Louise Hathersage.'

Five

Herbert Hathersage rose to his feet in the long hall of his country mansion and glanced about him. The tables had been positioned so that the top table lay horizontally to the foot of the wide staircase, with three tables running the length of the hallway at right angles to the bridal party table.

At first-floor level the staircase divided and ran in a gallery around the hall, the ceiling high above them in a skylight at third-floor level. At the far end of the gallery, musicians played *pianissimo*, a genteel background to the muted chatter of the guests.

Catching the eye of the trio, Herbert nodded and the music stopped, but not until he had tapped the table with a spoon, did conversation cease and faces turn expectantly towards him.

'Dear friends, may I welcome you all to our home on this happy occasion which unites not only two young people, but two families and . . .' he paused for effect, 'the two major trawling companies in this part of the British Isles. I'm sure I speak for Hayes-Gorton's family,' he gave a small bow towards Samuel and his wife, 'when I express my delight at the union of our companies. In due time, it will be our mutual grandson at the helm of a great business empire . . .' His voice droned on and Robert bowed his head and suppressed a visible shudder. Oh, what had he done? He hardly knew the girl at his side. They had spent no more than a few hours alone together during the whole of their supposed courtship.

He didn't like to think of himself as weak so how had he allowed himself to be carried along on the tide of his father's enthusiasm for the match? He was not even twenty-one and Louise was only eighteen. There had been no reason to oppose the match, and yet . . .

He became aware of his surroundings again. '. . . And so dear friends, I ask you to be upstanding and to drink a toast to the bride and groom.'

There was a scraping of chairs on the marble floor and a murmuring like a breeze wafted around the hall. 'The bride and groom . . . bride and groom.'

And then it was Francis's turn, as Robert's best man. He made a few of the usual jokes, though Robert was relieved that he did not descend into crudity as he was wont to do in men-only company. Francis proposed the health of the four bridesmaids and then Robert found himself on his feet, and, to much laughter, heard himself say, 'My wife and I . . .' Dutifully he thanked everyone for coming, for their good wishes, paid tribute to his new in-laws and a lavish compliment to his bride, but inside his mind he was thinking, Yes, my wife and I. I am a married man. It's done and now I must make it work. As he sat down to the polite applause, he turned towards the girl at his side. She really did look very pretty, he told himself, beneath the chiffon veil and its headdress of wax orange blossom. Now he noticed that she was wearing his wedding-day gift to her; a pearl necklace and drop earrings.

Taking her hand in his, he raised it to his lips and she turned and smiled at him, her blue eyes sparkling, her nose wrinkling daintily.

Yes, he really would try to make this marriage work,

Robert promised silently, but first, there was just one thing he had to do.

'Edwin.' Robert gripped his younger brother's arm. 'I must talk to you. Come out on to the terrace. We shan't be overheard out there. Louise is upstairs changing and we won't be missed. I've got to talk to you.'

His brother grinned. 'What? Cold feet already? Or do you want a pep talk about the facts of life?'

But Robert did not even smile in return. 'Please, Edwin.'

'Let me get a drink first then. One for you?'

Robert shuddered. 'No, thanks. I reckon I've had enough to last me a lifetime,' he said with bitter irony.

Edwin laughed. 'Well, I'd not argue with that. Be with you in a minute.' He pushed his way through the throng to where the solemn-faced butler stood with a tray of drinks while Robert skirted the mingling guests, submitting *en route* to handshakes and kisses and good wishes until he came to the front door, which was standing open to the bright sunlit day. He blinked as he stepped outside and then drew in deep breaths of fresh air. Nodding to the footman who stood sentinel at the side of the door he moved along the paved terrace and leant on the parapet looking out over the lawn stretching down to a lake and beyond that a copse of trees. Behind him towered the square Georgian house; the Hathersage mansion, as everyone called it.

He was part of all this now, he told himself, but the thought gave him no joy. He groaned aloud and leant his elbows on the stonework.

'Still got a hangover, old chap?' came Edwin's voice at his elbow.

'A bit.' He straightened up and turned to face his brother. 'But it's not that. I must know what happened last night. Francis keeps making snide remarks and I really don't know what he's talking about.'

Edwin sighed. 'I wish you wouldn't worry about it, it's—'

'Edwin, I've got to know. I keep remembering flashes but not everything and it's driving me mad.'

His brother shrugged. 'If you insist then.' Briefly he recounted the events of the previous evening.

'. . . Then suddenly there was this girl, like an avenging angel, fists flying and shouting at the top of her voice. It must have taken some courage, you know, to wade in amongst the lot of us. For all she knew she could have ended up being – well, you know – too.'

'Raped, you mean?' Robert's voice was a hoarse whisper. 'You mean I was party to a rape?'

'Oh, you didn't actually do anything,' Edwin gave a wry laugh. 'You weren't capable.'

'That's not the point. This is terrible. What about that poor girl? And what if the police had come along?'

'Oh, one did,' Edwin said, as Robert groaned again. 'But luckily it was PC Parsons and he just sent us on our way. Advised me to get you home, which, incidentally, I was trying to do anyway.'

'And the girl?' Robert persisted.

'Which one?'

'The one – the one . . .' Robert gulped painfully. 'I attacked.'

'You didn't attack anyone. It was all Francis's doing. He's a vicious sod when he's had a drink.'

'But what happened to her?'

'Oh, the other girl – the one who came to her rescue – took her off. Home, I expect.'

'Who was she? The – the other girl?'

Edwin shrugged. 'By her accent, one of the fisher lasses. Nobody who matters.'

Nobody who matters. The phrase jangled around Robert's battered mind. Oh she mattered all right. For it was that girl whom he could not forget. Whose accusation still rang loudly inside his head.

'You should be ashamed of yourself.'

He was, oh he was, he answered her silently.

'The boats are leavin'. Shall we take our jilly piece and watch them go?'

It was the time when the girls took a brief respite. Jeannie smiled at Grace who stood on the far side of the farlane, holding jam sandwiches – their 'jilly pieces' – wrapped in a cloth. Grace Lawrence might not be Scottish born but with Nell for her mother there was some of the breeding there, the words and phrases of Jeannie's homeland.

Jeannie nodded, unable for a moment to speak. Standing all morning amongst her own kin had made her feel homesick and heart-sore for the loss of her own folks.

Linking arms, the two girls walked along the quay, eating as they went. Standing in the same spot where Jeannie had stood the previous night, they watched the ships easing their way out of the dock, heading for the open sea.

'There they go,' Grace murmured. 'Safe home,' she added like a prayer.

'Which one is your father and brother on?'

'Dad skippers the *Gorton Sea Spray*. But I can't see it. Maybe they've gone already.' She screwed up her eyes against the glare of the sunlight glittering on the water.

As they walked back, Jeannie glanced about her. 'Isn't that your father? Talking to that woman?' The figure of the stranger stood out in sharp contrast to the working fisher lasses. The woman wore a blue and white striped ankle-length dress made in a shiny fabric. Silk, Jeannie supposed, though she could not quite be sure from this distance. The woman's hair was covered with a close-fitting cloche hat trimmed with two white feather pompons that rippled in the breeze. She wore white silk stockings and pointed shoes.

'Where?' Grace asked and, following the line of Jeannie's finger as she pointed, added, 'So it is. And me mam'd go daft if she saw him talking to her.'

'Why?'

'That,' Grace said, nodding towards where the tall, broad figure of George Lawrence stood laughing down into the upturned face of the woman, 'is Aggie Turnbull.'

'Aggie . . .?' Jeannie began and then she remembered. 'Oh yes. The woman whose house you'd been to last night.'

Grace nodded.

'I ken your mother doesna like her?'

Grace gave a snort of laughter. 'You could say that.'

'Why?'

The girl smiled impishly. 'Me mam ses she's "Nae better than she should be".' Grace mimicked the Scottish accent perfectly, even though her own speech normally held no trace of it.

Jeannie laughed, throwing her head back so that the scarf tied around her head slipped down letting her red hair fly loose in the wind. George Lawrence turned away from Aggie Turnbull and walked along the quay towards them.

'My, my, that's a pretty picture for a man to take to sea with him,' came his cavernous chuckle.

Self-consciously, Jeannie touched her hair and then tried to pull the scarf up over her head again.

George put out his huge hand and touched her curls. 'Don't cover it up, lass. It's such pretty hair.'

'You – you dinna mind, then?'

George looked puzzled for a moment and then he laughed. 'Oh, old Billy McBride and his superstitions, eh? Nell been telling you, has she?'

Jeannie just smiled. She had known of the superstition from childhood.

'Well now,' George put his arms about both girls' shoulders and steered them down the jetty towards where his own boat was moored. 'I respect a man and his beliefs. We've got a few of our own, but red hair on a pretty girl isn't one of them, not in these parts anyway. Now, come and see me off. It's high time I was aboard.'

They couldn't stay until the boat nosed its way from the jetty towards the dock gates but they watched him climb the ladder and jump aboard the *Sea Spray*.

As they turned away they saw Tom hurrying towards them.

'I can't stop,' he said. 'I should be aboard, but . . .' He turned to Jeannie. 'You'll still be here when we get back?'

'I dinna ken,' Jeannie said quietly and her glance flickered beyond Tom's shoulder across the grey water to the Havelock boats moving out into the mouth of the Humber and towards the sea until they became distant specks on the horizon.

Tom, misreading her thoughts, said, 'If you're looking for the Scottish drifters, they were first out on the tide this morning. But they'll be back. They'll be using this port for a week or two yet, I reckon.'

'Uh?' She dragged her wandering thoughts back to the young man standing in front of her. 'Och no, it's no' that.

47

I mean, I wasna looking for the herring boats. At least,' her voice dropped to a mere whisper, 'not the ones that have just left.'

She said no more and avoided meeting Tom's eyes until his deep voice, the disappointment evident in its tone, asked gently, 'What are you watching for then? Or is it some*one* you're watching out for? Is that it, Jeannie?'

Now she had to meet his gaze and, though she tried to smile, she knew the haunted look was deep in her eyes.

Tom put out his huge hand and suddenly gripped hers. 'Tell me? What is it?'

There was a shout from a man standing midway up the gangway leading on to a ship. 'The gates'll be closing in half an hour, Tom.'

Jeannie heard his sigh. 'I'm sorry. I'll have to go . . .' Again he gave her hand a quick squeeze. 'I – I hope you're still here when we get back. And Jeannie, there's just one more thing. Look out for my little sister here, while I'm gone?' He smiled down at Grace and tweaked her nose playfully. 'I wish we weren't sailing today but I can't let me mates down. I'm just glad I've managed to get on a Hathersage boat this trip and not a Gorton.' Suddenly there was a dark anger in his eyes. 'That bastard is going to pay for what he did. Me dad – nor me – aren't going to forget.'

And then he was gone, striding along the quay and running up the gangway and on to the *Hathersage Enterprise*.

She was still standing watching when Grace touched her arm and said, 'We'd best get back to work, else you'll lose your place.' She gave a wry laugh. 'There's allus plenty of local lasses without steady work trying to get into a team while the herring girls are here.'

48

Jeannie gave one last glance towards the trawlers and then hurried after Grace. 'Doesna your mother come down to see them away?'

Grace shook her head. 'She's too busy. She's got to braid a net – part of a cod net, that is – in two days. She'll still be at it when we get home tonight. You'll see.'

And Jeannie did see, for when she unwound the ties from her fingers and walked wearily through the gathering dusk to Baldock Street, it was to find Nell Lawrence standing before the kitchen wall from which hung a fishing net, growing longer under her nimble fingers. Jeannie watched in fascination as the braiding needle flashed in and out of the mesh.

'I'm sorry, hen,' Nell said, her hands never slowing in their task. 'I havena had time to get you a meal ready.'

Grace winked at Jeannie. 'That's all right, Mam. You carry on. Me an' Jeannie'll get the supper, but you must stop and have a bite.' The girl, now fully recovered from her ordeal of the previous night, wagged her finger play-fully at her mother. 'I bet you've never stopped all day to eat, have you?'

Nell chuckled and shook her head. 'This net willna braid itsel', hen.'

Jeannie moved closer, watching, and when Grace went from the kitchen into the back scullery, Nell asked in a low voice, 'Has she been all right today, Jeannie?'

'What? Och aye. She seems fine now. She seems to have got over it very quickly.'

Nell's lips compressed into a tight line. 'Only thanks to you coming along in time, hen. It might have been very different if . . .' She stopped and then shrugged her shoulders and said, 'Well, let's just be thankful you did. We'll think no more of it now and I just hope it'll all be forgotten by the time the men come home again.'

Margaret Dickinson

Jeannie turned away, anxious that Mrs Lawrence should not see the doubt in her eyes. She was sure that Tom would not forget Mr Robert Hayes-Gorton and his friends and what they had tried to do to his sister.

Six

News of the grand wedding was the talk of the fish dock
for days. Gossip filtered back from the domestic staff who
worked at the Hathersage mansion.

'It was a lovely wedding,' Mary told them dreamily.
'And they've gone away on honeymoon now. For a whole
month.'

'How do you know?'

'The daughter where I'm lodging is a maid at the
Hathersages' place and she was telling her mother all about
it. Their servants have been run off their feet for weeks
before, but she said it was worth it. Miss Louise looked a
picture, Annie said. She wore a cream ankle-length gown
with gold embroidery and beading round the neckline and
hems. And she had a long train from the shoulders . . .'
Mary swept her hand down the length of her own body to
demonstrate. 'The edges were decorated to match the
dress. And white silk stockings.' She sighed. 'Och, what I
wouldna give to wear white silk stockings.'

'Dinna forget, Mary, that Aggie Turnbull and her like
wear white silk stockings,' put in a voice at the next trough
and Mary shot a venomous glance at the girl, who only
laughed and nudged her companion. 'Our Mary gets carried away with herself and her dreams of living in high
society.'

Mary sniffed contemptuously and turned her gaze
away, determined not to let anyone spoil her romantic

fantasies. Then she looked down wistfully at her rough clothes and at her hands bound with the ragged tapes. 'I dinna think anyone will ever say that about me. That I look "a picture".'

Flora sniffed. 'Shouldna think little Miss Louise has ever had to lift her dainty fingers to do a stroke of work in her life. 'Tis nothing to be proud of, leading such an idle life.'

'I could get used to it,' Mary grinned, her natural resilience and good humour rising to the surface once more. 'Married to Robert Hayes-Gorton, I could get used to anything,' she added, rolling her eyes comically so that all her workmates laughed.

Only Jeannie Buchanan did not join in their laughter, pressing her lips together to keep them from opening and spilling out exactly what she thought about the man who seemed to hold such a fascination for Mary Fraser.

On the second morning of their honeymoon, Robert Hayes-Gorton stood at the bedroom window overlooking Lake Windermere. The pale, early sun was just rising over the hills filtering gentle streaks of light across the water. The lake was peaceful, so opposite to the tumult going on inside the unhappy young man's mind. His gaze was upon the tranquil scene, yet he hardly took in the view.

He was reliving the night. The horror of it. Inside his head he could still hear Louise's hysterical screaming that had not subsided until he had given his solemn pledge never to try to touch his wife again.

It had begun with such promise. The previous night – their first as man and wife – had been idyllic. As they had driven away from the reception in Samuel Gorton's motor car, Louise had been laughing and flirtatious, waving happily to all their guests as the motor rounded the bend in the driveway of her home and turned into the road. Then she had tucked her arm through Robert's as his hands rested on the wheel and snuggled her head against his shoulder. 'My husband,' she had murmured. 'My handsome husband.'

That evening, they had dined in the small hotel where they were to stay for the first night. There were few other guests in the dining room, but Louise had sparkled and chattered throughout the meal.

'Weren't the bridesmaids pretty? Did you like my friend, Madeleine?' Robert opened his mouth to reply with a dutiful compliment, but Louise carried on, almost without pausing for breath. Her questions, it seemed to Robert, did not require an answer.

'She's my very best friend. She's asked us to go up to London and stay with her any time we like. Won't that be fun, darling? And Francis made a wonderful best man. He's very handsome, isn't he, with that fair hair and pointed moustache? Has he got a girlfriend? I'm surprised he wasn't the first to get married.'

'He's not the marrying kind,' Robert put in, 'so he says.'

Louise's laugh tinkled merrily. 'Oh, they all say that, but he'll change his mind, once he meets the right girl.' Coyly, she put her head on one side. 'Just like you.'

Robert smiled and reached across the table to touch her hand.

Later, as he slipped into bed beside her, she nestled against him. Knowing how tired they both were, he held her, kissed her gently but tried nothing more. Time enough, he told himself, even though the feel of the girl aroused him.

But last night, here in the hotel overlooking the lake where they were to spend the first two weeks of their honeymoon, he had taken her in his arms, his kisses becoming more passionate. His trembling fingers tugged at the front of her nightdress and at once she shrank from him.

'What are you doing, Robert?'

'You're my wife, Louise. You know what happens, don't you?'

'What do you mean "what happens"?'

'When a man and woman are married. You know about – well – that?' There was a silence until he added, with a growing sense of disappointment, 'Don't you?'

'I don't know what you're talking about.'

He released her then and rolled on to his back, letting out a great sigh. 'Oh,' was all he said, his voice flat.

There was silence as they lay side by side in the huge bed. Then she stirred beside him, raising herself on one elbow and leaning towards him, she said softly, 'You can show me, if you like.'

Hope surged within him and he reached out for her again, pulling her to him. 'I'll not hurt you,' he murmured, kissing her gently. 'I promise . . .'

His kiss became more urgent as his ardour heightened. He unfastened the front of her nightdress and buried his face in the soft fullness of her breasts and he moaned with pleasure, kissing and caressing. Then he was tugging at her nightdress again, pulling it up, his hand seeking her private place, his fingers searching.

'No, no, you mustn't do that. It's . . .'

But his urgency was too far gone now for him to pull back. He was astride her, lying on top of her, spreading her legs apart with his knees.

'No, no, Robert. You're hurting me. No, no!' She was pushing against him and her voice was loud and frightened.

54

And then suddenly it was as if he were back in the alleyway and beneath him someone was screaming. He almost felt the hand on his shoulder once more pulling him away.

His passion died and he was still, lying heavily on top of Louise, who was crying hysterically, 'You're hurting me.'

He rolled off her to his own side of the bed and lay staring up into the darkness, listening to his child-bride sobbing beside him.

And out of the blackness of the night, yet again, came the voice. 'You should be ashamed of yourself.'

55

Seven

'What were you doing at Aggie Turnbull's place that night anyway?' After a few days when Grace seemed to have recovered from the incident, Jeannie felt able to ask the question.

The girl glanced at her quickly and then her gaze fell away. 'I'd – er – just been round to see Aggie. Y'know.'

'Are you friendly with her then?'

'It's – it's . . .' Grace hesitated and Jeannie had the feeling that she was trying to scrabble around her mind for some plausible excuse. A defensive note crept into Grace's tone. 'Aggie's all right. Really she is. She's kind and friendly and – well – fun.'

'But your mother doesna approve.'

Grace looked at her and then suddenly she moved closer, glancing about her to be sure they could not be overheard. 'If I tell you summat, will you promise not – not to tell me mam?'

Jeannie studied the girl's young face, but she could not be less than honest. 'I canna promise you that until I know what it is.'

Grace blinked and faltered, 'Oh. Oh, then it's best you don't know.' She half-turned away, but Jeannie caught hold of her arm. 'Be careful what you're getting into, Grace. Aggie's house may seem like good fun, but . . .' Suddenly, Jeannie felt older than her eighteen years and much older than the naive sixteen-year-old standing beside

56

her. Surely, she thought, living in this area, knowing Aggie Turnbull all her life, Grace could not be so ignorant? If she were, then Nell had kept her unenlightened deliberately. But there were consequences to be paid for for being overprotective. That ignorance could lead Grace into danger.

The young girl shook her head and at her next words, Jeannie knew a sense of partial relief. 'Oh, I know what Aggie Turnbull is.' A small smile twitched at the corner of her mouth. 'Everybody round here knows that. It's a wonder there isn't a pathway worn in the road by the number of fellers who make a beeline to her door when the boats come in. Aye, an' not only the single fellers either. There's married ones an' all whose wives don't . . .' Mischief danced in Grace's eyes. 'Make 'em welcome home, if you get my meaning.'

So, Jeannie thought with amusement, Grace was far from being as naive as she had imagined.

'But,' the girl went on, giving a mock shudder of disapproval, 'don't think I'm getting into anything like that. It's just that – well – I can meet me friends at Aggie's.'

Jeannie frowned, her mind racing and, quick to understand the underlying meaning to Grace's words, she said, her mouth tight, 'You mean, friends your mother wouldna approve of?'

Again the quick glance and then away again. 'She doesn't approve of me having boyfriends. Ses I'm too young.' Now Grace flapped her hand at Jeannie, 'Oh, now look what you've made me do.' Angry tears shone in her eyes. 'You've wheedled it out of me and you'll go and tell me mam and . . .'

'Only if I think you're – well – in danger of getting yoursel' into trouble.'

'No, no, it's not like that. It's – it's only a boy. He's not

57

from round here. I – I only see him now and again. When . . .' Again she seemed to be searching for a credible story. 'When his boat's in.' Now Grace seemed to be warming to her theme. 'Mam'd like him, if only she'd let me bring him home.'

'Mm.' Jeannie was thoughtful. It was an old problem and one that was hardly likely to change. When girls and boys got to a certain age and thought of themselves as grown up yet their parents still treated them as children, it could lead to this kind of deceit.

'You won't tell me mam?' Grace begged.

Jeannie sighed heavily. She had the uncomfortable feeling that whilst Grace may not be actually lying to her, she was sure the girl was not telling her the whole truth. 'I'm not making any promises, Grace,' she said. 'But just you mind what you're doing.'

Impulsively the girl hugged her new friend. 'I will, Jeannie. Honest I will.'

'They're back. Have you heard?'

The fisher lasses were once again standing at the troughs. Today they were all well wrapped up, for the wind lashed through the docks, rippling the surface of the water and whistling along the quays. Then it began to rain, soaking the girls, stinging their faces but still they stood there, working with no easing of their speed, stoically trying to ignore the cold.

'Back?' Flora said, never lifting her eyes from her flashing blade. 'Who's back?'

'The bride and groom.'

'Already? I thought you said the other day that they'd gone on honeymoon for a whole month?'

'So they had, but they're back. And that's not all.

They've gone to bide at the Hathersages' place and . . .'
Mary paused to achieve the most dramatic effect. 'And
they've got separate bedrooms,' she finished triumphantly.

There was a moment's silence until Jeannie said, 'Well,
don't a lot of the upper classes sleep in separate bedrooms?'

The other girl seemed nonplussed for a moment but
then said stoutly, 'Well, you wouldna think newly-weds
would want that, would you? Not even in the upper
classes. And what about coming home early from honeymoon then? Besides, I got it from Annie. She works as an
upstairs maid there and she ses . . .'

The girl prattled on whilst Jeannie was busy with her
own thoughts. She felt sorry for the child-bride. No doubt
Robert Hayes-Gorton had forced himself upon her on their
wedding night in the same way that he'd attacked Grace.

Oh yes, she felt very sorry for the poor girl and she
hadn't a moment's sympathy for him. Not one moment.

'Come in and close the door.' It was a command rather
than an invitation.

Robert did as he was bade and stood before his father-
in-law's huge desk in his study.

'Now, young feller, you'd better tell me what's going
on between you and my daughter.'

Robert felt himself blushing uncomfortably, making
him feel even more gauche and foolish than he already
felt.

'Well?' came Hathersage's bark. 'I'm waiting.'

'It's personal and – and delicate.'

'Oh, so Francis was right, was he?'

Robert's head jerked up to see his father-in-law nodding
knowingly. 'Francis? What has he been saying?'

'When you arrived back from your so-called honeymoon far earlier than expected, your brother guessed that you haven't – er – consummated the marriage yet, eh? Only Francis didn't put it as politely as that.'

I bet he didn't, Robert thought morosely. He was rapidly beginning to see his elder brother in a very different light recently. If it hadn't been for Francis, he wouldn't have been involved in that disgraceful incident the night before his wedding and now, it seemed, his own brother was not above tittle-tattling to Robert's new in-laws about what was a private matter between the newly-weds.

Robert lifted his head, squared his shoulders and faced the man across the desk. 'Your daughter, Mr Hathersage, is only eighteen and doesn't seem to have been told what to expect of married life.'

'What?' Now the red-veined face opposite him was growing purple. 'What are you insinuating?'

Calm now, Robert said, 'I'm not insinuating anything. She didn't know anything about the – well – you know what I mean.'

Hathersage let out a grunt of anger. 'I left all that sort of thing to her mother.' For a moment he was silent and thoughtful, as if he were thinking back and remembering. Slowly, he said, 'Mm, well, it's not as unusual as you might think, m'boy. You'll just have to be very patient with her.' Standing up he added, 'But I wish you hadn't come back so soon. It's set the servants gossiping. And the separate bedrooms hasn't helped either, but I'll have a word with her mother.' He moved round the desk and patted Robert on the shoulder with what was intended to be a fatherly gesture but to the young man it had the feel of condescension about it. 'Yes, yes, that's the best. I'll speak to her mother. It'll be all right.'

Eight

Robert weaved his way amongst the fish troughs ignoring the raucous shouts from the girls until he found himself standing opposite a tall, slim girl with her bright red hair tied back. Her hands never slowed in their movements, yet he was aware of her glances. He could not fail to see the anger and resentment in the flash of those green eyes that told him she knew exactly who he was and what he had done.

Surely this couldn't be the girl he had supposedly attacked? She looked too feisty, too spirited to have . . . And then suddenly he knew. She was the one who had flown to the other's rescue. This was the girl who had shouted at him and hauled him away.

Ever since the day of his wedding he had promised himself to come down to the docks to seek her out. But now, standing before her, Robert's mouth was suddenly parched. He ran his tongue around his lips and when he tried to speak his voice was little more than a hoarse whisper. 'Excuse me. Might I – er – have a word with you in private?'

'I canna leave me work,' was her curt reply.

Robert was immediately aware that close by all the chatter and noise had ceased and though the work never slowed, he knew that all who could overhear were listening hard.

He swallowed and tried again. 'I would like to speak

to you. Could I meet you somewhere when you finish work?'

'Meet me? Meet me?' Suddenly the sharp blade of the knife she was wielding with such effect on the fish, was being held threateningly only inches from his face. 'Like to meet me in a dark alley, would you?'

He stepped back to find himself up against one of the girl packers at the next trough.

'Mind where yer treadin', mister.'

There was laughter all round. 'Aye, he wants to mind where he's treadin' all right.'

His face reddening, Robert turned and blundered away, the sound of their suggestive taunts following him.

'I'll meet you round the back, mister, if she won't.'

'Fancied a bit of rough, did you?'

Jeannie bent her head over her work, thrusting the blade into the fish with a vicious delight. How she would like to have slashed at his face; marred those godlike good looks, that smooth, boyish skin.

Then suddenly a wave of shame swept through her. She had always known she had a quick temper, but until this moment she had never experienced such a passionate hatred for anyone. The violence of her feelings shocked her.

She paused a moment and glanced up to watch him hurrying away, his shoulders hunched.

She felt Flora's elbow dig her in the ribs. 'That the one who attacked Grace Lawrence, then?'

Jeannie turned wide eyes on her team-mate. 'How on earth . . .?'

The girl laughed. 'Och, news travels fast on the fish dock, Jeannie. You canna keep a secret round here for long.'

Jeannie said nothing until Flora prompted again, 'Well, was it him?'

In a quiet, flat tone, Jeannie answered. 'Aye.'

Flora nodded towards the corner of the building around which Robert had disappeared from their sight. 'You should have given him a chance to explain, maybe to apologize even. He's only a wee laddie, Jeannie. You should have given him a chance.'

'Him and his friends weren't giving poor Grace "a chance",' Jeannie retorted bitterly. Yet she was honest enough to admit that now she had seen him close to and in daylight, he was much younger than she had expected.

'Aye well,' Flora was saying, her tone philosophical. 'From what I heard, if Grace Lawrence goes visiting Aggie Turnbull's, then she can expect all she gets.'

'You two goin' to gossip all day,' came the truculent voice of their packer from behind them. 'I'm waiting.'

Jeannie guessed that Mary had seen what had happened and overheard every word, had learned the truth about the young man she had so admired from a distance. And Mary didn't like it.

'Sorry,' Jeannie said at once and again her knife blade flashed, but this time only upon the fish.

He was waiting in the shadows on the corner of Baldock Street when Jeannie and Grace made their way home.

'Excuse me . . .' When he stepped out in front of them, both girls jumped and Grace gave a little scream.

He glanced briefly at Jeannie but now it was upon Grace that his gaze rested.

'Please . . .' He put out his hand to catch hold of her arm and Grace screamed again, the sound echoing along the street.

'Don't you dare to even touch her,' Jeannie hissed and stepped between them.

63

'Please, you've got it all wrong. I've come to apologize
– to explain—'

'What is there to explain, mister? You attacked an
innocent young lass. A gang of you. What chance had she
got, eh?'

Even in the fading light, she could see that he turned
white. 'I was drunk. I can't even remember clearly what
happened. I would never – ever – have done such a thing
in my – my right mind.' He swallowed painfully and again
he looked directly at Grace. 'Did – did I hurt you?'

Mutely, Grace shook her head but fiercely Jeannie said,
'Only frightened her out of her wits. And who's to know
what might have happened . . .' She didn't add 'if I hadn't
come along' for even to her own ears, it would have
sounded boastful.

He was putting his hand into the inside pocket of his
jacket. 'Please, let me . . .?' He opened a leather wallet and
extracted a five-pound note and thrust it towards Grace,
but before the girl could even reach out, Jeannie wrenched
the piece of paper money from his fingers and tore it into
shreds, casting it into the gutter. 'How dare you? How
dare you insult her like that?'

'I'm sorry. I only wanted—'

'We ken what you wanted.' She grabbed Grace's arm
now and hauled her along the street, calling back over her
shoulder, 'You and your like! Think the fisher lasses are
good for only one thing.'

Robert stood staring after them whilst, as Jeannie
dragged her away, Grace twisted her head round to watch
the little pieces of white paper float along the gutter and
disappear down a drain.

Jeannie was still seething about the incident when they
arrived home but Nell, her fingers still busy braiding a net,
seemed to accept the news calmly. In fact, to Jeannie's

annoyance, Grace's mother seemed almost to be taking the young man's part.

'I canna understand you.' Jeannie spread her hands, palms upwards, in a gesture of exasperated disbelief. 'Any of you. Just because he's the son of the owner of the ships, you're going to allow him to get away with what he did to Grace.'

'He didna do anything to Grace, did he? Not really?' And as Jeannie opened her mouth to retaliate, Nell held up her hand. 'Och I ken, lassie, what he – and all the others – might well have done if you hadna come along when you did.' For a moment, Nell actually dropped the length of sisal she was holding and moved towards Jeannie. Taking her hands between her own, Nell said gently, 'I ken how you feel, hen, and what you'd like to do to those – those . . .' The word to fit the description of what she felt for them defeated her and her sentence ended in a sigh. 'And I feel just the same . . .' She balled her hand into a fist and smacked her own plump chest. 'In here. Really I do. But there's nothing – *nothing* we can do. It's best left.'

'But to come down to the dockside today. To seek her out in front of everyone and offer her money. The final insult. How could he do that?' Jeannie burst out.

Grace, who had stood nearby quietly listening to every word, spoke up now. 'He was going to give me five pounds, Mam. A whole five-pound note, but – but Jeannie tore it up under his nose and threw it into the gutter.'

For a fleeting moment even Nell blinked and glanced from one to the other, a moment's unguarded hesitation on her features. Five pounds to a fisherman's family, even a skipper's family, was a lot of money. She gave a little sigh and a tiny shrug of her shoulders as if to dismiss it from her mind and then, looking once more directly into Jeannie's eyes, she said softly, 'Have you stopped to think, hen, what courage it must have taken for that young man to come amongst all the lassies on the docks today? They're the salt of the earth, all of them, I'll never say different, but they wouldna have been beyond turning on him if they'd all known the full story. He could easily have found himself rolling in the mud, his clothes torn from his back. They might even have thrown him into the water. Son of an owner or not, if they'd all done it, there'd have been precious little anyone, including the police, could have done about it.'

Jeannie, still unforgiving, her mouth a straight hard line, leant a little closer to Nell and said, with quiet deliberation, 'Aye, an' if I'd known that this afternoon, Mrs Lawrence, I'd have led them on mysel'.'

Nell gazed at her for a long moment and then nodded slowly. Her eyes softened as she smiled. 'Aye, I do believe you would have done, hen. For you're a brave, feisty girl, and I'll thank God every day of my life that you came along at that moment. But you know something, Jeannie lass . . .?' The older woman patted the hand she still held. 'You're always going to be the one that others lean on. Because you are so strong, you're always going to be the one they all come to. All your life, lass, you're going to have to carry the burdens for those nearest to you.' For another moment she held Jeannie's gaze and then she turned away, bustling back to her work. 'What am I doing standing here blethering on as if next week'll do. I've this net to finish by the morning and I'll be up half the night as it is.'

'I'll help you, if you like,' Jeannie volunteered and Nell glanced at her again, this time with surprise in her eyes.

'You know how to braid?'

Jeannie nodded and a lump came into her throat as she

said hoarsely, 'I had a very good teacher. The best. My father taught me.'

Aware that the girl was perhaps reliving painful memories, deliberately Nell pulled a comical face. 'Is there anything you *canna* do, lass?'

Now Jeannie laughed as she moved towards the net to watch Nell's quick fingers for a moment. 'Plenty,' she said and added wryly, 'I'm no great shakes in the kitchen. The man who takes me on'll have to have a strong stomach.'

The two women laughed together and behind them even Grace smiled as she turned away, the one, by the sound of it, to cook the meal again that evening.

Nine

'Tell me about your home, hen,' Nell said softly. 'Your mother and father and where you come from.'

They were sitting by the fire late one evening, just the two of them, waiting for Grace to come home.

'We lived in a small fishing village on the Fife coast,' Jeannie began and suddenly she could almost feel again the wind on her face as she had stood on the wall watching her father's boat becoming a mere speck on the horizon as he sailed away. A wave of homesickness for the white-washed, gabled cottages that clustered around the harbour, the ever-open doors of friendly neighbours in the tiny community where everybody knew everyone else, washed over her.

Faltering a little at first, Jeannie went on to tell Nell's sympathetic ear about her childhood, the loss of her mother, but when she spoke of her father there was a catch in her voice. 'My father's sister took care of me when he was at sea but I used to live for his time ashore. He'd take me into Kirkcaldy and buy me clothes and presents or even to Edinburgh. Och, he used to spoil me rotten. Once he took me on a real holiday to the Trossachs. D'you know, if I close my eyes . . .' she did so to demonstrate, 'I can still see the wet rocks and hear the rushing water of the Falls.'

She sighed and opened her eyes bringing herself back to the tiny, cramped kitchen that was miles from her homeland. She forced a smile and said, 'Mr Lawrence reminds me of him in so many ways. He even looks a bit like him.' She laughed. 'He has a beard like him.'

'Aye, he's a good man is my George,' Nell said dreamily as if she too were thinking back. 'The first time I laid eyes on him, Jeannie, I knew he was the man for me. I just never went home.'

'Have you ever been back to Scotland? For a visit?'

Nell pressed her lips together and shook her head. 'We couldna afford it, specially when the bairns came along. And now all ma family in Scotland are gone. There's no point in going home. I've been homesick many a time. But you see, hen, I loved George Lawrence. And he,' she ended simply, 'was here.'

'But you still call Scotland "home"?'

The two women exchanged a glance. 'Aye well,' Nell said. 'You never forget your roots, do you, hen?' She paused a moment and then asked gently, as if already half-guessing the answer, 'And your father?'

Mutely, Jeannie shook her head and then the words came haltingly. 'He – he didna come back from his last trip. He was with the fleet – the herring fleet. He has . . .' She hesitated and then deliberately said, 'Had – his own little steam drifter.' She bit her lip and fell silent.

'How long since his boat went missing?' Nell's soft, lilting voice was a balm to Jeannie's tormented heart. The sound of home and yet far enough away to lend a remoteness that in itself was a comfort.

'It's – it's been four months now. I know it must sound foolish, but that's why I came further south. I thought he might have put into another port for a wee while for repairs and then maybe moved on, following the herring fleet, y'ken . . .? Her voice trailed away. Then Jeannie pulled in a deep breath and with a determined effort, she said, more strongly, 'But I know I ought to face the fact that he – he's gone. If he'd been all right, I'd have heard by now. He wouldna have let me go this long without a word from him.'

'Aw lassie, I'm sorry.' Nell had reached out and gripped the girl's hand, but she probed no further.

The room was silent for a moment save for the ticking of the clock and the spitting of a log on the fire.

'How long was it before you married Mr Lawrence? After you'd met him, I mean?'

'Och well, I went on with the fisher lasses right down the coast to Yarmouth, but instead of going back home at the end of the season, I came back here and we were married on his next shore leave.' She smiled impishly at the memory. 'There were a few too many local girls with their eye on George Lawrence for my liking.' A slight shadow crossed her eyes as she murmured, 'One in particular . . .' Then she cleared her throat and was smiling again, 'And I couldna let him escape *my* net, now could I?'

As they laughed together, Nell glanced up at the clock and her expression sobered. 'It's time Grace was home. Surely she can't be working as late as this again?'

'Would you like me to go and look for her?'

'No, no, Jeannie. I'll wait up. You be away to your bed. Tomorrow's a big day . . .' Her face was wreathed in a happy smile again. 'The men will be home again.'

As Jeannie rose Nell reached up and patted her cheek affectionately. 'Sleep well, hen.'

When George Lawrence stepped into the house, Nell came alive. The big man brought light and laughter into the little terraced house and even the ever-present net lay limply, half-braided, against the wall whilst Nell bustled about after her husband. It wasn't that she was miserable when he was at sea, but the moment he came home there was a sparkle in her eyes, a smile on her lips and an extra spring to her step.

'Get yar bonnets on, girls. I've been for me settlings . . .' He spilled a bundle of notes and coins on to the table. 'It was a good trip, so I'm taking you into the town. You too, Jeannie.' He reached out and gathered most of the notes together. 'Here's your housekeeping, Nell. And this . . .' he picked up the remaining money, 'is to spend.'

He took them to Main Street, Nell, Grace and Jeannie.

'It's lucky there were no herring boats in today, else you'd have missed this,' Grace said, linking her arm through Jeannie's, but her new-found friend's reply was a heavy sigh.

'The shoals of fish are moving south. The girls will be going too soon.'

'Shall you go?'

Jeannie shrugged. 'I dinna ken.' Then she smiled. 'Let's no' think about it today. Let's enjoy ourselves.'

'Yes, let's,' Grace agreed.

And enjoy themselves they did. They had dinner in a fancy restaurant and George took them round the shops and insisted on buying each one of them a new winter coat.

'Och no,' Jeannie resisted. 'I couldn't possibly.'

'Go on, hen.' Nell nudged her and winked. 'Our Tom'll be home soon and I know he wants to take you out. You'd look lovely in that dark green coat with your pretty hair.'

Jeannie felt a lump come into her throat.

Spending lavishly after a good trip, George Lawrence reminded Jeannie even more of her father. Thinking of him, she felt the familiar ache in her chest. The only difference was when he spoke, for George's Lincolnshire dialect was nothing like the brogue of Angus Buchanan. But for today, she could imagine she had her father back with her, so she lifted her chin, smiled and thanked the big, generous man.

'I told you, didn't I?' Flora said. 'There he is.'

'Who?' Jeannie looked up, her gutting knife still for a few seconds.

'Francis Hayes-Gorton.' Mary nudged her from behind. 'Look, over there. Oh, but he's handsome. Just look at his fine clothes.'

Jeannie's eyes narrowed as she studied the man. He was, as Flora had predicted, strolling about on the edge of the area where the girls worked, idly swinging his cane, his thumb hooked into the pocket of his waistcoat.

'I wouldna trust that one,' Flora put in. 'Now, if you'd told me that he was the one who had attacked Grace Lawrence, I'd have believed it.' She shook her head. 'But, you know, I still canna believe it was the other one. Robert.'

'He was there.' Jeannie nodded her head towards Francis.

'Was he trying to stop what was going on then?' Flora probed.

'Well . . .' Jeannie hesitated. 'I think it was him who was the ringleader but, to be truthful, I dinna ken. I just waded in. I didna wait to see who was doing what exactly.' She grinned ruefully. 'Me and my temper.'

'There,' Flora said triumphantly. 'I didna think it would be Mr Robert. I've always thought he was rather nice. Though I'm not,' she added sharply and, with her knife, indicated the girl behind them, 'as smitten as Mary.'

Jeannie was thoughtful for a moment before she said,

slowly, 'There was one of them who tried to be, well, helpful.' She gave a sniff of derision. 'But only afterwards, when I'd broken it up.'

'Who was that?'

'I'm not sure.' She paused again, dredging back through the fleeting images and voices of that night. Then she asked, 'Is there another brother?'

'Yes, we told you. Edwin. He's the youngest.'

Jeannie nodded. 'I think it was him, then.'

'I still dinna think it was their fault. Not any of 'em.' Mary was still determined to defend all the brothers. 'She led 'em on, if you ask me.'

Jeannie half-turned and opened her mouth to make a sharp retort in Grace's defence when her attention was caught once more by Francis Hayes-Gorton. He was standing by the corner of a building, talking to a girl. His head was tilted to one side and he was looking down at her, a sideways, slightly sardonic smile on his thin mouth. Then he reached out and touched the girl's cheek with his fingers.

Jeannie drew breath sharply and then clamped her mouth together to stop the words she had been about to utter.

'There,' came Mary's triumphant voice from behind her. 'What did I tell you? See that?'

The girl, looking up into Francis's face and blushing prettily, was Grace Lawrence.

When the work was finished for the day, Jeannie went in search of Grace. As she moved amongst the throng of girls making their weary way home, she felt a touch on her arm and turned to look down upon Billy McBride.

'A word with you, lassie.' His face was serious and for

one moment Jeannie's heart leapt in her breast. He had news. News of her father.

'Jeannie, I'm sorry, but there's not enough work to warrant taking you with us on to Yarmouth. The catches are dwindling already. They've not been what they used to be for a few years now.' He sighed heavily. 'I reckon soon there won't be any Scottish lasses coming this far south. And besides, the lass who's usually with Flora and Mary will be well enough to work when we get to Yarmouth and back to take her place in the team.'

Jeannie nodded and smiled. 'It's all right, Mr McBride, I . . .'

'I could have a word with a few of the local employers, if you like, lassie. I know several of them. And you're a good worker . . .' He nodded and smiled, showing broken, uneven teeth. 'I've been watching you.'

It was a rare compliment, Jeannie thought, and her smile broadened of its own accord. Billy McBride was a hard taskmaster. That much she had seen. His recommendation would certainly be worth having. She thought quickly. She had been about to say, before his interruption, that she would go home, back to Scotland. But now, with the promise of a job here, she held her tongue. At least, for the present, it might be worthwhile staying in Havelock. She was overcome by a sudden longing for home and her resolve almost weakened. But news, her head told her, if any came at all, was far more likely to come here, to Havelock, for her father's vessel had been following the boats southwards.

Quickly, she made her decision, she would stay here. She would write home to one of their neighbours to make sure there had been no news there, but she would stay in Havelock at least for a while longer.

Her attention came back to the wiry little man and what he was saying. '. . . There's the kippers. There's work there for a while longer. Or the filleting, alongside Nell's lass. Maybe she could help you find employment.'

Ah yes, Jeannie thought, Nell's lass indeed. Grace Lawrence. Now there was another problem. It wasn't really any of her business, of course, but she meant to say something to the girl. She could not begin to understand how Grace could even speak to Francis Hayes-Gorton after what had happened. It seemed to Jeannie that she was far more angry and resentful about the incident than Grace. Wisdom told her that she should catch the first train back north of the border. And yet, she liked the Lawrence family. She felt drawn to Nell, who was one of her own, and to George. And to Tom Lawrence too. One day he would grow into a fine man like his father.

Jeannie felt herself being lured into the mesh of this family, like a fish entangled in one of their nets. Instinct told her to go; she ought to leave, right now, and yet something held her here.

It was more than just the vain hope that her father would one day come sailing into this safe haven. Now, it was more to do with the Lawrence family and, in particular, in saving Grace from her own foolishness.

So when the other Scottish girls moved southwards following the herring fleet, Jeannie stayed in Havelock.

'You'll easily find work in the fish docks, hen,' Nell had assured her. 'And you're welcome to stay here as long as you want.'

'But you havena the room when the menfolk are home.'

Nell gave a snort of laughter. 'And how long are they

at home? You tell me, as if I didn't know. Thirty to forty days out of a whole year, so you'll hardly be in the way, now would you?'

Jeannie laughed. 'No, I suppose not, if you put it that way.' Her eyes took on a faraway look, as she murmured. 'I should like to stay here a while longer.'

So, when Tom Lawrence came home, Jeannie was still there and his expression, when he saw her, left Jeannie in no doubt as to his pleasure at seeing her again.

'My word, what have you got, Jeannie, that the rest of the girls round here haven't?' Grace teased her archly as they undressed and got into their shared bed that night. 'He's never stayed away from the pub and his mates on his first night ashore. And taking you out for a walk, just the two of you.'

In the flickering light from the candle, Jeannie smiled grimly to herself but said nothing. She could hardly tell Grace that they had spent most of the time talking about her and that the conversation had almost turned into a quarrel.

'Have you been looking out for our Grace, then?' had been Tom's first words. 'Has she been behaving herself and keeping away from Aggie?'

The familiarity with which Tom spoke of Aggie Turnbull was not lost on Jeannie, but she made no comment. 'She's been out once or twice – to see friends – but she didna stay out late.'

Tom gave a grunt. 'Where did she go?'

'I've no idea, Tom. I promised you I'd look out for her, but I'm not her keeper.' Her anxiety about the girl made her tone sharper than she had intended. She had tried to keep a watch on Grace, but the girl was as slippery as one of the fish Jeannie gutted each day. Always, it seemed,

Grace had a plausible excuse. 'I was on an errand for me mam,' or 'I had to work late . . .'

When Jeannie had probed about seeing her talking to Francis, even then Grace had had a ready retort. 'I can hardly snub him if he chooses to speak to me, now can I? His company employs my father.'

'I'm sorry, Jeannie, but I worry about her,' Tom was saying now. 'She's only sixteen and a naive sixteen at that. And me mother, well, I think she sees no wrong in her.'

'Och, I think your mother knows more than you think,' Jeannie said, remembering the immediate reaction of Nell Lawrence on the night of the attack when hearing Aggie's name mentioned. 'I think she knows exactly what Aggie Turnbull is. And so does Grace.'

Tom stopped and turned to face her, catching hold of her arm and turning her to face him. 'What do you mean by that? "What Aggie Turnbull is"?'

She looked up into his face, seeing his fair eyebrows drawn together in a frown. The square of his jawline suddenly hard and his mouth down turned at the corners. For a moment Jeannie stared up at him and then with deliberate pointedness looked down at the huge hand still grasping her arm. Quickly, he released her and gave a quick, rueful, smile. 'I'm sorry, Jeannie . . .' He ran his hand through his thick, springy fair hair. 'But I get so wound up when I think about our Grace getting 'ersen into trouble.'

Jeannie felt her head reeling. For a moment, his quick spurt of temper and the sudden disarming apology had reminded her yet again of her own father; the loving, generous man with a heart of gold had nevertheless had a swift temper but it had always died just as quickly as it had flared.

Now she was just as quick to forgive Tom. 'It's all right. I do understand. It must be very difficult for you – and for your father – being away so much, to look after your womenfolk.'

'It's a strange life,' Tom murmured. 'Me dad always ses that when you're at sea you long to be home and when you're ashore you can't wait to get back to sea.'

Jeannie smiled, but the smile was tinged with sadness for his words still reminded her of her father. 'Yes,' she whispered, a little catch in her voice. 'That's what ma father always said too.'

And suddenly she found herself confiding in Tom, telling him everything that she had told Nell.

'I used to count the days off on the calendar to him coming home,' she said softly and her throat constricted at the memories. 'And then all too soon, he'd be gone and the counting of the days would start all over again.'

'And now?' Tom prompted gently.

Jeannie shook her head and said flatly, 'He – he hasna come back. Since May, on his first trip out with the herring fleet this year, the – the counting has never stopped.'

'Aw Jeannie . . .' Now the touch on her arm was surprisingly gentle. 'I'm sorry. Sorry about your dad. I – I thought it was – I mean – I thought you were waiting, watching for someone special . . .' He faltered. 'Y'know – a boyfriend.'

My father was special, she wanted to say, very special, but she said nothing. They walked on together for a while before Tom asked, 'What are you going to do?'

Jeannie lifted her shoulders in a shrug and there was reluctance in her tone. 'Go home, I suppose. Eventually.'

'Is that what you really want to do? I mean, is there someone back home. A feller?' Again, disappointment clouded his eyes.

Now Jeannie laughed. 'No, no feller. But there are a lot of friends. People who took care of me when my father was away. Although,' she hesitated again, 'my aunt died last year. Very suddenly, from a stroke.'

'Do you want to go back?'

There was a pause before Jeannie said slowly, 'I dinna ken. It's my home and yet – without my father . . .' She left the sentence unfinished for she was muddled in her own mind as to exactly what her feelings really were. Part of her was homesick for Scotland and yet another part of her dreaded having to go back to the house knowing he would never come home again.

'Then stay here, Jeannie, with us. Me mam'd love to have you and you'd be a friend for our Grace and . . .'

She looked up at him, a sharp retort on her lips that she had no intention of staying just to be nursemaid for his sister, but then she caught the look in his eyes and there was no mistaking the sentiment in his next words. '. . . And I'd like you to stay too.'

Ten

The screams echoed through the house bringing Mr Hathersage and his wife, dressed only in their nightwear, running to the bedroom which Robert and Louise now shared at her parents' insistence. Yet it was only to stop the servants gossiping, Robert thought resentfully. No one seemed to be making any real effort to help Louise act like a real wife towards him.

His blustering father-in-law flung the door open without even knocking. 'What on earth is going on?'

It was like a scene from a farce, yet no one was laughing. Louise lay on one side of the huge four-poster bed, drumming her heels and wailing whilst Robert slipped from beneath the sheet and reached for his dressing gown. As he pulled it on to cover his nakedness, Mrs Hathersage rushed forward to gather her child to her ample bosom. Rocking her, she crooned, 'There, there, my precious. I'll not let him hurt you again.'

As the girl's crying lessened to a hiccupping sob, the mother glared at the two men until they moved away and left the room.

'Huh, such a carry-on. Come down to the study, boy. I could do with a drink . . .' Henry Hathersage led the way downstairs, his bare feet and ankles poking out comically from beneath his white nightshirt.

In the book-lined study that reeked of its owner's stale tobacco smoke, Robert sat in one of the leather armchairs.

His father-in-law poked the fire into life. 'Doesn't look as if you're going to give me a grandson at this rate, m'boy. What are we going to do about it, eh?'

When Robert made no reply, the older man turned towards the array of bottles on the sideboard. 'Mind if I make a suggestion, young feller?'

'No,' was Robert's toneless reply.

Mr Hathersage came and stood in front of him holding out a glass with a inch of amber liquid in the bottom.

'Go and see Aggie.'

'For heaven's sake!' Robert burst out without pausing to think. 'You're as bad as my brother.'

'Eh?' The older man sat in the chair opposite. 'What's that supposed to mean?'

Robert sat forward, placed his drink on the small side table and leant his elbows on his knees. With a groan he dropped his head into his hands. 'Oh hell, what a mess!'

'Come now, my boy. It's not as bad as all that. Why, I remember . . .' Mr Hathersage made a coughing noise and changed the direction of his sentence. 'I've told you before, this is a common thing with the ladies, especially a young, sheltered girl like our Louise.'

Slowly Robert raised his head and looked at his father-in-law with a haunted, haggard expression in his eyes. 'Does she know nothing? About – about that side of married life?'

Mr Hathersage cleared his throat again noisily. 'Evidently not. My wife – er – finds such matters indelicate and could not bring herself to talk to the girl. Pity. It's hardly fair on you.' He shot Robert a keen glance. 'You – I take it – have little experience with women?'

Robert gave an involuntary shudder, remembering.

'What did you mean? About your brother?' Mr Hathersage persisted. When Robert did not reply, the older man's tone became coaxing. 'Come on, my boy, this is man to man stuff. It'll go no further than these four walls. I promise you.'

Still Robert hesitated. It seemed ironic to confide such a thing to the father of his bride. And yet, the young man thought, it would be a relief to speak of it. He let out a huge sigh and began to relate the shameful details of the night before his wedding.

'Ha!' Mr Hathersage slapped his knee with the flat of his hand. 'Francis took you to Aggie's, did he? Didn't I say that's what you ought to do. She knows a thing or two about how to please a man, does Aggie.'

Slowly Robert raised his head and was appalled to see his father-in-law give him a broad wink.

'And as for the girl, well, if she wasn't one of Aggie's girls then she should have known better than to be in that street, specially at night.' Mr Hathersage dismissed the whole incident as being of no consequence.'Your brother had the right idea, m'boy. You go back to Aggie's.' He tapped his forefinger against the side of his nose. 'But not a word to our ladies, eh?'

Sickened, Robert got to his feet, sorry now that he had foolishly confided in his father-in-law. 'Thank you for the drink, sir.'

'All right, m'boy. All right. And think about what I said, eh?'

Robert nodded, turned and left the room, closing the door quietly behind him. He had no intention of going anywhere near Aggie Turnbull's. Instead, he decided, he would try to talk to his wife. Perhaps, if he was very gentle with her, they could learn together. It was worth a try.

And she was not the only girl he wanted to talk to. He had still not had a chance to explain everything to that red-haired beauty, Grace Lawrence's avenging angel, Jeannie Buchanan.

'The boats are in. The boats are in.' The cry, and the excitement that the words always brought, rippled around the docks and the neighbouring streets. No one ever quite knew how it happened, but the news spread like a tidal wave, bringing wives, sweethearts, children, sometimes whole families, to the dockside to watch the armada of boats coming home with the tide.

It was not the herring fleet now that had appeared on the horizon this time, for they had moved southwards, but the home fleet of Havelock trawlers. Since Tom had last been ashore, Jeannie had found work alongside Grace, as a filleter, and now the two girls, in their break, stood watching the ships draw near.

'Me mam's still busy with a net, so I've come to see me dad's boat come in. And Tom's too.'

Jeannie was looking forward to seeing them both, the big man with his loud laugh and bluff affection, but especially Tom with his lopsided grin.

'Are they on different boats again?' Jeannie asked.

'Yes. Tom's still on the *Hathersage Enterprise*. He ses he won't go back on a Gorton ship.' Her face expressionless and without a trace of emotion in her voice, Grace nodded towards a building behind them. 'But they're all here today. I wonder why?'

Jeannie turned to see five men standing on the steps. They were all in formal suits with high-standing collars and black ties and the two older men had moustaches, twisted into points at either side.

Involuntarily, Jeannie felt her jaw harden. 'Two I

know,' she said, her voice tight as she recognized Francis and Robert Hayes-Gorton. 'The third young man must be their brother, Edwin.'

'That's right.'

'Who are the two older men?'

'The one standing next to Mr Robert is his father, Mr Samuel Hayes-Gorton. The other is Mr Hathersage.'

Jeannie turned her gaze away from the men for a moment and looked at Grace. Bluntly, she said, 'I saw you talking to Mr Francis a while back?' Sarcasm crept into her tone. 'Was he apologizing?'

Grace's face was suddenly bright red as colour flooded it. 'Oh Jeannie, please don't make any more trouble. It was nothing. Honest. He's always around the docks, specially when the fisher lasses are here. He's just a flirt. We all know what he is. And don't say anything to me dad. Please? Or to Tom.'

'We-ell,' Jeannie said slowly, trying to stop the teasing smile twitching her mouth. 'Just so long as you do as your mother says and keep away from Aggie's.' Then she allowed her generous mouth to curve in a mischievous smile. 'But d'you know, I keep hearing about this Aggie Turnbull. Her name seems to keep cropping up. I've seen her, but only at a distance. One of these days I'll have to meet her. I'm quite looking forward to it.'

'Oh you!' Grace said good-naturedly. She linked her arm through Jeannie's. 'Come on, let's go and meet Tom. That's his boat just coming in now.'

Tom was first off the boat, clambering down the ladder almost before the ship had settled its prow gently against the side of the jetty.

'He seems in a hurry,' Jeannie murmured, puzzled by the young man's haste. There seemed an air of agitation about him and his face was set in a grim frown.

'I don't think he's seen us,' Grace said in surprise. Obviously she had thought that her brother's haste was because he had seen them waiting for him, but as his feet hit the solid mass of the quay, he began to run, a little unsteadily at first, towards the dock office.

'Tom. Tom!' Grace shouted and began to push her ways towards him, with Jeannie in her wake.

The young man halted and turned to face them. At once, Jeannie could see the anxiety in his eyes.

'Jeannie, oh Jeannie. You're still here.' Tom came to her and put his arms about her, burying his face in her neck, not caring who saw.

'Tom, what is it?' Jeannie tried to ease herself from his embrace, but the young man held on to her fiercely.

Now Grace was tugging at the sleeve of his jersey. 'What's the matter?'

Against her, Jeannie felt Tom drag in a shuddering breath and then he lifted his head, loosened his hold on her and stepped back a pace. But he did not let go of her hands, still clinging on tightly as if he would never let her go.

'I'm that glad to see you still here.' And he gave her hands an extra squeeze. 'Has there been any news?'

'News, Tom?' Grace said. 'We don't know what you're talking about?'

Still his gaze was on Jeannie. 'You mean, you haven't heard anything?'

'Heard what . . .?' Then, as understanding dawned, Jeannie heard Grace draw in a sharp breath. 'Oh no, you don't mean Dad's ship?'

Wildly, Tom shook his head. 'That's the trouble. I just don't know. There was a terrific storm three nights ago and we heard that a boat had gone down. But I can't seem to find out which one. I don't know what to do.'

Gently, Jeannie pulled herself free of his grip. 'Won't the dock office know?'

Tom ran his hand through his hair. 'Yes, yes. They might. I suppose I'd better go there.'

Jeannie took hold of Grace's arm and said, 'We'll come with you, Tom.'

But Grace held back. 'You go. I – I'll wait here.'

Jeannie turned to look at her in surprise. 'But don't you want . . .?' she began and then noticed that Grace's gaze had gone beyond her, beyond her brother, to the building that housed the Gorton offices.

'I bet that's why they're here.' Grace nodded her head in the direction of the five men and as Tom turned his gaze and noticed them for the first time, Jeannie saw his body stiffen. 'I couldn't understand it. I've never seen all of 'em come down to the dock 'afore. That'll be why.'

'Right,' he said grimly. 'We'll see what Hayes-Gorton himself has to say.'

'Oh no, Tom,' Grace cried, catching hold of his arm. 'Don't make trouble. You know Dad wouldn't want that.'

Her brother turned to face her, whilst Jeannie looked on silently. 'I'm not going to make trouble, Grace. I just want to know what's happened to me dad's ship.'

'But you said yourself, you don't know that it is his. Not yet. Why don't you . . .?'

'Have you seen it come in?' Tom flung his arm out wide to encompass the steady stream of trawlers nosing their way through the narrow dock gates and towards their assigned positions.

'No, but – but – they're not all home yet. Not even all the ones that are due today. Likely his boat's just late. Maybe tomorrow . . .' Her voice, and her argument, fell away.

Tom's voice softened. 'There's no harm in me asking.

They can't do anything to me for just asking, can they?' But now it was as if he were seeking reassurance too.

Jeannie stepped in. 'Then I'll go. There's nothing they can do to me . . .' and added bitterly, 'at least, not in broad daylight.'

Robert saw the girl pushing her way through the people milling about on the dockside, coming directly towards them, and his mouth was suddenly dry. Surely, she wouldn't make a scene? he thought and then answered himself at once. Oh yes, she would. He felt his breath coming faster and then she was standing before them, on a lower step, looking up at them, her bold, green gaze resting on each of their faces in turn. And when she came at last to him, Robert saw the contempt in her eyes. But her glance flickered away from him and turned instead to his father.

Becoming aware of her scrutiny, Samuel Hayes-Gorton looked down and said, 'Well, young woman? What do you want?'

'Sir, there's a rumour going around the dock that one of the boats has gone down.'

Her tone was polite, but firm, deferential but certainly not fawning. At his side, Robert felt his father stiffen.

'Nonsense,' Mr Hayes-Gorton growled. 'There are several not back yet. Whatever makes you think that?'

Jeannie opened her mouth to say that the son of one of the men aboard the *Gorton Sea Spray* had heard it even whilst still at sea, but she closed it again. The reason she was standing here was because Tom himself did not want to be the one to enquire.

'Then you're saying,' she said, 'that you have not had word that a boat's gone down?'

'I've already given you my answer, young woman,' Samuel Hayes-Gorton said, but neatly avoiding answering her question, whilst, beside him, Robert cringed. He saw the girl glance again into the face of each of them as if she were trying to read the truth written there. As she turned away, his father muttered, 'Get down there, boy, and scotch this rumour. Edwin, you get back to the office. We must make sure word doesn't get out.'

'But I can't tell them nothing's happened when we know it has,' Robert said, aghast to think that his father cared so little for the families of the men aboard the *Sea Spray* that he would lie to them, just to ensure that, in two days time, his fleet would sail again, unhindered by the knowledge that a tragedy had befallen one of their boats.

'You can't . . .' he began, but his father cut short his protest.

'Don't you tell me what I can or can't do, boy. Get down there . . .' And without waiting to hear any more Mr Hayes-Gorton turned and stamped up the steps into the building.

'You'd better do as Daddy says, old chap,' came Francis's smooth voice whilst Mr Hathersage gave a grunt and turned to follow his fellow trawler owner up the steps.

For a moment Robert made no move but, from his vantage point, he watched Jeannie make her way back to where a young man and a girl stood together, obviously waiting for her. He ran lightly down the steps and followed her. As he neared the three, they turned to face him. Robert nodded briefly to Jeannie and then to Grace, feeling once more as he did so, the flush of shame creep up his neck. He cleared his throat with a nervous sound and turned to face the young man. Strangely, both Tom and his sister refused to meet Robert's eyes. Only the red-haired girl's green eyes met his challengingly. Despite his father's orders, he could not lie to these people, so instead he said quietly, 'If I promise to let you know, myself, immediately we have news, would you – I mean – could you, please, say nothing to anyone else for the present?'

Jeannie, quick on the uptake, said, 'Aye, I thought your father was avoiding answering my question.'

Keeping his voice level, Robert found himself replying to her, for the other two had not opened their mouths. 'Well, in a way, yes, he was, but I think . . .' He hesitated, for he was in danger of lying too now and he hated being forced into doing so. 'The truth is,' he began afresh, 'that we ourselves know very little at present and we don't want rumours to spread before we know the truth.'

Now Tom spoke, his tone deferential. 'But you think something has happened then, sir? To the *Sea Spray*?'

Robert swallowed again, conscious the whole time of Jeannie's steady, unforgiving gaze upon him. 'Something's happened, yes, but – but we don't know what. Yet.'

The young girl was crying now, clinging to her brother's arm. 'Oh no, not Dad. Not our dad.'

Robert's eyes, full of sympathy and contrition, turned towards her. 'I'm so sorry. So very sorry,' he whispered and, as the three pairs of eyes now looked upon him, he knew that they were all aware that he was not only apologizing for the tragedy which may have befallen the Lawrence family, but also for his part in the disgraceful incident on the night before his wedding.

He saw Tom Lawrence give a brief nod. 'Yes, sir, I do believe you are.' And Robert felt that the young man too was referring to both events. He felt himself relax a little, believing that his apology had been tacitly accepted, but when he turned to look directly at Jeannie he saw in her fine eyes that her understanding was not forthcoming.

Abruptly, he turned away, saying over his shoulder, 'I'll keep you informed. I promise,' before he strode away.

As he ran back up the steps and into the building, Robert Hayes-Gorton was still thinking about the girl with the fiery hair.

More than anything, he had wanted her forgiveness.

Eleven

'What are we to tell your mother?' Jeannie asked.

Tom hesitated and glanced at his sister. 'I don't think we should tell her anything. Not yet. What do you think, Grace?'

'Not tell her?' Jeannie was scandalized. 'You mean we're going to walk into that house and act as if – as if nothing's happened?'

Now Tom would not meet her eyes. 'There's no point in upsetting her. Not till we know for certain. We'll just say his boat isn't in yet.' He spread his hands. 'After all, we don't really know that anything has happened. Do we?'

'But you heard what *he* said?' Jeannie could not bring herself to refer to Robert by name. 'Something's going on.'

'Yes, I heard,' Tom said with quiet patience and resignation. 'And I heard him promise to let us know as soon as he knew more himself. And he will.'

Jeannie gave a snort of contempt. 'You think so?'

She made to turn away with an angry movement, but now Grace caught her arm. 'Please, Jeannie, don't say anything to Mam. Let's do what Tom says.'

Jeannie shrugged her shoulders, but her mouth was still tight. She hated deceit of any kind and what was happening now, to this family, was all too close to her own tragedy for her to think rationally. Had they all known back home that her father's ship was missing? Had they, too, all kept the secret from her, just leaving her to come

91

gradually to the realization that he was not coming back? She hoped not. She didn't want to think that of her own people, her own kin. She knew herself well enough, her own strengths and weaknesses, to know that she would have dealt far better with the honest truth than this dreadful not knowing. Maybe never knowing.

Now, her words clipped by her anger, she lifted her shoulders as if shrugging off their problems. 'It isna my business, anyway. I'll be leaving soon. I'll be going home – to Scotland.'

And with that, she pulled free from Grace's hold and marched away.

'What do you mean, you can't find out?' Robert leant on his knuckles over the desk, towering over his brother.

Patiently, though with the anxiety evident in his voice, Edwin said, 'We'll find out when we've had time to talk to the men.'

'Who? Which men? Let me talk to them. I'll go. But tell me who?'

'Calm down, Robert,' Samuel Hayes-Gorton's voice boomed as the door to Edwin's office was flung open and their father, followed by Henry Hathersage and a languid, bored-looking Francis. 'We'll know soon enough if the news is bad. And if it isn't, I don't want you spreading fear amongst the crews unnecessarily.'

Robert straightened up and turned to face his father but the older man put out his hand, palm outwards, to stave off further argument. 'You know what might happen when we lose a ship. It makes no difference to the real fishermen, they're hardened to it. Accept it as part of the life, but the youngsters, well . . .' He glanced at his son's face and seeing the puzzlement there, added, 'A lot of them might not report for duty when the boats are ready to sail. They take fright or—'

'Or their dear mamas will try to keep them safely tied to their apron strings at home,' came Francis's sarcastic tone.

'What utter nonsense. Fishermen and their families have always accepted the hardships and dangers as part of the job. If you ask me, the women are every bit as courageous as their menfolk. More so, in a way. They have to sit at home waiting. Just waiting.'

Francis laughed sarcastically. 'Oho, all of a sudden we're the expert on women, are we?'

Robert felt himself colour at the innuendo in his brother's tone, but it was more from anger than embarrassment. He stepped towards the door, but passing Francis, he paused and thrust his face close to his, saying hotly, 'And even if they did try to keep their menfolk at home, can you blame them? I don't see you joining a ship, my dear brother, and learning what this trade – the trade that buys you all your luxury – is really all about.'

Francis smirked and raised his left eyebrow. 'Oh yes, and how many trips have you done, old boy?'

Robert clenched his teeth, 'None,' then he added ominously, '. . . yet.'

'Now, now . . .' came his father's voice, but Robert waited to hear no more and left the office slamming the door so hard behind him that the frosted glass in the upper panel of the door cracked.

He ran down the stairs and once outside stood again on top of the flight of steps, his glance taking in the busy fishdock in front of him. He must speak to the skippers of the vessels which had already docked. Surely someone must know something. For a moment, he paused. He didn't want to spread alarm through the community without just cause. It was a hard life for the fishermen and their families and whilst they all lived with the constant fear of disaster, he didn't want to be the one to make things worse. At least, not until he knew for sure.

He could not get the picture of the Lawrence family out of his mind: of the young girl's wide, fearful eyes, of the deep anxiety on the young man's face. And the other one, Jeannie, with her feisty spirit and her strength. He could see her so clearly; that glorious red hair flying freely in the breeze, wayward curls framing her face, her cheeks faintly pink from the cold and the tiny peppering of freckles across the bridge of her nose. He sighed as he thought about her. Such a lovely mouth, yet when she looked at him it was tight with disapproval and those wonderful green eyes held such contempt. Yet even though her look made him cringe in shame, he was sure he had seen sadness deep in those eyes.

He wanted to make it up to Grace Lawrence, but more than anything else, he wanted to see the look in Jeannie's eyes soften towards him. He wanted to see her smile.

Oh yes, more than anything else he wanted her to smile at him.

In their shared bed that night, Grace snuggled close to Jeannie and whispered, 'Don't go away, Jeannie. At least not yet. Not till we know – about Dad.'

In the darkness, Jeannie sighed thinking over the day's events.

Returning to work after leaving Tom and Grace standing on the quayside, Jeannie had regretted her sharpness. Her angry retort to them, saying that she intended to return home, had been said in the heat of the moment. The truth was, Jeannie acknowledged, that she didn't

94

really want to go home. Who was there, back in Scotland, who really needed her now? Oh yes, kind friends and neighbours, but no kin. No one who would care for her and whom she could care for.

The brother and sister had looked so young and forlorn standing there on the bustling dockside as she had walked away from them. And lost. They needed someone, she told herself. Someone like her.

And you should know how that feels, Jeannie Buchanan, she reminded herself, if anyone does. She felt a shudder run through her, imagining the long hours the young brother and sister may stand, looking out to sea, watching the horizon in vain for the sight of their father's ship.

As long as she had watched until, at last, all hope was gone.

She had been unable to concentrate properly on her work and had incurred a reprimand from the foreman and now had a tiny cut on her little finger as a result of her own carelessness when allowing her mind to wander.

Arriving home had been the worst, seeing Nell bustling about her tiny scullery, red faced from a day's baking and cooking to welcome her man home from the sea.

'Hello, son,' had been her greeting to Tom as he had bent to kiss her cheek. Jeannie had watched as Nell had reached up and patted his muscled shoulder. 'How was your trip?'

'Good, Mam,' Tom replied and Jeannie marvelled that he was able to keep the anxiety from his tone. 'We had a good catch and there should be a fair pay out.'

'Aye well, you'll be needin' it if you're away to the Fisherman's tonight.' Nell's eyes twinkled mischievously behind her steel-rimmed spectacles as she had placed his meal before him. 'Or are you staying home?'

'Eh?' The young man looked up, startled. It was obvious to Jeannie that for one moment he thought his mother must have heard something and expected him to stay with the family until they heard news instead of joining his mates drinking and making merry. His tone was suddenly high-pitched as he asked, 'Why? Why, should I stay home?'

'No reason, son.' Nell shrugged her shoulders and winked at Jeannie. 'I just thought you might find something to keep you at home.'

'Such as?' he asked brusquely, picking up his knife and fork. He did not begin to eat but kept his questioning gaze upon his mother.

Careful, Jeannie wanted to say, you're going to give the game away yourself if you're not careful, and she found she was holding her breath.

'Well, I just thought . . .' Nell was saying and then suddenly Jeannie realized what the older woman was thinking. The last time Tom had come home from the sea, instead of going to the pub that first evening, he had taken her, Jeannie, for a walk. She remembered how Grace had teased her about it and she had understood that it was not Tom's usual behaviour.

Now she laughed aloud, trying to save Tom from falling into the trap that his mother was unwittingly setting. 'Och, I'll no keep a man from his drink, Mrs Lawrence.' She nodded towards Tom. 'You go, Tom.'

Tom looked at her and blinked and then, seeming suddenly to remember too, he gave her a quick, grateful smile.

'Och well now,' Nell was saying, 'I'm no' so sure I agree with you there, hen. It's all very well, these traditions, but when they've wives and families. Now, you take their dad, he's never gone out to the pub the minute

96

he sets foot on land. The next day, well, maybe so, but he always liked to stay with his family . . .' Nell prattled on, busying herself between the back scullery and the range but Jeannie felt a cold spasm of fear clutch her heart. It was an unfortunate choice of words on Nell's part, in the past tense, and Jeannie prayed that they were not prophetic.

But she was very much afraid that perhaps already the sea had indeed taken George Lawrence.

Even with Tom gone from the house, the tension did not lessen. Not for Jeannie. She was aware all the time of Grace casting surreptitious, nervous glances at the clock above the fireplace. For a while Nell returned to her endless braiding against the wall, but by nine o'clock even she looked towards the clock and said, 'Well, it doesna look as if your dad will be home tonight. Away to your bed now, hen.' This to Grace, but her glance seemed to include Jeannie too.

'Are – are you going to bed, Mam?' To Jeannie's ear, Grace's voice seemed high-pitched with the anxiety she knew the girl was feeling.

'No, no, I'll sit by the fire a while longer, just in case.'

Oh no, Jeannie thought. The waiting's begun. Counting the hours, then the days and the weeks.

Oh no, not again.

She took a deep breath, rose from her chair and said as cheerfully as she could, 'Shall I make us all some cocoa?' And forcing a smile, she added, 'Even I can manage that.'

Minutes later as the three women sat sipping the hot liquid, the silence deepened between them until Grace sprang up from her chair, slopping the last of her cocoa over the side of the mug. 'I'm going up,' she said and Jeannie knew instinctively that the girl could not bear the suspense any longer, could not bear sitting there knowing that she was deceiving her mother and unable to shed the huge burden that was growing like a heavy weight in her chest.

'All right, hen,' Nell was saying calmly and lifting her face for her daughter's dutiful goodnight kiss.

As Grace left the room and they heard her footsteps mount the stairs, Jeannie too rose, but before she could move away, Nell's hand touched her arm. Softly she said, 'A moment, hen.' She waited, holding her head on one side, listening until her daughter's footsteps sounded in the room overhead.

With her right index finger, Nell pushed her spectacles higher up her nose and looked straight at Jeannie. 'I'm a wee bit concerned about George, but I don't want Grace to worry. And Tom, maybe tonight the pub was the best place for him. He'll think nothing of it, just that his father's boat is late. And even if he does, well, the drink'll dull his wits. But I know George. He always tries to beat the Hathersage boats back to Havelock. He should have been here on this morning's tide along with Tom's. Or at worst, tonight's.'

Jeannie said nothing but swallowed painfully, debating quickly within her mind whether or not she ought to tell Nell Lawrence what she knew. She felt caught in the middle now, between the family members each trying to keep their fears from the other.

She leant across and patted Nell's hand. 'If you've heard nothing by the morning I'll go to the offices mysel' and find out.'

'Thank you, Jeannie. I'd be grateful if you'd do that for me, hen. Very grateful.'

Jeannie stood and then she too bent and kissed the woman's cheek. A look of surprise crossed Nell's face and for a moment her keen glance searched Jeannie's face. She gave a slight nod of the head as if to indicate that she knew Jeannie understood what she was feeling only too well.

'Away to your bed, hen.'

As Jeannie opened the door leading to the stairs, she turned back once to look at the lonely figure sitting before the fire, gazing into its glowing depths, but every so often her glance would go to the clock on the mantelpiece. Without looking round, Nell said softly, 'You know, I canna believe the sea has taken him. Not my George. When he was a young deckie, he was washed overboard, but the next wave washed him back on board again. Twice that happened to him. They always say . . .' there was a catch in her voice now, 'that if that happens, the sea doesna want them.'

Jeannie could think of no reply and, quietly, she closed the door unable even to bring herself to say, 'Goodnight.'

Hours later, snuggled against her, Grace slept, but Jeannie found rest impossible. Through the long hours of the night, she waited, listening for the sound of Nell coming to bed or Tom returning home from the pub.

But the house was silent. Just waiting . . .

Twelve

Breakfast at the Hathersage mansion five miles beyond the outskirts of Havelock was a tense affair, at least between the two men, Robert and his father-in-law.

Louise, however, was in a frivolous mood, prattling endlessly about her plans for her nineteenth birthday the following week.

'I had such a marvellous time in London last year staying with Madeleine. She took me to all the smart balls and social events. Can I go back again this year, Mummy?'

Mrs Hathersage cast a coy glance at Robert. 'It's not up to us now, darling. You're a married woman. You must ask your husband.' But there was a sly insinuation in her tone that left Robert realizing that he really had no say in the matter.

Louise gave her tinkling laugh and leant towards Robert seated next to her. 'Can we go to London, Robert? For my birthday. We'd have such fun.'

Robert opened his mouth to say that he could not leave at present because of the uncertainty about the *Sea Spray*, but before he could speak, Mr Hathersage's voice came down the length of the table. 'Of course you can go, my princess. It would do you good . . .' He glanced at Robert as if suddenly remembering to include him and added quickly, 'Both of you.'

Louise clapped her hands in delight and cried, 'Oh thank you, Daddy.' She pushed back her chair and rushed to the end of the table to fling her arms about her father's neck.

How could they be thinking about such matters, Robert thought bitterly, when one of their trawlers may be lying at the bottom of the ocean with all hands? With a jerky, angry movement he stood up, turned and left the room, without dutifully kissing his wife's cheek, nodding to his father-in-law or giving a polite bow of his head and murmuring 'Mrs Hathersage'.

'Well, really!' he heard his mother-in-law say loudly as he marched across the hall towards the front door. 'That young man really has a lot to learn as a husband.'

And your daughter, Robert would liked to have said bitterly, has a lot to learn as a wife. As he drove down the wide sweeping driveway towards the wrought iron gates, Robert's anger cooled a little. He drove his own motor car into Havelock each morning. He had no intention of keeping the same office hours as Mr Hathersage who was chauffeured into his company offices at ten in the morning, took two hours for lunch and returned home to his mansion at three thirty each afternoon.

He sighed as he pulled the motor to a halt outside the Gorton offices and sat a moment. Perhaps, for once, the Hathersages were right. Perhaps a little time away together in London would be good for both Louise and him. Away from the influence of her parents, maybe he could talk gently to her and they could take time to get to know each other. Maybe . . .

As he walked towards the entrance to the building, other thoughts now pushed these plans aside. There were more urgent and important matters to be dealt with and as he ran lightly up the steps, Robert's mind was full of foreboding about the news this day might bring.

*

Jeannie awoke to the sound of frantic knocking on the back door. Slipping a shawl around her shoulders over her flannelette nightgown, she padded on bare feet down the stairs, through the kitchen and into the scullery in time to hear Nell's voice raised indignantly.

'And what right has the likes of you to come knocking on my door at this time of the morning? Or any morning, if it comes to that, Aggie Turnbull?'

Jeannie gasped aloud. Aggie Turnbull? Here? It couldn't be! But as she came to stand behind Nell and peer over her shoulder she could see at once that it was indeed the woman she had only before seen at a distance. Yet now she saw her close to, Aggie's appearance was not what she had expected. For one thing she was older than Jeannie had believed her to be. She was hatless and her coat looked as if she had pulled it on in a great hurry. Her blonde hair was dishevelled and though she wore bright lipstick, it seemed to have been applied with a shaky hand. The outline around her perfectly shaped mouth was smudged. Her skin, though smooth, was blotchy and when Jeannie looked into the woman's eyes, she saw why. Aggie's clear blue eyes were brimming with tears.

'Oh Nell. I'm sorry. I had to come. It's not true, is it? For God's sake tell me it's not true. They're saying – that George – that his boat is missing.'

'*My* George is a fine skipper. He'll no' be losin' his ship,' Nell said, her mouth prim and tight. Was it Jeannie's fancy or did Nell really emphasize the word 'my'?

'But it's all round the docks . . .'

'Well, I'll no' believe any tale you bring to ma door, Aggie Turnbull. Good-day.' And Nell made as if to close the door.

'Please, Nell.' The woman clasped her hands together

as if in prayer and Jeannie could see that her fingers were shaking. 'For pity's sake . . .'

But Nell shut the door and leant her back against it. She closed her eyes and let out a deep groan. Jeannie stood watching her.

'What was all that about?' she asked.

Nell opened her eyes, pushed her glasses up her nose with an irritated gesture. 'Dinna ask, hen. Just dinna ask.' But as Nell bustled away, Jeannie heard her mutter, 'The impudent begger, coming to ma house . . .'

'Are you sure? Are you absolutely sure?'

The bearded fisherman, standing before him, nodded gravely. Robert had come down to the fish dock to seek out the men from the other Gorton trawlers.

'As sure as I can be, sir,' the man was saying. 'The storm was dreadful. So bad that our skipper stopped trawlin'. And it takes a fair blow to do that. Before dark, the *Gorton Sea Spray* was alongside us, well, you know, fishing 'aside us.' He flung out his arm to the left as if indicating that the two vessels had been fishing parallel with each other. 'Then in the morning, she'd gone.'

'But maybe she'd moved. Maybe the storm had driven her away, out of your sight.'

The man shrugged. 'Possible, sir, I'll not deny it. But . . .' He hesitated and then shook his head. 'Not very likely.'

'Why?'

The fisherman looked kindly at the well-dressed young man and explained patiently. Son of a trawler owner, he might be, but Robert had little experience at sea. 'There were a lot of ships in the same area, sir. We'd found a

103

good ground. And they,' he paused as if for dramatic effect, 'were all still there the following morning. All, except the *Sea Spray*.'

Robert felt his heart sink. 'I see,' he said heavily. 'Thank you for telling me what you know, but I still don't know if it's enough that we ought to – well – say the ship's missing.'

'There's one other skipper you ought to talk to, sir.' The man glanced around him, searching amongst the boats lining the quay. 'He's on a Hathersage ship, the *North Sea Spirit*. Hewson, they call him. There's a tale going about that he picked up a body from the water. Could be . . .' The man's voice faded away, as if he too didn't want to believe what might have happened.

Robert swallowed hard. 'But that still wouldn't mean the ship had gone down. It might be that he got washed overboard in the storm.' Robert was now like a drowning man clinging to the wreckage. And he knew it. And the skipper knew it too. Soberly, the man said, 'Could be, sir, could be.' But there was little hope in the wise old fisherman's tone.

It was Jeannie who opened the front door to find Robert Hayes-Gorton standing on the pavement outside. She knew at once, by the look on his face, that the news was bad.

Pulling the door wider, she said curtly, 'You'd better come in.'

Nell, standing before the net on the wall, her fingers never still, called, 'Who is it, hen?'

Receiving no immediate answer she looked up as Jeannie ushered the man into the kitchen. Then Nell's eyes widened, her glance flickering from one face to the other. And now, deep into her eyes, came the fear.

Robert stood, an awkward figure in the cluttered room. He was taller than Jeannie had remembered and, closer now, she could see that his slim build belied a strength in his shoulders. He removed his hat and smoothed back his dark wavy hair. In his brown eyes Jeannie could see there was a haunted expression. Twisting his hat round and round in his hands, he said, 'Mrs Lawrence . . .'

His voice too, was deeper, though perhaps that was because of the difficult news he was trying to impart. Jeannie could sense, though she was reluctant to acknowledge it, that there was sympathy and genuine concern for these people in his tone.

'Mrs Lawrence . . .' His glance went briefly towards Tom who was rising from his seat by the fireplace. 'I am so sorry to come with – with some bad news.'

For a fleeting moment, Jeannie felt a flash of sympathy for the young man, but remembering again the night she had first encountered him, her pity died and she stood, jaw clenched, as he dragged out each painful word.

Nell dropped the ball of sisal and the net flapped idly against the wall. She turned slowly to face Robert, her gaze now intent upon his face.

'The *Sea Spray* has not – not returned. Of course, there's still the chance that she's late. That . . .' He could add no further words, because he could think of none.

Tom spoke now. 'Have you asked around?'

Robert turned his glance towards him, with a sense of relief. He could deal better with another man, a fisherman. 'Yes, I've spoken to several of the other skippers from both our boats and those of the Hathersage company, and the last one, he – he had picked up a – a body from the sea

105

and it was . . . I'm so sorry . . .' Again his glance came back momentarily to Nell. 'It was one of the crew from the *Sea Spray*.'

For a moment there was silence in the room and then Tom gave a groan, sat down heavily in his chair and dropped his head into his hands, resting his elbows on his knees.

With a slow, wooden movement, Nell turned back towards the wall and picked up the half-finished net. Her fingers grasped the braiding needle so tightly that her knuckles showed white. It was left to Jeannie, the comparative stranger in their midst, to say, forcing politeness into her tone, 'Thank you for coming, sir. I'll see you out . . .' and led the way to the door into the street.

Back on the pavement, he turned to face her. 'If there's anything I can do – anything, you will let me know?'

She leant towards him, her eyes flashing, no longer needing to hide her feelings. 'Go. Just leave them alone. Havena you and yours done enough damage to this family?'

He jerked backwards as if she had struck him physically. He stared at her for a moment and now she could see the tightening of his mouth and the anger in his eyes.

He put on his hat, gave an exaggerated bow and said in a low, tight voice, 'I'll bid you "Good day", Miss Buchanan.' Then he turned and walked swiftly away.

Turning back into the house, Jeannie closed the door, leant against it for a moment and gave a low groan. She shouldn't have spoken to him like that. Not now, not at a time like this. He was the very person, probably the one and only person, who could help this family in their hour of need and now she had driven him away. She sighed heavily and moved back into the kitchen to find the two people there just as she had left them; Nell braiding the

net and Tom sitting with his head in his hands making no
move to comfort his mother nor to go out and try to find
out more news for himself.

Without stopping to think, Jeannie said as much. 'Are
you going down to the dock to see what you can find out?'
When there was no answer, no response of any kind from
him, not even a movement, she said, more sharply, 'Tom?'

Slowly, like a man in a trance, Tom lifted his head and
looked towards her, his eyes suspiciously wet. Jeannie
gestured towards his mother. 'Tom, hadna you better do
something?'

'What? What can I do?'

'Well, go out and ask around. Get more news. Anything.' She held her lower lip between her teeth, biting
back the words, 'anything instead of sitting there looking
sorry for yoursel''. 'You should be thinking of others,' she
wanted to shout at him. 'Of your mam and Grace, who
doesna ken yet.'

But all she said aloud was, 'I'll make a cup of tea,' and
went into the tiny scullery to busy herself.

Minutes later she returned with a tin tray with three
mugs on it. Nell was still braiding rapidly, her fingers
steadier now and the net growing.

'Come on, let me finish that for you.' Jeannie tried to
coax Nell away from the net. 'Sit by the fire and drink
your tea.'

But Nell's fingers held fast on to the sisal like a drowning man clinging to a lifeline.

'Leave her be,' Tom said quietly. 'She's better keeping
'ersen busy.'

Jeannie moved away from Nell towards Tom to say
softly, 'But she doesna seem to have taken the news in.'

He gave a shrug. 'It's just her way of coping, that's all.
She's strong . . .' He glanced up at her. 'You women are a

lot stronger than us men when it comes to coping with tragedy, you know.'

'Och now, I don't believe that for a minute.' It seemed ironic that she should be plunged into the midst of another family's tragedy. Perhaps, she thought, in staying to help them, she could come to terms with her own loss too.

As if reading her thoughts, Tom looked up at her and said softly, 'Jeannie, will you stay with us a while longer. Please?'

Jeannie did not answer at once but looked across the room at Nell, seeing the bent head and the busy fingers threading and twisting and knotting as if her life depended upon it.

Slowly, she nodded her head. 'Aye, Tom, I'll stay.'

He reached up and grasped her hand tightly, hanging on to it. 'Thank you,' he said hoarsely. 'I knew you would.'

Embarrassed by his display of emotion, she handed him a mug of tea and said brusquely, though not unkindly, 'Here, drink this and then go and see some of your mates. Maybe they've heard more.'

'He's gone,' Tom said brokenly, reaching out for the tea with a trembling hand. 'He's gone. I know he has. Oh how am I going to tell Grace?'

But Tom did not have to tell Grace anything for though he and Jeannie sat beside the fire far into the night and Nell refused to come away from her work at the wall, Grace did not come home.

And still, Nell's fingers twisted and knotted and the net grew longer.

Thirteen

Robert strode along the dock towards the company's offices. How dare that slip of a girl speak to him like that, he raged inwardly. Well, that was it, he wouldn't help that blasted family any more. He'd apologized for that other incident and, shameful though it had been, the young girl had not been hurt. Shocked and frightened, yes, but not physically harmed.

But even as he thought about that night again, guilt twisted at his stomach and his anger died. Sighing inwardly as he ran up the steps and into the building, he knew that despite Jeannie's rudeness, he would still do what he could to help the Lawrence family and that he would go on doing so.

One day, he promised himself, I'll make that red-haired firebrand smile at me.

As he opened the door to Edwin's office, his father came towards him. 'And where the hell have you been? Spreading the news, I suppose, to all and sundry.' He stepped closer to his son and thrust his face so close that Robert could smell the whisky on his breath. Eleven thirty in the morning and already he could smell it.

'Do you know what you're doing, boy? Losing us money, that's what. Half the crews won't turn up to sail tomorrow night, or if they do, they'll go on Hathersage boats. Just because you've married into the Hathersage family, don't forget your loyalty to this one.'

109

Robert stood unflinching as the older man's spittle rained upon his face. Three weeks away from his twenty-first birthday, it came to him now as he stood facing the blustering man that it was time he, Robert Hayes-Gorton, grew up. Time he took on the mantle of maturity, time he started acting like a man. And it was time too that he started to earn the respect of others. He was under this man's thumb, they all were, the whole family, even, to some degree, Francis. It was high time someone stood up to Samuel Hayes-Gorton.

How he wished with all his heart, that he had done this weeks, months ago. Then he would not be tied in marriage to a woman he did not love, nor she to him.

Thinking of his child-bride, he said with a calmness he was not feeling inside, lacing his words with sarcasm, 'I thought we were supposed to be in partnership with the Hathersage family since you so conveniently arranged a marriage between the two companies.'

'Arranged? Arranged? What are you talking about, boy?'

'Oh come on, Father. You know very well what I mean. You and old man Hathersage have planned a union between the companies for years and how better than by marriage.'

He was feeling slightly sick now, not only listening to the callous manner in which his father thought nothing of the loss of a ship and all its crew, save what it would mean to his company in lost revenue, but also realizing just to what depths he and his like would stoop. The two men, Hathersage and his father, had had no compunction in sacrificing the happiness of their own children for the sake of business.

From behind them, as if trying to break up the scene

110

that promised to grow ugly, Edwin's mild voice said, 'I have to say, Father, it seems definite now that the boat is lost. I think it behoves us to be open about the matter.'

Hayes-Gorton swung round, pointing his finger at his younger son. 'Don't you start. You just do as you're told . . .'

Slowly, Edwin rose from his chair behind the desk, leather topped and scratched with years of wear. 'I will do,' the young man said slowly, 'what I think is right. The same . . .' now every word was deliberate, 'as my brother obviously intends to do.'

For a moment, their father, standing between them, appeared stunned. Then he let out a loud bark of laughter, but there was no humour in it. 'Oho, the cubs are turning on the old fox, eh? Well, you're not too old for a whipping and this fox is not too old to give you one . . .' His glance went from one to the other. 'Either of you.' A malicious gleam came into his eyes. 'I can change my will, you know. Leave everything to Francis. If you're not careful, I'll cut the pair of you off without a penny. And you'll find yourself without a job too.' He glanced from first one to the other and back again watching what effect his words were having.

The two brothers exchanged a glance and Robert felt a warm glow spread through him as he read the support in Edwin's eyes.

'If that is what you want,' he said, 'so be it . . .' There was the slightest of pauses before he added, 'sir'.

There was silence and then with a swift unexpected movement Samuel Hayes-Gorton raised the ebony cane he carried and brought it down with a resounding crack upon the surface of the desk. His sons flinched but did not move.

'Damn and blast the pair of you then,' the older man

thundered. 'It's your own inheritance you're throwing away.' He paused and then barked, 'Where's Francis? Francis will handle this properly.'

Again the two younger brothers exchanged a glance and Robert said quietly, 'Try Aggie Turnbull's, Father.'

For a moment he thought he had gone too far, for Samuel's face grew bright purple and the veins on his forehead stood out.

'Damn you, boy,' he muttered, 'damn you to hell and back.' Then he strode to the door, wrenched it open, was through it and slamming it behind him so that the frame rattled leaving the two brothers staring at each other.

'Actually, he is right, you know,' Edwin said, leaning back in his chair. 'I don't agree with his attitude, mind you, but he is right when he says we might be short of crews tomorrow night.'

'Well, I don't go along with that. I'll grant you some of the young lads may use it as an excuse to stay ashore and miss a trip, but the older fishermen – well, sadly they're all too used to it.'

Edwin stood up. 'You're right, of course, but I'll have a quiet word with our ship's runner.' He tapped the side of his nose and winked at his brother. 'Jackson's just the man to round up the youngsters.'

'You see,' Samuel thumped his fist on the desk. 'I told you to keep your blasted mouth shut. We're short of crews. One ship can't sail.'

'It's affected our crews too.' Hathersage stood with his back to the coal fire burning brightly in Samuel Hayes-Gorton's office. 'What have you to say to that, young feller-me-lad?'

Robert glanced at Edwin and raised his eyebrows. The

other smiled and gave a slight nod and held out a hand-written list to his brother. They had both known that this confrontation would occur and were well prepared. Now Robert was able to face the two older men with equanimity.

He glanced down at the piece of paper between his fingers and began to reel of the list. 'There are precisely seven men whom our ship's runner has not been able to sign on. One has been ashore for three weeks with a broken arm, sustained, incidentally whilst at sea on a Hathersage boat. One is in hospital with pneumonia, another with a suspected appendicitis. That's three. Tom Lawrence will, of course, miss this trip—'

'Why "of course"? There's no "of course" about it.'

Robert glanced at his father-in-law and asked quietly, 'You really expect the man to put to sea for a three-week trip, leaving his mother and his sister . . .' to say nothing of Jeannie Buchanan, he added silently to himself, 'to cope alone?'

Mr Hathersage gave a grunt and twisted the tips of his moustache. But he made no answer.

Robert continued with the list of absentees and their reasons. 'That leaves three more. Abel Johnson, a cook, is retiring. It was his last trip anyway and we knew that. And lastly there are two brothers, aged fifteen and sixteen and, yes, it is their mother who is adamant that they shall not go to sea again.'

'Ah, there!' Samuel boomed with triumph. 'I told you so. Well, she needn't come running to me begging for shore jobs for them.'

Calmly, Robert went on as if the interruption had not occurred. His tone was deceptively soft. 'I don't think anyone with any feeling could possibly blame her. She lost her husband and her eldest son three years ago on the

Hathersage Evening Star when it went down in Arctic waters.'

There was silence in the room now as the two older men glanced at each other a little uncomfortably.

'Of course,' Robert went on smoothly, 'what is missing is a Gorton ship with all hands. The *Sea Spray* will never set sail again, nor will any of her crew.'

With that parting shot, he turned on his heel and left the office.

At breakfast the following morning in the Hathersage household, Mr Hathersage spread his newspaper and disappeared behind it, not even wishing his son-in-law 'Good morning'.

Robert stared down at the kipper on his plate, quite unable to eat a mouthful when he thought of the appalling price that men had paid with their lives to bring such fish ashore. He was about to ask the maid to fetch him something else when the door opened and Louise, her face more animated than he had seen it since their marriage and holding a letter in her hand, burst into the room.

'Oh listen everyone ... Morning, Mummy ... Daddy ...' she added hastily but she was so excited and happy as she smiled at Robert and waved the letter towards him. 'You'll never guess. Madeleine has invited us to stay with her in London. I was so hoping she would. We can go the day after tomorrow. Oh Robert, isn't that wonderful?'

She was looking very pretty this morning, in the frilled morning dress and her hair neatly dressed. Her round cheeks were delicately pink with excitement and her blue eyes sparkled and, looking at her, Robert felt a wave of tenderness for her and hated to be the one to have to say that at present such a visit was out of the question.

'I'm sorry, my dear. I cannot possibly leave just now. The whole town will be in mourning for the loss of the *Sea Spray* and all its crew. And I must – I must see to the family . . .' Swiftly he added as a hurried afterthought, 'All the families.'

But in his mind was only one family: the Lawrence family and their visitor, Jeannie Buchanan.

Louise's pretty face crumpled and the ready tears spilled over. 'You don't love me,' she cried in a childish voice. 'Else you'd want to make me happy. What do I care about some silly boat?'

Appalled by her callousness, Robert rose from the table and went from the room, leaving his breakfast untouched.

'Have you heard any more news?' Grace came in at the back door, her hair awry, her clothes dishevelled.

'Where on earth have you been?' Jeannie flashed at once. 'And why didn't you come home last night? Where were you?'

Twenty-four hours had passed since Robert had brought the only news so far. Since then, they had heard no more. A steady stream of neighbours had knocked on the back-door, but when they saw Nell refusing to leave her net and Tom sitting gloomily by the fire, they patted Jeannie's hand and whispered, 'If there's owt we can do, lass, you just let us know.' But then they left, unsure how to deal with the strange reaction of each member of the Lawrence family.

Weeping, they could have handled, or even rage from the lost fisherman's son, but it was their silence they could not understand. A silence that seemed to rebuff their good intentions.

'Oh come on, Florrie,' Jeannie heard one woman mutter as she stepped out into the back-yard. Their voices drifted back to her as they waddled down the passageway between the neighbouring houses. 'Leave 'er be, if that's 'ow she wants it.'

'But I don't like to, Wyn,' her companion said, her voice high-pitched with distress. 'When my Charlie's ship were missing for a time, Nell were that good to me. I want to help her now, like.'

'Well, you can't,' Wyn said bluntly, 'if she dun't want your help.' She sniffed. 'Nor mine neither, it seems, and we've lived next door for years.'

'Seems she only wants that lass that's just come – the one that answered the door to us. What do they call 'er?'

'Jeannie summat.'

'She's a nice enough lass, but they hardly know her, do they?'

'She's a Scottie though, ain't she? Like Nell.'

'A relation, y'mean?'

'Don't think so.' The woman paused and then said, with an insight that was beyond Florrie's comprehension, 'Mebbe Nell finds it easier because the girl *is* a stranger.'

Jeannie sighed and closed the door as the voices faded and became indistinct. Returning to the kitchen, she said, 'Tom, I'll need to go to ma work to see the foreman. Will you take a walk?'

But Tom shook his head, not even looking up at her. He had sat before the fire during the whole of that time, moving only to answer the call of nature or to stoke up the fire and Nell had continued to work, non-stop, at her braiding.

So Jeannie had been the only one to leave the house.

'Take as long as you need, lass,' the foreman had said. 'We all know what's happened and we know Grace, and you too since you're staying with the family, will need a little time off. The other girls have said they'll cover for you.'

A lump came into Jeannie's throat. 'That's very kind of them. Please thank them for me, will you?'

'I will.' The man, usually so brusque, was showing a kindness Jeannie had not seen in him before. 'George Lawrence was a good skipper and a fine man. I feel for his family. Give Grace and her mam my best, will you?'

Jeannie looked at him, puzzled. 'You mean Grace isna here? At work?'

'No. She didn't come in this morning.'

'Oh.' Jeannie could not prevent the surprise from showing in her face. She had been worried enough when the girl had not come home the previous evening, but since neither Tom nor Nell had even mentioned it – in fact, they hardly seemed aware of it – Jeannie had waited until the morning to look for her. She had been so certain that Grace must have just stayed the night at a friend's but that she would be at work today. Now the young girl was missing from her workplace too.

Swiftly, Jeannie gave the foreman a weak smile. 'I expect she's gone down to the dockside. To – to watch . . .' Her voice faded away.

Poor Grace, she thought then. I must find her.

Excusing herself, Jeannie hurried away towards the docks. It was still early, yet the fish market was in full swing. Row upon row of kits of fish lined the pontoon and buyers, resplendent in black suits and bowler hats, moved amongst the freshly landed fish whilst the incessant drone of the auctioneers' voices could be heard above the general rabble. Men with barrows rushed backwards and forwards, carrying the sold fish ready to be transported to inland markets.

Jeannie pushed her way through the throng, past all the jetties where now the ships were making ready to set sail once more in a few hours' time. But there was no sign of Grace, no sign of a lonely figure far out at the end of one of the piers.

Jeannie searched everywhere she could think of, but she could not find the girl.

And now, standing facing Grace in the small back scullery, she felt both relief at seeing her safe but an overwhelming desire to shout at her for causing so much worry and at a time like this too.

The girl's face was suddenly mutinous. 'You sound like me dad.' The words were out before she thought and now Grace's eyes filled with tears as she stared at Jeannie. 'I – I'm sorry. I didn't mean to worry you, but – but I couldn't bear it here. I stayed the night with – with a friend . . .' She lifted her head again. 'Me mam didn't know, did she?'

'That you never came home at all? She must have done, but she's never said a word. Not all night.'

'What do you mean "all night"?'

'She never went to bed again. Grace,' Jeannie's tone softened, 'you should have been here to look after her. You're her daughter. It's you she needs. Not me. I'm a stranger.'

Grace shook her head. 'No, no, you can help her more than me. Really. Maybe it's because you're from her homeland and she still feels the pull. You know?'

Oh yes, Jeannie knew. She felt the pull of home even more strongly now, and yet something still held her here and even now she couldn't be sure that it was just because she wanted to stay and help these people who had befriended her.

'Where is she?' Grace whispered and Jeannie gestured with her head into the neighbouring room as she said grimly, 'Still braiding the net. She's been at it all night. Just standing facing the wall and braiding.'

Grace's mouth dropped open.

For the second time in two days, it was Jeannie who opened the door to Robert Hayes-Gorton.

'I presume you've heard the most recent news? That they've found some wreckage from the *Sea Spray*?' he asked gently.

Jeannie nodded and said shortly, 'One of the lumpers came to tell Tom.' She hesitated and then added, 'So it's definite then?'

'I'm so sorry, but yes.' He paused and then said, 'He – Tom – didn't go back to sea then?'

'No, but he's expecting to be ignored by the ship's runner for the Hathersage company because of it.'

Robert sighed, realizing that Henry Hathersage had more than likely already given instructions to his runner that 'that idle bugger, Tom Lawrence, is not to be given a berth on any of my ships again'. Aloud, Robert said, 'I'll make sure he doesn't suffer. That he finds a ship when he's ready to go back.'

Jeannie knew she ought to thank him, but the words stuck in her throat, so she merely gave a curt nod as if to say, 'That's no more than you owe this family.'

They stood there, an awkwardness between them for it was obvious that she had no intention of inviting him inside. His dark brown eyes troubled, Robert asked, 'How are things?'

Jeannie lifted her shoulders. 'How do you expect them to be?'

He sighed and said heavily, 'If you – they – need anything, please let me know?'

Again she nodded, then stepped back and closed the door.

Standing in the doorway leading into the kitchen, she watched Nell, still at her work on the net. Sadly, Jeannie shook her head. Just what were they to do with Nell? She clicked her tongue against her teeth in a noise of exasperation. Tom and Grace were little or no use.

After sitting by the fire for a full night and the following day, now Tom seemed to be out all the time, probably, she suspected, in the Fisherman's Rest. He'd no doubt be coming home the worse for the drink.

And Grace. Well, she was out again too and, at this moment, Jeannie did not like to begin to think where she might be.

Why am I bothering with them all? she asked herself. They're nothing to me. I should be on my way home, back to Scotland. But she knew exactly why she bothered. The Lawrence family reminded her of her own, the family she had lost.

No, she couldn't leave now. Not yet. Not till things were better.

She moved forward to say gently, 'Please, won't you rest?'

'I must finish this, hen. George will be home soon and wanting his tea.'

Jeannie's hand fluttered to her mouth to stifle a startled gasp. 'Oh no, Nell, no,' she breathed.

Fourteen

On the Sunday morning, Nell finally left her net and put on her black coat and hat. 'I'm away to the kirk.'

'I'll come with you,' Jeannie offered but Nell held up her hand.

'No, no, hen. I'll be fine. Sunday morning I always go to the kirk. George'll know where I am.'

Jeannie watched her go with a heavy heart. The little woman walked briskly along the street, nodding to her neighbours as she passed by. Jeannie bit her lip and hurried up the stairs.

'Grace, Grace . . .' She shook the sleeping girl by the shoulder. She had been very late home the previous evening, but at least she was now coming home each night and had not, since Jeannie had rebuked her, stayed away overnight again. Even so, Jeannie intended to question her about where she was going so often, but now she had a more urgent worry. 'Grace, wake up. You've got to get up. Your mother's gone out. To the kirk. You ought to go after her. See that she's all right. Grace, will you get up.'

But the girl shrugged her off, turned over and buried her head beneath the bedclothes. Exasperated, Jeannie dragged the covers off her. 'At least tell me where the kirk is and I'll go.'

Grace sat up and tugged at the blanket, but Jeannie held on and the two girls glared at each other. 'Just tell me where it is, then you can go back to sleep.'

'Two streets away, at the far end.' And Grace yanked the bedclothes from Jeannie's grasp and lay down again.

The church was almost full and when Jeannie arrived they were singing the first hymn but she slipped into a pew at the back, her glance darting around the congregation for sight of Nell Lawrence. Then her lips parted in a startled gasp for there, sitting in the third row from the front, his head bent solicitously towards Nell, was Robert Hayes-Gorton.

Jeannie could hardly believe what she was seeing, but there was no mistaking the slim build nor the dark brown hair that curled, just a little, over the edge of the stiff, white collar. Nor, as he turned and she saw his profile, the straight nose, the curve of his eyebrow just above those deep, dark brown eyes. His mouth was serious, yet when he bent towards the older woman, Jeannie could see the merest hint of a smile that uplifted the corner of his mouth and deepened the line running from nostril to chin.

Jeannie dragged her gaze away, picked up a hymn book from the ledge in front of her and rifled the pages to find the place. Glancing up towards the list of numbers on the hymn board, her glance again found the top of Robert's dark head and she allowed her gaze to rest upon it once more. Whatever was he doing here? Surely this was not the church where the Hayes-Gortons, nor the Hathersages, would normally worship? And he was alone too. She could see no other member of his family amongst the congregation.

She bent her head and tried to concentrate on the words, but the print danced before her eyes and her heart was still racing from having run all the way here.

The service continued, but Jeannie could not have told anyone what prayers were said, apart from the one that

122

mentioned the *Sea Spray* and prayed for all those aboard, nor what the vicar said in his sermon.

Just before the end of the final hymn, Jeannie slipped from the pew and out of the church door. She walked swiftly across the grass between the gravestones and away from the main pathway to the gate. In the shadow of the yew tree she stood to watch the worshippers leaving the church and when Robert appeared, leading Nell on his arm, Jeannie shrank back even further beneath the low branches.

She could see now that Nell had a handkerchief to her face, a large, white, man's handkerchief. She was dabbing at her eyes and Robert was still leaning towards her speaking quietly and patting her hand that lay on his arm. As they passed among the other worshippers, Jeannie could see that it was Robert who nodded to them, or acknowledged their greetings, protecting Nell from their intrusive sympathy.

It should be Tom with his mother, or even Grace. Not him. Not Robert Hayes-Gorton. But then, the truthful, honest side of Jeannie's nature answered her. Neither Tom nor Grace were being a comfort or support to their mother. That had been left to comparative strangers, herself and now Robert.

When they reached the gate, Jeannie saw them stop and Robert gesture with his arm towards his motor car standing by the kerb, but Nell shook her head firmly. Jeannie guessed that he was trying to offer to take her home and Nell was, understandably, refusing.

Yet his action was a kind one, Jeannie admitted grudgingly as she watched them move off down the road, walking past the car as if intending to leave it and walk the distance to Nell's home.

Jeannie moved forward to the path and through the gate. She had almost reached them when she saw Robert look up and catch sight of her.

To her surprise, her smile as she went towards him was quite genuine. She had witnessed for herself his gentleness towards Nell. Whilst the cynical side of her nature, still smarting with resentment against him, might have said that it had been his guilty conscience making him act so attentively towards Nell, the more generous part of her character was, for once, willing to give Robert Hayes-Gorton the benefit of the doubt.

'I came to meet you, Mrs Lawrence,' she said as she came up to them. 'Grace told me where the kirk was.'

'Oh Jeannie . . .' Nell began and as she turned to glance at her, Jeannie could see that her eyes were red and that she still dabbed at them with the handkerchief, pushing the cloth beneath her glasses and almost dislodging them. 'Mr Robert has been so kind.'

Jeannie nodded towards him and smiled again. 'Thank you,' she said briefly, but now it was Jeannie who linked her arm through Nell's and drew her gently away.

Over her shoulder Nell called, 'Goodbye, Mr Robert – and thank you.'

They walked for some time in silence and then Nell said suddenly, 'You must have thought me a bit daft, hen. Going on about George as if – as if he was – well – still here.'

Involuntarily, Jeannie stiffened and she found she was holding her breath.

Nell's voice was low and flat, but quite steady as she went on. 'I know he's gone, Jeannie. I know that now, but I didna want to believe it – wouldna believe it until today.'

Jeannie said nothing. There was nothing she could say. For she knew exactly how Nell Lawrence was feeling because it was how she had felt about her father. But Nell had accepted the truth more quickly than she had.

Jeannie took a deep breath. Well, it was time she did the same then. Angus Buchanan was never coming home from the sea again and neither was George Lawrence.

As they walked along, Jeannie hugged Nell's arm closer to her and feeling it, Nell tightened her hold on Jeannie in response. Together, they would come through this.

Watching them walk away from him, Robert was thinking, she smiled at me. And her eyes lit up until they sparkled. Jeannie Buchanan actually smiled at me. And, despite the sadness of the day, the thought made him smile too and for a brief moment he felt ridiculously light-hearted.

Fifteen

'Jeannie, I don't know what we would have done without you these past weeks. You – you've been marvellous.'

She was standing with Tom on the edge of the jetty, below the ladder leading up on to the boat on which he was about to sail. He had stayed at home for two weeks to be with his mother and sister, but now, he had to go to sea again. He had lost his place on the Hathersage boats, but Robert Hayes-Gorton had been as good as his word and had found him a berth on the *Gorton North Star*.

It had been a difficult time for all of them and Jeannie, keeping her own private battle just that – private – nevertheless found that helping the Lawrence family come to terms with their loss helped to ease her own heartache. It was strange, she reflected, standing once more on the quayside, the wind lifting her hair, how each of them dealt with their grief in a different way. After her visit to the kirk, Nell had at last accepted that her husband's ship had been lost at sea though she still turned to her work, standing before the wall in the kitchen, her fingers working automatically, her need to keep occupied an unconscious therapy.

Tom found his salvation in the Fisherman's amongst those who were, not hardened, but resilient to such tragedies. It had always been part of the fabric of their lives. As a miner lives with the knowledge that he may one day be entombed, as a steeplejack knows he may, sometime, fall, so a fisherman knows that one day the sea may take him. They live with the knowledge but rise above it, not allowing the might of the ocean to humble that inner core of courage that makes them men.

And Grace. Jeannie sighed whenever she thought of Grace, for the girl sought her comfort outside the family home with friends about whom Jeannie had serious misgivings. But when she tried, gently, to broach the subject with the girl's mother, Nell just lifted her shoulders in a shrug. 'Let her be, hen, for a while anyway. She'll come to no harm and if it helps her . . .'

She did not finish her sentence and Jeannie let the matter drop but it did not stop her worrying for now when Grace crept into their shared bed at night, Jeannie could smell the liquor on her breath. It seemed strange to her that Nell seemed unconcerned when, at their first meeting, she had been so strict with her daughter.

But since then, Jeannie reminded herself, the star by which Nell steered the course of her life had gone from her firmament.

So now Jeannie smiled up at him and said, 'Safe trip, Tom.'

His blue eyes were earnest as he looked down at her. 'Jeannie, you will stay? You will still be here when I get back?'

Jeannie sighed. Part of her longed to go home, back to Scotland and yet another part of her shrank from doing so. She nodded and said hoarsely, 'Yes, Tom. I'll be here. There's – there's nothing for me to go back home for. Not just now, anyway.'

Suddenly his huge hands reached for hers and he held them tightly. 'Jeannie, I want to know you're waiting for me to come back. I want to know you'll always be waiting for me. I need you. We all need you. Please, will you think about something while I'm away? Jeannie – will you marry me?'

'I hear your dear little wifey has gone to London to stay with her friend again.'

'How do you know so damned much about my life? You seem inordinately close to my father-in-law,' Robert growled.

Francis laughed aloud. 'Old man Hathersage and me . . .' he crossed two fingers and held them up to show his brother, 'we're like *that*.'

'Then maybe . . .' for once Robert resorted to the sarcasm that Francis so often employed with enjoyment, 'you should have married his daughter.'

Francis tweaked the sharp points of his fair moustache. 'My dear fellow,' he drawled, 'I am not the marrying kind. You know that. I prefer to love 'em and leave 'em.'

Robert stared at him. For many reasons he admired his elder brother. There was no denying his astute business acumen which, though perhaps a little too ruthless, far outstripped anything that Robert himself, or even Edwin, would ever attain. Francis always dressed elegantly; his suits were made of the finest materials and tailored expertly. He was a handsome devil. The trouble was, Robert thought, he knew it. He knew how attractive he was to women, yet he treated them with a callous disdain that seemed to have them hanging on his every word even more. Even amongst their parents' small circle of friends, Robert was certain there were one or two unmarried girls who had 'hopes' of winning Francis Hayes-Gorton.

'Even so,' Robert replied smoothly, 'I'd have thought

that it would have been much safer for the business if *you* had married her. I mean, as the elder brother, you stand to become head of the Gorton company. Who's to say whether I will even stay.'

For a brief moment there was an unguarded look of incredulity in Francis's eyes. Then the gleam of certainty was back. 'Oh you'll stay, Robert, my boy.' Maliciously, he added, 'You're trapped. There's no way out now. Besides, you'd be cut off with the proverbial shilling.' As he passed close beside Robert, heading for the door, he paused briefly to pat his younger brother's cheek. 'So be a good boy and let's have no more of such talk.'

He opened the door to leave, but then paused and said briefly, 'Oh, I'll be away for a few days. I've business in London. I'm sure you and Edwin can cope between you.'

When the door closed behind Francis, Robert stared at it for a moment and then moved towards the window of the office to look out across the docks that lay below. He could see the *Gorton North Star* nosing her way out of the harbour. Tom Lawrence would be on that ship – three weeks of backbreaking labour with little rest and icy, bone-freezing conditions. Three weeks of living every minute knowing that one freak wave, a storm or even an accident with the machinery could end a life in a second. Living with the knowledge that out there somewhere in the depths of the icy seas Tom's own father, George Lawrence, had lost his life.

Yet, despite all this, Robert Hayes-Gorton envied Tom his life. It seemed, to Robert, one of glorious freedom. And that was not the only reason he envied Tom. For as his gaze dropped and he watched the figures on the quayside, he saw her. Striding along, her hair blowing in the wind, her face lifted to the breeze, was Jeannie.

Robert leant against the window and watched her weaving her way amongst those thronging the quay, saw her turn and wave once more to the ship leaving the dock. Then she turned and hurried around a corner and was gone from his sight.

Even so, Robert stood staring at the place where she had disappeared for a full minute.

Jeannie Buchanan. The name seared itself into his heart and her image was indelibly imprinted upon his mind.

When she entered the house that evening, Jeannie was surprised to see the net hanging limply against the wall. She knew a moment's fear until she saw Nell sitting in the rocking chair at the side of the range, her head resting against the wooden back of the chair, her eyes closed, her hands idle in her lap.

Jeannie made to turn and tiptoe away, back into the scullery, but Nell opened her eyes. 'It's all right, hen. I'm no' asleep. But I just felt – all of a sudden, you know – so very weary.'

Jeannie came and sat down opposite her. 'It's time you had a good rest. Time – time you let go, Mrs Lawrence.'

'Aye.' Nell nodded slowly and her voice was heavy. 'Aye, you're right, hen. But I never thought the sea would take him, y'ken? Not after casting him back on board those times. I really though the sea didna want him. Ah well . . .' She paused and then asked softly, 'And have you "let go" too, Jeannie?'

The girl pressed her lips together tightly but nodded.

They sat in silence for a while, each with their own thoughts, but it was a companionable silence born out of a shared grief.

It was Nell who broke it at last. 'Has he asked you, then?'

Jeannie's eyes widened as she stared at her. 'You knew?' She felt suddenly cheated that Tom had discussed his proposal with his mother before even telling her of his feelings.

'I suppose,' Nell was saying slowly, her gaze on the flickering embers in the grate, 'a young man usually talks over such things with – with his father. But now . . .' She did not finish her sentence and Jeannie was a little ashamed of her spurt of anger against Tom and was thankful she had not voiced her feelings.

In answer to Nell's question, Jeannie now said slowly, 'Aye, he has.'

'And?' Nell prompted.

Jeannie sighed. 'I like Tom. Of course I do. He's a fine man and he's so like his own father but – but I've known him such a short time and in rather . . .' she allowed herself a small, rueful smile, 'strange circumstances.'

'I know, hen. But it's the same for all fishermen's sweethearts. And wives, if it comes to that. They're away so much that each time they come home, it can be like another honeymoon.' Nell's eyes misted over at her own memories and Jeannie was silent. 'And that's what makes it so difficult to accept what's happened now. You get so used to waiting for them to come home that you can't believe that this time they're not going to. That – that they're never going to come home again.'

Wordlessly, Jeannie reached out to lay her hand on Nell's arm. The silence lengthened between them; the only sounds the ticking of the clock on the mantelpiece and the settling of a log in the grate. For a moment, flames shot upwards, illuminating in its flickering light the pensive faces of the two women sitting close beside it.

'Think about it, Jeannie,' Nell said softly at last. 'Tom loves you, I know. And he needs someone like you. Someone steadfast and loyal and strong. We all do, Jeannie.'

Jeannie did think about it, long and hard. Though she loved her homeland and always would, there was really no one left for her to go back to in Scotland. Kind friends and neighbours certainly, but no family. No kin of her own. No house, for that had been rented. Not even any furniture that was worth very much. There were a few bits and pieces of sentimental value only to Jeannie to be packed and sent to her by carrier or rail. Mrs McTavish, who lived next door, would do that, Jeannie knew.

No, she decided, she wouldn't even go back at all.

There was no one there now who wanted and needed her like the Lawrence family did.

Sixteen

'It's been hard not to have a proper funeral for him,' Nell said, 'but George wouldna have wanted us to spend our life greetin' for him. He'd have wanted us to enjoy Hogmanay the same as ever. What do you think we should do, Jeannie?'

More and more Nell was leaning on Jeannie, deferring to her for decisions, almost as if she were now the wife of the house and Nell herself already the dowager.

'Whatever you would normally do.'

'We used to have Christmas when they were both home. Even if it's the middle of January, but we always keep Hogmanay. After all, you canna move that so easily, can you now?' She thought for a moment. 'We should get a dark man to first-foot for us. Do you know any dark-haired men, hen?'

Unbidden, the image of Robert Hayes-Gorton was in Jeannie's mind. Now why, she thought, angry with herself, should she think of him? And then jumped, almost guiltily, as Nell said, 'There's that nice young man, Mr Robert. He's got lovely dark wavy hair, hasn't he?'

Jeannie glanced at her sharply. Was Nell Lawrence a mind-reader? Deliberately casual Jeannie said, 'I can't say I'd noticed, but I doubt the likes of him would first-foot for us, do you?'

'No,' Nell said. 'But he's been very kind, coming to see us two or three times a week ever since George . . .' Her voice trailed away but Jeannie was thinking, aye, he has, but it's more likely a guilty conscience. Then inwardly, she castigated herself. A young man of his position had no need to bother with a fisherman's family, even if that fisherman had been one of their company's skippers. He had been good, but no doubt that would soon end. To her surprise and chagrin, the thought that she would not see Robert Hayes-Gorton so often saddened her.

'There must be a dark-haired neighbour, surely?' she suggested, deliberately trying to steer the conversation, and her own unruly thoughts, away from Robert.

'Aye well,' Nell sighed, seeming to lose interest. 'We'll find someone.'

Christmas was quiet. With Tom away at sea and the very recent loss of the man of the house, the three women found the festive days very difficult. Once more, Grace disappeared on Christmas Eve.

'Let her go, Jeannie,' Nell said tiredly. 'There's no merry-making in this house this year, now is there?'

'She shouldna be merry-making so soon after . . .' Jeannie began to say, but stopped when she saw the tears in Nell's eyes.

'She's only young,' Nell murmured.

'But where's she going? Do you know?'

'She said she away to Jane's. An old school friend who lives three streets away. She'll be fine. And she's asked if she can stay the night.'

'And you've agreed?' Jeannie was startled. 'You mean, she'll no' be here in the morning? Christmas morning?'

Nell shrugged. 'She'll be home for Christmas dinner.'

Jeannie felt her mouth tighten. She could not help wondering if young Grace was being entirely truthful. It isna my business, she tried to tell herself. But it was. As long as she stayed here, she was, like it or not, involved.

During the week between Christmas and New Year, Nell seemed more like her old self. She bustled about baking, cleaning and dusting the tiny house, neglecting even the ever-present net on the wall. Every night when the two girls came home from work there was a tasty hot meal awaiting them. Although the outward signs were good, Jeannie began to be a little fearful that Nell had perhaps slipped back into thinking that George was coming home for Hogmanay.

But when Tom's ship docked on the morning tide on New Year's Eve, Nell said, 'Tom's the man of the house now.'

'Will he go first-footing to the neighbours?' Jeannie laughed. 'We'll have to black his hair with boot polish.'

Nell's sad expression lightened a little as she smiled and said, 'Like they black the bridegroom's feet at a Scottish wedding?' Then she actually gave a little chuckle as she said, 'Well, if I'm not mistaken, we might be blacking his feet soon anyway. Oh Jeannie, hen . . .' She reached out impulsively and caught hold of both Jeannie's hands. 'He'll be wanting his answer this time. Please, Jeannie, do say yes.'

'Oh Mrs Lawrence . . .' Jeannie began, but at that moment the back door flew open and Tom was home.

On the morning of New Year's Day 1925, Robert stood at the bedroom window and looked out across the smooth lawn. It was trying to snow; the sky, pearl grey, was laden with it. Behind him, Louise still slept on in their bed. Their virgin bed, he thought bitterly. He turned his head and watched her for a few moments. She was even pretty when she was asleep. Her lips curved in a gentle smile, her smooth blonde hair unruffled. Her skin, smooth and still shiny with cream, was flawless. How sad, he thought objectively, that such a lovely creature was so spoiled, so selfish, so – he searched for the word and found it – so unloving. He turned back to look out of the window, watching the birds pecking at the lawn, digging with their beaks to find a morsel, a worm, anything in this bleak, winter weather.

Dare he go? he asked himself for the hundredth time. Dare he take a bottle of whisky to the little terraced house in Baldock Street and ask them to 'tak a wee dram' with him? He didn't want to risk Jeannie's wrath again. He had deliberately not gone at Christmas for several reasons. One being that he felt it would be an intrusion on their grief at such a time and for another, he knew Tom to be at sea. He felt Hogmanay was different. All Scots celebrated the New Year with a fervour that the English sometimes found incomprehensible. But Robert thought he understood it. It was a new beginning; a time to look forward and hope for better things. And the Lawrence family, if anyone did, deserved better things in the coming year.

And now, too, Tom was home. It would look better if he visited when Tom Lawrence was there.

He washed and dressed quietly in his dressing room and slipped away without waking Louise. She would no doubt sleep until lunch time. She had not arrived home until almost three o'clock. He had feigned sleep and did not want a confrontation this morning.

He too planned a new beginning for a New Year.

The front door was opened to him by a surprised Nell. 'Why, Mr Robert. How did you know?'

Robert frowned for a moment, puzzled. Was there something he should have heard? Had something else happened to this benighted family that he should know about? Oh no, it wasn't Jeannie, was it? Oh pray God nothing had happened to her.

'Och no, I'm being silly,' Nell went on. 'How could you? Come away in.'

He stepped over the threshold straight into the best parlour, removing his hat and setting the unopened bottle on the table. Tom, Jeannie and Grace all rose from seats beside the fireplace and looked at him in surprise. Under their scrutiny, he felt a blush creeping up his neck and deliberately he kept his glance away from Jeannie.

'I just wanted to wish you – well – to hope that the New Year is better for you.' He touched the bottle. 'For you all, but . . .' His gaze rested upon Nell. 'Has something happened, I mean, what you said just now?'

Nell smiled. 'Och no, sir. It was just that I'd said to Jeannie that we should ask you to first-foot for us. You being so dark.' She gestured towards his brown hair. 'And then, when I opened the door and saw you standing there, well, I didna think what I was saying. But of course you couldn't have known about my wee joke.'

Robert too smiled. 'Oh I see.' He glanced at the others, his gaze coming to rest – as he had known it would eventually from the moment he had stepped into the house – upon Jeannie. 'Well, I would have come,' he said quietly, as if he were speaking to her alone, 'if you had asked me.'

She was returning his gaze steadily and for a moment there was no one else in the room, no one else in the world for him except her.

Tom's voice broke in harshly, breaking the spell. 'We first-foot for each other around here. My mother had no right to even think of asking anyone else. What would folks think? And besides, I'm sure,' he added and there was a hint of sarcasm in his voice now, 'that you had your own family celebrations . . .' There was a calculated pause before Tom added, '. . . sir.'

Robert looked at the young man, at the glowering face, the spots of angry colour against the tan of his skin and the blue eyes, icily polite yet unable to conceal resentment.

'Of course. I wouldn't dream of intruding,' Robert said tightly. 'I'll bid you "good day".' He gave a little bow to them all and turned towards the door. He replaced his hat carefully on his head and reached for the door knob. Then he hesitated and glanced back over his shoulder and looked now directly at Tom and only at Tom. 'I shall not be calling again, but if you need anything, just let me know.'

He raised an eyebrow and was rewarded by a quick, reluctant nod. He was gratified to see too that the young man's colour had deepened.

Robert stepped out into the street and as he pulled the door to close it behind him, he heard Nell say, 'There was no call to be so abrupt with him, Tom. He's been good to this family.'

'Well, there's no need,' Tom fired back, his voice raised so that Robert could hear him plainly. 'I'm the man in this family now. And I'll work to keep it. We're not a charity case.'

'Tom . . .' Robert heard Jeannie begin, but at that he had to pull the door shut and walk away up the street.

'Tom.' Jeannie laid her hand on his arm and said quietly, 'He was only trying to be kind.'

'I thought you didn't like him? Not after what he did.'

'I don't. But he has tried to be good to your mother. I watched him in the church that first Sunday after we heard about – about your father.'

Nell was shaking her head over the bottle of whisky.

'How kind of him. How very thoughtful . . .' But Tom's frown deepened.

Jeannie put her hand through his arm. 'Come, let's go for a walk. I could do with some fresh air.' She could feel the tension in the room rising and wanted to get him out for a while. Nell wanted to cook the dinner today, had insisted on doing it all. 'Just like I've always done.' So Jeannie was not needed. Misreading her words, Tom's face brightened. 'So could I, after that visit.' He sniffed the air. 'Phaw! What on earth had he got on? Perfume? Give me the stink of fish any day.'

'You coming with us, Grace?' Jeannie asked. 'The fresh air will do you good.'

Grace was looking peaky, Jeannie thought, but the girl merely huddled closer to the fire. 'No thanks. It looks like snow. I'll give me mam a hand.' She glanced at her brother and Jeannie intercepted a wink.

'Come on then, Jeannie,' Tom said. 'Get yar best bonnet on and let's be off.'

They walked a long way, skirting the docks and taking the coast road towards Farleston, a seaside town that was spreading so rapidly, its borders now adjoined Havelock. Here the sandy shore was a favourite place for holiday-makers and bathers.

Jeannie lifted her face to the breeze. Despite the cold and the threat of snow, she felt happier than she had done for many months. It was the start of another year and she was striding along in her smart new coat that would for ever remind her of George Lawrence. She was wearing, for the first time, the close-fitting matching cloche hat that Nell, Tom and Grace had joined together to give her as a Christmas gift.

Tom took her hand and pulled her arm through his as they walked. They didn't speak much, for the wind whipped their breath away and smarted their cheeks. But reaching the seafront at Farleston, Tom drew her into a sheltered spot and turned to face her.

'Well, Jeannie Buchanan. I'm waiting for my answer.'

Feigning ignorance, Jeannie teased him. Widening her eyes, she said, 'Answer, sir? And what answer might that be?'

'D'ya want me to go down on one knee in the snow, woman?'

Jeannie threw back her head and laughed. 'There's no snow yet.' But as if the heavens intended to defy her words, a delicate white snowflake drifted down and settled on her nose. Gently, Tom flicked it away with his fingertip. 'If you keep me waiting much longer,' he said softly, 'we'll be buried in a snowdrift. So, please, Jeannie Buchanan, will you marry me?'

She had thought about it constantly ever since he had first asked her and until this moment, she had still been unsure. Now, as she looked up into Tom's eyes that were suddenly serious, he said, 'I love you, Jeannie. It would be so wonderful knowing that you were here to come home to. I'll make you happy, I promise. Maybe one day, I could get a job ashore and then – and then you wouldn't have to spend your life watching and waiting.' He paused and then added, 'I'll look after you, Jeannie. We'll look after each other.'

She felt part of this family now, even whilst it was still coming to terms with a loss of its own. Perhaps that was the reason she felt such a kinship with the Lawrences.

She had a future to plan alongside this good man. He was offering her everything he had to give. What more could she ask?

Smiling, Jeannie said softly, 'Aye, Tom, I will marry you.'

Seventeen

'I hear that Scottish lass who's been staying with the Lawrences is to marry the son. Tom, is it?' Edwin said, not realizing what an effect the piece of news would have on his brother.

'What?' Robert stared at him and before he had thought to stop the words, he said, 'Jeannie is to marry Tom Lawrence?'

'Well, yes, if that's her name.' Edwin paused and then added, 'You seem to know her well?'

'Er – oh – I – er . . .' Robert stumbled and avoided his brother's shrewd glance. 'I got to know her – and the family – after George Lawrence's ship went down.'

Edwin nodded. 'I know. Tom explained how you'd found him a berth aboard one of our ships since he lost his place with the Hathersage boat. I presume you spoke to Jackson?'

John Jackson was the ship's runner employed by the Gorton Company. He was responsible for signing on the crews for each trip on every one of the fleet of fifteen vessels which the company now owned.

Robert nodded. 'He was amenable enough. He liked and respected George, but he did say . . .' He paused briefly, but then continued, 'He did say that the son was not the born fisherman his father was. He reckoned young Lawrence would jump at the chance to have an excuse to miss a trip.' He was thoughtful for a moment. 'Personally,

I thought Jackson was being a bit harsh. I mean it was natural, wasn't it, that Tom wanted to wait for news of his father?' Slowly Robert shook his head. 'I sometimes wonder where our humanity is, Edwin? I don't think our grandfather would have treated men like we sometimes treat them now? Do you?'

'No, Rob. And *we* won't, either.'

Robert smiled thinly, but without humour. 'Maybe. Maybe not. We're not going to be head of the company, are we?'

There was a happy, confident grin on Edwin's face. 'No, but there's two of us to keep Francis in line. We'll have a say. Don't you worry.'

'Mm.' Robert was only half listening.

'In fact,' Edwin was saying, 'I've already taken a managerial decision without asking either our dear brother, or father, if it comes to that. Tom Lawrence asked if he could miss the next trip to get married and have a bit of a honeymoon, so I said he could.'

Now Robert was all attention as he frowned at his brother. 'You did what?'

'I said he could have time off,' Edwin repeated patiently. 'To get married. It seemed only fair.'

'Well, you shouldn't have given him any more time off, whatever the reason,' Robert snapped, but even as he spoke he knew he was now guilty of being unreasonable. 'Not when we're short of crews as it is.'

'Hey, wait a minute. A moment ago you were saying you could understand him missing a trip when his father was feared lost and yet now—'

Robert interrupted harshly. 'Maybe Jackson was right after all. Maybe Tom Lawrence will jump at every opportunity to stay warm and cosy at home. No doubt he thinks that I'll intercede for him every time he condescends to go to sea again. Well, I won't.' He jabbed his forefinger in the air towards his brother. 'So just tell Jackson to watch him in future. He's to have no more time off. No more missed trips, else he'll find he hasn't a berth on a Gorton boat either.' With that, Robert turned on his heel and left the office slamming the door behind him.

The thought filled his mind and clouded his reason. Jeannie Buchanan – that lovely, red-haired, feisty girl, with green eyes and a wide, smiling mouth – was to marry Tom Lawrence.

He must talk to her. She couldn't marry Tom. She couldn't marry anyone. He must stop her.

'Can I be your bridesmaid then?'

Jeannie smiled at the excited young girl, pleased for once to see that Grace had something to interest her other than disappearing every night to be with her friends. Remembering an earlier conversation, she was now beginning to worry that Grace was meeting some boy. Someone of whom her mother would disapprove.

'Of course you can,' she said aloud, 'but we're not having a fancy white wedding. I thought you knew that. We've planned a very quiet affair. Just – just family. I mean, just you and your mother. It wouldn't be right, in the circumstances,' she said, referring to the fact that the Lawrence family were still within the expected period of mourning. Flatly she added, 'And there'll be no one from my side, anyway.'

'Yes, yes, but you'll have a pretty new dress surely and carry flowers? So, couldn't I too?'

'We'll see. We'll see what your mother thinks.'

But Nell agreed with her daughter. 'George wouldna have wanted us to spoil your day, hen,' she said and added wistfully, 'and he'd have been so pleased to see his son wedding a Scottish lassie.'

'Are you really sure, Jeannie? I mean, you haven't known him very long, have you?'

Jeannie stared up into the face of Robert Hayes-Gorton and her lips parted, the angry retort ready to spurt out. But she bit back the words, quite literally for she felt the sharpness of her teeth on the tip of her tongue. His dark brown eyes were looking into hers with such impassioned intensity that it was impossible for her to doubt that his concern was genuine.

Had she really misjudged this young man? Already, before today, she had seen his little acts of kindness but she had closed her mind and hardened her heart against him. Now, close to him, looking up into his face, she felt her resolve to hate him begin to crumble.

Before she had time to form a reply he was speaking again. The words came haltingly, as if he were voicing aloud, perhaps for the first time, his innermost feelings. And that he found it difficult and painful was obvious. 'Jeannie. I couldn't bear to see you make a terrible mistake. If – if I tell you something, it's just between the two of us?' He waited until she gave a slight nod in assent. Then she heard him let out a long deep sigh.

'I've made the most dreadful mistake in marrying Louise. It's not her fault,' he added hastily, 'or mine. But we've both allowed ourselves to be pushed into a marriage of – of convenience. A marriage our families wanted. I thought I did too. At least – what I mean is – oh this is dreadfully difficult . . .' He ran his hand distractedly through his hair. 'I don't even know if I should be saying this to you, but you see, from the moment I saw you . . . What I mean is, if I were still free, then – then I could speak, say all the things that are in my heart. But I'm not, and I – I can't. And now you're going to be married too.' Now his voice faded away and he just stood gazing at her helplessly.

And Jeannie just stood there too, looking back at him, for she could not think of a word to say.

Now, his voice hoarse with emotion, Robert just said, 'Please, Jeannie, just be sure. Very sure.'

And then he was gone, leaving her just staring after him.

Jeannie told no one of the incident. There was no one in whom she could confide such a thing. Maybe if Flora or Mary had still been here in Havelock, but they were long gone. They'd likely be back home in Scotland now. Aye, back home. Jeannie sighed at the thought. Was she really doing the right thing in marrying Tom? Mr Robert's strange, almost impassioned plea, had at least made her stop and think. His words had forced her to take stock.

She was sure that Tom loved her in his own bluff way, but he was not a demonstrative man. She didn't expect him to be. To Jeannie, men were like her father; strong, courageous and hardworking and they showed their love for their families in their actions. In going to sea and doing a very dangerous job to earn a living.

Jeannie was not used to the manners of a gentleman who, in her opinion, did little or nothing to earn his own living, but prospered on the toil of others. She had never encountered a man who made flowery speeches or showered a woman with expensive gifts. To her mind, Robert had no right to speak to her as he had done, though she did acknowledge that his words were genuine.

The thought that he felt something for her shocked her.

Not so much from a moral standpoint as that she could not believe that a man in his position should even notice someone like her.

He's just feeling guilty still, she told herself and tried to put the incident from her mind. But for many nights leading up to her wedding, her dreams were troubled by Robert's face, his dark eyes and his voice saying 'Are you really sure, Jeannie?'

On the eve of their wedding day, Jeannie was mystified by Nell and Grace.

Nell spent the early part of the evening forever glancing at the kitchen clock and then, on the stroke of seven, she said suddenly, 'Awa' to the Fisherman's, son, and give us women a bit o' peace. We've things to do for the morrow that you shouldna be seeing.'

Tom grumbled, but he got up, put on his jacket and left the house.

Jeannie eyed the two women suspiciously. They seemed to be sharing a secret, whispering and giggling and trying, yet failing, to stifle their amusement

'What's going on?' she said at last. 'I hope you're no' planning tricks on me. Sewing ma nightdress up or something.'

Mother and daughter exchanged a glance and then burst into laughter. 'We hadn't thought of that, Mam,' Grace said.

'We should ha' done, hen.' Again, they smiled at each other. 'Shall we tell her now he's gone?'

Grace nodded.

'The lads at the pub are going to have a wee bit of fun with your bridegroom. He'll no' be coming home in the state he went out.'

Jeannie groaned. 'Och, you dinna mean he's going to get drunk?'

'Aye well, a little merry, maybe. But no, they're going to wash his feet . . .'

'But first,' Grace gasped between peals of laughter and holding her side as if she had a stitch, 'they're going to smear his feet with shoe blackening, just to make it worth the washing.'

Nell chuckled. 'And if I know the lads round here, it won't stop at just his feet.'

'Oh, oh, stop it, Mam. Me side's aching wi' laughing so much.'

Jeannie felt the corners of her own mouth begin to twitch. Their laughter was infectious.

'Wait a while, till they bring him home,' Nell said. 'There'll be plenty to laugh at then.'

At ten thirty, they heard the commotion out in the street and hurried to fling open the front door and stand watching the merriment. Jeannie glanced at Grace, wondering if she were remembering the last occasion when they had witnessed the antics of a stag night, but the girl was convulsed with laughter watching her brother being borne down the street, plastered with black polish and covered from head to toe in flour. His tormentors had been thoughtful enough to remove his jacket and trousers, so Tom was being carried, shoulder high and amid much shouting and laughing, along the street in his shirt and long-johns.

'There you are, Jeannie lass.' A burly fisherman, who Jeannie knew was the third-hand on the same ship as Tom, came to stand in front of her. 'Here's your handsome bridegroom.'

Entering into the fun, Jeannie said, 'Thanks, but I'll no' be wanting him now. You can keep him.' Mischievously, she linked her arm through the big man's and said, 'Are you doing anything in the morning, Jack Brightman?'

The man's eyes twinkled and he laughed loudly. 'Don't temp' me, lass. Don't temp' me.' He winked at her. 'Shame, like, but I reckon the wife'd have summat to say about that, don't you?'

'Bring him in,' Nell was saying. 'We'll strip him down and wash him properly, now.'

'Oh,' Jeannie shrieked and, feigning coyness, she put her hands to her cheeks. 'Oh pray, spare my blushes.' She turned and hurried away into the house, the sound of their laughter following her.

It was all good, if not quite 'clean' in the literal meaning of the word, fun, and Jeannie was grateful to Tom's pals for helping to lighten what was, in part, going to be a poignant occasion for the Lawrence family. And for her too, she thought soberly, for on her wedding day there would be no father to give her away.

But he'll be there in spirit, she comforted herself. I know he will.

At the window of his office, Robert stood staring down into the bustling docks below him. To the west he could see the spire of the church where he knew, at this very moment, Jeannie was making her vows to love and to cherish Tom Lawrence and to remain his wife until death do us part.

He had realized, when Edwin had told him of their marriage plans, that he had fallen in love with Jeannie Buchanan and he had not been able to stop himself going to see her. Remembering his halting, puerile babblings, he groaned with embarrassment. How foolish and weak she must think him. Though she had said very little, in fact now he thought about it, she had said nothing at all, but he had read in the depths of those beautiful green eyes, her puzzled expression.

Perhaps she had even believed him to be drunk again. Perhaps she had not even understood what he had been trying to say. No doubt she had just dismissed him from her mind and thought no more about his near declaration of love. In fact now, standing here looking across at the church, he could not really remember what he had said. All he could remember was that he had wanted her to be absolutely sure that she wanted to marry Tom.

Tom Lawrence. How Robert envied him at this moment.

He sighed and turned away from the window and picked up his hat and cane. He would walk to the church in time to see them come out. He patted the inside pocket of his jacket, feeling the rustle of the white envelope that contained a cheque. It was his wedding present to Jeannie. He could neither write nor say the words that were in his heart but with this gift would go all his loving wishes that at least she would be happy.

Sadly, he knew now that he would never find happiness in his own marriage.

As Tom and Jeannie emerged from the dim interior of the church, they both blinked in the brightness of the January sunlight.

Nell and Grace came to stand on either side. 'Ha' you some coppers in your pocket, Tom, ready for the bairns?' Jeannie heard Nell ask her son.

Tom looked about him. 'I don't see any . . .' he began and then stopped.

'Not here, maybe, but back at the house, the bairns in our street'll be waiting. You can be sure of that.'

149

But Tom was not listening to her now, 'Look,' he said quietly, 'there's Mr Robert standing at the gate.'

Jeannie's lips parted in a little gasp of surprise as she watched Robert walk up the path towards them. Stretching out his hand towards Tom, he shook it warmly.

'Congratulations, Tom. You're a very lucky man.' His voice was firm and he was smiling as he wished them both well. From his pocket he took out an envelope and pressed it into Tom's hands. 'Please – just a little personal gift. And I hope you have a lovely honeymoon. Where are you going?'

'Across the river, Mr Robert. On this afternoon's ferry and then on to Scarborough.'

Robert nodded and there was a moment's awkward pause before he said, 'Well, then. I'll – er – not keep you . . .' He nodded at Tom and then turning to look at Jeannie said, his voice deep and low, 'May I be the first to kiss the bride?'

'Of course, sir,' came Tom's dutiful, though reluctant, reply.

He was standing before her, looking down at her once more and now he leant forward and his lips touched her cheek in the most gentle, almost reverent kiss, that Jeannie could ever have imagined. Close to her ear, he whispered so softly that even she scarcely heard the words, 'Be happy, my dearest Jeannie.'

Then Robert straightened up and stepped back from her, smiling and raising his hat to them both. He turned and, with long strides, walked swiftly away from them.

Eighteen

They were walking along the seafront at Scarborough. Jeannie paused to watch the breakers far out to sea.

'Do you wish you were back at sea?' Jeannie asked him.

Tom laughed, the wind whipping away the sound. 'Fancy asking me that, Mrs Lawrence. On our honeymoon.'

He put his arm about her waist and they walked on in companionable silence, until at last Tom broke it by saying, 'Why did you ask me that question?'

'I remember ma father,' she said quietly. 'Whenever he was ashore you could see it in his eyes, a faraway look whenever he looked out to sea. He could hardly wait to get back aboard his ship.'

'Huh, more fool him, then.'

'Tom!'

'Oh, I'm sorry, Jeannie, but I've never been able to understand it. Me dad was just the same. Me . . .' he shrugged, 'I'd as leave be ashore.'

Jeannie was silent but she watched him now and saw that he hardly glanced out across the water, nor took any notice when the grey shape of a ship appeared on the distant horizon.

She thought back to the previous night, their first as man and wife. She had known what to expect. Her aunt, God rest her, Jeannie thought, had been a sensible, down-to-earth woman, who had, at what she considered an appropriate age, explained the facts of life to her niece. A no-nonsense, practical explanation of the workings of a woman's body, and of a man's, it might have been, but it had left Jeannie with a well-balanced view, with no fears born out of ignorance and certainly no romantic expectations that were unlikely to be fulfilled.

She had been surprised to find, however, that Tom was a gentle and considerate lover, and a practised one too. Tom Lawrence knew exactly what to do and how to do it, and even when he entered her for the first time and she felt the pain of the breaking of her maidenhead – as her doughty aunt had warned – he was thoughtful for her.

If she had expected the inexperienced fumbling of a boy, then Jeannie was either pleasantly surprised or acutely disappointed to think that for him, it was not his first time.

At this moment, she was not quite sure what she did feel. The matter, she decided rationally, was best left unspoken of, at least for the moment. Later in their marriage, perhaps.

What had surprised and definitely pleased her was that Tom had not – as her aunt had also led her to expect once the lovemaking was over – turned over and fallen sleep. He had held her gently in his arms and he had talked to her, telling her of his life at sea.

'I suppose there are some good things about it. The comradeship and the sight of a net coming up over the side, fair bursting with fish. And in the Icelandic waters, the views are magnificent. You feel as if everything's so clean and pure, the icebergs sparkling and the blue of the sea and the sky. It's as if no man has ever seen that part of the world before. As if you're the very first to ever see it. But that's about all that's good. For the rest, it's hard labour. Eighteen hours non-stop when we're fishing.

Longer, if the skipper's a greedy bastard and the hauls are good . . .'

She had nestled against him listening to his voice rumbling in his chest as he spoke. She was drowsy, scarcely taking in what he was actually saying. She drifted into semi-consciousness and imagined that it was her father once more telling her stories of his voyages. The same stories that George must have told his son, Tom. And now Tom was a fisherman too and experiencing all the wonderful sights for himself. Tom was like his father and her father. She believed that he, too, was a fisherman, born and bred.

So her question this morning had seemed quite a natural one to ask. 'Do you wish you were back at sea?'

But his answer had shocked her and left her with a disconcerting feeling of disappointment.

'Louise. My dear, I've booked a room for us at your favourite London hotel. I'm so sorry I couldn't go when you wanted me to, but there were problems at work. You know—'

'Oh, I don't want to go now, Robert.' Louise waved her slim hand, with its perfectly manicured nails and its soft skin that never saw a moment's drudgery. 'I've only just come back from Madeleine's. I don't want to go again.'

'I've booked theatre tickets and I thought you might like to go shopping for a new spring outfit.' He paused then added pointedly, 'But if you're too busy . . .'

He watched as the gleam came into her blue eyes.

'Well, I suppose,' she said slowly, but he could see that in her butterfly brain she was already in the Knightsbridge stores, 'I could re-arrange my plans, seeing as you've gone to so much trouble.'

What, Robert thought to himself, did his wife ever have in her life that would prevent her accepting the chance of shopping in the London stores and the round of social parties they would soon find themselves caught up in once they arrived there? He was quite prepared, before he had even made the suggestion, that their weekend would become a week-long holiday.

But Robert stretched a smile. It would be worth it if he could salvage their marriage. He was determined now to do everything he could to make it work. He was in it for better or worse. And it couldn't get much worse, he told himself wryly. So there was only the 'better' to hope for. And he really meant to try. He had resolved to put all thoughts of Jeannie out of his mind. He was married and, now, so was she. He almost wished that she had gone back to Scotland, that she could have become just a distant memory of a girl he had once seen.

Now, however, he was going to be faced with the prospect of seeing her, of knowing what went on in her life and her family. Yet part of him longed for that very thing; to know that he could see her, that he could, in a way, look after her from a distance – and without her knowing it.

Pushing thoughts of the beautiful firebrand to the back of his mind, he smiled at his wife and said, 'When shall we go then?'

To his surprise, Louise jumped up, threw her arms about his neck and kissed him on the cheek. 'Tomorrow. I can be ready tomorrow.'

*

Jeannie had never in her life known such idleness, at least not for so long a stretch at any one time. From quite an early age, she had to do household chores to help her invalid mother. After her mother's death Jeannie had, with the help of her aunt, kept the house always in readiness, waiting for her father coming home from the sea. The only holidays she could remember were the occasional trips with her father; each an idyllic time that she held in her memory amidst a lifetime of waiting.

And now she had let herself in for another life of waiting for her man to come home. But it was a life she was quite happy to accept. She would be proud of Tom, she knew, whatever he did. So she tucked her hand through his arm, and smiled, determined to store the memories of her honeymoon that she could live and relive in her mind. The beach in winter and, further up the coast, quaint villages and coves. Inland, the moors seeming to stretch for ever, broken by streams and vales with water-falls tumbling over craggy rock faces.

'It reminds me of home,' she murmured once, without thinking.

'Lincolnshire's your home now, Jeannie,' Tom reminded her and then laughed. 'All flat land and sea and sky. That's your home now.'

Maybe it was, Jeannie thought, for now. But one day I'll go back, she promised herself. One day I'll see my homeland again.

'Not more parcels, Louise.' Robert smiled as he teased his wife. Louise glanced at him and seeing that his expression belied the words, gave her tinkling, joyous laugh.

'Oh darling, I've bought the perfect dress for tonight's

155

party at Madeleine's. It's the very latest fashion. It's blue silk with a low waist and a tiered skirt. Just wait till you see it.'

'You're pretty to me whatever you wear,' he said and moved closer to her.

'Oh sweetie, you say the nicest things.' She patted his cheek and made a kiss in the air at the side of his face, but moved away before he could reach out for her and draw her to him. Stifling a sigh, he said, 'Shall we have a look round St Paul's or the Abbey after lunch?'

Louise made a little moue with her perfectly painted mouth. 'I want to rest this afternoon, Robert, if I'm to look my best. And then I want to have a long lovely bath in that gorgeous bathroom.' She waved her elegant hand towards the adjoining bathroom with its deep bath and gold taps in the shape of dolphins. 'But don't let me stop you, darling. You go, if you want to, but you will be back in time to be ready for eight o'clock, won't you?'

'Of course,' Robert said, hiding his disappointment. Dutifully, he held out his arm to her. 'Shall we go down for lunch.'

'In a minute, I must just renew my lipstick.'

'Jeannie, it's such a pretty hat. Let me buy it for you?'

'Oh no, Tom, it's far too expensive and frivolous. When would I wear a hat like that?'

The item under discussion was displayed in the centre of a shop window; a broad brimmed straw hat decorated with pink silk roses.

'Well, I don't know,' Tom said, wrinkling his forehead. 'Does it matter? Can't you wear a hat like that any time? On a Sunday?'

Jeannie laughed. 'To the kirk? Oh Tom, really. It's

more the sort of hat . . .' She bit back the words swiftly, for she had been about to say, it's the sort of hat that Aggie Turnbull would wear, but she turned the moment into a joke and hugged his arm to her side, and said, 'To wear at a wedding. Now, if you'd bought me it last week, then I could have worn it on my wedding day.'

'Well, I'm sorry I didn't see it in time. But won't you let me buy it for you now?'

'It's sweet of you, Tom, but really it isn't practical. It would be a waste of your hard-earned money.'

'You let me dad buy you that coat.'

'Yes, and the three of you bought me this hat for Christmas to go with it, didn't you?'

Tom's mouth turned down at the corners petulantly. 'I bet it's the sort that Mr Robert would buy *his* wife.'

Then his face brightened as he thrust his hand into the inside pocket of his jacket. 'Of course! I was forgetting. Mr Robert's cheque.'

He waved the envelope in the air. 'We'll need most of this to pay the guest house at the end of the week, but there should be enough left over. I'll get it cashed and then we'll buy that hat. You'll look a treat in it, Jeannie.'

She sighed inwardly. She didn't want to upset him by throwing his generosity back in his face and this was, after all, their honeymoon. 'Well, if you're really sure you can afford it . . .' she began and before she had finished speaking, she saw that his face had brightened and all sign of little-boy surliness had gone.

Tom grasped her hand and pulled her towards the shop. 'Come on, Jeannie. By, you'll be grand in it.'

Alone in the echoing vastness of a city church, Robert stood looking at the sweet face of the Madonna. In his imagination, the carved figure became not his own wife, but Jeannie.

The trip to London had not been entirely unsuccessful, he told himself. At least he and Louise were now friendly and she did not entirely rebuff his gentle advances in their bed at night. But she would only allow him to hold her in his arms and cuddle her and talk about the theatre play they had just seen or the party they'd just been to and what everyone had been wearing. If he tried a bolder move, she would move away, out of his arms and say, 'I'm tired now. Good night, darling.'

As he looked now at the mother figure, saw the love and devotion etched even into those carved features, he knew that it was very unlikely he and Louise would ever have children. But now, Jeannie, he could see her as a mother, an earth mother devoted to her husband and his children.

Swiftly, Robert turned on his heel and walked the length of the aisle, his footsteps echoing eerily in the silence. He hurried from the holy place, feeling guilty that he could have had such irreverent thoughts in this place. That he had dared, in the Lord's House, to covet another man's wife.

Nineteen

'Just where is it you're going, Grace, nearly every night?'

They had been married a month and Tom was away at sea on his first trip since their honeymoon. He'd had to go. There had no longer been any choice. He had no money left to give Jeannie during her first weeks as a housewife.

With her mouth set in a grim line, Jeannie had wrapped the pretty straw hat in tissue paper and placed it in a box on top of the wardrobe. She no longer wanted to set eyes on it, for it was a reminder that, until Tom came home from the sea again, the only money coming into the household would be earned by the three women in it.

With Tom away and Nell still mourning, Jeannie felt she should find out just where it was that Grace was going night after night. Besides, it was what Tom wanted of her.

She had been a little hurt by his parting words. She had gone to the dockside to see him off. 'You will take care of yourself, Tom, won't you?' she had said, sudden fear gripping her.

'Don't you worry about me, Jeannie. I'll be fine. Now I've got something – or rather someone – to come home to.' The smile had begun on Jeannie's mouth but it froze as Tom spoilt the loving words by adding, 'And knowing you're there to take care of Mam and Grace, well, I shan't worry so much when I'm at sea.'

So now, Jeannie told herself, she had every right to question Grace.

'It's none of your business,' the girl snapped back.

'Well, I'm making it my business. You're not being fair to your poor mother. Nor Tom either, now he's head of the family.' She knew it was cruel to make a reference, even a veiled one, to George Lawrence's death, but desperate situations required desperate measures. 'He feels responsible for you. You're still only sixteen.'

'I'm not doing anything wrong. I'm just going to a friend's, that's all.'

'Who? Who is this friend?'

'It's none of your business,' Grace said again.

'Is it Jane?'

There was a guarded look in the girl's eyes and she avoided meeting Jeannie's gaze. 'It might be.'

'Oh well, if that's how you feel, you'd better get on with it.' Exasperated, Jeannie turned away. Deliberately, feigning disinterest now, she made up her mind to follow the girl the very next time she left the house. She was worried about Grace and now it was more than just Tom's request that she should look after his sister. Just lately the girl had seemed thin and pale.

'Are you sure you're not sickening for something?' she'd asked her countless times, but each time Grace shrugged off her concern.

'I'm just tired, Jeannie. I feel the cold so at work, you know.'

Jeannie did know. For anyone not as healthy as herself, she could well understand how the cold seeped through the fingers until there was no feeling left and the slicing and filleting became merely a series of repetitive movements that they could do in their sleep.

That evening when Grace went out, Jeannie waited a few moments and then followed her. Pulling her shawl around her head and shoulders, Jeannie bent her head against the wind whipping down the wet street and hurried after the figure ahead of her, yet minding to keep her distance.

At the end of their street, Grace turned to the right and then, passing by the next turning, turned right again. Jeannie hovered on the corner. This was the street where she had first encountered Grace, where the attack had taken place.

This was Harbour Road where Aggie Turnbull lived. Surely . . .? In the darkness, Jeannie squinted to see where Grace went. She saw the girl hesitate about half-way down and glance around her as if to make sure no one was watching. Jeannie drew further back into the shadows of the house on the corner. Then, as she watched, she saw Grace bend her head and scuttle into a passageway between two houses. Leaving her hiding place, Jeannie walked swiftly down the street in time to hear, in the stillness of the damp night, voices and laughter coming from the back-yard of the house as the door was opened to let Grace in.

Jeannie stood in the darkness, biting her lower lip, uncertain, now, as to what to do next. She was sure that this was Aggie Turnbull's house. What could she do? What ought she to do? Should she knock on the door right now and demand Grace to come home? Should she go back and tell Nell just where her foolish, wayward daughter was? But her mind shied away from that. Nell was still mourning the loss of her beloved husband. Jeannie could not bear to bring further trouble to her unless it became absolutely necessary. And with Tom now away at sea again, the burden of responsibility fell upon her.

As she stood debating, Jeannie heard the sounds of a motor car in the distance, but for a moment she took little notice. Then she realized that the sound was coming closer, that the vehicle was turning into this street. Anxious not to be thought loitering, especially outside the house of Aggie Turnbull, Jeannie bent her head and hurried back to the corner where once again she paused in the shadows and peered round the end house to watch.

The motor drew to a halt outside Aggie's house and the noise died away. As the man stepped from it, Jeannie inched forward, but she could not see him clearly, only his shape. Tall, with a slim build, the man was dressed in an evening cape and top hat. He went towards the front door of the house and rapped smartly on it with his cane, the sound echoing along the street.

Has he no shame, she thought, to be seen knocking at the door of that house? Obviously not, she answered herself, as she crept closer. The door opened and light and laughter from the house flooded into the street. Nearer now, and with his features illuminated in the seconds before he stepped into the house and the door closed behind him, Jeannie recognized him.

Francis Hayes-Gorton.

That did it! Now, without a moment's hesitation, Jeannie marched up to the front door and banged on it with her fist. 'Open this door. Open this door at once, d'you hear me.'

The door was flung back and Jeannie, her arm raised to knock upon it again, almost fell forward. She clutched at the door frame to steady herself and blinked in the sudden light. Before her stood Francis in the action of taking off his cloak and hat. He turned and a smile twisted his mouth. 'Oho, Mrs Jeannie Lawrence, if I'm not mistaken. Come to join the fun whilst your man is away at sea. Come in, my dear, come in . . .' He made a motion towards her with his hand inviting her to step inside but Jeannie stood resolutely on the doorstep. Then her glance went beyond him to where the staircase rose behind him. At the top, dressed in a shiny, red satin evening gown, with diamonds glittering at her throat, stood Grace. She was descending the stairs, her gaze upon Francis Hayes-Gorton and seeing the look on the girl's face, Jeannie gasped.

Grace had the rapturous look of a young girl hopelessly and helplessly besotted by the young man standing at the foot of the stairs.

Francis shrugged. 'Oh well, if you won't join in the fun, then . . .' He turned towards Grace and took her out-stretched hand in his. Raising her fingers to his lips, he kissed them and then glanced, with a sly, triumphant look, over his shoulder at Jeannie. 'See what you're missing.'

Then Jeannie lunged forward. 'I see what I'm missing, all right,' she muttered and grasped Grace's arm, dragging her away from Francis. Because her move had been so swift and unexpected, she managed to pull the girl towards the door and almost had her across the threshold and out into the night, before anyone realized what was happening. But then, Grace resisted, pulling against Jeannie's grasp and at the same moment Francis stepped forward and gripped Jeannie's wrist so fiercely that the feeling went from her hand and her hold on Grace slackened.

'Trying to play the avenging angel again, are we, Mrs Lawrence?' he said through thin, tight lips. 'I think you should let Grace decide whether she wants to go or stay, don't you?'

In the red heat of anger, Jeannie faced him boldly. 'No, I don't. She's only a girl. Scarcely more than a bairn.' She became aware that others had appeared at the top of the stairs, and behind them, emerging from the front room, was Aggie herself. Now, Jeannie turned on her. She opened her mouth to scream a tirade of abuse at the woman, but instead she found herself forestalled as Aggie smiled and, stepping forward, put her arm about Grace's shoulder. In a husky voice, she said, 'I think you should go home with your sister-in-law, my dear.'

But Grace interrupted. 'No,' she shouted, pulling herself free. She stepped close to Francis, putting her cheek against his chest and her arms about his waist. 'No, I want to stay here.' She stared boldly at Jeannie and added defiantly, 'All night.'

Jeannie knew her mouth dropped open. She was shocked and, suddenly, very afraid.

Now she tried the softer approach, making her tone a gentle appeal. 'Grace, please. Just come home. Your mother will be worried.'

For a moment there was a haunted look of doubt in the girl's eyes. And guilt. Yes, Jeannie could see it. Guilt. Suddenly, with a woman's intuition, Jeannie knew there was something very wrong. Her voice low, she held out her hand towards Grace and said, 'Grace, we'll help you. We'll stand by you.'

The girl's eyes widened and she whispered, 'How – how did you know?'

Jeannie's heart was heavy within her chest. She hadn't known, not really. But she had guessed and sadly, it seemed, she was right.

She saw Francis stiffen as he looked down at the girl snuggling so close to him. 'What? What do you mean?'

Grace looked up into his face and Jeannie saw again the look of adoration and she groaned inwardly. Grace idolized this man. Her face was shining with happiness now as she said, 'I'm to have your child, Francis. Isn't it wonderful?'

All around them there was a silence, as if everyone

listening were holding their breath. Although her gaze was upon Grace and Francis, Jeannie was aware that Aggie gave a little gasp and her hand fluttered to cover her mouth. She, too, was staring at the couple and Jeannie was sure she heard the woman breathe, 'No, oh no.'

Well, at least we're in agreement on that, Jeannie thought grimly.

Francis's eyes narrowed and his mouth was hard. Suddenly, his handsome face was ugly. He pushed Grace from him and then gripped her wrists savagely, shaking her and bending towards her, hissing in her face, 'Don't you try to pull that one with me, you little whore.'

Grace's eyes were wide, her mouth dropping open. 'But – but Francis . . .'

With a vicious movement, he flung her away from him so that she fell backwards, losing her balance, and before anyone could move to help her, she had fallen heavily against the wall, cracking her head. Slowly, she slithered down into an ungainly heap on the floor. Her head lolled forward and she tipped to one side.

At once, Jeannie and Aggie rushed forward and knelt either side of the girl. Aggie ran her fingers over the girl's scalp. 'There's no cut,' she said, 'but she'll have a nasty bruise.'

Grace moaned and her eyelids fluttered.

'Let me help you up—' Jeannie began, but Aggie said at once, 'No, don't move her for a moment.'

Suddenly, they felt a draught of cold air and heard the front door slam behind them. The two women glanced at each other.

'Good riddance,' Aggie muttered and bent over Grace, stroking the girl's face with such a gesture of tenderness that Jeannie was mystified.

'Here,' a voice spoke behind them and Jeannie turned to see that one of the other girls was holding out a glass of water.

'Thank you.' Gently Aggie raised the girl's head and shoulders. Cradling her against her breast, Aggie took the glass and held it to Grace's lips. The girl's face was deathly pale, the bright red lipstick a smudged gash across her mouth.

As consciousness returned, she drank the water and then she pressed her face into Aggie's bosom and wept.

Twenty

'Tom . . .' She put her hand out towards him.

'Jeannie!' The smile spread across his face to see her standing there, waiting for him, and he dropped his bag to the ground and held out both his arms. Jeannie went into them, but, whilst submitting to his kiss of greeting, she held herself back a little from him. Feeling her reserve he looked down at her and said at once, 'What is it? Is something wrong?'

'Tom, I'm sorry to greet you with bad news . . .'

His eyes darkened with anguish. 'What is it? Not Mam? Oh she isn't . . . She hasn't done something silly?'

Jeannie blinked and looked up at him in astonishment. 'Do something silly? Your mother?' she countered sharply. 'Never! She's a Scot, Tom Lawrence, and dinna you forget it.'

For a moment a wry smile twitched his mouth and he made a fair impression of the Scottish brogue. 'Och, Ah'm no' likely to, the noo.' But then his face sobered again as he asked again, 'Then what is it?'

'Two pieces of news, really. One is, I'm sorry to say, bad news. The other – well – I hope you'll think it good.'

Tom sighed. 'Don't keep me in suspense, woman. Let's have the bad first then.'

'It's – it's Grace. She's expecting.'

Tom's mouth dropped open and he stared at his wife without saying a word. When he did speak his voice was a hoarse, strangulated whisper. 'Pregnant? Our Grace has got 'ersen pregnant? Oh, no . . .' He shook his head violently now, as if the very idea was unthinkable. He pulled away from Jeannie. 'No, no, I don't believe it.' He paused a moment and then said viciously, 'I bet it's him again, isn't it? She's been attacked, raped. That's what'll have happened. By God, if only me dad was still here, he'd . . .' He turned and took a few steps forward and then stopped, swaying for a moment as did most fishermen when they stepped on to firm land after weeks at sea. Then Jeannie saw his shoulders slump as if in defeat. The drive to do something, to take some action, lasted only seconds with Tom Lawrence.

He half-turned back towards her. 'Who is it?' He asked flatly. 'Do you know who the father is? Will he marry her?'

'I do know who he is, but no, he won't marry her.'

His haunted eyes met her steady gaze. 'Who is it? Is it him? Hayes-Gorton?'

Jeannie swallowed. 'Not the one you're thinking. It's the other one, Francis.'

He stared at her and then repeated incredulously, 'Francis? Francis Hayes-Gorton. You mean he – he attacked her?'

'No – no.' Swiftly, Jeannie shook her head and then looked down at the ground. This part was even more difficult than the first, awful news. 'Grace fancies herself in love with him. She's been meeting him secretly.'

'Meeting him? How? Where?' And then before Jeannie could speak, Tom answered his own question. He gave a nod of his head and said flatly, 'Of course. Aggie's.'

Mutely, Jeannie nodded and they stood staring at each other for several moments oblivious to the hustle and bustle of the dockside going on all around them.

Wearily, Tom held out his hand towards her. 'Come on, we'd best go home.'

'Don't you want to hear the other piece of news?' she asked, a trace of sadness in her tone now that the bad news had obliterated any chance of joy and excitement at her own.

'Of course,' Tom said, but she could sense that whatever it was, he was scarcely interested.

'Tom, we're going to have a baby. I'm expecting too.'

In the intimacy of their bed that night, Tom took Jeannie in his arms and held her close. 'I'm so sorry,' he whispered against her hair, 'that your wonderful news was spoilt by – by Grace.'

Jeannie snuggled closer but said nothing. She was not about to say, 'It's all right' because it wasn't. Her happy surprise had been spoilt and she felt cheated.

'What are we going to do?' came Tom's deep voice.

Jeannie lay perfectly still, wondering, for a moment, if she had misunderstood. He, Tom, the man of the house, was asking her what they should do. The realization came slowly, creeping into her being like icy water, then flooding through her like a tidal wave of disappointment.

The man she had married was not the man she had thought him to be. His father, yes, now George Lawrence had been a strong, steadfast man. Mistakenly she knew now, she had thought that his son would take after him.

But Tom's outbursts were not those of a strong character, determined and sure, but the bluster of a man who had perhaps always lived in the shadow of a more dominant man. And even though that man was gone now, the son had not the personality to step into his shoes. Yet Tom was a good man, she would not deny. And that he loved her, she was sure. But she knew that it was she who was the rock to which they all clung. Even Nell, since George's going, had floundered helplessly in the raging torrent of her loss and had turned to Jeannie for strength and fortitude. It was odd, Jeannie pondered, how the whole family had so readily leant on her, the girl who had come as a stranger into their midst. Why did Nell have no friends amongst her neighbours? Was it merely because she was the wife of a skipper and perhaps set slightly apart from them? Or was there something more?

And now Grace. Jeannie sighed. Silly, foolish, gullible Grace. Now she would have to see to Grace too.

With her cheek still against his chest, she let out a long sigh. 'We'll take care of her, of course. And the child.'

His arms tightened about her in unspoken gratitude, but again his voice rumbled deep in his chest against her cheek. 'But ought we to do something? I mean, about the father?'

'What can we do? A Hayes-Gorton will never the marry the likes of us . . .' As the words came out of her mouth, in her imagination it was not her husband lying by her side, holding her, but Robert Hayes-Gorton, with his gentle smile and his dark, brown eyes and his deep voice whispering in her ear. The feeling was so overwhelming that Jeannie pulled back, frightened by the power of her emotions and the wickedness of her imagination.

'Jeannie? What is it? What's the matter?'

Overcome with a sudden rush of affection and guilt that she should even think of being unfaithful to this good man, she reached for him and pulled him into her arms. 'Let's forget Grace,' she whispered softly. 'Just for tonight, the one night you're home.'

*

170

When Tom went back to sea, anxious, for once, to be gone and away from all the trouble at home, Jeannie marched to the house two streets away and rapped sharply on Aggie Turnbull's door.

'Jeannie—'

'Dinna you "Jeannie" me,' she snapped as the woman she had come to see opened the door herself. 'How could you let her do it? How could you encourage her to come here? She's no more than a bairn. Sixteen—'

'Seventeen next month,' Aggie countered swiftly.

'Och aye. Old enough to become one of your whores, I suppose?'

'She came here for one thing only—'

'Aye, and we know what that was.'

Aggie, two pink blotches of anger showing in her cheeks, took a step towards Jeannie. 'She came here for a little fun. To dress up in pretty clothes and escape from the stink of fish. Just for a few hours. And she came to escape from the endless cod net on the wall and Nell always working—'

'Good, honest work.'

Aggie continued as if Jeannie had not spoken. 'And to try – just for a while – to forget about her dad.'

For a moment, Jeannie was silent and then it appeared that Aggie had taken in exactly what Jeannie had just said, for she went on, 'And as for Nell being a good, honest woman. Well, I could tell you a thing or two about Nell Lawrence. Oh yes, indeed I could.'

'There's nothing that you could tell me about that family that I'd want to hear.'

Aggie shook her head. 'No, Jeannie, I don't suppose you would want to hear anything that I might have to say. I don't think you would like it.'

'My name's Mrs Lawrence to you,' was Jeannie's only reply as she began to turn away.

'Mrs Lawrence,' Aggie said softly, seeming to almost savour the name on her lips. 'Mrs Lawrence.'

Glancing back, Jeannie was shocked to see sudden tears in the woman's eyes. All her anger had evaporated, leaving only a pensive, wistful expression. 'I am sorry about Grace,' Aggie said gently now. 'More sorry than you'll ever know. I tried to warn her, but she wouldn't listen.'

Jeannie stopped and twisted round to face her again. 'Tried to warn her? Well, you didna try very hard. You could have stopped her coming to your house very easily. Stopped her meeting him here.'

'I could, yes.' Surprisingly, Aggie agreed. 'But she would only have met him some other way. She loves him, really loves him.' She paused and then added, 'Watch over her, Jeannie. Please. I'm so afraid of what she might do now he has deserted her.'

'Och, the Lawrences wouldna let the likes of him bring them down.'

'Are you sure, Jeannie?' Aggie said softly.

But as Jeannie now turned away finally, she was not so sure herself of her own vehement statement.

It was not the first time she had been to the offices of the Hayes-Gorton Trawler Company. She had come to collect pay due to Tom, lining up with all the other fishermen's wives to be sure that they had enough money to feed their family before it all disappeared behind the bar at the Fisherman's Rest. She would not so easily forget the incident over the hat and, in future, she intended to hold the purse strings.

But it was the first time she had ventured beyond the

pay window and further into the building to find the offices of the partners. Her heart beat a little faster and her hands felt clammy.

The woman in the outer office was middle-aged and spinsterish. Small, round, steel-framed spectacles and straight, grey hair cut short with a heavy fringe did nothing to enhance her appearance. Her thin-lipped mouth did not even stretch itself into the pretence of a smile.

'I would like to see Mr Hayes-Gorton, if you please? Mr Francis Hayes-Gorton.'

The woman looked up and then slowly her gaze travelled down to Jeannie's shoes and then up again, assessing her from head to toe. 'Do you have an appointment?' The voice affected superiority but far from intimidating Jeannie, it only made her more determined and icily polite.

'No, I dinna have an appointment, but if that is the way things are done, then I would like you to make one for me.' She paused ever so slightly and added again, 'If you please.'

Languidly the woman flickered over the pages of a diary. 'He's very busy just now. I really don't know when he would be able . . .'

Jeannie heard the door open behind her and without needing to turn round, she knew who had entered the room. She could feel his presence, feel him close to her. Resolutely, she licked her dry lips and continued to stare at the woman in front of her.

'Jeannie?' Robert began as he closed the door and came around her to stand to the side of the secretary's desk. Then, hastily, he corrected himself. 'Mrs Lawrence? What brings you here? Is there anything wrong?'

Jeannie opened her mouth to reply but the woman forestalled her. 'She's requesting an appointment to see Mr Francis, sir, but I really don't think . . .'

Robert held up his hand. 'It's all right, Miss Forbes, I will attend to this. Please . . .' He turned towards Jeannie and spread his hand in a gesture of invitation to precede him from the room. 'Won't you come into my office? Maybe I can help?'

'But I dinna think . . .' she began and then, glancing briefly at the tight-lipped expression of disapproval on the secretary's face, with a spark of devilment Jeannie nodded agreement and turned in the direction he indicated.

Closing the door of his office behind them, he gestured towards a chair. 'Please, sit down. May I get you a cup of tea – or anything?'

Jeannie shook her head but took the seat he offered whilst Robert went around the desk and sat down in the swivel chair on the opposite side. He leant his arms on the edge of the desk and bent forward a little towards her.

She's here, he was thinking, she's really here, in my office, sitting opposite me and I can't think of a sensible thing to say to this woman who has become the object of my every waking moment and even most of my sleep too. It is her I think of when I wake in the morning and she is the last face I see in my mind's eye in the darkness of the night before I sleep, hoping to dream about her too.

Now here she is. Sitting in front of me and I am like a tongue-tied schoolboy. And she looks so calm, so dignified, so in control. But then, he reminded himself sadly, why shouldn't she? She dislikes me, perhaps even hates me. The thought saddened him so that when he spoke, his voice was devoid of all emotion, flat and almost unfriendly.

'How may I help you?'

Jeannie tried to still the rapid beating of her heart, tried to sit facing him calmly and without a trace of the tumult of emotion inside her from showing on her face. How could she be so foolish as to even allow herself to feel like

174

this when she was married to another man and expecting that man's child? How could she let herself think such wild, wicked thoughts? Why did she keep wondering just what it would be like to be held in this man's arms, to feel the touch of those lips on her mouth, to dig her fingers deep into that thick, dark brown hair and pull his head down on to her breast and hold him close . . .

Aloud, her voice harsh, she said, 'It's Mr Francis I need to see.' She licked her lips and added deliberately, 'Sir.' His smooth forehead puckered in a frown and his brown eyes were unfathomable depths.

Robert felt his heart plummet and there was a pain in his chest. There was a cold edge to his voice as he said, curtly, 'I see. Then I can't be of assistance?'

Jeannie swallowed. Now she had made him angry. She could see it on his face. 'I'm sorry. It's a delicate, personal matter. I must see him.'

He could hear the urgency that was almost a desperation in her voice. And deep in her eyes was a haunted look that tore at his heart. What the hell had his dear brother been up to now to make Jeannie look like that?

Robert stood up suddenly. 'Please – stay here a moment. I'll see if he's in the building.'

'Oh – I . . .' She made as if to rise when he did, but at his bidding she sank back into her chair.

Whilst he was out of the room, Jeannie looked about her. Though her mind was occupied with the problem and she thought that she hardly took in her surroundings, later she was to find that she had remembered Robert's office in minute detail. An antique mahogany desk with polished brass handles and a green leather top. The walls were lined with mahogany bookcases and over the fireplace hung a portrait of an elderly man dressed as the skipper of a trawler. Jeannie guessed he was Robert's grandfather and supposed he must have dressed up like that for the painting. But then she remembered Flora's story of the Gortons. This was the man who had started out with one boat, which he had skippered himself. She looked again at the picture. He wore the clothes with a comfortable familiarity. This was no upper-class gent dressing up. The man in the painting was a genuine, born and bred fisherman.

The door opened and Robert appeared. 'He's in his office. Come along, I'll show you the way.' Now she rose and followed him along a corridor and passed into a similar office as he held open the door for her, though here the furnishings were modern, sleek lines of wood and metal that, for Jeannie, had neither warmth nor soul.

Francis was sitting behind the desk, leaning backwards, his hands linked behind his head. 'Well, well, well, if it isn't Mrs Lawrence. Protector of the young and innocent.' He laughed, a cruel sound. 'Though they're not so innocent as she'd like to believe. Eh, my dear Jeannie?'

Robert had closed the door but had remained in the room. Now he came and stood between them, to one side of the desk so that he glanced first at one and then at the other.

Jeannie took her gaze away from Francis for a brief moment and said, 'This is between me and Mr Francis, sir.'

At once Robert made as if to leave. 'I'm sorry—' he began but Francis interrupted. 'There's nothing you can have to say to me that my brother shouldn't hear.'

For a brief moment, Robert and Jeannie stared at each other, the one mystified, the other embarrassed by what she was being forced to say in front of him.

Tight-lipped, she turned her bold, green gaze upon Francis Hayes-Gorton. 'Very well,' she said in a voice that was deceptively quiet. 'You must ken why I'm here. What are you going to do about Grace Lawrence?'

For a moment there was complete stillness in the room until Francis, still rocking gently back and forth on two legs of his chair, said with a calculated indifference and a glitter of malice in his eyes, 'Absolutely nothing.'

'But you are the father. We all heard her say so.'

Now Francis let his chair drop forward with a crash and at the same moment brought his fists down on to the desk in front of him with a thump that startled both Jeannie and Robert. 'How dare you! How dare you come into this office with your malicious tales! Just because one of Aggie Turnbull's trollops gets herself . . .'

Now Jeannie was angry too and she leant across the desk, bending her face close to his, forgetting now in the white heat of her ire, that this man held the Lawrence family's livelihood in his hands. But at this moment, even if she had thought about it, she did not care. Right now, this was about a young girl brought low by this man.

'She's no' one of Aggie's girls, and you know it. She's a silly, naive, yes, foolish, girl, but she is not – not a whore.' Her voice dropped. 'She imagines herself in love with you, and in her stupidity, believes you love her.'

'Ha!' Francis threw back his head and laughed aloud, but the sound had no humour. It was cruel, mirthless laughter. 'Then you are right about one thing, Mrs Lawrence. She is stupid and deserves all she has brought upon herself.' He leant closer again. 'And whilst I make no secret of the fact that I visit Aggie and her – er – friends, I most certainly make no admission as to fathering the girl's bastard. It could,' he said with slow deliberate malice, 'be any one of a number of men.'

Jeannie's lips parted in a gasp and slowly she straightened up. 'I see. So that's how it is, is it?'

Francis rose to his feet and leant on his knuckles across the desk. 'That is exactly how it is. I'll bid you "Good day", Mrs Lawrence.'

Jeannie wagged her forefinger in his face. 'You,' she said slowly and with emphasis on every word, 'have no' heard the last of this, Mr High n' Mighty Hayes-Gorton.'

Smiling sarcastically, he said smoothly, 'Oh, I think I have. I think you will find, dear lady, that your husband will not approve of today's little visit, never mind any further trouble-making on your part.'

'Are you threatening me? Threatening that Tom will lose his job if I—'

'That's enough.' For the first time, Robert spoke, his deep voice breaking into the quarrel.

Jeannie tore her gaze away from the man before her, gave one swift, furious glance at Robert then turned and in one quick movement dragged open the door and marched from the room.

'Jeannie – Jeannie, wait . . .'

She heard him clattering down the steps behind her, but he did not catch up with her until they stood side by side on the steps outside the building.

She stood a moment, gulping fresh air into her lungs, almost as if to clear herself of the putrid air of Francis's presence.

Giving full vent to her anger, she turned on Robert, spewing out her wrath, yet even as she did so, she knew she was being unfair. He was not to blame and yet she could not stop herself. 'Leave me be. You and your family have caused us enough grief. She's no' what he says. There've been no other men. I'd stake my life on it. It's him. Just him.'

'I believe you.' Touching her arm briefly, Robert spoke with a quietness that was such a direct contrast to her angry words, that she immediately felt ashamed. Then the anger that had carried her here, buoyed her up to confront one of their 'masters', died and she felt suddenly exhausted.

'I'm sorry,' she said at once. 'It's no' your fault.' She could not resist a fleeting, wry smile as she added, 'At least, no' this time.'

Robert too gave a slight smile of regret. 'I've wanted to tell you so often, Jeannie, to explain about that night.'

She gave a gesture of dismissal with her hand but he went on, haltingly at first and then with greater assurance as he realized that for the first time she was ready to listen to his side of the story. 'I remember very little of what happened. Please believe me. I'd been drinking, and yes, I admit it a little too much. But not *that* much. Not enough to make me so paralytic that I didn't know what I was doing. I found out later,' he added grimly, 'that my dear, caring . . .' here the word was heavy with sarcasm, 'brother Francis had mixed my drinks with rum. It always makes me ill and he knows that. And it was certainly he who led our party to Aggie's house. What I don't understand . . .' his brown gaze was now searching Jeannie's face for her side of the story, 'is what a nice girl like Grace Lawrence was even doing at Aggie's.'

Jeannie sighed, seeing for the first time how the events of that night had really been. Young men out on a stag night, intent on causing the greatest embarrassment to the young bridegroom that they could. And the ringleader had been his own brother.

Jeannie sighed. 'She shouldna have been there. I know that now. But still, she's not what your brother calls her. She's just young and silly and gullible, bowled over by fancy clothes and parties.' She shook her head slowly. 'I suppose, in a way, you can't blame her either. She just wanted a bit of fun and didn't realize what it would lead to.' Now she looked at him full in the face. 'She does love him, you know.'

'Oh Jeannie.' Her name was a whisper on his lips as they stood on the steps together just looking at each other.

Then becoming aware that they were standing in full view of passers-by, of the whole dockside area if it came to that, Jeannie said, 'I must go.'

'Just one more thing . . .' he said softly. 'Would you please not – this time – take it as an insult if I say that I will try to see what I can do for Grace? In – in the way of money, I mean.'

Jeannie stared at him for a moment, reading so many emotions deep in his eyes. Shame, regret, concern, even . . . She turned away, shutting out the one feeling she could see there that threatened to overwhelm them both.

Nodding, she said heavily, 'Aye, I'll no' refuse you this time, Mr Robert. For she'll be needin' all the help she can get.'

She walked down the steps and, though she was aware of him standing watching her, she did not look back.

Twenty-One

Jeannie sailed through her pregnancy hardly noticing her condition. She was lucky that she had good health, but wryly she admitted to herself that there was precious little time for her to indulge herself.

In contrast, Grace was ill throughout the following months. Whilst her stomach swelled, the rest of the girl's body grew thinner, until her face was pinched and her skin, devoid of colour, was stretched tightly over the bone structure of her features. Unable to face the gossip, she gave in her notice at work and sat all day hunched in the chair at the side of the fire. Whilst Nell continued to work at her net on the wall, not a word, as far as Jeannie could hear, passed between mother and daughter. Shattered by the loss of her husband, her daughter's downfall seemed to have robbed Nell of her last ounce of strength. She turned to the only comfort she knew: work. As the weather improved, Nell took her net into the back-yard and hung it from the rail fastened across the kitchen window. During the summer days the back-yards were filled with the sound of laughter and chatter as neighbours, their hands busy with the braiding, called to each other. Only this year, Nell worked in silence whilst Grace stayed indoors, even on the warmest days.

'You must eat, Grace, for the sake of the baby. You're no' eating enough to keep a bird alive.' Jeannie tried to coax her gently.

But Grace would not answer.

'Will you talk to her?' Jeannie asked Nell.

Tight-lipped, Nell said, 'There's nothing I can say to her, Jeannie. I never thought my Grace would shame us in this way.'

Jeannie pleaded the girl's cause. 'She's no' the first and she willna be the last. She loved the man, worthless though he is.'

Nell glared at Jeannie, stung to anger. 'You might be married into this family now, Jeannie, but you dinna ken everything about us. Grace knew that she shouldna go to Aggie's and not only for the obvious reason. There are other reasons too.'

'What?' Jeannie demanded, but Nell turned away and though she said no more, her action spoke loud and clear: 'Mind your own business'.

Annoyed, Jeannie turned and marched along the alley-way running between the back-yards of the houses. Tom's ship was due in on the next tide.

He would help her, she told herself, he would talk to Grace.

'She's a little whore and a bloody liar and if you so much as breathe a word of this to Father, I'll kill you.'

Robert watched the face of his elder brother contorted with rage, his blue eyes bulging, his face white.

Calmly, Robert murmured, ' "The lady doth protest too much, methinks".'

'What? What are you burbling on about?'

'I should have thought you, of all people, would have known your Shakespeare. You, with your public school education. Edwin and I were not so – er – fortunate.' The sarcasm was evident in Robert's tone. 'But perhaps the local Grammar School was not so bad after all.'

'Huh, you think a good education is being able to spout the Bard?'

'Oh no.' Robert shook his head. 'I think a good education is learning how to lead a good, honest, decent life. And that . . .' he paused for emphasis, 'includes standing by your mistakes.'

Francis's eyes glittered and his lips curled. 'Just like the Honourable Robert in his farce of a marriage.'

Robert felt the colour begin to creep up his neck, but he kept his tone level. 'My marriage is nothing to do with you.'

'Ah,' Francis said slowly. 'You think not, eh?'

The brothers stared at each other for a long moment before Robert said once more, 'What are you going to do about Grace Lawrence?'

'I've told you. Nothing. Absolutely nothing. I shall deny everything. I might even, if you don't stop meddling in my affairs, start a few rumours that the child is yours. So I should be very careful what you do, dear brother.'

'Your threats don't bother me,' Robert snapped.

'Really? Well, I don't think Father or your father-in-law would be too pleased to hear that you have a bastard child by a little whore when you can't even provide the company with a legitimate son and heir.'

Robert opened his mouth to retaliate, but anything he said would be disloyal to Louise. And despite everything, he could not descend to that.

'Oh go to hell, Francis,' he muttered, but his brother only laughed. 'Since you're so fond of quotations and sayings, dear boy, how about this one: "The Devil takes care of his own".'

*

183

Jeannie stood on the jetty, pulling her coat around her. The buttons would scarcely meet now over the bulge of her stomach and the wind, whipping along the quay, found its way inside her coat and made her shiver. It was a blustery day and cold for July.

'Come on, Tom, for goodness sake!' she muttered, her gaze on the distant gates for sight of his ship nosing its way into the dock. She walked up and down, more to keep herself warm than searching for sight of his ship, but when she came near to the end of the jetty, she saw the *Gorton North Star*, its nose tight against the wall and the lumpers already unloading the kits of fish. She went nearer. 'How long has she been in?' she asked one of the workers.

'Two hours, missis. One of the first in when they opened the gates.'

'Do you know Tom Lawrence? Did you see him come ashore?'

The man shook his head and, as a yell from the boat caught his attention, he turned back to continue his work.

Jeannie hurried away down the length of the quay, annoyed with herself. Here she was standing in the cold and all the time Tom was already ashore at home or in the Fisherman's.

She went home first but he was not there.

'No,' Nell said. 'He's no' been home.'

'But his ship came in two hours ago.'

The two women stared at each other, fear for a moment in their eyes.

'Oh no.' Jeannie shook her head. 'We'd have heard by now if . . .' She left the sentence unfinished and Nell turned away, back to her braiding.

'I'll go to the Fisherman's,' Jeannie said, 'but he'd best not be in there, else I'll skite his lugs for him.'

Tom was not in the pub on the corner nor had he been to the pay office to collect his money. She was turning away from the narrow window when she heard someone call her name. Looking round, she saw Robert striding towards her.

'How are you?' he said and she could see at once that he was trying hard not to glance down at her stomach.

'I'm well, but at this moment, rather angry.'

'Oh? Can I help?'

'Only if you can tell me where my husband is. His ship's docked, but I can't find him anywhere.'

For a moment, Robert looked uncomfortable.

'You know where he is, don't you?' Then as a thought struck her, she shook her head. 'Och no, he wouldna . . .'

Misunderstanding her, Robert said swiftly, 'He's all right. Nothing's happened to him, I promise you.'

'I wasna thinking it had,' she said wryly. 'I was thinking he might have gone to Aggie's.'

'Tom?' The surprise on Robert's face was genuine. 'Go there?' He could not believe that the man lucky enough to be married to Jeannie could even look at another woman, let alone frequent the house of Aggie Turnbull.

Jeannie sniffed and before she had stopped to think, she said, 'Well, it was no' the first time for him on our wedding night . . .' Then she clapped her hand over her mouth in horror. 'Och, what am I saying.' She could not believe that she had confided such a thing to anyone, especially to a man and, more especially, to Robert. 'I'm sorry,' she said at once. 'I shouldna have said that.'

She had seen the spark of anger in his eyes and had misinterpreted its meaning for Robert was by no means offended by her confidence, but he was angry on her behalf. 'No, *I'm* sorry, Jeannie. The man's a fool if . . .'

185

In her confusion, Jeannie reached out and touched his arm. 'Please, don't say any more. Just – just tell me if you know where he is.'

Robert sighed. 'Jackson said he came off the *North Star* and went straight out again on the *Arctic Queen*. She was just waiting to sail and they were a deck-hand short. Jackson said that Tom jumped at the chance.'

Jeannie stared at him. 'Tom? Tom went straight out again on another boat?' She couldn't believe what she was hearing.

Robert nodded. 'Yes, I have to admit, it surprised me a little. He's not exactly got the name for being a "born fisherman". Not like his father.' He paused and then added, 'You'll be all right, won't you? I mean, the office will let you have his money.'

Jeannie nodded. 'Och aye. I suppose,' she added with wry amusement, 'there's one good thing about it. Half his pay won't disappear across the bar at the Fisherman's.'

As Jeannie walked home she realized that far from being the courageous act it appeared on the surface, Tom would rather brave the perils of the ocean than face the problems at home.

Robert called at the Lawrences' house in Baldock Street the following day and thereafter, regularly every week, running the gauntlet of the gossips in the street and the tales that would be told.

'It must be him, that's the father of Grace's bairn.'

'No, no. It's the other one. Mr Francis. One of the girls from Aggie's told me. She used to meet him there. Daft over him, she was. But, of course, he denies it.'

'Mebbe she ain't sure which of 'em it is.' And the

raucous laughter would echo around the fishdocks, tearing Grace's reputation into shreds.

Now, Jeannie did not refuse Robert's help and, whilst it went against her proud nature to accept money from him, this time she took it and spent it on titbits to tempt Grace's appetite or things for the coming baby.

When he stepped into the tiny, stuffy kitchen on his first visit and sat down on the opposite side of the fireplace to Grace, Robert was appalled by the change in the girl.

Later, outside, he said, 'Oh Jeannie, I can't tell you how sorry I am about this.'

She looked at him keenly and could read the haunted look in his eyes. There was more there, she thought shrewdly, in those brown depths than just sorrow at the downfall of a fisherman's daughter. In that moment she was sure, now, that there was some truth in the servants' gossip that his marriage was not all that it might, or should, be. And he had told her as much himself.

Overwhelmed by a sudden feeling of pity for him, she reached out towards him and touched his arm. 'We appreciate your kindness, Mr Robert, all of us. But even I, this time, have to say that the fault is as much Grace's as – as the man concerned.'

He gazed long into her eyes and murmured, simply, 'She loves him, Jeannie.' His voice dropped to a whisper as he added, 'You – you should know how that feels.'

It was as if a gigantic wave had hit her, carrying her on its crest in a flood of emotion. The blood was pounding in her ears and she felt suddenly giddy. She felt an over-whelming desire to reach up, to cup his face between her hands and to kiss his mouth.

'What is it?' she heard his concerned voice say as if from a great distance.

Swiftly, her voice hoarse, she managed to say, 'Nothing – nothing. I . . .' But she could say no more, for there was such a tumult of emotions going on inside her that she was robbed of her power of speech.

'Jeannie, what is it? Are you unwell? Here, let me take you back into the house.'

Solicitously, he took hold of her arm and made as if to lead her back indoors, but she resisted. 'No, no. I'm fine. I'm better out here. In the fresh air.'

'Let me fetch you a chair, then?'

'No, no, really. Thank you. You go. Dinna let me keep you. I'll be all right.'

She didn't want him to go and yet she couldn't bear him to stay. She needed to be alone. To control her riotous emotions and castigate herself sternly for them.

'I don't like to leave you like this.'

'Please, I'll be fine. It's just the heat, I expect.' The July weather was capricious and today was hot and oppressive.

'Well, if you're sure?' She nodded and he stepped back from her but he did not turn away and leave her immediately. He saw her glance about her as if looking to see who of their neighbours in the street might be watching. He followed her glance and saw that there were two or three women further down the road who had found it imperative that their front steps needed scrubbing at this very moment.

'You're right,' he said, giving her a quick, understanding smile. 'I'd better be going.' Then glancing down briefly towards the now-obvious mound of her stomach, he said huskily, 'Take care of yourself, Jeannie, won't you?'

She watched him go, walking up the street away from her towards his motor car.

I love him, she thought and the knowledge made her ridiculously happy. I've fallen in love with him. But then as realization of her true situation crept into her mind, she felt plunged into the depths of despair.

But I shall never, she told herself, know what it is to be loved by him.

Twenty-Two

Jeannie's baby was due about a month after Grace's, but when the expected date of the younger girl's confinement came and passed by, Jeannie became concerned.

'I wish Tom was home.' A tiny vestige of hope still remained that he would help her shoulder the burden of worry. But, more than that, Jeannie needed to see her husband, needed his reassurance that he loved her and to prove to herself that she still loved him.

'The men are best out of the way, hen,' Nell was saying. 'This is women's work.' It was the first time during the long months of waiting that Nell had shown any concern for her daughter.

At once Jeannie decided to try to encourage Nell's involvement. 'Was your husband away at sea when your two were born?'

Nell's expression softened. 'My George was different. Very different.' She glanced at Jeannie and then away again, almost apologetically. 'He was a fine man. One you could lean on, lass. But I'm afraid, Tom, though I love him dearly, mind, well, he's not quite got the strength of character his father had.'

Jeannie stared at her mother-in-law. She had never thought to hear such words from a mother's lips. But she could not think about that now. Grace was more important. 'Do you think we should get the midwife?'

Nell pushed her spectacles up her nose. 'Aye, you could.'

'Please, won't you go up and look at her. She hasna even got out of her bed all day.'

'We'd soon know if it was coming, hen,' Nell said. 'We'd hear her down here.'

Jeannie sighed and levered herself up from the chair by the range and reached up to the lamp to turn down the light.

'Leave it, hen. I must stay a while and do a little more braiding.'

Jeannie glanced over her shoulder at the older woman and shook her head. 'You shouldna be staying up half the night at the nets. It isna right.'

Nell sighed heavily. 'I've got to do something, hen. It's not fair to expect Tom to keep the lot of us.'

'Then I'll stay and help you.'

'No, no . . .' Nell now rose stiffly from the chair. 'No, you away to your bed. I promise I'll only bide an hour or so.'

'We-ell . . .' Jeannie said slowly. 'Mind you do.' And she wagged her forefinger in mock admonishment.

At half past two in the morning Jeannie awoke to find Grace sitting up in bed beside her and moaning. When Tom was away, they shared the double bed in the front bedroom, Nell sleeping in the back room.

'Is it the bairn, hen?'

'I – think so.' The girl leant back against the pillows, her face, in the low night-light they had kept burning through the dark hours for the past few nights, was wet with sweat.

Jeannie heaved her bulk from the bed and began to dress hurriedly.

'Don't leave me, Jeannie,' Grace gasped.

'I must fetch the midwife. Mrs Jackson, isn't it? The ship's runner's wife? I'll wake your mother before I go.'

'No, no, don't. She only came up half an hour ago.'

Jeannie clicked her tongue against her teeth in annoyance. 'So much for her promise, eh?'

'What?'

'Ne'er you mind, hen. Lie back and try to keep calm.'

Ten minutes later she was banging on the door of number twenty at the bottom of the road. The window above opened and Mr Jackson, his bald head shining in the moonlight, his mouth shrunken in, squinted down into the street below.

'Who's that?'

'Jeannie Lawrence, Mr Jackson. Could you ask Mrs Jackson to come to Grace, please? It's her time.'

'She ain't here.' He jerked his thumb over his shoulder. 'Gone t'other side town. Midwife there's ill and she's 'ad to tek her place.'

'Then who can I get?'

The man shrugged. 'Dunno. The doctor, I suppose.'

Jeannie bit her lip. It would be costly, but they'd have to have someone. She had no idea what should be done. And by the look of Grace already, the birth was not going to be easy.

But the doctor, too, was out on a call and when she returned home, she found Grace in a distressed state. Her cries had awakened Nell, who was standing beside her daughter's bed, wringing her hands.

'Jeannie, get help. We must have help.'

Swiftly, Jeannie explained and added firmly, 'There's no one. We'll just have to help her ourselves.'

'If only George was here,' Nell wailed and she pushed her fingers behind her glasses to wipe away the tears.

'We can do it,' Jeannie said. 'You must tell me what to do . . .'

The woman looked up with startled eyes. 'Me? I don't know what to do.'

'But you've had two children of your own.'

'Yes, but . . .' She watched helplessly as Grace writhed in agony now. 'But George was here. He fetched the midwife and stayed with me.' The tears flowed afresh. 'All the time.'

Then the two women standing either side of the bed looked down at the girl in surprise as Grace gasped, 'Aggie. Fetch Aggie. She'll help me. She'll know what to do.'

Jeannie looked across at Nell, the question in her eyes.

Nell was shaking her head vehemently. 'I'll no' have that woman in ma hoose.'

'But there is no one else and we need help,' Jeannie argued.

Nell leant across the bed. 'If you fetch that woman in here, I'll no' speak to you again, Jeannie Lawrence, as long as I live.'

Jeannie's lips parted in a gasp of surprise. She had not realized that Nell's hatred of the woman and all that she was supposed to be went so deep that she would put her own daughter's life at risk. For, as Jeannie looked down at Grace, at the sweat running down her face, at the dark shadows of suffering beneath her eyes and the gaunt hollows of her cheeks, she knew it was exactly that. If they didn't do something quickly, Grace's life was ebbing away.

Jeannie made her decision. 'I'm sorry, but I must think of Grace. If Aggie Turnbull is the only hope we have, then . . .' She said no more but turned swiftly away and hurried down the stairs again as quickly as her own cumbersome bulk would allow.

Dawn was breaking as Jeannie hammered on the door of the notorious house two streets away from the Lawrence home. It took some minutes before the door was opened by a bleary-eyed Aggie herself.

'Heavens!' the woman uttered. 'What on earth brings you to my door?'

'It's Grace. She's come to her time and – and there's something wrong. The midwife and the doctor are both out and – and—'

'I'll come at once,' Aggie said and was already turning back towards the stairs.

'I'll go back now, but please, hurry.'

The woman turned, resting her hand for a brief moment on the newel post at the foot of the stairs. 'Does Nell know you've come for me?'

Jeannie nodded. 'Aye, but she doesna like it.'

Again, the small smile. 'No,' she said softly, 'I don't expect she does.' Briskly then, she said, 'You go back, I'll be as quick as I can.'

'Thank you,' Jeannie said simply.

To Jeannie's horror when she reached home again, Nell was standing in front of the net on the wall, seemingly calmly braiding and completely ignoring the desperate cries of the girl in the room above.

Jeannie shook her head in disbelief but said, 'She's coming. I'll get clean sheets ready and towels. What else do we need?'

Nell made no sign of having heard. Her mouth tight, her shoulders rigid, her fingers worked faster and faster, only pausing to push her spectacles up the bridge of her nose every so often.

Jeannie set the kettle to boil and a large pan of water too. Somewhere she'd heard about boiling water at such a time, but she didn't know exactly what it was for. Back upstairs, she sponged Grace's brow and stood helplessly whilst the girl gasped and groaned.

Suddenly, Aggie was beside them, bending over Grace and saying gently, 'Now then, my dear. Let me look at you.' Swiftly, and to Jeannie's inexperienced eye, Aggie examined the girl knowledgeably. Then she looked up at Jeannie and said quietly, 'It's not coming normally. You'll have to get a doctor. I think it's breech and with her being so small, it could be dangerous. She's already weak.'

Jeannie waited to hear no more but was already lumbering down the stairs again. Nell had drawn back the curtains and now Jeannie saw that it was full daylight.

'I must find a doctor,' she told Nell. 'Something's wrong. Please, go up to her, Mother.' It was the first time Jeannie had used the name to Nell and she did it deliberately, trying to force Nell to overcome her prejudice and help her daughter. 'She needs you.'

But Nell continued to move between pantry and kitchen setting the table for breakfast as if everything within the household was just as normal. Exasperated and fearful of wasting any more time, Jeannie pulled on her coat and rushed into the street.

The midwife was still not home, nor was the doctor.

'Do you know of another doctor?' she asked the maid who answered the surgery door, but the girl shook her head.

Jeannie was almost frantic with worry and as she hurried down the steps and on to the pavement to cross the road, she almost stepped in front of a motor car. There was a squeal of tyres as the driver swerved to miss her. She stepped back and lifted her hand in apology, but the driver had drawn his motor to the side of the road and the noise of the engine died as he leapt down and came towards her.

Oh no, Jeannie thought abstractedly. This is all I need.

Some man giving me a telling off for not looking where I was going.

But as she lifted her eyes and looked at the man coming towards her, her heart leapt with thankfulness. It was as if her prayers of the last few hours had been miraculously answered. Striding towards her was Robert.

'Jeannie – are you all right. I didn't hit you, did I?'

'No, no.' She managed to smile tremorously. Without consciously thinking what she was doing, she reached out with both her hands towards him and he took hold of them in his.

'What is it?' he said at once. 'Something's wrong, isn't it?'

'It's Grace. She's been in labour half the night and – and the baby's the wrong way round. The midwife's away and so's our doctor. Oh Mr Robert . . .' Unaccustomed tears threatened to overwhelm her. She was exhausted and frightened.

'I'll find you a doctor.'

As Jeannie opened her mouth to protest, Robert said quickly, 'Please, at least let me do this. I can find one for you much quicker in the motor. And besides, it is my nephew or niece who's about to be born, you know.'

Jeannie closed her mouth and nodded swiftly. 'Thank you. That would be kind of you.'

For a brief moment they stared at each other and then he was running back towards his car.

So, thought Jeannie, as she stood watching as Robert steered the car away from the pavement and sped down the road, at least one member of the Hayes-Gorton family is willing to acknowledge that the child is Francis's.

Twenty-Three

It was while she was still bending over poor Grace, mopping the beads of sweat from the girl's forehead, noticing how the girl's face was now grey with fatigue, how the dark shadows beneath her eyes deepened to black rings, that Jeannie felt the first pain low in her groin.

'Oh not now, please, not now.'

She said nothing to anyone else and the pains, whilst persisting, were only at half-hourly intervals. For the moment her whole attention was upon Grace. The girl, weak with exhaustion, could no longer help Aggie and the doctor – the Gorton family's own – bring her child into the world.

'There's nothing else for it,' Jeannie heard the doctor mutter. 'She's slipping away from us.'

Dimly, she was aware that the doctor had flung his instruments aside, rolled up his sleeve and – though she couldn't quite be sure afterwards – seemed to delve into Grace and pull the infant from her with his bare hand. The young mother, now almost unconscious, gave only the faintest of gasps, though Jeannie imagined that the pain must have torn her apart.

In contrast, four hours later, in Nell's bed, Jeannie gave birth to a fine, lusty squalling boy who slipped into the world with the minimum of fuss and trouble. The doctor, returning on Robert's insistence, examined her and pronounced Jeannie 'as strong as an ox' before shaking his head sadly and returning to the other bedroom that was strangely and ominously silent. There was not even the sound of a newborn baby's wails.

As Jeannie put her son to her breast for the first time, Aggie, standing watching, said, 'It's a good thing you've plenty of milk already, Jeannie. I'm very much afraid . . .' her voice broke as she added, 'that you're going to have to feed two now.'

Tired and triumphant, but certainly not exhausted, Jeannie looked up at her noticing, for the first time, that Aggie's face was distraught.

'What is it?' Jeannie whispered, suddenly afraid. 'Tell me?'

'It's Grace . . .' The older woman's face crumpled and tears welled in her eyes and trickled down her cheeks. 'She's gone, my dear. Too weak to fight any more. And I don't think she had the will.'

Jeannie closed her eyes and bent her head over her tiny son, who, oblivious to his mother's tears falling on to his downy head, sucked noisily at her breast. Then Jeannie raised her head and said, 'Bring the child to me. Bring me Grace's son.'

A smile flickered briefly on Aggie's face. 'I knew you'd do it. I told Nell, you would. Salt of the earth, I told her. Jeannie'll cope with the two of them.'

'You've spoken to Nell?' Jeannie asked in surprise. 'How is she? Is she – all right?'

Aggie lifted her shoulders. 'I've tried to talk to her, but she won't speak to me. Won't leave that net on the wall to look at the babies.' Harshly, she added, 'Who knows what Nell Lawrence is thinking. She's a hard woman.'

But Jeannie was shaking her head. 'No, no. It's just her

way of coping.' And privately she thought, once Aggie was gone, out of the house, Nell would come up the stairs to see her two grandsons.

But Nell did not mount the stairs, did not even come to see if there was anything Jeannie needed. She did not even come to see her still and silent daughter.

Tom did not arrive home in time for his sister's funeral though Jeannie waited as long as she could before arranging the ceremony. Robert came with the news. 'The *North Star* has put into a small fishing port on the Scottish coast for urgent repairs. They're all safe,' he added hastily, reaching out in his concern to touch Nell's hand, 'I promise you, but they're landing their catch there so they'll be going straight back to sea. We have an agent in that area who's arranging everything, so Tom won't be home for a while. Although I could . . .' he appeared to be thinking quickly, 'send word for him to come home by train.'

Quickly Nell shook her head. 'No, no, sir. You've been very kind, but it would leave the crew short.' Even amidst her own troubles, a small smile touched her lips. 'And I know what trouble that causes. My – my George used to tell me that if they could stand, they had to be on deck.' It was the first time Nell had spoken in the two days since Grace's death.

Robert smiled gently down at the woman who, over the past few months, had had so much tragedy to bear.

And Jeannie. His Jeannie, as he thought of her within the secrecy of his own mind. She was still so young and yet womanhood had been thrust upon her. His glance went to her now as she bent over the two cradles, her beautiful hair falling around her face as she tucked the coverlet

199

gently around her sleeping son. As she straightened up, her gaze met his and she gestured towards the other crib.

'Would – would you like to see him?' she asked quietly and Robert knew she was pointing to the child that was his brother's son.

Robert nodded and moved forward to look down upon the tiny sleeping form. 'Is he all right?' he murmured. 'I mean – I know the birth was very difficult and in the circumstances . . .' His voice trailed away as he felt himself on delicate ground.

'He's fine. A little small, especially considering he was overdue, but poor Grace had been . . .' She sighed. 'Well, she didn't look after herself properly. She was thin and ill even before the birth.'

'I am so sorry.'

Gently, she said, 'It's no' your fault, nor ours either. We – her mother and me . . .' Deliberately, she glanced at Nell not wanting the older woman to be excluded, trying to convey to her that she bore no grudge towards her mother-in-law for what had passed in this house on the day of Grace's death or during all the months preceding it. She could understand how Nell had felt even though she did not condone her behaviour towards Grace. 'We did all we could,' Jeannie said, firmly including Nell and deliberately sharing in whatever emotions Nell must now be feeling. 'But we both feel guilty for all that . . .' She left the words hanging in the air. As Aggie had said, the poor girl had not had the will to go on living, not even for the sake of her child.

Robert bent over the cradle and reached out with a gentle finger to touch the baby's head. Wordlessly, he straightened up but stood looking down at the tiny scrap of humanity for a long time. Then he cleared his throat, turned to Jeannie and asked, 'May – may I see your son?'

'Of course.' She gestured towards the other cradle

where the infant also lay sleeping. Robert felt a moment's surprise. Despite the fact that they had been born on the same day, this child looked much bigger than the other one. The fair, downy hair that covered his scalp already had a touch of ginger in it. Robert felt a fond smile twitch his mouth in spite of the sadness that was in this house. Already, he could tell which was Jeannie's child.

How he wished with all his heart that this child were his. He glanced back at the other cradle. But he did have a connection now to this family. A genuine reason for involving himself in their welfare. From his pocket, he took out two small silver coins and placed one on each pillow beside the sleeping baby boys.

'Thank you,' he heard Jeannie whisper, and knew that the gratitude in her eyes was more than for the money itself. He knew it was a Scottish custom and guessed that it was one Jeannie would hold dear.

He turned to face both women and said, 'I hope you will allow me to – to see my nephew from time to time and I hope also that if there is anything – anything at all you need – you will let me know. I can only once more express my sorrow that my family has treated yours so – so shabbily.'

There was nothing more to be said, nothing more he could say, but he would have been gratified if he had heard the conversation in the kitchen after his departure.

'He's a kind young man,' Nell said, speaking to Jeannie directly for the first time since her stony-faced rage at Aggie Turnbull being asked into her home.

'Yes,' Jeannie said slowly. 'I think, perhaps, in the past, I have misjudged him.'

'Sit you down, hen. I'll get us a bite of dinner. You must rest, y'ken, if you're to feed both bairns.'

Jeannie, with a small smile on her mouth, did as Nell said. It had taken Robert Hayes-Gorton's visit to melt the ice around Nell's heart and Jeannie was more than ever grateful to him for his visit.

'And what, pray, is the attraction in Baldock Street?' Louise asked and Robert looked up to see his wife's lip curl with distaste on the last two words of her question.

They were seated at the Hathersage family breakfast table and it seemed to Robert that if Louise wanted to pick a quarrel – as indeed she so often did these days – she always chose a time when she had the support of her doting papa. And meal times were an ideal opportunity.

Robert felt the muscles in the back of his neck tighten with tension as he decided prevarication was not the answer. Boldly, and without even glancing towards his father-in-law yet knowing both Louise's parents were listening intently, Robert said, 'It's where the Lawrence family live and – as you may recall . . .' he bit back the sarcasm that threatened to line his words, 'they've had more than their fair share of trouble just lately.'

Louise cut her bacon and slanted her glance across the table as she did so. 'Most of it brought on by themselves, I don't doubt. But, if what I hear is true, I understand you are not entirely blameless.'

Robert swallowed. Surely Mr Hathersage had not betrayed his confidence and told his daughter? he thought, but at her next words it was obvious that was exactly the case, particularly as Hathersage himself began to bluster. 'Now, now, my dear, this is hardly the sort of talk for the breakfast table and in front of your mother too.'

Louise's blue eyes flashed towards her father and her lips pouted petulantly. 'If what you said to me last night is true, then it's all my mother's fault that my husband seeks his comfort elsewhere.'

To Robert's consternation, tears brimmed her eyes. He leant across the table towards her and started to say quietly, 'Louise, we should talk about this in private—' but he was interrupted by Mrs Hathersage's voice from the other end of the table rising shrilly. 'What? Henry, what on earth have you been saying?'

Now, even her father cast a half-despairing, half-exasperated glance at Louise. He rose from the table, leaving his half-eaten breakfast, flinging his morning paper to the floor. 'I'm going to the office. I won't be in for lunch and probably not dinner either. I, too . . .' Now he wagged his forefinger down the length of the table towards his wife. 'I, too, will find my *comforts* elsewhere, though I make no secret of the fact.'

'Well, really,' Mrs Hathersage said as the door slammed behind her husband. 'What is the world coming to when a man speaks like that to his wife.' With delicate fastidiousness, she pressed her napkin to her lips.

Robert stood up. 'I must go. I have a funeral to attend this morning.'

'In Baldock Street, I take it?' was Louise's parting shot.

There were two people who stood apart from the family members at Grace's funeral, though they did not stand together. A little way off, but in no way trying to hide his presence there, stood Robert. Beneath the trees and deliberately trying to keep herself from being seen was Aggie Turnbull.

But Jeannie spotted her. Jeannie saw them both, though she hoped that Nell had not seen Aggie. It was a pathetically small gathering around the grave side, Jeannie thought. Just Nell and herself and one or two neighbours. It seemed so few for a young girl whose loss should have been mourned by many.

As the committal ended and the mourners moved away, leaving only Nell and Jeannie looking down into the grave to take their last sight of the coffin, Robert moved forward.

'Mrs Lawrence,' he said softly. 'I'm so very sorry.'

Nell, her arm tightly through Jeannie's and leaning against her, looked up at him. Her face was drawn, pinched with sorrow, but her eyes behind her steel-rimmed spectacles were dry. It seemed, however, that she could not speak, for she just nodded in answer to his condolence and Jeannie felt her arm squeezed even more fiercely.

'Would you allow me to take you home in the car—' he began but Jeannie cut in sharply.

'No . . .' Then realizing her brusqueness she added, 'No, thank you. It's kind of you, but it's not far and . . .' She glanced around at the neighbours who were still lingering in the churchyard, still watching.

'I understand,' Robert said at once. 'I'll be going then, but I just thought you might like to know,' his brown eyes were full of sympathy as they turned back to Nell, 'we've had word that your son's ship is at sea again and all is well, but – I am sorry – it's as I thought. They're going back to the fishing grounds again before they come home.'

Wordlessly, Nell nodded again but it was Jeannie who said, 'Thank you for letting us know.'

Robert gave a slight bow, put on his black hat and said, 'I'll call to see you in a day or two, if I may.'

Now it was Jeannie who merely nodded and did not speak.

As the funeral party dispersed, Robert to his motor car, Nell and Jeannie to walk back home to offer tea and sandwiches to those neighbours who cared to call in, only Aggie Turnbull still stood beneath the shadows of the trees, watching everything that went on.

Twenty-Four

When Tom first saw his son, the child was almost a month old. It was a difficult moment, Jeannie realized, for although he had already been told of his sister's death and knew her funeral had taken place, the joy in the birth of his son was marred by his sorrow. As he stood looking down at the sleeping boy, he said, 'He's like me dad.' A slow smile spread across his face. 'I'm glad about that.'

'Grace's bairn is fair too,' Jeannie said softly. 'They're very alike. At least, at the moment.' She gestured towards the other cradle where the baby made snuffling, whimpering noises.

'Aren't you going to move it away? It'll wake *him*.' There was a harshness, a strange belligerence in Tom's tone.

'They don't wake each other. Not often, anyway.' She watched Tom's face as his gaze remained firmly fixed upon his own child.

'Aren't you going to look at your nephew?'

She saw him stiffen and glance up at her. 'I aren't interested in it.'

Jeannie stared at him. 'What on earth do you mean?'

He shrugged his huge shoulders. 'What I say,' he said curtly. 'It's nowt to do wi' me. Anyway, what's going to happen to it? Mr Francis Hayes-Gorton going to look after his bastard, is he?'

205

'No,' Jeannie said sharply. 'We're going to look after it – him.' She altered her words quickly.

'Oh no, we're not.'

Jeannie stood facing him, anger welling up inside her. 'What on earth do you mean?' She leant closer to him, her glance raking his face, trying to read the meaning behind his words. 'If you think the Hayes-Gortons are going to do anything, then you're mistaken. Mr Robert's been very kind, but even he . . .'

'Oh aye. Mr Robert. Mr bloody Robert Hayes-Gorton's nearly worn a path in the road leading to this door whilst I've been away, by what I've heard.'

Jeannie stepped back suddenly, as if he had physically hit her. She found, to her surprise, that she was defending Robert. 'He was genuinely sorry. He's been trying to do something to help Grace's bairn.'

'Trying to help himself, more like.'

She shook her head, bewildered. She did not think herself naive or stupid, but she could not guess what Tom meant. 'What *are* you talking about?'

'He's been coming here, hasn't he?'

'Yes, but I've told you—'

'To see *you*.' Whilst she knew herself innocent of his accusation, Jeannie could not help a quiver of embarrassment. Perhaps, she thought suddenly, perhaps Robert was visiting a little too often. In the dark recess of her mind she remembered her wedding day and almost felt again the touch of his lips on her cheek. Because she had secretly acknowledged the change in her own feelings towards Robert, now she could feel the colour creeping into her face.

Tom jabbed his finger into her chest. 'Aggie ses—'

'Aggie? You've been to see Aggie before you even came home to see your wife and your bairn for the first time?'

'No, no, of course, I didn't.' Now Tom was on the defensive and Jeannie knew intuitively that in his temper he had said more than he had intended. 'She – she was on the dockside when the boats came in.' He spread his hands in a gesture of appeal. 'Jeannie – you know she always is.'

In this Jeannie knew he was speaking the truth. Mollified a little, she said, 'Aye well, maybe so. But you shouldna have listened to her gossip. For all that she helped us at the births, she's still a blether.'

'Eh?' Now it was Tom's turn to look mystified. 'Here? She was here? I don't believe it. Me mam would never let her across that threshold.' He flung out his hand towards the door to emphasize his words.

'She had no choice,' Jeannie said and told him all that had happened, ending by adding, 'and she came to Grace's funeral, though she kept well out of sight. But I saw her there, standing beneath the trees.'

Tom said, his voice quieter now, 'I think she was very fond of our Grace.'

'Aye well,' Jeannie sighed. 'Maybe so, but it was at her place that Grace's troubles started. Aggie condoned what was going on. Encouraged it even. Never forget that.'

Now Tom looked a little sheepish. As if wanting to change the subject he glanced again towards the other cradle. 'So, you want to keep him, eh?'

Jeannie's anger flared. 'You sound as if you're talking about a kitten or a puppy, Tom. The wee man is your nephew and your mother's grandchild. Her first grandchild, as a matter of fact, for he was born a few hours before our own son.'

For a long moment, there was a heavy silence between them, then the man turned away with an angry, defeated movement. 'Have it your own way then, but don't expect me to treat him like I'll treat me own.'

207

He slammed out of the house, leaving Jeannie staring after him wondering how a man could be so callous towards the tiny mite.

She had thought Tom like his own father, and so consequently, like her own.

But the man she was seeing now was nothing like the kind-hearted Angus Buchanan.

'We're going to have to decide on names,' Jeannie said, forcing a brightness into her tone. 'We really can't go on calling them Grace's bairn and young Tom, can we?'

'What does Tom say?' Nell asked.

Jeannie sighed. 'He's leaving it to us.'

Nell glanced at her over the top of her spectacles. 'Don't let him worry you, Jeannie. We'll take him at his word. Now then . . .' Nell came and sat down at the table. 'Make us a cup of tea, hen, and let's think.'

Jeannie set the kettle to boil and laid the cups out. 'Well, of course, our way . . .' she began, referring to the Scottish custom, 'would be to call Grace's bairn Samuel and ours, George.'

Nell nodded. 'After their paternal grandfathers.' She was thoughtful for a moment. 'I wonder what Grace would have wanted,' she murmured sadly.

'Probably "Francis" but I don't think we should do that. It would look a bit pointed, wouldn't it?'

Nell sighed. 'Aye, I dinna want any more trouble or bad feeling. Tom's got to keep his livelihood.'

Jeannie felt the older woman's sharp eyes on her. 'Not happy about Grace's bairn, is he?'

'No,' Jeannie said shortly, 'but I told him, the wee man bides here.'

'Thank you, hen,' Nell said simply. Jeannie said nothing but marvelled at the change in the woman since Grace's death and the birth of her two grandsons. Nell bore none of the resentment towards Grace's child that she had shown to his mother in the final months of her life. Jeannie thought the saying that 'they bring their love with them' was very true in this case. How she wished Tom could feel the same. And now, the poor woman must be feeling overwhelmed with remorse for the way she had treated her daughter.

Jeannie reached out and touched the wrinkled hands, lying, idly for once, on the table. 'So,' she asked softly, 'what are we going to call them?'

'We-ell,' Nell said slowly. 'I rather like Samuel and . . .' She pushed her spectacles up her nose. 'And my George's second name was Joseph, and it was my father's name too, but do you like it?'

Jeannie's smile widened. 'We'll christen him George Joseph then, just like his grandfather, but call him Joe. And yes, we'll call Grace's boy, Samuel, after old man Hayes-Gorton.' She laughed, her green eyes glinting with mischief. 'You never know, he might inherit a fortune.'

Now Nell laughed too. 'I shouldna hold your breath, hen. That'll no' happen as long as there's fish in the sea.'

So, on Tom's next time ashore the two little boys were christened in the church where Jeannie and Tom had been married and this time, Jeannie was relieved to see, Robert Hayes-Gorton did not put in an appearance.

Robert was restless and he knew why. He was aware that at this very moment his nephew and Jeannie's son were being christened and he was finding it difficult to resist the urge to go to the church.

Instead, he went in search of his wife. 'Louise, are you busy?'

Considering she was lying on a sofa, a box of chocolates at her elbow and a book lying open on her knee, it was a silly question, but he had learnt not to presume. Amused, he watched her glance up at him with a mixed expression of coyness and suspicion. 'That depends,' she said archly. She, too, had learnt not to be too hasty with her replies. Whatever it was he wanted, it might of course be something distasteful to Louise, but on the other hand, her husband was capable of nice surprises now and again. Robert hid his smile, realizing that his wife had learnt caution.

'My dear, I'd like to take you for a drive. I have something I'd like to show you. Something I'd like your opinion about.'

'Really?' At once, Louise's interest was aroused. She flung aside her book and swung her shapely legs to the floor. 'Is it something nice?'

'I'm hoping you'll think so,' he replied mysteriously.

'Oh, you tease.' Louise pecked him on the cheek before running from the room. 'I'll just get my coat.'

Half an hour later when Louise had not only 'got her coat' but had renewed her lipstick, powdered her face and changed her dress three times before she found one that suited an outing in the motor car, they were driving from the Hathersage mansion towards the town.

'Are we going shopping?' Louise leant against his shoulder and twisted her head to look up at him.

'Sort of,' he laughed, 'but not quite the sort of shopping you mean.'

Louise pouted prettily, but for once it was deliberate pretence. She was still intrigued.

Just before they reached the outskirts of the town,

Robert turned to the left down a country road for a distance of about half a mile and drew to a halt outside a square Georgian house set in an acre of gardens bordered by trees. It was nowhere near the proportions of the Hathersage home but it was an elegant country house.

'Now,' Robert said, leaning forward, his arms resting on the driving wheel. 'What do you think to that?'

'It's nice, but . . .' Louise looked at him and her eyes widened. 'Oh! For us, you mean?'

'Well, only if you like it?'

'But we're all right at home, aren't we?'

He thought he detected a little note of fear in her voice, as if she were afraid to leave the protection of her parents' home. As if, once in their own home, she was afraid of what her husband might demand of her.

Carefully, Robert took her hand in his. 'Louise, my dear, I know certain aspects of being married are – well – difficult for you.'

'Robert, please, I . . .' She made to pull her hand away but he held it firmly.

'No, my dear, listen to me, please, because we need to talk about this.'

Reluctantly, she left her hand in his, but her pout was no longer a teasing pretence.

Quietly, as if talking to a child, he said, 'And I do understand, really I do. It's – not altogether your fault. But we are married and even if – if, well, we can't be man and wife in that way, there's no reason why we can't have a home of our own. Louise, we can be friends with each other, can't we?'

Her blue eyes were large in her perfect doll's face. 'You mean, you mean you're not going to ask me to . . .? You know?'

He looked down at her, their faces, for a moment, close

together. 'My dear, I'd like nothing better than for us to be man and wife in every sense, but I am not going to force myself on you. I – I'm not that kind of man.' As he spoke the words he blotted out the shameful memory and yet he knew he spoke the truth, for that dreadful night had not been of his making.

He was startled to see tears well in Louise's eyes. 'Oh Robert, you are perfectly sweet and you make me feel so awful.'

Now he felt pity for her overriding his own disappointment. He patted her hand tenderly. 'I don't want you to feel awful. I just want us both to make the best out of this marriage that we find ourselves in.'

She nodded and with a sudden flash of wisdom that he had never before credited her with, Louise said, 'Yes, we were rather pushed into it, weren't we? I – I am sorry if you feel, well, let down. I – I am very fond of you, Robert.'

His only answer was to lay his lips gently against her forehead, trying to blot out thoughts of a red-haired girl with sparkling green eyes. Then, forcing gaiety, he said, 'I've got the key to the house. Shall we go inside and take a look?'

Like an excited child, Louise clapped her hands. 'Oh yes.'

Half an hour later, when they had gone from room to room, Louise running ahead, exclaiming each time, 'Oh yes, yes. Oh Robert, it could be such a beautiful house. It needs redecorating throughout, but it's got such promise. Just look at these lovely French windows leading out on to the terrace. What summer parties we could have out there. Oh darling, it's perfect. Do let's buy it. Daddy will help us, I know he will.'

Robert smiled. 'There's no need, my dear. On my twenty-first birthday, I inherited a legacy from my maternal grandfather. It was divided equally between the three of us and my share should be enough to buy this house and for you to be able to have it decorated and refurbished just as you wish.'

Louise stood perfectly still for a moment. 'Oh Robert,' she whispered, 'you do spoil me. I – I don't deserve it.' She came towards him and put the flat of her palms on his chest. Looking up into his eyes, she stood on tiptoe and gently kissed his mouth. 'I'll try to be a – a good wife to you, Robert. Truly I will.'

Automatically, he returned her kiss gently, but he felt no stirrings of passion. All he could think of was the little christening party that would be coming out of the church about now.

'Weren't they good? No' a peep out of either of them all the time.' Back in the terraced house, Nell was bustling about her kitchen more like her old self than at any time since the death of her husband.

Jeannie smiled as she sat down before the fire and opened her blouse to feed the two babies. 'I thought they were supposed to bawl lustily to drive out the devil,' she laughed and Nell joined in.

As Jeannie put Sammy to her breast she glanced up to see Tom watching her with bitter resentment. Harshly he said, 'Shouldn't you feed Joe first?'

Anger flashed in Jeannie's eyes but she managed to keep her voice calm as she said, 'I haven't enough milk for both now, so they take it in turns and the other one has the bottle.'

Tom gave a grunt. She saw his gaze on her breasts and saw the desire leap into his eyes. And there was something else there too. Jealousy, she supposed. Abruptly, he turned away and blundered towards the door. Sighing, she watched him go and, as the door slammed behind him, she wondered briefly whether it was the pub he was heading for – or Aggie Turnbull's.

Twenty-Five

Robert came rarely to Baldock Street now and, whilst part of her was pleased that Aggie no longer had reason to spread vicious rumours, Jeannie found she missed him.

It was from Nell that she learnt the possible reason. 'Have you heard, hen, about the big house that Mr Robert has bought?' Nell was sitting in the wooden rocking chair, nursing Sammy, gently moving backwards and forwards. 'They say he's letting his wife have a free hand in all the renovations.'

Jeannie lowered her head over Joe, whose sturdy legs were kicking so strongly that she found changing his nappy difficult. 'My, who's a strong boy then.' Keeping her voice level and making it deliberately disinterested, she said, 'No, I hadna heard.'

'That'll be why he's not been down to see the bairn.' Nell glanced down at the sleeping infant in her arms. 'But he's still sending the money every month, just like he promised. He's as good as his word, I'll say that for him. And it was kind of him to send that big pram so that you can wheel them both out together. Do you think he chose it himself?'

Now Jeannie laughed. 'No. He'd send one of their employees. Someone from the office, I expect.'

Nell was quiet for a moment, then she said slowly. 'At least he's taking more of an interest than the bairn's father.

You – you dinna think that . . .?' She stopped and Jeannie prompted, 'What?'

'Well, that Grace might have been protecting him. That it was Mr Robert after all and not the other one?'

'No,' Jeannie said sharply and when Nell glanced at her in surprise she realized that her denial had been too swift. 'No. Dinna forget, I saw them together. I was there when she told Mr Francis. If you could have seen the way she looked at him, there was no mistake that it was him she was in love with.' Jeannie sighed and muttered, 'Poor Grace.'

Now there was silence between the two women, each busy with her own thoughts, and the only sounds in the kitchen came from the two babies.

'We must have a party to celebrate your twenty-first birthday, Robert and the completion of all the renovations to the house. Mr Portus,' Louise referred to the builder, 'says we can move in as soon as we like. Everything's finished.' She linked her arm through his. 'You must come and see it. I'm dying to show you everything. I just hope you like it.' She pulled a face like a little girl pretending to be fearful of his displeasure.

He patted her hand. 'Of course I shall like it, my dear, if you're happy with everything.'

When he saw the house, Robert was hard pressed not to blurt out his disappointment. He could see at once that his wife had been heavily influenced by her London friend and everywhere he could see Madeleine's hand in the choice of decor.

Louise led the way across the new parquet flooring in the hall. 'I wanted to achieve a feeling of spaciousness and elegance,' she said.

Robert glanced wryly at the only furniture in the large hall; a small table set against the wall with a mirror above it. For 'madam' to check her appearance just before going out, he presumed. Two chairs on either side were the only other items.

'Where's the hat-stand?' he murmured.

'Oh darling! There's a teeny cloakroom through that door. I don't want hats and coats cluttering the place.'

She threw open a door to the left. 'This is the morning room, and this . . .' the door to the right of the hall, '. . . the dining room. And this, next to the dining room, is the sitting room.'

As Robert stepped into it, he imagined for a moment that the store had not yet delivered the furniture. But then he realized. This was all there was. A large sofa and two armchairs, a small table and a cocktail cabinet.

'I thought we might have a baby grand piano in that corner, darling.'

'But neither of us play.'

'I know, but they look so elegant with silver framed photos on the top, don't you think? Besides,' she waved her hand, 'when we have parties, *someone* will play.' Louise fluttered her eyelashes and added, 'Your brother, Francis, plays, doesn't he?'

'Mm.' Robert was only half listening, his glance still roaming around the room.

He said nothing more until he had toured the whole house, even the kitchen.

'You don't like it, do you? I can see you don't.' Louise's voice was high-pitched.

Setting a smile on his mouth, Robert turned to face her. 'Of course, I do. It's wonderful. Very – tasteful.' But try as he might, he could not feign the enthusiastic praise she wanted to hear. Her voice rose hysterically,

'You don't like it. Oh, you've spoiled everything. *Everything*.'

Louise burst into tears and rushed from the room whilst Robert stood helplessly listening to the sound of her wild crying as she ran up the stairs. Then he heard the slam of the door of the master bedroom and heard the key turn in the lock leaving him standing alone amidst the cold, stark emptiness of the newly decorated house.

Unbidden, came the picture of the tiny terraced house in Baldock Street; overcrowded and never free of the reek of fish from the nearby docks and the ever-present net on the wall to remind them of the constant need for work. But that house, Robert thought, was more of a home than this palace would ever be.

'I'm just taking the boys for a walk. They'll soon be too big to go out in the pram together.' Winter had given way to spring and summer once more and the two boys, at nearly eight months old, were growing rapidly.

'Aye. They'll be walking before ye ken.' Nell nodded fondly towards her two grandsons. 'Then we'll be needin' eyes in the back o' our heeds! But I have to say, Jeannie, you've been a grand lass rearing them both. It's been like having twins for you.'

'It's perhaps a little unfair to say so,' she said, thinking of Grace. 'But to be honest, I do think of them both as my own now. Perhaps I shouldn't.'

'Aye well,' Nell said. 'Grace wouldna have minded. And the bairn needs a mother's love.'

'And a grandmother's. I couldna cope without you, you know,' Jeannie said softly.

Nell flapped her hand as if to dismiss the compliment

but Jeannie saw the pink flush of pleasure on the woman's face. 'Och, awa' with you and have your walk.'

It was a bright blustery June day and Jeannie walked through the streets scarcely noticing the distance she was covering until she came to the outskirts of the town and found herself in a country road.

The two boys, their heads at either end of the pram, were fast asleep. Jeannie smiled down at the round little faces, soft in repose. She was wandering aimlessly, enjoying the fresh air of the countryside away from the ever-present stink of fish, feeling the warmth of the sun on her back. It seemed so quiet, so peaceful out here and reminded her sharply of the fields behind the village back home.

As she heard the sound of a motor car approaching from behind she pushed the pram on to the grass verge and waited until the vehicle should pass her. But it did not. The motor stopped and the engine died. When she turned to look over her shoulder, she saw Robert emerging from behind the wheel. She felt the colour pink in her cheeks and glanced away from him, suddenly shy as if she had been caught in a place she should not be.

He came close and said simply, 'Jeannie.'

Then she looked at him, screwing up her eyes against the sunlight behind him.

'Mr Robert. I . . .' There was so much she could say, so much she wanted to say and yet, now, the words would not come.

It seemed as if he felt the same; for a long moment they just stood staring at each other. Then he removed his hat and swept his hand through his hair.

'How are you?' His voice was deep and gentle. 'And how is Samuel?'

It seemed strange to hear the child called by his proper Christian name.

'He – he's fine.'

'And your boy? Joseph, isn't it?'

Now she smiled but there was a tinge of sadness in her tone as she said, 'They are both my boys, Mr Robert. I never think of them as being anything else. Not now.' Silently, she thought, I just wish Tom would feel the same.

'Of course not,' Robert said swiftly. 'I'm sorry.' He smiled ruefully. 'It's a word I often seem to be saying to you, isn't it, Jeannie? Sorry.'

'There's no need, not now,' she said gently. 'That's long forgotten.'

'And,' he said, his voice suddenly so deep and quiet that she scarcely heard, 'and forgiven?'

Her throat was suddenly strangely constricted and all she could do was nod.

'You don't know how very happy that makes me, Jeannie.'

There was an awkward pause and then he cleared his throat and said, more briskly, 'Would you like to come up to the house? The gates are just here . . .'

She turned to look over her shoulder at two huge black wrought-iron gates and the sweeping drive that led up to a house nestling against a background of trees.

Startled, she said, 'Is this your house? Och no, I couldna. I mean . . .' In the shaded lane, with the sun beating down, she was suddenly hot. 'It wouldna be right.'

'My wife's away in London and there are no servants here today.'

'Then it certainly wouldna be right,' Jeannie said crisply. Though her heart was traitor to her words and beat faster at the very thought of being alone with him.

'I didn't mean to offend you. I'm sorry . . .' he began

and then laughed at himself. 'There I go again.' And the tension between them lightened.

From the pram there came a whimper as Sammy stirred and began to wake.

'I must be getting back. It's quite a walk.'

'Let me drive you.'

'No, no.' Now her voice was sharp again at the thought of the Hayes-Gorton motor car pulling up outside the house in Baldock Street and all the gossip that would cause. 'It's kind of you, but I'd rather not.'

He nodded. 'I understand,' he said and she knew that he did.

They talked for a few moments longer and then, when she turned the pram around and said again, 'I really must go,' he turned back to his motor, swung the starting handle, climbed up and in a moment was driving through the gates and up the driveway towards the house.

Jeannie stood at the gates watching him go. Then she turned and began to push the heavy pram back towards the town feeling suddenly lonelier than she could ever remember feeling in her life before this moment.

Part Two

Twenty-Six

'Those two lads are always fighting. Can't you handle them, Jeannie?' Tom complained irritably.

'Well, you're their father. You do something.'

He glared at her. 'I'm Joe's father,' he said pointedly.

'Canna you spare a mite of affection for the wee man? Sammy is your nephew, whether you like it or no',' Jeannie snapped, weary of his attitude that had never softened in the thirteen years since the birth of the two boys.

Tom leant back in his chair, put his feet on the brass fender and wriggled his toes. 'Ah,' he said with satisfaction. He opened his newspaper. 'Maybe so,' he said, grudging to acknowledge even that much. 'But I don't see enough of my own son when I'm hardly ever here, never mind me sister's bastard.'

'You're ashore more than most.' The words were out of her mouth before she could stop them.

The paper was crumpled to his lap in a fierce, angry movement. 'And what's that supposed to mean?'

Jeannie sighed, wishing sometimes that she could hold her runaway mouth in check. Now they were heading for yet another row.

'You should try it on a bloody boat out in the Arctic ocean in a force nine gale and still expected to gut fish on deck. You don't know you're born, woman. Nice, cosy little house you've got here with only two lads to look after . . .'

And your mother, she wanted to retort, whose mind's beginning to wander now. But she held her tongue. She had not yet told him that she was worried about Nell's health. The woman was not old and yet some days she acted like an old lady, just sitting staring into the fire, her hands lying idly in her lap.

Nell was no longer the bustling little woman Jeannie had known when she had first arrived. Now it was Jeannie who stood hour after long hour braiding the nets against the kitchen wall.

Tom leant towards her, his mouth twisting. 'I s'pect you dream about living in a fancy house just outside town, eh? Still coming here, is he?'

Jeannie's heart lurched, but she managed to return his glare calmly and steadily. 'Who?'

But as Tom opened his mouth again, she realized that it would look more suspicious than ever if she made out that she did not understand that he was referring to Robert. Jeannie gave a wry laugh and said, 'Oh Mr Robert, you mean. We never see hide nor hair of him these days.' Now she deliberately laced her own voice with sarcasm for she still felt bitter towards the Hayes-Gorton family, if not so much at Robert himself now. 'I expect he feels he's discharged his duty towards his nephew.'

For a moment Tom looked nonplussed. It was not the calm reply he had expected – nor probably wanted – from her. 'What? What do you mean?'

'I told you that he'd set up a monthly payment into a post office account for me . . .' She altered her words swiftly. 'For us. Just as a gesture. He didn't have to. Mr Francis has never even acknowledged the boy as his.'

Tom gave a grunt and his scowl deepened. 'I've always had me doubts as to that anyway. I reckon it's him –

Robert. I've always thought it was him. It was him that attacked her that time, weren't it?'

No, no, no, she wanted to shout at him. I know the truth now, but you'd never listen, would you, Tom Lawrence? You're so tied up with bitterness and hatred that you can't bring yourself to hear the truth. So twisted that you take it out on a young innocent lad for the circumstances of his birth. But the words, reeling around her mind, remained unspoken. She said nothing but was glad that his train of thought had at least moved away from accusing her. But she was mistaken. 'So you haven't seen him lately?'

Her heart was thumping as she said casually, 'I canna remember when I did last see him.' She hated telling Tom a deliberate lie for she could remember very well exactly when she had last seen Robert. The day she had told him not to visit Baldock Street again.

The back door crashed open and both Tom and Jeannie looked up, startled. Tom opened his mouth to bawl at Sammy who stood in the doorway but when he saw the boy's face, even he, for once, held his anger in check.

Jeannie rushed forward. 'Oh whatever's happened, son?' Sammy's face was covered in blood from a cut on his left eyebrow. His right eye was so swollen that it was completely closed and blood and mucus oozed from his nose.

'Is it true?' He was breathing heavily through his mouth, pulling in great gasps of air. His injuries seemed not to concern him; there was something far more important on the boy's mind.

Jeannie leant down towards him and put out her hand towards his face. But he leant backwards away from her. 'What is it, Sammy?'

'Is it true?' he said again, 'that he's . . .' he flung out an arm towards Tom, 'not me dad and you're – you're . . .' the young boy's voice faltered a little, 'not me real mam?'

'Who's been saying such things?' Jeannie began angrily. 'Just you tell me . . .'

But from the hearth came Tom's voice. 'Oh tell him the truth, Jeannie, and let's be done with it. He's old enough now to know.' He turned away back to his newspaper, dismissing the whole thing as being none of his concern.

Jeannie rounded on him. 'You don't care, do you? You don't care that someone's been opening their mouth and . . . Just wait till I get ma hands on whoever . . .' She turned back again to look down at the boy who was staring up at her with his bright blue eyes. His fair curling hair was rumpled and speckled with dirt and blood. His knees were scraped and there was a tear in the elbow of his jacket. 'Who told you?' she demanded.

'Is it true?' he said doggedly, yet again ignoring her question. His voice was calmer now but there was a quiet determination in his tone that demanded to be told the truth

Jeannie put her arm about his shoulders and urged him towards the kitchen sink. 'Let me sort that cut and then we'll sit down quietly and I'll explain.'

'Oh, for God's sake,' Tom exploded. 'Just tell him. Tell him the truth. That he's my sister's bastard and that she was no better than a whore and that we're not quite sure who his father is. Mebbe it is one of the Hayes-Gorton brothers, but which one . . .' He shot a venomous look at his wife. 'Well, your guess is as good as mine.'

Tom stood up from his chair, flung the paper to the floor and marched out of the back door. 'I'm away to the Fisherman's,' he said, quite unnecessarily, and slammed the door behind him leaving a stricken young boy and an angry woman staring at each other.

Sammy stood stoically silent whilst Jeannie bathed his cuts and bruises and then allowed her to lead him towards the fire. Still he said nothing as she sat down and pulled him close to her so that he was standing beside her knee, their eyes on a level. She left her arms draped loosely around his waist. The boy made no protest but stood waiting patiently for her to explain.

First, Jeannie had a question of her own. 'Who were you fighting with? Who was it who told you?'

His voice was scarcely above a whisper. 'Joe.'

'Joe!' She was shocked. They had always squabbled and she knew that now they were older, they resorted to fisticuffs now and then. But she had still thought that it was just boyish quarrelling between two brothers. She had not realized that feelings went much deeper than that. For they were not brothers, but cousins, and now, they both knew it.

She sighed. 'Your father's . . .' she began and then stopped. Even this was not true. She began again. 'Tom had a sister called Grace. She was your mother, but she died giving birth to you and later the very same day, Joe was born.'

'So you and Dad . . .' there was the slightest hesitation over his reference to the man he had always believed to be his father, 'are Joe's Mam and Dad?'

Jeannie nodded. 'Yes, but to me, you've aye been my son too. I suckled you as a bairn and I've never treated you any differently to Joe. I've always thought of you both as my sons. My twin sons, really.'

He appeared to be thinking for a moment, then Sammy shook his head. 'Yeah, I know you have. But . . .' His blue eyes gazed earnestly into hers. 'He hasn't.'

Her arms tightened around him. 'I know,' she said softly. 'And it's never been fair. It wasn't your fault you were born, but you're the only one left for him to take it out on.'

There was silence again. Jeannie didn't need to ask how Joe had found out. People round here had long memories. Children overheard adults gossiping and so . . .

'Joe said I ain't got a dad,' Sammy's voice was small, barely audible even standing so close to her.

Jeannie almost smiled despite the emotion of the moment. 'Of course you've got a dad. Everyone has. But – well – because your mam and dad weren't married, he doesna acknowledge you as his. See?'

The boy thought for a moment and then nodded. 'I think so. But – but who is he? Do you know?'

'Mr Francis Hayes-Gorton.'

'The man who used to come here sometimes?'

Jeannie winced. Another piece of common knowledge that had obviously found its way to the boys' ears as it had to Tom's.

'No, that's his brother, Mr Robert. He's aye shown an interest in you.'

'But he doesn't come now.' The boy's voice was accusing, suggesting that the man's interest had waned.

Jeannie sighed. 'No. But that wasna his fault. I had to stop him coming.'

'Why?'

Her mouth was tight. 'Same reason that's caused today's trouble, son. Bloody neighbours blethering.'

The boy blinked. Jeannie never swore and the fact that she did so now, underlined her bitterness.

Sammy was silent for a moment and then gently he pulled away from her embrace. 'Thank you for telling me,' he said, with an unusual adult courtesy. Then he turned and walked towards the door, a defiant bearing in the set of his shoulders and a dignified carriage of his head that had not been there before. Sammy, Jeannie realized, had in the last hour, grown up. The shock he had just received would not defeat him. It would be the making of him.

Twenty-Seven

Robert stood at the long window of the drawing room and looked out upon the neat garden realizing that he was a lonely, unhappy man with little to look forward to in a desolate future. Even his visits to Baldock Street had ceased long ago.

He thought back to the last time Jeannie had opened the door to him. It was the little boys' fifth birthday and he had come loaded with presents. A new blazer for each of them for school, a pencil case and a satchel. All well-meaning gifts, yet he had learnt, many years later, that they had never been used. His middle-class offerings would have set the children apart from their peers, and Jeannie, swift to protect them, had waited to see if the boys themselves chose to use them. They never had.

But Robert remembered that day. If he closed his eyes he could still see her so clearly. Her unruly red hair twisted up onto the top of her head, her green eyes troubled and a dab of flour smudging her nose. He had longed to reach out and brush it away with a tender, loving action. But as he had taken his leave, he had stood on the doorstep listening to her words that would extinguish the only bright spot in his life.

'I'm sorry, Mr Robert,' she had said. Had it been fanciful imagination on his part, or had there been a tearful catch in her voice? 'But I'll have to ask you not to come here any more. There's been gossip.' She had given an exasperated toss of her head towards the street outside her home. 'You ken what they're like . . .'

She had not needed to say more. He could guess the rest. And now, eight years later, standing alone in the empty house, he still remembered the moment with regret for his own reaction to her words. To hide his disappointment, he had behaved like a pompous oaf, he told himself. He had raised his hat to her, given a stiff little bow, and said, 'As you wish,' then turned and walked out of her life.

As she had watched him walk away, Jeannie had thought her heart would break. But she had had no choice. After Tom's last time ashore, when he had made snide remarks about Robert's continuing visits, she had known that she would have to stop him coming to the house.

'Aggie ses Mr Robert still comes here on a Thursday afternoon, even though the lads have started school now. And that's the afternoon me mam goes out. That right?'

'No, it isna,' Jeannie had replied shortly. 'And Aggie Turnbull'd do better to mind her own business.'

'But he does come here?' Tom had refused to let the matter drop.

'He comes to see Sammy,' Jeannie had said, trying to keep her voice level, though she was fast losing patience.

'What, when he's at school? Pull the other one, Jeannie. It's you he comes to see.' He jabbed a finger towards her. 'Well, I aren't havin' it! He might let his wife mek a cuckold out of him, but I aren't. Not even if he is me boss.'

Jeannie swung round, her temper flaring now. 'How dare you accuse me of any such thing!' She advanced towards him, her own finger now wagging in his face, only inches away. 'He comes here to see the boy. Let's face it, he's the only man who does take any interest in the wee man. His father doesna and neither do you.'

For a moment Tom had looked ashamed. 'I can't help it if I can't feel the same about him as I do about our Joe.'

'Well, you could at least act it,' she had snapped back, but even as she had said the words she had known it was useless. Tom would never change in his attitude towards Sammy, nor in his jealousy over Robert Hayes-Gorton.

It was not until later, after she had spoken to Robert and told him not to visit any more, that Jeannie remembered Tom's words again and wondered what he had meant about Robert being made a cuckold. Well, she wasn't going to be able to solve that little bit of gossip and besides, it wasn't really any of her business.

She had thought her action would stop the chatter but no, even eight years after that day, it was still going on. And now wagging tongues had rocked young Sammy's world.

Well, this was her business and there was something she could do. There was only one person to blame: Aggie Turnbull.

In the years since she had come to Havelock that woman had seemed to intrude upon Jeannie's life in all sorts of ways; ways that she did not fully understand. Mention of the woman's name would upset Nell for the rest of the day and yet Tom had no compunction in talking freely about her.

It was time, Jeannie decided, that she had words with Aggie Turnbull herself.

When the door opened, Jeannie felt a smug satisfaction at the surprise on the woman's face.

'Well, well.' Aggie smiled and held the door wider, tacitly inviting Jeannie inside. 'Who'd have thought I'd ever see you on my doorstep again, Mrs Lawrence. Not requiring my midwifery services again, are you?'

'No,' Jeannie said shortly, feeling the familiar stab of disappointment that there had been no more bairns for her and Tom. 'But there is something you can do for me.'

'Do come into my drawing room.' Aggie led the way and Jeannie found herself sitting down on a silk brocade covered sofa. Aggie sat down in a matching easy chair, crossed her slim, white-stockinged legs and said, 'Now, my dear, what can I possibly do for you?'

Jeannie stared at her. It was thirteen years since she had seen Aggie close to. Not since the night the two boys had been born when, she had to admit, she had been thankful for Aggie's help. Remembering, some of the anger that had carried her here faded.

She was still much as Jeannie remembered her except that now the cosmetics could not cover the passage of the intervening years. Beneath the blonde hair, the bright lipstick and the silk dress, Aggie was growing old. She must be nearly as old as Nell, Jeannie thought, as Aggie serenely submitted herself to Jeannie's scrutiny without a trace of embarrassment, a small smile on her mouth.

Jeannie said bluntly, 'I dinna like you blethering about me. It's no' true and every time Tom comes home, he still—'

'Ah yes, Tom,' Aggie said smoothly. 'Poor Tom. Such a dear, but a little, what shall we say, weak, don't you find?'

'Weak?' Jeannie was startled.

'Mm. Isn't that what you would call it? He goes to sea for one or two trips and then suddenly there's some excuse for him to miss the next one and languish ashore for the

235

following three weeks. Then back to sea he'll go, one or two trips and then . . .' She leant forward. 'Don't tell me in all these years, you hadn't realized?'

Jeannie was silent, staring at the woman. Oh yes, of course she'd realized it. But to hear it from someone else's mouth, particularly from the likes of Aggie Turnbull, shocked her.

Aggie leant back amongst the brocade cushions and sighed, waving a slim, elegant hand in the air. 'Of course, he's not the man his father was. Now, there was a man.'

Jeannie levered herself to her feet. What on earth had possessed her to come here and why was she sitting here allowing this woman to talk about the Lawrence menfolk as if she knew them both – intimately?

Well, if she did, then Jeannie had no wish to hear about it.

'Going already?' Aggie looked up, amusement in her eyes. 'So soon?' She stood up too and now her face was suddenly serious. 'Jeannie, I know what everyone round here thinks about me and I expect you share their opinions. Well, some of it's probably true, but a lot of it isn't. One thing I will tell you, I do not spread gossip. Oh, I hear a lot. I know just about everything that goes on around here. But it wasn't me who spread the rumours about Mr Robert Hayes-Gorton and his visits to see his nephew when Tom was at sea. Nor did I tell young Joe about young Sammy's – er – origins.'

Jeannie gasped and her eyes widened. So, Aggie knew even this.

'Your gossip-monger, Jeannie, is closer to home. Someone in your own street whose lace curtains twitch every time someone sneezes.'

'Who?' Jeannie said, disbelieving.

'Well now, I'd be gossiping too if I were to tell you, now wouldn't I?'

'Och, dinna be so aggravating, Aggie Turnbull.'

At this the woman threw back her head and laughed. 'Oh Jeannie, I like you. I really like you. How I wish I had a friend like you.'

As Jeannie opened her mouth to make a sharp retort, Aggie held up her hand. 'Don't worry,' she said and, suddenly, Jeannie detected a note of wistfulness in her voice. 'I know it can never be. Just, my dear,' her tone was softer, gentler, 'as there can never be anything between you and Mr Robert.'

'There is nothing between us,' Jeannie retorted hotly, her face fiery red.

'I know, I know. But you'd both like there to be, wouldn't you?'

'No!' The denial was like the crack of a sail, yet both women knew it to be false.

'Why else,' Aggie asked quietly, 'would you bother to come here, to risk visiting a woman with my reputation, if there was absolutely nothing to feel the tiniest bit guilty about?'

Jeannie blundered from the room and out of the house, knowing that she had made a dreadful mistake in coming. Aggie Turnbull was nothing like the woman she had imagined her to be. She was intelligent and sharp and she had neatly turned the tables upon Jeannie.

Robert turned away from the window as he heard the rattle that heralded the arrival of the evening newspaper. Automatically, his mind still preoccupied, he walked across the tiled floor of the hall and pulled the paper from the jaws of the brass letterbox. He unfolded it and stood in the middle of the hall, staring down at the paper. The newsprint blurred before his eyes and then suddenly, it sharpened as he read the headline. A headline so dramatic that at once his thoughts were pulled back with a jolt from the events of eight years ago to the present.

'HITLER MARCHES INTO CZECHOSLOVAKIA'.

The answer to his boredom was staring up at him. With more energy and enthusiasm than he had felt for years, he flung the newspaper to the floor where it lay in a crumpled heap on the otherwise immaculate and sterile floor. Robert picked up his hat from the table and left the house, pulling the door closed behind him with the satisfied air of a decision made.

Twenty-Eight

'You are going to do what?' Samuel Hayes-Gorton rose from his swivel chair and leant on his desk towards his son standing on the opposite side.

'I said,' Robert repeated calmly, 'I am going to join the Royal Navy Volunteer Reserves.'

'Edwin,' the older man roared. 'Get in here this instant.'

A moment later the communicating door between two offices opened and Edwin poked his head round it. 'Hullo, old chap,' he beamed at his brother. 'Nice to see you back. Feeling better?'

Robert felt the colour rising in his neck and felt guilty about the small lie he had told for his absence from the family business during the past week. 'I've got the bost dreadful co'd,' he had said into the telephone five days earlier, holding his nose as he did so. 'I can't bossibly come in.' He remembered sniffing loudly and had even manufactured a sneeze.

'Of course not, Mr Robert,' Miss Jenkins, secretary to all the senior partners, had gushed. 'I do hope you'll soon be feeling better.'

And now he was back with not so much as a red nose to lend credence to his pretence. 'Fine. Didn't last long, as it happens.'

'Fine? Fine, he says?' their father boomed. 'The boy's taken leave of his senses.' He snorted derisively. 'If he ever had any.'

Edwin's puzzled glance went from one to the other. Then Samuel Hayes-Gorton flung out his arm. 'Only says he wants to join the Royal Navy. That's all.'

'The . . .?' Edwin began and then said, 'Whatever for?'

'Exactly!' Samuel bellowed again. 'Whatever for?'

'The Volunteer Reserves,' Robert corrected. 'And I shan't be going away. There'll just be training sessions once or twice a week, I expect.'

It had all seemed so easy, that spur of the moment decision standing in the empty loneliness of his house – and he used the word 'house' deliberately for it never had been and never would be a home. Not without a woman who . . . He sighed again. Not without Jeannie there. And that was another reason. Maybe if he could find some direction for his energies, he might be able to stop thinking about her every waking moment.

'Robert?' Robert heard Edwin's gentle voice interrupting his thoughts. 'Why, old chap?'

Robert lifted his shoulders. 'I just need something positive to do with my life."

'Something positive?' their father roared again. 'You don't regard running the Gorton-Hathersage Trawler Company as something positive?'

Since the alliance of the two companies through marriage, the ties had become even stronger and following the death of Henry Hathersage the two companies had merged and become the Gorton-Hathersage Trawler Company Limited. Samuel Hayes-Gorton took the Chairman's position and Francis, Managing Director. With Edwin as Company Secretary, Robert had only a seat on the Board as a Director. There was no useful position and little for him to do in the day-to-day running of the business. His role, he thought bitterly, was, and always had been, merely a means to an end.

Well, they all had the 'end' they had wanted now.

Even Louise was quite happy with the money she received as a major shareholder, though she had never bothered to attend so much as one meeting of the Board.

'Of course, Mummy's got an annuity for life but everything else comes to me,' Louise had informed Samuel Hayes-Gorton and his three sons after the reading of her father's will. 'But I don't want anything to do with the business.' She had fluttered her eyelashes and looked at each of the men in turn. 'What does silly little me know about boats and the price of fish. So, Robert is to have – what did the solicitor man call it, darling?'

'Power of attorney.'

'Oh yes. It means Robert can sign anything on my behalf. All I want,' she giggled prettily, 'is the money.'

'My dear Louise,' Francis had risen from his chair behind his desk and come round it to take her slim hand in his and raise her fingers to his lips, 'your business could not be in safer hands than your husband's and his fellow board members.' He waved his hand to encompass himself, Edwin and their father. 'You leave everything to us, my dear, and you just enjoy yourself spending the money we make for you.'

'Oh Francis, you say the sweetest things. You must come to dinner on Friday. Mustn't he, Robert?'

'Of course,' Robert murmured dutifully.

'That's settled then,' Francis said as he opened the door for her. Louise, clad in a suit with a fur stole around her shoulders and a hat with a pheasant's feather, kissed the air beside her brother-in-law's cheek.

'See you Friday,' she trilled as she left the office, but Robert had the distinct feeling that Francis had not been referring to her invitation to dine, but to the official amalgamation of the two companies which had long been his ambition.

Since then, Francis had set about systematically acquiring not only all the other small shipping companies in Havelock, but he had begun also to buy out the service industries including engineering and ship repairing, coaling and even cod liver oil production and net making.

Net making, Robert thought, immediately reminded him of Jeannie. If his brother had his way, all the nets would be made in one of his factory units and the women who worked in their own homes would lose a valuable source of a little extra income for their families.

'By God, the ingratitude.' Samuel was still shouting, bringing Robert's wandering thoughts back to the present and the bombshell he had just dropped. 'After all I've done for you, this is the thanks I get. Your duty is here with the family business and even more so if there is going to be a damned war.' He paused, waiting for some response from his son. When none came, he threatened, 'Well, if you go, boy, you go without my blessing. You'll have no part in this company ever again. I'll have you voted off the Board and I'll cut you out of my will.'

'Father, I'm superfluous in this company and you know it.' Robert's mouth tightened. 'The only useful purpose I have ever served was to be the means of an alliance between the Gorton and the Hathersage companies.'

Samuel's face turned purple. 'You make it sound like a business transaction, boy, instead of a marriage between two people, who—'

'It was,' Robert said curtly. 'You and old man Hathersage concocted the idea between you. She was his only daughter, his only child, and more than anything he wanted a grandson. You saw your chance to build your empire. But why me? Why the second son? Why not Francis?'

His father glanced away now, suddenly embarrassed

under the scrutiny of his two sons. He cleared his throat and said gruffly, 'Francis would have broken the poor girl's heart in a fortnight. The – er – kind of life he leads. You knew that at the time.'

Robert nodded slowly. 'The only trouble is, we weren't in love with each other. Not then, not now. You know she spends nearly all her time in London. Has done for years. She's there now, has been for the past week. That so-called home I bought was a last-ditch effort to try to make the marriage work. Well, I failed.'

Samuel, still belligerent, wagged his finger towards his son. 'You should have given her a child, boy. That'd've made her stay at home instead of gallivanting to the city every five minutes. You should have—'

'I tried, oh I tried, believe you me. But she wouldn't let me near her. Never has. Why do you think we came back from honeymoon early? Why do you think I spent the whole of my inheritance from my grandmother on a house for her? Why do you think I indulge her every whim?' Robert leant towards his father and slowly and deliberately, said, 'The marriage has never been consummated.'

Now Samuel's mouth dropped open. 'What?'

'You heard,' Robert said bluntly. 'And now it never will be, because I've no taste for it either.'

'Really?' Now there was sarcasm in his father's tone. 'Maybe not with your wife, but from what I've heard you're not above trips to a terraced house in Baldock Street.'

It felt as if a knife had been driven in just below his ribcage and Robert almost gasped aloud at the force of it. He stood rigidly still for a moment and then let out a long breath. So, he thought, Jeannie had had good reason to stop him going to her home. If the rumours had even reached his father, then they must certainly be rife around the docks. He pulled in a breath now and then sighed heavily. 'Like I said, I'm not much use around here anyway. You're still head of the company. Francis, for all his dissolute ways, has a superb business sense. He's proved that over the last few years. He just about controls the whole of the fish docks. And Edwin here, well, he runs the office side of things like clockwork. So what exactly is my role? Tell me, because I'd really like to know.'

For a moment Samuel blustered, refuting Robert's words, but then his voice trailed away leaving unfinished sentences.

'Precisely,' Robert said quietly and calmly now. 'Even you can't define my usefulness, can you? Look, Father, I don't want to quarrel with you. That's the last thing I want, but I want to do something useful with my life. And if,' he added sadly, 'you don't want me to be a part of the family business in the future, well,' he paused before saying, 'then so be it.'

'That's not going to happen,' Edwin's quiet voice put in now, with such a firmness in his tone that both Samuel and Robert looked at him in surprise.

'Now, don't you start—' Samuel began, but Edwin said, 'Father, the company, one day, will come to the three of us. The three Hayes-Gorton brothers. Nothing is going to change that. Francis and I wouldn't want it any different.'

'Don't you try to tell me how to arrange my own affairs.'

'I'm not,' Edwin said. He remained unruffled and there was even a small smile on his lips. 'I'm just saying that whatever happens, whatever Robert decides to do . . .' He lifted his shoulders. 'Whatever you leave in your will, Robert will always be a part of this company. Francis and I will see to it.'

'Well, I'll be damned,' Samuel sat down suddenly and heavily in his chair and rocked backwards. 'The young cubs ousting the old fox, eh?'

Edwin laughed. 'Oh, I think there's plenty of bark still left in the wily old fox yet, don't you?'

Robert looked on in amazement. His younger brother was really showing his mettle these days. Edwin turned and laid a hand on Robert's shoulder. 'I don't want you to leave the company, old chap, but you must do what you want to do. And – and I'm sorry if I've taken the role that should rightly be yours.'

Robert shook his head. 'You haven't. You're brilliant at the administration side. You've a head for figures and accountancy that I've never had. I couldn't do it anyway. Any more than I could wheel and deal like Francis does. I haven't got his – er – business acumen.' The two brothers exchanged a glance and smiled slightly at one another.

'Have you told Francis?' their father put in, glaring at Edwin. 'Are you sure he feels the same way?'

'Not yet,' Edwin said and added confidently, 'but he will.'

Samuel grunted. 'Where is he, anyway?'

Again the two brothers exchanged a glance.

'In London,' Robert said and he could not keep the edge of bitterness from his tone as he added pointedly, 'he's been there the past week.' Then, with the deliberate intention of giving his father food for thought, food that might well give him indigestion, he said slowly, 'Perhaps Francis should have been your chosen bridegroom for Louise, after all.'

'So, your fancy man's running away to sea, is he?'

Jeannie glanced quickly at her husband and then away

again. 'What are you talking about?' Then deliberately she added, '*Who* are you talking about?'

'As if you didn't know,' Tom sneered.

She turned to face him now. 'Aye, I ken. And I'm tired of it. You shouldna listen to the neighbours' blether. Mr Robert used to come here to see his nephew or to bring money for his keep. But he hasna been for years. You know that, yet still you accuse me of all sorts of dreadful things that are . . .' she stepped towards him and thrust her face close to his, 'that are not going on. D'you hear me?' She tossed her head and added, 'And whilst we're on the subject, why is your first port of call when you come ashore always to see *her*? Not quite the actions of a devoted husband, is it?'

Tom was visibly flustered. 'I don't. I mean, it isn't.'

'Really?' Now it was Jeannie's turn for sarcasm.

'I do see her. Now and again . . .' he blustered and as Jeannie's eyes flashed resentment he put out his hand as if to fend off an expected attack. 'Not for that, Jeannie. I promise you. Never for that. I never have. But – but . . .'

'But what then?'

'There's things about Aggie Turnbull and this family – our family – that you don't understand.'

'Eh?' Now Jeannie was surprised. 'What things?'

'I can't tell you. Maybe some day, but not now.'

'Huh,' Jeannie snorted. 'Well, I've heard some excuses in my time, but that's a new one. I'll ask your mother.'

'No,' Tom was shouting now. 'No, you won't. I forbid you to.'

'Forbid me?' Jeannie retorted. 'How dare you say such a thing to me?'

'Jeannie, please, don't say anything to me mam. It'll hurt her too much.'

Slowly, Jeannie nodded. 'Very well then, but only for that. And one day you'll tell me what you're on about.'

He shrugged. 'Maybe.'

'Och there's no "maybe" about it, Tom Lawrence. You will.' She paused and then asked, feeling in control now, 'So, what was it you were saying about Mr Robert?'

'He's joined the Royal Navy, they reckon. Gone away to sea. Though why he didn't just ship aboard one of his own trawlers, beats me. He could have pulled rank, as they say, and skippered a Gorton boat if he'd been so desperate to go to sea. More fool him, I say.'

Jeannie turned away hardly listening to Tom now. He didn't even come to say goodbye, was all she could think.

Twenty-Nine

A few months later, at the beginning of 1939, Tom startled Jeannie by announcing that he, too, was going to join the RNVR.

'You?' she said unable to keep the surprise from her tone. 'But if war is declared, you'd be one of the first to have to go.'

'I know.' Tom, now approaching his mid-thirties, ran his hand through his hair. He had never achieved promotion, not even to third-hand status never mind mate or skipper, but had remained a deckie all his working life. It was, Jeannie knew, because he was unreliable.

'But why?'

'All the lads are joining. You know, a sort of "Pals Battalion". A bit like they did in the last lot. And it's the obvious choice for fishermen. They reckon if the balloon does go up, the Navy will be commandeering our ships anyway. I s'pose it makes sense,' Tom shrugged. 'There won't be much point in us trying to fish in the North Sea when it's alive with enemy submarines. And there's no point in the trawlers lying idle if there's a useful job for them to do.'

'Tom,' she said, placing her hand on his arm and looking up into his face, 'don't – don't let yourself be pushed into doing something you don't really want do. I mean, just for the sake of – of how it looks.'

He stared down at her, his blue eyes troubled, his

mouth tight. And then he put his arms about her and drew her to him, resting his chin on the top of her head. 'Oh Jeannie. You know, don't you? Have you always known, how I fear the sea?'

She moved her head against his chest in a tiny movement of denial. 'No,' she said, her voice muffled against him. 'Not at first, but I began to realize.'

'When I missed a trip at the slightest opportunity, you mean?'

'Aye, something like that.'

Close to him she heard the sigh deep within his chest. Then he pulled away from her and held her at arm's length looking down into her face. 'I just wanted to be like me dad,' he said simply.

'And you went to sea because of him?'

Tom nodded. 'And now,' he said slowly, 'I'm going to get involved in this blasted war just because I still want him to be proud of me.'

'Your father would be proud of you whatever you did, Tom.'

'You think so?'

'I know so. You dinna have to keep proving yourself over and over again.'

Quietly he said, 'Maybe I do, Jeannie. Maybe I do, even if only for myself.'

'Oh Tom.' She shook her head and there were sudden tears in her eyes. 'I dinna want anything to happen to you.'

He touched her cheek with calloused fingers. 'You mean that? You really mean that?'

'Of course I do,' she said, now with a trace of impatience. Then, more gently, she added, 'But you do what you want to do for yourself. I'm not going to stand in your way, but please, Tom Lawrence, just come home safely.'

As he drew her against him and wrapped his arms about her again, now with a fierce intensity, Jeannie buried her head against his chest and closed her eyes, knowing a sudden fear for her husband.

Robert'd be safe, she told herself. With his connections, Robert would get a desk job. With his father's influence, he'd be bound to be in a safe, shore job. He wouldn't be sent to sea. At least Robert would be safe, Jeannie told herself.

But what about Tom?

On 26 August 1939, Robert, in London on business, received a telephone call. The voice on the other end of the telephone said, 'You're to report to Lieutenant-Commander Walsh at Lowestoft, Gorton, at 0.700 hours tomorrow. That's where the Royal Naval Patrol Service has been set up. Bit of a hotch-potch at the moment, but the chaps down there will soon sort it all out. Walsh asked for you personally. He'll be mustering his crew and wants you as his first lieutenant aboard a minesweeper . . .' The man went on with travel details and finished by saying, 'Walsh says you have particular knowledge of trawlers. A fisherman, are you? I know a lot have volunteered.'

'Not exactly,' Robert replied, not wanting to explain fully. 'But I do have a knowledge of trawlers, sir, yes.' He wanted, in this war in which he was obviously going to be involved now, to be treated on his own merits. Without deliberately lying, he intended to conceal the fact that he was a trawler owner with the distinction of the name Hayes-Gorton. He had considered using the name Hayes only, and dropping the Gorton, but instead had decided to drop the double-barrelled bit and become plain Robert Gorton. It was doubtful now that the Gorton-Hathersage

Trawler Company would have many ships left by the end of the conflict. He wondered what would happen to his family's business and if there would be any company left for his father to cut him out of.

He listened as the voice crackled down the wire giving him further instructions ending with the words, 'You'll be going to a place called Havelock. Ever heard of it?'

'Oh yes, sir.'

'Oh good. Can't say I have, but there you are. A chap can't know of all these little fishing villages round the coast.'

As Robert replaced the receiver, he was smiling to himself, and murmured, 'What a pity my father couldn't have heard that last remark.'

'Jeannie, I'm to report to Lowestoft along with a lot of the other lads.'

'Oh Tom. So this is it, then?'

'Looks like it.'

She watched him. There was apprehension in his eyes but something else too. Was it, could it possibly be, excitement? At his next words, Jeannie began to understand a little of what Tom was feeling.

'Me dad never went to war. He didn't serve in the last lot. I'm doing something me dad never did.'

Was that it? Was that what Tom had needed all along? The chance to emerge from the shadow of the big man and be himself? Smiling, Jeannie went to him and put her arms about his waist, saying again what she knew he needed to hear. 'We're all proud of you, Tom, and your dad would be too. Just take care of yoursel' and get home whenever you can.'

He was back in a few days and the exhilaration was gone already from his eyes. 'You'll never believe it. I've not only got drafted back to me own home town but on bloody trawlers turned into minesweepers. I'll be serving on the same bloody boats I've been on all me life. I thought at least I'd get chance to go on a proper warship or summat. But a bloody trawler . . .'

'Will you be minding your language, Tom Lawrence,' Jeannie snapped, disappointed that the first tentative signs of a change in Tom had already been swept away.

'And that's not all.' His expression was resentful, full of loathing. 'Jimmy the One on my ship is none other than Mr bloody Robert Hayes-Gorton. Lieutenant Gorton, as he wants to be known now.'

'Jimmy the Who?' Jeannie asked.

Tom clicked his tongue against his teeth with exasperation and waved his hand. 'Oh, it's the nickname they give to the first lieutenant on board ship. And do you know what I'm to be called? Sparks.'

'Sparks?' Jeannie repeated and then started to laugh. 'What on earth does that mean?'

With a sudden change of mood, Tom puffed out his chest proudly. 'I took a course to be a wireless operator when I joined the RNVR. And after the war, I could become a sparks aboard a trawler. No more eighteen hours – and longer – on deck guttin' for me, Jeannie.' He rubbed his hands together. 'Nice cosy little room for me from now on. The most important people on a trawler, is the sparks. A skipper relies on his wireless operator, he does.'

Jeannie glanced at him and then looked away. He was forgetting she was a fisherman's daughter and knew that every man aboard a trawler was just as important as the next, from skipper to galley boy. Poor Tom, she thought with sudden sympathy, always trying to prove himself and never quite managing it.

Aloud, she laughed, wanting to hold on to his sunnier

temper. 'Well, sit down to your dinner, laddie, else there'll
be sparks flying in this hoose if you let this meal go to
waste.'

'So, dear boy,' Francis said languidly, 'you're going to play
the hero at last, are you? Well, just mind you take care of
our ship and don't let her get blown up by the enemy.'

Robert grinned. 'Thanks, Francis, for your concern
about *my* safety.'

They were all gathered together to dine at Samuel
Hayes-Gorton's home, Louise and her widowed mother
being present too.

'I must say, you look awfully handsome in your uniform, darling, doesn't he, Mummy?'

Conscious that she was a guest, she smiled politely, but,
Robert noticed, the smile never reached her eyes which
remained as cold as they had always been when turned
upon him.

'We'll go to London when you come home on leave,
darling, and I can show you off to all Madeleine's friends.
Her husband's joined the RAF and they all make such a
fuss about the glamorous boys in blue, but I think the
Royal Navy uniform is even smarter.'

'Louise, it won't be safe in London from now on. You
really shouldn't go there any more.'

'Not go? Not go to London?' Louise was plainly horrified. 'Oh Robert, you know I couldn't stay and stagnate in
this place for months on end.'

'She'll be safe enough,' Francis said. 'It'll not last long
and I doubt even Herr Hitler would dare to bomb
London . . .'

*

253

Robert and Tom had been going to sea for almost two months, four or five days at a stretch then returning to Havelock for thirty-six hours or so, out of which they were allowed about eight hours ashore. On 13 November, the first bombs were dropped on British soil: the Shetlands. Jeannie read the news with horror, at once imagining part of her beloved homeland to be laid waste. People dead or dying and beginning interminable days and nights of living with constant fear. Later that same month, specially designed enemy U-boats began to lay a devastating new type of mine, the magnetic mine, around the coast of Britain. And so began a game of cat and mouse between the scientists on both sides. The one to invent newer and deadlier mechanisms, the other to find ways of destroying the mines before they blew up the convoy ships.

Already the war was a devastating reality and the two men were now engaged in trawling the icy waters of the North Sea for a far more deadly fish.

Thirty

'Why can't we go and join up like Dad?' Joe asked mutinously.

She could not remember ever having seen the two boys so united, standing shoulder to shoulder to argue with her, the common enemy. Though she had to admit that since the time Sammy had found out the circumstances of his birth, he had not allowed Joe to dominate him. The realization that Joe was his cousin, and not his brother, had strengthened the boy's character rather than weakened it. Sammy's new stance had for a time resulted in some bloody-nosed battles between the two of them. But Jeannie thought that the best way was to allow them to sort it out between themselves. Now, as they stood before her, she knew she had been right, but, she thought wryly, maybe to her own detriment.

'You're no' old enough,' she said firmly. 'You have to be eighteen at least.' She wasn't sure if that was exactly right but she was relying upon them not knowing either. 'You're only just sixteen.'

'We could sign on as cabin boys, couldn't we?' Sammy stood beside Joe. 'We're old enough for that, aren't we?'

She glanced at each of them in turn, deliberately making sure that her glance did not rest longer upon Sammy than it did upon her own son. Why was it, she thought, that fight it though she did, she could never stop feeling more for the boy that was not flesh of her flesh, bone of her

255

bone, than she did for the one who was? Just the same, her conscience pricked her, as she worried more about Robert Hayes-Gorton than she did about her own husband.

'Well, I'm signing no papers to let you go anywhere. Either of you.'

'But we look old enough.' It was Sammy who was persisting.

They did. She had to admit that. They both had fair hair and blue eyes, but there the similarity ended. Joe was the taller; he was going to be a big man like both his grandfathers as he matured and broadened out. Even now, his shoulders were muscular and his slim hips belied his strength. Already he had been at sea for a year as a deckie on one of the few battered old trawlers that still ventured into the mine-ridden waters of the North Sea. Sammy, too, was a deck-hand on a Gorton-Hathersage ship that was too old and dilapidated to be of interest to the authorities.

'Dad'll clear the channels for us,' he'd say jokingly, but Jeannie knew he was only trying to reassure her. 'He'll know where we're going.'

For the most part Joe was jovial and outgoing. The life and soul of the party, Jeannie heard him described by his pals in the Fisherman's. But his temperament was volatile; he could switch from laughter to rage in a second. And, to Jeannie's disappointment, though he was more of a born fisherman than Tom, he seemed to have inherited his father's streak of jealousy and resentment. Throughout their childhood it had always been Joe who had started the fights with Sammy, rather than, as one might have expected, the other way about.

Sammy was smaller, but stockily built. He was the quieter of the two with a placidity that belied his strength of character. He would never begin a quarrel, but once challenged he would defend himself ferociously and usually, to everyone's surprise, emerge the victor. A deep thinker, Jeannie judged him, who would weigh up the pros and cons of a situation before making his decision. Yet once that decision was made, he would not waver, despite whatever pressures were put upon him.

Jeannie suspected that this trait was inherited from his natural father. She was thankful, though, that whilst the boy vaguely resembled Francis Hayes-Gorton in looks, she was sure he had none of the man's cold, ruthless streak. When Sammy smiled, his eyes twinkled with warmth and merriment and his face creased disarmingly. A fact that had not escaped the notice of the young girls in the neighbourhood.

So she still found herself turning towards Sammy, for she knew instinctively that whereas Joe would be caught up in the glamour of being a hero, Sammy would have been the one to think it out carefully.

'We won't be in that much more danger than we are now, Mam,' he said quietly and she knew he could read the anxiety in her face.

Jeannie sighed inwardly and tried another tack. 'How would I manage Grandma without your help? At least you're home fairly regularly now.'

Nell needed constant supervision, for though she was physically well, her mind wandered so badly now that she scarcely seemed to know where she was, what time of day it was or even that there was a war going on all around them. Getting her to the Anderson shelter which the boys had constructed in the back-yard was as big a battle as any fought in the front line and without Sammy's patient coaxing and wheedling the old lady when he was home, Jeannie thought, she'd never get Tom's mother to safety.

The boys said nothing now but exchanged a glance that

spoke more than words could. 'And dinna you go planning to run away to sea together . . .' Jeannie began and as they both glanced at her with the same guilty look, she knew she had been shrewd in her guess.

But they went anyway. Four days later she found a note on the kitchen table saying that they had done just that.

'We're sorry, Mam,' the note said in Joe's untidy scrawl, 'but me and Sam have got to go.' And in Sammy's neat handwriting were the words, 'Take care of yourself and Gran. Please don't be cross. Love Sammy.'

She crumpled the note. She wasn't cross, she thought as she bit her lip to try to stop the tears from flooding her eyes and spilling down her cheeks.

Just so terribly alone.

'I wouldn't have believed it possible,' Tom was still complaining. 'After two years sweeping the bloody North Sea, we're still on the same ship. I thought at least when that mine blew our ship up we might get drafted to different ships then. But no, here we are still the same happy little band. We even got into the same lifeboat.' His voice dropped to a low growl. 'Given half a chance, I'd have let the bugger drown.'

'What on earth are you talking about?' Jeannie was exasperated now and only half-listening. Nell had wandered out in the street and had gone missing and all Tom could do was rant on about how badly life was treating him.

'Mr flaming Robert Hayes-Gorton. That's who I'm talking about. Only he's a bloody lieutenant now, ain't he? I'm still taking orders from him.' He punched one fist into the palm of his other hand. 'If there'd been any justice in the world, *I'd* have been over *him*. Bloody trawler owners! Reckon they rule the bloody world.'

Calmly Jeannie said, 'I expect it's because he joined the RNR sometime before the war started.'

'How do you know that?' Tom rounded on her and, at once, Jeannie realized her mistake. Luckily she remembered how she had come by the information.

'You told me.'

'Oh. Did I?' Tom was fazed for a moment and muttered, 'Mebbe I did, but I still think he's done it on purpose.' He glowered at Jeannie as if the whole thing were her fault. 'Mebbe he's going to pick his moment when no one's looking and toss me overboard.'

'Never mind all that just now and do stop swearing. Help me find your mother. If she gets into the town, we'll never find her.'

'Then you should look after her better. You've nowt else to do all day now me and the boys have gone.'

'I'm doing a bit of war work like all the other women round here.'

Tom gave a humourless laugh. 'Oh aye. I've heard that one before. Supplying comforts for the troops. Aye . . .' His face darkened. 'Comforts for the troops billeted in the town, I don't doubt. Setting up in opposition to Aggie Turnbull, are ya?'

Her hand flew threw the air of its own volition and her palm met the side of his face with a loud smack. He gripped her wrists and for a moment they stood glaring at each other, breathing heavily, their faces only inches apart.

'What the hell did you do that for?'

'I'm sick of your snide remarks, Tom Lawrence. I havena done anything – you hear me – anything to deserve them.'

He stared at her and then his face seemed to crumple and he flung his arms about her and pulled her to him in a fierce embrace that was more like a child clinging to its mother than the embrace of a husband for his wife. His cheek was against her hair. 'Jeannie, oh Jeannie. I'm sorry. It's just . . .' His voice dropped to a whisper. 'I'm so bloody scared, that's all.'

Jeannie did not answer him but just held him tightly. Knowing what he must be feeling, she tried to comfort him, tried to give him strength and courage. But who was there to comfort her? Who was there to help her cope alone with Nell and the worry of the men of her family who were in the front line of the war.

And then there was her secret worry. Always, in a special corner of her heart, there was Robert.

It was more than eleven years since he had last stood on this doorstep. And now he felt like a nervous schoolboy, or a young bashful cadet instead of a lieutenant in the smart uniform with the wavy rings around his sleeves. He found he was holding his breath as she opened the door.

At once he could see the changes. There were a few strands of white amongst the still thick and luxuriant hair. Though there were tiny lines around her eyes and dark shadows of strain and tiredness beneath them, they were still bright and sharp as they widened at the sight of him. She was as slim and lithe as ever and the smile that Robert had so longed to see for him alone was on her mouth. And now, after all this time, it was for him.

'Robert . . .' She said the name by which she always thought of him before she could stop herself. Swiftly, she said, 'I'm sorry, Mr Robert . . .'

He was smiling down at her, saying softly in the deep

voice she remembered so well, 'I prefer it without the Mr.'

Her smile faded and anxiety clouded her eyes. Her joy at seeing him – private joy though that must be – was obliterated by the thought that he was the bearer of bad news.

'What is it? Is it Tom?' It dawned on her, swiftly now, that whilst Robert was obviously on leave, Tom had not arrived home at the same time. 'Has something happened to him?'

'No, no,' Robert said quickly, suddenly realizing what she must be thinking. 'He's fine. I've been granted compassionate leave because my father's ill. He's dying, Jeannie.'

'Och, I'm sorry. Please, won't you come in.' She opened the door wider.

In the front parlour, he perched awkwardly on the old couch.

'Can I get you anything? A drink or . . .?' she began, but he shook his head.

'No, no, thank you.' He cleared his throat in embarrassment. 'Jeannie, this is very difficult, but I've come to ask a favour of you. At least, if it's possible.'

She said nothing but her gaze was on his face and he was having trouble remaining in his seat, when what he really wanted to do was to take her in his arms and tell her just what he felt about her. He cleared his throat and said, 'Does Sammy know the truth? About his birth and – and who his father is?'

'Aye,' she nodded. 'He found out when he was about thirteen.' Her tone hardened slightly. 'Joe told him.'

'Really? But he's never – I mean – doesn't he want to meet us? His family. I mean, the other side of his family?' he amended swiftly.

Jeannie shook her head. 'No. He's adamant he wants nothing to do with the Hayes-Gortons.'

'Oh,' Robert said and his tone was flat with disappointment.

'Why, does it matter?' she asked and then allowed herself a wry smile. 'I'd have thought you'd've all been quite relieved that you weren't facing a paternity suit or that he was trying to lay claim to the Hayes-Gorton millions.'

Now Robert smiled too. 'Scarcely millions. But in fairness, he ought to have a share in the company. If only Francis would acknowledge him.' He sighed heavily.

'I dinna think he ever will,' Jeannie said bitterly.

'But young Samuel's his all right. Oh, you haven't known, Jeannie, but even though I had to stop coming here, I've still watched the boy grow up. I used to make some excuse to visit the school where he was, just so that I could see him. He never knew,' he added hastily. 'I'd make a point of talking to all the children so that it never looked as if I was singling out Samuel – Sammy you call him, don't you?'

He even knew that, she thought, as she nodded in answer.

'I never wanted to be the cause of him learning the truth.'

There was silence between them for a moment as they sat gazing at each other. Only a few feet lay between them and yet the gulf that separated them was as wide and as deep as the Humber and the currents were as treacherous as those of the river.

'So why,' she said softly at last, breaking the spell their silence was casting around them, 'are you here?'

'My father always wanted a grandson. More than anything he wanted to know that there was another generation for his company to pass on to.' Robert sighed. 'He doesn't see that perhaps at the end of this war there might be precious little company left for anyone to inherit.'

Surprised, Jeannie asked, 'Do you mean he knows about Sammy?'

Robert nodded. 'Over the years he's heard rumours that the boy you're bringing up as your own could be his grandson.'

There was a tense silence before Jeannie said, 'And?'

'He's asked to see him.'

Now her mouth dropped open in a gasp of surprise. 'You're not serious?'

Solemnly, he nodded. 'Very.'

Bluntly, she said, 'I don't think Sammy'll agree. Besides, he's not here. They're at sea. Both of them.'

'I know. Their ship docks in Hull the day after tomorrow and I could arrange for Sammy to be granted compassionate leave.'

'Is there anything you don't know about this family?' she asked tartly.

'Not much,' he admitted and grinned with such disarming boyishness that Jeannie found herself smiling too.

'Well, you can try,' she said slowly, but the doubt was evident in her tone. 'Just so long as you make sure he knows straightaway that his compassionate leave has nothing to do with this family. You see,' she added, glancing towards the ceiling indicating the bedroom above where they were sitting, 'Mrs Lawrence is not well now and he would immediately think . . .'

Robert stood up. 'Of course. I'll go myself to meet him off the ship and I'll mind I'm the one to explain everything to him.'

'He might not want to come even then.'

'That's a risk I'll have to take. My father has set his

heart on seeing the boy. In fact, he seems to be hanging on to life just for that. I must do what I can.'

'Be sure to tell Sammy that,' Jeannie said quietly. 'He's a good boy at heart.'

'I'm sure he is, if you've had the raising of him, Jeannie. But I have to remember that he has Francis's blood in his veins too. And my dear brother can be quite ruthless when he's a mind. As we all know to our cost.'

To this remark, Jeannie had no answer.

Thirty-One

Robert had waited a long time whilst the ship went through its docking procedure and the crew were allowed to step ashore. But at last he was standing on the quayside as the young sailors ran down the gangway, hit the solid ground, staggered for a moment, and then rushed forward to greet their loved ones waiting to meet them.

Then he saw them, almost the last to leave the ship, coming down the gangway, Joe in the front, leading the way.

Robert stepped forward. 'Excuse me. Might I have a word?'

The two young men stopped and, recognizing him at once, Joe said, 'What's wrong? Is it me dad?'

'No, no,' Robert said swiftly. 'All your family are well.'

Mystified now, Joe and Sammy glanced at each other and then both turned their gaze back upon Robert, who took a deep breath and said, 'I have a favour to ask of Sammy.'

'A favour? Of me?' His surprise was evident and again he glanced at Joe.

'Look, would you allow me to take you to lunch? Both of you.'

'If it's Sammy you want to talk to, you don't want me along.' There was a hint of belligerence in Joe's tone.

'Perhaps you should be involved, Joe. I can see how close you are to each other.'

'Close!' The two laughed aloud and Joe punched Sammy playfully on the shoulder, and added, 'We fight like cat and dog. We were both in trouble last week for fighting.'

Sammy, too, grinned and pointed to his chin. 'See. I've still got the bruise to prove it.'

But Robert was smiling too. 'Maybe so. But just tell me one thing. Just suppose your ship was torpedoed and sinking and you could save only one other person from the whole ship. Tell me,' he asked quietly, 'who would it be?'

The boys' faces sobered now and with one accord they both jerked their thumbs towards the other and said in unison, 'Him.'

'I thought as much,' Robert murmured and then, more briskly, he said, 'Now will you *both* have lunch with me? Please?'

Seated in the restaurant, Robert could see that both boys were ill at ease. Not only were they sitting with a superior officer, but also with the man who had been and still was, in a way, their employer. Only because of the war did they all three find themselves in the same service.

Robert did his best to put them at their ease, but until the food was served the conversation was stilted, the older man trying to open lines of communication only to be met by monosyllabic answers.

It was when they picked up their soup spoons and took the first mouthful that, suddenly, the atmosphere changed.

'By heck, this is like me mam's Tattie Soup,' Joe said. 'I ain't tasted anything as good as this since I was last home.'

Robert chuckled. 'The chef here is a Scotsman, a kinsman of your mother's.' He saw the young men glance at each other again and thought, for two who are supposed not to get along together they have a remarkable affinity between them.

Robert cleared his throat. 'Talking of your mother . . .'

An identical closed look was immediately on both their faces. 'My mother, ya mean,' Joe said and jerked his head sideways towards Sammy. 'She in't his.'

'I know,' Robert said at once and now he looked straight at Sammy. 'I know all about your parentage, Sammy. That's the reason I'm here. You're my nephew. The son of my elder brother, Francis.' When the boy made no answer, though his face was stiff with resentment, Robert went on. 'I believe you did know that, didn't you?'

Sammy gave a quick nod as if he were loath even to acknowledge the fact. Joe was smirking. 'I telled him years ago.'

Robert pushed away his empty soup bowl and leant his elbows on the table. 'I'll come straight to the point. My father is dying.'

The boys looked uncomfortable, not knowing quite what they should say, but Robert continued, not expecting any reply from them, 'He has no other grandchildren except you, Sammy. And he wishes to see you before he dies.' He paused a moment to allow this to sink in and then added softly, 'That is the favour I have come to ask of you.'

'You want me to come to see him?' Sammy blurted out. 'To meet him? Me?'

Robert nodded.

'Don't go, Sam,' Joe put in at once. 'They're up to summat.'

Robert spread his hands, palms upwards. 'No catch, I promise you. No strings – nothing. I'll even arrange it so that you don't run into Francis, if that's what you're afraid of.'

'He ain't afraid of nothing, mister,' Joe shot back. 'You tell 'im, Sam.'

'Shut up, Joe. I'm thinkin'.'

Piercing blue eyes that were so like Francis's were regarding Robert, who felt a shiver like a cold dousing of water run down his spine. There it was, the likeness he had been looking for. There was that same calculating reasoning going on in the boy's mind as he had witnessed so often in his brother. Yet, he was thankful to see, it stopped short of ruthless cruelty.

'He's not wanting to have me become part of the family, is he?' Sammy asked, putting his head on one side. 'Not wanting me to come into the company?'

Robert gave a wry laugh. 'There's little of the company left at the moment for you to come into. We won't know until after the war whether we'll still have a fleet of trawlers. We're only fishing the North Sea now with the few ancient ships we have left and the crews are made up of old men and young boys. No, I promise you I'm just asking you to come and see him before – before it's too late. Obviously, it's more for his sake than for yours. Nevertheless . . .' He paused and then added, 'You never know, there might come a time when you'll be glad you at least met your grandfather.'

There was silence now around the table as Sammy considered. 'All right,' he said at last. 'I'll come.'

'Fine.' Robert stood up. 'I think I've got enough petrol to get us back via Goole. I'll drop you off at home if you like, Joe?'

'Thanks, but I can walk from your place.'

'My parents are at my house. Their own was bombed two months back.' He sighed. 'I think that's what brought on my father's heart attack.'

'Well, just drop me in the town then, please,' Joe said, and Robert had the feeling that the young man was doing everything he could to prevent Robert having any reason to visit Baldock Street.

Driving to the outskirts of the town, having left Joe in Main Street, Robert asked carefully, 'Are you concerned about running into Francis?'

Sammy pulled his mouth down at the corners and shook his head. 'Not really. In a way, I suppose, I'd quite like to see him. It might be quite funny to come face to face with him.'

The boy even had the same sarcastic sense of humour, almost the same turn of phrase. Whilst he didn't speak in the same way, didn't use such lofty wordage – Francis would have said something like, 'it would be most amusing to encounter him' – nevertheless the sentiment expressed was exactly the same.

There was certainly no doubt in Robert's mind now – if there ever had been – that Samuel Lawrence was indeed his brother's son.

As he swung into the driveway, he said, 'Here we are, then,' and drew the vehicle to a halt.

As he opened the front door and ushered Sammy inside, Louise's high heels came tapping across the hall floor. Even in wartime, Louise managed to dress in the latest fashion: a knee-length tan wool dress with padded shoulders. However did she do it, Robert thought, and couldn't help feeling a pang of guilt for all those women who were having to 'make do and mend', including, he suspected, Jeannie.

Her high-pitched, affected voice echoed shrilly through

the hall. 'There you are, Robert. I've sent for Francis and Edwin. Your father's worse. Your mother's with him now. Who's this?' she said, without seeming to pause for breath.

'This, my dear, is Samuel Lawrence. My father's only grandson.'

Louise's face was scandalized. 'You've brought him here? Now? You're not thinking of taking him upstairs to see your father, are you? Oh surely not.'

'I am about to do exactly that, my dear. At my father's express wish.'

'But you can't. What about Francis? He'll be here at any moment.'

'Francis can go to hell for all I care,' Robert muttered and then, looking her straight in the eyes, added, 'and probably will.'

He saw the colour suffuse her face as her glance darted from him to the young man at his side and back again.

'If you'll excuse us, Louise . . .' and Robert gestured towards the staircase.

He led the way into the bedroom realizing that the moment for the boy must be very difficult. Even he was unsure of what his mother's reaction towards Sammy would be. But the woman who was sitting on the far side of the bed as they entered rose with difficulty from her chair and came round the end of the bed to meet them. 'Robert, oh my dear. You've brought him. Thank goodness. He's been making himself worse with fretting.'

She turned then to Sammy and studied him intently for a moment before stepping in front of him and putting her hands on his shoulders. She did not, Robert was relieved to see, make any attempt to kiss the young man, but contented herself with smiling at him and saying softly, 'I am your grandmother, my dear. I am very pleased to meet you.'

For a moment Sammy's cool composure seemed to crumble and Robert caught sight of a side of his nature that came from the Lawrence genes. After all, poor Grace had been a gentle creature and his other grandparents were George Lawrence and Nell. Robert almost smiled at the thought of his maternal grandmother. Why, there was even a drop or two of Scottish blood in young Sammy's veins. How could he have believed that Sammy would be just like Francis, as ruthless and selfish and . . .

But there was a likeness for his mother was commenting upon it now.

'You're just like Francis was at the same age. Come.' She laid her hand on Sammy's arm and urged him to step closer to the bed. 'Come and meet your grandfather. He has been waiting for this moment.'

Thirty-Two

'Did you know about it, Mam?' Joe demanded as soon as he set foot across the threshold. 'About Sammy going to see old man Gorton?'

Jeannie answered him with another question. 'Where is he?'

'I've just said, gone to see the old man. He's dying. Did you know?'

'Aye. Robert – Mr Robert came here to ask me if Sammy knew about . . .' She gestured with her hand. 'Well, everything.'

'He met us in Hull.' Joe put on an affected tone. 'Took us to a fancy posh restaurant for lunch.' Then he relaxed into his normal way of speaking, adding, as if reluctant to give praise even when it was deserved, 'Mind you, it were good.' Jeannie felt his glance upon her. 'He's been here again then?'

'Och now, dinna you start. I've had enough all these years with your father seeing things that aren't there.'

'Oh well, you know what they say? There's no smoke without fire.'

'The only fire that's here is the one in the grate there and it's nearly out, so you'd best be fetching the coal in,' she snapped and turned away, afraid lest he should see the flames that smouldered within her, so deeply banked down that they were not even allowed to smoke. She picked up the tray to take it upstairs to Nell, who, more often than not these days, stayed in bed. But her thoughts were a couple of miles away inside another bedroom, unknown to her, but where she imagined old Samuel Hayes-Gorton lay dying.

Robert watched as Sammy approached the bedside to stand looking down at the old man. His namesake was a shadow of the rotund, bewhiskered gentleman he had once been; the proud owner of the Gorton Trawler Company of Havelock. Since his illness, he had shrunk to a skeleton. Coming home each time on leave, Robert noticed the difference more markedly than those who were with him every day.

He knew, before anyone else, that his father would not live much longer and the thought had prompted him to broach the subject of young Sammy's existence. The day they had first spoken of it, the old man was still able to sit out of bed for part of the day near the window with a rug over his knees. Robert had broached the matter carefully, sensitive to his father's feelings.

'You know, I'm sorry, Father, that I have not given you the grandson you wanted.'

Samuel Hayes-Gorton had grunted, his eyes watery, still bright and certainly sharp and knowing. He'd smoothed his white moustache and then squinted up at Robert.

The words had come haltingly. 'Not altogether your fault, m'boy.' There had been a long pause whilst Samuel had gone back to gazing out of the window. Then, very quietly, he had said, 'I do have a grandson though, don't I?'

'Yes, Father. You do.'

Another long silence before the old man had said, 'I have a mind, Robert, to see the boy before . . .' He'd

looked up then, straight into his son's eyes, and Robert had
seen the knowledge there. Much was said in that exchange
of a long look even though no words were spoken. Samuel
had let out a long sigh and said, 'Well, soon.'

Robert had touched his shoulder. 'I'll see what I can
do.'

And now they were here, standing in the room, almost
too late for the sick old man to know. Already his breathing was laboured and every few moments it seemed to stop
and everyone held their own breath, fearing they had heard
the last of his. But then the stubbornness to hang on would
return and he would pull in a breath once more.

As he stood watching, Robert saw his father, propped
up against several pillows, open his eyes. The voice issuing
from the shrunken form was still remarkably strong. 'Has
he come? Is he here? My grandson?'

Mrs Hayes-Gorton bent closer. 'Yes, yes, my dear.
Robert has brought him. Young Samuel is here.'

The tired eyes focused and the mouth sagged and then
old Samuel gasped, 'My – God!'

'Yes, my dear.' His wife took the words from him,
saving him the labour. 'I thought just the same. He's so
like Francis was at the same age, but not quite so tall,
don't you think?'

She turned then and whispered to Sammy, who was
standing rigidly beside the bed, not knowing quite what
was expected of him. 'Say something to him. Speak to
him.'

Sammy half turned towards Robert as if seeking reassurance of some kind. Robert nodded and the boy turned
back towards the old man again. 'Good afternoon, sir. I'm
– I'm sorry to see you ill. Mr Robert, he came to meet the
ship. He said – he said you'd like to see me.'

A great sigh escaped the old man's lips and his whole body seemed to relax and sink into the pillows. 'I am glad to see you – Samuel.' The struggle to speak was supreme but no one present thought to tell him to rest. They knew that although this effort may well be his final one, it was important to him. For what else was there for him to reserve his energies now? 'You've – been to – sea?'

'I'm in the Navy, sir.'

The watery eyes squinted up at him. 'Ah, I see now – your uniform.'

His breathing rasped again for a minute as he gathered strength to ask, 'You love the sea?'

'Yes, sir,' Samuel said and added with unmistakable pride, 'When we've won the war, I'll still go back to sea. On a trawler, more n' like.'

'Gorton trawlers, my boy. Make sure – it's on a Gorton trawler. One day – one day they'll be yours . . .'

The eyes closed and the hands on the coverlet were motionless now. Mrs Gorton knelt by the bedside and bowed her head. Clutching at her husband's hand, she wept quietly whilst Robert touched Sammy's shoulder and led him from the room.

'Is he – did he . . .?' the boy began.

'No, no, he isn't dead, but I fear it cannot be much longer. He's been drifting in and out of consciousness for a couple of days now.'

They had reached the hallway, when the front door flew open and Francis marched into the house, for all the world as if he owned the place. Robert saw him stop in surprise as he saw the young boy standing there.

'What the hell . . .?' he began and then his cold eyes narrowed. 'So, dear brother, you thought to bring your bastard into the family fold, did you?'

Beside him, Robert felt Sammy stiffen, yet he held his head proudly and returned Francis's disdain with a steady, composed look.

Robert cleared his throat. 'Father wished to see his grandson.'

'Only because you . . .' Francis jabbed his cane at Robert, 'put him up to it.' The smirk on his face was malicious now. 'Still afraid he's cut you out of his will as he threatened? Thought you'd get back in favour by the back door, eh? Well, no bastard's going to inherit the Gorton company, let me tell you . . .'

'I want nowt to do with your company.' Sammy's voice rang out, cool and calm. 'Except perhaps to work aboard one of your ships after the war.'

Robert watched in a kind of horrified fascination as father and son stared at each other, the nearest they had ever been. He could see now that each was assessing the other, each searching for – and finding at once – the likeness to one another.

Quietly Robert said, 'He's your son, Francis. You know full well he is.'

Francis let out a bark of laughter. 'Ha! Never. His mother was nothing but a slut, a whore. One of Aggie Turnbull's trollops. I doubt she even knew who this brat's father was. But she saw a chance to lay the blame at my door and you . . .' again he jabbed his ebony cane towards Robert, 'were fool enough, besotted by that red-haired bitch, to believe their tales. Been paying for it all these years. Well, I hope you got your money's worth when Lawrence was away at sea.'

Robert heard Sammy make a funny noise in his throat and then the boy ran towards the door, pulled it open, leapt down the steps and flew down the driveway.

Through clenched teeth, Robert spat, 'You're the bastard, Francis . . .' With two strides he came close to his brother, drew back his arm and punched Francis on his chin. The man fell backwards, sprawling on the floor and as Robert left the house it was to the sounds of Louise running across the hall, crying, 'Oh Francis, oh darling, what has he done to you?'

Thirty-Three

Though Robert climbed at once into his motor car and drove after him, he was unable to find Sammy. And once he reached the town, he knew his search was fruitless. He could be in any one of a dozen pubs. At last he turned towards Baldock Street and knocked upon Jeannie's door.

'He's not here, is he?' he asked, without explanation, when she opened it.

'Who? Sammy?' Jeannie said and then shook her head. 'What happened?'

Robert ran his hand through his hair and said, 'Everything was fine, well, as fine as it could be in the circumstances, if you know what I mean?'

Jeannie nodded and then, swiftly, he recounted the events. 'He just ran out and by the time I'd thumped Francis on the jaw and gone after him, he'd just disappeared. Jeannie, I am sorry.'

'You hit your brother?' she asked, scarcely able to conceal her laughter.

'Oh yes.' He grinned at her. 'We used to fight as kids. I suppose sometimes the feeling never goes away, not even when you're grown up.'

'Just like Joe and Sammy,' she chuckled.

Robert put on his hat. 'Well, I'd better go, seeing as you're obviously not going to invite me in.'

Jeannie grimaced and said, 'I can't. I'm sorry. Nell is having a bad morning. I daren't leave her.'

'She's ill?' Robert frowned in concern.

'Not physically. It's her mind. She seems to live in a little world of her own these days. I daren't leave her for a minute. If she wanders off, I'm searching the streets for her.'

Robert nodded in sympathy. 'I've just found out what that's like.'

'Och, dinna worry about Sammy. He'll come rolling home, drunk as a lord, when he's ready.'

As he turned to go, she called after him, 'I'm sorry about your father. It's – it's a difficult time for you.'

He glanced back at her, taking the picture of her into his memory. 'Thank you, Jeannie.' Very softly, he added, 'Goodbye, my dear.'

Samuel Hayes-Gorton lived another week after meeting his grandson for the first, and only, time. The news of his death soon spread around the local community and the subject of his will was general speculation for days though only the family were, at first, aware of its detailed contents.

He had not, as he had threatened, cut his middle son off with the proverbial shilling, but had left his company to his three sons, although Francis Hayes-Gorton had a 49 per cent share. He had, of course, made generous provision for his wife for her lifetime, but the codicil to the will, made only six days before his death and the day after his meeting with his grandson, altered the share of his two younger sons. Instead of the remaining 51 per cent being divided equally between Robert and Edwin, it was split into three parts of 17 per cent each to the two brothers and to '*Samuel Lawrence, of Baldock Street, Havelock, being my eldest son's natural son and, therefore, my grandson.*'

279

'This is outrageous!' Francis jumped to his feet as the lawyer read out the will to the family gathered together after the funeral. 'I shall contest it. He wasn't of sound mind. This is your doing, Robert.' He pointed his finger towards his brother, who sat calmly with a slight smile on his mouth. 'I won't have it. I won't be outvoted by the two of you and some slut's bastard who imagines he's a claim on this family. I've never acknowledged him as mine and I never will. If he's anybody's, then he's yours.'

Again he jabbed his finger towards Robert, who said calmly, 'Then in that case, he still has a right to his inheritance. He's still Father's grandson.'

For a brief moment Francis's handsome face twisted into ugliness. He picked up the chair he had been sitting on and hurled it against the wall, causing a picture to fall, shattering the glass. 'You'll pay for this, Robert. I'll ruin you, I'll . . .'

'Francis, control yourself,' came their mother's imperious tones. 'Robert had nothing to do with your father changing his will. He knew no more about it than you until this moment. If anyone's to blame, then it is me. I witnessed the codicil and approved its terms. But the suggestion came from your father. It was what he wanted, and, I'll have you know, he was in complete charge of his senses almost until the end. Physically, yes, he was very weak but his mind was clear and . . .' her gaze upon her eldest son was unflinching as she added, 'I would be prepared to stand up in court and say as much.'

Now Edwin, who had not spoken, rose. 'There will be no need for that, Mother. We shall resolve this between the three of us. The young man in question is not old enough yet, I believe, to take an active part on the Board anyway. His shares – if I understand the terms of the will correctly – are to be administered by Robert until young Samuel attains the age of twenty-one. Is that correct, Mr Paige?'

The lawyer nodded.

'I don't care for all the legalities,' Francis spat. 'I won't have any of it. You'll be hearing from *my* lawyer on the matter.'

With that parting shot, he strode from the room leaving his mother shaking her head sadly and murmuring, 'Oh dear.'

'Don't worry, Mother,' Edwin said. 'We all know Francis. He has a brilliant mind and has every right, not only as the eldest son but also because of his business acumen, to the major share of the company. But that doesn't mean we're going to let him ride roughshod over us. Does it, Robert?'

Robert smiled. 'Well, at the moment I'm reeling from hearing that I am still a part of the business. I thought I was to be – er – cut off.'

Mrs Hayes-Gorton chuckled. 'Your father thought he could bring you to heel by his threats.' She leant forward across the polished surface of the mahogany dining table. 'But I'll tell you something now. He was secretly rather proud of you for having the courage to decide your own future. Even I knew he never meant to cut you off.'

'Didn't I tell you so, Robert old chap.' Edwin, too, was smiling as he put his hand on Robert's shoulder. 'And Francis will come around too. Just give him time.'

To that, Robert made no reply.

The legal-looking letter arrived for Sammy long after he had returned to his ship. Jeannie put it on the mantelpiece, unopened, but often over the following weeks her glance would go to the long, white envelope wondering what lay inside it.

But then other matters demanded her attention and she forgot all about the letter addressed to Mr Samuel Lawrence.

Thirty-Four

Lieutenant Robert Gorton stood on the bridge. They were nearing the end of a sweep and his eyes were sore, red-rimmed with tiredness from gazing out across the grey waters. They had completed four days at sea and were returning to Havelock for replenishment and a few brief hours ashore before coming out again to sweep the same area of sea again and again and again to clear a safe channel for the convoys.

They were searching for acoustic mines now as well as the magnetic type.

Would it never end? Robert asked himself. Almost four years already and still the war raged on. At least now, he thought, the Americans were in too. Surely with their might, the end could not be in doubt. Yet, when would it come? And how many more young men would lose their lives before it was all over?

Robert blinked, trying to focus his attention once more upon the water. It was so cold that he couldn't imagine ever feeling warm again. Not for the first time, did his thoughts turn to the trawler men who spent most of their lives at sea. And he had been one of the privileged few – an owner – who had sent those men out here. Well, now he was one of them and no longer an owner of very much.

Since the Gorton trawlers had been commandeered, half of that number had already been blown up by the very mines they were attempting to clear or had been attacked and destroyed by enemy fighter planes. Two had succumbed to U-boats.

Now he and the men the Hayes-Gortons had once employed were – quite literally – in the same boat. Fighting not only a common foe, but the wind and the sea and the terrible cold.

And what, he wondered, would there be for any of them who did manage to survive to go back to?

Some fishing in the coastal waters still went on and if he knew his elder brother – his scheming, devious, yet clever brother – Francis would already have transferred his business interests to war work of some sort. But it would undoubtedly be an effort for the war that would be profitable for him too. Oh yes, thanks to Francis, there would be something for Robert to go back to. But for what?

Here on this ship, a battered old trawler turned mine-sweeper it might be, he had earned the respect the men gave him. He had earned his place as 'Jimmy the One'. Now, when they called him 'sir', it was more than because he was the son of their employer.

Maybe, Robert thought, as he passed his hand over his tired eyes once more and squinted at the clouds above, raking the sky for the tell-tale signs of enemy aircraft, maybe, he mused, if he survived, he'd stay on in the Royal Navy.

His brothers would run the company, or what was left of it. His wife would spend most of her time in London with her smart friends as she still did, despite the dangers.

And Jeannie? His heart contracted at the thought of her. She would be waiting for her Tom to come home from the sea.

Thinking of her, as he often allowed himself to do

through the long cold hours, Robert promised himself that after the war, he'd see what he could do for Tom.

During their time together aboard this ship, the man had never once let his animosity for his former employer show, had never let slip to the ship's company just who and what Robert Gorton had been before the war. He had kept the pact they had made.

When Robert and Tom had come face to face for the first time aboard the minesweeper, he had seen the surprise in the other man's face, not only for the ironic twist of fate that out of all the ships on the ocean they should end up serving on the same one, but also when he first heard his superior officer addressed without the 'Hayes' to his name. And Robert had seen something else in the man's eyes: a wariness that he himself was feeling too. Later, Robert had come to Tom's radio operator's room.

He'd come straight to the point of his visit. 'I suggest we leave any differences we have ashore, Lawrence, don't you? And the circumstances of our backgrounds. It's known I had some connection with trawlers before the war, as I'm sure that's the case for you too. But no one knows exactly what. I prefer it that way.'

There was a note of command in Robert's voice. 'Are we agreed?' he prompted when Tom made no reply.

When Tom had looked at him, he had seen the insolence in the man's eyes, but all Tom had said was 'Aye, aye,' and had added, with the slightest hesitation, 'Sir.'

Robert stretched his face and blinked again, forcing himself to concentrate. It was one thing to let his thoughts wander when on watch, but not for one moment must he relax his vigil even though they were on their way home.

They passed Spurn Head and entered the mouth of the Humber, anchoring until the high tide made their passage through the dock gates possible. With the outline of the buildings on the fishdock clearly visible against the skyline, the whole atmosphere aboard the ship seemed to relax.

Robert watched Tom Lawrence walking along the deck, the slip of white paper he was holding fluttering in the breeze. The man seemed to be hesitating about what to do and now Robert saw him glance up and look directly at him. For a moment their glances met and held, then Tom moved forward and began to climb the ladder to the bridge.

As the captain half-turned and held out his hand for the piece of paper, Tom saluted and said, 'Message for Lieutenant Gorton, sir. Of a personal nature, sir.'

The senior officer's eyebrows rose and he glanced at Robert with a slight frown of disapproval on his forehead. At sea, such an occurrence was strictly against regulations, but here, almost home, even the skipper relaxed a little too. When he said nothing, Tom persisted, 'With your permission, sir?'

The sub-lieutenant due to take over the watch from Robert, had arrived on the bridge a few moments before Tom and so, released from his duties, Robert turned towards Tom and saw at once that in the man's eyes now was a mixture of anxiety and sympathy.

'Sir . . .' Even his voice was hesitant. 'I am very sorry, but I have some bad news for you.'

Robert swallowed but said nothing. He was glad that Tom Lawrence could not read his thoughts, wild and irrational as they were. All he could think of at this moment was, it can't be Jeannie else he would be the one receiving the bad news, not me.

Tom was speaking again and Robert forced himself to listen. 'It's your – your wife, sir. She's been killed in an air raid in London.'

Poor Louise, poor little girl, was Robert's first thought.

The pretty, bright, pleasure-seeking child, who had not been able to resist London even when the Blitz had been at its height, was gone, her butterfly life crushed. He felt a deep sorrow, not so much because he loved her, for he did not and never had, not in the same way that he loved . . . No, no, he must not think of her, not now. Poor Louise, he thought again, she hadn't deserved to die in that way and so young too.

Tom Lawrence was still standing before him, making no move to leave him alone with his supposed grief. 'I'm sorry, sir, but there's something else. Your brother, Mr Francis . . .'

Robert's eyes bored into the other man's, his voice harsh and abrupt. 'What about him?'

'He was killed too, sir. In – in the same air raid.'

Now Robert turned away abruptly before Tom could read anything in his face. Robert knew that Tom Lawrence was editing the truth. He could have said, so easily, that they were together, maybe even in the same bed. For without being told, Robert knew, instinctively, that was the case. He had felt for some time, though he had no proof, that he was being cuckolded by his own brother.

What a shame, he thought dispassionately, that Francis had not been the chosen one to unite the two companies by marrying Louise Hathersage.

Then he realized and the sudden knowledge hit him like a forty-foot wave.

He, Robert Gorton, was now not only the senior partner and head of the Gorton-Hathersage Trawler Company, but he was also Louise's next of kin and consequently would inherit her shares too. It was an awesome responsibility.

Now briefly, he turned back to face Tom. Quietly, he said, 'Thank you for taking it upon yourself to be the one to tell me. It can't have been easy for you.'

Tom gave a quick nod, saluted and turned away. As Robert watched him go he thought, I wonder if he realizes just how very lucky he is to have Jeannie as his wife.

'So, your fancy man is free now and head of a giant company.'

Two days later on a brief shore leave, Tom faced Jeannie across the kitchen table, a sneer in his tone and bitter resentment in his eyes.

Calmly Jeannie continued kneading the dough for the bread she was making, though deep inside she sighed. She glanced at him and, her mouth tight, said, 'I've more things on my mind than listening to your jealous imagination running riot. What are you going to do about the boys running away to sea? Can't you do anything to get them brought home?'

Tom shrugged. 'They're eighteen in a few months. Hardly worth it now, anyway. I still haven't worked out how they could have got away with it. Didn't you ask *him* to pull a few strings to get them out?' When Jeannie did not answer, he added, resentfully, 'I bet it was Sammy's fault. He'll have shamed our Joe into going. Made him feel a coward if he didn't.' Tom fell silent and Jeannie glanced at him, wondering, fleetingly, if that was what had made Tom volunteer for the Reserves. He wouldn't have wanted to be branded a coward when all the other fishermen were joining up.

'They went together,' Jeannie said aloud. 'I think it was mutual agreement.'

Tom gave a snort of derision. 'Huh, pull the other one, Jeannie. They don't get on. You can't tell me they've gone together. They were always fighting.'

'Well, they have and now they're fighting side by side

instead of each other.' Her fear for their safety lent a bitter sharpness to her tone. 'War makes strange bedfellows of folk.' She looked at him meaningfully now.

Tom sat down in the chair by the fire. 'It does that,' he said heavily. Softly, he added, 'It was me told him, y'know?'

The time for pretence was over. There was no point in feigning ignorance for Jeannie knew full well who Tom was talking about.

'About his wife and his brother?'

'Yeah.' He paused and then added, 'First time I've ever felt sorry for him, y'know? Fancy being told that your wife's been killed in bed with your brother.'

Jeannie gasped. 'You told him that?'

'Not in so many words, but he knew. Oh he knew all right.' He looked up at her then. 'Jeannie, just tell me. Please. Is there anything going on between you and him?'

Jeannie set the bowl of dough beside the warm fire to prove and knelt down on the hearthrug. Leaning her elbows on his knees she looked into his face and said, 'Tom, there is nothing between us. Never has been and never will be. I was brought up a good, God-fearing Scottish lassie and the vows I made in the kirk to you I have kept and I always will.'

There was silence for a moment. 'Till death us do part, eh Jeannie?'

Jeannie swallowed the lump in her throat for every day death was very close to both of them. She reached up and touched his cheek. 'You're a good husband, Tom Lawrence, and a good father, I'll never say otherwise. But I just wish you'd stop imagining things that aren't true.'

He leant down and gathered her into his arms, holding her tightly and burying his face in her hair. Hoarsely he said, 'I'll try, Jeannie, I promise I'll try. But you're everything to me. I love you so much, I just couldn't bear it if . . .'

'And I love you, Tom,' she said and stroked his hair.

She closed her eyes tightly and pressed her face against his shoulder and prayed silently, may God forgive me for this lie.

Thirty-Five

Another legal-looking letter arrived addressed to Mr Samuel Lawrence and joined the first behind the clock on the mantelpiece to await his next leave. And whilst speculation ran rife, no one, this time, seemed to have definite knowledge as to the contents of Mr Francis Hayes-Gorton's will.

'They'll have to pay a lot of death duties, won't they?' went the gossip. 'Two of 'em dying so close together like that.'

'Dunno. Shouldn't think the company's worth all that much just now. More'n half the trawlers have been converted to minesweepers and fishing's difficult even in the near-waters.'

'Aye, ya could be right.'

But the person who could have told them what was in Francis's will, was far out at sea, serving on a destroyer. On his eighteenth birthday, Samuel Lawrence had no idea that he was now a major shareholder in the Gorton-Hathersage Trawler Company.

Aboard the minesweeper, the alarm bell shrilled and the order 'Action Stations' was given. Immediately, they heard the whine of enemy aircraft overhead and Robert looked up to see six screaming down towards the ship. The seven guns on board were given leave to fire independently and the splatter of bullets arced skywards.

291

Two bombs hurtled from the bellies of the planes swooping low across the deck. They splashed into the sea on the starboard side, sending a plume of water into the air. The ship rocked under the turbulence.

Robert, standing beside the skipper, dispatched a rating to report any damage. The young lad was running along the deck when it took a direct hit. Helplessly, Robert watched as the blast blew the youngster off his feet and over the side of the ship. Several others were lying injured on the deck now, but the guns above the bridge swung to follow the path of the plane, the rapid fire never faltering.

'Fire!' The cry went up as flames erupted from the hole in the deck and, with growing horror, Robert realized that just below where the bomb had fallen was not only a crew room, but the radio operator's room too.

Jeannie's husband could be dead or dying, but though Robert's whole being cried out to scramble down the ladder and run in search of Tom, duty kept him on the bridge, calmly carrying out the orders of his commanding officer.

The next few chaotic minutes seemed to take an eternity to live through until, with the ship burning fiercely and listing badly to port, the captain was forced to give the order to abandon ship.

Only then, when it was an 'every man for himself situation', could Robert go in search of Tom. The heat almost defeated him, singed his hair and scorched his arms as he held them up to shield his face. But desperation drove him on. Jeannie, Jeannie, was all he could think. He must find Tom for Jeannie's sake.

He was slumped over his radio, his fingers still grasping the dials as if he had been trying to send a last urgent message. Robert hauled the inert figure on to his shoulder in an ungainly kind of fireman's lift and, finding a strength he hadn't known he possessed, staggered towards the hole in the side of the ship. Then he pushed Tom through it and followed him into the water below.

For a moment, he thought Tom had sunk beneath the waves, but suddenly, there he was, bobbing up beside him. Robert grabbed at him and began to swim, dragging Tom away from the ship that looked as if it would go to the bottom at any second.

At what he considered a reasonably safe distance, Robert trod water, holding Tom's chin up. 'Hold on, man,' he kept saying. 'Think of your family. Think of Jeannie. For God's sake, hold on.'

At last, with the help of some of the crew, Robert managed to have Tom hauled out of the water before willing hands pulled him into the life-raft too.

They were in range of the coastal lifeboat, but it was four hours before they were found and picked up. Four hours in which Robert held Tom to him, trying to keep him warm, trying to keep him alive.

As the lifeboat man climbed down into the life-raft to help the cold, oil-covered men aboard, one said, 'Let him go, sir. He's dead.'

But Robert clung on to Tom's still form, whispering hoarsely through cracked lips, 'No, oh no. How will I tell her?'

'Come along, sir. We'll have to leave him.'

'We must take him back. We must take his body . . .'

'We can't, sir. The lifeboat's already overloaded. We must think of the living.'

Robert's reason, for a moment, had deserted him, but the calm, rational tones of the lifeboat man brought him to his senses.

'You're right, of course. I'm sorry. I don't know what I'm thinking of.'

Still with reluctance, Robert and the lifeboat man gently tipped Tom's body into the waves. Robert crossed himself, bowed his head and muttered a short prayer.

'Friend of yours, was he, sir?' the man asked kindly.

'Sort of,' was all Robert could say, for all he could think of was, how am I to tell Jeannie?

As Robert stood outside the door of the Lawrence home, part of him wanted so much to see her again and yet his heart quailed at the news he must bring her. He glanced briefly over his shoulder up and down the street and saw a lace curtain fall back into place.

Within minutes, all the neighbours would be aware of his visit. He knew that. But this time, it was different. This time only he could be the bearer of this news, painful though it was.

The door opened and she was standing before him and as he said swiftly, 'May I come in . . .' she pulled the door wider and gestured for him to step inside.

Almost before she had closed the door, shutting out the inquisitive gaze of the neighbours, he turned to face her and said, 'I'm sorry to come with bad news.'

Her hand was still on the door knob and now she leant against the door, staring at him. 'It's Tom, isn't it?'

He nodded. 'I'm afraid so. We were attacked by enemy aircraft and the ship took a direct hit just above where he worked. It caught fire and he was badly burnt even before I got to him. We began to take water fast and we had to abandon ship. I kept him with me, tried to keep his spirits up, but his injuries and then being so long in the water, well, I'm so sorry, Jeannie. He died in my arms.'

She moved woodenly to sit in a chair and rest her arms on the table. Robert followed her. He did not sit down but went towards the range where he reached up for the tea caddy on the mantelpiece above, catching sight as he did so of the two unopened letters. He spooned tea into the pot and poured boiling water into it from the kettle which always stood on the hob. Then he took two cups and saucers down from the dresser and set them on the table.

'Milk?' he enquired gently and Jeannie gestured towards a pantry where the milk stood on a cold stone slab.

Moments later he pushed a steaming cup of strong tea towards her and ordered gently, 'Drink it.'

Automatically, she obeyed him. He noticed, as she put the cup back on the saucer with a clatter, that her hands were trembling. 'You – you tried to save him?'

He said nothing, merely nodded.

Her eyes filled with tears. 'Thank you. Whatever you did, thank you.'

He looked at her directly then, stared at her for a long moment before he said, 'Anyone would have done the same.'

She nodded, but hoarsely she whispered, 'Oh yes, I know that. But only *I* know what it must have cost you.'

He closed his eyes and shook his head slowly. 'Oh Jeannie. I would do anything to spare you pain. I would even – even have sacrificed my own life if it would have brought back the man you love.'

She could not tell him, she could not say the words, for it would have felt so wrong, would have been wicked at this moment. But never before had she loved him quite as much as she did now, sitting opposite him, watching the lines of sadness etched deeply upon his face knowing that he had fought with a desperate bravery to save Tom, risking his own life, not so much for the man himself, but to bring her husband back to her.

How very much at this moment she loved Robert

295

Gorton. But her mouth remained closed and the words unspoken.

The boys were given compassionate leave and they stood either side of Jeannie and Nell during the memorial service in the church where she had married Tom and where too, years before, Nell had married George. Jeannie mourned her husband deeply and sincerely. He had been a good man and she had loved him, perhaps in the way that one loves a brother or a good friend, but not, she knew now, as a lover with a searing, consuming passion. She had never felt the trembling of her knees nor the pounding of her heart nor the sudden dryness in her throat for Tom as she felt when she saw Robert.

He was standing behind her now. A little way back from the family mourners, keeping a respectful distance. As they came out of the church and into the grey November day, Jeannie made as if to move towards him, but Joe, his arm firmly through hers, steered her towards the curving pathway leading to the gate.

'What's he doing here?' Sammy, on her other side, muttered.

'He has a right to be here,' Jeannie said. 'He tried to save your father and he was his employer. He's just come to pay his respects. And another thing. That medal they've awarded Tom, well, who do you think put in the recommendation, eh?'

Joe, from his lanky height, looked down at her. 'Well, it wouldn't be him. If you believe that, Mam, then you've not the sense you were born with.'

'Joe!' She looked up at him and despite herself, angry tears filled her eyes.

'Don't talk to Mam like that,' Sammy put in. He was

still smaller than Joe and always would be, but he had taken up boxing and now iron muscles rippled beneath his uniform. Jeannie had the feeling that in the future Joe would not be so ready to pick a fight with his cousin and wondered if that was the very reason that Sammy had taken up the sport.

But Joe was not awed by Sammy's new-found strength. 'I'll talk to *my* mam any way I want, thank you very much.'

Suddenly Jeannie was angry with the pair of them. 'Don't start. Not here. Not now. Look to your Gran, both of you.' She glanced at them, leaving neither in any doubt as to her feelings as she said pointedly, 'She is grandmother to you both, after all.'

Then she pulled her arm from Joe's, turned deliberately around and marched back towards Robert. Defiantly, she held out her hand towards him and said clearly, 'I want to thank you for all you did to try to save my husband. Please excuse my boys. They are too distressed today to know their duty.'

Then before giving him chance to reply Jeannie turned away again, back towards her family. She took hold of Nell's arm and said kindly, but firmly, 'Come, Gran, it's time we were away home.'

As they left the churchyard, she did not look back towards Robert, but beneath the trees near the wall she suddenly spotted another figure, dressed from head to toe in black, a veil over her face.

Aggie Turnbull.

Thirty-Six

'So, are you going to open your letters, then?'

Sammy scowled towards the mantelpiece. 'There'll be nowt I want to read in them,' he muttered.

'Aw, go on, Sam. At least see what they say,' Joe encouraged, but Sammy's scowl only deepened.

'Oh well, in that case . . .' Jeannie said, stepping towards the hearth and reaching up for the two envelopes. 'I left them for you because they're addressed to you and even though you are still underage legally and I have every right, I thought . . .' She held the letters in her hands now, turned one over and made as if to open it. 'Seeing as you're doing a man's work now, you'd a right to handle your own affairs. Seems I was wrong.'

As she slid her finger under the flap to tear it open, Sammy lunged forward and snatched the letters from her hands. 'I'll open them mesen when I'm good an' ready.'

Jeannie shrugged. 'Well, they've been sat there for weeks now. You'd best get on with it.'

Glowering, Sammy slit open the envelopes and unfolded the letters, smoothing them out on the table. Then, reading the dates, he picked up the first one. Jeannie and Joe watched the expression on his face alter as he read. First there was surprise and disbelief, then a brief delight. Then as he scanned the second letter, his face grew red with anger. Suddenly, he picked up both letters and tore them into shreds.

298

'Wait a minute . . .' Jeannie reached out. 'Whatever are you doing?'

'I want none of it,' Sammy muttered through clenched teeth. 'I want nowt to do with any of them. You're me family. Not them. I don't want to be a – a Hayes-Gorton.'

He stepped towards the range as if to throw the pieces of paper on to the fire, but Joe barred his way. 'Oh no, you don't. Not till you've told us properly what's in them letters.'

They began to struggle, gripping each other's shoulders, wrestling to gain supremacy, whilst the fragments of the paper fluttered to the floor.

'Stop it, both of you, else I'll bang your heads together . . .' And when they didn't stop at her bidding, Jeannie did just that, their two skulls coming together with a crack.

'Ow!'

'What did ya do that for, Mam?' Joe said ruefully, rubbing his head.

'If you behave like bairns, then I'll treat you like bairns. Now then, son . . .' She turned to Sammy. 'You just sit down at that table and piece those letters together and tell us what's in them that's made you so angry.'

Grudgingly, Sammy picked up the scraps of paper and began, like tackling a jigsaw puzzle, to sort out the pieces.

'The first letter said that old man Hayes-Gorton . . .' he still refused, Jeannie noticed, to refer to Samuel as his grandfather 'left me 17 per cent of the shares in the Gorton-Hathersage Trawler Company.'

Joe whistled. 'Blimey, Sam, you're rich.'

Sammy's mouth tightened. 'Huh, that's not all. The second letter, would you believe, ses that Francis Hayes-Gorton left the whole of his fortune divided equally between Louise Hayes-Gorton and his natural son . . .'

Jeannie saw Sammy raise his eyes and look straight at her. 'Samuel Lawrence.'

Now Jeannie felt her legs give way beneath her and she sat down heavily on a chair, resting her arms on the table. 'He acknowledged you? After all this time of denying your existence, he actually says that – that you're his son?'

'Seems like it.' Sammy was still tight-lipped.

'Why did he leave the other half to her?' Joe put in, puzzled. 'She's Mr Robert's wife, ain't she?'

Jeannie saw Sammy look up at Joe. Now there was a smirk on his face. 'Bit of gossip that's missed those flapping ears of yours, our Joe? Mr Francis and Mr Robert's wife were . . .' He glanced swiftly at Jeannie. 'Well, y'know.'

Joe blinked for a moment or two and then his face cleared. 'Oh, I get yer. My God! Were they really?' He thought for a moment and then with a sly glance towards his mother said, 'Well, suppose you can't blame her if her husband went visiting elsewhere . . .'

It did not go unnoticed by Jeannie, but for once she chose to let the innuendo pass.

'So, Sammy,' she said instead, 'you're a man of means now, are you?'

He stood up, shoving all the pieces of paper into a heap again, though this time he made no effort to burn them. 'No, I aren't. I don't want none of it. You hear me? Not one penny.'

He left the room and they heard the back-door slam.

'Silly bugger!' Joe muttered. For once Jeannie did not reprimand him.

Robert came to see her later the same afternoon, knocking on the door and standing hesitantly outside on the street, until she persuaded him to step across the threshold. She ushered him into the front parlour and invited him to sit down. He declined and instead stood awkwardly in the centre of the room twirling his cap between restless fingers.

'I'm not going back to sea yet. I have what they call survivors' leave.' He paused and she guessed that he was feeling guilty because he was a survivor and Tom was not. He cleared his throat and went on. 'I just came to see if there was anything I could do. If there was anything you need.'

'We're fine. At least,' Jeannie smiled sadly, 'as fine as we can be.'

'I know. It must be very hard for you, especially with the boys away too. Very hard. And the old lady?'

His words were like a jolt. Old lady! Was that how he thought of Nell Lawrence? Perhaps it was how everyone thought of her now? Well, she supposed with a shock, Nell was old now and she probably looked older than her years anyway.

Jeannie sighed and shrugged. 'I'm not even sure she understands what's happened. That Tom has gone.'

Robert nodded and said again, 'It must be very difficult for you.'

There was an awkward silence between them and a tension too. Jeannie felt it and knew he must feel it also. She had the overwhelming desire to fling herself into his arms, knowing that he would hold her and comfort her and take care of her.

But she could not. He would be going back to sea. He was leaving and there was always the possibility that he would not return. In that moment, she knew that she had to tell him. She could not let him leave her not knowing how she felt about him.

'Please, won't you sit down a moment.'

'I must go, I . . .' Then she saw him hesitate and knew

that there was something in her face that made him move to a chair and perch uncomfortably on the edge of it. She sat down opposite him and clasped her hands so tightly in front of her that her knuckles were white.

'I'm going to say something to you now. I should not be saying it. Not now. Not so soon after Tom's death and on the very day we've held a service for him. I'll probably be condemned to eternal damnation for it.' She gave a wry smile and hurried on. 'And I don't want you to say – or do anything – when I've said it. I just want you to go. But it has to be said. I – I can't let you go back without you knowing – how – how I feel about you.'

She saw him start physically, saw the flame of hope leap into his eyes. He breathed her name, 'Jeannie.' Just that. Just her name. 'Jeannie.'

'I was very fond of Tom,' she went on. 'He was a good man. A good husband and father and I – I thought I could love him.'

She thought back now in her own mind, but not saying the words aloud, how she had believed that Tom Lawrence would be like his father who had reminded her so much of her own beloved father. She had been disillusioned and yet she was still able to say quite truthfully that Tom had been a good man.

'I loved him but I was never *in love* with him. I never knew what it was to fall in love until . . .' She licked her lips nervously. 'Until I met you.'

'Jeannie . . .' He was up and out of his chair and taking the two strides that it took to reach her.

'No, no,' she cried and held up her hands, palms outwards, to fend him off. 'Please, don't. Don't say or do anything. It wouldn't – wouldn't be right. It's bad enough that – that I'm even saying this at all. Please . . . don't.'

Reluctantly he sank back into the chair.

Flatly now, she said, 'I just had to say something. I couldn't let you go back without – without telling you. I mean, Havelock could be bombed or you could . . .' The words stuck in her throat.

His face was serious but there was more life and hope in his eyes than she could ever remember seeing. 'I'll come back to you, Jeannie. I promise you. And you – you take care of yourself.'

He rose from his chair. 'And now I must go or I shall be guilty of an action that I might well feel ashamed of.' They looked at each other, their eyes meeting as they both remembered. He smiled and said softly, 'And I wouldn't want that to happen. Not again.'

As he passed close to her on his way to the door, he touched her shoulder gently. 'Remember I love you, Jeannie, as I have never loved another woman in my life. It feels as if I have loved you for ever.'

And then he was gone, closing the door behind him. As she heard the back-door close too, Jeannie picked up a cushion from the sofa and buried her face against it to stifle the sobs that would no longer be held in check.

Robert felt guilty at feeling so happy. It didn't seem right that he should be so full of hope and actually, for the first time for as long as he could remember, looking forward to the future. Not when that future was only going to happen because of the death of two people: his wife Louise and Tom Lawrence. And yet, he couldn't help it. But for a while he must keep his happiness in check. He was still supposed to be mourning his wife and paying respectful tribute to a man who had been his employee and a shipmate in wartime.

But privately Robert dreamt of a future with Jeannie

and he couldn't stop himself from making plans. After the war was over – and it must be soon – he would return home. He would pay court to Jeannie properly and openly and after a decent interval they would be married. He would sell the house Louise had furnished and decorated with her own individual taste. It had never, for a moment, been his and he would buy Jeannie another home. No, no, he corrected himself, this time they would buy one together.

So it was with a happy heart and bounce in his step that Robert strode up the gangway of the minesweeper with an air of 'Let's get this damned war finished and get home again'.

Thirty-Seven

Now why, Jeannie questioned over the following days, had Aggie attended Tom's funeral? She was deliberately trying to keep her thoughts from straying to Robert and at least the puzzle gave her something else to concentrate her mind on. The boys had returned to sea and the house, with just her and Nell in it, was lonely. Nell was no company now for she spent her days lost in a little world of her own. Jeannie wondered if she even realized that she had now lost every member of her family except her grandsons.

So, with the figure of the black-clad woman still in her thoughts, the day Jeannie opened the back-door to find Aggie standing there was no surprise.

'May I come in?'

Jeannie hesitated, glancing over her shoulder. Nell was in the front room, asleep on the couch. There could be no harm, Jeannie thought, in Aggie stepping into their kitchen. Just for a moment.

She nodded and held the door open.

Aggie stood in the centre of the homely kitchen and looked about her, as if drinking in the scene and committing it to memory. Slowly she pulled her gloves from her hands and moved towards the wooden chair near the fireplace and ran her fingers over its smooth high back.

'Was this George's chair?' she asked and as she turned

to look at her, Jeannie was shocked to see tears shimmering in her eyes.

Jeannie nodded and then said, 'Won't you sit down? Would you like a cup of tea?'

But Aggie seemed not to be listening. She was still standing looking down at the time-worn chair and then, very slowly, she moved round and sat down in it.

Jeannie set the kettle to boil and a few moments later she held out a cup of tea to the woman without even asking further if she would like it.

Taking it, Aggie said, 'You must be wondering why I've come?'

'Aye, well. I suppose I am.'

Jeannie sat down in the chair opposite and waited.

'Where's Nell? I don't want to upset her.'

Jeannie gestured with her head towards the next room. 'Asleep. Besides, I shouldna worry. Her mind's . . . Well, let's just say she might not even remember who you are.'

'Poor Nell,' Aggie murmured. 'To come to this. I wouldn't have wished this on her, not even though I've detested her for years.' She smiled wryly. 'Though not, I suspect, as much as she has hated me.'

Once more, as she had been on the few occasions she had come into contact with Aggie Turnbull, Jeannie was surprised at the cultured tones of this woman.

'And I don't hate her now. Not any more,' Aggie was saying. 'She hasn't deserved all the tragedy that has befallen her. To lose her husband . . .' the voice quavered a little, 'and both her children.'

Jeannie said nothing but she was thinking, the nerve of this woman! To sit here in Nell's kitchen and talk of her loss as if they had been bosom friends, when in fact Aggie had played a part in Grace's downfall. The very nerve . . .

The blue eyes were now regarding Jeannie steadily. 'I'm not as black as I'm painted, you know. I loved Grace like my own daughter.' The smile on her mouth was wistful now. 'If things had been different, she might well have been *my* daughter. She should have been my daughter. Not Nell McDonald's.'

'What – what do you mean?'

Aggie leant her head back against the chair. 'George Lawrence and me. We were walking out together. We'd talked about getting engaged to be married. A proper engagement, you know. For a year or so. Not like now when they're rushing to the altar. Living for today because they don't know if there's even going to be a tomorrow.'

Jeannie stiffened and gripped the arms of her chair. But she did not interrupt Aggie.

'Yes, we were going to be married. Me and George.' There was a pause and then a bitter note crept into her tone as she said, 'And then the herring girls came and with them, Nell McDonald.'

For a long moment there was silence and as Jeannie opened her mouth to prompt Aggie in her story, there was a sudden noise and both women in the kitchen jumped as the door opened and Nell stood there, as if on cue.

Nell glanced from one to the other and then her gaze rested on Aggie. Jeannie watched in amazement as recognition flared in Nell's eyes. Gone, in an instant, was the vacant look of the past months. Nell's eyes flashed and her mouth tightened.

'What is she doing in *my* kitchen?' she asked and her tone spat venom. Already Aggie was rising from the chair, setting her cup on the table and reaching for her gloves. 'I'll be going, Jeannie. I don't want to upset her.'

'Her? *Her?* I have a name.'

307

'I know your name. Only too well.' Now Jeannie could see that Aggie's patience was at an end. 'Oh yes, I know your name all right, Nell McDonald.'

'Lawrence,' Nell screeched. 'And dinna you be forgetting it.'

'I'm not likely to do that, Nell. Since you're the one who wrecked my life.'

'Oho, so it's ma fault you became a whore, is it? But you took revenge right enough, didn't you? Taking my daughter down the way you did.'

Softly now and sadly, Aggie said, 'I would never have harmed a hair of her head. Grace was the daughter I never had. The daughter I should have had. *His* daughter.'

Nell seemed about to speak, but Aggie had control now and held up her hand. 'No, Nell, you shall hear me out. After all these years, you shall know the truth. When George fell in love with you and left me, it broke my heart. And my heart never mended. Oh, I was foolish, I admit that. I went a little mad for a while. I thought I could fill my life with fun and laughter and – and other men. By the time I came to my senses, it was too late. All too late. My reputation was in shreds.' She nodded towards Nell. 'Aye and you did your share in spreading the gossip. So, I did become what everyone said I was. But there was no one, not any man, who could ever fill George's shoes. And then Grace came into my life. A little piece of the man I loved. I had watched her grow, and Tom, too, from a distance, and then suddenly, she came to my house one day. She came for a little fun. To dress up and look pretty for while.' She leant forward. 'For a few hours she wanted to get away from the stink of fish and the net on the wall and the worry of wondering whether her father and her brother were going to come home again from the sea. She just wanted a little harmless fun, Nell. That was all.'

'All? All, you say? To become a – a whore, like you? To – to . . .' Nell spluttered, her mouth unable to form the dreadful words.

Aggie was shaking her head. 'Now that is where you're wrong, Nell. Grace never lay with any other man than Francis Hayes-Gorton. And that only because she loved him and believed he loved her.'

Nell advanced towards Aggie threateningly. 'How dare you even speak of my daughter in that way!'

'Oh I dare, Nell, because it's the truth. I've only come here today because I wanted Jeannie to know the truth. I no longer hate you, Nell. I feel sorry for you . . .'

'I'm no' needin' your pity,' Nell spat, but Aggie carried on as if she had not spoken. 'I feel sorry that you have lost them all now. You don't deserve that. And no mother should go to her grave believing her daughter a bad woman. She wasn't, Nell, truly she wasn't.'

For a moment Nell stared at the woman and then suddenly her features crumpled and she covered her face with her hands. Swiftly, Jeannie moved to her and put her arms about her, holding her close. Over her shoulder, she said, 'I think you'd better leave,' but the words of dismissal were not spoken harshly but with more understanding than Jeannie had ever thought she would be able to use towards Aggie Turnbull.

'I'm sorry,' Aggie whispered and she made to leave. 'I didn't mean to upset her.'

With head bowed, Aggie passed through the back door and closed it quietly behind her.

Thirty-Eight

They spent a restless night. Jeannie lay awake listening to Nell tossing and turning in the next room, anxious lest Aggie's visit would tip the elderly woman completely into the realms of confusion. In the morning she was surprised to find that Nell was up early and downstairs in the kitchen, singing. When Jeannie descended the stairs, her head aching behind her eyes after only brief snatches of sleep throughout the night, she was startled to find Nell standing at the kitchen wall, braiding the net.

For a moment, time took a tilt and she thought she was back in the early days when she had first come to this house.

'The porridge is on the hob, hen,' Nell said and glanced up briefly. She turned back to her work, but not before Jeannie had noticed that her eyes were unnaturally large and bright, though her fingers were working with the easy rhythm of old.

'Right,' Jeannie said, moving forward, glancing at Nell warily for she did not know quite what to make of this sudden change, this recapturing of her old vigour. Then Jeannie shrugged. Oh well, she told herself. Perhaps it had needed a shock to jolt Nell from her lethargy.

Jeannie fervently hoped so.

The day continued as it had begun. Nell even hummed softly to herself as she worked.

'You should rest now,' Jeannie said in the middle of the afternoon. 'It's lovely to see you back to your old self, but don't try to overdo it.'

Nell cast her a puzzled glance. 'My old self? Why, haven't I been?'

'Well.' Jeannie cast about in her mind for words that were not a lie, but would not tell the whole truth. 'We've both been a bit under the weather recently, haven't we?'

Again, a quick glance and a smile, but Nell's fingers never stopped.

Jeannie longed to question Nell about Aggie's visit and the meaning behind all that had been said. But she dared not take the risk.

Maybe I'll go and see Aggie myself sometime and find out, Jeannie promised herself. Maybe tomorrow, when I've seen Nell up and about, I can slip out. But today, I don't want to leave her.

Jeannie's glance rested again upon the woman who was her mother-in-law, her son's grandmother and Sammy's too. How good it was to see her back to her old self.

The following morning Jeannie was first down to the kitchen, half an ear listening for signs of Nell moving about upstairs. When eight thirty came and she had not appeared, Jeannie went up the stairs and tapped on the bedroom door. 'May I come in?'

There was no reply, so Jeannie opened the door. 'Gran?'

In the half light shining through the drawn curtains, it seemed as if Nell was still asleep, lying on her back, her arms resting above the covers. Jeannie moved across the room, opened the curtains and then came back to stand beside the bed. She touched Nell's shoulder and bent over her. 'Gran?' she said again, but already she knew.

Nell had died, quite peacefully, in her sleep.

The boys got compassionate leave once more only a few weeks after Tom's death.

'I got a bit of flak from my skipper.' Joe grimaced. 'Asked me how many more relatives I'd got who were likely to pop off so that I could wangle more leave. I told him, there's only me mam and even Hitler wouldn't dare to bomb her.' He tried to grin, but it was an effort. Both boys had been very fond of their grandmother and she had never been a cause of animosity between them.

'I've only got forty-eight hours,' Sammy said quietly. 'Mine was quite good about it, surprisingly, 'cos he can be a right bastard about everything else.' They were serving on different ships now and saw little of each other.

'Sammy . . .' Jeannie said warningly.

'Sorry, Mam, but he is. Anyway, I explained about Dad and told him I thought probably the shock had affected Gran worse than we knew. I mean, when we came home for his funeral service, I thought it was all sort of – well – passing her by.'

Jeannie smiled sadly. 'I wish you could have seen her that last day. She was just like her old self. Giving Aggie Turnbull a piece of her mind . . .'

'Aggie Turnbull?' Both young men spoke at once. Then Joe said, 'She was here? In this house?' and Sammy asked, 'Why?'

Jeannie shrugged and said slowly, 'There's a mystery somewhere. Something to do with years ago and George –

312

your grandfather. But whatever it was, it certainly roused Nell out of her – well – whatever it was she was in.'

Joe glowered. 'More than likely that's what killed her.'

Jeannie stared at him. 'Oh no, dinna say that. It's no' fair. She died of a stroke.'

'Exactly,' Joe said grimly. 'Brought on by the likes of Aggie Turnbull daring to set foot in this house. I'm surprised at you, Mam, even letting her across the threshold.'

Jeannie stared at him. Standing there, a scowl on his handsome features, she had never seen Joe look so very like his father. It was almost as if Tom had come back to life.

And then Sammy spoke in his gentle voice in a tone so reminiscent of his Uncle Robert, that Jeannie was forced to reach out to the nearest chair for support. 'Aggie's not so bad. She . . .'

Joe turned on him viciously. 'Oh aye. Know her well, do ya? Been visiting her whorehouse?' Then he turned and slammed out of the room, leaving Jeannie and a red-faced Sammy staring at each other.

'I've come to see Sammy, really,' Robert said, as he removed his hat and stepped into the house by the front door. His voice dropped to a whisper as he added, 'But it's a good excuse to see you.'

'Ssh, they'll hear you,' Jeannie said and felt herself blushing.

She led him through the front room and into the kitchen, raising her voice to say, 'They're both in here. You've only just caught them. They're away in an hour.'

Both young men rose to their feet as Jeannie said, 'Mr Robert's come to see you, Sammy.'

Jeannie beckoned Joe to follow her from the room, leaving Robert and Sammy alone, but Robert held up his hand. 'No, no, please don't go. That is unless Sammy has any objections?'

He looked towards the young man whose face was set in mutiny. 'I've nowt to say that they don't know already, mister.'

'I see,' Robert said slowly and cast a look at Jeannie, raising his eyebrows slightly in a question. But Jeannie lowered her gaze.

There was a tension in the room already as Robert sat himself at the table opposite Sammy. 'It seems I've left it a little late if you're leaving shortly, but Edwin and I would like you to come to the office to discuss the future of the company. As you know . . .'

Sammy stood up with such a sudden, jerky movement that his chair fell backwards. 'I aren't coming anywhere, mister. Not now, not ever. I want nowt to do wi' you or your company.'

'Sammy,' Jeannie said, 'think what you're saying.'

'You keep out of this, Mam.'

'That's right,' Joe agreed, moving nearer Sammy. 'He's a right to choose what he wants to do.'

'Not until he's at least twenty-one, he hasn't,' Jeannie snapped.

Sammy was quick on the uptake. 'Then I can't be involved in decision-making either.' There was a sneer on his face as he spoke directly to Robert. 'I aren't old enough.'

Carefully, Robert said, 'No, we realize that, but we want you to feel involved. We want you to be involved.'

'Why?' Joe demanded. 'Why should you want him – a bastard who's only just been acknowledged by his own father *after he's dead* – to have a hand in running your company?'

Robert spread his hands. 'It was his grandfather's wish. I admit, Francis's turn-about has surprised us just as much as it has you, but we all know that this is what old Samuel wanted.'

'Oh aye, an' he took his time acknowledging him too, didn't he?' Joe was vociferous. 'Eighteen years, to be exact.' He paused, his eyes narrowing. 'If you ask me, you only want *him* . . .' Joe jabbed his finger first into Sammy's shoulder and then towards Jeannie, 'because it'll give you an excuse to keep seeing *her*.'

'Joe, how dare you? Apologize at once.'

'I won't, 'cos it's true, ain't it, mister?'

Calmly, Robert said, 'Actually, no, it isn't. This has nothing to do with Jeannie . . . your mother and me.'

Careful, Jeannie wanted to say, careful what you say.

Quietly, in his own way, Robert was trying to explain, trying to win the two young men over, but Jeannie knew it was a hopeless task. 'Our two families have been intertwined for many years. Your Grandfather Lawrence worked for the Gorton Trawler Company all his life, first as a deckie-learner, then as a deck-hand, mate and lastly, for many years, as a skipper. Don't you think he would have been proud to know that you, Sammy, were an important part of that company now?'

'No, 'cos he wouldn't have been proud of his birth. He wouldn't have been proud of the likes of you bringing his daughter down and causing her death, if it comes to that.' It was surprising how Joe was suddenly Sammy's mouthpiece and even more surprising that Sammy himself seemed content to let his cousin speak for him.

'George was a good man who would have stood by

Grace and would have brought up Sammy and loved him. Just as we have done,' Jeannie put in.

'Oh aye,' Joe flashed at her, the bitterness of years suddenly surfacing. 'You've certainly done that. You treat him more like a son than you do me.'

Still Sammy said nothing, but a slow, burning redness crept up his neck.

'So, Sammy,' Robert said, trying to steer the conversation away from dangerous currents. 'Do I take it that you want nothing to do with the company and that, when you're old enough, you intend to sell your shares?'

'Ah, now I see. You want his shares.' Still, it was Joe speaking.

'No,' Robert said quietly, holding on to his temper. But only just, Jeannie thought, as she saw the impatience flicker in his eyes. 'What I want, is for Sammy to take a full and active part in the running of the Company in any way he wants.'

'How generous,' Joe said sarcastically.

'Shut up, Joe,' Sammy muttered at last. 'I'll say what I'm going to do – or not do.'

'Well, get on an' say it then, instead of standing there like a piece of wet fish.'

'I don't want the shares,' Sammy said. 'I don't want anything to do with the Gortons or their ships. When I come back from the war – if I do – I'll get a berth with another line. Mebbe the Hathersage Company or . . .'

Joe gave a bark of wry laughter. 'Don't be daft. They're all one now.'

Sammy's mouth dropped open and he turned back to Robert. 'Is that true?' and when Robert nodded, he said, 'Oh well, that's it then. There'll be no job for me here after the war.'

'Now don't be so hasty,' Robert tried one last time.

'Think it over. None of us can do anything until after the war anyway. My brother's keeping things going as best he can, but with more than half the fleet requisitioned by the Navy, well, there's not a lot of fishing being done anyway. Will you at least promise me, Sammy, that after the war's over you'll see how you feel then?'

'All right,' the young man said stiffly. 'But I aren't going to change me mind.'

Thirty-Nine

'If you marry that man, I'll – I'll never speak to you again, as long as I live. Oh I saw him lookin' at you.' His lip curled. 'And you at him.'

Jeannie stared at Joe and her mouth tightened. 'And who are you to tell me what I should or shouldna do?'

'I'm your son, that's who. Though you seem to have a job remembering which of us is.'

Robert had left and now the three of them stood facing each other in the cramped kitchen.

Jeannie stared at Joe and shook her head sadly. 'So, you'd condemn me to a life of loneliness? And for why? What have you got against him?'

'Me dad hated him and that's good enough for me. He made Sammy the excuse to keep coming here, didn't he?' He glanced at Sammy and then away again. 'It were him, Mr Robert, who attacked me dad's sister. And isn't *he* the result?' He flung his hand out towards Sammy.

Aghast, Jeannie said, 'No, no, you've got it wrong. Mr Francis is – was – his father. Grace loved him.'

'If you believe that, Mam, then you're daft,' Joe sneered. 'After she died, I 'spect Mr Robert thought he'd have a go at you, did he?'

Jeannie was incensed. 'How dare you speak to me like that! Or say such things about your brother . . .'

'He's not my brother. He's my cousin.'

'Well . . .' For a moment Jeannie was confounded.

318

'Well, yes, that's true, but I still won't have you saying, or believing, such things.'

'If I'm old enough to fight in a war, I'm old enough to say what I like in my own house. And yes, it is my house. I am head of it.'

'Not while there's breath in my body, you're not,' Jeannie retaliated.

'Then,' he said slowly. 'I'll leave.'

'No,' Sammy spoke up. 'If anyone should go, it ought to be me.'

He stood between them, looking at each of them in turn. 'We've never got on, have we, Joe? So, we'd best be going our separate ways. And Mam – for I shall always think of you as me mam, even though I know the truth now—'

'Don't be silly, Sammy,' Jeannie said sharply. 'There's no need to be talking of leaving. This is your home and always will be. All brothers fight.'

'I tell you, he's not my brother,' Joe roared. 'He's a Gorton bastard. And he's too stupid to take what's handed to him on a plate.' Now he turned to face him. 'God, Sam, you are stupid. Turning down all that money.'

'Oh aye, I'm stupid all right. Stupid to stand here and let you be me mouthpiece. But me mind's made up. I'll make me own way in the world. But one thing I do know. I'm not the result of a rape, nor am I Mr Robert's bastard. Like Mam has always said, I'm Francis Hayes-Gorton's son, 'cos there's no way a man like him would have left his will the way he did, if I weren't. Besides, I asked someone who really knows the truth.'

'Oh yes, there is,' Joe said maliciously, referring to the will and ignoring the last part of Sammy's remark. 'He left it like that to get back at his brother, Mr Robert.'

'What do you mean?' Both Jeannie and Sammy spoke at once.

Joe smirked triumphantly. 'Stands to reason, dun't it? We all know – now – that Mr Francis was having an affair with Mr Robert's wife. So, he left his shares in the business between her, what was her name . . .?'

'Louise,' Jeannie murmured, without stopping to think.

Joe cast her a glance but went on, 'Aye, Louise and Sammy. Sammy already had 17 per cent of the shares from the old man, so together him and Louise owned 66 per cent of the company. Between 'em, they had enough to outvote both Robert and Edwin every time, if they wanted.'

Jeannie gasped. 'How do you know all this? How do you know such exact figures?'

Joe grinned. 'It was all set out in Sammy's letters. I pieced 'em together again and read 'em.'

'But that's not the case now, is it?' Sammy said. 'She's dead so Mr Robert's got all her shares too.'

'I know that. I'm just saying that I reckon that was the only reason Mr Francis left *you* anything. Because he wanted to get back at his brother.'

'You could be right, I suppose,' Sammy said, and Jeannie was sure she detected a note of disappointment in his voice. 'But why bother leaving me anything at all? Why not leave the whole lot to her?'

'Because he wanted to get back at 'em all. At Mr Robert by proving all the rumours true. That he had been having an affair with her and also making it that the Hayes-Gorton family had to accept you. You still own forty-one and a half per cent of the company. You could make life difficult for them if you wanted. By heck, I wish it were me. I'd mek 'em all sit up and take notice of me.' He thumped his chest as he said it.

'Well,' Sammy said again. 'I still don't want any part of it. Though he's right about one thing. I'll make up me mind when the war's over. A lot can happen 'afore then.'

'Sammy,' Jeannie was frantic now. 'You didna mean what you said? You will come back here. This is your home.'

The two young men glanced at each other and suddenly Joe grinned and put his arm about Sammy's shoulder. 'Course he will, Mam. Don't worry. I'll see we both come back safe and sound.' He stepped forward and suddenly kissed her cheek. 'You'd not know what to do with yarsen, if you hadn't us to keep sortin' out and getting between us when we start scrapping.'

She hugged them both swiftly. It was time they were leaving now, but before she let go of Sammy she said, 'What did you mean when you said you'd been to see someone who knew the truth about your birth?'

For a moment Sammy looked embarrassed. 'I went to see Aggie Turnbull.'

Now Joe let out a huge guffaw. 'Find you a girl, did she? Or do you fancy an older woman?'

He glanced briefly at Joe. 'Don't be disgusting, Joe. She's old enough to be me grandmother. And no, she didn't find me a girl. I can do that well enough for mesen.' Then he turned back to Jeannie again. 'Mam, she's very ill. She took bad the day after she'd been here. The day Gran died. She told me everything. Even about her and me grandad and then about me own mam and Mr Francis. I know the truth now, but I still don't want anything to do with that family. The Hayes-Gortons. I'll earn me own living.'

'I still bet you'll go to sea on one of his boats, though,' Joe put in slyly. 'Ne'er mind what you say now. Work'll be hard to find after the war. You'll be glad to take what you can then, I bet.'

'Mebbe I will,' Sammy said quietly. 'But if I do, it'll be honest labour and I'll be paid for the job I do.'

'Aye, an' they earn plenty of the sweat off our backs,' Joe said. 'You don't see them going out on them trawlers, putting themselves at the mercy of the North Sea. Oh no, but they're quite happy to buy their fancy houses and live like lords on the money we earn for them. And I suppose that's what you want now, is it, Mam? Living out of town with Mr Robert in his fancy house and dressed in furs and dripping jewellery. Well, if ya do, you won't see me any more, I'm telling you.'

'Joe—' she began but then Sammy cut in, saying, 'Mam, I'm sorry, but I'm with Joe on this. If you have owt to do with Mr Robert, then you won't see me either.'

She was stunned into silence.

'Well, I'll be damned.' Joe was beaming and he slapped Sammy on the back.

'And there's another thing.' Sammy was going on as if she had nothing to say nor comment to make on their organization of her life. 'Aggie was asking for you.'

Wordlessly, Jeannie nodded and sat down heavily in the chair. For the first time in the whole of her life she was speechless. She could say nothing.

There was nothing to be said.

Forty

She sat beside Aggie's bed and took the frail, wrinkled hand into her own.

'Aggie, it's me. It's Jeannie.'

She could hardly believe that the woman lying in the bed was indeed Aggie. In just a few days, the woman looked as if she had aged twenty years. The meeting with Nell had taken its toll on Aggie too.

'Jeannie?' Even the voice was different. 'Oh yes, Jeannie. I'm glad you've come. I'm not long for this world and . . .'

'Oh now, don't say that, Aggie.'

The smile was wistful. 'I'm tired and I'm ready to go. There's no one left now to even mourn me.'

Jeannie felt the tears smart her eyes.

'So many memories. So many regrets . . .'

Now Jeannie was silent as Aggie continued, her voice a little stronger as she did so. 'I wanted to see you. There's something I need to tell you, Jeannie. I suppose I'm looking for a kind of absolution.'

'You want to see a priest?'

'No, no . . .' Now the smile was almost mischievous again and yet there was still a tinge of regret. 'No, I'm afraid me and priests haven't had much to do with one another for a long time.' She paused and then went on quietly. 'I'm sorry for what happened to Nell. Sorry if I caused it.'

'Nobody could ken that, Aggie. There's no point in taking the blame.'

Aggie cast her a glance of wry amusement. 'One more burden of guilt won't make much extra weight for me.'

She sighed and nestled back against the pillows, glancing away from Jeannie, out of the window at the grey clouds scudding by, though she let her hand lie in Jeannie's.

'I wanted to tell you about myself. Do you know, Jeannie, out of all the folks around here, you were the only one I ever wished could be my friend?' Her smile was wistful as she added quietly, 'I knew it was impossible, of course. Not only were you married into the Lawrence family but you were, by nature, a good woman. Not the kind who could ever consort with me and my sort.'

Jeannie desperately wanted to deny that she had ever judged Aggie, but her innate honesty kept her silent. She knew, to her shame, that she had played her part in shunning Aggie and her like, had physically dragged Grace from her 'house of ill repute' without knowing either what really went on there or anything about the woman everyone was so eager to malign. Unable to say anything, Jeannie merely patted Aggie's hand and settled back to listen. That was the very least she could do for the dying woman.

'I was born in this house, you know,' the frail voice began, but as she talked, Aggie became more animated, almost as if she were reliving her early years and some of the youthful vigour crept into her tone just once more. 'My father was a fisherman, a hard worker, I'll give him that, for it's a tough life.' She paused. 'But that's about all I can say good about him. He was a brute of a man. When he came home from sea he was straight to collect his settlings and into the Fisherman's Rest. If my mother didn't waylay him somewhere between the two, there'd be no money till the next trip. Then he'd come home roaring drunk, knock Mam about – and us kids, too, if we got in his way – and then he was off to sea on the evening tide the next day. We used to dread him coming back.'

'How did your mother manage? Were there many of you? Bairns, I mean?'

'Six. Well, eight really, but two died in infancy and I think she had a miscarriage somewhere in amongst us all. And she worked. Braided the nets and took work on the docks if she could find it. I tell you, Jeannie, if it hadn't been for her, we'd have starved. We damn well nearly did as it was.' Now there was a bitter twist to her mouth. 'But she was a hard woman. Understandable, I suppose, when you think what she had to put up with, but she never showed us any affection. Never hugged us or praised us. She loved us in her way, I suppose. Certainly, she worked hard for us, but . . .' Aggie sighed. 'Kids need to feel affection, don't you think? They need to be told they're loved.' Again there was a pause before she said softly, 'I never knew what it was to be loved or what a good man was until I started courting George Lawrence. I'd always known him, of course. We'd been kids at school together, though he was a couple of years older than me. I'd adored him then. Ever since the age of seven. You know how little girls talk, well, I was always going to marry George Lawrence when I grew up and have two children, a girl and a boy.' Her voice faltered a little.

'When did you start courting?'

'George went to sea as soon as he could. I think he even stowed away his first trip, he was that mad keen to be a fisherman. He was eighteen and I was sixteen when he first asked me out. When I got home, my mother leathered me with Dad's belt. I couldn't understand what I'd done

325

wrong. We'd only gone for a stroll around the docks. He
loved looking out to sea, watching for the boats to come
in on the evening tide. "I won't have you hanging round
the docks like a woman of the streets," she yelled at me.'
Aggie chuckled. 'Do you know, Jeannie, I didn't even
know what she meant? Well, the next time George was
home, I met him in secret and we went on meeting like
that for months, almost a year. That was the happiest time
of my whole life. I loved George and I knew he loved me.
At least, he did then. Just for a year . . .' The voice faded
away as she remembered. She closed her eyes and Jeannie
thought she had dropped to sleep but then her eyelids
fluttered. She sighed heavily and began to speak again but
now her tone was flat with sorrow. 'It was the middle of
August and that was when the Scottish fisher lasses arrived
every year. It's more than forty years ago now, Jeannie,
but I remember it as if it was yesterday. George was a
young deckie then. On the day his boat was due in, I'd
dress in my prettiest dress and go down to the docks. Of
course the girls working on the fish docks called me names.
Names that weren't true. Not then. I was just prettying
myself up for my feller. You know?'

'I know,' Jeannie said softly.

'They were hard workers those fisher lasses, all of them,
and it wasn't an easy life, not by any means, and I suppose
when they stood there day after day with the stink of fish
on their clothes and in their hair, well, the sight of a girl
with time to dress up and stand idly on a corner waiting
for her man, it riled 'em I suppose.'

'Aye, I suppose I could understand that,' Jeannie said
softly. 'They'd be jealous of you, with time to spare and
nice clothes to wear.'

'When he came ashore, George came straight to me, of
course, and we went off together, but they called after us,

shouting things. He just turned and waved good-naturedly at them. Just a lark, he said, that was all it was.' She paused again and now a note of bitterness crept into her tone. 'But the next day, it wasn't a lark. I went to the quay to see him off, but before he came a group of the girls surrounded me, dragged me into an empty warehouse and kept me there until his ship had sailed.'

She was silent for so long, that Jeannie said, 'What happened?'

'I was upset, of course. I cried a bit that I'd missed seeing George off, but I daren't say anything to my family. They still didn't know I was even meeting him. I was only seventeen, remember. And I think, at that stage, if I'm honest, the fisher lasses didn't mean any real harm. They were only having a bit of fun, y'know, taking me down a peg or two for showing off.'

'But surely, it was all right the next time he came home, wasn't it? The fisher girls would have moved on by then.'

'That's what I thought, but it wasn't to be, Jeannie. Yes, they had moved on, but the boat that George was on had engine trouble and put into Yarmouth for repairs. And that's where that same team of girls had gone. And of course, when they recognized him . . .'

Jeannie was beginning to piece the story together now. 'You mean that Nell was one of those girls? That she was one who locked you in the warehouse?'

'No, no,' Aggie said swiftly. 'I'll not accuse her of that, because I don't think she was. No, she was a young lass, only a year older than me and down here on her first trip with the herring girls. Some of the older girls teased her a bit about George, told her he'd followed her down the coast. Come looking for her especially. He felt a bit sorry for her, all those miles from home, learning the trade. It is hard work, I know that. And she'd cut her finger badly.

He told me years later that he'd said, straight up, that he had a girlfriend back in Havelock but then – then . . .'

Her voice broke and tears threatened. Though she longed to hear the end of the tale, Jeannie said at once, 'Aggie, dinna say any more.'

She drew in a shuddering breath. 'No, no, I want to tell you. I need to tell you, Jeannie.'

'Then the girls told him that the time I'd not gone to see him off, they'd seen me go off with another feller whose boat'd just come in. They implied, you see, that I was there waiting for the fishermen to come ashore, collect their pay and then – then I'd go off with them.'

'And George believed them?' Jeannie was scandalized.

Aggie sighed. 'You couldn't blame him, Jeannie. He was only eighteen. We were both so young, so innocent. And I mean that, Jeannie, 'cos we were.' She paused and added meaningfully, 'Then.'

'Do you mean to tell me that Nell made up that story about you?'

The white head moved from side to side on the pillow. 'No, I don't think so. I think the girls – the older girls, that is – were just having a bit of sport with the two of them. Maybe they didn't even mean to cause the trouble they did, though the story about me was unkind.'

'To say the least,' Jeannie murmured.

'George's boat repairs took a week. In the life of a fisherman, Jeannie, a week is a long time. He was far away from home with nothing to do. And so was Nell. Not able to work for a few days because of her cut finger.'

'So, they spent a lot of time together?'

'Yes. And they fell in love.'

From the recesses of Jeannie's memory, into her mind came Nell's words when she had been telling Jeannie a little about herself. 'I just never went home,' she had said.

'But – but when George came home from Yarmouth, didna you tell him what had happened? What they'd done?'

'I tried, but I could see it was too late. Nell had hooked him and he was as helpless as a fish on the end of a line. I suppose in that week, they'd spent more time together than George and I had managed in almost a year.'

'Oh Aggie, I'm sorry.'

'Ah well, it's all a long time ago now,' Aggie said, but Jeannie could detect that the hurt and the loss were as keen as ever they had been. 'And then, I suppose, you can guess the rest. I left home to escape my domineering mother. I just wanted to be loved by a strong, kind man. A man like George Lawrence. But, I never found him, Jeannie . . .' The voice was fading now as Aggie drifted into sleep. 'I never found another George.'

For a long time, Jeannie sat there, imagining how it must have been. Imagining how the practical joke a group of young girls had played had led to the ruining of this poor woman's life. And yes, she was a 'poor' woman, for she had been misunderstood and maligned the whole of her life.

Over the next few weeks until the day that Aggie Turnbull slipped into unconsciousness from which she never recovered, Jeannie visited her daily, even sitting with her throughout that long, last night.

And Aggie's last words were to remain with her. 'If you find happiness, Jeannie, take it. Grasp it with both hands and never let it go.'

Forty-One

He was going home. The war was over, in fact it had been over for almost five months. Whilst there would be work for the minesweepers for some time to come, Robert was no longer needed. He could go home. And now there was something – or rather someone – to go home to. A new year – 1946 – and a new life.

Of course, there was still the company, such as it was now. He and Edwin would run the family firm together and one day Sammy would inherit it from them. Robert was sure Edwin wouldn't mind. Maybe even Tom's boy, Joe, would come into the company too. Jeannie would like that. Her son and the boy whom she had always looked upon as her own, running the Gorton-Hathersage Trawler Company. Then he could retire and he and Jeannie could travel the world. He could take her to all the most beautiful places. Oh, they were going to be so happy, he and his Jeannie . . .

When she opened the door to him, he saw at once the anxiety in her face. That she was pleased to see him, he could not doubt, for even on the doorstep in full view of the whole street, she flung her arms about him crying. 'You're safe. Oh thank God, you're safe.'

But as she drew him into the house and closed the door upon the world and they sat together, their arms about each other, Robert said gently. 'Something's happened. What is it?'

They had not written to each other, nor had he come to see her again, since the day of Nell's funeral service. Deliberately, he had stayed away, confident in the thought that when the war was over, she would be waiting for him. Then, he had promised himself, there would be nothing and no one to stand in the way of their happiness.

She told him of Aggie's death, not sure whether he had heard the news. When she fell silent, he said, 'But there's something else, isn't there? Something to do with us?'

She looked at him then and, as she did so, Robert felt a stab of fear, for her eyes were brimming with unshed tears. 'What is it?'

'I'm sorry, Robert, but I can't marry you.'

For a moment he could not speak. He just sat there, staring at her and gripping her hands tightly. At last, he said hoarsely, 'Why?'

She dropped her gaze, shook her head and then rested her forehead against his chest. His arms were about her. 'Just tell me why, Jeannie?'

'It's the boys. They – they're both so – against the idea. I could understand Joe, but not Sammy. I mean, you're his uncle. But even he . . .' Her voice trailed away.

'I'll talk to them . . .'

'No!' She pulled away from him then. 'Please, let me handle it.'

'Jeannie, I love you. I want you to be my wife.'

She was shaking her head slowly. 'I know, but . . . I'm not sure myself. Now.'

'You mean – you're not sure if you love me?'

'Oh no, not that. I love you. Please don't ever think that. Maybe it's because I do love you so very much that –

331

that I'm not sure. I'm so afraid. I mean, you live in such a different world. You're from a different class . . .'

Robert shook his head, his voice a gentle whisper. 'Don't talk like that. Not about me. Not about us.'

'But it matters. I wouldna fit into your world.'

'We'll make our own world.'

'But your family. It's not true what they say, you know.'

'What do *they* say?' He traced the outline of her face gently with the tip of his finger. He wasn't taking her seriously. He couldn't believe that she could say she loved him and yet allow her boys to dominate the rest of her life. His life too. Their life together.

'That you don't marry a person's family. You do. You marry into the whole family.'

Suddenly, he felt cold, colder than he had ever been out in the North Sea. She was serious. She did mean it. She was afraid of losing her own son and Sammy too. Trying, still, to make light of it, he said, 'But there's only Edwin left now and he's the most easy-going chap in the world. A good business man, mind you, but . . .'

'But there are friends, the circles you move in. Even the world of business. Your wife would be expected to be a – a hostess.'

He laughed. 'Louise never once hosted a business dinner for me.'

'Really?'

'Really.'

'Oh.'

'So, you've not a thing to worry about with my world, as you put it. The problem,' he sighed heavily, 'seems to be with your boys. What is it? Just that they don't like me or . . .?'

'I think it goes deeper than that. I think Joe is carrying on Tom's resentment against you and your family.' She glanced at him apologetically. 'Tom never made a secret of it.'

'Because of Grace you mean?'

Jeannie said nothing. She didn't want to tell him the full extent of Tom's bitterness that concerned not only Grace but Jeannie herself. Robert sighed. 'And I suppose Sammy's resentful for the very same reason.' He was quiet for a moment then asked, 'And do they blame me for Tom's death?'

Carefully she said, 'I think that comes into it.'

'Oh.' Now his tone was flat with despair. 'Well, there's going to be no way I can win them over then. Not if their reasons are as deeply rooted as that.'

'No.'

'So, you're going to have to choose, aren't you? Me – or your boys.'

Again tears filled her eyes and she nodded wordlessly, unable to speak.

He closed his eyes and gave a deep-throated groan. 'I can see you've already decided. But, oh my darling, please be sure you're doing the right thing. They'll marry, have families of their own. Are you really sure that you'll be content to live your life through them? Don't throw away the rest of your own life, Jeannie.'

She shook her head. 'I'm sorry. So sorry. But I love them both as my own sons. I couldn't bear to lose them. Not now, when they've come through so much.'

Robert picked up her hand, traced the tiny scars on her fingers, the hardened callouses. Then he pressed it to his lips and murmured against her palm, 'I thought you were made of stronger stuff, Jeannie.'

That hurt. Oh, how that hurt her. She snatched her hand away, angry now, and pulled herself free of his embrace. She stood up. 'How would you know what it feels like to be a mother? Or even a father? You've never had children of your own.'

She saw at once by his bleak expression, how much she had now hurt him. But there was no taking back the words. They were said and could not be unsaid. He rose and gave a stiff little courteous bow towards her. 'If that is your final answer,' he said, his words clipped, 'I will take my leave of you.'

'Robert, please, try to understand. I'm sorry, I didn't mean to hurt you.'

'But you are hurting me, Jeannie. And, worse still, you're hurting yourself just for the sake of two selfish young men who don't know the meaning of love yet.'

He turned away then and left the house without another word, leaving her bereft and empty, with a pain inside her too deep for tears.

Three days later, she received a letter from him. '*My darling, I can't bear to part with you in anger. I just want you to know that I will always love you and always be here for you. If ever you should need me, you know where I am . . .*'

The loving, forgiving words brought tears to her eyes, tears that now spilled over and ran down her cheeks. Impatiently, she brushed them away. He was right, she thought. She was made of sterner stuff than this. She had never been the weepie sort and yet here she was, allowing others to dictate her life.

I will go to him, she decided. I will marry Robert. Joe and Sammy will come around to it in time. Without stopping to think any more – she had done enough thinking over the past weeks, she told herself – she hurried to put on her hat and coat.

She caught the bus to the outskirts of town and then marched purposefully along the road until the houses petered out and she was in the countryside, heading for the lane where she remembered Robert's fine house lay. Frost lay on the hedgerows and the February wind was bitter, but Jeannie scarcely felt the cold.

She couldn't wait to see him now, couldn't wait to tell him . . .

She came to the gate. A wooden, five-barred gate had replaced the fancy wrought-iron one she remembered seeing on the last occasion she had come here. The war effort, she supposed, had taken them. It seemed so long ago now, since she had last stood on this spot. The two boys had been but bairns. She paused, her hand resting on the top of the gate. She was staring at the house set against a backdrop of trees, the long windows leading out on to the front terrace, the heavy oak front door, yet she was not really seeing it or the beautiful, well-kept gardens or the surrounding countryside with its flat, panoramic views.

She was remembering Joe and Sammy as babies and reliving the feel of their chubby arms clasped tightly about her neck or a sticky kiss planted on her cheek. She remembered the day they walked for the first time, those first faltering steps, the wide grin on their faces at the sense of achievement. Joe had been first and a week later, not to be outdone, Sammy had followed suit. In those first few years they had grown together believing themselves to be brothers. Oh, they had squabbled like any siblings, but not until the day Joe had told Sammy about the circumstances of his birth, had the resentment between them begun to fester.

Yet now, they were the closest they had ever been, united in their hatred of the Gorton family and so fervently opposed to her involvement with Robert.

They were so passionately set against him with the sureness of youth that they were right, that she knew they would never come around.

If she were to marry Robert Gorton and come to live in this grand house, she would lose her boys for sure.

There was a lump constricting her throat as she let her gaze wander over the house for the last time. She knew now that she would never live there. Much as she loved Robert, the heartbreak marrying him would bring would blight their love and cast a shadow over their lives. In time, it would eat into their love like a canker. Of course, she was sensible enough to realize that in time, resentment might creep into her relationship with the boys for they were forcing her to make the most difficult decision of her entire life. But now, at this moment, she could not guess to what extent that might happen.

Tears blurring her vision, she turned away. As she did so, she thought she caught sight of a figure standing at one of the first-floor windows. This time she made no effort to wipe away her tears.

This time she had good reason to weep.

Forty-Two

'Mam, this is Thelma.'

Jeannie rubbed her hands down the front of her overall, held out her hand and smiled a welcome towards the girl who was standing nervously in the doorway. She was tall and thin, so thin that Jeannie could have believed the girl hadn't eaten for days. And she stooped slightly, her shoulders rounded. Her dress was faded, the type a smart woman might have worn before the war and Jeannie guessed it was either a hand-me-down from a better-off relative or maybe even from the second-hand clothes shop. But her eyes were bright and sharp and her long fair hair curled around her face.

'I'm pleased to meet you,' Jeannie said kindly. 'Come in, hen.'

The girl's eyes widened and she giggled at the unfamiliar endearment. 'Oh, you're Scotch.'

Jeannie bridled at the misnomer but let it go. 'And you're a local lass?' she said instead.

'Oh yeah. Born an' bred in Havelock. Me dad's a fisherman, just like Joe.' The girl's eyes turned towards Joe and Jeannie could see at once the adoration in her expression. 'He's a skipper, just like Joe's going to be one day. Aren't you, Joe?'

Joe grinned, his arm about the girl's shoulders. 'I reckon.'

Jeannie smiled at the young man's confidence.

337

'The sea's me life,' he was saying, 'Always will be. Thelma understands that, bein' brought up in a fisherman's family. She won't mind being a fisherman's wife.'

'Wife?' Jeannie was surprised.

'We're getting engaged, Mam. There's a little house come up for rent at the end of Wessex Street. Just ideal. We don't want to miss it. If we get it, we'll be getting married straight away.'

'This is a bit sudden, isn't it?' She felt aggrieved. It was only five weeks since she had turned her back on Robert. Then, Joe had been ecstatic, picking her up bodily and dancing around the kitchen with her. 'We'll look after you, Mam. Me an' Sammy,' he had said. 'You've done the right thing. It'll be just the three of us. You'll not regret it, I promise.'

She was regretting it already. He had the audacity, she thought, only weeks later to waltz into her kitchen and calmly announce that he was leaving home to get married.

She looked at him keenly. 'Is that the only reason or is there something else you should be telling me?'

Joe's brow met in an angry frown. 'No, Mam. She's not expecting, if that's what you're meaning.'

Beside him the girl gasped and turned bright red.

'I'm sorry, hen,' Jeannie said swiftly, gesturing towards the girl. 'But you've got to admit that it all seems a bit of a rush. How long have you been walking out together?'

The couple glanced at one another.

'A month?' Joe muttered.

'A month!' Now Jeannie was scandalized. 'And you've been away at sea for the past three weeks.'

'But we've known each other a lot longer than that,' the girl put in. ''Aven't we, Joe? I'm a barmaid at the Fisherman's and—'

'A barmaid?' This was getting worse by the minute.

Once upon a time, Aggie's girls had worked behind the bar at the Fisherman's.

'What's wrong with that?' The girl bridled. 'It's hard work there and long hours.'

Jeannie pursed her lips and said nothing, but she knew her expression would give away her disapproval. Then she realized she was being unfair. She should not judge this girl by what had happened years ago. She turned away, shrugging her shoulders. 'Well, there doesna seem to be anything I can say. You seem to have made up your minds, but I hope . . .' she turned back briefly to face Joe once more and knew that he would understand the meaning behind her words, 'I hope *you* know what you're doing.'

It all happened so fast that Jeannie hardly had time to draw breath. Joe and Thelma got the house and were married on Joe's very next shore leave. And, as if not to be outdone, Sammy produced a girlfriend and, whilst he made no announcements of engagements or impending marriage, when he was home from the sea he was hardly ever in Jeannie's home.

In the once bustling, over-crowded Lawrence household, Jeannie was now alone and all the days of the rest of her life stretched before her, empty and meaningless.

Oh she had neighbours, and soon, she would no doubt be a grandmother, but was that all she could hope to look forward to?

It wasn't enough. Not for Jeannie.

On a fine spring morning, Jeannie locked the door of the terraced, back-to-back house in Baldock Street and walked away from it. In her handbag was more money than she had ever carried before. From the wooden box under her bed she had taken her life savings. Shillings and sixpences scrimped and saved over the years. Saved for a rainy day or for that promised trip back to her homeland.

Well, the rainy day had never come nor had the trip to Scotland. Today was a bright, glorious morning and she was going to spend the lot on herself. What was that saying she'd heard someone say once? 'Today is the first day of the rest of your life.'

Oh yes, indeed it was. And from now on, this was how it was going to be.

'Are you sure, madam?' The sales assistant sounded very doubtful. 'I mean, are you going to a wedding? That's the sort of dress and coat and hat that you'd wear as – well – the mother of the bride.' The woman's face cleared. 'Is your daughter getting married, madam?'

'No,' Jeannie said shortly and offered no further explanation but inside she was laughing, hugging the secret to herself. 'No, I just thought I'd spoil mysel'.'

The woman eyed Jeannie's own sober, serviceable coat and hat lying across the chair in the fitting room. 'Come up on the pools, have we, madam?' There was an edge of sarcasm to the woman's tone, almost of jealousy. But nothing could ruffle Jeannie's feathers today.

'No, it's my savings.'

Now the woman looked worried and eyed Jeannie suspiciously.

Maybe she thinks I've been to the Fisherman's, Jeannie thought. She'll be sniffing my breath next. Then she almost laughed out loud as another thought struck her. Maybe she thinks I've stolen the money. But the woman merely said, 'And I thought the Scots were supposed to be mean.'

'No' mean, hen, just canny,' Jeannie countered, still not offended. She twisted this way and that, eyeing the new Jeannie Lawrence reflected in the long mirror. 'Aye, I'll take it.'

Now the woman brightened. It would be, Jeannie sur-mised, her best sale of the week.

'Thank you, madam. Shall I wrap everything for you?'

'No, no. I'll keep it on. If you'd just remove the labels.'

'Then shall I – er – wrap your own garments?' There was a distinct look of distaste on the assistant's face now.

Jeannie chuckled. 'No, hen, you can throw them away.'

And with them, she thought, would go the aroma of fish that she had lived with for the whole of her life until this moment.

'But you can do one more thing for me?'

'Yes, madam?'

'Where is the underwear department?'

Jeannie spent the rest of the morning and half the after-noon in the store. In the hairdresser's, she had her hair restyled, curled and wound up on to the top of her head. It was the most sophisticated style she had ever had and, though she doubted she could repeat it herself in front of her own bedroom mirror, just for today she felt as if she had stepped off the front cover of a fashion magazine.

As she left the store, Jeannie's step was light. Clad in new clothes from the silk underwear that felt deliciously smooth against her skin to the new dress and coat that fitted snugly against her still slim figure, and her new hat set at a jaunty angle, she walked the full length of Main Street with a smile on her mouth. She could still turn a few heads, she thought.

She caught the bus heading out of town and within half an hour she was walking down the lane towards Robert's house. As the sun dropped behind the far horizon, she approached the gate once more. Her heart was beating rapidly. She stood again with her hand resting on the top bar and let her gaze roam slowly over the house. Twice before she had stood here and then turned away, back to her life near the dockside.

But this time was different. Now she took a deep breath, pushed open the gate and walked through it.

Forty-Three

'We'll buy another house, my darling. I'll put this on the market and . . .'

But Jeannie was standing in the centre of the huge drawing room, her hands clasped in front of her, turning slowly, taking in everything around her. Then she walked to the long French windows and stood looking out across the smooth stretch of lawn to the copse at the end of the garden. He came and stood beside her, putting her arms about her waist and resting his chin on her shoulder.

She leant back against him and sighed dreamily. 'But it's a beautiful house. Surely you don't want to leave it. It's your home, Robert.'

'It's never been a home, Jeannie. Louise decorated and furnished it in her own ultra-modern style. And then, she hardly ever lived here.'

Jeannie turned in his arms to face him. 'So what are you saying? That you don't want to live here because it has unhappy memories for you?'

'No, no,' he said swiftly. 'The house is right enough. I just thought that – well – you wouldn't want to live where I'd lived with Louise.'

Jeannie wrinkled her nose. 'Well, I dinna like some of her choice of decor.' Then she laughed impishly. 'Well, to be truthful, I dinna like any of it.'

'Nor me,' Robert put in with heartfelt fervour.

'But,' Jeannie was more serious now, 'I'm not jealous of

Louise so I'm not afraid of her ghostly memories in this house.'

'My darling, you have no need to be. I have only ever loved one woman in the whole of my life and she is now here in my arms.' He sighed as he added, 'But I have to admit to being jealous of your Tom.'

Jeannie blushed a little. Even now she was not quite ready to lay open her soul to Robert about the truth of her own marriage. It seemed to her that she would be dishonouring Tom's memory if she did so. And she would never want to do that for he was the father of her son and the closest to a father that Sammy had known.

They were married very quietly with Edwin the only family member present.

Neither Joe nor Sammy came to her wedding.

The day she had returned to the house in Baldock Street to meet the two boys, due home for a day and a half, had been very painful. She stood at the open front door and watched them walking down the street. Her heart contracted at the sight of them. Two good-looking young men, laughing and joking and pushing each other. They were arguing already, she thought, even though they'd stepped off different boats and hadn't seen each other for three weeks. Then they saw her standing there, dropped their bags and ran towards her.

'Mam! You look smart. Been into town?' Joe gave her a bear hug, lifting her and swinging her round. Sammy, as always, kissed her cheek and asked, 'You been all right, Mam?'

'I can't stop,' Joe went on, without giving her chance to speak. 'I must get home to Thelma. She'll be waiting for me.' He gave a suggestive chuckle and nudged Sammy. 'I'll see you in the Fisherman's later – if I've still got the strength.'

Trying to keep her voice calm, Jeannie said, 'There's something I must tell you.'

Joe grinned. 'Well, make it snappy, Mam. I ain't seen my lovely wife for three weeks, y'know.'

No, she thought, you're impatient to see your wife and that's only natural, but you think nothing of condemning me to a life of loneliness. 'Come in, just for a moment.'

The house was cold for she had not lived there for a week now and as soon as the two men stepped into the kitchen, she saw them glance at the cheerless grate and then at the wall, empty now of a half-braided net. Eyebrows raised, they looked at each other and then, with one accord, turned towards her.

Jeannie stood facing them, the kitchen table that had once been the hub of the crowded family home, between them.

'Joe,' she began, 'you're married and have a home of your own. Sammy, although you dump your washing here, you dinna sleep here even when you're ashore. You're with Sally or Sarah or whoever the girl of the moment is—'

'Helen, as a matter of fact.'

'With Helen, then,' she went on calmly, though she was aware of the fluttering just below her ribs. She clasped her hands tightly together to stop them trembling. 'I've thought things over very carefully and decided that I'm not prepared to spend the rest of my life alone.'

Joe was frowning, as if half-guessing already what she was about to say. 'You're not alone. We always come to see you. We come here *first*,' he added belligerently, as if they were bestowing a great favour upon her.

'Yes,' Jeannie agreed, 'And how long do you stay? Five minutes? Ten minutes? Long enough,' she glanced at Sammy, 'to drop your washing off?'

There was a moment's silence and then as she opened her mouth, Joe took the words from her lips. Pointing his finger at her, he burst out, 'I get it. You're going to him, aren't you?'

Silently, she nodded.

'Aw Mam, no,' Sammy said. 'No, don't do it. Please.'

'She already has,' Joe snarled. 'Just look at her fancy clothes. She didn't buy them hersen'.'

Resolutely, though her insides had turned to jelly, Jeannie said, 'You can apply for the tenancy of this house, Sammy, and you can have everything that's in it, apart from any bits and pieces that Joe might want. I'm sure,' she added with a hint of sarcasm, 'it won't be long before you follow Joe's example and get married.' She paused and then, mentioning his name for the first time, she said, 'Robert and I are getting married in three weeks' time to coincide with the next time you are both due ashore. We hope you will come to the service. It's at—'

'Never! Never in a million years. In fact . . .' Joe leant towards her, all the resentment and bitterness that had been his father's as well as his own, clearly etched into his twisted features, 'I don't want to see you again. Not ever!'

With that, her son turned and left the house slamming the door behind him so hard that the window next to it rattled.

'Oh Mam,' Sammy was saying sadly, shaking his head. 'How could you? How could you do this to us? I thought you loved us.'

That, more than Joe's anger, had been the cruellest shaft of all.

Forty-Four

'Where are you going, Jeannie?'

Robert came up behind her as she pinned her hat on to her head. 'To see Thelma.'

'Thelma?' Robert repeated, surprised.

'Aye, ma daughter-in-law.' Her mouth was tight, her words clipped with disapproval. 'If what I've been hearing is true, she's about to get a piece of ma mind.'

Robert put up his hands, palms outwards. 'Oho, I wouldn't be in her shoes, not for all the fish in the sea.'

Jeannie turned and gave him a wide smile, but her eyes still sparkled with the light of battle.

She and Robert had been married for three months and during all of that time she had not seen, nor heard, from her boys. Instead, she had heard gossip about Thelma.

Intrigued now, Robert leant towards her. 'What exactly have you been hearing?'

But Jeannie only tapped him on the nose and said, 'Never you mind. This is women's business.'

'Ah.' He asked no more but offered, 'I'll drive you, if you like.'

'You can take me into the town, but not to her door. I'll walk from the end of their road.'

He smiled knowingly. Jeannie didn't want to be seen by the neighbours drawing up in the fancy motor car. He glanced down at the grey coat and hat she was wearing. Although of good material and fine cut, they would not attract the attention that some of the items now in her wardrobe would.

'Shall I wait for you?' he asked half an hour later as he opened the car door for her and helped her to alight.

'Are you going to the office?'

'Yes.'

'Then I'll walk from their house to the dockside and meet you there.' The corners of her mouth lifted slightly. 'It'll be nice to see Edwin. We should ask him to dinner soon. Do you think he'd come?'

'Of course, he would. He likes you, you know.' He closed the door as he added, 'See you soon, then. Good luck!'

Jeannie's smile broadened. 'It'll be her needing the good luck.'

Chuckling to himself, Robert got back into his car and drove away as Jeannie set off to walk the length of Wessex Street until she came to the terraced house where Joe and his wife lived.

Rapping smartly on the door she stood and looked about her, tapping the toe of her shoe whilst she waited. Across the street, she saw the net curtains twitch. Further along the road, two women stood, their arms folded beneath their ample bosoms, their hair tied up, turban-style, in headscarves. They watched her, their heads bent towards each other as they gossiped.

Thelma opened the door. She was still in her dressing gown though it was gone eleven in the morning. 'Oh, it's you,' was her only greeting.

'Well, are you no' going to ask your mother-in-law in?'

The young woman pulled the corners of her mouth down, but left the door open and led the way, scuffing along on worn-down slippers, through to the back kitchen. Jeannie wrinkled her nose in disgust as she entered the stuffy room. There was a stale smell of cabbage water. The floor did not appear to have been swept for a fortnight, nor the windows cleaned.

Jeannie flicked the chair with her glove before sitting down. Turning to look at the girl, she asked, not unkindly, 'Are you ill, hen?'

Thelma looked up in surprise. 'Ill? No, course I aren't. Why d'you ask that?'

Jeannie's glance around the room spoke volumes and the girl reddened though more from anger than embarrassment. 'Oh I see. Not posh enough for you, now?' Her lips curled.

Jeannie's own mouth was tight. 'I've never lived in fancy houses, not until now,' she admitted. 'But I've always kept my home clean and tidy. There's no excuse for this.' She waved her hand to encompass the whole room. 'It's not what Joe's used to.' Thelma opened her mouth again, but Jeannie forestalled her. 'But that's not what I've come about. If you want to live in a pigsty then that's up to the pair of you.' She leant forward. 'But what I don't like, is hearing gossip about you while my son's away at sea.'

'Eh?' The girl looked startled.

'Aye.' Jeannie nodded slowly. 'From what I hear, you're fast taking over from where Aggie Turnbull left off.'

Thelma sprang up out of her chair so suddenly that Jeannie jumped, her spine coming up hard against the back of the wooden chair. Thelma leant over her, raining spittle on Jeannie's face. 'How dare you? How dare you come into my house and say such things?'

Jeannie rose slowly and stood facing the younger woman. 'I dare because I care about my son.'

'Well, he dun't care about you. Not since you married *him*. He dun't want anything more to do with you. So, you can get out of this house and stay out.'

'Very well. But I shall be on the dockside the next time his ship comes home.'

A look of sudden fear passed over Thelma's face. 'He won't believe you,' she said, though now there was a tiny sliver of doubt in her tone. 'He'll not believe anything *you* tell him.'

Jeannie made to turn away towards the door, but glanced back to say calmly, 'He'll believe me, because he's the jealous type. Just like his dad. He believed the gossip about Mr Robert calling at the house when he was away. Never mind that Sammy was his nephew and he was trying to help him. Never mind that he was the one who kept Tom at sea when other ships' runners would have passed him over for the times he missed a trip. Oh no, Joe's just like his dad in that. He believes what he wants to believe.' She shrugged. 'And even if I don't tell him, you can bet someone from around here will. I've heard the gossip about you as far away as my posh house.' She raised her eyebrows and put her head on one side. 'Haven't I?'

Before her eyes the girl's bravado crumpled. 'Oh please, don't tell him. Please. He'll kill me.'

As she burst into noisy tears, Jeannie stepped forward and put her arms about the girl. 'There, there, hen. Whatever's been going on, must stop. I'll say nothing, but I canna promise he won't hear from others.'

The sobbing only increased as, muffled against Jeannie's shoulder, Thelma said, 'It has stopped already. It was – it was only the one time. There was this sailor. Swedish, he was. He kept coming into the Fisherman's. I know it was stupid of me, wrong of me, but he was so handsome and charming and Joe'd been away at sea so long, longer than usual.'

She drew back and looked up into Jeannie's face now. 'I swear it was only him used to come to the house, but there was one time when some of his mates called round here for him. I suppose that was when the neighbours . . .'

'Och aye, the neighbours,' Jeannie said with a sudden, heart-felt sympathy. 'What they don't know they'll make up, hen. That's why you've got to be so careful. But if it's over, then we'll say no more about it. And, as I say, Joe will hear nothing from me. Forget all about it. Put it behind you and get yourself prettied up for when he comes home.'

The tears were still flowing down Thelma's face. 'I – can't forget all about it. I'm – I'm pregnant. And – and I don't know whose it is. Joe's or – or Olaf's.'

'Och no,' Jeannie whispered. 'No, hen.'

'I canna be pregnant. I'm forty-one. It's no' decent at my age.' Jeannie, wide eyed, faced the doctor. She was appalled at the very thought of becoming a mother again and a grandmother almost within the same month.

'Well you are, Mrs Gorton. A good three months gone, I'd say. Had you really not thought that could be the case?'

Jeannie shook her head. 'After my son was born I thought there might be another bairn or two, but it just never happened. I only came to see you because I thought – I thought maybe it was the change starting early.'

The doctor smiled. 'No. A late baby, my dear, not the menopause.'

Jeannie was silent, just staring at him.

'I'd have thought you would be pleased. An heir for the Gortons, eh? If it's a boy, of course.'

A legitimate heir she was thinking. Would he oust Sammy? She didn't know the law well enough to know. But he would be a threat to Sammy. Maybe when he was old enough, he would fight Sammy in court and win.

Maybe Sammy would just hand everything over to him without a fight. He had never shown any sign of even wanting the share of the company that he already had, let alone one day playing an active part in the running of it. He had climbed down far enough to work on a Gorton trawler, but, Robert had told her, Sammy left the money that came from his shares just sitting in the bank account into which it was paid twice a year.

'He's never even touched it,' Robert had said. 'Not even when there's been a bad trip and he must be short of cash. It's as if he denies, even to himself, that it's even there.'

'Does he know about it?'

'Oh, yes, statements are sent to him regularly.'

Remembering the previous times, Jeannie said, 'Perhaps he doesna even open the letters.'

Robert had laughed, unable to believe such a suggestion. 'Oh, he'll come around one day.' And then referring more to her than to the company or to money, he had added, 'They both will.'

'I don't want it,' she heard a voice saying now and realized it was she who had spoken.

'Oh come, my dear,' the doctor said. 'It's a shock, I've no doubt but . . .'

'I'm too old. It – it could be born, well, no' right.'

The doctor spread his hands. 'The risk is higher when you're older, but really there is no reason to talk like that. You must talk to your husband. Robert, I'm sure, will be delighted.' Suddenly the kindly doctor was disapproving. 'I do hope you're not contemplating doing something very silly.'

Mutely, Jeannie shook her head and stood up suddenly. She needed to get out of this stuffy consulting room. She needed to think.

She walked the length of Main Street and found herself

at the docks. She did not stop but kept ⌐
out past the dock master's office, right out ⌐
the pier. The very place where she had stood ⌐
night in Havelock watching for her father's boat. ⌐
night she had met Robert and Grace and all the people
who were to change her life for ever.

All at once she was very homesick. Homesick for
Scotland. For years she had promised she would go back.
Visit the cottage where she had lived as a child, see if there
was anyone still left in the village who remembered her or
her father.

The wind whipped at her hat and tore it from her head.
She watched it whirling high, born on the wind, tossed
and blown then dropped lower and skimming the surface
of the river below her until it flopped into the water and
lay there for a few minutes bobbing like a tiny craft. Then,
as the water soaked the fabric it slowly sank beneath the
surface and disappeared from her view. It was like watching a boat sink. Her father's boat had been just as helpless
against the might of the ocean as her smart hat. She missed
him still. She wished Joe had been more like him, but Joe
was like Tom, given to bitterness and resentment, though
he was, Jeannie admitted, more courageous than his father.

How would he feel when he heard that he was to have
a half-brother or sister? And what would Sammy say if she
were to produce a legitimate heir to the Gorton inheritance? Would he change his mind about becoming part of
the company?

Jeannie gazed down at the water lapping against the
pier and then she turned away.

As she walked back, she was aware of the glances. She
was out of place here now, dressed in her fine clothes. She
knew most of the men must recognize her; some as the
'Mester's Missis', others as Tom Lawrence's widow. A few

touched their caps to her, some turned away, deliberately ignoring her. That didn't worry her. Inwardly she smiled to think of the days when they would call after her, trying their chance with a pretty girl. Now, their deference was to an older woman of position. Yet her mature body was still trying to act like that of a young woman, allowing itself to become pregnant.

When she told him, Robert was ecstatic.

'Jeannie, oh Jeannie, that's the most wonderful news I've ever had in the whole of my life – except,' he smiled broadly, 'the day you walked through that gate.' His gaze searched her face. 'Aren't you happy about it?'

'I can't help worrying that, at my age, something might go wrong.' She avoided looking directly at him. She was afraid to look into his happy face, afraid that he would read the truth in her eyes.

She did not want this child.

'I'll take you to London,' Robert was saying. 'You shall have the best doctors . . .'

Jeannie was shaking her head. 'No, no, I don't want that. Dr Walker is quite capable.' And besides, she was thinking in the secret recesses of her own mind, if something were to go wrong then . . .

'Are you thinking of the boys and how they might react to the news?' Robert was probing gently.

Jeannie shrugged. 'I don't see them anyway.' She sighed heavily and she knew she could not hide the hurt from showing in her eyes. 'I don't think they'll care one way or the other, to be honest.'

'They will. They'll come around. They'll both be related to him.' Hastily, Robert added, 'Or her,' but Jeannie knew how much he was hoping for a son. 'They won't be able to resist seeing him,' he went on. 'He'll be Joe's half-brother and cousin to Sammy, just in the same way that Joe is.'

Jeannie wrinkled her brow, working it all out. 'Yes, you're right about that, but I don't think you're right about them coming around. I don't think . . .' she said and there was no mistaking the catch in her voice, 'that they ever will.'

'One day, they will,' Robert said, 'and besides, Joe's wife is expecting a baby too, isn't she?'

Jeannie's heart felt as if it skipped a beat. So, that news was out too. She hoped not every secret surrounding Thelma's child was common knowledge. She nodded, wordlessly.

'That'll bring you closer together. They'll come around, I promise.'

But it was a promise – the only one – that Robert was not able to fulfil for his beloved Jeannie.

Forty-Five

'Have you told Joe the truth?'

Jeannie was once again sitting in the kitchen in Wessex Street, but this time the atmosphere was much different. The room was clean and warm, the net curtains freshly washed and the windows sparkling. A fire burned in the grate and the kettle sang on the hob. On the table lay Thelma's knitting: a white matinée jacket. So, Jeannie thought, at least she's making preparations for the coming baby. That's more than I am doing.

'Oh Mam,' Thelma began and Jeannie realized with a shock that it was the first time her daughter-in-law had ever addressed her that way. 'I couldn't. I just couldn't. He was that pleased, I couldn't spoil it for him. And besides . . .' she bit her lip and glanced at Jeannie, 'it could be his. So what's the point in telling him something that might not be true.'

Jeannie was silent, wrestling with her own conscience. She was remembering how differently Tom had always treated Sammy, who was not his own son, even though Jeannie had always been able to treat the boy as if he had been her own. She thought, too, about how Joe had seemed to carry on that resentment, one moment fighting with Sammy, the next defending him against outsiders. She shook her head slightly. Joe was a funny mixture, just as Tom had been. But there was one thing she did know.

Joe would never accept another man's child as his own.

As the weeks passed, Robert became desperately anxious about Jeannie. She seemed tired all the time and uninterested in the coming child. She refused to buy baby clothes or a new pram or even to redecorate one of the bedrooms as a nursery.

'It might not live,' she blurted out one day to a horrified Robert.

'Oh, my darling.' At once he put his arms about her and drew her to him. 'Is that what's troubling you?'

She clung to him, afraid that now he would guess the truth. That it was not what she believed would happen. It was what she hoped.

'What does Dr Walker say? You're in good health, aren't you?' He held her from him, searching her face. She shrugged listlessly and avoided looking at him.

'I'm fine, Robert.' But as Jeannie turned away from him, he stared after her, hurt and puzzled.

'Come in, Mr Gorton. What can I do for you?'

Sitting down, Robert said, 'It's about my wife.'

'Ah.'

He looked straight at the doctor. 'I do realize there are questions you may not be able to answer, but I'm worried about Jeannie. It's – it's . . .' Helplessly, he cast around in his mind for the right phrase. 'It's almost as if she doesn't want the baby.'

When the doctor did not answer, but picked up his pen and played with it, turning it end over end and tapping his desk with it at each turn, Robert felt a cold fear run through him. 'Is that it?' he asked hoarsely, unable to believe that Jeannie, his Jeannie, would be even capable of such feelings. Why, she was a devoted mother to Joe and to Sammy too.

'Ah,' he said slowly, thinking aloud. 'Could it be because of the two older boys? Joe and Sammy? They've cut her off, you know, because she married me.'

The doctor wrinkled his forehead and pulled down the corners of his mouth. 'Could be, I suppose. Physically, she's very well. Remarkably so, considering her age.'

'That's another thing. She keeps on about her age. That the baby might not – survive. She won't even discuss names.'

'Women of her age are often – well – embarrassed about being a mother again in their forties. And of course that feeling may be compounded because she's going to become a grandmother around the same time.'

The doctor paused and glanced at Robert, who nodded.

'Of course,' Dr Walker went on, 'you understand that I must insist that she goes into the hospital for the birth but I'm afraid that will only add to her feelings of being, well, something of an oddity. All the other mothers there will probably be young enough themselves to be her daughters.'

Robert winced. 'Oh dear.'

The doctor spread his hands. 'The only advice I can give you is that you should just bear with her moods. It's not long now, only another two months and once the child is born . . .'

'But what if she rejects it then? I've heard of that happening.'

'It can, yes, but all you can do now is be supportive towards her. And don't keep questioning her. The last thing she wants is for you to know what she's feeling

358

about the baby.' Dr Walker smiled sympathetically. 'For the next few weeks, Mr Gorton, you are going to have to be a very good actor.'

Jeannie knew nothing of Robert's visit to the doctor's, she was just so thankful that he had stopped fussing over her and asking her questions. He was still as loving as ever, kind and concerned for her welfare. And that he was joyfully anticipating being a father was never in any doubt.

But it only added to her feelings of guilt.

'Jeannie! Jeannie, where are you?'

She heard him calling from the hallway and then his feet pounding up the wide, sweeping staircase.

'In the bedroom,' she called and as he came in, she stood up and turned to face him. He was breathing heavily and she could see at once by his expression that something was wrong.

Her hand flew to her throat. 'What is it? Is it the boys?' Joe and Sammy now sailed in the same Gorton ship.

'No, no, it's Thelma. One of her neighbours came to the office today. It's the baby . . .'

'Oh no. It can't be. It's too early . . .' Already she was rushing to the wardrobe for her coat.

'I'll take you there, Jeannie.'

This time he took her right to the door and even stepped into the house with her, though he waited below whilst she rushed up the stairs.

As Jeannie stepped in through the bedroom door, she stopped in horror to see the blood-soaked sheets and the white face of the girl against the pillows. Her eyes were closed and she seemed scarcely to be breathing. The midwife, a stranger to her as Mrs Jackson had long since retired, was bending over her patient. 'The doctor will be here presently. You may have to go into the hospital, dear.' She looked up as Jeannie tiptoed to the bedside. 'You are Mrs Lawrence's mother?'

Jeannie shook her head. 'Mother-in-law. What's happened?'

'She's lost the baby, I'm afraid,' the midwife said in low tones. 'Stillborn.'

'Will – will she be all right?'

'I think so. She's young, but . . .' She paused, glanced at Thelma and added, 'It's not for me to say more than that. The doctor, or the hospital if he sends her there, will tell you more.'

Jeannie sat by Thelma's bedside until the doctor arrived half an hour later. Whilst he examined Thelma, she went downstairs to sit with Robert who was still pacing the kitchen.

'How is she? Do you want me to radio Joe's ship?'

'Not at the moment. Let's wait until the doctor comes down.'

They spent an uncomfortable, worrying twenty minutes until they heard him descending the narrow, dark staircase.

'She should go into hospital. There's still some bleeding. A surgeon should take a look at her. I'll call the ambulance. It shouldn't be long. Perhaps,' he glanced at Jeannie, 'you could get a few things ready for her to take. The midwife was unable to stay. She had another urgent confinement.'

Robert repeated his question to the doctor. 'Should I let her husband know?'

'Fisherman, is he?' When Robert nodded, the doctor asked, 'When's he due back?'

'Two days' time.'

'Leave it until then. She's not going to die, if that's what you're worried about. Better to tell him when he's safely back on dry land than have him worried to death out at sea where he can't do anything about it.'

There was reasoning and good common sense in his words and both Robert and Jeannie knew he was used to dealing with this community and its particular problems.

As he left the house, Jeannie went back upstairs to sit by Thelma's bedside once more and hold her hand. A tumult of emotions was going on inside her and she was glad that the girl was sleeping and she didn't have to speak. Not at this moment. Not now when she was trying to quell the overwhelming guilt she was feeling.

She had wished to lose the child she was carrying and instead, in a cruel twist of fate, poor Thelma had lost hers. Yet perhaps, in the circumstances, it was a blessing. Joe might, some day, have heard ugly rumours. She looked at Thelma's white face, at the blue smudges beneath her eyes and the colourless lips, her hair spread over the pillow and wondered briefly if the girl had done something to herself to bring this about. As, she reminded herself sternly, she had contemplated.

Much later, Jeannie asked Robert to drive her to the church where in the quiet, deserted sanctuary, she knelt and begged forgiveness for her own wickedness and for the soul of her still-born granddaughter.

'I'll come with you, if you like, to meet his ship,' Robert offered, but Jeannie shook her head.

'No, no. I must do this alone.'

And so, as the *Arctic Queen* nosed her way to the jetty

and the gangway from ship to quay clattered into place, the deckies were the first ashore. Jeannie stepped forward and put out her hand towards one of the men. 'Please, would you fetch Joe Lawrence for me. Tell him, it's urgent.'

The man looked at her for a moment and then as if reading something in her face, he nodded, 'Right, Missis.' He turned and ran lightly back up the gangway and she heard him calling as he went, 'Joe, Joe . . .'

She glanced up and saw Joe looking down at her standing there on the quayside. She could not read his expression from this distance, but she knew he would not be pleased to see her.

She saw the deckie climb aboard again, saw the exchange of conversation between him and Joe, saw the deckie gesture towards her. Then Joe was standing at the top of the gangway and coming down towards her.

He nodded in greeting but said nothing as he stepped, a little unsteadily, on to firm ground.

'Joe, it's Thelma. She's in hospital, son. I'm sorry, but she's lost the bairn.'

He stood staring at her for a moment. Then, she saw him glance down at the mound beneath her own coat and his mouth twisted with bitterness. Still without a word, he turned and walked unsteadily away from her.

'Joe,' she called after him, but he did not look back.

She turned and glanced up at the ship to see Sammy standing at the top of the gangway, but instead of coming down to speak to her he, too, turned away and disappeared from her sight.

Jeannie, her eyes blurring with tears, walked back along the quay to the Gorton offices where she knew Robert was waiting for her.

*

When the child – the boy that Robert so wanted – was born Jeannie was surprised how quick and easy it was. She had expected a difficult confinement considering her age and the fact that it had been twenty-two years since she had given birth to Joe.

She was given a room on her own in the hospital with the child in a cradle at the side of her bed. When Robert came to visit her and she saw him standing in the doorway, his arms full of flowers beaming like a Cheshire cat, Jeannie burst into tears.

'Oh darling . . .' He flung the flowers down and sat on the edge of the bed and drew her to him.

'You're not – supposed to sit on the – bed,' she hic-cupped, her words muffled against his chest. 'Sister will have a fit.'

'Never mind the sister. I'll buy her a whole new bed if I have to. Now, come, dry your tears. Show me my son, Jeannie.'

Still leaning against him, she glanced down towards the cradle, saying nothing.

'He – he is all right, isn't he?' Robert asked anxiously.

She nodded. 'He's perfect. Just perfect. He's even . . .' her voice became high-pitched as fresh tears threatened, '. . . got my red hair. That's why I feel so guilty.'

'Eh?' Robert said, trying to make light of what she was saying, trying to sound as if he did not already understand what meaning lay behind her words. 'You feel guilty because he's got your red hair?'

'Oh Robert . . .' She clung to him then, fiercely like a drowning person. 'You're going to hate me. I didn't want him. I kept wishing that . . . that . . . Oh it was so wicked of me. I'll never forgive myself. And then when poor Thelma lost hers . . .' She was babbling, the words pouring out in a tumult of pent-up emotion. 'And

363

now, I love him so much if anything were to happen to him . . .'

'Nothing's going to happen to him. I promise you.'

A shudder ran through her. He meant it, she knew he did, but that was something outside the power even of Robert Gorton.

He had not been able to fulfil that other promise he had made her. That one day she would be reunited with Joe and Sammy.

Forty-Six

'You spoil him.'

'So do you.'

They laughed and then put their arms about each other standing looking down into the cot and the sweet face of their child. Jeannie and her son had been home from the hospital a week and every day Robert had returned from the office with yet another toy or a tiny new outfit for the little chap. But he never omitted, too, to bring flowers or perfume or chocolates for the new mother. During that first week, Jeannie had barely left the nursery, even though Robert had employed a capable nursemaid. She even hovered close by whilst the child slept.

'He's perfect,' she murmured. 'I just canna believe I've been so lucky. I dinna deserve to be . . .'

'Now, now, stop that,' Robert remonstrated gently and tactfully changed the subject. 'Edwin has asked if he can come and see him tomorrow.'

'Of course he can.'

He thought for a moment and then said, 'I was thinking that we should ask Edwin to be godfather, but we could ask Joe and Sammy instead, if you like. If you think it would help?'

'It's sweet of you to suggest it, Robert. But I don't really think it would. Besides, I want to ask your brother to be his godfather. I like Edwin.'

'But you could ask Joe and Sammy as well, you know.'

365

'I'll see. I'll think about it.'

'So, are we decided on his name then?'

Jeannie smiled as she looked up at him. 'If you're really sure you dinna mind?'

'Of course, I don't. Angus Buchanan Gorton, it is.'

Since the birth of her own child, in robust health, Jeannie had found it difficult to bring herself to go to see Thelma. But when she had been home three weeks, she realized she could not put the moment off any longer. Taking fruit and flowers, she knocked once more on the door of the house in Wessex Street.

Thelma's eyes widened when she saw Jeannie. 'You can't come in,' she said bluntly. 'He's home. At least, he's at the Fisherman's. He could come back at any minute.'

'That's all right,' Jeannie said calmly, stepping over the threshold. 'I want a word with Joe anyway. How are you feeling, hen?'

The girl shrugged listlessly. 'All right.' She paused and then glanced keenly at Jeannie. 'You aren't going to tell him, are you?' Her eyes were brimming with tears as she whispered, 'He must never know. Never. I was a fool. I love Joe. I couldn't bear to lose him.'

Jeannie swallowed the huge lump that rose in her throat. No more can I, she wanted to say, but it looks as if I already have. Instead she said aloud, 'No. I gave you my word. I won't break it, whatever happens.'

The girl seemed to relax. 'Would you like a cuppa?'

'I'd love one, but I thought you didna want me to stay?'

Thelma smiled suddenly and her young face lost some of its misery. 'Oh sod 'im, for once,' she said. 'You've been good to me, Mam. He's a fool, the way he's acting, if you ask me.'

'Well, I dinna want to cause trouble between the two of you.'

Again she shrugged. 'Oh I can handle Joe,' she said, more confident now that she had extracted Jeannie's promise. 'Dun't you worry.'

Jeannie placed her gifts on the table, wondering at the sudden change in the girl's attitude towards her. Wondering if it would last.

As she set a cup of tea in front of Jeannie, Thelma said, 'You'd better have all the baby clothes I'd got ready. I shan't be wanting them.'

'Of course you will,' Jeannie tried to say briskly. 'You're young. There'll be more bairns.'

Thelma shook her head. 'The doctor seemed to think I didn't ought to have any more. It might be dangerous.'

'Och, what do they know?' Jeannie tried to reassure her, but in her heart she knew that the medical advice would not have been given lightly. 'Give yourself time to heal and then see, eh?'

There was silence between them before Thelma said suddenly, 'I told Joe you'd been here. I told him how good you'd been to me. Stayin' with me an' that and getting me to the hospital.'

'But – he still doesna want to see me?'

Thelma pressed her lips together and shook her head. 'He . . .' she began, but at that moment they both heard the back door open. There was only a chance for the two women to exchange a glance before Joe lurched into the room.

He stood in the doorway, swaying slightly and blinking as if to focus his gaze. 'What the hell is *she* doing in my house? I thought I told you . . .'

Before the girl could speak, Jeannie rose. 'I'm going. I came to ask you to be godfather to your brother, but it seems I'm wasting ma breath.'

'You are,' her son said. 'I want nowt to do wi' any of that family. Nor you, now you're a part of it. Far as I'm concerned, I have no brother.'

'I'm sorry you feel that way, son. I'll no' be coming here again. But if ever you need me . . .' she paused fractionally as her glance flickered briefly towards Thelma to include her too, 'you know where to find me.'

'Not afore the North Sea freezes over,' Joe muttered through clenched teeth as he moved away from the door to allow her to leave.

As she walked up Wessex Street, Jeannie felt the tears burn behind her eyelids and the lump grow and grow in her throat. She longed to rush home to Robert, to feel his arms around her and to stand with him and look down upon their child. But there was one more place she must visit first.

'Mam!'

She saw the surprise in Sammy's eyes as he opened the door and the fleeting pleasure, but it was gone so swiftly that she wondered if she had fondly imagined it. Now the veil of disapproval had come down once more. He seemed edgy, too, for he glanced over his shoulder and made no move to invite her into her old home.

Then she understood as a girlish voice called out, 'Who is it, Sammy?'

Jeannie's mouth twitched with amusement. 'Och I'm sorry, I wouldna want to spoil your homecoming.'

He gave a swift grin and for a moment his eyes danced with mischief. 'Just me girlfriend. That's all.'

'Aye.'

They stood in awkward silence for a moment and then both spoke at once.

'What was it . . . ?'

'Sammy, I just wanted . . .'

They both stopped and then Sammy gestured that she should continue.

'I've been to see Joe. He's still adamant. I just wondered. Are you?'

The young man sighed heavily and closed his eyes a moment. 'I don't want it to be like this, Mam. I never did. If only you hadn't married *him*. If it'd've been anyone but him, we'd have understood. I don't think even Joe, in time, would have expected you to spend the rest of your life alone, you know? But to marry that man, after all that's happened. Well, we just can't handle it.'

'Oh Sammy.' Her heart was heavy. 'I'm sorry too.' There was another pause before she said sadly, 'If that's all you've got to say, then I'd best be on ma way. But I'll always be there for you, son. If you need me. Whatever you feel about me now, I'll always be your "Mam".'

For a moment, she thought she had broken his resolve. Sammy's face crumpled and, for one heart-stopping moment, she thought he was going to fling his arms about her and bury his head against her shoulder.

But in that instance the plaintive voice from inside the house came again. 'Sammy . . . ?'

He turned away and quietly closed the door in her face.

Forty-Seven

So Joe and Sammy never saw Angus grow up. They were not around to witness the surprise on the child's face the first time he found he could roll over, nor the delight when he fathomed out how to crawl and reach the things he wanted. They were not there to teach him his first words nor to hold out their hands to him as he tottered to his feet, for all the world like a fisherman coming ashore. They were missing from his christening and his first birthday party.

In the early years of his life, Angus, knowing no different, was unaware of the lack of their presence in his life. His father doted on him and his mother, compensating for the guilt she felt, idolized him. She channelled all the love that she could no longer show towards the two older boys into this one tiny infant. That he grew into a sunny-natured, unspoilt child, was nothing short of a miracle. Anything he wanted, he got; anything he wanted to do – within reason on the grounds of safety – he did. Even his uncle was bowled over by the red-haired, mischievous little rascal.

'Wouldn't old Samuel have been tickled pink by him,' Edwin would say, sitting on the lawn with Robert and Jeannie watching the boy's first faltering steps. As he sat down with a thump, each one of the grown-ups made a start forward, hands outstretched towards him. But the child merely chuckled, turned a beatific smile upon them and hauled himself upright to try again. 'He's a real charmer with that smile of his,' Edwin murmured, never taking his eyes off his nephew and godson.

At a year old Angus was walking sturdily. At two, he was saying several words clearly and once he learnt how to string words together, he never stopped talking. From morning until he fell asleep at night, he chattered.

'He's so clever,' Jeannie would say, her fond gaze following him everywhere. And then, briefly, her eyes would cloud. 'I do so wish Joe and Sammy could see him.'

'I saw them last week,' Robert told her gently and, when the hope flared in her eyes, he wondered if he had been wrong to mention it. Quickly he said, 'My dear, I'm sorry, but they're still resolute.'

'You talked to them? How are they? Are they well? Is Joe a father yet?'

'They're fine,' Robert said carefully. 'Rumour has it . . .' he paused and Jeannie held her breath, 'that poor Thelma can't have children now. It's a shame, not only for them, but for you too. Perhaps, if Joe were to become a father, he might soften in his attitude a little. Towards you, I mean, if he knew what it was like to have children of his own.'

She sighed and then asked, 'And Sammy? Is he married yet?'

'No. He's still living in the house in Baldock Street. He has some lodgers, I believe, so that the house is occupied whilst he's at sea.'

'And Helen? Is he still with Helen?'

Robert shook his head. 'Lord, no. By all accounts, he has a different girlfriend every shore leave.'

'Huh, just like his father,' Jeannie said bitterly. 'I hope he's not as cruel and unfeeling as Francis was, Robert. I hope there's a little of you and Edwin in him.'

'And Grace,' Robert murmured. 'Don't forget Grace.'

'No, no,' Jeannie said. 'I willna forget Grace.' But guiltily she realized that she often did forget that poor Grace had been Sammy's mother and not her.

'Take me to see the ships, Dad.' Every weekend when his father was not at the Company's office, Angus would make the same request. He was besotted by the sea and everything to do with it. All the toys he asked for were boats, all the picture books and later, reading books, were about the sea or ships. When his parents took him on a day trip to the nearby seaside town, he would smile and say, 'But can we go to the docks on the way back home? Please?'

When he started school and began to read and write, the teachers despaired. 'Can he think about nothing else, Mrs Gorton, other than trawlers and fish? I know we're a major port and justifiably proud of our fishing industry here, but there are other things that Angus should be learning.'

But neither Jeannie nor Robert could do anything.

'Where is he? Robert, I canna find Angus.' As he grew older and learnt to ride a bicycle, the boy would go missing. In the school holidays Jeannie's anxious telephone calls to the office punctuated Robert's working day.

'My darling, you know where he'll be. But I'll find him.' And Robert would leave his desk to walk along the jetties until he saw his son watching the latest catch being landed. Some mornings Angus even crept out of the house before dawn to be in time to see the first fish sold in the auction on the dockside.

He would still be there late at night when the trawlers were being coaled up and supplies taken aboard for the ship to go out with the next tide.

'One of these days he'll really go missing. He'll stow away. I know he will,' Jeannie would say distractedly, but Robert would only smile.

'Darling, he has the sea in his blood from both sides of his family. If ever there was a born fisherman, Jeannie, then it's our son.' His glance roamed lovingly over his wife's face as he added softly, 'I'm sorry if it's not what you want for him.'

'Maybe we should have sent him away to boarding school,' Jeannie mused. 'Put some distance between him and the sea. But I just couldna bear to let him go.'

Robert snorted. 'What? And have him turn out like Francis? No fear, Jeannie. Besides, I'm proud of the lad.'

Jeannie glanced up at her husband, a mischievous look on her face. 'Despite my smothering him, so am I. But dinna tell him I said so.'

They laughed together.

Robert put his arm about her and she leant against him. 'Just so long as you know, my darling, that one day he's going to want to go to sea.'

'Aye,' she whispered. 'Aye, I ken.'

Forty-Eight

The moment Jeannie had been dreading came soon after Angus's fourteenth birthday.

'I'm off to sea,' he announced.

'You can go in the school holidays,' she said, valiantly trying to stave off the moment even though she knew it was hopeless. 'I don't mind that. Just for one trip.'

His eyes were twinkling with mischief and he was smiling broadly. 'And then when I leave school, I can go to sea as a real fisherman.'

Now she came to stand before him and place her hands on his shoulders. Already he was almost as tall as she was. As she looked him straight in the face, her heart turned over. He had her red hair but in so many other ways he reminded her of her father. He even smiled in the same way and laughed in that big, head-thrown-back, hearty manner. He was the image of old Angus. And now it seemed, sea water ran in his veins the same as his grandfather had always joked it ran in his.

'Angus, I couldna bear to lose you. I've already lost a father and a husband to the sea.'

'I know, Mother,' the boy said gently. 'But Joe and Sammy are fishermen. And they're all right, aren't they?'

Jeannie nodded, biting on her lower lip. 'Aye, I pray every night to keep them safe . . .' And then she added in a whisper, 'But they're as good as lost to me, for I never see them.'

Now Angus's smile broadened. 'Well, you might soon, Mam, because in the Easter holidays I'm going to sea on the *Arctic Queen II*, the boat Joe skippers.'

Jeannie gasped. 'On Joe's boat? You're going to sea with Joe and Sammy?' It was a Gorton boat, she reminded herself, but even so . . .

At that moment, Robert walked into the room and Jeannie whirled around to face him. 'Did you set all this up?' she demanded.

His glance went from one to another. 'Now what am I supposed to have done?' he asked.

'Did you ask Joe and Sammy to take Angus to sea on their boat?'

But Robert looked genuinely startled and glanced at his son, who spoke up before his father could answer her question.

Angus drew himself up. 'No, Dad knew nothing about it. I asked 'em.'

'You? But – but you dinna ken them.'

'Course I know them.'

'But – how?'

'Every time they dock, I meet the ship. Joe's a great bloke.' He smiled at his mother and added gently, 'I think my half-brother's beginning to like me. And I know Sam does.'

Jeannie opened her mouth to say, of course Joe likes you. But in this family, that was no guarantee. She had not spoken to them since the day she had gone to ask them both to be godfather to Angus. Fourteen long years ago, and since then not a day had gone by that she hadn't thought about them. But until this moment she had had no idea that Angus had even met them, let alone spoken to them. The revelation came as a shock. And yet, rationally, if she thought about it, he had spent such a lot of his young life down at the docks, it would have been odd if he had not run into them. But it sounded now as if he had deliberately sought them out.

'How – how long has this been going on?'

The boy wrinkled his forehead. 'Oh about six months I suppose. I've known for a long time that I wanted to go to sea and I thought the best way would be to go with Joe. And Sammy, too, of course. He's my cousin, isn't he?' He looked towards his father for confirmation. All Robert could do was nod.

They had never tried to keep the fact a secret. Indeed, from an early age, Jeannie and Robert had spoken openly about Joe and Sammy in front of Angus and, when he was old enough, Robert had explained gently all that had happened in their families to cause the rift between them. He had even, Jeannie thought with admiration, told their son of the very first time he had encountered Jeannie, hiding none of his own shame at the memory.

Now Angus took his mother's hands into his own and, looking straight into her eyes, he said quietly, 'I thought I might be able to bring the family together at the same time.'

Tears blurred her eyes and she reached out and touched his cheek with the tips of her fingers but no words would come. He was a deep thinker, this youngest son of hers, with a kind and generous nature. He knew that her dearest wish was to be reunited with Joe and Sammy and, to try to bring it about, he was willing to go to sea with them. All three would be on the same ship at the mercy of the mighty ocean.

No, no, she couldn't let it happen. She must talk to Robert alone. He must stop Angus going.

*

'Now you are being silly, darling,' Robert said. 'This isn't like you at all. Where's my strong Jeannie? The girl who once brandished a gutting knife under my nose? Not that I didn't deserve it,' he added hastily.

'But how do you know they will look after him? How do you know that they're not taking him to sea to – to . . .?'

Even she balked at putting her deepest fears into actual words.

'To tip him over the side in a gale, you mean?' Robert said bluntly, bringing her worst nightmare into the open. 'Oh come now, Jeannie. You're talking about your own son and about my nephew. I know Francis was a bad lot but I don't think even he would stoop to something like that. And as for Joe, well he's your son and Tom's.'

Jeannie faced him. 'Aye, and Tom carried a hatred for you and your family all his life. A resentment that Joe seems to be carrying on. As for Sammy, well, he's his own particular bitterness, hasn't he? I always used to fear for you when you and Tom served on the same minesweeper in the war. More than just the enemy's aircraft and the mines you were clearing.'

Robert stared at her. He opened his mouth to argue but then he remembered. Remembered, suddenly, the times he had felt Tom's antagonism. It had been real, very real. So real that on the odd occasion – strange how he had forgotten it until this moment – the thought had crossed his own mind that he might be in physical danger from the man.

Quietly he said, 'And now you fear for Angus's safety if he should go to sea with Joe and Sammy?'

Wordlessly, because to say it aloud seemed so awful, she nodded.

He was thoughtful for a moment before he said slowly, 'Then I'll go with them. No one would misinterpret that.

He's only fourteen. And after all,' he gave a half-smile, 'I am in the happy position of being able to "pull rank". I own the ship.'

She rushed to him and flung her arms about him. 'Oh Robert, would you? Would you really go?'

He put his arms about her and sighed against her hair. 'You know, Mrs Gorton, that I would do anything in this world for you.'

The day they left, Jeannie refused to come down to the dockside to see them off. Childhood superstition was still strong within her and though her hair now had more strands of white than of the rich, red colour, her fear was still there. 'It might make things awkward if I come with Joe and Sammy there.' She made the excuse that they could not deny, but when she saw Angus's crest-fallen face, she forced a brightness into her voice to promise, 'But I'll come and meet you the day you come back.'

So she did not go down to the dockside, but, unknown to them all, from the window of the Gorton-Hathersage Trawler Company's office, Jeannie watched the *Arctic Queen II* nose its way out of the dock and head for the open sea. Beside her stood her brother-in-law, his arm about her waist.

'Oh Edwin,' she sighed, resting her head against his shoulder for a moment. 'They're all aboard that one boat. The four most important people in my life, and I've let them all go together into the treacherous Icelandic waters.'

'They'll be all right.' Edwin squeezed her waist, still as lithe and trim as a young woman's. 'Joe's a fine skipper. He may be the youngest we've ever had on our boats but he's one of the best. And Sammy too. Not skipper material, maybe, but he's a good seaman. They'll be all right,' he said again, but she had the uncomfortable feeling that he was trying to convince himself as much as comfort her.

Forty-Nine

The 1950s had been a boom time for the Gorton-Hathersage Trawler Company of Havelock. Having weathered the economic problems of the '30s, it had seemed ironic that a world war should smash all that they had built up. At the end of the war, Robert believed he had little to return home to in the way of the business. Caught up in his love for and hopes for the future with Jeannie, he was not too concerned, but after her rejection of him, Robert's only salvation was to plunge himself into work.

Under Edwin's steady hand on the financial side of the business and with Robert's natural flair for dealing fairly with the men in their employ, the company began to flourish. Whilst the brothers themselves might have missed Francis's leadership, amongst the fishermen there was little regret.

By the early 1960s the Gorton-Hathersage Trawler Company of Havelock was reckoned to be the biggest trawler-owning company on the north-east coast of Lincolnshire, and the most modern thinking. And some said they even rivalled the owners in the port of Hull on the opposite bank of the Humber.

'An old man and a boy? Dead weight they'll be. The skipper must be out of his mind teking 'em.'

'He hasn't got a lot of choice, has he? Seeing who it is?'

'Why? Who is it?'

'Don't ya know? Mester Robert Gorton and his young son.'

'Never! I dun't believe you.'

'True.'

'Well, the skipper has lost 'is marbles then.'

The other man laughed. 'Like I said, he ain't much choice seeing as 'ow Mester Robert's the owner of this ship.'

'And I suppose . . .' there was a note of comic horror in the man's tone now, 'you're going to tell me next that I'll get the brat working with me as galley boy?'

The other man laughed. 'No, the young 'un wants to be on deck, so they say. No, old son, you've got the mester as your "galley boy".'

The choice words that followed made even Robert's ears burn. He hadn't meant to listen to the conversation, but had found himself trapped in the tiny cabin stowing his gear when the two men, passing by, had spoken in such loud voices that it was impossible for him not to overhear. He held his breath, hoping they would not step into the cabin and only let it out when the footsteps went on.

The final words Robert heard were, 'Mind you, I dun't reckon the skipper does like it – the old man coming along, I mean. They say he dun't have nowt to do with any of the family even though his mother's married to Mester Robert.'

'What about the lad?' At this point the voices became indistinct and Robert could not hear the reply but he could have told them. Oh yes, he could have told them about the lad.

'The lad' had been in a turmoil of excitement ever since the trip had been finally agreed upon. At first he had argued about his father coming too. 'What'll the crew think? It'll make me look a baby.'

But, credit due to the boy, Robert thought, when he had seen his mother's genuine anxiety, Angus had given her a bear-hug accompanied by his engaging grin of capitulation.

And now he was aboard, his belongings stowed and already he was on deck demanding of Sammy – the third hand – what he could do.

The first two days at sea were awkward. The crew were ill at ease. Conversations stopped abruptly whenever Robert or Angus approached and were virtually non-existent when they all sat together in the messroom. But then, forty-eight hours out to sea, the natural hierarchy aboard ship took over. Though the men all had work to do on the voyage out, there was nevertheless a relaxed atmosphere. When the nets and all their gear had been made ready and the skipper sent down the first tot of rum to 'wet the net', Robert and Angus felt themselves accepted.

'You watch it, Dad, you know what rum does to you,' Angus teased, knocking back his own tot like an old hand.

'And you just wait till I tell your mother about you!'

'Skipper's keeping himself to himself, ain't he?' was the only other remark Robert overheard, though he guessed there were plenty went on out of his hearing.

'Aye, well, awk'ard for him, ain't it?'

'Oh aye. I s'pose it is,' came the reply and Robert, as he carried two mugs of tea and two plates of bread and butter along the rolling deck, felt their glance upon him. But by the third day, they were taking their tea and saying, 'Thanks, mate.'

Ted Gutteridge, the cook, had been blunt. 'Well, Mester Gorton, I can't say I'm pleased to have you aboard, but since you're here and we've got to rub along for the next three weeks, that's the last time I'm going to call you that. From now on, you're Rob and you take your orders from me.'

'Right you are, Mr Gutteridge . . .' Robert had begun, but the man had stuck out his hand, grinned and corrected, 'Ted.'

Robert took his hand. 'Ted, it is.'

Ted had seemed to relax a little. 'It's a dangerous place, the galley. Specially in a force nine gale.' He jerked his thumb upwards. 'Oh I know it's rougher up there, but they don't have a pan of boiling soup slopping over their legs if the ship gives a lurch.'

Robert nodded, respecting the man's trade. 'You just tell me what you want me to do, Ted, and I'll do it.'

Ted slapped his new galley boy on the shoulder. 'Good man.'

Trying not to make it noticeable, Robert still tried to keep a watchful eye on Angus, though it was not easy since he was in the galley most of the time whilst the boy was on deck.

Over the next few days, once the tension had eased, 'Rob' was surprised to find that in a masochistic kind of way he was actually enjoying himself.

He saw little of Joe and nor did Angus, though Robert was thankful to see that Sammy had taken the boy under his wing. In fact, Angus became the third hand's shadow.

'When we get to the grounds,' Ted told Robert, 'he'll have to keep out of his way a bit then. Dangerous job, Sammy's got, y'know. He's the one who releases the knot when the trawl net comes aboard. I've seen a man killed doing that.'

Robert said nothing, but he was wondering if he had been right to go against Jeannie's instincts and allow their son come to sea. Even though he was aboard too, he couldn't watch the boy every minute, nor could he be sure of being able to keep the lad out of potentially dangerous situations.

The moment the ship had nosed its way out of the mouth of the Humber, past the lightship and into the treacherous waters of the North Sea to begin its eight-hundred-mile voyage to the fishing grounds off the north-east coast of Iceland, there was danger.

Suddenly, with a stab of fear, Robert realized, strangely now only for the first time, that the four men who mattered most in the world to Jeannie were all aboard this vessel.

Fifty

With both Robert and Angus away, Jeannie felt lost. Although she saw Edwin every day, either visiting him at the Gorton offices or inviting him to dine with her in the evening, there were still too many hours when she was alone. He took her to the theatre twice in the first week but afterwards Jeannie could not have said what the plays were about; her thoughts were out at sea.

There was one person who would understand how she felt. Thelma. On the first morning of the second week since they had sailed, Jeannie stood outside the terraced house in Wessex Street.

'Hello, Mam. What are you doing here?'

'I hope you don't mind . . .' Jeannie began, stepping into the kitchen but then she stopped as she glanced round in amazement. Every surface gleamed and sparkled. From the scullery came the smell of freshly baking bread and the girl herself was smiling at Jeannie. She had gained a little weight and her face had lost that gaunt, discontented look. Thelma was no longer a girl, Jeannie reminded herself, but a young woman. She must be in her mid-thirties now, Jeannie calculated. As she looked around, everything so tidy and in its place, Jeannie felt a stab of pity. It was too tidy. Immaculate – and childless.

'I'll mek you a cup of tea, Mam, but I'm ever so sorry, I've got to go out at eleven. I've got mesen this little part-time job in Yorks in Main Street.' It was the major department store in the street, the shop where George Lawrence had bought Jeannie the coat all those years ago.

Jeannie nodded. 'That's nice, hen. It's a beautiful shop.'

'It's only part time.' The young woman giggled. 'I wouldn't want owt to interfere with the times Joe's at home, y'know. But it's nice to have summat to do when he's not here. A little bit extra money's handy and it keeps me out of mischief.'

Jeannie made no comment but the two women exchanged a smile.

'Don't let me keep you then.'

'No, no, it's nice to see you. I've half an hour. I'm all ready except for putting me coat on. Sit down, Mam, do. I'll get the kettle on.'

Thelma bustled about, lay a tray with a dainty cloth and reached for delicate china from a cupboard. Jeannie could scarcely believe her eyes. The change in the girl was incredible. She wondered if there was more to it. Surely, oh surely not. Had Thelma got another man whilst Joe was away? Then firmly, she shook herself. I'm getting as bad as Tom in my suspicions, she told herself sharply.

Thelma sat down at the table and poured the tea. 'Do you know, Mam, I'll always be grateful for what you did for me that time. You brought me to me senses. I love Joe and he's a good man. A bit moody at times, maybe, and he gets jealous . . .' She pulled a face. 'Even when there's no need.'

Jeannie knew at once that her fleeting fear had been groundless. She smiled. 'Dinna let's talk about that any more, hen. It's forgotten.'

'Well, I just wanted you to know, that's all. I am grateful, really I am.' Thelma sighed. 'I just wish Joe would see sense and mek friends with you again. He's missing so much, but he's so stubborn. Mind you,' she added, and there was a more hopeful note in her tone. 'I reckon he's coming round to his little brother. And Sammy thinks the world of young Angus, y'know?'

Jeannie's eyes widened and she felt her heart thumping and she could not prevent the tremble in her voice as she said, 'Does he? Does he really?'

Thelma nodded. 'I reckon Joe'll come round, given time. He just doesn't want to admit it, y'know.'

Jeannie smiled, remembering the fights between Joe and Sammy and then the sudden switch to brotherly, or rather cousinly, affection. Maybe Joe was feeling the same towards Angus. He just couldn't decide exactly what he did feel towards his half-brother.

'I just wish I knew what was happening out there,' Jeannie murmured, sipping her tea. 'I just wish I was with them all.'

Thelma laughed. 'Oh, you're best out the way, Mam. The Arctic Circle in a force ten is no place for you an' me.'

Despite the warm cosiness of the room and the hot tea she was drinking, Jeannie shuddered.

As they sailed northwards, Robert pointed out the hazy outline of hills on the port side. 'That, Angus, is Scotland. Somewhere over there is the Fife coast where your mother was born.' He paused and murmured more to himself than to the boy, 'I've been promising to take her back for a visit.'

'We'll take her when we get back,' Angus shouted above the throb of the diesel engines beneath his feet. 'She'd like that.'

The ship passed between the Orkneys and the Shetlands and on past the Faeroes towards Iceland.

As they neared the fishing grounds, Robert went up on

deck. He thought he had never seen such a beautiful sight in the whole of his life. For a moment, he wished Jeannie were standing beside him, seeing what he was seeing.

'It's a rare sight, ain't it?' Sammy said at his elbow. Without taking his gaze away, Robert murmured, 'It certainly is. I wouldn't have missed seeing this for the world.'

They were silent, standing together, watching the small pack ice drift by as the ship nosed her way carefully further and further northwards. The sea was calm, sparkling in the spring sunlight and already sea-birds circled above their heads waiting for easy picking when the fishing began.

'It all looks so – so untouched,' Robert murmured. 'As if no one's ever been here before us. Just look at the blue of the sea and the sky and the whiteness of the ice. It's magnificent. Oh, I'm glad I came – if only for this.'

'It's certainly picture-postcard scenery when it's like this. But get a freezing force ten blow and it's a fearsome place. Mind you,' Sammy nodded towards the bridge, 'I don't know how far north he's planning to go this time. Sometimes he . . .' Sammy stopped suddenly and glanced at Robert in embarrassment.

'It's all right. I'm not on board as The Boss, Sammy,' Robert said quietly. 'Anything you say goes no further.'

'Well, sometimes he goes right to the edge of the ice field, y'know. Fish are often plentiful there.'

More confident now, Sammy grinned impishly, puncturing Robert's romantic image of the magnificent scenery all around him and bringing him back to stark reality.

'You'll be sick of the sight of ice before we've done and so will Angus. He's been down in the ice-room all morning, breaking it up ready for our first trawl. But we've let him up on deck for a bit now, though.' Sammy pointed to where Angus stood on the fo'c'sle, eagerly scanning the horizon. 'He can't wait to get started, can he? But he shouldn't have much longer to wait now.'

'Are we nearly there, then?' Robert asked.

Sammy nodded towards where Joe stood in the wheel-house, a pair of binoculars to his eyes. 'He's got Sparks listening in to the radio to see if he can track the other ships.'

Robert glanced around him, the blue water stretching emptily as far as he could see. 'I don't see any others.'

'You will,' Sammy said, confidently. 'Sparks'll find 'em. Good lad is our Sparks. He listens in to all the radio conversations. He's even picked up a smattering of German and can listen into them, an' all. And he's fath-omed out some of the others' codes. Them that don't change their codes regular like we do. Mind you, Skipper won't join the other ships. He hates bein' in a crowd. But he uses them as a marker, y'know. He's a good skipper, is Joe, and a lucky one. He seems to have an instinct for where the fish are. It's usually us the other ships follow.' Sammy glanced sideways at Robert. 'Course he shares the info with the other Gorton boats . . .' He paused almost waiting to see if Robert would refute his words. Robert managed to keep his face straight, though inwardly he was thinking, pull the other one, Sammy.

The Gorton fleet used a system of codes which their skippers could use to help each other find the good grounds, but Robert knew from overhearing the other skippers as they came ashore that Joe Lawrence was a loner. Rather than fish in a crowded area, he would deliberately steam off and trawl in waters ignored by the other skippers. More often than not it paid off. As Sammy said, Joe was a 'lucky' skipper. But sometimes the gamble failed and Joe had a poor haul.

But now, as they neared the grounds, Sammy was full of confidence. 'If we get a good catch,' he was saying, 'Skipper has everyone on deck. All except the cook. He even has Sparks boiling the livers. So get yer gutting knife ready, he'll mebbe not let you stay warm an' cosy in the galley.'

Robert's expression must have been comical for Sammy laughed and slapped his shoulder just as Angus came running along the deck, sure footed as a goat on a slippery mountain side. 'There's a ship to the north west. Have you seen it?'

Sammy glanced around and squinted in the direction the boy was pointing. 'Where? I can't see. By heck, lad, your eyes must be sharp. Away and tell the skipper. I don't reckon he's spotted it, even with his glasses.'

Robert watched as Angus climbed the ladder to bridge. He saw Joe turn briefly as the boy stepped inside the wheelhouse. Then Angus was pointing and Joe was putting the binoculars to his eyes once more and training them in the direction the boy pointed. The two watching from the deck saw him search the skyline for a few moments and then, dropping the binoculars momentarily, he gave the lad a brief nod and a quick smile and then his attention was once more on the trawler on the horizon.

Angus left the wheelhouse and clambered down the ladder. 'He ses he can see several ships. We're there, Dad, we're there.'

'Right then,' Sammy said. 'There's work to be done. 'You come with me, Angus. I've a job for you.'

Happily, the boy trotted after his cousin.

Robert watched them go. It was the longest conversation he could remember having with Sammy, he thought, and certainly the friendliest. If only they could carry this camaraderie back to shore, back to Jeannie, how happy she would be.

And work there was in plenty. From the moment they reached the fishing grounds and Joe turned his ship portside to the wind to shoot the first trawl over the starboard side, Robert lost all account of time and only the cook seemed to keep a tally of whether he should be serving breakfast, dinner, tea or supper.

'You go up on deck whenever you want, Rob,' Ted said. 'I know you want to keep an eye on that lad of yours.'

'You sure, Ted? I'm supposed to be helping you.'

The man grinned, showing a broken front tooth. 'Yer more of a hindrance than a help down here, but I'll give you a shout if I need a hand.'

So Robert was able to watch as they shot the first trawl. When the shout went up, 'Pay away', over the side went the net, bobbins, trawl doors and lastly several hundred feet of three-inch steel cable. As the net sank below the surface to the bottom of the sea, Joe turned the vessel in the direction he had chosen to fish. For the next three hours the ship would trawl at a steady four knots.

Angus was beside him. 'Sammy ses I'm to get summat to eat and some kip, 'cos once the first haul comes up, we're going to be busy.'

Robert smiled at his son. 'Then I'd better go below and see if I can be of any help to Ted if it's "grub up" time.'

'D'you know, Dad,' Angus chattered on as they clambered down the ladder, 'Sammy ses Joe hardly ever lets the mate tek over the ship whilst they're fishing. Once he only had four hours sleep in six days. I can't imagine that, Dad, can you?'

'No,' Robert replied soberly, but in his mind he was thinking, but you may well be about to find out, son.

There was a sense of excitement throughout the ship the first time they hauled in the gear. Everyone was waiting to see if the skipper had got it right. The deckies were all there, some operating the winch whilst others stood by to secure the doors as they came on deck. Up came the metal bobbins and then they heaved on the net itself, leaning down over the side as the ship tilted and rolled and the waves lashed on to the deck. As the cod end floated they could see that the catch was good. Now the cod end was lifted aboard by the derrick. Sammy dodged beneath the water gushing from the mass of fish, jerked the knot undone and, in a second, fish of all shapes and sizes cascaded on to the deck. Robert watched the figure of his son, almost hidden beneath his yellow oilskins, yet he could see the boy's face wreathed in smiles and even above the throb of the engines, he could hear his jubilant shouts.

The boy was a natural, a fisherman born and bred. There was no denying it. Whatever he or Jeannie might do, Robert knew now, they were never going to stop Angus coming to sea.

Despite his size and youth, the boy worked alongside the experienced deckhands. He was quick to learn and, with no serious repairs needed to the net, the trawl was soon back at the bottom of the ocean once more. Then began the hours of work to gut and put away the fish.

Angus, standing close by Sammy now, who was in charge of this operation, watched closely as the man took a cod into his hands, slit open its belly and removed its guts, separating its liver which he dropped into a basket. Then he lobbed the gutted fish into the washer from where

391

it would slide down a chute into the fish-room below. There, the mate, with a deckie to help him, packed the fish in ice and stowed it away.

Robert found he was holding his breath as he watched Angus pick up a sharp knife and take a fish into his left hand. It took the boy a dozen or so fish before he was gutting like an old hand. Robert suspected that this was not the first time young Angus had tried his hand at gutting. Obviously, his hours spent haunting the Havelock fishdocks had not been wasted. Not that he worked with the speed of the other men yet, but that would come. Robert smiled to himself as he remembered, years ago, watching Jeannie at the farlanes. It seemed that young Angus had not only inherited his grandfather's seamanship, but also his mother's dexterity with a gutting knife.

It was a good catch so there was only half-an-hour for deckies to eat and snatch a short rest before the next cod end swung on to the deck and deposited its silver haul.

'Take this to the skipper, Rob, will you,' Ted asked. 'He'll not leave his wheelhouse for the next ten days.'

'You're joking.'

Ted wasn't. 'No, I'm serious. It's his job. He'll stay up there now until the job's done and we make for home.'

'What about sleep?'

The toothy grin was evident again as Ted said, 'Sleep? What's that, mate?'

Six trawls in twenty-four hours with snatched meals and even less sleep had Robert worried for his son. He was only a boy, only fourteen. Surely he couldn't keep up this pace? But Angus was determined and it wasn't until Sammy himself ordered him below for a six-hour period off, that the youngster gave in.

392

Robert followed him down to help him take off his oilskins, but the boy said, 'Don't, Dad, I can manage.' And Robert was obliged to stand and watch while Angus, reeling with exhaustion, pulled off the stiff, unyielding clothes. Blood and fish guts streaked his pale face. His hands were blue with cold and he winced as he flexed the fingers of his right hand that had held the knife. But the grin on his face was still stretched from ear to ear and even though his eyes were large with tiredness, there was still in them the sparkle of excitement.

'Did you see that huge plaice that came up? "Dustbin-lidders", they call them. Wasn't it huge?'

'It's certainly the biggest I've ever seen.'

'Isn't this great, Dad?'

Robert had to swallow the lump of sheer pride that rose in his throat before he could say, 'Yes, son, it's great. Now, come and eat your supper and away to your bunk.'

It was the first time on board Robert had come face to face with Joe. The skipper, with his own cabin directly behind the bridge, rarely came down to the lower deck and never during the time at the fishing grounds.

'Thanks,' Joe said, taking the meal Robert had carried up to the wheelhouse. As he turned to go, Joe mumbled, his mouth already stuffed, 'He's a good lad, that.'

As Robert turned back to face him, he was amazed to see a grin spread across Joe's face. 'I can tell he's my brother. He looks a bit like me an' all, dun't he?'

Robert smiled, anxious to meet Joe half way, yet at the same time careful not to appear over-eager.

'Your mother always says you both take after your Grandpa Buchanan both in looks and in your love for the sea.'

'Aye well, there's worse to tek after than him.'

Robert wondered if it was a veiled reference to the Hayes-Gorton family, but he said nothing.

Her name was between them now. She was almost a physical presence here in the cramped quarters of the wheelhouse on this heaving ship eight hundred miles from home. And yet she was here with them both. He could see the same hurt mirrored in Joe's eyes that he had seen so often in Jeannie's. He tried to think of something to say, something that could heal the breach yet at the moment he opened his mouth, Joe turned away, his attention once more upon the job in hand. The moment was lost.

But at least, Robert thought, Joe seems to be coming around to Angus.

It was a start.

Fifty-One

'Have you had no word at all from them, Edwin? Don't they keep in touch regularly with their position?'

Edwin smiled at her. 'Not Joe, Jeannie. He's a law unto himself when he's fishing. But,' he shrugged philosophically, 'we've learnt to trust your son. Oh, he'll radio in when he feels like it. And if there's any trouble . . .'

'Trouble?' she said sharply. 'What sort of trouble?'

Edwin swallowed swiftly, realizing his slip. He smiled again. 'That's what I mean, Jeannie. No news is good news, where your Joe's concerned.'

'Oh,' she said, a little mollified, but her shrewd glance at Edwin left him wondering if he had entirely convinced her.

'We'll maybe get a message when they're on their way home,' Edwin said. 'Cheer up. Only one more day and they'll be turning for home. That's if Joe's fish-room is full.' He laughed. 'If it isn't, he'll stay out there as long as he's catching fish and as long as his supplies hold out.'

'But if they've had a good catch, they could be home in four to five days?'

When Edwin nodded, the light came back into Jeannie's eyes.

*

'Last day's fishing today, Dad.' Robert heard the disappointment in the boy's voice.

Sitting beside Angus in the messroom, one of the deckhands shovelled the thick white flakes of fish into his mouth, anxious to snatch a few minutes' sleep before the next haul. It was a shame, Robert thought as he placed bread and butter and a mug of tea in front of the man, that they hadn't time to savour the meals Ted cooked. What that man couldn't do with haddock, wasn't worth knowing. He could teach the chefs in smart hotels a thing or two. That was for sure. Fresh bread buns baked every day. Three main, three-course meals and plenty of snacks in between, to say nothing of gallon after gallon of strong tea. The food was good, Robert was pleased to see, but if only the crew had time to enjoy it.

Picking up on Angus's remark, the deck-hand laughed. 'That's if he can stuff another six hauls into yon fish-room. Have you taken a look down there? We must have got fourteen hundred kits down there.' Grinning at Angus, he added, 'That's almost ninety tons to you, laddie.'

Much too polite to tell the deckie he knew very well the weight of a kit, Angus merely smiled and nodded. 'There doesn't seem much room left.'

The man swallowed his tea and stood up. 'Best trip we've had this year.' He touched the boy's shoulder and winked. 'You must 'ave brought us luck, lad. I have to say it, I thought at first you might be a Jonah, but you're not, you're a good 'un. You can come again.'

The smile on Angus's mouth threatened to split his face in two.

As the final day's fishing began, the weather, which had been kind throughout the whole trip, deteriorated. When the third haul came up over the side, the wind lashed the deck and the ship tossed from side to side in the mountainous waves.

The cod end swung in over the deck and Robert could see at once that it hung limply, devoid of its usually bulging weight of fish.

'What's happened?' he mouthed to Angus. The boy shrugged as together they watched Sammy duck beneath it and release the knot. A pathetically small catch of fish slithered on to the deck. Sammy was issuing orders, pointing and shouting to the men close by and then he was running along the deck towards the bridge.

'He's going up to see Joe.'

Though he passed close by, they did not try to detain him. They'd find out soon enough what had gone wrong.

On his way back, Sammy said briefly, 'We're turning for home. The net's badly torn and it'll take an hour or more to repair. With the weather worsening, it's a sensible decision.' He grinned suddenly, his face drenched beneath his sou'wester. ''Sides, he's got enough fish, if only he'd be satisfied.'

Robert had experienced rough weather during his years at sea aboard the minesweeper, but it was nothing compared with the ferocity of the storm they ran into as they left the Icelandic waters.

The ship was tossed and thrown as the winds, ever changeable, whipped the waves in every direction, so that one moment they were on the crest of a sixty-foot wave, the next being plunged into the trough below.

Grasping Robert's arm, Sammy bellowed into his ear, 'Get the lad below. The mate's going up on to the bridge to help Joe. He's close to exhaustion now. This is all he needs.'

Robert took hold of Angus's arm and was about to pull him towards the ladder when they all felt the ship plummet into a kind of vacuum created by the turbulence of the ocean. Robert and Angus looked up as a huge wave hovered above them and almost in slow motion came down upon them engulfing the ship in a deluge of water.

He put his arms about his son and clasped him to him as they fell together on to the deck. It seemed to last an age that they were tossed and thrown about the deck, bruised and battered. Robert was praying like he'd never prayed in his life before, not even when he had been under enemy fire aboard the war-time trawler. Never, ever had he known such fear. But all the while, he clung on to his son and prayed that they would both live to see Jeannie again.

He was fighting for air and then strong arms were lifting him up and he found that Angus and Sammy were hanging on to him.

'Dad, it's all right,' Angus was panting, gasping through the water and the spray. 'Feel that?'

As he spoke, Robert felt a tremor run through the whole of the ship.

'We're going to be all right, Dad. We're all right.'

Much later, Robert asked Angus what he had meant.

'That shudder, you mean? If you feel that, then the ship's buoyant. I just knew we were going to be all right. That's all.'

Robert stared at his son, marvelling yet again at the boy's instinctive knowledge and understanding. But the dangers were not over yet for the bad weather did not let up. Through the driving rain and sleet, now ice began to collect on every part of the surface of the vessel, but not so much that the crew were called upon to chop it away.

Robert was as busy as when they'd been trawling, carrying tea and food along the heaving deck and up to the wheelhouse.

'This is a bad 'un. I'm sorry you and the lad are having to go through this,' Joe said.

His eyes were dark-ringed with tiredness and the anxiety never left his face. He had the ship and the whole crew, to say nothing of a hold full of fish, for which he was responsible. Grimly, Robert said, 'No apology necessary. I'm glad I came. No, I mean it,' he added firmly as he saw Joe's look of scepticism. 'And you might not believe me, Joe. But it's been an eye-opener for me. I thought I knew about ships and going to sea when I served in the war, but this.' He shook his head. 'My God, this is hell on earth out here. Oh, it's all fine when the weather's good and the fish are there. But face this weather?' He shook his head slowly. 'Joe, I never realized.'

They stared at each other for a moment whilst beneath their feet the ship heaved and rolled.

'So,' Joe said slowly, 'you'll not be letting young Angus come to sea again, then?'

Robert allowed himself a quick, wry smile. 'I shan't be able to stop him. Nor shall I try.'

'You won't?' Joe was obviously surprised.

'No. If he wants to make the sea his life, I shan't try to stop him. Though,' again he smiled, with a tinge of sadness, 'I don't doubt his mother and I will worry every moment he's away. Just,' he added softly, 'as she has always done about you and Sammy.'

The man was silent and he looked away, out of the screen overlooking the deck, unwilling to meet Robert's eyes.

Robert cleared his throat. 'You may not believe me, Joe, but I promise you something. When we get home, I'm going to do everything I can to improve the lot of the fishermen, at least in our fleet. And you know something else too, Joe?' Though he waited a moment, there was no response from Joe, but Robert knew by the rigid set of his shoulders that the skipper was listening to every word. 'Sammy – and you as well – could do so much to help us. If only you would.'

He turned then and left the wheelhouse, clambering down the ladder and along the deck with the waves like walls on either side.

As he was about to go below, he turned and glanced back towards the bridge. Even through the driving rain, he could see that Joe was watching him. Then he glanced sideways to where Angus stood on the deck alongside Sammy. He saw Angus look round and grin at him, but then, as Robert watched, the boy's gaze went beyond him and a look of horror spread across his young features.

As the wave swept on to the boat, lifting Robert high in the air and carrying him over the side, the last thing he remembered was the stricken look on his son's face.

Fifty-Two

'Edwin, you must have heard something? They were due home today. Surely Joe's radioed in by now?'

She could see that Edwin was worried too and she was convinced he was holding something back.

'Even if you've had bad news, I'd sooner know.' All the old fears were crowding in on her. The terrible waiting, the awful not knowing . . . 'Please, Edwin.'

'Dearest Jeannie.' He took her hands in his. 'Try not to worry. Look, let me take you out to lunch and when we come back—'

'No, no, I couldn't eat a thing.' She pulled free of him and began to pace up and down his office coming back each time to stand before the window overlooking the docks. 'You must have heard something.' Jeannie was too knowledgeable to be put off so lightly. 'Are any of the other ships that went out at the same time, back?'

Edwin cleared his throat. 'Er, well, yes.'

'How many?'

He hesitated a moment and she could see the tortured expression in his eyes. Reluctantly, Edwin admitted, 'Most of them.'

Jeannie put her hands to her cheeks and stared at him. She took a deep breath and, her gaze never leaving his face, she asked, 'Edwin, what is it you're no' telling me?'

He sighed and said heavily, 'There was a storm—'

'What! You dinna mean their ship's missing?'

'No – no,' he said swiftly.

'What happened then? Are they all safe?'

But all her brother-in-law would say was, 'Joe's a fine skipper, Jeannie. I promise you. Just put your trust in Joe.'

She turned back to look out of the window once more, across the docks towards the river. Like a figure turned to stone, she stood there the whole day, just watching and waiting . . .

Jeannie refused to leave the office until, at almost midnight, Edwin insisted on driving her home. She lay awake for most of the night, tossing and turning, debating whether she should get in touch with Thelma. At about four o'clock in the morning she fell into an exhausted sleep. Then, as dawn broke over the North Sea, the telephone shrilling in the hall below dragged her back to consciousness.

'Jeannie, that you?' Edwin's voice came down the line.

'Yes. What is it? Tell me quickly.'

'It's all right. Their ship's coming in. She'll be docking on the morning tide in about an hour . . .'

Before he could say any more, Jeannie said, 'I'll be there.' And she dropped the receiver into its cradle and was running back up the stairs before Edwin, at the other end, could draw breath to ask her if she wanted him to come and pick her up.

'Oh well,' he said aloud to his empty office. 'I'll go anyway.'

'Oh Edwin, they're a' right? All of them? You've spoken to them?' She drew him into the kitchen and poured him a cup of coffee.

'This is most welcome, Jeannie. I went back to the office after I dropped you here.'

'You promised me you were going home,' she scolded, but she was laughing, light-headed with relief.

He smiled up at her, but she could see that the anxiety was still not entirely gone from his eyes. 'It was the only way I could get you to come home and try to get a little rest. I knew, if I didn't say that, you'd have stayed up all night at the office too.'

'Aye, I would.'

She watched as he drank his coffee, standing impatiently before him, almost willing him to finish it quickly so that they could leave for the docks.

'What time will she be in?'

'As soon as the dock gates open, I don't doubt. Joe likes to land his fish first to get the best prices.'

'And they are a' right?' she asked again, but Edwin avoided her eyes now. Standing up, he said, 'Come on, time we were going.'

She stood once more at the window of Edwin's office, feeling now as if she had not moved away from it at all in the last twenty-four hours. She squinted towards the place where the dock gates still remained closed, any ships waiting to dock were still drifting on the Humber's tide.

'When will he open the gates?' Jeannie asked for the third time.

'Another five minutes or so, I reckon.'

It was the longest five minutes of Jeannie's life until she saw the gates open and the first ship came nosing her way through.

'Is that the *Arctic Queen II*? I canna see . . .' She almost pressed her nose to the pane in her anxiety.

'Come on,' Edwin said. 'We'll go down. I'll find out where she's berthing.'

Jeannie was waiting on the quayside with Edwin when the first of the deck-hands came down the ladder.

On the bridge she saw Joe and, shading her eyes to look up at him, she knew that he had seen her. He seemed to look down on her for a long moment and then he turned away and disappeared from her view. Several other men came down the ladder and walked away without glancing in their direction. And already the lumpers were gathering near the ship.

Then she saw them. First Sammy came down the ladder followed by Angus. Jeannie sent up a whispered prayer of thankfulness.

Next came Joe. As he stepped ashore, they seemed to hesitate for a moment, standing together, the three of them, as Jeannie's glance went back to the top of the ladder, expecting to see Robert swinging his leg over the side and coming down to join them.

But there was no one else.

They were walking towards her, just the three of them.

Jeannie pulled in a breath and held it. Her hand fluttered nervously to her throat. Oh no, not Robert.

Her glance was darting between them as they came towards her. And then she was aware that Joe's arm was about Angus's shoulders. She looked into their faces, trying to read what she most feared to learn. Her legs felt weak beneath her and, blindly, she stretched out her trembling hands towards them. Towards her three boys.

But Angus was smiling, calling out to her now. 'Mother, Mother, it's all right. Dad's all right. At least . . .' They reached her now and surrounded her, hugging her. All three of them.

'He's safe, Mam,' Sammy said quickly. 'But he's had an accident . . .'

'We had some foul weather, Mother, and a huge wave washed Dad overboard.' Angus was determined to be the one to tell her. His grin widened. 'But, you'd never believe it, the very next wave washed him back on board again.'

'He was badly bruised,' Joe explained, his deep voice calmer than the other two. 'And his leg's broken. He tried to come right home, but we could see he was in a lot of pain. When we got off the coast of Scotland, we radioed ashore to one of the company's agents and he arranged for the local lifeboat to come and take him ashore. He's in hospital in Kirkcaldy.'

Jeannie gasped. 'My home? Near my home?'

'Aye.' Joe grinned and imitated her Scottish tongue. 'You're awae hame, Mam. We're putting you a train . . .' He put his arms about her, holding her close to his chest and resting his cheek against her hair. Huskily, he said, 'You're going home, Mam, just like you always wanted.'

Her eyes brimming with tears, Jeannie looked up into the face of her first-born, unable to speak for the lump in her throat. She wanted to say something, but the words would not come.

'There's just one thing.' He was smiling now, his eyes teasing. 'We're sending my brother, Angus, with you.' There was only the merest emphasis on the word 'brother' but hearing it, the lump in her throat swelled. Again Joe put an arm about the younger boy's shoulders and, as Angus grinned up at him, Jeannie could see the hero worship in his eyes.

'Just to make sure,' Joe was still speaking, his voice sounding a little husky now, 'that you come back to us.'

Now the tears overflowed and ran down her face as she held out her arms, trying to envelop them all.

405

She'd come back. Oh yes, she'd come back. That was what she wanted to say to Joe, to say to them all. Home was not in Scotland now. Home was here in Havelock. With Robert and her three beloved boys.